CROOKED PARADISE

THE COMPLETE SERIES

EVA CHANCE
& HARLOW KING

Crooked Paradise: The Complete Series

First Digital Edition, 2022

Cover design: The Pretty Little Design Co.

Ebook ISBN: 978-1-990338-65-6

Hardcover ISBN: 978-1-990338-66-3

SCORNED PRINCESS

Crooked Paradise #1

1

Mercy

Just one more day until I'm free.

I held onto that thought as I looked around the restaurant. The light of the brass chandeliers glanced off the long table that stretched down the middle of the room, covered in a white tablecloth and set out with fine china and silverware. Soft jazz spilled from the speakers through the chatter of the arriving guests.

This was a classy place, about as nice as you could expect to get in the Bend. Colt had picked it, since his family was hosting the rehearsal dinner. I liked it, which felt like a good omen.

"There you are, Mercy." My aunt Renee adjusted the pendant on my neck before flashing a grin at me. "You look beautiful, honey."

That was all that was supposed to matter in our kind of life—if you were a woman. But as much as I hated that fact, I couldn't exactly have shown up in one of my typical tees and beat-up jeans. I smoothed my hands over the silky turquoise dress that fell to just past my knees and smiled back at her. She meant well. "Thanks. Turns out I don't clean up so bad, huh?"

She scoffed. "Anyone could have seen that. Your husband-to-be should consider himself very lucky."

I glanced toward Colt automatically, but my gaze caught on another man first. The one who made my stomach tighten.

My father was easily the tallest man in the room—and the most intimidating one. Tyrell Katz held the kind of ruthless magnetism that made even the toughest men shake in their boots. That was how he ruled over the Claws, one of the most powerful gangs in the Bend, without challengers.

That was how he'd ruled over my life for the last twenty-one years. But tomorrow, I wouldn't be *his* anymore. I couldn't wait to be out of his iron-clad grasp.

And I would be out, thanks to the man poised next to him right now.

Colt Bryant stood only a little shorter than my father, laughing politely at some probably off-color joke dear old Dad had told. I let myself smile again, watching him. He filled out his dark suit to impressive effect, and the chandeliers' light brought out the gold in his pale hair.

What I really liked about him, though, was that he acted like he gave a damn about more than how I looked in a dress. Over the year of our engagement, we hadn't gotten into the deepest of conversations. We both knew this was primarily a business arrangement, after all, and the truce between his gang and the Claws had still been shaky. But he listened when I talked and had intelligent things to say back instead of spending the whole time ogling my boobs, unlike the other two assholes Dad had brought around before him. Thank God Dad hadn't liked their terms.

Colt could make me laugh. He'd spent more time considering my comfort during the dates we'd gone on than Dad had in my entire life. So I'd call this a win. Tomorrow's wedding would solidify the truce between the Claws and the Steel Knights, and I'd stop being Dad's bargaining chip and become Colt's partner.

Maybe it wasn't a perfect kind of freedom, but it was the best I could hope for given Dad's insistence on using me to expand his reach through the Bend—and, he imagined, to bring about the male heir he'd always wished I was.

Colt caught my eyes across the room. He excused himself and strode over to me. "Hey, you okay?"

I nodded, shoving aside all thought of my father. Just the fact that Colt had come over to check on me proved he was the better man. He'd been leading the Steel Knights since he was just nineteen, after his father had died several years back. He knew what it was like being underestimated and having to prove yourself to doubters.

Soon he'd see I was just as capable as the guys who helped run things for him—that I could be a *real* partner in every way. We could call the shots together.

And who knew? Maybe someday this battered heart of mine would even feel love again. If it was going to happen with anyone, I had to think it'd be him.

"No wedding jitters, then?" Colt asked in a teasing tone.

"Not yet," I shot back. "Just stay on your best behavior."

He laughed and clinked his wine glass to mine. Honestly, I wished we could skip all of this family nonsense and get married straight away. The celebratory buzzing felt like it was for everyone but me.

Or maybe that was just me being cynical. Grandma was walking over to me with tears in her eyes. She dabbed at them with a tissue. "You'll be the most beautiful bride when you walk down the aisle tomorrow."

I wagged a finger at her. "Hey, hey, no crying until the ceremony. There are rules about these things, you know."

"The first rule is no telling your grandma what to do," she informed me with a light swat.

I laughed and hugged her, and she hugged me back tightly. Grandma had always been there for me in the periods when Dad switched from training me like the son he'd wanted to pretending I didn't exist at all—or punishing me for being a daughter instead. She hadn't stood up to him over how he treated me, because everyone knew telling Tyrell Katz he was wrong never went well, but she'd done her best to make up for it.

My two uncles, Dad's right-hand men, ambled over. Their swagger seemed a tad subdued—possibly they felt a little naked without their usual weaponry. In recognition of our newfound alliance, both sides had agreed to attend the dinner unarmed, other than the bodyguards posted at the door for protection.

There was still plenty of testosterone to go around. Aunt Renee's husband, Uncle Steven, bumped his elbow against Colt's. "You've gone all out for us here. It's a nice place. Say, I've heard you've got quite the MMA tournament running these days. Now that we're relatives, maybe you can score us ringside seats."

Aunt Renee rolled her eyes, but Colt chuckled. "Sure. We've got a new fighter who's become a real talking point—a woman who's been taking on the men, and she's good enough to topple them. You should see her."

One of the servers called out over the chatter that dinner was about to be served. As I walked toward my seat by the foot of the table across from Colt at the head, Dad caught my arm. He leaned to speak gruffly by my ear. "Let's see more of that smile. Remember this is a *happy* occasion."

I gritted my teeth behind the grin I plastered on. "I know." I'd been a lot happier *before* he'd spoken to me. My hatred unfurled like tendrils in my chest.

Just one more day.

I wasn't getting away from him just yet. He sat down next to me, and I let my fingers curl around my fork. Imagining stabbing him with it also made me happier.

You could do a lot of damage with a fork. I knew from personal experience when one of the lower-level Claws lackeys had tried to get handsy with me.

Everyone had taken their seats except the servers, who were standing back as if waiting for permission to fetch the food, and Colt, who'd stayed on his feet at the head of the table. His cousins and a few other close associates from his gang had turned toward him. He raised his glass, and everyone quieted down. Even the music stopped.

"Thank you for coming, everyone," my fiancé said. "I'd like to make a toast. Here's to the beginning of a new era for the Steel Knights!"

Something twitched in my stomach. Why would he mention the Steel Knights and not the Claws too?

That was all the warning I got before the servers around the table whipped guns from beneath their aprons.

Colt's men jumped up from the table, drawing their own concealed weapons, and the room exploded with ear-splitting booms of gunfire. Uncle Steven caught two to the chest in mid-yell. Aunt Renee's scream was cut off by a bullet to her neck. As I sprang out of my chair, her blood splattered all over my dress. I looked down at it with shaking hands.

Colt's eyes were pure ice as he pulled out a pistol of his own and aimed it at my father. His first shot caught Dad in the shoulder.

Dad lurched and more shots rang out around us. My heart racing, I dropped down beneath the level of the table. My knees jarred against the tiled floor.

"You traitor!" Dad shouted, heaving to his feet.

"It's only business, Tyrell," Colt replied, crisp and even.

With another bang, Dad fell to the floor, his eyes staring. Blood streamed from a circular wound in the middle of his forehead.

He was dead. They were *all* dead.

I stared numbly at the bodies scattered around the table, limp and blood-splattered. Oh, God, *Grandma* was lying there just a few feet away from me, one last gurgle working its way out of her throat. The front of her dress was drenched with red.

No, no—this couldn't be happening—

"Make sure you get *everyone*," Colt said in the same awful voice, and my own blood turned cold. He meant me too.

Grief and horror constricted my chest, but my heart was still pounding, my fingers still clutching the damn fork. A searing haze closed in on my mind.

I'd been so close to claiming my freedom. So goddamned close. Just one more day...

I was *not* going to fucking die here.

My head jerked around. The two bodyguards had left the door to join in the carnage. At the same moment as I marked their positions, one of them caught sight of me.

I flung myself toward one of the smaller restaurant tables, ricocheting this way and that as years of tumbling and parkour practice guided my body, trying to keep some kind of furniture between me and the various attackers while my pulse thundered on in my head.

There must have been a couple of people on the Claws side still living, because a few more shots rang out behind me, followed by a thump. I dove right under another table and sprang out the other side, hurtling toward the door—

Another *bang* rattled my eardrums, and a blazing pain cut across my upper arm. *No.*

Swallowing a gasp, I threw myself onward. One of the servers charged at me, and I whirled to the side just long enough to stab the fork as deep as I could into his gun hand. Then I burst past the door into the night.

Pain kept throbbing in my arm. Shouts carried after me. I dashed along the sidewalk, stumbling and then kicking off my stupid heels. My bare feet pushed me faster, but footsteps stomped out of the restaurant behind me.

At the end of the block, a guy was standing next to his car, one hand resting on the open door. He tossed his keys into the air with the other as he chatted with friends at a patio table lit by café windows.

I summoned a fresh burst of speed. The guy and his friends all whipped around at the sound of my feet, but I was close enough. I snatched the keys and dove past the open car door.

The guy yelped, but I'd already yanked the door shut. Jamming the lock in place, I tossed myself into the driver's seat, pushed the key into the ignition, and slammed my bare foot down on the gas pedal.

The car tore down the street, tires screeching as I avoided a parked truck just ahead. I sped around one corner and then another, weaving back and forth, nothing in my head except getting the fuck away from the guns and the blood.

Well, the guns, anyway. There was plenty of blood here, spilling down my arm from where the bullet had gouged it. My head started to spin.

Where the hell did I go now? What the hell had just *happened*? Colt and his men—they'd just killed my whole family—he'd tried to kill *me*—

Had this been his plan all along? Some kind of long game to wipe out the leadership of the Claws? He'd been playing me—and Dad—for the entire year of our engagement?

My stomach churned, but only some of the nausea was thanks to the pain burning through my arm. I'd trusted Colt. Not completely, but enough to be willing, even happy, to tie my life to his. He'd acted as if he cared about me. I'd pictured a whole future with him.

And now it was gone in a hail of gunfire.

I'd had no love for my father, and I couldn't say I'd liked most of the rest of my family either, but I hadn't wanted them *slaughtered*. And Grandma... A lump swelled in my throat, my vision blurring with tears.

As I blinked them away, anger crept up through the grief. It expanded through my chest, searing almost as hot as the gunshot wound.

How *dare* he? How dare that snake turn this night into a massacre, steal my entire family from me—shitty as most of them were—and for what? If I got my hands on Colt...

My knuckles ached from gripping the steering wheel. My arm throbbed, more blood streaking down it. I blinked harder and refocused on my surroundings as well as I could through my growing wooziness. I'd been driving without paying attention for who knew how long.

I'd ended up in Paradise City, the jewel of Paradise Bend County. Skyscrapers towered on either side of me. And up ahead loomed the big hill at the north end of town with its massive white mansions, aglow now with the gleam of their security lights...

When I was a kid, Dad had driven me up there sometimes to point out the biggest mansion, smack in the middle. "That's where the people who rule all of Paradise Bend live, Mercy. The Nobles. Play our cards right, and one day we might be half as posh as they are." Then he'd laugh.

I'd never been sure what the joke was.

A plan formed in my pain-addled mind. I turned at the next intersection and cruised past polished storefronts followed by increasingly overblown houses.

People who figured they were somebody lived in Paradise City. The rest of us got stuck with the Bend, the sprawl of grungy suburbs and smaller towns that bled into one another in a loose arc around the city—so close and yet so far from Paradise. But I'd bet there were just as many assholes here as there. At least we knew what we were.

As I aimed the car up the steep slope that led to the peak of the hill, a wave of dizziness swept over me. I clenched my jaw against it and rammed my foot farther down on the gas. The engine grumbled, but we made it to the top.

My father had battered enough sense into me that I parked three houses down from the Nobles' grand mansion rather than right out front, because at this point the car was basically a moving crime scene along with being stolen. My thigh stuck to the seat for a second before I peeled myself out; the whole side of my lovely dress was soaked with my blood. I staggered a little on the asphalt.

There wouldn't have been anywhere to park in front of the Nobles' house anyway. Sedans and sports cars cluttered the broad driveway and both sides of the street almost as far as my car. Tuning out the pain in my arm and the trickle of blood over my skin, I gathered myself as well as I could and strode across the expansive lawn to the front door, which stood half open.

These were the people who ruled all of Paradise Bend. If anyone could crush Colt into the smithereens he deserved, it was the Nobles.

The faint bass of a rock song thumped through the doorway, hitting me at full force the moment I stepped into the foyer. People milled around—men and women bobbing with the music, waving glasses around, mashing their faces together and sometimes their hips too. A few older guys stood stern-faced watching the crowd.

I avoided them, melding into the mass of bodies. None of the partiers seemed to notice my seeping wound or the blood saturating my dress. Too caught up in their posh, powerful lives, huh?

These idiots couldn't help me. I needed the actual Nobles. Dad had pointed the father and heir out to me once a few years back when we'd crossed paths with them at a distance. Fancy suits, fiery auburn hair, faces like carved marble. *Rich pricks*, I'd thought at the time, but I'd also committed their names to memory. You never knew when a stray tidbit Dad or any of the other Claws dropped might come in handy.

I dragged those names out of my whirling head. Ezra. Ezra Noble. He was the big boss. And the son—

I stepped through another doorway, and my gaze latched onto a head of tousled auburn hair. Speak of the devil. My lips curled into a wobbly smile.

Wylder. That was him. He was bent over a pool table right now, lining up a shot. No suit jacket tonight, just a navy-blue button-up with the sleeves rolled up over his muscular forearms, brawny shoulders flexing in a way that would make a lesser woman want to run her hands all over them. I had more important things to take care of tonight.

As I wove through the spectators to the table, the guy landed his shot and straightened up into a cocky pose. The man next to him, a handsome hulk with cropped black hair, shot him a grin. A skinny blonde in a dress that covered more of her arms than her boobs shimmied where she'd decided to dance stripper-style on the edge of the table. The guys didn't seem to be paying much attention to her, but she glowered at me.

I ignored her too and marched straight up to Wylder. Or maybe it was more a sway. The floor was getting tipsy on me.

"Wylder Noble," I demanded, prodding him in the arm with a determined finger.

The guy turned, his eyebrows rising. Fuck, he was stunning up close. Blazing green eyes, sculpted jaw, nose just a tad crooked so he was perfectly imperfect. That kind of face should be illegal.

"You want something?" he said coolly, and another surge of dizziness rose up over me, fogging the edges of my vision. Wylder's gaze dropped to my dress, and a flash of something beyond calculated boredom crossed his expression. Probably peeved I was bleeding all over his swanky floor.

"I need to talk to you," I announced. "*Now.*"

Which might have gotten me farther if the world hadn't closed in on me completely then. My legs gave, and everything went black.

2

Mercy

THE VAGUE FEELING OF BEING CARRIED IN SOMEBODY'S ARMS crept over me. Groaning, I instinctively curled into a hard chest, seeking its warmth. The arms tightened around me as I was carried up a flight of stairs. A door banged open, and a few moments later, I was laid down on a bed while a voice barked orders to someone nearby.

I tried to open my eyes, but they felt heavy. I faded out again.

When I really came to, somebody was prodding the side of my arm. Whatever they were trying to do, it stung like holy hell. Adrenaline jolted through me, and I kicked out blindly. Someone—a man—cried out in pain.

"Holy shit." Strong hands descended on me, pinning me down. I screamed and thrashed, my mind flashing with the images of the bloody slaughter. My father, Grandma, my entire family, sprawled and savaged on the restaurant floor.

"Stop," a voice commanded with an unshakeable air of authority. My body stilled as if keyed to his wish. Blinking hard, I slowly brought the world around me into focus.

Bright green eyes stared down at me. A gorgeous man who was

familiar in ways my hazy mind couldn't quite identify yet was poised right over me, his knees bracketing my hips. The weight of his body pinned me to the bed.

The sense of being trapped made me squirm again. The guy's grip on my wrists tightened, his eyes darkening. Something unfurled deep in my stomach, and all of a sudden I wasn't completely sure I did want him off of me.

"Wylder," a voice warned behind him, shattering the bizarre impulse.

Right. Wylder Noble. My would-be savior—at least, I'd thought he could be. So far he was mostly being a criminally handsome menace.

I heaved at him as well as I could, but he didn't budge. "Kitten's got claws," he said and then chuckled darkly. "The irony."

"Get off me," I snarled.

"Wylder," came the voice again.

This time he listened and finally his weight lifted off me. On the other side of the bed, a man was cradling his arm, looking at me like I was a psycho. He must have been the one I'd kicked. Wylder jerked his head toward him.

The brawny guy with the dark buzzcut who'd been with Wylder at the pool table stepped into view. "Frank was just trying to stitch you up. From that gouge on your arm and the way you bled all over the living room carpet, it looks like you didn't quite manage to dodge a bullet."

The faint thump of dance music carried from beyond the door. Apparently I hadn't been out too long—and it took an awful lot to shake up one of the Nobles' parties.

"That's one way of putting it," I said a little faintly.

Come on, Mercy, get a grip. But my arm was throbbing again, and my thoughts kept jumbling with images of the massacre.

Wylder motioned to the man at the end of the bed. "Can you finish the job?" A few smears of blood marked his bare forearm where he must have held me. He picked up a rag someone had left on the end table and gave it a brisk wipe. I'd probably gotten some on his shirt too, although it was hard to tell against the dark fabric.

"Yes, Mr. Noble," Frank said, still eyeing me uncertainly.

"Not even properly shot and you passed out," the brawny guy remarked. "Not your usual scene?"

I didn't speak. If my father hadn't been dreaming of grandsons, *he* would have put a bullet through my head years ago.

Frank eased closer. "I have to finish cleaning the wound, and then you're going to need stitches."

"Fine, fine," I muttered. "Just be quick."

The guys' stares burned into me as their doctor—or whatever he was—dabbed more antiseptic around the raw flesh. I clenched my jaw and refused to let out a sound, no matter how it burned. They thought I was enough of a wimp already.

My lips might have twitched a few times from holding back the pain while Frank closed the wound with a needle and thread, but the antiseptic seemed to have numbed the spot a bit. When he'd taped a bandage over the injury, he offered me a bottle of blue liquid.

I eyed it suspiciously. Any woman in the Bend learns at a very young age not to accept drinks from strangers. "What is that?"

"It's an energy drink. It's the best option I've got on hand for your blood loss."

I didn't take it. Wylder stepped forward and swiped the bottle from Frank's hand, twisting the lid open. "Drink up."

I stared at him stonily.

"Drink, or I'm going to throw you out of my house. I don't care why you turned up here bleeding half to death."

Well, if he'd had nefarious intentions, he probably wouldn't have waited to see me stitched up first. And I was a lot more likely to get into a bad situation while my head kept whirling.

I snatched the bottle from him and chugged the blue liquid down. The sour taste of it made me wince, but I managed to finish it.

Frank stood up, clearly in a hurry to get out of there. "That's the best I can do. As long as you keep it clean, it shouldn't get infected or need further treatment."

After he was gone, the brawny guy started to laugh. "You scared the doctor away."

A cool voice spoke up from behind him. "To be fair, Frank does scare pretty easily."

Another guy came into view at Wylder's other side. His hair was dyed a bold, sapphire blue and jaggedly cut as if he'd done it himself. He considered me with narrowed eyes so sharply intent I had to resist the urge to squirm.

"I wasn't trying to scare anyone," I said, taking in the room more thoroughly now that I could focus better. I was sitting on a queen-sized bed in a small room with no other furniture except the ebony bedside table and a matching chair in the corner. It had the blank impersonal vibe of a hotel room. No one had bothered to shut the gauzy curtains on the window, which showed total blackness outside.

Wylder glanced at the brawny guy. "Did anyone see us bring her in here, Kaige?"

"Oh, maybe a few," the other guy—*Kaige*—answered. He winked at me with a flex of his massive biceps. Tattoos of vines climbed up his muscular forearms, disappearing beneath the sleeves of his V-neck tee. "But they were too out of it to remember tomorrow. Most of the drinks have been laced with the good stuff."

Ah. No wonder nobody had paid attention to me. Drunk and high without a care in the world. No doubt the Nobles had enough cops under their thumb to ensure they didn't get so much as a noise complaint.

Wylder returned his attention to me. I met his gaze head on, even though it felt like his striking green eyes could see right down to my deepest, darkest secrets. He cocked his head. "All right, spill. Why did Princess Katz of the Claws show up at my door looking like this?"

My mouth fell open in surprise. "You know who I am?"

He chuckled. "It's kind of my job to keep tabs on all the gangs that operate in and around Paradise Bend, Princess."

I made a face at him. "Don't call me that."

"Don't like the nickname? I could call you Kitty Cat instead, because you've sure got some claws."

I ignored him. I wasn't about to take his bait again.

The pain in my arm grounded me. My body felt stiff, and I shook my feet to bring some flow of blood to them. At my movement, my dress rode up to my thigh, and all three pairs of eyes turned to my bare flesh like it was a flaming beacon. My spine tingled with apprehension—and maybe the tiniest bit of heat—under their collective attention.

I was in a room with three guys who belonged to the most dangerous outfit in all of Paradise Bend. Time to get on with the plan that had propelled me here, even if that plan was seeming foolhardier by the second.

I swallowed, clenching my fists at my sides. The basic idea hadn't been bad. If anyone could take Colt and the Steel Knights down for what they'd done, it was these guys, gorgeous assholes or not.

"You look like you're about to stab me in the eye," Wylder said, giving me an amused look.

"I'd be interested to see her try," the blue-haired guy said in the same coolly detached voice as before.

Wylder snorted and elbowed him. "Of course you would, Gideon. We can hold the battle royale later. Come on, Princess. Cat got your tongue?"

I dragged in a breath. "I was engaged to Cole Bryant—the leader of the Steel Knights." The words made bile rise up my throat. For a second I couldn't go on. The screams echoed in my head alongside the blare of the merciless shots of the guns. The memory of the bodies dropping in quick succession flashed behind my eyes. My grandmother lying dead in a pool of her own blood...

The bedroom door burst open. "I heard that you—"

The new arrival stopped mid-sentence when he caught sight of me on the bed, and my world tilted sideways.

I was hallucinating, right? No way could Rowan Finlay, my first love —and my last, after the way *he'd* betrayed me—be standing just a few feet away from me in Wylder Noble's house.

It *was* him, though, even if he wasn't the skinny boy with an adorable dimple I'd met in junior high. He'd cropped his once floppy ash-blond hair short and spiky, and he was wearing a suit as if he'd just stepped out of a meeting. He had grown into his height, his shoulders broadened. But seeing him shocked me back five years to the last time I'd seen him as if no time had passed at all.

We stared at each other as if challenging the other to look away first. Could he see the fury and pain in my eyes?

Our unspoken exchange could hardly go unnoticed. Wylder frowned at me. "Do you have a problem with the company I keep?"

I blinked. Rowan looked uncomfortable for a moment before smoothing his face to be expressionless. Of course, I meant nothing to him. He had made that crystal-clear all those years ago.

Shaking my head, I pushed any lingering hurt and confusion out of my mind. The past should stay in the past. It—*he*—didn't matter anymore. "No," I said flatly.

I inhaled slowly. Once. Twice. I needed to remain calm and coherent. "Cole Bryant killed my entire family tonight."

All four pairs of eyes widened. Rowan took a step toward me and then seemed to check himself.

"The Claws are all dead?" Kaige asked, gaping openly.

I nodded. "Everyone who had any kind of authority—my dad, my uncles, their top men. I'm the only survivor. It was supposed to be our rehearsal dinner." A laugh with no humor at all in it sputtered out of me. "I was supposed to walk down the aisle tomorrow to marry Colt. But it turned out to be a trick to lure us in without weapons."

The first time I'd met Colt, his easy smile and kind eyes had seemed like a breath of fresh air. He'd spoken to me respectfully and with warmth that I hadn't received in a long time. And all of it had been a lie.

How long had he been playing me? I'd been so blinded by the hope of the life he'd allowed me to dream of that I hadn't seen the truth right in front of me.

"Why the fuck would you walk into enemy territory without weapons?" Wylder demanded.

"Both sides agreed, as a matter of honor. Our marriage was supposed to solidify an alliance. We thought we weren't enemies anymore."

He scoffed. "Honor means shit when you end up dead."

I bunched the bedsheet in my palms in an effort to not punch him right where he stood. He spoke so carelessly, not giving a flying fuck that my entire family had been murdered tonight.

"It's a dog-eat-dog world," Wylder went on. "Or should I say Knights-eat-Claws. This is a game of survival, and if your father couldn't protect what was his, then he deserves to be dead."

None of the other guys argued on my behalf. But why would they? I was some blood-drenched stranger who'd showed up at their door. This wasn't a fairy-tale, and they were definitely not any kind of Prince Charmings, despite their terribly handsome facades.

But I couldn't lose hope. I was Mercy Katz, and for all his flaws and torments, my father had honed me into something stronger than he'd ever imagined. I could do better than this.

"Colt went back on his word," I said firmly. "He betrayed us. And for that he needs to pay."

Wylder raised his eyebrows. "And how do you figure I come into that?"

"He took down one of the most powerful gangs in the Bend. What if he gets ideas for more? You Nobles are supposed to have all of Paradise Bend at your beck and call, aren't you? How's it going to look if you let some upstart get away with shit like that and walk free?"

"I'm not getting involved in some lovers' spat," Wylder said, but I had the sense I'd gotten more of his attention.

I fixed him with a glare. "We weren't in love. It was a business transaction, and more for my father's benefit than mine—although yes, I was happy enough with what I thought I'd get out of it. Clearly Colt wasn't. What if he still isn't happy? He could be coming for Paradise City next."

"And if he does, he'll regret it. So far it sounds like all he's done is removed a weak link. If you think I'm going to jump at the command of some small-time gang princess who came begging for help, you're sorely mistaken, Kitty Cat."

I held back a snarl at the nickname. "I didn't come here to beg. I came to call on you to prove that the Nobles really do rule—that this kind of backstabbing won't get a pass under your watch."

Wylder shrugged. "I'm still not convinced the Claws didn't get what they had coming to them. Look at you, barely making it two steps into my house before fainting from a bullet wound."

"Bullet wound?" Rowan spoke for the first time and then snapped his mouth shut.

Wylder ignored him. "You're weak. It's going to take more than batting your pretty lashes at me to prove your case."

"I. Am. Not. Weak," I said, biting out each word. "I'll be right there with you every step of the way—I want to watch him ground into the dirt. I can hold my own."

A speculative gleam lit in Wylder's eyes. "And what if I said I'd need you to prove that first. Follow my orders, show what you're made of. Are you ready for that, Princess?"

Follow this prick's orders? Every nerve in me resisted the idea—especially when I remembered how my body had briefly responded to his own pressed against it.

But this was my opening—the only one I was likely to get. I had to take it. There was nothing he could throw at me that was worse than what I'd already been through.

I lifted my chin and held his gaze. "Whatever it takes if it means Colt Bryant burns."

Rowan

Of all the places I could have come face to face with this ghost of my past, I'd never have expected it to be one of the Nobles' spare bedrooms.

Mercy Katz's gaze cut to me again, her words ringing in the air, the pale blue eyes that had once gazed into mine shining with love now filled with pure venom. Of course she hated me. All she knew was that I'd broken my promise, abandoned her… I'd never meant to look back.

It shouldn't have affected me now. I wasn't the boy she'd known anymore. I'd quickly climbed the hierarchy within the Nobles and stood at the right hand of Wylder Noble despite joining only a few years ago. There were many people other than her who hated me.

But none of the others had ever bothered me like this.

Her dress had ridden dangerously close to her upper thigh where she sat on Wylder's bed. It clung to her body, damp and darkened with… blood? Wylder had mentioned a bullet wound, and someone had bandaged her arm.

The outline of her underwear showed against the thin fabric. My cock twitched in spite of everything. Tendrils of her hair had come loose from a carefully made chignon that spilled down her neck. But most dangerously tempting of all was the fire burning inside her. She commanded attention.

From the way both Wylder and Kaige were watching her, I didn't think I was the only one who'd noticed. My jaw clenched.

"We should talk about this," I said to Wylder. There was no fucking way I was letting her into my life again. If I'd ruined hers, then my relationship with her had ruined mine just as much. I wanted her nowhere near me ever again.

Wylder glanced at me. "I haven't agreed to help her yet. I just want to see what the kitty's made of. If you've got ideas on that score, I'm all ears."

He jerked his head for the rest of us to follow him and strode out of the room without a backward glance.

I gave Mercy one last look before I turned on my heel and followed. Fury flashed in her eyes at the brisk dismissal. For a second, the thought of the loss she'd just endured, the horrors she must have witnessed, gnawed at me.

But I had no choice. I had to protect what was mine, including the life I'd so carefully built in the years since I'd parted ways with her. I couldn't let it all go to hell all over again.

Music from the party trickled upstairs, the noisy, nonsensical beat of it grating on my nerves. It was past midnight already, but the festivities weren't showing any sign of dying down.

Wylder came to a stop on the landing, looking down over the partygoers in the main foyer. Writhing bodies danced to the music. A few of them were singing along to it in off-key voices that made me want to take my gun out.

Was I upset at them or Mercy?

"She isn't good news," I said. "Forget testing her—just get her out of here."

Beside me, Kaige shrugged with the flirty smile that always came out when he was about to put a move on some chick. My hackles rose before he even spoke. "I don't know. She seems like she could be a lot of fun."

Gideon leaned against the banister with his hip, his analytical gaze as penetrating as always. "We do have to consider the territorial implications. Colt Bryant took down the entire Claws. That's going to have an impact."

"Is that necessarily a bad thing?" Kaige said. "Haven't we been getting news of them stirring up trouble?"

"The Claws were the most powerful force in the Bend, and Colt massacred them in one night. He's cold and precise," Gideon replied levelly. I'd never witnessed the guy raise his voice, but he always managed to get his point across nevertheless. "That makes him a potential threat, one we have to consider."

Wylder turned to me. "How do you know the girl?"

The question caught me off-guard even though I should have seen it coming. There were rarely things that Wylder didn't catch. He had a crazy knack for making people spill, which was why his father used him for most of the interrogations.

I cleared my throat. I knew lying wasn't an option. He would catch my bullshit right away. "She and I dated for a while back in high school. Before I moved to the city. I was surprised to see her—and vice versa—that's all."

He nodded, but I could tell he wasn't exactly satisfied with my vague answer. "I'm not saying I trust her, and it sounds like you know her better than we do. But Gideon's right. She raised some fair points about the Bryant prick getting out of hand. And *she* knows him better than any of us do."

I sucked in a breath, but Wylder's eyes were still trained on me, as if he were waiting for some reaction. He obviously suspected something else was going on between Mercy and me, but I wasn't going to give him any more information. That was completely unrelated to the gang, and I kept my private life out of this business.

Before I could protest, a flash of limbs and pale skin threw herself at Wylder. He scowled down at the girl who was now practically hanging off him.

"Wylder, I was looking for you all over the place." Gia's voice was slurred from all the alcohol she must have consumed. The skimpy outfit that she was wearing threatened to fall off any second, and the mounds of her breasts were all but exposed.

All the sight did was make me think of Mercy in that bloody dress.

Wylder shook her hands off him and stepped away. "Gia, I think it's better that you sleep it off. You're drunk."

Gia pouted in response and then turned her attention to Kaige, running her finger along his jaw. "What about you? You want some of this?" She thrust her hip out at him.

Kaige rolled his eyes, but he took her by the waist and leaned in. "No," he said, loud enough for us to hear.

Gia's lower lip wobbled. "I just want to be good to you," she slurred and then scampered away, stumbling in her high heels.

"Is it just me, or is she more annoying when she's drunk?" Kaige asked.

Gideon sighed. "Don't even pretend that you don't like the attention."

Kaige grinned in answer.

"I think it's time we pull the plug on this party." Wylder put his hands on the balustrade and raised his voice. "Everybody gets out in five minutes, or I'm going to start shooting."

The music stopped abruptly. Everybody stared up at us in horror, Wylder's words cutting through the haze of alcohol and drugs in their system. There wasn't a person in the room who didn't know they were looking at the second most powerful figure in the Nobles.

He raised a brow and motioned to the outline of the gun at his hip. "Do I need to repeat myself?"

People started rushing out of the foyer immediately, their urgency to get away almost comical. Wylder shook his head at them and returned his attention to us, swiping his hands together. "Always an effective way to break up a party fast."

As the last of the partiers hustled out, we walked down the stairs, examining the aftermath. Throwing a party was one thing, cleaning up afterwards was a whole lot of trouble.

I stepped on what looked like a used condom and winced in disgust. Kaige toed the pizza crusts and the crumpled paper cups out of his way. "People are such fucking pigs."

"Thank God for the cleaning staff." Wylder paused, and a smirk that set off warning bells in my head curled his lips. "Although I say we tell them to leave one room untouched for the time being."

What was he up to? I studied him and couldn't stop the question from tumbling out. "What about Mercy?"

"What about her?"

I knew I was pushing it, but I had to give it one more shot. "Even if Colt is a problem, we don't need her to tackle him. We're the Nobles. You just cleared a hundred people out of the building by pointing at your gun. Why keep her around?"

Wylder shrugged. "I don't believe in throwing away a useful tool that's fallen into our laps. Colt Bryant could become a problem for us in the future. And Mercy Katz has the inside scoop on him. Maybe she'll even prove herself somewhat useful in other ways. It's been a long time since high school, Rowan."

I bit back any retort I might have made to that. I'd worked my way into Wylder's inner circle by doing whatever he needed me to do, being whatever he needed me to be, and I was still a relative newbie here. He'd been counting on the other guys way longer. If I made a single misstep, I wasn't totally sure he wouldn't be casting *me* out of the house at gunpoint.

Kaige snorted. "Do you think she'll have any idea who her fiancé really is? He murdered her family in cold blood and then tried to kill her. He obviously wasn't the most upfront dude ever."

"No," Wylder said. "But they had been engaged for a year. They'll have talked. She'll have seen things. I don't get the impression she's the type to wander around with her head in the clouds."

"At the very least, she'll have some idea of his schedules and habits," Gideon said in his familiar analytical tone.

Kaige frowned. "There's something I don't get though. Why would he go to all this trouble for a whole fucking year? He couldn't have found an excuse to get enough key Claws members together sooner?"

"Maybe it took him that long to build enough trust?" I suggested.

Gideon nodded. "Tyrell Katz wasn't an idiot. It would have taken a lot for him to agree to go in without weapons."

"Well, his loss is our gain." Wylder's smirk came back. "If there's anything the kitty cat hasn't told us yet, we'll get to the bottom of it. And if she's a rat as well as a Katz, *she'll* be the one we're crushing."

"We shouldn't go easy on her," I said quickly. "Whatever our history, I won't." If Wylder wouldn't kick her out right away, then I'd just have to make sure she decided leaving of her own free will was better than staying.

It might even be better for her. Her dad was dead—Tyrell Katz was gone from this world. Part of the reason I'd started on this path was with the vague idea that someday, *I* might be in a position to end that villain's life, and now it was already done. It felt weirdly anticlimactic, like it wasn't quite real.

This bastard from the Steel Knights had screwed Mercy over too, and I couldn't condone what he'd done to her entire family or tried to do to her, but at least she didn't have to live in fear of Tyrell anymore. She could go anywhere, do anything... The last thing she should have wanted was to get dragged down into even more violence.

Why the hell had she had to come here when she'd had so many other options?

As I grappled with the clash of concern and anger inside me, Wylder's gaze slid to Kaige. "Anyway, having her around might distract attention from *you* while Anthea's still working her investigation."

Kaige's shoulders stiffened, but he couldn't argue with that.

Wylder motioned toward the staircase. "Get to bed, all of you. I want you sharp in the morning when we get to work on this new development."

I didn't like the sound of that at all, but I dipped my head in agreement and set off for my bedroom.

As soon as the door was closed behind me, the frustration that'd been building inside me overflowed. I slammed my fist against the doorframe. "Goddamn it."

I walked to the bed and ripped the mattress off it, throwing it against the wall. It wasn't enough. I pummeled it a few times, but the motions only made me feel more ineffectual. In the end, I sank to the floor, my hands still fisted.

For years, I hadn't let myself think of her. And now Mercy Katz had shown up at my door, stirring up all kinds of trouble.

And the worst part was, something in me still wanted to save her.

4

Mercy

DARK FIGURES CHASED ME IN MY NIGHTMARES, GETTING closer and closer. It didn't matter how fast I ran, they caught up to me, swirling around me, choking me, cutting off my breath until the shadows materialized into the grinning face of Colt Bryant. He was drenched in blood.

I woke up damp with sweat. At some point in the night, somebody had turned off the air-conditioning, and the room was stifling hot. I wiped the beads of perspiration that rolled down my neck to my cleavage as I struggled to catch up to reality.

It was just a bad dream.

But I hadn't outrun my nightmare. I had just woken up to another one. I closed my eyes and saw the lifeless faces of my grandma and Aunt Renee lying beside her. They were dead. Every person who'd had much of any impact on my life growing up was dead.

Desolation crept up inside me followed by a surge of rage so powerful I had to bite back a scream. No, I wasn't going to freak out or break down. I'd tamp down all my emotions, just like Dad's drills had forced me to.

"One step at a time," I muttered to myself. I wasn't going to take down Colt in a day. I would have to work up to it.

My head throbbed with what felt like the beginning of a headache. I swung my legs over the side of the bed, and my bare feet hit the pooled fabric of last night's dress where I'd left it on the floor. The blood had crusted over, the silk utterly ruined. I grimaced at it, a shudder running through me.

At least I wasn't wearing it anymore. While I'd been sitting here wondering what to make of that conversation with Wylder and his men, a woman who must have been part of the household staff had bustled in with a clean T-shirt and sweats for me to change into—and clean sheets for the bed I'd gotten a fair bit of blood on too. She hadn't even tutted over the stain that'd seeped into the mattress, but then, in this household blood was probably a common sight.

That'd seemed like a clear enough invitation to spend the night. Now the sun was beaming through the thin curtains. I rolled my shoulders, testing my wounded arm. A shallow ache ran through my bicep, but I'd felt worse. Seemed like the doctor guy had known what he was doing.

My eyes fell to the gold engagement ring with its glittering diamond on my finger. A fresh surge of rage rushed through me, sudden and desperate. I yanked at the ring, but it stuck on my knuckle. Gritting my teeth, I pulled harder. It felt as if my skin was melting under the cursed thing. I finally ripped it off and hurled it at the wall next to the door.

The door that was now opening. My engagement ring clattered to the floor and rolled in front of a pair of steel toe boots.

I raised my eyes, my gaze skimming beefy thighs outlined against tight jeans, hips with a perfect V, and then the heavily muscled chest above. The guy Wylder had called Kaige was watching me with an amused smile. "Woah, easy there."

My temper flickered, but I wasn't likely to get Wylder's help by pissing off his inner circle before I'd even started proving myself. "I wasn't aiming at you."

He bent down and picked up the ring. "Considering what that asshole did, I get the sentiment, but you might not want to throw this away just yet. From the looks of it, you could get a few K for it easily. Might as well make the bastard pay for his sins, right?"

He could've easily pocketed it himself, but he walked over to me, turned my hand up, and rested the ring in the middle of my palm. Heat spread from his fingers into mine. His gaze slid down my body like a caress, lingering briefly on my chest.

I'd have been more annoyed if I hadn't just been checking *him* out a minute ago. And if the approval in his eyes hadn't sent a tingle of sharper heat through me.

"Like what you see?" I found myself saying.

His smile widened. "You know what, I do."

Okay, that was enough of that. I jerked my hand away from his, my fingers closing around the ring, and stood up, stepping away from him in the same motion.

Kaige held up both of his hands as if in surrender, but I knew better than to trust him. Wylder hadn't agreed to help me yet. They were probably still debating on my usefulness. Nobody was my friend here.

"I'm just supposed to collect you for breakfast," he said with a twinkle in his deep brown eyes. "Do you need me to show you to the facilities first?"

My bladder said yes. I crossed my arms and raised my chin. "Lead the way."

Kaige led me down the hall at a casual stroll. Of the four guys I'd met last night, he seemed the most easygoing, but he was awfully intimidating without even trying. I wasn't a shrimp at five foot six, but this guy had nearly a foot on me—both in height and probably more than that in width with all that muscle. Pretty easy to guess what his job in the crew was. No attacker was likely to get at Wylder through him.

He swept his arm toward the bathroom with a jaunty little bow, and I held back a glare as I strode past him. Inside—with the door *firmly* closed—I looked at myself in the mirror and grimaced. My eyes were bloodshot, and my hair had turned into a bird's nest. I wasn't going to generate a lot of respect like this.

I splashed water on my face and under my arms, and combed my fingers through my hair, wishing I had an elastic to pull it back into one of my typical ponytails. The pins that had held it in its updo for the rehearsal dinner had all fallen out. After a couple more tugs at it, I ventured back into the hall where my new shadow was waiting.

"Twice as gorgeous without the bedhead," Kaige said with a wink.

I glowered at him, but my stomach chose to gurgle at the exact same time. Gee, thanks. "You mentioned something about breakfast?" I said pointedly.

My lack of responsiveness to his charms didn't appear to bother Kaige one bit. He offered me one of his brawny arms. "I'll give you the tour along the way."

I declined to be led along like a lady in one of the historical melodramas Grandma had loved, as tempted as I might have been to find out just how solid those muscles were, but I fell into step beside him.

Everything about this place screamed money, from the gilded windows that looked out into the sprawling lawn to the slew of framed paintings scattered along the hallway. Kaige waved toward the doors we passed. "Guest bedrooms here, Wylder's part of the house farther down. Including my bedroom, if you ever want to drop in on me."

"Noted," I said dryly.

We emerged into a larger section of hall overlooking a winding staircase and the huge foyer I'd stumbled into last night. On the way down, Kaige pointed at the set of huge oak doors. "The main entrance. Kitchen's this way. Plus various sitting rooms and living rooms and I-don't-know-if-they-even-have-a-name rooms. You need to get something done, there's probably a room for it here."

As we entered the kitchen, an expansive space full of shining stainless steel and marble countertops, the smell of frying sausage and eggs hit my nose. My mouth watered, and my stomach outright roared.

"You took your time," Wylder remarked from where he was standing just inside the room, his head cocked to the side. He was dressed in black jeans and a black shirt that I couldn't help noticing fit him snugly, showing off his well-defined chest.

Kaige aimed his grin at the other guy, apparently unperturbed that he might have pissed off the Noble heir. "Hey, I like to make sure a lady's treated right."

I wandered farther into the room, ignoring them and any

amusement I might have had at the idea of me being a *lady* while I chased the delicious food smells. Gideon and Rowan were leaning against an island in the middle of the kitchen. Whatever conversation they'd been having trailed off as they both glanced at me, Gideon coolly and Rowan hesitantly. Rowan's gaze stopped on the bandage over my gunshot wound, but he didn't comment on it.

Beyond them at the stove, a woman I hadn't met yet was flipping something in a pan. Her red hair, a more vibrant version of Wylder's and his father's auburn, cascaded to halfway down her back. She was petite, maybe half a foot shorter than me, but when she turned, I guessed from her face that she was around her late twenties. With her blue paisley dress and pearl hair pins holding the ruddy waves back from her temples, she didn't look like she belonged here at all.

She slapped a piece of French toast and some bacon on a plate and motioned me over to the island. "I assume you're hungry."

I was starving, but I didn't admit that. Warily, I stepped forward and took a seat as far as I could get from Rowan. This felt like some kind of a trick.

The woman poured orange juice into a glass and pushed it toward me. I was parched too. I'd never gotten to eat much of anything and hadn't drunk anything but a few sips of wine last night before...

Gunfire and blood splatter flashed through my mind. I shoved those memories aside and grabbed the glass to take a swift chug, as if I could wash last night away completely with the tartly sweet liquid.

"I feel introductions are in order." Wylder took a seat next to me at the island, so close the scent of him, like leather and brandy, filled my nose. I resisted the urge to inhale deeply as he gestured toward the woman at the stove. "Meet Anthea Noble, my aunt, babysitter, and proxy mother. She's kind of the all-in-one package."

Anthea rolled her eyes. "Mother? I'm only, what, five years older than you?"

"Six," Wylder said, causing her to shake her head.

I relaxed a little. She was family, not a business associate. That made more sense. Although the two factors did often end up pretty mixed up in our line of work.

Wylder gestured to me. "And Anthea, here we have the only living representative of the Claws' leadership in our kitchen. Say hi to Mercy Katz."

Anthea's gaze roved over me with cool efficiency, and I got the impression she'd known about my arrival long before I'd actually stepped in here.

"Anthea's here to keep our asses in line while Wylder's dad is away," Kaige said. As if to make a point, he wiggled his butt. I had to bite my cheek to stifle a laugh.

How had this guy ended up with the rest of this bunch? Or Rowan, for that matter? Back when I'd known him, he'd been on a fast-track course to get into an Ivy League college.

But then, obviously I hadn't known him anywhere near as well as I'd thought.

Gideon was easier to figure. He might not have packed anywhere near as much muscle as Kaige on that slender frame, but he had the detached gaze of a stone-cold killer. "Some people are harder to manage than the others," he remarked with a pointed look at Kaige.

I took a bite of my French toast—slathered with the perfect amount of syrup—and had to muffle a moan. Embarrassment turned my ears red hot.

Wylder chuckled. "I don't blame you. Anthea is a great cook. That's one of her specialties—along with concocting the perfect poison, of course."

I almost choked on my mouthful. Wylder thumped his hand against my back. I took a big gulp of the juice to push the bread down my throat.

Anthea smiled at me but without much humor. "You don't have to worry about deadly poisons this morning. If we wanted to kill you, you'd be dead already and not know any better."

I guess she had a point, but I remained on guard as I took another bite. The guys shifted around the island. They were watching my every move, and after a while my skin started to prickle with their attention. It didn't help that even if they were assholes, they were undeniably attractive assholes—ravish-me-in-the-dark attractive.

"So, tell me about Colt," Wylder said, studying me as intently as the others.

I drained the last of my juice before answering. "What do you want to know about him?"

He shrugged. "Let's start with the basics. What do you know about his business?"

"It's typical Bend stuff, mostly. Moving drugs and stolen goods, collecting from the local businesses—you know the score. And he runs regular MMA fights, collects bets on them. Those have gotten pretty popular since he started them up."

Gideon nodded, tapping the screen of a tablet he'd pulled out while I was talking. "I've heard about those."

Wylder picked up a fork and twirled it between his fingers. I couldn't help thinking of the one I'd stabbed into one of Colt's men. "And that's what appeals to the Katz princess in a husband?"

I glared at him. "I told you, it was a business arrangement. My father's more than mine."

"What made your father so eager to give away his only daughter to a rival gang?"

A strange heaviness was spreading through my head, like the grogginess just before a cold sets in. I rubbed the back of my neck. "They'd had a few clashes. Disputes over territory, interrupting deals. The kind of thing that's inevitable. It didn't have to be Colt. Dad would have been happy to expand his influence with any of the gangs in the Bend he could have connected me to."

I shut my mouth before even more words could tumble out. I didn't need to tell the guy my entire life story, for fuck's sake. What was wrong with me?

Wylder tapped the fork against the countertop. "That's all you were worth to Tyrell Katz? A bargaining chip?"

"And a broodmare," I muttered without thinking, and nearly bit my tongue. I sure as hell hadn't meant to say *that.*

Something was wrong. I tried to push myself off of the stool, but my balance wobbled. I couldn't even stand up straight.

My gaze shot to Anthea. "You—you *did* poison me." I snatched at the knife I'd used to cut my toast, but Wylder grabbed it first and sent it spinning across the counter to his aunt. Then he put his hand on my shoulder and sat me down on my seat. My body obeyed, just like my mouth had answered his questions automatically. My stomach listed.

Anthea set her elbows on the counter and propped her chin on her folded hands. "I said I didn't want to *kill* you. This is just a little concoction to loosen your tongue and make it harder for you to lie. Most of the symptoms will recede in a bit, and you'll barely feel anything at all."

She was right. The heaviness in my head was easing already. My stomach was settling. But my thoughts drifted with a floating sensation, as if my mind had been cut off from the rest of my body.

These pricks. Like I would have lied to them anyway. I was the one who'd come to *them*—had they forgotten that?

Of course, maybe they saw that as suspicious.

Wylder glanced over at Gideon. "Where were we?"

Gideon flicked at his tablet's screen. "The reasons for the engagement."

"Right." The Noble heir turned his bright green gaze back on me. "So your father wanted any alliance he could get within the Bend to strengthen his power base, and... grandkids?"

"An heir," I bit out, irritated with myself but unable to hold back the words. "I didn't count, seeing as I don't have a dick."

Kaige made a sound as if he'd choked back a snort. Wylder moved smoothly onward. "And you went along with this because...?"

"Because it was a chance to have some kind of life he wasn't totally controlling. Colt seemed like he'd be open to a real partnership, even if it was more business than love to begin with. You don't know—" I managed to cut myself short before I got into the messed-up sob story of my life under Tyrell Katz.

But of course Wylder wouldn't let it rest there. "I don't know what?"

I forced myself to look at him head on, directing the words as well as I could while they spilled out. I could talk without telling him *everything*. "He wasn't shy about his dissatisfaction with my dickless state. It was not a happy home. Zero sunshine, zilch roses. Do you really need the gory details?"

"I think I get the picture," he said casually, as if we were talking about a day at the park and not twenty-one years of horror. Well, fuck him.

Except no, I really shouldn't do that. Or want to. Oh, God, how long was this brain-melting "concoction" going to last?

Gideon looked up from his tablet again, all professional cool. "Walk us through what happened last night. You said it was your rehearsal dinner?"

"Yes. Colt made all the arrangements. It was supposed to be his contribution since my father was paying for most of the wedding." I dragged in a breath. "He picked the venue. I'm assuming now that the supposed staff were actually members of the Steel Knights. To avoid any old tensions bubbling over, both sides agreed not to bring weapons, other than a few bodyguards posted around the space who were meant to be a joint hire."

Wylder sighed, and I remembered his disdain for that idea last night. I barreled on.

"As soon as we sat down at the table, the servers, the bodyguards, and Colt and his men pulled guns on everyone on the Katz side and just opened fire. I saw most of them dead with my own eyes—my dad, my aunts and uncles, my grandmother..." I paused, swallowing hard. "Colt ordered them to take me down too, but I managed to get to the door and grab a car outside."

"That lines up with the official reports, as much as has been reported," Gideon said.

I peered at him. "You've got access to the police files?" Maybe I shouldn't be surprised. A sudden spurt of hope rose in my chest. "Was anyone at all from my—"

He shook his head before I could even finish the question. "Twelve dead. Your father, your grandmother, two aunts and uncles, and miscellaneous figures I believe were close associates of your father's."

I sank back down on the stool. "Yeah." He'd brought them along to show off the union he'd arranged. Lucky them.

Wylder drummed his fingers, eyeing me again. "Now we get to the important questions. Starting with, why did you come to me?"

"I didn't have anywhere else to go," I blurted out, the stupid drug from the drink still keeping my tongue loose. Damn it. I sucked in a breath and tried to make the best of it. "Colt wanted to kill me. He'd have checked my house. And I didn't want to just go into hiding. I want him taken down for what he did. I want him to *suffer.*"

The last word came out more emphatically than I'd intended. The guys all stared at me for a moment. Then a smirk stretched across Wylder's handsome face.

"Bloodthirsty. I can appreciate that. But why *me,* Kitty Cat?"

Did he really need to ask? "Everyone knows the Nobles run things in Paradise Bend. All the gangs in the county operate only as your family permits. Who better to crush that asshole?"

"Ah, so all you see when you look at me is a ticket to vengeance, huh?"

"And a prick who's too hot for his own good," I muttered, and almost chomped on my tongue when I realized what I'd said.

Wylder threw back his head with a laugh, twice as hot now that he was amused. I definitely wasn't watching the perfect curve of his throat and wondering if he tasted as good as he smelled.

Kaige rolled his eyes, while Rowan looked at me with a tense expression. If I didn't know any better, I'd think that he was trying to hide his annoyance, which didn't make any sense. He was the one who'd essentially dumped me.

Gideon broke in, his voice as flat as ever. "Why do you think Colt turned on the Claws? Did he ever seem unhappy with the arrangement?"

Deciding the best course of action was to pretend I'd never let the slightest compliment toward Wylder slip from my mouth, I focused on his friend instead. "No. If I'd had any idea, I'd never have walked into that restaurant in the first place. We'd been engaged for a year. I thought... I thought we were at least something like friends at that point."

Wylder and Anthea frowned. Gideon fixed me with a stare. His pale gray eyes were impossible to look away from once they'd homed in on their target. Something about him both unnerved me and made me deeply curious about what made that mind tick. Out of the four guys, he was the hardest to read.

"And how do you feel about him now?" he asked.

Hadn't I already laid that out? "I think he's a rat bastard who deserves to drown in a pool of blood," I said. "Preferably while also choking on his own testicles. If you want to get even more creative than that, I won't argue."

Kaige let out a low whistle that sounded impressed, but Gideon held my gaze. "Is that *all* you want?"

"Yes," I said. "Other than for this conversation to be over so we can get on with hunting him down already."

Without realizing it, I'd started shredding a paper napkin that'd been left on the island. Kaige leaned over and tipped his head toward my hands. "What happened to your fingertips? Did you try to remove your fingerprints like some kind of super spy?" He only sounded half joking.

I dropped the napkin, my fingers curling toward my palms. I didn't have to look at them to know what he'd noticed: the pads at the ends were mottled with tiny crisscrossing scars that'd cooled over time from angry red to faded white.

"Looks like the kitty cat almost got declawed," Wylder remarked, his tone playful but his gaze searching.

The light-headed sensation was dwindling. I found I could control what I said a little better than before. "I scraped them up pretty bad during a job for my father. He didn't go easy on me."

Rowan shifted in his seat, and my pulse hiccupped. He knew the truth—I'd told him in a moment of weakness and never regretted it until this moment. I looked up and caught his eyes. He met my gaze but didn't open his mouth to speak.

Why not? His loyalty was obviously with the Nobles now. He hadn't given a shit about my feelings before. But maybe he just didn't see how it was relevant, so he wasn't going to distract from the real issues by bringing it up.

I glanced around the island at my audience. "Listen, I'm here for only one thing—getting justice for me and my family. I know you're the only people who can help me deliver it. I've given you all the answers you asked for. What else do you need from me?"

To my surprise, Gideon closed his tablet. "I think we're done here. Wylder?"

Wylder observed me for a few beats before he said, "Yeah, I think we are."

I knew he didn't quite trust me yet but I was getting closer. Relief rushed through me. I'd passed his first test.

Anthea cleared her throat. "I'll just remind you that the serum only makes lying *harder*, not impossible."

There was no emotion at all in Wylder's voice when he replied. "And if she has been lying to us, I'm sure she knows I won't hesitate to put a bullet through her head." A smile curved his lips. "But for now it's time to put the princess to work."

5

Mercy

IGNORING MY IMMEDIATE CRINGE AT THE "PRINCESS" nickname, I turned to Wylder. "Put me to work how?"

He beckoned me with a curl of his index finger. "Come with me."

I followed him out of the kitchen and down the hall. Partway along it, he halted in his tracks and swiveled toward me. In that moment, his eyes looked as fiery as his auburn hair.

"Just so you know, Gideon is like my brother and Kaige will willingly carve out his chest to prove his loyalty. I don't expect anything different from Rowan."

I stared at him. "Why are you telling me that?"

He shrugged. "Just making sure you don't get any ideas. You may look like sin incarnate, but you're never going to sway my men."

As if to prove his point, his gaze slowly traveled down my body. It felt as if he'd touched me instead, lighting up flames all across my skin. He looked at me as if I was standing bare in front of him instead of wearing sweatpants and a loose tee that showed only the slightest hint of cleavage. My pussy clenched.

I found my voice. "I've already taken your test."

Wylder laughed. "Only the first part. You said you'd do whatever it takes to earn my help."

"So what's next?"

"I volunteered you for cleaning duty." He took a few more steps and pointed through a doorway.

As I reached him, I recognized the room where I'd found him last night—the one with the pool table off to one side. All traces of the party had been wiped clean from the rest of the house, but this large space was still littered with trash. A sickly smell like stale alcohol and... vomit? turned my stomach.

Wylder rested his hand on the small of my back. Despite the stink and my wariness of him, my nerve-endings lit up where he touched me. So much that I almost didn't process the words when he leaned close to my ear and murmured, "Well, get to it."

I blinked at him. "Pardon?"

"You heard me." He stepped back, waving to the room. "Clean the whole thing. I want it spick and span."

Was he kidding me? "I'm not your *maid*."

"Oh, no? Wasn't that you begging me for my help last night? Are you backing down so easily, Princess?"

"I'm not backing down. I'm just saying this has nothing to do with how strong I am or whatever it is you want me to prove."

Wylder moved toward me again with an air of menace, but I stood my ground. I realized the error in my judgment when he stepped right up to my face, close enough that he could have kissed me with just a little tilt forward.

"You are going to clean this room for me," he said, emphasizing every word. "Because I told you to, and while you're here, what I say goes. If you can't learn that lesson, you can forget about getting anything from me."

My eyes dropped to his mouth and the quick flick of his tongue as he spoke, and another flare of unwanted heat washed over me. Wylder smirked as if he knew exactly what I was thinking about. "No questions, Kitty Cat?" he said in a low, husky voice that made my stomach tighten. Suddenly, the nickname didn't sound half bad.

I snapped myself back to reality. What was wrong with me?

I *had* said I'd do anything. If this was what he wanted, I sure as hell wasn't throwing in the towel over a messy room. "Fine. Get out of my way, and I'll get to it."

I ventured farther into the room, my gut lurching as the smell thickened. Empty chip bags, half-eaten pizza slices, and bones leftover from sticky chicken wings lay in total disarray. Apparently Wylder's guests hadn't been familiar with the concept of garbage cans. There *was* a pool of vomit dried into the carpet in one corner, and... had someone taken a *shit* on one of the chairs? What kind of drugs had been in the drinks last night, exactly?

And now it was up to me to get rid of all this crap to the Noble heir's satisfaction.

Wylder propped himself in the doorway, his bright eyes tracking my every move. "What are you doing?" I asked, annoyed both at him and at me for being affected at all by his presence. "Don't you have more important ways to spend your time?"

"I don't know. I think supervising you for a bit should be both important and incredibly entertaining." He folded his arms in front of his chest. "Go on. There are cleaning supplies in the closet at the end of the hall."

Girding myself, I stepped past him and marched to the closet. From the shelves inside, I grabbed a box of garbage bags, a pair of rubber gloves, a package of bristly sponges, and a heavy bottle of cleaning fluid. I lugged it all to the pool table room and then went back for a bucket that I hauled to the kitchen to fill with water.

Wylder watched the proceedings with no shift in his faintly amused expression. I resisted the urge to claw his eyes out like the cat he kept saying I was and tugged up my shirt collar to cover my nose. It wasn't enough protection from the stench to prevent me from wanting to gag every five seconds.

It also left a band of skin around my waist bare. "Love it," Wylder called out teasingly. "Getting a bit of a strip show too."

I'd have stuck my tongue out at him, but he wouldn't have seen it anyway through the shirt. Tuning him out, I concentrated on my work as well as I could, humming a soft tune to distract myself.

Bit by bit, I worked through the disgusting mess. I let my mind detach, paying no attention to what I was putting my gloved hands on, just getting through this chore. Everything I could easily pick up went into a garbage bag until three were stuffed full.

Beneath a pizza box that'd been wedged under a chair, I found one treasure amid all the trash: two tightly rolled fifties with a faint dusting of white powder. Fucking rich assholes who could afford to snort coke with a bigger bill than some people in the Bend ever had in their wallets —and to forget those bills on the floor. But hey, their loss was my gain.

When I looked up, Wylder was gone. I guessed watching me wiggle my ass in the air while grabbing junk off the floor hadn't been so exciting after all. I definitely wasn't disappointed to have lost his company. I wiped the powder off the fifties and tucked them into my pocket.

Then it was time to get down to scrubbing.

For a little while, my nose had gotten numbed to the horrendous stink. As soon as I started working the worst of the offenses out of the carpet and the furniture, the smell rose up twice as strong. Only now it was combined with the pungent tang of the cleaning fluid.

My stomach lurched, and I nearly lost my breakfast to add a second pool of vomit to the room's décor. Gritting my teeth, I pushed through the nausea. Why not imagine that with every rub of the sponge, I was throttling Colt's neck? Bashing his arrogant face in. He'd deserve nothing less.

Less than twenty-four hours ago, I'd still thought I was going to marry him. The idea seemed so foreign now I almost laughed.

In the most horrible of ways, he'd given me what I'd wanted, hadn't he? I didn't have to answer to Dad anymore, that was for sure. But—God, as much as I'd hated my father sometimes, as many times as I'd pictured pulling a gun or a knife on him myself just to make the torment stop, I hadn't enjoyed seeing him go down.

Colt had killed him without provocation while under a treaty of peace most people even in the Bend would have considered sacred. There was no justification for that, let alone what he'd done to every other Claws member in that building. What he'd tried to do to me.

It wasn't even just killing them. Who would have been left to mourn any of them if he'd succeeded in taking me down too? Even with me still alive, it wasn't as if I could organize a dozen wakes, say a full farewell to any of them. If no one else, Grandma should have gotten a proper send-off.

But Colt's people would be searching for me, I was sure of it. He wouldn't take the chance that I'd come back for revenge. I was a loose end, and men like him didn't get where they were without learning to stamp out every one of those they came across.

I thought back to our last couple of dates—the lunch we'd grabbed at that new café he'd recommended, the chick flick I'd dragged him to less because I was eager to see it than because I wanted to see how well *he'd* endure it. Colt had laughed with me, held my hand, looked at me as if he couldn't wait to discover more of me on our wedding night.

And it had all been a lie. Even if he hadn't been planning the massacre all along, he must have known by then, right?

How could I have been so *stupid*?

I wrenched my hands against the rug in a particularly brutal motion, and the last of the vomit stain disappeared. Sitting back on my heels, I let out my breath and surveyed the room.

There were still a few splatters of what looked like cola to deal with and a scattering of crumbs I'd take the vacuum over later, but I was getting there. And Wylder had thought this request would be enough to send me running.

Rolling my eyes, I got to work on the next stain. I'd zoned out so deeply that the voice that broke through my thoughts practically gave me a heart attack.

"Who the hell are *you*?"

I startled and lost my grip on the sponge. Three beefy middle-aged guys with polos tucked into their jeans were standing by the door. Tattoos edged up their necks from beneath the folded collars. Nobles men, and pretty high up in the pecking order from their slightly posh clothes.

The man who'd spoken, a bald guy with another tattoo decorating his scalp, stepped toward me with a scowl. "I asked you a question, girl."

One of the other men snickered. "Just look at her, Axel. She must be one of the groupies." His open leer sent a wave of disgust through me. Suddenly I missed Wylder.

I kept my gaze steady. The trick with every gangster I'd ever met *other* than my father had been to show no fear, not even any concern. If you outdid them in boldness, they stopped seeing you as prey and decided it was easier not to see you at all. "Wylder told me to clean up this room. I'm just about finished."

The first man—Axel—narrowed his eyes at me as if he had expected me to simper. But now that my initial shock had faded, I considered the layout of the room and how easily I could dodge around these jerks to the door if they came at me. It never hurt to be prepared.

The guys turned away from me, muttering to themselves. "Why the fuck did Wylder even let an untried chick in here?" the leering dude said in a voice not quite hushed enough. "It hasn't even been two weeks since the Titan bit the dust."

The Titan? Was that one of the Nobles' people—he'd died? Here? I frowned. If it'd been bad enough for these guys to be disturbed about the death two weeks later, it mustn't have been a typical loss while on the job.

"Who knows what goes through the kid's head," Axel said. "He's a loose cannon."

The third guy shot me a dark look and grumbled to the others. "Not as much as that hulking thug of his we all know did Titus in. First he brushes that off, then he's hauling more trash in here?"

I scrubbed the carpet very emphatically, torn between wanting to remind them loud and clear that I could hear them and knowing I was probably much better off if they thought I wasn't listening at all. Just some ditz at Wylder's beck and call. A "groupie." I restrained a shudder.

That hulking thug of his. Did they mean Kaige? I couldn't see anyone describing Gideon or Rowan as hulking or a thug. They thought Kaige—flirty, laid-back Kaige—had killed some dude named the Titan or Titus?

Axel let out a huff. "I hear you. Hopefully Ezra will too when he gets back. By now, the kid should be more careful about who he lets into his quarters."

They walked away, and I realized I'd been scrubbing a spot that was already clean for the last minute. I paused, catching my breath.

Either those assholes were wrong… or Kaige was the kind of guy who'd murder one of his own colleagues. I'd better keep that in mind—and be a little more careful how I dealt with Mr. Flirtatious going forward.

6

Mercy

By the time I was done, my shoulders were aching, my bandaged wound burning, and the weariness seemed to have sunk into my bones. It wasn't as if I'd gotten the best of sleep last night. As I straightened up and stretched, my back protested. I collapsed on the sofa that I'd just finished wiping off.

I looked down at my borrowed T-shirt. I'd gotten water splashed on it, bits of debris were sticking to it, and I was pretty sure the stink from the room had sunk right through it all the way to my skin. I needed a shower, stat.

I gave the room one last look before I left. The carpet was unmarked, if a bit damp, and all the furniture clean, the garbage bags set to the side since I didn't know where they went. I couldn't see any reason for Wylder to complain. No, I enjoyed imagining the smirk falling off his face when he realized I'd handled it all without faltering once.

As I climbed up the stairs, Gideon stalked right past me, his eyes glued to his tablet screen. I was abruptly aware of just how tightly—and kind of see-through-ly—my shirt was clinging to my chest. I folded my arms over the most questionable spots, and the movement drew his gaze.

He glanced at my arms over my chest and then at my face, with a distant air as if he wasn't totally sure who I was. Without speaking, he walked on. Alrighty then. It wasn't as if I needed his attention.

The bathroom Kaige had shown me before contained a narrow but perfectly serviceable shower stall. I soaked under the steaming hot water for several minutes, rubbing the expensive-smelling soap someone had left in a cabinet all over me, until I was sure I'd gotten the last traces of grime off.

My bandage ended up soaked—oops. I peeled it off carefully and examined the stitched-up flesh underneath. The line of the gunshot wound glared starkly red against my pale skin, but a scab was already forming along it. I dug through the drawers until I found a half-empty tube of antiseptic and a roll of gauze, smeared most of the rest of the tube over the wound, and then wrapped a few layers of gauze around my arm. That'd have to do.

I grimaced, tugging my still-grimy shirt back over my head, but when I returned to the guest bedroom Wylder had set me up in, a fresh tee and sweats lay on the bed. I looked around, but there wasn't anybody here.

The only people who might have noticed the state of my clothes were those leering jerks who'd been talking smack about Wylder and Kaige... and Gideon. Had he sent someone to make sure I had something halfway decent to wear? The thought that he'd have bothered was flattering and uncomfortable at the same time. I didn't like accepting favors any more than Wylder liked giving them out.

Too often, it turned out there were strings attached.

Since I'd fled the restaurant last night, I'd been living moment to moment. I had to start thinking more clearly about the future. And part of that meant figuring out how to take care of myself so Wylder wouldn't have any grounds to call me a burden.

As I changed into the clean clothes, I moved my engagement ring and the cocaine-scented fifties from one pocket to another. The sight of the ring made my jaw clench, but Kaige was right. I'd left my purse behind in the restaurant; everything else I owned was in the Katz house that Colt would have thoroughly swept by now. This was the only thing of value I had left, so I had to use it. It'd definitely give me enough cash to buy plenty of essentials so I wasn't relying on Noble charity or scavenging drug money.

There was just one thing I couldn't replace with cash. I'd find a way to get that back as soon as I could. The fifties should even pay my way. The rest... The less I thought about my old life, the better.

My stomach rumbled. It had to be way past lunch, and I'd recovered enough from the stink to rediscover my appetite.

I made my way back to the kitchen without running into any of the guys. Sighing with relief, I headed for the fridge. I wouldn't be surprised if Wylder walked in and demanded I get started on his next task for me. If I didn't get anything into my stomach first, I'd probably hit him in his stupidly perfect face.

I found some leftover pasta in the refrigerator and put it in the microwave to heat. While I waited, a girl I vaguely remembered from the party walked in. It was the blonde who'd been shimmying on the edge of the pool table I'd just cleaned.

The look on her face was of absolute fury. As she came to a stop in front of me, planting her hands on her hips, I could feel the venom coming off her in waves. How the hell could she hate me that much when I had no idea who she even was?

"What the fuck are you doing here?" she demanded.

I blinked at her innocently. "What do you mean?"

She sneered. "I mean *here*. In this kitchen, in this house. You were at the party last night, weren't you? Why didn't you leave? Do you want me to show you the way out?"

"As a matter of fact, I'm a guest," I said.

She looked down at my modest T-shirt and smirked. Her own deep V-neck top was skintight and dipped practically to her nipples. "If you're going to try and seduce the guys, that's not going to work."

I rolled my eyes. "Good thing I have no interest in seducing them then."

She scowled. "I know girls like you. But trust me, they don't last here very long."

What exactly was her problem? "I don't give a flying fuck about what you think of me," I said. "You're welcome to try to kick me out, but somehow I think you'll find yourself *knocked* out instead. Give it a shot."

The girl gaped at me in disbelief. The microwave pinged, announcing my food was ready. I dipped into the slightest of mocking curtsies. "Now if you will excuse me..."

I tried to move toward the microwave, but she blocked my path. "No way."

Annoyance crept in. She was wasting my time—and getting between me and my food. I'd dealt with plenty of girls like her all through high school: all talk, no action. If she really wanted a fight, I was happy to give her one. But I didn't think she'd enjoy the result.

"You're blocking my way," I said coolly.

"Oh yeah? What are you going to do about it?" Her voice had grown increasingly high-pitched through our short conversation. And man, she was standing so close to me I could smell her strong perfume. How much of that crap had she doused herself with?

I shrugged. "Oh, I don't know. Maybe I should ask your boyfriend why you're so obsessed with defending his honor. Which one of them is it? I mean, you must be dating at least one of them if you're getting this worked up about it, right?"

Her expression twitched. With savage satisfaction, I knew I had hit a nerve.

The girl got right up to my face, her straw-pale hair swinging, spit practically flying at me. "I protect what's mine. And I don't let any bitch just walk in here and pretend she knows what she's doing. So you better take the fuck off with that attitude or else..."

Instead of finishing her threat, she poked me on my arm, right over my bullet wound. I winced at the needle of pain that shot through the muscle.

I balled my fists at my side. "Wrong move, bitch."

I was about to punch the living daylights out of her, consequences be damned, when a voice spoke from behind me. "Gia, back off."

The girl who was apparently named Gia looked toward the door and faltered. "Oh. I was just— Wylder wouldn't want her—"

Rowan ambled into the room, his expression mild. "Wylder knows she's here. He told her she could stay, for now." Had an edge come into his voice with those words? "Do you want to take it up with him?"

Gia stepped away from me. "I don't trust her. You can tell him that. I've met enough girls to know trouble when I see it."

"Right now I'm pretty sure you're the one making the trouble," Rowan said. "Get out of here, and leave Mercy alone."

His voice stayed casual, but there was a hint of steel underneath it that I'd never heard before. Whether because of his own authority or simply his association with Wylder, Gia shut her mouth. She gave me one last look and surreptitiously flipped me off before scampering out of the kitchen.

Rowan stopped in the middle of the room as if he thought it was better not to get any closer to me. "Gia's a bitch to pretty much everybody who isn't Wylder," Rowan said. "It's nothing personal. She's annoying but mostly harmless."

Was he seriously trying to make conversation? After everything that had happened? "Thanks for the tip," I replied with dripping sarcasm and returned to my meal.

I expected him to leave, but he stayed there, watching me take the plate of pasta out of the microwave. I set it on the island and found a fork, but I couldn't just dig in with him as an audience. "*What*?"

"I didn't say anything," Rowan said, but he stepped closer. His eyes were hooded, his expression almost unreadable.

For a second, I found myself searching for the guy I'd known all those years ago, the boy with eyes that sparkled the moment they found mine in the crowded hall of the high school and the easy smile grazing his lips that made me want to know everything about him. How much of him was left under that nonchalant façade he was putting on?

How much of him had ever been real to begin with?

"If you don't want anything, you could let me eat in peace," I said.

He snorted. "Is that what you came here for? To find *peace*?"

"You know why I'm here. Why *you're* here, I don't have a clue. But frankly, I don't care. So run off to your master, since we both know you never gave a shit about me."

His eyes flashed, but I forced myself to focus on my food, jabbing a piece of penne with a little more force than was strictly required. I'd eat, and then I'd get out of here if he wouldn't.

"I only came in because I saw how Gia was going at you," Rowan said after a moment.

"I wasn't worried about Gia," I said. "So if you're waiting for a thank you, it's not coming. I was handling her by myself just fine, and I most definitely didn't need your help."

"Right," Rowan said in a voice that held far too much meaning. "Because Mercy Katz never needs *anyone's* help."

I glared at him, but images from the seventh-grade field trip when we first started talking rose up in my mind despite my best intentions.

My classmates hadn't known everything about my father, but they'd gotten enough of the gist over the years to be nervous of me—and resentful of the fact that I made them nervous. At the museum that day, someone had dared me to climb inside an antique wardrobe. Refusing to show any fear had mattered more to me than the fear I had very definitely been feeling.

As soon as I'd climbed inside, they'd jammed something to hold the door shut. I could still remember the snickering, the footsteps fading away, and the expanding realization that I was trapped, in the dark, just like—

The walls had begun to close in on me. No amount of shoving got me out, and after what felt like an hour, I curled into a ball, muttering to myself to try to hold back the terror sinking its talons into my mind. I'd been crouched there, shaking, when the door had yanked open and a head topped with ash-blond hair had appeared in front of me.

Rowan had come to the junior high from a different elementary school. I'd barely noticed him before. But when I couldn't stop rocking, he'd squeezed in there with me, grasped my hand, and talked about all the ridiculous things he could say about the kids who'd locked me in until my panic attack receded.

I'd never trusted anyone at school before. Never really trusted *anyone*, full stop. But Rowan... Rowan had convinced me he was worth it.

And then he'd thrown all my loyalty and love in my face.

Rowan took another step toward me, the movement bringing me back to the present. There was something in his eyes, a low kindling fire, one that might have been anger or desire or both.

"You shouldn't be here," he said, his voice low.

"Really?" I said. "And who the fuck are you to tell me what I should or shouldn't do?"

He flinched. As if *I'd* hurt him. Me, the one who'd given him everything from my first kiss to my virginity. The one who'd spilled all my darkest secrets to him, always expecting him to run away, more reassured every time he didn't. I'd thought his love meant I was more than just my father's daughter, a worthless girl.

But he'd run away after all. He had no claim on me now, no right to try to tell me anything about how to live my life. He'd thrown that away when he threw *me* away.

"It's for your own good, Mer," he said.

"My good or yours?" I stood up, my food forgotten. I'd lost my appetite.

Rowan's eye swept down my body and then up again as if he'd been looking for something he hadn't found. Like him, I'd changed too, a lot of it in ways he couldn't see.

"This isn't going to end well," he said finally.

I snorted. Yeah, it was definitely himself he was worried about. What did my being here cost him? "What are you so afraid of?"

"I'm not afraid," he snapped. "Not anymore."

What did he mean by that?

Fuck it, it didn't matter. I didn't have to play his games. I brushed past him. "You just don't want to deal with the fact that I'm here or to face up to what you did all those years ago."

"That isn't true," he said as I headed for the door. "I did what had to be done. I don't feel any regret."

My heart stuttered at his words. It turned out Rowan Finlay still had the ability to hurt me.

When I didn't speak, he kept going. "Walk away from all of this. Your dad is gone; you can start fresh. Maybe this is a good thing for you, just what you needed."

He had some fucking nerve. "My freedom shouldn't have come at the cost of innocent lives. Besides, you lost any right to give me advice when you vanished on me." I spun to face him again. "I never had a normal life, and I never expected to get one. Who says I'd want one anyway?"

I turned on my heel and stalked out of the kitchen.

7

Kaige

I COULDN'T SLEEP. AGAIN. OF COURSE, THAT MIGHT HAVE had something to do with my drinking habits. The staff kept the mini fridge in my bedroom well-stocked with energy drinks, and I was in the habit of guzzling them throughout the day whenever I had the urge. My last one had been just before dinner, and a restless buzz was still tickling through my veins.

At least it was a pleasant night to be up. A warm summer breeze licked over me where I lay swinging in the hammock tied between the trunks of two of the biggest trees around the side of the Noble mansion. Crickets chirped in an erratic melody. A smattering of stars and a half-moon peeked between the leaves overhead. Ridiculously peaceful. Maybe I'd manage to drift off for an hour or two right here.

The shadows around the edge of the house shifted, catching my attention. I sat up slowly, my eyes narrowing, my instincts kicking into gear. The unmistakable form of a body darted past the shrubs lining the front walk. Was somebody trying to break in?

But no—the figure was headed away from the house. Whoever it was moved stealthily, folding into the shadows so deftly that if any of the men who patrolled the grounds at night had looked that way, they must have missed it. Interesting. A worthy opponent.

I smiled to myself, all possibility of sleep vanishing under a jolt of adrenaline. I hadn't had a mission in weeks, and honestly I'd been dying for an assignment. I missed the rush that came with it, but Wylder had me keeping a low profile after what had happened with Titus. He didn't want to give anyone the chance to accuse me of screwing up a job until my name was cleared.

I clenched my teeth at the thought. I didn't care about proving anything to anybody except him, but it would be nice if people didn't think I went around murdering my colleagues—no matter how much of a prick they were—for no good reason.

Tracking the figure's movement, I stayed still on the hammock. When the person dashed from the bushes toward the brick wall that framed the sides and back of the yard, I squinted to get a better look.

It was a woman. Her hair was tied back in a braid, and she was wearing clothes that covered all of her body except her arms, but there was no missing the shape of the perky mounds on her chest outlined against the faint moonlight.

I was so arrested by that delightful sight that it took me a second to recognize who it was.

Mercy Katz cast a glance up and down the road before jogging out of sight past the wall. Huh. Where was the Claws' princess heading in such a hurry and so secretly? I got to my feet, itching to find out.

I couldn't deny that Mercy had caught my eye the moment she had walked into the party, her chin raised, fearless and demanding Wylder's attention. There weren't many people in this county who'd talk to the heir to the Nobles that way. Most of the women around here started babbling or simpering the second he was in their vicinity. If I hadn't respected the guy so much, I might have found it annoying. But hey, there was always plenty of action for me too.

Loping after Mercy, I reached toward my phone. Should I alert Wylder that his "Kitty Cat" was on the prowl? Maybe she'd given up all hope of him joining her revenge plan after all. I wouldn't really have blamed her after the mind-numbing chores he'd been putting her up to. Just today, he had made her pull out the weeds in the back lawn using just her hands. I shook my head, my mouth twitching with amusement when I remembered the death glare she'd shot his way.

But she'd followed through, as gorgeous and defiant as ever. She seemed pretty serious about proving herself.

What if all that had been for show, and she had ulterior motives after all? She could be sneaking off to meet some co-conspirator.

After a moment's debate, I left my phone in my pocket and continued after her. I'd look like an idiot if I raised the alarm for no reason, and half of Ezra Noble's staff saw me as an idiot already. Anyway, I'd find out more if I saw where she went first.

And a chase would be more fun.

Around the fence, I caught sight of her farther down the street, heading toward the corner. I hustled after her, setting my feet as quietly as I could and keeping close to the trees at the edge of the neighbors' lawns so she wouldn't notice me.

It was harder to hang back far enough heading down the steep slope that led to the busy downtown streets below the hill. I let Mercy get more of a lead, but my gaze never left her.

Just as she reached the bottom, where traffic was whizzing by, she raised her hand. My muscles started to tense with the thought that she might have had plans to meet someone behind our backs, but a moment later, a striped car pulled up to the curb. She'd only been flagging a cab.

Of course, that cab could be taking her somewhere Wylder would want to know about. As she popped into the back seat, I hustled the rest of the way down the hill.

Thankfully, there were plenty of taxis cruising around downtown at this time of night, hunting for bar-goers who needed a safe ride home. I spotted one about to zip right by me and dove into the street in front of it.

The tires screeched, the hood tapping my thighs as it just barely stopped without knocking me over. I grinned at the driver through the windshield, my adrenaline spiking just the way I liked it.

"Y-you almost died," the cabbie stammered.

"But I didn't." I bounded around to dive into the back. "I need a ride. Follow that yellow-and-green taxi that just stopped at the lights up ahead. I'll pay you double if you step on it."

Money could grease plenty of wheels. The driver got over his shock just like that, and in moments we were rumbling after Mercy without her any the wiser.

To my surprise, Mercy's taxi headed out of the city and into the Bend. Wouldn't Colt's men be on the hunt for her there? My suspicions prickling to the surface again, I leaned forward in the seat as if I could figure out Mercy's intentions if I stared at the car hard enough. What was she doing walking back to the den of the tiger?

Wylder didn't bother doing much business directly in the Bend, but I was pretty sure the part we'd ended up in was former Claws' territory. Mercy's taxi stopped in a residential neighborhood, and I asked my cabbie to pull over at the other end of the street. After handing him a wad of cash, I got out and covered the rest of the distance on foot.

Mercy had disappeared into the backyard of a big brick house farther down by the corner. I frowned, venturing closer. Movement flickered in the shadows, and then suddenly she was bounding off the high branch of an oak tree onto a second-floor balcony.

All right, so the girl had some climbing skills. She was part-cat after all.

Smirking, I stayed in the shadows to watch. She landed on the balcony railing so lightly I couldn't hear the impact and sprang toward the door there without hesitation. From the looks of it, she'd done this a million times. With a quick jiggle of the handle, she disappeared inside the house.

I eased into the yard. The house looked empty, no lights on, no vehicles in the driveway. An obvious explanation occurred to me—and was confirmed a moment later when I spotted a beefy guy lurking by a car on the other side of the cross-street in front of the house.

No one was home, but the place was under surveillance. Why had Mercy figured it was worth the risk of coming back here?

But she'd managed it without the heavies staked out in front noticing her. After about fifteen minutes, she reappeared and launched herself back onto the tree. I couldn't see exactly how she made it down. Stepping back against the hedge next door, I let her hustle past me, a leaf she hadn't noticed snagged in her dark hair. Then I stalked after her, a smile curling my lips in anticipation.

Probably looking for a busier spot where she could hail another cab, she set off at a brisk pace. After a couple of blocks, I figured we were far enough from the house to avoid the notice of what I assumed were Steel Knights sentries.

With several swift strides, I caught up to her, tucking my hand around her elbow as I reached her. "Well, fancy running into you here."

She startled, slamming her hand against my chest before her gaze had found mine. Recognition lit there, followed by a mixture of wariness and irritation. Not exactly the response I'd want to provoke in her, but we could work on that.

"Fuck, you scared the living daylights out of me," she hissed, jerking her arm out of my grasp. "What are you doing here?"

Still smiling, I stepped closer, forcing her back against the wooden fence of the nearest yard. I set one hand on either side of her, just an inch from her shoulders. Her eyes darted to the side, and I could see her calculating her chances of escape: very slim.

I hadn't been quite this close to her before. Her scent hit my nose, like some kind of wildflowers that had caught on fire. Pretty and fierce at the same time. Perfect for the woman in front of me.

"I should be asking you that," I said casually. "You came to the Nobles for help. Of course your movements are going to be monitored, especially when you leave the house in the middle of the night like some kind of thief."

She scowled at me. "I had no idea that place had become my prison or that I wasn't allowed to leave."

"I wouldn't say it's a prison, but we have to take precautions. A lot of people would like a piece of the Nobles." I cocked a brow at her. "Why on Earth would you come back to the Bend in the middle of the night when somebody is trying to assassinate you? Whatever brought you here must be nothing short of world-ending."

"It's none of your fucking business," she spat out.

I leaned closer. "I think it *is* my business. You made it mine when you came to us for help."

Mercy huffed in response, but I could see her pupils dilating. She shifted, visibly swallowing, her body just inches from mine. Was that a tiny tremor running through those delicious curves?

My grin widened. "Does the kitten like to be dominated?"

"Fuck you," Mercy said, but she didn't make any move to struggle. My hands slid down the fence, brushing the sides of her arms, and her breath caught just slightly. Ah ha. She might be pissed off about that, but she liked it too.

I resisted the urge to see how she'd react if I trailed my fingers over the mounds now straining against the thin fabric of her T-shirt. As much as I was enjoying the moment, I did have a job to do. "Now tell me, what are you doing here? Or do I need to haul you back to Wylder and let him ask the questions?"

At first she didn't answer. My hands skimmed down to the level of her waist, and I gave into the impulse to splay my fingers over the sides of her full hips. She tipped toward me just a bit before reining her response in. Jesus Christ, this girl was built generously in all the right places.

"So, hauling it is?" I said, both teasing and serious.

"We don't have to bring anyone else into this," she bit out. "I was just stopping by my house—or at least, what was my house. I had something there I wasn't willing to leave behind."

"Didn't we talk about this? You don't need to stick your neck into harm's way—just use that bastard's engagement ring to get whatever money you need."

She grimaced. "There are some things money can't buy, you know." She was quiet for a beat before she rummaged in her pocket and then held up something in her hand. I inspected it under the moonlight. It was a silver bracelet, too tiny to fit Mercy's wrist and cheap-looking—the kind you'd give a kid. The words *Little Angel* were engraved into the plate clasped to the chain.

I blinked at her with genuine confusion. "You risked your life for *that*?"

Mercy stuffed it back into her pocket with a scowl. "I don't expect you to understand. My mother gave it to me. It's all I have left of her."

I stared at her for a few seconds, and she didn't flinch away from my gaze. She was telling the truth. I took a step back, giving her a bit of space, a twinge of guilt running through my stomach.

I'd been playing around, trying to provoke her, when this whole expedition meant a hell of a lot more to her than I could have guessed. Now I felt like an ass.

Silence stretched between us. I groped for words and said the first thing that came to mind. “I do understand.”

She snorted. “Right.”

“No, really. I—I didn’t have the greatest relationship with my dad, but I’ve still worn his dog tags since the day he died.”

Her gaze dropped to my chest. “Are they invisible dog tags?”

I glowered at her. “No. I fucking lost them somewhere a couple of months ago. But until then— Anyway, the point is I get it. If I knew where they were, even if it was behind enemy lines, I’d go for them too.”

Her tone softened but stayed wry. “Maybe you should look harder then.”

I didn’t like the direction this conversation was going in. I’d wanted to get under her skin, not the other way around. I took another step away and raised my chin toward the road. “Let’s head back before people start questioning where you went.”

Her eyebrows arched, but her tone turned hesitant. “You’re not going to rat me out?”

I laughed. “Do you want me to?”

She shook her head, looking unconvinced.

“Come on, let’s get some sleep. Not together of course. I mean, unless you really beg.” I added the last part with a chuckle, and she punched me in the arm.

“Fat chance of that,” she muttered, but right then, I knew I was going to find a way to have her.

8

Mercy

A SCRAP OF THE CURTAIN BEING JERKED ASIDE WAS followed by a blare of sunlight on my closed eyelids. I groaned, shielding my face against the sudden brightness, and rolled over on the bed.

When I looked up, I found myself staring right into Wylder's striking green eyes. He was leaning over me, his face just inches from mine. At the sight, I woke up completely, with a jolt that made me hit my head hard against the headboard. I winced.

"What the hell do you think you're doing?" I snarled, rubbing the sore spot.

"You seem to have forgotten, so I'll politely remind you. This is my house." Wylder offered a lazy smirk and stepped back. "If you don't enjoy my hospitality, you're welcome to shack up somewhere else overnight."

I made a face at him. "I don't exactly have anywhere else to go." Not even my own house really belonged to me anymore, not with Steel Knights thugs staked out on the street outside. "And shouldn't you be happy to have me at your beck and call?"

The edge in my voice didn't appear to faze Wylder at all. If anything, his smirk widened. "Oh, don't worry, I am."

"Rise and shine," Kaige declared from behind him. Before I knew what was happening, he'd scooped me right out from under the covers and up into his arms. As he carried me toward the door, I squirmed in his arms, twisting this way and that until his grip loosened.

Landing a solid kick, I spun from his hold and onto my feet—a little too easily considering his bulk. Annoyed by the suspicion that he'd let me win and by that cocky grin he was now aiming at me, I shook a fist at him. "Try to carry me off again and the next thing getting carried will be your ass into a morgue."

A laugh exploded out of him. That wasn't the reaction I'd been going for. "You'll think it's less funny when you find out how serious I am," I informed him.

Wylder tsked. "Careful, the kitty cat hasn't been declawed after all."

I bristled all over again. "Don't call me that."

Wylder just kept smirking. "Come on, you've made us late for breakfast. And I, for one, am absolutely starving."

I followed them to the kitchen where Gideon and Rowan were waiting, talking to Anthea. Rowan was wearing one of what seemed to be his usual suits, looking overdressed next to all the other guys in their jeans and casual button-ups.

Gideon had a cup of coffee in his hand, stroking the handle as if he was protective of it. His tongue flicked out over the silver ring that protruded from one side of his lower lip. I couldn't help tracking the movement. There was something weirdly sensual about it that provoked a response I didn't entirely like low in my belly. Even with his bizarre blue hair and cool eyes, Gideon was just as good-looking as the others in a remote, alien sort of way.

I looked up to see Anthea observing me like a hawk and quickly averted my gaze.

There was nothing cooking on the stove yet. Even though I was wary of her, Anthea was a damn good chef, and the thought of her French toast was making my mouth water. I glanced around. "What's for breakfast?"

"I don't know," Wylder said. "Why don't you tell us, since you're the one cooking today?"

I took a few steps back. Abso-fucking-lutely not. "I can't cook. At all." That wasn't technically true. I had to make myself food all the time, but only basics like a PB&J sandwich. No way was I up to Anthea's level. And I could just tell she'd jump on any reason to criticize my efforts.

Wylder shrugged. "Too bad. You're going to today. So, chop, chop. Get to it."

I suppressed a sigh. The ache in my fingers after the many weeds I'd yanked out of the lawn yesterday were all the reminder I needed that what Wylder wanted, Wylder got—unless *I* wanted to forget my whole revenge plan and spend the rest of my life in hiding, stewing ineffectually over Colt's betrayal. Fuck.

Well, if he didn't like my breakfast, he'd have no one to blame but himself, now would he?

I reluctantly stepped behind the stove, even grabbing a polka-dotted apron that was hanging from a hook on the wall. Everything in the kitchen seemed so harmless and homely, it almost didn't feel that it belonged in a house belonging to Ezra Noble, the gang boss revered by everybody in Paradise Bend.

"I think I want bacon," Wylder said after he seemed to ponder over it for a few seconds. "What about you, Kaige?"

The brawny asshole grinned with a gleam in his eyes that suggested he was remembering our secret adventure last night. At least it seemed like he'd kept his mouth shut about that like he'd said he would. He tapped his chin cheekily. "I like the sound of an onion and cheese omelet."

"I've already eaten," Anthea said with a hint of disdain.

Gideon didn't bother looking up from his coffee. "Whatever they're having. Food is just fuel."

"I thought *I* was deciding what's for breakfast," I said. "Who said anything about taking orders?"

"Rowan?" Wylder asked, ignoring me.

Rowan shrugged. "Bacon and eggs works for me too."

Somehow it irritated me that he hadn't asked for anything else, like he was trying to cut me a break I hadn't asked for. Gritting my teeth, I stomped over to the fridge and retrieved an onion, a block of cheese, a carton of eggs, and a package of bacon. I knew at least enough to figure out that the onion should go in first.

I found a cutting board and a knife and started chopping away. It took all of three seconds before my eyes stung with tears.

Wylder stepped up behind me. "That's not how you do it."

I scowled. "Will you let me work?"

Wylder smiled, feigning innocence. "I'm just trying to be helpful, since you said you weren't much of a cook and all."

I nearly rolled my eyes out of my head. "No thanks. I'm sure I can figure it out on my own."

The asshole reached for my hand anyway. For one instant, I thought he would pry the knife right out of my hand. Instead, his fingers curled around mine over the handle. A thrum ran through my body as his strong hand flexed, adjusting his grip, holding me in place with his other hand settling on my waist. Warmth washed through me all down my side.

"I don't think you can, Kitty Cat," he said in a sexy, bossy voice that left me breathless despite myself. My insides clenched. He was trying to take charge... and I kind of wanted to let him, damn it.

From the corner of my eye, I noticed Rowan straightening up to get a closer look. When I glanced at him, daring him to say something, he went back to fiddling with a delivery menu someone had left on the island.

Wylder's breath tickled hot down my neck. "I think I need to teach you how to chop up onions nicely. You see, cooking is an art."

I contained the shiver that ran down my spine at his proximity. I wanted to turn around and shove him away, while another insane part of me had the urge to pull him even closer just so I could soak up all of his heat.

"If you don't create the perfect base, nothing you make is going to taste good." As he spoke, he directed my hands back to the cutting board and slowly chopped the first few slices, his actions almost sensual. I bit my lip as his hips brushed mine. He practically had me locked in an embrace. His leather-and-brandy scent filled my nose, and I might have leaned into him just the slightest bit—

Wylder stepped away with a sly look on his face that I wanted to smack right off it. "See, not that hard, right?"

I glared at him. He knew exactly what he'd been doing to me. Still grinning, he took a seat on the kitchen island next to Kaige, who was watching me appreciatively.

"I could get used to seeing you in an apron," the bigger guy said.

I waved the knife at him. "In your dreams, maybe."

Once the onions were sizzling, I cracked the eggs one by one, trying to remember how I'd seen my grandma cook for me whenever I went to her house. I was aware of everybody's stare on my back—especially Kaige's, whose hot gaze made my stomach knot. Anthea seemed to be studying my every move as if she were going to write a report on my performance.

Rowan and Gideon stayed in the periphery. Any time my gaze slipped over Rowan, he was scowling almost as if he was annoyed to be there, spinning a pen between his fingers.

After I'd beaten the eggs with a fork, I rummaged in the kitchen cabinets, searching for the pepper and salt. Then I scrambled to turn down the heat, since the onions were quickly heading from lightly browned to blackened. I'd never hear the end of it if I burned this meal.

"For somebody who doesn't know how to cook, you're doing it quite well," Anthea observed dryly. I didn't quite know what to make of her. I definitely didn't get friendly vibes from her.

Somehow I didn't think she meant her words as a compliment. It was hard not to wonder what tricks she had up her sleeve that were deadlier than her little truth serum. "Thanks," I muttered.

As I started to toss the eggs in the pan, Kaige took a deep sniff of the air. "Smells great."

"It's just onions and eggs."

"With a hint of you," he said with a wink. "That's what makes it better."

A smile tugged at my lips despite myself. First Wylder was getting to me, then Kaige—what the hell was wrong with me? I wiped the smile off my face, replacing it with a frown.

These guys were my potential allies—nothing more than that. They sure as hell weren't my friends. I'd been slaving away for the past two days without much sign of anything changing.

When the omelet was done, I scraped it onto plates in four portions. Then I popped several strips of bacon onto the pan. Feeling pleased with how well I'd stayed on top of things so far, I threw a few pieces of bread into the toaster oven for good measure.

Anthea came around the counter to inspect me. I pushed the bacon around the pan with the spatula, trying to fry it as evenly as possible. That was the goal, right? If I remembered right, Grandma's trick had been to hold the pan a bit higher than the flame and then toss it with a flick of her wrist.

I grasped the handle, but for a moment the memory of my grandmother in her kitchen gripped me so vividly I couldn't move. A burning sensation crept up through my chest to the back of my eyes.

Before I could get a hold of myself, Anthea brushed past me, her shoulder hitting mine. The force of it made me stumble. A few drops of hot oil splashed into my skin. I hissed in pain and almost dropped the pan.

I shoved it back onto the stove and flipped on the tap. The cool water washed over the stinging of the much more literal burn, making me wince.

"I'm sorry, I didn't realize you were so distracted," Anthea said, not looking even a little bit apologetic. No way had that been an accident. She'd been trying to screw with me. What had I done to her to make her hate my guts?

Rowan was on his feet, but he stayed by the island as Kaige, who'd also hopped up, offered me a towel to dab at my sensitive skin.

"Thanks, but I'm fine," I said, keeping my voice even.

"You need ice?" Kaige asked.

Wylder yawned. "Didn't you hear her? She said she's fine. I think you burnt the bacon, Kitty Cat."

What an absolute asshole. I immediately switched off the stove and worked at prying up the over-fried bits of the bacon.

"I'm starving. Serve the breakfast," Wylder ordered as if it wasn't his aunt's fault I'd gotten sidetracked. When I glared at him, he raised his eyebrows. "What are you waiting for?"

I turned away. I couldn't let his heckling bother me. Nothing that happened here mattered as long as it led to Colt getting crushed under an onslaught of Noble rage.

I slapped the plates down on the island in front of each of the guys and stepped away, grabbing a piece of toast and slathering peanut butter on it for myself. Wylder pretended to gnaw on a particularly difficult piece of bacon. "I've had better."

"It's not totally awful for a beginner," Kaige offered with a smile.

Rowan looked a little pained, which might have been because of my presence or his feelings about my cooking. Gideon wolfed everything down between delicate sips of his beloved coffee without a word. At least the food appeared to have been edible.

Just as they were finishing up, the big guy with the shaved head who'd hassled me while I was cleaning two days ago appeared at the door. He was carrying a lit cigarette on his lips which he slowly took a drag of.

A cloud of annoyance appeared on Wylder's face. "You know no one's supposed to smoke in here, Axel."

"Says who?" Axel asked with a challenge in his voice. "This isn't your part of the house."

Wylder remained unfazed. "The rule is no smoke around me and my men, *anywhere* in *my* house. If you're in the mood for criticizing, why don't we talk about how you still haven't gotten Trent back in line?"

Axel muttered a curse and threw the cigarette to the floor, where he crushed the butt with his shoe. Instead of leaving, he stepped farther into the kitchen.

"You're one to talk. What have you done to solve the issue?" The older man's gaze fell on me. "Meanwhile you're letting strangers walk all over the house."

"Why should I do your work for you?" Wylder said. "And she's here for a reason. As a matter of fact—" A slow smile came over his face. "It might be your lucky day after all. I know just the way I'm going to fix that little problem."

I eyed him, already knowing he was going to drag me into some new scheme I wasn't going to like. He grinned back at me. "How'd you like to get out of the house for a bit, Princess?"

"To do what, exactly?"

"Patience, patience. All will become clear." He stood up. "Stay here and clean up while I get the details sorted out."

Just like that, he walked out of the kitchen, beckoning for the other three guys to follow him. Prick. I aimed my middle finger at his retreating back. Kaige chuckled, but he left his plate on the island like the others did as they all headed out at their boss's bidding. Anthea shot me one last narrow look and stalked after them.

Axel's phone rang, and he walked to the far corner to talk in a low voice. I liked his company even less than the others', but whatever.

When I went to grab the plates, my hand stopped over the flyer Rowan had been toying with. He'd been doodling on it too. A little pen sketch had expanded the flower logo for the restaurant into a whole garden of blooms trailing around the border.

He'd always been so good at drawing. Apparently a few things hadn't changed. Before I could second-guess the impulse, I snatched up the flyer and folded it into my pocket.

Instead of washing the dishes, I just dumped them in the sink and ran some water over them. Let Wylder complain if he wanted to.

Axel ended his call and looked around the room, glaring at me as if annoyed that I was the only one left. "Where the hell did Wylder head off to?"

Did he think I was somehow the Noble heir's keeper? "I don't know. He said he'd be back." Of course, he hadn't mentioned whether whatever details he had to sort out would take minutes or hours. I wouldn't put it past him to leave me sitting here waiting for the rest of the day.

But looking at Axel, a light bulb went off inside my head. I needed all the information I could gather to get myself an edge around here, and he definitely knew a few things I'd be interested to hear more about.

People tended to say more if they figured you already knew what they were talking about. I forced a smile way sweeter than he deserved. "Hey, no hard feelings about the other day. I get how concerned you'd be about strangers after what happened to the Titan."

Axel's expression stayed wary, but he didn't bite my head off for bringing up the subject, which was a start. "What's it to you?" he growled.

"I just mean it's kind of hard for me not to worry when people are going around killing each other around here. Why the heck would Kaige go off on one of Ezra's own men?" I shook my head disapprovingly.

Axel didn't correct me, which meant my guess that he'd been talking about Kaige being the culprit was right. "Good question. Maybe you should ask the kid who's covering for him."

I tipped my head like the ditzy girl he no doubt saw me as. "As if Wylder's going to tell *me* what really went on. He obviously cares more about protecting his friends."

That remark seemed to hit the right spot. Axel let out a disgruntled sound. "It's clear as day who must have done it. Who else could have tossed Titus over the goddamn fire escape?"

So the Titan—or Titus—whatever his name was—had been thrown off the fire escape to his death? What a way to go. "Yeah," I said carefully, leaving space for him to fill in the blanks. "I mean, after all, Kaige is just so..."

"No one else could have overpowered him," Axel burst out. "The young guys and their stupid tempers—all riled up because Titus laid it to him straight about what the rest of us think of his 'boss.' Kaige practically killed him right then. Threatened to put him in a grave for daring to speak up, and guess what? He did."

9

Mercy

Axel's last words had barely faded from the air when Wylder strode back into the kitchen. He glanced from me to Axel and frowned. "Having a little chat?"

"She's smarter than she looks," Axel said, nodding at me. I groaned internally. Obviously he was happy that I seemed to agree with his theories about Wylder and Kaige, but why the hell did he have to say that?

Now that he'd dropped that little bomb, Axel ambled out. I hoped at the next party he stepped in vomit *and* sat on someone's chair turd.

"I see you've made friends," Wylder said dryly.

I folded my arms in front of my chest. "So, what, I can't talk to people?"

"Talk to my men as much as you like. Axel is an idiot. But I'm guessing you could tell that. What were you hoping to get out of him, Kitty Cat?"

I swallowed hard. Wylder definitely wasn't an idiot, no matter how big a prick he was. Or how big his prick probably was.

Focus, Mercy.

I couldn't tell him that I was asking questions about Kaige and how he was involved in this Titus guy's death. That was obviously a sore spot for him. I groped for the most obvious answer. "I was just asking him about your father. I haven't gotten to meet the old man yet, after all."

"He's out of town on business," Wylder said coolly. At the mention of his father, his eyes turned frosty. Okay, another sore spot. Clearly we had plenty of awful parents to go around between the two of us. No big surprise. If there was a Venn diagram of qualities that made for great gang leaders and fantastic fathers, the circles would barely overlap.

"Where did he go?" I asked.

"What's it to you?"

"I don't know. I figure if I'm asking for the Nobles' help, I should probably loop in the man in charge at some point."

Wylder snorted. "Trust me, you don't want to be anywhere near Ezra Noble. *If* I decide your cause is worthy, I'll handle that side of things. Forget about that for now. I have something for you."

I studied him suspiciously. "Does this have something to do with whatever new job you dreamed up for me?"

"So quick to catch on." Wylder stalked up to me like a tiger on the prowl, stopping just a little too close for my nerves—or my hormones—to stay quiet. "You're tired of cleaning duty, aren't you? Ready for some real action? Well, you're getting your wish. There's an important meeting in a couple of hours. I'll have a dress sent to your room. Wear it and be ready."

I scowled. Was he about to dress me up and parade me in front of people? "I'm not going to a party as your escort."

A laugh spilled out of him. "Trust me, Princess, that's not what I had in mind." With that he whirled around and left, leaving me seething. What was he up to this time?

I went back to the guest room and paced the length of it. Before long, somebody was knocking at my door. I threw it open to reveal the same woman who'd brought me the tee and sweats the first night. Today she had a sequined dress in her hands. Even without seeing it unfolded, I could tell it was absolutely hideous.

"Mr. Noble says to wear this," she said and thrust it and a cosmetics bag at me. Before I could ask any questions, she scurried away.

When I opened the bag, lipsticks, glitter, and mascara fell out of it. Despite Wylder's sarcastic assurance, this stuff definitely had an escort vibe. Holding up the dress to my frame, I shuddered. The thin strips of fabric would cover my nipples and crotch and not a whole lot else.

But he wanted me to say no. This was yet another test. I wasn't here to cater to my dignity, but to avenge all those bodies bleeding out on the restaurant floor.

I discarded my casual clothes, slipping my childhood bracelet and the flyer with Rowan's sketch out of the pants pocket. After a moment's hesitation, I tucked them both into the make-up bag, which was the closest thing I had to a purse. I didn't want to leave the bracelet out of my reach again, and the doodle, well... Call it silly, but there was something vaguely comforting about the idea that I hadn't been *totally* wrong about the guy I'd thought I'd been so close to.

Standing in front of the full-length mirror, I shimmied into the dress. When the silver of it caught the light, it gave a glow to my otherwise pale skin. Unfortunately, way too much of that skin for my liking was on display.

Might as well make the best of it. Aunt Renee had given me lessons in make-up until I'd been able to pull off the kind of look that could stop a man in his tracks, if that was what I was going for. These might not have been the exact cosmetic items I'd have picked, but I could work with them.

When I was done, I stepped back to inspect myself in the mirror again. With the deep red lipstick and my hair falling in loose waves across my shoulders, I could have given a lesser goddess a run for her money, if I did say so myself. Even the bandage around my upper arm looked almost like part of the costume. It was a fierce, avenging warrior goddess they'd get.

I smirked to myself. Wylder's intention of humiliating me was going to backfire on him big time.

Just then, the door burst open and Kaige strode in.

"We can't be late—" He broke off mid-sentence when his eyes landed on me. His feet stalled just inside the doorway, his jaw going slack. If I didn't know any better, I'd think I'd left him speechless.

I waved a hand in front of his face. "Earth to Kaige."

He blinked, and a smile crossed his face that was both sexy and predatory. "I don't know—from the looks of things, I've landed in heaven instead."

When I scoffed at the cheesy line, he walked right up to me. His fingers skimmed down my back, only just grazing my skin but leaving a trail of heat in their wake. Suddenly all sorts of parts of me were waking up in ways I didn't like. *That* wasn't how this was supposed to go.

Kaige tugged a lock of my hair, twisting it around his finger possessively. "You look...wow."

I shook off my body's reaction to him as well as I could. "Thanks."

He held up a pair of heels. "I brought shoes. If you don't like them, blame Wylder."

They were stilettos, the spikes at least three inches high and sharp as needles. Lovely. I made a face but took the shoes from him. Looking on the bright side, if somebody decided to get handsy with me, I could get in both a kick and a stabbing at the same time.

Thankfully I'd gotten in my practice with towering heels at my father's various formal events. When he bothered to bring me along, he wanted to be able to show me off. The heels clicked against the floor as I followed Kaige downstairs to the foyer where Wylder and Rowan—but not Gideon, I noted—were waiting. They looked up simultaneously.

Rowan's stance stiffened. Instead of looking at me, his gaze seemed to latch onto Kaige, whose hand had settled on my upper back. I was deeply aware of it, along with the other pair of eyes watching me.

Appreciation lit on Wylder's face, his gaze roving over me. He inspected every part of my body as if he could see right through my skin-tight dress.

"Look at that," he said in a husky voice. "Kitty Cat cleans up well."

A rush of pleasure climbed up my spine at his compliment. I clamped down on it, mentally cursing myself. I'd have been happier that I'd clearly struck the mark with him if my stupid body wasn't betraying me at the same time.

I walked toward the boys, flipping my hair behind me. "Here I am. What's the big event?"

Rowan turned toward the door, tearing his eyes away from me. "The people we're going to meet today will be mouthy and defiant.

Talking nicely hasn't worked so far. This is going to take force. Are you sure you want in on this?"

Force? With me dressed like this? What the hell were we actually doing here?

But Rowan's tone made me raise my chin. All my life, I'd never backed down from anything. He knew it well. "Of course. I'm ready."

Wylder explained everything in his car. He drove a deep-blue Mustang, which even though it was obviously an older model was sleek and pristine. "Trent has been causing a lot of trouble lately. Your job will be to go in and rile him up, giving us an excuse to step in."

"What's he done?" I asked curiously.

"He hasn't paid his tithe," Kaige said from the seat next to me. Wylder drove the car while Rowan sat beside him. "And he's been mouthing off, acting like he shouldn't have to pay tribute to the Nobles. We need to stamp out his little rebellion before others get ideas."

My father had a special room in our basement, made for people he wanted to punish. Old images flashed in my mind's eyes, souring my mouth.

Wylder was nodding. "You go in, ask for the money, and get him to lose his shit. He won't take you seriously—"

I rolled my eyes. "Why? Because I'm a woman?"

Wylder raised his eyebrows at me in the rearview mirror. "You're a woman, and you're dressed like a hooker. I think the second part is what'll really do the trick."

I glared at him and noticed Rowan watching me surreptitiously. The set of his mouth told me he was annoyed for some reason. I reached into the make-up on my lap and pulled out the doodled-on flyer.

Yeah, it reminded me that the boy I'd loved hadn't all been a lie, but right now I just wanted to get a reaction out of him.

I waved the paper carelessly. "Found this in the kitchen. Hey, Kaige, what's your favorite animal?"

Rowan turned fully in his seat, his jaw tightening even more as he must have recognized the paper. Kaige rubbed his square jaw, pretending to think hard. "I would have to go with a cat." He gave me an impish smile.

I rolled my eyes. "Something else."

"Fine. Can I say dragon, or are mythical creatures not allowed either?"

"I can do that." Making a few swift creases, I tore the flyer into a square. Rowan almost flinched. Just a doodle, but he didn't like me manhandling it, now did he?

"What are you—" he began, and then he seemed to catch on.

I deftly formed a series of folds, smoothed the sides to give it a final shape, and then held it up. "Ta-da!" I offered the origami dragon to Kaige.

"Damn, girl," he said, taking the fragile figure out of my hand. "You'll have to teach me how to do that."

"What will I get in return?"

He waggled his eyebrows. "Anything you want."

"It's a childish game," Wylder announced.

I wrinkled my nose at him. "Let's see you do it then."

He met my gaze in the mirror, and I had to keep myself from squirming at the look in his eyes. "I'm good at everything I do, so I'd imagine I could handle twisting around a bit of paper if I wanted to bother."

I had the itch to kick the back of his seat but controlled the flicker of anger. Instead of giving in to it, I leaned back into the seat. "So where are we headed?"

"People call it the Park," Rowan said tersely.

"And where is that?"

"It's the covered parking lot of a mall," Wylder filled in. "Trent and his main bunch like to hang out there. He's decided to make us come to him. We're going to make him regret that."

Right. And I was the bait. I held back a grimace and peered out the window. A question that'd been niggling at me ever since I'd come down to meet them rose up again. "Where's Gideon?"

Wylder's eyes narrowed. "Fights aren't his strong point. He doesn't normally come along for these kinds of jobs."

"The great Wylder Noble has someone on his team who can't hold his own in a brawl?" I said in mock disbelief.

"What Gideon can or can't do is none of your business," Wylder snapped as if I'd gravely offended him.

Kaige chuckled and ignored the evil eye Wylder shot at him. "Don't mind him. He's just over-protective. Gideon helps out plenty in his own way, with the computers and everything. He gets more done with his brains than I do with these guns." He flexed his biceps. "He's got a lung condition; it acts up if he pushes himself much physically."

"I did say it's none of her business," Wylder reminded him.

I remembered his grousing at Axel over the cigarette. "Is that why nobody's allowed to smoke in the house?"

"You're damn right." Wylder clenched the steering wheel harder. "I protect my own."

"We're here," Rowan announced with what sounded like trepidation.

We pulled into one of the empty parking spots in the lot. This end of the space clearly didn't get used much by your average mallgoer. A few abandoned cars stood sprawled across more than one spot, one missing a door, another with its roof dented in. Spray-painted graffiti mottled the concrete wall nearby. The sound of raucous voices carried from the other side of a couple of parked vans farther across the lot.

"Trent and his crew will be over there." Wylder pointed to the vans and then turned to me. "You know what you have to do?"

"It's not exactly a complex plan. Go in, ask Trent to pay up, listen to him insult me a bit, and then watch the three of you swoop in and kick his ass."

"Right," he said, a hint of sarcasm in his tone. "Trent isn't dangerous, but he thinks he is, which makes him a little unpredictable. So stick to that plan."

I glowered at him. "Like I said, I've got it."

Rowan jumped in. "The first sign of trouble, and you—"

I cut him off. "I *am* here to cause trouble, aren't I?"

Before any of them could lecture me more, I shook out my hair and pushed open the door. I was aware of the three pairs of eyes watching me in the closed space.

"See you boys later," I said as I stepped out of the car.

The guys followed me, moving more quietly. They'd hang back by the vans out of sight until they had all the excuse they needed to take their target down several pegs. I took brisk steps, my stilettos rapping away on the concrete.

The faint notes of hip-hop music drifted toward me. The smells of cheap weed and cheaper beer saturated the air.

As I came around the vans, I found a loose circle with half a dozen guys in ripped jeans lounging in plastic chairs. A woman in a short dress was sitting on one man's lap, batting her eyelashes.

"Which one of you is Trent?" I demanded, jutting my hip out for good measure. If I was going to play a role, I'd damn well sell it.

I'd already guessed the leader of these goons was the dude with the goatee and the beer gut whose chair was just a little larger than the others. He looked me up and down with an open leer while a couple of the other guys let out whistles of approval. "That'd be me. What are you looking for, honey?"

As I sauntered over, I added a little sway to my stride. I planted myself right in front of him. His eyes lingered on all those gaps in the dress, his tongue slicking over his chapped lips with a lecherous grin. Ugh.

"I'm looking for money, Trent," I said, giving him a sickly-sweet smile. "You owe the Nobles quite a lot, and you haven't been paying up."

A rush of murmurs and a little laughter spread through the crowd. Trent scoffed at me. "And they sent *you* to collect it?"

"Damn right, they did. Now are you going to hand it over or what?" I made a grabby gesture with my hand.

"Forget it." Trent leaned back in his chair, propping his feet up on a crate. "I don't owe the Nobles shit. I'm my own man now."

I cocked my head. "I don't give a crap about your delusions of grandeur. I just want the money you owe. Now stop acting like a pussy and pay up."

That riled him up good. His eyes flashed, and the others fell silent. He kicked aside the crate and sprang to his feet. "Talk to me like that again, bitch, and you'll be the one having delusions."

I wondered if he had any idea what that even meant, because that threat hadn't made a whole lot of sense. I sighed. "Well, if you want to do this the hard way, that can be arranged. But are you sure you want me embarrassing you in front of your dickhead friends?"

One of the guys let out a grunt of protest. Trent held up his hand, openly seething. "What exactly do you think *you're* going to do, you trumped-up whore?"

I let another smile, much sharper, cross my lips. "Let's not get to that. Imagine what your master will say if he hears that one of his lapdogs has forgotten who's in charge? If that ego inflates any more, your head might explode."

"I'm not a lapdog," Trent roared. He reached into his jeans, and before I could blink, he was pointing a gun at me. "You're going to die, bitch."

Did he think he was the first man to ever aim a pistol at me? I eyed it calmly, my pulse only stuttering momentarily.

I could handle this. I'd faced so much worse than he could imagine.

Trent jabbed the gun at me. "What do you have to say about me now, huh?"

I fluttered my eyelashes at him. "Now you're a dog with a gun."

Wylder was probably intending to rush in here the second the asshole released the safety. But I had other ideas. He wanted to see what I was made of? I could kick plenty of ass all on my own.

Before Trent could react to my insult, I snatched his wrist and twisted so swiftly the gun tumbled from his fingers. As the men around him leapt to their feet, I finished him off by yanking him toward me—right into my knee, which happened to be ramming straight at his crotch.

He started to crumple, and I bashed my elbow into his nose for good measure. The bone crunched with a spurt of blood.

Oh dear, I'd stained this pretty dress. What a shame.

When I shoved him away, Trent fell to his knees with a groan. One of his men charged at me, but before I could give him a taste of the medicine I could deliver, a huge form barreled into him.

Kaige toppled the guy with a swift body-check. "Thought you might need some help," he tossed over his shoulder to me as he spun to face another incoming attacker.

Around me, a larger fight had broken out. Rowan tackled a man to the floor while Wylder took on two at once. I watched as his well-built body shifted from side to side between them. He knocked one to the ground, and when the other came for his shoulder, he turned and grabbed him by the neck. With one quick heave, he slammed the other guy into the hood of one of the vans.

"Don't you fucking dare," he snarled.

My pussy clenched as I watched him. There was something undeniably hot about Wylder dominating his enemies. Not that I'd ever admit that to him.

Kaige looked down at Trent, who was still hunched on the ground. Blood flowed down from his nose onto his T-shirt. The other guys stumbled off.

Wylder spit on the ground next to Trent in disgust and then looked up at me again, his face twitching. With surprise, I realized he was trying not to smile. He actually looked impressed for a change.

"That was fucking *hot*," Kaige said. "Don't mess with Mercy." The gleam in his eyes made my stomach wobble in a way I wasn't sure was totally wise.

I cleared my throat. "I'll let you guys clean up," I said, and spun toward the car.

Kaige caught my arm before I made it two steps. "I think I need a little more inspiration first."

Before I could ask what he meant, he slid his fingers along my jaw and tugged me into a kiss.

The press of his firm lips sent a flare of heat through my entire body. I clutched his shirt instinctively, my mouth already moving against his, urging him on.

Kaige's tongue teased over the seam of my lips and slipped into my mouth. Fuck, he was good at this. It was definitely unwise. It was a horrible idea. But I couldn't bring myself to shove him away.

Kaige started to ease back, and I yanked myself away too, my cheeks flushing. His sly smile made me wish we hadn't stopped. "Wow," he murmured.

Yeah, that about summed it up. Hell. That definitely hadn't been part of *my* plan at all.

10

Mercy

As I took another step away from Kaige, still reeling from the kiss, I noticed Wylder watching us with narrowed eyes. His fists were balled at his sides, his body pulled taut, radiating tension. But if he had something to say, he just walked right past us.

Part of me felt relieved that he hadn't acknowledged the kiss. At least he wasn't accusing me of trying to make a move on Kaige.

I hadn't been the one to initiate the moment, after all, despite how much I'd liked it. Kaige was still grinning. "Damn," he said. He swiped his thumb across his lips and sucked on it as if savoring the lingering taste.

My cheeks flushed like I was some kind of naïve virgin. For fuck's sake.

But maybe it was a little understandable. Other than a few brief pecks, I hadn't done anything with Colt during the year of our engagement—or with any other guy, since it hadn't seemed smart to treat our impending marriage *that* much like it was only business. He hadn't pushed, and I'd been happy to wait to get more intimate after the knot was fully tied. We'd still been building the trust between us.

But he'd probably been laughing it up with different girls every night while I'd been stuck in a dry spell. I was certainly thirsty now.

Rowan walked over with a stack of bills in his hand, providing a welcome distraction. Wylder glanced at him. "You got everything he owed?"

"And a little extra in asshole tax," Rowan said.

"Well, now the prick knows better than to bite the hand that feeds him. Or a cat that's baring her claws." Wylder's gaze slid to me, and I'd have sworn that impressed look flickered in his eyes for just a second before he pointed everyone toward the car.

He reached it first and tugged open the front passenger seat. "In you go, Kitty Cat. You sit with me."

Was he trying to keep me and Kaige apart? The bigger guy came up behind me, cocking his head. "Everything okay?"

Maybe I'd rather not be sitting too close to that buff body anyway. I hopped in as if it'd been my idea anyway. "Yeah, fine."

Kaige's expression darkened, but he didn't argue. Rowan accepted the change in seating with a pursing of his lips. As Wylder started to drive, the silence hanging over us felt thick enough to spread on toast.

I sank back into the seat, which was annoyingly comfortable, and pretended not to notice the awkwardness. When Wylder turned up the hill to the mansion, I couldn't take it any longer. "So, you saw what I can do. I held my own. Can we get on with making my ex-fiancé pay already?"

Wylder gunned the engine to roar up the steep slope and swerved neatly around the corner. He parked the Mustang in the driveway and stalked toward the house without a word.

I had half a mind to throw one of my heels at his head as I scrambled after him. "Aren't you going to say something? I swear to God if you've changed your—"

He whirled around so suddenly that I crashed into his hard chest. He caught my arms to steady me and just as quickly let me go with a jerk. His smile was stony. "I didn't promise anything, Kitty Cat."

The nerve of this asshole. "Listen, you—"

Just then the skinny blonde who had confronted us in the kitchen pranced out of the house. I racked my brain to remember her name: Gia.

"Wylder, I've been looking for you all over," she said, clinging to his arm. He looked annoyed but didn't ask her to let go.

Gia glanced toward me, eyeing my dress with malice. "Where are you coming from wearing a dress like that? Are you that desperate for attention?"

I rolled my eyes. Her dress wasn't much better, and she'd picked that one out herself. "FYI, it isn't very nice to slut-shame other girls. It's almost like *you're* the one begging for men's approval."

Gia scowled at me. "Why do you always have to be a bitch?"

"I'm simply reflecting back what you've given me to work with," I replied with mock sweetness.

The girl's eyes narrowed and she looked about ready to throttle me. I almost wanted her to try.

"I don't think you want to start a fight with Mercy, Gia," Kaige said, walking up beside me. He put his arm around my waist, and Gia stiffened. Jesus, did she think she owned Wylder *and* Kaige? Did this girl have a thing for all the guys here? "She just came back from breaking a man's nose. Possibly also his balls—we didn't stop to check."

Gia's eyes widened, and she seemed to shrink against Wylder as if seeking his security. Drama queen. "Yeah, I don't want any of that," she said in a shrill voice.

Wylder actually looked at her as if she were some kind of wounded animal. Jeez, did men really buy into that?

Kaige grinned at me, stretching his arms to admittedly impressive effect. "I feel like this calls for a raid into the liquor cabinet." He poked Wylder's shoulder. "You've been promising that Grey Goose for a while now."

Wylder rolled his eyes. "Fine, but only if the princess retrieves it."

I set my hands on my hips. "You still haven't made good on your word."

"What word exactly did I give you?"

I let out a huff of frustration. He hadn't said exactly that getting the money from Trent would be what it took to finally get his help, but what more proof could he possibly need of my "worthiness"?

Anger surged up inside me. I'd had enough of this shit. "Do you want me to prove myself as the gang princess or your freaking maid? If you even for a second mistook me for the latter, let me remind you that—"

Wylder spoke over me. "Spare me. You know you need my help—you're a desperate little kitten. That's why you're here following my orders like the good girl you are."

"You have no idea what I am or what I can do."

"I think I've got a pretty good idea." Shaking off Gia, he took a step toward me. He might not have been quite the hulk Kaige was, but he still towered over me. As if I was going to let him scare me.

His eyes flickered down to my mouth, and he wet his own lips as if in anticipation. I found myself following the path of his tongue. Okay, maybe fear wasn't the emotion he was trying to strike here.

I balled my hands into fists, my glare daring him to try me.

"Woah, woah, woah," Kaige said, stepping in between us. "No brawling until I get the drink I was promised."

Wylder just chuckled. He spun on his heel, and I didn't have much choice but to follow him and the other guys into the house.

Wylder led the way to a lounge room near the kitchen. To my annoyance, Gia followed us to the doorway. He turned to her there. "Don't you have anywhere else to be?"

She peered at him coyly through her eyelashes and reached for his arm again. "I'd rather be here."

He pried himself out of her grip, much to my satisfaction. "We've got work to do. Take a hike."

Gia made a face, but she couldn't exactly argue with him. She gave me one last dirty look before she pranced away. Good riddance.

Kaige was already standing in front of a liquor cabinet behind a built-in mahogany bar, rubbing his hands together eagerly. It was packed with bottles of just about every kind of liquor I could imagine and then some. The Nobles kept a nice stash, I'd give them that.

"Go on," Wylder said. "Find the Grey Goose."

I brushed past Kaige to step behind the bar, running my hand along the smooth surface of the polished wood. Even more bottles were stashed under its countertop. There was enough classy booze in this room to party for a year straight without feeling your face.

I spotted the bottle easily and held it up. "Just vodka straight? I could do something more interesting with this."

Wylder looked faintly amused. "So you know your liquor too, huh? What was that about being a good girl? Maybe I'll have to revise my opinion."

"Like I give a shit about your opinion on that subject," I retorted mildly, grabbing a couple more bottles and a few of the glasses stacked off to the side of the bar.

"Kind of a shame to cut that stuff with anything else," Kaige said.

"Fine, you can have yours neat. I'll save my skills for the boss." I let sarcasm drip from that last word.

There was a little fridge with lemons and an icemaker, a saltshaker perched on top of it. I was set. With several brisk motions, I poured Kaige his Grey Goose, slid the glass across the bar to him, and got to work on my concoction for Wylder.

I was freestyling, but that was how I'd found I worked best after I'd branched out from learning all the typical cocktails the people at my father's gatherings would want to inventing my own. No one had ever cared that most of that time I'd been too young to legally drink myself.

People's lips got pretty loose around the bartender, even an unofficial one. It'd been one more way to glean all the secrets I could, searching for an advantage. For a way to ensure Dad never got to lay a finger on me again.

The guys watched, Wylder still looking amused, Kaige practically swooning as he savored his vodka, and Rowan's expression mildly surprised. I'd picked up this hobby not long after I'd parted ways with him.

As I tossed a dollop of this and that into the glass, Anthea and Gideon walked in. Her eyes narrowed. "What's our runaway princess doing now?"

"Repaying my host for his kind hospitality," I said tartly. I finished mixing and nudged the glass toward Wylder. "Drink up."

He considered the drink with obvious curiosity and picked it up to swirl it in his hand. Just as he was about to take a swig, I called out. "Wait."

He froze. Kaige and Rowan looked at me, their bodies tensed as if they were about to spring on me any second, like I was the one who concocted poisons around here.

I extended a saltshaker toward him with a smirk of my own. "I think I forgot to add the salt."

Kaige laughed, and I felt the tension leave the room. Even Wylder chuckled. He threw back a gulp and then blinked with obvious surprise. "I've never had that before, but it's good."

"My own recipe," I said, propping my elbow on the bar.

He raised an eyebrow at me. "What's it called?"

"Hadn't named it yet. Just made it up five minutes ago." I tapped my finger against my lips. "In honor of its inspiration, how about we call it an Asshole on the Rocks?"

Kaige snorted so hard I thought a little Grey Goose might have shot up his nose. Wylder glowered at me. He did throw back more of the drink, though. Point to Mercy.

"Anyone else?" I asked, already putting together another.

Gideon ambled over, his gaze mild. "I'll give it a try."

Anthea stayed noticeably silent, hanging back from the bar. I had no problem simply ignoring her. As I mixed Gideon's drink and one for myself, because I'd like a taste too, Wylder drained the rest of his glass and leaned his elbow on the counter. "I wonder how your fiancé dealt with that tongue of yours. Or maybe the problem is that he didn't?"

He was close enough that his breath tickled over my hand when I poured out a splash from a bottle of gin. "What do you mean?" I asked, as if I couldn't already tell this was going in a bad direction.

He shifted even closer, trailing a finger down the side of my arm. I resisted the urge to flinch backward like a coward, gritting my teeth at the heat his touch stirred up.

Wylder's eyes gleamed. "You're practically drooling for it. Couldn't Colt Bryant satisfy you in bed? Although I guess a woman like you would be hard to please."

"Oh, and I suppose you figure you're the man to do it?"

He leaned back with his typical smirk. "Maybe that's why you really came here, begging for my help." His voice was full of innuendo, sending more heat through my body even though he wasn't touching me now. I couldn't help but think of how he'd fought the guys back at the parking lot, so swift and powerful. Imagine that strength put to work on my body in much more enjoyable ways...

I jerked myself out of the reverie. All this game-playing had gone on long enough. I drew the one ace I had. "You know what I think? You're just making me merry-go-round in an attempt to distract yourself from the real problem."

"And what's that?"

I looked him straight in the eyes. "Titus's death."

I was taking a hard gamble, one that could go very, very badly. Farther down the bar, Kaige stiffened.

Wylder's eyes turned cold. "What do you know about that?"

"You think word doesn't get around? I've heard things." I turned to Kaige with a flicker of sympathy for his obvious discomfort. "Things I find hard to believe, as convincing a case as certain parties might have made."

"Kaige had nothing to do with it," Wylder snapped. I'd hit a nerve, just like I'd meant to.

I shrugged. "There's no point dancing around it. If you tell me your side of the story, maybe I'll have some insights."

Wylder scoffed. "What kind of insights?"

"I figured out plenty already without even trying, didn't I?"

Wylder grimaced as if he didn't want to give me credit. "You found out some. Not even half of it, I'd bet."

I shrugged. "Then why don't you fill me in while I make you another drink? What could it hurt?"

Wylder stayed silent, but he didn't say no, which meant he was coming around. I grabbed another glass. This time I added a more generous amount of vodka, tweaking my recipe slightly. All the better to loosen his tongue.

Anthea pushed into the guys' midst, her arms crossed. "Are you sure getting her involved in this is wise?"

Kaige studied me warily for a moment, but his shoulders had relaxed. "I don't see the harm."

Wylder finally spoke, his voice light but with a hint of an edge. "It *has* been two weeks since you started investigating, Aunt Anthea, and we're nowhere near the answer as far as I can tell."

Anthea bristled. "There's little to no evidence. I told you, I need more time." Then she looked up at me accusingly as if I were the one questioning her competence.

But Wylder had made his decision—in my favor. As I passed him his second drink, he nodded to Gideon. "Why don't you do the honors?"

Gideon tapped his fingers against the bar counter as if counting out the facts. "Titus, also known as 'the Titan,' was one of Ezra's best men. Two weeks ago he was found dead on the back lawn. He appeared to have fallen from the fire escape platform on the third floor after the railing broke."

Axel hadn't mentioned the railing. "Then why does everyone seem to think he was murdered?"

"The railing *was* broken, but on closer inspection, it was clear it'd been sawed through and treated with chemicals to make it look as if it'd rusted out instead." Gideon's tone stayed totally matter of fact. "Oh, and he was dead before he even hit the ground anyway. His neck had been snapped first."

He pulled out his phone and turned it toward me. The photo on the screen showed a guy sprawled limply on his back. Axel crouched next to the body with an angry expression. Even in his prone position, Titus was obviously huge—at least six and a half feet tall and a good two hundred and fifty pounds minimum, all muscle. His veiny arms looked ready to pop. Like Axel, his head was shaved.

Shock rippled through me. Somebody had managed to break this giant's neck.

"That must have taken one heck of a powerful person," I said.

"It sure as hell wasn't me," Kaige muttered. After a pause, he couldn't seem to help adding, "If it'd been a fair fight, I wouldn't have minded taking credit. To date, no one's beat Titus in a brawl."

"But *someone* did. Someone who managed to kill him." Possibilities were already running in my head. It had to be somebody with massive upper body strength. As narrow as the neck was, it took a lot of effort to snap it, not to mention getting access to that area in the first place unless his attacker was equally tall.

Without thinking, my eyes drifted to Kaige. He was the picture of innocence. But could I really trust him? It was true that I hadn't seen anyone else who came close to the Titan in size and strength around here so far.

"People are pointing the finger at Kaige because just a few days before Titus's death, the two of them got into a spat," Rowan said, speaking up for the first time.

Kaige smacked his fist on the counter. "I had no choice. The bastard decided to come after Wylder, questioning his authority, getting right up in his face. I'm not going to stand around while anyone disrespects him."

Wylder nodded. "Kaige was standing up for me."

"By going ballistic?" Anthea said. "And it wasn't just that. Multiple people heard you threaten to *kill* the guy."

Kaige frowned. "Whose side are you on exactly?"

"I'm just stating the facts."

"It was an empty threat," Kaige said. "I was pissed off, but I'm not a big enough fool to go after one of Ezra's men. That'd be a death sentence for *me*."

"Titus had threatened to kill you too," Anthea pointed out.

"Just spouting off like I was. I forgot about it by the next day." Kaige grimaced at her. "I told you already, I didn't kill Titus. I hated the old bastard, but he didn't die at my hands."

The circumstantial evidence against him wasn't exactly hope-inspiring, though. Was he annoyed by the discussion because he really had nothing to do with it or because he knew what a proper investigation would unearth?

Wylder was observing me as closely as I was watching Kaige. "So, what do you think of all this, Kitty Cat?"

"It's a strange case," I admitted.

Kaige groaned. "I'm sure everything will be fine if Anthea stops pointing out the reasons it could be me and actually manages to exonerate me."

Anthea scowled at him. "Ezra gave me a job, and I intend to do it to the best of my abilities. Stop doubting my judgment."

Wylder shook his head. "It's not enough. We're running out of time. Dad will be home soon, and Axel and the others will be pushing for retribution as soon as he does. Maybe that means it's time to bring in reinforcements." He arched his eyebrows at me. "What do you think, Kitty Cat? Are you up for the job?"

I blinked at him. "What?"

"You wanted a proper deal, right? Well here, I'll give it to you. You figure out who actually killed the Titan, and I'll take down Colt Bryant for you, no further services required."

11

Gideon

At Wylder's words, the girl's piercing blue eyes widened. In my head, I referred to her as the girl because she was a temporary guest in our life. When she was gone, I would simply delete her from memory like I did most useless information.

Or at least that was what I told myself.

My gaze drifted over the silvery lines of the dress Wylder had forced her to wear—and the copious amounts of smooth, pale skin that showed through the gaps in the fabric.

"You're serious?" she said to Wylder. "No changing your mind once I've done what you asked me to, yet again?"

My best friend looked back at her with the kind of calm I knew hid a whole storm of emotion inside him. "If you can clear Kaige's name, I'll make Steel Knights' blood rain from the sky for you, no questions asked."

She raised her chin. "Forgive me if I'm not sure I can just take your word for that. You're asking me to go after a known killer, without any idea who that killer is. That's a little more dangerous than confronting some dork with a gun."

Wylder walked around the bar until he was standing toe to toe with her. The girl, to her credit, didn't even flinch. Wylder frowned, as if he had wanted her to cower, but when she stood her ground, he simply reached for the paring knife she'd cut the lemon for our drinks with. When he held it up, she still didn't try to move away. She didn't break eye contact for a second.

There weren't many people Wylder couldn't manage to scare when he wanted to. She definitely wasn't much like the other girls around here.

He flipped the knife in his right hand and carefully punctured the skin of his left thumb so that a bead of blood trickled out of it. I hissed under my breath before I could catch the sound. What the fuck was he doing? A blood promise among criminals like us wasn't something you could walk away from, not without losing all faith in your word going forward. But Wylder was offering one anyway.

"I mark my words with the honor of my blood," he said.

The girl's eyes widened for a second. She knew he wouldn't make an offer like that without meaning it, and we all stood here as witnesses. I wanted to haul Wylder's ass out of the room and ask him if he knew what the hell he was doing giving the word of his blood to this unproven quantity.

Finally, she nodded and shook hands with him. It was done.

"Wow," Kaige said, sounding bewildered. Wylder had done this for him, in the hopes of establishing his innocence. I just hoped he knew where to draw the line.

The girl took a step away from Wylder. "I'll try my best to find out who the killer is."

"Just don't get murdered in the process," Wylder said casually as if he hadn't just given her the most solid oath any of us could make. He turned on his heel and walked out of the kitchen.

The others followed suit. The girl paused to put away the alcohol, ignoring the empty glasses we'd left on the bar. I guessed cleaning up wasn't her job anymore.

When I moved to go too, she cleared her throat meaningfully. "Hey."

I glanced back at her. "Yes?"

She paused, looking a bit awkward, which wasn't unusual. No one ever seemed to know exactly how to talk to me—except Wylder. He never acted like there was anything to be uncomfortable about. Like there was any reason to think that I didn't belong here.

Then she raised her eyes, and the full force of that bright blue gaze burned into mine. "You had someone bring me a clean outfit the other day, didn't you?"

The wheels in my head spun, but I knew she was right before I'd even quite remembered it. She'd looked so bedraggled coming up from the first task Wylder had given her... It hadn't been fitting for anyone who was running with the Nobles even on a small scale. I'd simply ensured she didn't tarnish his image through his association with her.

"It was nothing," I said evenly.

"It wasn't." She held my gaze, no awkwardness left, and it occurred to me that her initial hesitation might not have had anything to do with me but with her own pride. No one who lived this kind of life tended to be very good showing open gratitude. "I appreciated the gesture, whatever reasons you had for making it. I just thought I should say that."

I didn't like the unexpected list of my stomach at her words. Why should it matter to me whether she thanked me over some brief remark to the staff or not?

"Don't mention it," I said, my tone coming out brusquer than I'd intended, and strode out of the room before I could dwell too much on the trace of disappointment I'd caught on her face at my response.

Back in my office, I sat down in front of my expansive computer setup, but the image of her face, those eyes pinning me in place, lingered in my head. Without any conscious direction, my mind produced another image—of her peeling the strips of that silvery fabric down her shoulders to reveal her breasts...

My cock stirred. Fuck. I swore under my breath and shook any thought of Mercy Katz away. To distract myself, I made my way to the complex espresso machine I'd had installed in my office. I couldn't work without caffeine—and it had to be caffeine done right. Maybe it would jolt me back to the mindset I needed.

With a meditative air, I set the machine running to my typical specifications and watched the dark liquid fill the mug. There was something grounding about the steady stream and the rising of the coffee against the pale sides. When it was finished, black, sugarless, and perfect, I sipped it while eyeing the aquarium that filled most of one wall across from my computer. The gliding motions of the fish grounded me too.

There was a knock on the door. Wylder peered in before I had a chance to answer. "Chess?"

I nodded. We kept up our running games a couple evenings a week, whenever Wylder wasn't too occupied with other work. I'd thought the girl's arrival might have put those on hold until the matter of her revenge request was settled. Apparently not.

Wylder sat down in one of the chairs by the table that held our partly played-out game, holding a snifter of amber liquid he'd brought with him. Kaige might salivate over the Grey Goose, but Wylder liked nothing more than the most expensive brandy he could get his hands on, drunk the old-fashioned way.

I raised a brow. "Haven't you had enough already?"

He chuckled. "Apparently not."

I shook my head and sat down next to him, considering the arrangement in which we'd left the pieces. I was winning. But then, I nearly always was. And if I wasn't, the tide turned soon enough.

"It was your turn," I reminded him.

Wylder rubbed his mouth, giving me a wry look. "Are you sure you're not giving me an extra turn in the hopes I'll offer a little more of a challenge?"

He'd need at least a dozen more moves for that. "Nothing's stopping you from studying up on the game a little more, you know. Or paying more than five seconds' attention to where you put your pieces."

He laughed. "I think even if I spent a year buried in chess books, you'd still beat me every time. That's okay. I like watching how you take me down."

Someone else might have seen that as a sign of suspicion. I knew Wylder had only admitted it because he trusted that I'd never turn on him in actuality. It was an honor, having that trust.

Beating him in chess once a week, not quite so much.

He took his move, shifting a pawn. I brought out my knight. Wylder squinted at the board for a second and then sent his bishop whipping several spaces.

I'd be able to take it now. I wasn't sure if he didn't realize or simply didn't care.

He watched me as I decided whether I wanted to bother or if there was an even better move available. "Do you have anything to say about what happened earlier?"

I shrugged. "You can make whatever promises you want to whomever you want."

Wylder snorted. "Come on, you obviously disapproved."

Fine. "We don't know her. Yes, we questioned her extensively, and her story has checked out so far, but we both know looks can be deceptive. She is the Katz heir."

"With no family left."

I shrugged. "Maybe that makes her even more dangerous. She has nothing left to lose."

Wylder paused. "I have considered that."

"Have you?"

"Yeah." He took a long, hard sip of his drink and put it on the table. "Concentrate on the game."

We played for several more minutes, Wylder's defeat becoming ever more inevitable, before he spoke again. "On a scale of one to ten, how likely do you figure she is to get to the bottom of the Titus thing?"

"Only the tiniest fraction more than zero," I said without hesitation. "Nothing is ever impossible, but she's a gang princess, not Sherlock Holmes."

Wylder chuckled. "That doesn't sound so promising."

"Well, it doesn't matter," I said. "We don't have anything to lose by letting her take a shot. She's just a tool anyway, right?"

"Right," Wylder said, but I could tell from his tone that wasn't entirely the truth. He was obviously more invested in her than I thought he should be. The knowledge that he was lying to me about that investment sent a prickle down my spine.

Of course, in a way I could understand his fascination. Her body with all its curves, as if it'd been made to lead men's minds astray. The way she let her hand linger against her skin now and then, I could already track which spots must be most sensitive.

A vision flashed through my mind of pinning her beneath me while I found every sweet spot that would make her moan. The side of her neck, definitely, right at the base where it met her shoulder. And the crook of her jaw just below her ear…

"What are you thinking?" Wylder asked, pulling me back to reality, and I realized I'd gotten hard beneath the table. A flush crept over my face that I fought to dispel.

"Nothing," I said, and made a hasty move that left a careless opening for Wylder. Not that he was likely to notice. As surreptitiously as possible, I adjusted my position in my chair, willing certain parts of my body to calm down.

Women didn't affect me like this. I couldn't allow this one to. My job was protecting Wylder in every way I could, and no one, no matter how pretty their bright blue eyes were, was going to threaten the security I'd worked so hard to construct.

12

Mercy

Standing on the back lawn not far from where Titus must have hit the grass, I peered up at the fire escape that zigzagged across the mansion's rear. I couldn't make out a whole lot from down here. The ladder to the second-floor section wasn't reachable from the ground, and the sun glared off the metal bars, stinging my eyes.

The promise Wylder had made came back to me, and with it the image of him slowly sucking the trickle of blood from his finger. My stomach fluttered at the memory. It was probably one of the sexiest things I'd ever seen, and there shouldn't have been anything even remotely sexual about it.

I shook my head to clear it. He'd given me his terms, and now I had to meet them. Even if I didn't have much of a clue how to accomplish that. Examining the scene of the murder had seemed like the most obvious place to start.

Heading inside, I got to enjoy the rush of the chilly air conditioning for the climb to the third floor. A large window at the end of one hall opened to the fire escape. I guessed that was how the Nobles' patrols climbed out to survey the yard from above. Titus would have had to squeeze to get out there.

I clambered through it back into the summer heat, grateful that the sweats and tee I'd put back on meant I wasn't flashing anyone who might have walked by below like I would have in that ridiculous dress. My shoulder twinged when the bandage brushed against the frame, but the bullet wound seemed to be healing nicely. It barely hurt when I moved now.

The third-floor section was only wide enough for three or four people to stand side-by-side. Maybe two if you were as big as Titus. A chunk of the railing *was* missing partway down.

I crouched next to it and examined the surface, running my fingers down the length of where the metal had broken off. Flecks of rust stuck to my finger. The broken ends definitely looked corroded. I checked the floor. There was a little sheen of dust but not enough to make a proper footprint. Well, by now a lot of people must have come out here to investigate anyway.

The lawn was a good thirty feet below me. Hardly anyone could survive that fall.

Especially with their neck already broken.

A loud screech behind me startled me so badly I nearly jumped out of my skin. My foot slipped, my body swaying dangerously close to the precarious drop.

A hand shot out and snatched the back of my shirt, yanking me away from the gap in the railing. I stumbled to the side and whirled around with a hitch of breath.

"Careful there," Anthea said. She climbed out of another, smaller window—its pane must have made that screech as she'd opened it—and onto the metal platform beside me. The thin smile that curved her lips suggested she was more amused than concerned by my near fall.

I narrowed my eyes at her. What the hell was she doing sneaking up on me? I curled my fingers around the more solid railing next to me.

Anthea hopped up and down a couple of times, managing to make the floor beneath us wobble. "It's a very old structure, you know," she said conversationally. "I'm not sure it was the wisest for Titus to be coming out onto it in the first place. Unfortunately, my brother isn't very keen on renovating. He doesn't want strangers on his property." She fixed her penetrating gaze on me.

I took a moment to study her right back. Other than the red in her hair and the proud slope of her nose, she didn't share a whole lot of features with her supposed nephew. But then, gang leaders had a habit of getting around. Especially with the age gap, chances were she and Ezra Noble didn't share a mother. Which made her, what, Wylder's half-aunt?

"What are you doing out here?" I asked, trying to keep the accusation out of my tone. I didn't want to seem like I was paranoid or show that she'd rattled me.

She shrugged. "I thought you'd need some help."

I highly doubted that she'd come here out of the goodness of her heart. But two could play at this game. I pushed my mouth into a smile. "That's fantastic. I had some questions, so I'm glad you're here."

Anthea looked surprised that I'd decided to take her up on the offer. She leaned back against the side of the house. "Shoot."

I ran my hand along the railing, tapping the broken edge. "How exactly did you know this wasn't an accident? Like you said, it's a pretty old structure, and it *is* obviously rusted."

Anthea tsked and pointed to a couple of whitish marks, so tiny I'd never have noticed them on my own. "You see that? Some kind of chemicals have been poured on the metal to accelerate the process of corrosion. They sawed out a chunk of the railing and doctored it afterward so it'd look accidental."

I examined the marks. "What does a person use to make metal rust just like that?"

Anthea shrugged. "The easiest would be a combination of hydrogen peroxide, vinegar, and salt. It'd take just a few hours."

"And who around here would know that?"

"Anyone who can run a quick Google search," she said dryly.

Okay, so that wasn't going to be my big clue. I glanced at the window Anthea had climbed through and then the one I'd used. "So, someone knew Titus would come out here on his patrol. They prepared the area ahead of time. Then they caught him while he was on the platform, broke his neck, and pushed him off."

"Right, simple as that."

I ignored her sarcasm, frowning. It *was* simple, actually. The real problem was how anyone had managed to do the "simple" task of overpowering Titus in the first place. Even if they'd snuck up on him like Anthea had with me, who could have gotten a good enough grip on his neck and managed to snap it without him tossing *them* over the edge instead first?

Maybe the real question wasn't who could have but why anyone would have wanted to.

I glanced at Anthea again. "Do you have any suspects?"

She arched a brow. "As far as I'm concerned, everybody is a suspect."

"Is Kaige included in that?"

"He's innocent until proven guilty."

Her voice tightened with those words, a hint of a frown creasing the corners of her mouth. I didn't think she liked that there was so much suspicion on him. "You don't think he did it, no matter how much evidence there is."

She aimed her frown at me. "He and Wylder are like brothers. I've practically seen him grow up. He can fly off the handle pretty easily, and he'd kill to defend Wylder in the moment, but I can't see him arranging some elaborate murder plan when no one's in immediate danger."

"Then why are you investigating him at all?"

She lowered her petite form to sit on the windowsill. "If I don't remain neutral, the investigation will be tainted. My brother wouldn't like that."

I worried at my lower lip. If she didn't think Kaige could have done it, I had to admit I was inclined to believe her. "Isn't there *anyone* else who could have taken Titus on? Who else was around that night?"

"It's a pretty busy house. Some of the top guys live here most of the time, and there are always associates coming and going. And then there are the groupies, not that they pose a threat other than by venereal disease."

I held back a laugh, picturing how Gia would have responded to that assessment. "Are there a lot of 'groupies' who hang around here?"

Anthea made a dismissive wave. "A few of them. It's a steady rotation as they realize no one here is going to want them for more than a quick lay and they move out to make room for the next round. But my brother lets them have a room so they're on hand should any of the men want to... partake of their services."

From the bitterness that had crept into her voice, I wondered if her mother had been one of the groupies. We might have had that in common. Whoever my mom had been, Dad definitely hadn't bothered to marry her or anything official like that. She'd been nothing more than a broodmare to him.

I wasn't trying to make an enemy out of Anthea—well, more than we already were—so I didn't pry on that subject. I was debating my next question when she spoke up again.

"You don't belong here."

"What?"

She stood up again, stepping close enough that I had to back up, starkly aware of how little space was left behind me. One quick push, and she could heave me over the railing just like that.

"Forget your revenge, forget vying for Wylder's favor, and get the hell out of this house," she said in a low voice. "Kittens don't last long in a place like this."

I snorted. "Is that a threat?"

"I could make it one. Let me be very clear: I don't want you here."

I folded my arms in front of me. "Oh yeah? So what's stopping you from showing me the door?"

Her jaw clenched. "It's not my house, and Wylder has decided to entertain your delusions. I have plenty of other resources at my disposal, though."

"You're a Noble too. You have seniority over him, don't you?"

A sharp guffaw spilled out of her. "And you're a woman too. I think you know well enough how men in this life see us."

"You have some kind of position here," I had to point out. More than my father had ever allowed me.

"Oh, sure, my brother makes use of my unique skill set. That doesn't mean he gives me any authority outside of that."

"And your job is poisons?"

She gave me a sharp little smile. "Any kind of killing that can fly under the radar as an accident or illness to prevent further investigation. Both identifying them and dealing them out."

The hairs on the back of my neck stood on end. But then, every man in this mansion was probably a killer several times over. Why not the main woman of the house too?

I forced my tone to stay casual. "That's how you knew about things like this rust concoction?"

"Exactly. My truth serum is only scraping the surface of what I can deal out, little girl."

I bristled automatically, but I held my tongue. She was trying to unnerve me, to get me to snap. I wasn't going to give her the satisfaction.

In my silence, she stepped closer again, stomping her foot hard enough to send a vibration through the platform. "As I said before, you shouldn't be here. We've already established that the railings don't hold, haven't we?"

If she wanted to intimidate me into running scared, it wasn't going to work. I held my position. "I actually like it up here." Sunlight danced on my skin, and the clean, fresh air filled my lungs. I didn't feel as caged as I did inside.

That was why I liked parkour too. Apart from the fact that I was naturally good at it, I could shut my mind off completely when I climbed and bounded, letting my body work on autopilot.

Anthea cocked her head with a knowing look I didn't like at all. "No, it isn't the sky you're afraid of but what lies beneath the ground, isn't it? No one likes being shut away inside a space they can't escape from." Her gaze dropped to my hands.

My arms froze at my sides. "What are you talking about?" Flashes of memory from years ago, images I had buried deep inside me threatened to cloud my vision. The rotting scent, the sting in my fingertips, my throat hoarse from screaming.

"You okay?" Anthea said innocently. "You look a little pale there."

She couldn't know. She was just taking whatever jabs she could. "I'm fine," I bit out.

"I suppose we'll see about that." She turned back to the window she'd come out through. "Well, this has been an enlightening conversation. Let me enlighten you a little more. The last person who really pissed me off was my former husband. Former because he's three years dead. And that's not a coincidence."

She shot one last smirk over her shoulder at me. "Wouldn't it be a horrible pity if somehow you ended up meeting the same fate?"

13

Mercy

My conversation with Anthea left my nerves jumping all over the place. Back in the house, I did my best to shake off the uneasy sensation crawling over my skin after her last words. She wouldn't come at me *that* hard while Wylder was still on board with having me around, right?

One thing was clear: if I was going to get to the bottom of this murder before she decided it was more important to get me out of the way, I couldn't do it alone. And I knew exactly the man who'd have the most answers at his fingertips.

It took me a while to figure out where Gideon's office was, even asking a couple of staff where he worked. The mansion was huge, and there were just so many fucking rooms here with ornate handles and oak doors. It was hard to pick one from the next.

I'd just tried another that led into a broom closet of all things when Kaige appeared at the other end of the hall. He held a steaming mug of coffee.

"Hey," he said. "I was looking for you. Thought you might need this after all the craziness this morning."

The craziness that had included our scorching kiss. My stomach did a little flip that had nothing to do with nerves. At least, not the nerves Anthea had provoked.

"Uh, thanks," I said, accepting the cup from him.

"You're very welcome." He flashed me a smile. Was he always this charming or was he simply trying to get into my pants?

If that kiss was anything to go by, maybe I shouldn't be stopping him.

"What are you thinking?" he asked with a sly grin as if he knew exactly what was going through my head.

I shoved away those completely unnecessary thoughts. "Uh, I was actually looking for Gideon."

Kaige frowned. "Why are you looking for him?"

"He seems to make a business of knowing everything about everyone else's business. I figured he might be able to fill me in on a few more details to prove your innocence."

"Well, I can't complain about that." Kaige beckoned me with a finger. "Allow me."

I followed him down the hallway to yet another door I couldn't have differentiated easily from any of the others.

It opened before he could knock on it. Wylder stood on the other side. When he saw Kaige and me together, an odd expression crossed his face. I remembered how he had looked when he'd caught us kissing this morning. Displeasure flitted across his face. "What are you doing here?"

Without answering, I walked past him into the room.

The office wasn't all that big, considering some of the massive rooms in this place. There was a desk with an elaborate set-up involving several monitors and two keyboards, plus a monster of a computer underneath. At the other end of the room, a huge aquarium covered the entire back wall.

"Jesus," I muttered under my breath. Colorful fishes swam around in the water, several of them as large as my hand, the rest just tiny slivers of bright reds, blues, and yellows. I wasn't a fish enthusiast, so I couldn't have identified any of them for sure... but the bigger ones with a metallic sheen to their scales and jutting lower jaws had a vicious look to them. Were those actual *piranhas*?

Why not? What else would a fucking gangster keep in his fish tank?

Gideon was sitting in a wheeled chair in front of his computer setup, Rowan leaning against the edge of the desk a couple of feet beyond him. My ex glanced away when I met his eyes. The guy I'd come to talk to hadn't bothered to look up in the first place.

I ventured farther in, tapping the surface of a small table beneath the narrow window between the desk and the aquarium, the only other furnishing in the place. A chessboard, several pieces still scattered across it, lay on the table. "Didn't finish your game?"

Kaige had stepped in behind me. He chuckled. "Wylder and Gideon always have a game going on."

Gideon still didn't look up, but he did acknowledge that point with his voice. "Wylder says it keeps his mind sharp."

"So far it hasn't gotten sharp enough for him to win a single game, as far as I know." Kaige grinned at his boss, who knuckled him half-heartedly.

"I'm pretty sure I could beat *you*," Wylder said.

Kaige held up his hands. "Which is exactly why I know better than to play."

It was kind of warming in a weird sort of way, watching them banter. I didn't think my father had ever been that comfortable even with his brothers. He'd seen everyone around him, even family, as a potential threat.

And the first time anyone had convinced him to let down his guard, that bastard Colt had made all of us pay for it. My teeth gritted, and I turned to Gideon. "I need some answers."

He finally raised his head, his expression unreadable. "To what questions?"

"For the investigation," I said. "Exactly who was here the night Titus died, what their role is, whether any of them other than Kaige might have had a beef with the guy."

His mouth twitched with what looked like annoyance. I guessed I'd probably interrupted him in the middle of something. "I've checked everything," he said. "So did Anthea. If there was anything that obvious, we'd have found it already."

"While I'm sure that's true, I need to start somewhere." I waved my hand vaguely. "Eliminate the obvious so you can see what remains, or something. Isn't that how detectives are supposed to work?"

Wylder snorted. "So now you're a detective?"

I jabbed a finger at him. "You're the one who put me up to this. If you want to skip that part and go straight to decimating the Steel Knights, be my guest."

"But why should I when it's so much fun watching your pert little ass scurry around at my bidding?" He smirked and tossed a remark to Gideon as he turned to leave. "Don't give up the goods too easily!"

Gideon eyed me for a long moment. I had the impression he might be staring right inside my skull—and that he wasn't all that impressed with what he was finding there. I shifted my weight from one foot to the other, and Rowan, naturally, decided to play hero.

"I can take you through—"

Gideon held up his hand with a jerk. "No. She should have the most accurate info, and I'm the one who can provide that." He blinked slowly, and a hint of a smile touched his lips. "But Wylder's right. She should have to work for it. We can't have someone messing around with Kaige's fate who isn't totally committed."

A shiver ran down my spine. "And what exactly do *you* expect me to do?"

He pointed past me to the aquarium. "Stick your hand in the tank with my school of piranhas. As long as it's fully dunked, I'll keep talking."

He kept the lights in here dim. The eerie glow of the computer screens lent his sharp features a grace that was almost angelic, but clearly he was just as devilish as the rest of these pricks.

"Are you kidding me?" I sputtered.

"Do I sound like I'm joking? Simply getting your hand wet shouldn't be too hard for the heir to the Claws."

I held back a growl and marched over to the aquarium. Stick my hand in the water. No big deal. He wouldn't ask me to if he really thought the fish would *eat* it, would he?

"Just so you know," he called after me with no apparent concern, "I can't remember whether I've fed them today. They might be a bit hungrier than usual."

Fan-fucking-tastic.

"Gideon," Rowan said, but his protest only hardened my resolve. He should see just what Mercy Katz was made of these days too.

"It's fine," I declared. There was a low step stool next to the aquarium cabinet. I stepped onto it so I could easily lift the lid over the tank.

The filter hummed. The piranhas swam by with flashes of their silvery scales. I swallowed hard and dipped in my hand.

The water was warmer than I'd expected. I watched the fish carefully, braced for a response to the disturbance.

The tiny, colorful fish scattered. The piranhas glided onward. I held my fingers as still as possible, wary of making any sudden movements. "Okay. I did it. Start talking."

Kaige and Rowan both stood frozen, looking nearly as tense as I was, but neither of them doing anything further to intervene. Gideon ran the show in this room.

The blue-haired guy had swiveled all the way around in his chair now. The reflected light glinted off his lip ring. He flicked his tongue over it and grabbed his tablet off the desk. "Ask away."

I tipped my head toward the hall. "Who was staying in or came by the mansion around the time of Titus's death?"

"Ezra, Wylder, Ezra's closest associates, and the three of us."

"And Ezra's closest associates would be..."

He rattled off several names that meant nothing to me, as well as Axel's. One of the piranhas flitted past my hand so close its scales slid against my fingers.

I clenched my jaw against a flinch. My fingers remained unchomped.

"Who else?" I demanded.

"Ezra had a meeting with a few of the lesser underlings." Gideon mentioned a few more names. "A couple of members from the Mont X crew came by. And, of course, the groupies and the cleaning staff are pretty much always around."

Mont X. I recognized the name—they were a small outfit on the fringes of the Bend. "What did the Mont X guys want?"

Gideon shrugged. "We weren't part of that meeting, but chances are they were offering Ezra more access to their territory in exchange for his backing in some business endeavor."

"And did he give them it?" Maybe Titus had intervened and pissed them off—

But Rowan's nod cut off that line of thinking. "They left looking happy, so I think that's safe to say."

Gideon cut a glance at him as if he resented anyone else intruding on his role as purveyor of all important information. At the same moment, another scaled body glided just beneath my fingertips, its upper fin tickling my skin.

Another piranha getting cozy with me, and I still hadn't lost so much as a nibble of flesh. My arm was getting a little stiff propped against the tank, but an unexpected thrill shot through my chest, like the rush I got when I pulled off a particularly dangerous parkour move.

Gideon had dared me, and I was rising to the challenge. Just like I'd keep doing until Colt and his men were nothing but crumbs crunched under my feet.

"That's everyone?" I asked, my head coming up a little higher.

Gideon eyed me. I couldn't tell whether he was pleased that I was passing his test or annoyed. "Those were all the people who could have had access to the fire escape, as far as we know."

Kaige nodded. "And some of them, like the Mont X guys—they left before the actual murder happened."

"There's always a chance someone we didn't know about slipped through our security," Gideon admitted with obvious reluctance. "No system is infallible."

Well, that didn't help me at all. "Okay, forget that, then. Who had Titus pissed off lately, whether you know they were near the house that day or not?"

"Plenty of people, I'm sure," Gideon said coolly. "He did a lot of work enforcing the Nobles' authority. But he was very good at it. I can't imagine many people would have thought it worth the risk of carrying out a grand plan to get revenge just on him, one that would have put them in far more danger than he ever threatened them with."

Kaige snorted in agreement. "Most of these crews are like Trent's. You saw what wimps they were."

"Hey, I'm trying to come up with a convincing story for how it could be *anyone* other than you," I reminded him. But I had to admit I was grasping at straws here. I snatched at another one. "Who was the last person who talked to Titus before the murder?"

"Other than the murderer, that appears to be Axel," Gideon said. "They were both on patrol that night, and they're friendly, so they talked a bit before setting off to cover their respective routes. He didn't tell Anthea anything useful, though."

Damn. Frustration raked through me, and my fingers twitched of their own accord. I snapped back to stillness, my pulse hiccupping.

Two of the piranhas swam closer. Were their teeth jutting even more avidly from their brutal jaws?

They flitted past my hand and continued through the tank. A rush of adrenaline replaced the fear in my gut.

What was the worst that could happen anyway? If they took one chomp, I'd just pull my hand out. The pain would only be momentary. There was a kind of power in knowing that I was tempting fate and doing it despite that, not letting the instinctive fear control me. *I* decided when I was done here.

"Do you know exactly when Titus died?" I asked. "I assume people noticed pretty quickly." A guy that big wouldn't have hit the ground quietly.

Gideon nodded. "People ran over to see what was going on as soon as they heard him fall. That was eleven thirty at night, from what they've reported. He started his patrol a little before eleven on the first floor, so he definitely couldn't have been dead all that long before he was shoved. I'd assume they happened nearly simultaneously."

That would make sense. Why would the killer want to hang around with his body, risking getting caught, rather than getting on with their scheme to make it look like an accident? I glanced at Kaige. "And you don't have any alibi for that time?"

He held up his hands with a crooked smile. "I was in my room asleep. Without company, sadly. I didn't even know the prick had kicked the bucket until I came down to breakfast the next morning. No one thought to accuse me until later that day once they got the autopsy and examined the railing by daylight."

Obviously if he'd had proof he couldn't have been there, this wouldn't be a problem to begin with. At least I had a small window of time to focus on now.

The water currents rippled against my skin. I glanced down at the piranhas, but my fear was completely gone now, replaced by the almost giddy sensation that'd been building in me. I found myself welcoming it.

Gideon was watching me closely, and I didn't know if he could tell that I wasn't afraid anymore. But there was something in his eyes that I could almost swear was grudging respect. I'd have enjoyed it more if the hint of admiration on his striking face hadn't sent a twinge of attraction right between my legs.

Damn these assholes and their ridiculous attractiveness.

"Anything else?" he asked.

I considered. "We're assuming the murderer must have come through the house, right? Because it'd be a lot easier to get out onto the third-floor platform of the fire escape that way, and it's not likely they could have run for it out on the lawn with everyone hurrying out to check Titus's body."

"We've found no evidence that anyone scaled the fire escape from outside, and no one saw anyone fleeing the scene."

Fair enough. I nibbled at my lower lip, with a flicker of satisfaction when both Gideon's and Kaige's gazes shot straight to my mouth. "I'd still like to see any surveillance footage you've got of the yard, just in case." I hadn't seen any cameras inside the mansion, naturally. Ezra wouldn't want his business activities being recorded, even by his own people. Too easy for someone to exploit that for their own gain.

"I've looked over it carefully, and so has Anthea," Gideon said, but he was already turning toward his screens. "You can take your hand out and come have a closer look."

"Thank you ever so much," I said with snarky formality, and closed the lid on the tank before wiping my wet hand on my pants. More adrenaline tingled through me as I shot the other guys a fierce smile.

They'd figure out soon enough that I could take anything they threw at me and still come out on top.

14

Mercy

THE SECOND TIME I LEFT THE NOBLE MANSION, I DIDN'T bother to sneak. No one had *said* I wasn't allowed to leave, and I was planning on sticking to Paradise City this time anyway. I needed to get out of that place to clear my mind and let everything I'd learned hopefully settle into something I could make sense of.

I also needed to stop relying on borrowed clothes. One less thing for Wylder to hold over my head as he was so fond of doing whenever he could.

I returned just as dusk pinkened the sky, carrying a few shopping bags. Kaige had been right: pawning off my engagement ring had given me a sizable chunk of change—and no small amount of satisfaction to boot. Thanks to a thrift store down the street from the pawn shop, I had a decent array of jeans and shirts I could call my own, as well as a wallet to keep the rest in. A convenience store farther down had supplied me with a burner phone I had to think might come in handy. That was all I needed for now.

I'd never been able to earn any money of my own without Dad taking it over. I wasn't going to spend this windfall all at once.

As I began to climb the staircase to the guest room, a screechy voice called out from behind me. "Well, well, well, look who we have here."

I turned around to face Gia, who was scowling at my bags. Great, my favorite person in the house. And considering Anthea was also living here, that was saying a lot.

I suppressed a sigh. "What do you want?"

She curled her painted-red lips in a sneer. "Whose credit card did you steal to buy all of that stuff?"

"News flash: I don't answer to you." I spun around and continued up the stairs, figuring we were done, but apparently she was feeling particularly irritating today. Her strappy sandals tapped against the hardwood. She caught up with me just as I reached the second floor.

"Don't think I don't know what you're doing here. Acting like the victim, trying to get the guys all wrapped around your finger."

Oh, she was one to talk. I whirled on her. "I have no interest in wrapping the guys around my *anything*, like I've told you before. The only person obsessed with them here is you."

She glowered at me. "You think you can steal them out from under the people who've been there for them so much longer, all because you have some stupid sob story. Please." She jerked her chin toward my bags. "And now you're stealing who knows what else from them. It's obvious trash like you can't afford these things."

My patience was fraying fast. Anger bubbled up inside me. I was *looking* at the trash, and I was starting to think it was time I took her out. "You have no idea who I am."

"Oh really?" Gia jutted her hip to one side. "Who are you exactly? A whiny little bitch who thinks she can sidle up to the guys and suddenly she'll be part of their circle? Doesn't matter what crazy ideas you have—a whore is still a whore."

I dropped my bags. "You—"

"Ladies!" Kaige ambled down the hall toward us. He looked between Gia and me. "What's this about?"

"Your groupie is accusing me of stealing," I said. In more ways than one, none of them true. "I think you need to put her on a leash."

"You bitch." Gia took a step toward me.

Kaige pulled her back by the arm. "That's enough."

Gia blinked at him, immediately looking like a lost puppy. I sputtered a laugh, remembering how just seconds ago she'd been accusing *me* of pulling a poor-me act. "But Kaige," she simpered, "she—"

He cut her off, clearly unmoved by her performance. "You've been hassling her since she showed up. Shouldn't dish it out if you can't take it, you know."

"Kaige, you don't understand." Her hair flipped over her shoulder as she turned to look at me. "This cunt was strutting around acting as if she owns you."

Any good humor in Kaige's voice fled. His eyes flashed, and he shoved her away. "Don't you dare call her that. You're lucky she hasn't already beat you down."

Gia hugged herself. "I was just trying to protect you," she insisted.

"Get lost, Gia. Now." Kaige gave her a look of utter disgust and turned away. "I don't want to hear another word."

An expression of dismay crossed Gia's face. Her lips quivered and then pressed together, her eyes closing for a second as if she was trying hard not to cry. Huh. I didn't think that was an act. He wasn't even looking at her now. She seemed to be... genuinely upset.

I almost felt bad for her. Almost. Gia was still a bitch, and if I wasn't going to put her in her place, I was glad someone else had.

She peered at Kaige a second longer and then darted away, swiping her hand across her face. Well, maybe if she hadn't been such a pain in the ass, he'd have liked her more.

"What the hell is her problem anyway?" I muttered as she disappeared down the stairs.

Kaige shrugged. "Don't mind her. Wylder was in a good mood the first night she showed up, and she thought him being a little friendly meant he was hers for life or something. Give 'em an inch..." He shook his head wryly, the usual sly gleam returning to his eye. "And how could she possibly help being jealous of a stunner like you?"

I rolled my eyes, ignoring his flirtation and the flicker of heat it sent through me. "So she's after Wylder, is she?" I said, grabbing my bags and turning toward my room.

Kaige ambled alongside me down the hall. "Pretty much all the girls are."

"Heir to the Noble legacy and the top prize," I said dryly, and considered what I'd just seen. "She seemed pretty upset having you tell her off, though."

"I suppose I make a decent second choice." He waggled his eyebrows. "And I can't completely blame her for being possessive about what she wants. We must protect what we intend to belong to us."

"What's that supposed to mean?" I looked up at him, practically having to crane my neck to meet his eyes when he was this close. He was just so freaking tall.

Which was why most of the people around here assumed he'd killed one of the Nobles' own. Who else was big enough to have a chance at taking on Titus? No real alibi, plenty of justification that even he'd admitted to, even if he'd dismissed their fight... *Could* he have done it? Was the charming smile a front for a ruthless killer?

I didn't want to think so, which was definitely a problem.

Kaige stopped, halting me with a hand on my waist. As he leaned in, his musky, manly smell washed over me, and my heart skipped a beat despite myself. His hand reached out to touch a strand of hair that had come loose from my ponytail. Instead of tucking it behind my ear, he played with it, twirling the lone strand between his fingers.

"Only that when I see something I want, I make sure I get it," he said.

It took me a second to remember what question he was answering. "Great," I said, willing my voice to stay steady and wincing inwardly at the breathiness that crept into it anyway. I wiggled the bags I was still clutching. "I've just got to put these away..."

"What's in the bags?" He refused to step away, his hand dropping to my jaw and then stroking a slow, sensuous path to my neck. I almost curled into his touch. Shit.

I forced myself to ease back a step instead, but I couldn't go any farther—my shoulders hit the wall. "Just some clothes. I took your advice about the ring."

"I have plenty of good advice on all sorts of topics." He grinned, prowling closer again. "Now I can't help wondering exactly what all is in there. You must have needed more than just T-shirts and jeans. Are you a plain beige girl or black lace? Or maybe you go for scarlet?"

My underwear, he obviously meant. I had actually popped into a store to grab a couple packs of new panties and new bras to match—because who wanted to buy those used?—one set beige, one set black. But I sure as hell wasn't telling him that. Especially now that his voice had dropped to that suggestive whisper. It seemed to dance on my skin, leaving goosebumps in its wake.

He tapped his finger under my chin, setting off even more sparks. "What's your favorite color, Mercy?" he asked, making the simple question sound unbelievably dirty.

I licked my lips unintentionally. "It is red, actually."

His rich brown eyes darkened with desire. "You know what they say about girls who like red..."

"I don't."

He leaned even closer, his warm breath washing over my cheek. "No matter what kind of front they put on, underneath they're dying to get it rough and hard. What do you think, Kitten? Under all that toughness, is there a little freak just waiting to be taken?"

My stomach clenched. Images of him dominating me in all kinds of ways flashed through my mind, and I'd swear lust momentarily short circuited my brain. So it wasn't really my fault that before I could form any kind of response, Kaige stole whatever words might have tumbled over my lips with his own mouth.

He kissed me slowly at first, easing me back until I was pinned between him and the hard wall. The bags slipped from my hands, but I didn't give a shit. His tongue traced my lips before seeking its way inside. As it twined with mine, he deepened the kiss. It was hot and insistent and oh, fuck, I could feel my insides turning to putty.

I clutched at the collar of his shirt to try and bring him even closer to me. He grabbed my hips, squeezing them as his tongue explored my mouth, making me moan against him. With a firm grip that sent an eager quiver through me, he nudged my legs apart and settled his thigh in between them. The pressure made me want to grind against him like a bitch in heat.

Damn, he was good at this. Good enough that I couldn't quite remember why I'd been so resistant a few moments ago. I dug my fingers into his shirt, plundering his mouth right back, and reveled at his groan. He rocked his thigh against just the right spot—

And a loud cough from farther down the hall brought me crashing back to reality.

Kaige pulled back just a few inches—which was far enough for me to see Anthea stopping a short distance away, her arms crossed and her fingers tapping the sleeve of her sundress. Somehow she looked as fierce as a tiger even in clothes that would have suited a '50s housewife.

"Got lost on your way to the bedroom?" she sneered.

I shook myself, recovering my sanity. Kaige offered Anthea a lazy smile, barely affected by the fact that she had stumbled on us making out. In fact, I was pretty sure he was enjoying it.

A flash of cold hit me at the thought of how this interlude would look to her, and I shoved him away from me. I hadn't been trying to seduce Kaige or any of the other three, but Anthea already had her mind made up against me. I'd probably just confirmed the worst of her assumptions.

Kaige stepped back at my push with a chuckle. "Woah, easy there," he said in that playful voice of his. It only set my temper more on edge. Why had I let his smooth, sexy talking get to me?

Anthea walked even closer, her heels clicking against the polished tiles. "Am I interrupting something?" She looked down at my shopping bags which had scattered around us, the clothes spilling out of them.

I bent down and began to collect them, stuffing the contents back in as quickly as I could.

Kaige winked at me. "We were just having a little fun."

I bit back a grimace. The movement of my lips brought back the memory of the kiss. They were still tender. God, if she'd waited just a *little* longer to come prancing down here—

No, it was better that she'd intervened. I needed a clear head, and Kaige certainly wasn't helping with that. Especially when he slowly wiped his mouth with a teasing swipe of his thumb.

"It isn't what it looks like," I said as I stood up.

Anthea scoffed. "Pretty sure I saw his tongue shoved down your throat. But okay, I'll hear your excuse anyway. What exactly is going on?"

"Nothing that was my idea. This guy started the whole thing. I was *about* to put a stop to it."

Kaige just continued to grin at me. It was obvious that he knew just how much I had enjoyed our interlude. "Aw, come on. I'm not that bad a kisser, am I?"

Not at all. I chose to ignore that remark. Turning away from Anthea's skeptical gaze, I marched the rest of the way to my room.

"We can pick up where we left off some other time," Kaige called after me, and damn if my pussy didn't twitch at the suggestiveness in his tone.

"What do you think you're doing?" Anthea snapped at him in a voice not quite low enough for me to miss it.

"She's helping clear my name," Kaige said, unperturbed. "Besides, a kiss never hurt anybody."

The thing was, it'd been more than a kiss. And it'd felt like a promise of many more things to come.

I closed the door to my room behind me and sank to the floor, bringing my fingers to my lips. They were tender to the touch. My panties were soaking wet.

I was in so much fucking trouble.

"What's wrong with you, Mercy?" I asked myself. "You can't let dick distract you."

So what if it had been over a year since I'd last gotten it on with anyone? I'd been around plenty of guys during that time without wanting to jump their bones in a fucking hallway.

"Fuck." I took off my shoes and then stalked to the bed, thinking maybe I'd let off some steam all on my own. I was about to flop down on the mattress when I noticed a piece of paper on the floor. It drifted closer on the breeze that slipped through the open window.

It was a lined paper like kids used in school, slightly crumpled, with a drawing covering most of its surface. The lines were haphazard, almost childish themselves, obviously not drawn by any great artist. Even Rowan's half-hearted doodle had shown more skill, so this definitely wasn't his. The rough sketch showed the face and shoulders of a girl with cat ears drawn over her hair.

Very funny. It was obviously meant to be me, Princess Katz the Kitty Cat. But who had drawn it, and why leave it for me to find?

I picked it up to get a better look at it, and my fingers tightened, creasing the paper. Any lust that'd still been coursing through my body vanished in an instant under a wave of horror.

At a glance, I'd thought the line by the girl's neck had been a shirt collar. Instead it was a gaping wound, blood pouring down from it. Someone had drawn me and then imagined slitting my throat.

And they'd wanted me to know it.

15

Wylder

Bam, bam, bam.

Every shot hit the target smack in the middle of the chest. I adjusted the gun in my hands, the feel of the butt heavy but comforting against my palm, and aimed at the head next.

Bam, bam, bam. Another perfect tattered hole. Smiling, I switched on the safety, removed my earplugs, and set the gun on the table next to the array of other weapons.

I picked up my phone and added the model to my list of mastered guns. Testing the new makes that came in, especially 9mms, on our personal range was one of my favorite activities. All the chaos that came with this life fell away with the muffled blare of the shots and the jolt of the kickback. Simple, direct, powerful. Exactly the way I aimed to be in all things.

A voice carried across the lawn from behind me. "Wylder."

I looked up to see Gia sashaying toward me. She almost tripped on a dip in the grass when she neared me, but I made no attempt to reach for her.

I let my expression darken. "What are you doing here? No one except the official crew is allowed on the range."

The ditz giggled and twirled a strand of her blonde hair. "It's fine. I'm not scared of guns." The way she eyed the weapons arranged on the table suggested otherwise. "Are you practicing?"

"Checking out some of the merchandise. I don't need practice." The first time my father had brought me out here, I'd been six years old. And he'd ridden me even harder after—

I dismissed that thought before it could rise all the way to the surface.

Gia giggled. "I'm sure you've got great aim. I'd love to watch you work."

"Sorry to tell you I was just finishing up."

As I moved to sweep the guns back into the crate, she sidled up to me, running a finger down my neck. I grasped her hand and pushed it away. I'd only tolerated her fawning earlier for Mercy's sake. The look on the Katz's princess's face when Gia had practically climbed onto me had been priceless.

She curled her lip into a pout she probably thought was sexy. "If you don't like that, why don't you tell me what you would like?"

I ignored that question. "What do *you* want, Gia?"

"I was just hoping to get to know you better," she said, putting both her arms around my shoulder.

I had the strongest urge to roll my eyes. I could see through her bullshit from miles away. She was no different from the countless girls who walked in and out of my life—just particularly desperate. She was after the power and protection that came with being a Noble woman, either as a mistress or something more permanent.

It was no good telling her that this life would slowly strip her of her dignity and respect—either they never believed it or they didn't give a fuck. It wasn't even *me* she wanted, just my proximity to power.

If I pushed her away hard enough, she'd find someone else to latch onto without more than a moment's regret. The whole thing left a sour taste in my mouth.

"Wylder!" somebody called out. Mercy was striding toward us, moving like a force of fury and spitfire. When she saw Gia hanging off my arm, her face tightened.

A twisted sort of satisfaction coursed through me. To piss her off, I pulled the other girl closer. Even Gia looked shocked for a second before she snuggled against me.

Unfortunately, Mercy didn't look fazed. And the defiant energy radiating off her was having way too much effect on my cock.

She slammed a piece of paper on the table with so much strength I practically hit half-mast just like that. "What the fuck is this supposed to mean?"

Down, boy, I thought at my least obedient body part, and frowned at the paper. It held a pen drawing, rough and amateurish. "Why am I looking at this?"

She set her hands on her perfectly curved hips. "The great Wylder Noble can't figure it out for himself?"

My gaze lingered on the cat ears and then the vicious gouge along the figure's throat. Hmm. Before answering her, I turned to Gia. "I need to deal with this, babe," I said with a smile. "See you later?"

Gia sighed. Beside me, Mercy's fists balled at her sides. Toying with her was fast becoming my favorite activity.

Gia unstuck herself from me reluctantly and sauntered away. When I turned to Mercy, she was looking at me with barely hidden disdain. It almost made me laugh, but I managed to keep a straight face. "That's the company you enjoy keeping?" she said.

I shrugged and picked up the paper. "Are you applying to be a cartoonist? I'll say you need more work."

"I didn't draw it," she snapped. "Obviously. But that's definitely supposed to be me in the picture." She pointed at the cat ears.

I pretended to be shocked. "The resemblance is astounding."

She let out a huff. "Wylder, I'm serious. I found it in my bedroom—someone left it for me to see. This feels like a threat."

I cocked my head at her. "What do you mean?"

"I mean someone wants me gone—most likely in a body bag."

"I hardly think we should take cartoons so seriously."

She ignored my jibe. "Think about the rest of the company you keep. Are any of them likely to toss sketches into people's rooms as a joke?"

She might have had a point there, not that I was going to admit as much to her. "All right, let's hear what you have to say then. Who do you think left it?"

"My best guess would be Anthea," she said without hesitation. "She's already all but threatened me to my face. I could see her wanting to intimidate me into leaving. Not that it'll work."

A frown crossed my face for the first time. My aunt had done *what* without checking with me first? I held my annoyance under wraps. "Whatever else she's done, this doesn't look like Anthea's work to me. She doesn't play kiddie games."

"Maybe it was Gia, then."

I snorted. "Then you really have nothing to worry about. You'd take her down in five seconds flat, Princess."

I probably shouldn't have admitted that thought out loud, but thankfully Mercy seemed to be too distracted to notice the compliment. She glowered at the drawing. "I don't like it, that's all."

An idea unfurled in my head, my smile returning with it. I let my voice drop lower. "I can think of something that would help you feel safer."

Her gaze jerked up, suspicious... but not without a certain heat. Oh, the Claws' princess might have had shields up all around her, but she wasn't unaffected by me, not by a longshot.

"What did you have in mind?" she asked tightly.

I motioned to the table. "Can you use a gun?"

Her gaze followed my gesture, taking in the array. Her posture stiffened slightly, but she nodded. "I haven't in a while, but I know the basics."

Of course she did. Her father would have been an absolute failure if he hadn't even given his daughter a basic grounding, whether he'd considered her a proper heir or not.

"No time like the present to refresh those skills." I picked up a smaller model of gun, checked to see if the clip was loaded, and handed it to her. "Go on, try it out."

Mercy blinked at me in surprise. "You're putting a gun in my hands while you're standing there unarmed?"

"If you even think of pulling it on me, you'll be dead in less than two seconds."

She ignored my words and instead peered down at the guns again. Her hands hovered over each before she set down the one I'd given her and grasped one that was bigger. "I think I'm going to go with this."

Interesting. Ambitious. I liked that more than I wanted to. "Are you sure?"

She shot me a baleful look. "I wouldn't have said it if I wasn't. Now what?"

I grabbed a pair of earplugs from the case on the table and handed them to her. "Assuming you value your hearing." Then I nodded at the targets on the opposite side of the range, each showing the outline of a head and torso filled with concentric lines narrowing in to a bull's eye on the chest and forehead. There were three other than the one I'd already blasted away. "Pick one and try to hit a bull's eye."

Mercy hesitated, but only for a second. She marched over to stand in front of one of the targets, giving me an excellent view of her ample behind. That body was all soft curves, a major contrast to her personality.

She fired the first bullet before I could stop her. The force of the recoil made her stumble. I caught her shoulders before she fell. She looked up at me and then at my hands where I held her.

"Your stance could definitely use some work," I said before she could shake me off. Of course, I *had* to lean especially close so she could hear me with the earplugs in. "Allow me." I fixed her arms and angled her body toward the target. "You must hold it firmly but not too tightly. All your muscles can't be engaged, or it'll kick you back harder than it has to. You need to be able to hold your ground."

"I know that," she said through gritted teeth, elbowing me.

I tsked at her. "Easy, Kitty Cat. You might know how to use a gun, but your technique still sucks. Your old man obviously slacked off in your training." I ran my hands down to her waist, something I'd been wanting to do for a long time. She went very still as my hands skimmed her body. Hell, she smelled fucking amazing, the acrid scent of gunfire mingling with something darkly floral.

My cock hardened in my pants all over again. It would be so easy to lay her flat on the table and take her right there. From the soft hitch of her breath, I wasn't sure she'd even protest before her normally hostile words turned into sighs of pleasure.

Reining in that urge, I slid my finger over hers on the trigger. "There you go. And then you fire."

We squeezed together. The first bullet hit the target at the edge of the chest bull's eye. Mercy stared in shock for a second.

I forced myself to let go of her and stepped back, letting her take charge. She promptly finished the entire round, firing five more bullets in quick succession, each closer to the center than the last. It was unbelievably hot, and my jeans were feeling way too tight. This girl—this *woman*...

Mercy lowered the gun and popped out her earplugs. I took on a smooth, unaffected tone. "Very good."

She shot a glare over her shoulder at me. "I don't need your approval. I'm glad to improve my skills for my own sake."

"And so you should be." I gave her a sly smile. "And since I helped you get there, that's why you should always remain grateful to me."

"Thanks," she said, giving me the middle finger at the same time. I held back a laugh. She placed the gun on the table and pointed to the paper drawing again.

"Are we still on that?" I asked, amused.

"This is important," she said. "Tell Anthea if she *is* the one who left this, to—"

"I already told you. Anthea had nothing to do with it."

"You can't know that for sure. What would it hurt to bring it up?"

I shrugged. "It's not my problem."

Her jaw ticked. "You're making this difficult on purpose."

"No, you are." I walked right up to her, grinning at the momentary widening of her eyes when I had her locked against the table by my body. "My patience is limited. If you really want my help, you'd better focus on the problem at hand instead of stupid pranks. Or is there something else you want from me, something that needed a silly excuse to seek me out?"

My eyes dropped to her pouty lips. I wondered how she would look with them closed around my cock, worshipping it.

She glanced up, her gaze zeroing on my mouth. Fuck, the heat in her eyes almost made me come undone. My hands itched to pull her up to the table and sink my tongue in her hot mouth. I wanted to know if she tasted like violets as much as she smelled like them.

Without realizing what I was doing, I reached for her face, grazing my fingers along her chin. For just an instant, she leaned into my touch, her eyelids fluttering.

The next second, she was yanking away from me, horror written over her face. Frustration shot through me, but I quickly replaced it with a sardonic smile. I didn't want to let her see just how much this small rejection stung me.

"What happened?" I taunted. "Did the Big Bad Wolf scare you?"

Instead of answering me, she turned and stomped back toward the house. My cock throbbed in my pants, reminding me that even if she hadn't won this round, I hadn't exactly won either.

"Don't worry, Kitten," I murmured. I wasn't one to force women or to chase after skirts. They came to me because they knew I'd deliver what *they* wanted. It was never the other way around.

I could play the long game. There'd come a point when she'd no longer be able to resist what so much of her was already begging for.

16

Mercy

Even though Gideon had said Axel hadn't offered any useful information about Titus's death, I'd seen for myself how invested the guy was in his friend's death. So when I spotted him out in the front yard the next day with a few of his buddies, drinking and smoking cigarettes Wylder wouldn't have allowed most places inside, I figured it couldn't hurt to talk to them. I couldn't exactly end up with fewer leads than I already had.

I made my way toward them, squinting in the hot late-afternoon sun. The sharp scent of nicotine-laced smoke tickled my nose.

Axel gave me an amused smirk when he saw me approach. "We're being joined by royalty. Here's the infamous Claws princess."

So word about my identity had spread around here. Wonderful.

I ignored his bait. "I need to speak to you. Ideally alone."

He snorted. "You can do it here. There's nothing I'd say to you that these guys can't hear."

The other men were practically leering at me. My knuckles itched to land square on somebody's nose, but I forced my voice to stay even.

"Fine. I wanted to ask you about Titus. I heard you were the last person who talked to him before he fell."

Axel's face tightened. He threw the cigarette butt to the ground and crushed it under his heel. "Before he was pushed after being murdered, you mean. What about it?"

"Did he say anything to you about any run-ins he'd had earlier that day? Anyone who'd been hassling him recently?"

"No one was stupid enough to hassle the Titan," Axel said. "That's why he was Ezra's favorite to send in when any of the lowlifes in the Bend got too cocky. But no, he didn't seem concerned about anyone in particular. The only person I know he'd had a beef with was that attack dog of Wylder's."

Kaige. I tried another angle. "He didn't seem at all distracted?"

Axel scowled at me. "He took his job seriously."

"I mean, he must have been at least a *little* distracted if somebody was able to ambush him."

Axel jerked around to fully face me, the veins practically popping out of his tattooed head. "I don't like you implying that he got killed through his own carelessness. If that hotheaded prick hadn't gone fucking crazy, nothing would have happened."

"Why are you asking so many questions?" one of the other guys asked.

I didn't think they'd respond well to the idea that Wylder had me investigating to clear Kaige's name, so I just shrugged. "I'm curious. Since it seems like I might be sticking around for a while, I'd kind of like to figure out how a person makes sure they *don't* get murdered."

Another asshole snorted. "Steer clear of Kaige Madden. And get any delusions about joining the Nobles out of your head. Just because your family kicked the bucket doesn't mean there's an opening for some ghetto princess. I wouldn't aspire to anything higher than the big man's bed."

The others snickered, and I gritted my teeth. "You definitely won't find me anywhere near yours," I retorted.

He took a step closer, purposefully looming. "You'd be *lucky* to get a taste of this."

It might have been four to one, and they might have all had a good fifty pounds on me, but I couldn't stop myself from making a gagging sound. The guy bared his teeth like he was going to bite my head off, and I readied my fists, adrenaline racing through my veins. Maybe I'd get a chance to introduce him to my mean right hook. At least that'd mean a little action.

Then a far too familiar voice called out from across the lawn. "Hey, let's all take a step back."

I whirled around to find Rowan walking toward us, his stance casual but his eyes intense. The other guy stiffened, but he didn't make a move. Obviously he knew better than to challenge Wylder's inner circle openly.

"Did Wylder tell you to babysit her?" Axel sneered. "You should do a better job."

"I just think we can give a better impression to one of the Nobles' guests than getting into a fight with a woman over a few comments," Rowan said calmly. "None of our egos are that fragile."

He did have a weird way with them that somehow deflated the tension. I guessed Axel couldn't exactly argue with his statement. Axel flicked his gaze toward me for just a second. "I've said all I'm interested in sharing. Beat it." He and his group ambled a little farther across the lawn, falling back into their original chatter.

Rowan reached as if to touch my shoulder and then drew his hand back. "Are you okay?"

I glared at him. "I was perfectly fine. I've spent more time around guys like this than *you* have." Why was he always annoyingly around just when I appeared to need help?

I turned toward the mansion, meaning to stalk back inside, but one of the things Axel had mentioned wriggled up through my mind. Ezra had sent Titus into the Bend to lay down the law when things got particularly bad. Gideon had mentioned something about that too. The start of a plan unfurled in my head.

Rowan was still watching me. "What are you up to now?"

"Just finding ways to fulfill the job your boss gave me," I said. "I'd rather do it without spectators."

He looked as if he might have said something more, but then he just shook his head and walked away. Good. I didn't want to find out what he'd say if he realized I was heading back to my hometown.

Technically, going into the Bend right now was dangerous. Colt probably still had the Steel Knights on the lookout for me. But I knew that place better than the back of my own hand. The streets were my home. I'd just stick to Claws territory, keep my head low, and there'd be nothing to worry about.

I slipped into the house just long enough to grab my new hoodie, which was a little hot for the current weather but would help me avoid notice, and a switchblade someone had left on a side table. Their loss, my gain. I tucked the knife into the hoodie's pocket and stuffed the hoodie under my arm for now. No need to draw attention around here before I was well on my way. Kaige had already spotted me taking off once before.

And speak of the devil, as I crossed the lawn, guess who came sauntering out of the garage, his gaze immediately zeroing in on me. Shit.

Kaige grinned when he saw me. "I hope you're not being a bad kitty and running off on us again."

Annoyance shot through me at his riff off Wylder's nickname, but I shook it off. I wasn't going to waste time here. Besides, just the sight of him made my lips tingle as the memory of our hot and heavy make-out session crowded my head. "I was just heading out to look into something that might help clear your name."

One corner of his mouth curled upward. "Need a ride? It'd save you spending your ring money on another taxi. I'm done with my car for the day."

I blinked, startled by the unexpectedly generous offer. The cab ride to my house the other night hadn't been cheap. "Yeah, that would be perfect, actually."

"Follow me," he said, and had to add one of his sly winks. "We could even warm up the engine before you go."

I rolled my eyes, but I followed him as he returned to the garage, which was a two-story building with a huge metal door. Kaige tapped in a code, and the door yawned open to reveal a sprawling bay. There were several cars haphazardly parked next to each other. I recognized Wylder's

Mustang. There was a night-black Jaguar next to it, which I wouldn't be surprised to find out belonged to him too.

"One of the few areas where I'd disagree with Wylder is his taste in cars," Kaige said as if he could read my thoughts. "He's more of a style over substance man."

I followed him into the bay. "So which one is yours?"

He pointed to a sleek dark blue Audi. I walked up to it and ran a finger down the hood. It looked like a car Kaige would drive, not too flashy but with an undeniable presence. Just like him.

He leaned against the car and eyed me with some interest.

"What?" I asked.

"I didn't say anything."

"You're really going to let me drive off in this thing, no further questions asked?" It was hard to believe it'd be that easy.

Kaige shrugged. "You're going to try to get me out of trouble. I kind of owe you, don't I?" A lazy grin crossed his face. "Anyway, Gideon has all our cars outfitted with his fancy tracking devices and all that shit. You wouldn't get far with it if you tried anything sneaky."

I hadn't been planning on it, but that was good to know in case I ever had the urge to turn car thief. I held out my hand. "All right then. Where's the key?"

He pointed to his jeans pocket. "Right here. Come and get it."

I narrowed my eyes at him, knowing exactly what he was doing. Undeterred, I hung my hoodie from a side mirror and marched up to him. He watched me through hooded eyes, his smoldering gaze tracing a path slowly from my legs to my face.

I made a grab for his pocket, but he dodged and snatched the key out before I'd gotten to so much as grope his muscular thigh. I raised an eyebrow. "Give it to me."

Kaige grinned and held the key up high. "You'll have to try harder than that."

I stood up on my toes and reached, but he was just too damn tall. I'd never win this fight fairly, so I made use of my own bodily assets. Leaning in, I pushed my tits against his hard chest and then did a wiggle so that his body was deeply aware of the soft mounds. Kaige froze.

I took the opportunity to yank his hand down and grab the key. But maybe that was all part of his plan too. Before I could skip out of reach, he closed his arms around me. "Where do you think you're going?" he rumbled. "I'm not done with you yet." Then he ducked his head and caught my mouth with his.

Some small part of me wanted to push him away like I had in the hall. But it was a *very* small part, and the rest of me was screaming to just enjoy this moment already.

I deserved this, didn't I? I sure as hell didn't owe my ex-fiancé anything. And maybe if I let loose some of the sexual tension that'd been building inside me, my hormones would quit going haywire over Wylder's antics. I didn't really trust him *or* Kaige, but between the two of them, I'd rather put my body in Kaige's hands any day.

Those thoughts whipped through my mind, and I gave in to my desire. As Kaige's mouth ravaged mine, I gave back just as good.

There was nothing gentle about the kiss. One of his hands reached up to grip my ponytail while the other grasped my waist, almost digging into my skin as he pushed me against the hood of the car. Without breaking the kiss, he put his arms under my ass and effortlessly pulled me on top of the firm steel.

My arms encircled his neck. Our tongues danced to gain control over the other, and nobody was ready to back down. His teeth grazed my lips and then nipped, with a pinch of pain that only made the pleasure of the kiss spike hotter. I moaned, my pussy clenching hard. Oh, we were going to heat up this engine all right.

I put my legs around him, tugging him closer. The feel of his hard cock digging into my inner thigh almost unraveled me.

Kaige abandoned my mouth long enough to mark a trail down my neck, kissing and licking. I gasped softly as his lips bit down on my earlobe before slowly sucking on it.

One of his hands reached up from my waist to skim along my side and finally cup one of my breasts. He massaged it greedily, sending giddy tingles all through my chest. "Fuck," he muttered. "I've got to have a taste of these."

Without wasting an instant, he picked up the hem of my shirt and pulled it up over my arms, almost tearing it at the seams. Kaige tossed the shirt to the side and turned to me. As his gaze roamed over my tits, his hungry brown eyes turned almost black with lust.

I hadn't had a lot of choice in the store I'd found, and my breasts were practically spilling out of the thing. My hard nipples pressed eagerly against the thin cotton material.

Kaige pulled on one before leaning over and sucking it into his mouth. I pressed my palms against the hood for balance. Even through the cotton, the feel of his hot mouth made my pussy impossibly wet.

He pushed the strap down to reveal one mound. Flicking the nipple with his finger, he looked up at me, his gaze scorching. Without breaking eye contact, he devoured the bare nipple as if it were the best meal he'd ever had.

Fuck, he was turning me on so badly. He kept shooting those lustful glances at me as he alternated between sucking on my nipple, nipping it between his teeth, and laving it with his tongue again. I growled at the myriad of sensations, each better than the other. My mind had lost the ability to think.

I pulled his face back up to me and kissed him hard. Kaige groaned into the kiss before pushing me away, panting. I blinked up at him.

"What?" I asked, my voice coming out so thick and husky I hardly recognized it.

Instead of answering, he pulled out a condom from his jeans, rolling the foil between his fingers. The question was clear in his eyes.

Despite my earlier resolve, I hesitated. But I knew my body needed this. It was practically screaming at me for release. What could a quick roll in the hay—or, well, the garage—hurt? Fate owed me a little distraction after everything that had happened in the past week.

Only an idiot would say no to it.

I took the packet from him and ripped the foil open. Kaige beamed at me before leaning in to kiss me again.

In a tangle of urgent movements, I yanked off his shirt and he started unbuttoning the fly of my jeans. Together, we helped him out of his own. I ran my hands along the hard planes of his chest, his muscles flexing under my fingers, the vines tattooed all across them rippling.

"Like what you see?" he asked. I chose not to answer.

His hand brushed against the sensitive skin of my thighs, skimming upwards. I held my breath as he reached my slick core. He stroked me and then slipped a finger in, and I practically exploded right there.

"You're so wet already," he whispered, curling another finger inside me. "So wet for me."

I'd be gushing in a moment. As the waves of bliss swept over me, I clutched hard at his shoulder so that I wouldn't slip off the car. He continued to kiss my neck as his fingers worked inside me. My eyes rolled up, and I ran my fingers down his bare back.

As his deft fingers flicked my swollen clit, I couldn't help crying out. My hips moved against his hand of their own accord, swaying with his rhythm.

"Easy, Kitten," he said gruffly, reaching down to roll the condom over his hard dick. I set my fingers over his and slid them along his length. His cock twitched in our combined grasp, as huge as the rest of him. I groaned at the size of it.

As soon as he was sheathed, he stepped between my legs and in one fluid motion, plunged into me. My body bucked against his. I stretched with his girth, shivering at the heady mix of pleasure and pain.

He thrust hard and rough, just the way I needed it. "Do you like that?" Kaige murmured. "Do you like my cock inside you?"

I gasped in answer, which was easier than admitting that yes, I did, very fucking much. With each thrust, he started swirling his hips so he hit the perfect spot inside. Damn, he was good at this.

Another moan slipped out of me, and Kaige brushed a teasing thumb over my lips. "Shhh, Kitten. You wouldn't want to get too loud. The walls echo, you know, and who knows who might come in to check on things."

The thought of somebody walking in on us—especially Wylder—shot a burst of excitement down my spine. A part of me wanted him to watch and seethe, knowing he would never own me like this.

Kaige eagle spread me on the hood, keeping a hand on my shoulder as he continued to pump inside me. Somehow the friction at my back heightened that between my legs.

He reached down between us and found my clit even as he continued to stroke into me harder and faster. My body jerked against his as both his finger and his cock found exactly the right spot at the same time. The orgasm climbed in me, careening toward a crescendo, and then I was flying on it.

My body sagged against the hard metal, but Kaige didn't let me recover from my first orgasm before he flicked my clit again, setting off another swell of ecstasy just like that. The crest of pleasure was even bigger this time. Everything around me hazed out with the blaze of bliss.

Kaige followed me with a guttural sound, his body jerking more erratically. He slumped too, almost collapsing on me, our labored pants intermingling with each other. A drop of sweat from his forehead rolled down to my body. He followed the trail to my tits, sucking on my nipple one last time before he pulled out of me.

Jesus fucking Christ. My legs still shook from the aftermath of the second orgasm, and my thumping heart was threatening to burst out of my ribs. When had sex *ever* felt that good?

Kaige tossed the condom away into a bin by the wall and pulled up his jeans. I dropped to the ground and almost lost my footing. I'd had good dick in my day, but I hadn't felt after-effects quite like this. Kaige knew his way around a woman.

And he was fully aware of that fact. "You okay?" he asked slyly as he caught my shoulder to steady me.

I nodded, getting a grip on myself. It'd just been sex—fantastic sex, but still only sex. And it'd probably only seemed so freaking fantastic because I was coming off the longest dry spell of my life.

Turning away from Kaige, I collected my clothes. He watched me lazily as I got dressed. His black hair stuck damply to his scalp, and he looked almost boyish as he stood, greedily drinking in the sight of me. My pussy started throbbing again as if it was ready for round two.

Oh, fuck no. It wouldn't do me any good getting hooked on this guy. We'd had a bit of fun, but I wasn't going to let it mean anything at all.

17

Mercy

Kaige tossed me the car key, which I caught easily. "That was one hell of a detour," he said with a grin.

"Thanks," I said, ignoring his innuendo. Yes, we'd just had mind-blowing sex, but his ego clearly didn't need any stroking on that score. It was time for me to get down to work.

Kaige gave me a strange look as I climbed into the Audi. You'd have thought he'd be happier about my easy-going approach. I mean, we'd just had our first hook-up on the hood of his car. Presumably he hadn't thought we'd be holding hands and whispering sweet nothings next.

I started the engine and smiled. This beat a taxi by a mile.

Kaige hit the button to open the garage door for me, and I thanked him with a little wave as I cruised past. I pulled out of the driveway and swung the car around the corner to careen down the steep hill that led into the center of Paradise City. As the car zoomed toward the bend, I leaned back in the buttery leather seat.

It smelled like Kaige—musky with a bit of a spicy bite, like ginger or something. To my annoyance, the scent set off a flare of heat low in my belly. When I squeezed my thighs, I could feel the lingering wetness between them.

Okay, maybe a *tiny* part of me hoped our hook-up would turn out to be more than a one-time thing.

As Paradise City's pretty streets gave way to the Bend's grittiness, a twinge of homesickness rippled through my chest. I knew each and every corner of the place. Before my formal education had even begun, Dad had made me memorize the street names and the by-lanes that ran past them. I'd made so many nooks and ledges my own, sneaking in my parkour practice when I could. This neighborhood had been *mine*, and now Colt had me running scared.

He'd pay for that like he would for so much else.

I found a quiet street in Claws territory and parked the Audi there out of view, because even if it wasn't especially flashy, a car this nice would draw the wrong kind of attention. As I stepped out, I pulled on my hoodie, yanking the hood up to hide my ponytail and shadow my face. The sun was starting to sink, thank God, because one minute in these clothes and I was already sweating.

There were a few bars in the neighborhood where disreputable types tended to gather. I headed toward the nearest one. Passing my favorite diner, Joe's Morning, a whiff of pancakes-for-dinner filled my nose and made my mouth water. Whenever I'd been feeling low, I'd stop by here.

Movement caught my eye. Up ahead, a grey car had stopped in the middle of the street. Three guys got out. One was swinging a baseball bat idly, though there definitely wasn't anywhere to play around here, and they all had red bandanas tied around their upper arms. Red bandanas with an emblem of a knight's helmet on them.

I froze. I hadn't expected to run into a whole squad of Steel Knights in the middle of Claws territory. With a lurch of my heart, I ducked into the closest alley, clutching the switchblade.

They didn't seem to be at all interested in a young woman walking down the street, though. They stalked right past my alley with a thrum of energy around them that told me something was about to go down. Frowning, I edged closer to the mouth of the alley to watch.

The guys marched up to the barber shop right across from Joe's. The leader rapped on the door with his bat.

A few moments later, a man poked his head out, his eyes wide. "What's going on here?"

"Where's our payment?" one demanded. "We sent out a message a few days ago. Now we're here to collect."

The man stared at them, bewildered. "I already paid my tithe to the Claws."

"The Claws are gone and dust," one of the Steel Knights replied. All three of them looked younger than me. That and their exaggerated swagger made me think they had to be new recruits. "These streets belong to us now."

My jaw clenched at his words. I was about to take a step forward when I remembered where I was—*who* I was. If I blew my cover, I was as good as dead. One little knife wouldn't do much good against the guns they were all undoubtedly packing.

But who the hell were these pricks to claim this territory as their own? The Claws leadership had barely been dead a week, and Colt was already mass-recruiting to fill the gap?

Not just recruiting but terrorizing the people who didn't fall in line as fast as the Steel Knights wanted.

"I—I don't know about this," the man stammered, and one of the guys grabbed him by the collar. As he dragged him out onto the sidewalk, the one with the bat smashed the shop's front window with a brutal swing.

I flinched at the shattering sound. Panicked people down the street started rushing away without making too much noise.

This wasn't exactly a new sight around here, but the streets were almost safe once each gang had established their territory. The Steel Knights were changing the very face of the Bend.

The guy who'd grabbed the shop owner shoved him down on his hands and knees. The man's shoulders shook. "I'll get your money. Please, this is my livelihood. Please."

His begging fell on deaf ears. When the guy with the bat stepped inside the barber shop, more smashing sounds followed in his wake. The third Steel Knight grabbed a can of gasoline from the car.

No. Anger built up inside of me like a whirlwind. My hands itched to find a gun or anything else to end this senseless violence, even if I had to use violence to do that.

The guy with the gasoline went into the shop and returned empty-handed with his bat-wielding colleague beside him. I knew what was going to happen, and I knew I couldn't stop it without risking everything, but I couldn't will myself to look away.

The apparent leader pulled a lighter from his pocket. "Let this be a warning to anybody who decides to cross the Steel Knights," he announced to the street at large. "We're the kings of this territory now. Everything here is ours."

With that, he flicked on the lighter and threw it through the store window. A terrible orange light spilled out, flames lashing at the frame and roaring higher inside. The owner, crouched on the pavement outside, started to sob.

The Steel Knights took turns kicking him. "Next time we ask you to pay up, you'd better have it ready or else."

After a few more jabs, they got back into their car and drove away. The sound of a fire engine's siren wailed in the distance. I knelt by the wall, trying to regain my breath as rage expanded inside my ribs until it felt like a splintering force.

My family hadn't even got a proper burial yet, and Colt's people were rampaging through my home, tearing it to shreds.

When I'd managed to calm the fury inside me enough, I walked across the street to where the fire was still raging. The man was weeping, beating his closed fist against the pavement. I crouched down next to him and took out a wad of money, most of what I had left from selling my engagement ring.

I'd bought everything I could use for now. He needed it a hell of a lot more than I did.

"Here," I said. "Take this."

He looked up at me with tear-filled eyes. He might have recognized me—Dad had made me a semi-public figure, dressing me up and dragging me to events. Showing off the daughter he sneered at in private.

"I'm going to make this right," I promised. The man nodded, but I couldn't tell if he believed me.

There was nothing else I could do but walk away. But I wasn't leaving it behind, not really.

The farther I went, the more evidence I saw of the Steel Knights claiming this territory. Fresh graffiti marked the walls. More guys with the knight emblem bandanas prowled the streets. There were plenty of people who'd pledged loyalty to my father still alive around here, but apparently no one was willing to push back without a leader.

I guessed I couldn't totally blame them. I'd gone running for help—they hadn't had the same option.

By the time I reached my intended destination, an old brownstone building in the warehouse district with a crooked banner that announced its name was Rookers, my stomach was churning with even more anger than before.

I entered the dimly lit room to the smell of old whiskey and smoke. The place was fairly crowded even though it was early in the evening. A few guys circled around a table were playing poker with chips, and others were occupied at the snooker table placed to the side. Twangy country music played over the speakers.

I walked up to the bartender, an old man who was cleaning the glasses. He didn't look like he was interested in serving anybody, but I took a place on one of the empty bar stools anyway. A guy sitting a few places down swirled a glass of amber liquid in his hand.

"What do you want to drink?" the bartender snapped.

So much for customer service. I considered the cash I still had on me, which wasn't much. But I definitely wouldn't make any friends here if I didn't cough up a little dough as a paying customer. "Gin and tonic. Strong." I needed it to drown out my fury over everything I'd witnessed outside.

A few moments later, he passed me a glass. I drank it slowly, letting the burn of the alcohol seep through my body. My other hand dropped to the pocket of my jeans, where my fingers traced the outline of my childhood bracelet.

Little Angel. Was that how my mother had seen me? I sure as hell wasn't an angel now, and that was a good thing. Bitches got things done. Angels… Maybe they ended up like her, either run out of town for fear of her life or buried in a grave somewhere.

Dad had never given me a straight answer about where she'd gone when she'd disappeared, but even at six, I'd been able to tell he was upset that she hadn't given him another kid. The boy he wanted that he'd never gotten.

Considering how many women he'd tried with, that'd obviously been *his* fault. Not that he'd ever have admitted it.

When I'd almost finished my drink, I tossed out a casual remark. "Say, I heard Titus used to stop by here now and then. Have you seen him lately?"

The bartender frowned. "Who?"

"A big guy," I said. "*Really* big. Some people called him the Titan. I wanted to talk to him about something."

The man grimaced. "From what I've heard, he's dead, girl. A pretty thing like you doesn't want to mess with that business."

"Oh my God." I pretended to be shocked. "How did he die?"

The man farther down the bar glanced over at me. Uneasiness made the back of my neck prickle. I turned my head so my hood would shield more of my face from his nosiness.

"From what I heard, he got drunk and took a fall," the bartender said. I guessed that was the story Ezra Noble preferred to have spreading around rather than that someone within the gang had murdered one of his top guys.

"Seems like a strange way to die," I ventured, watching the bartender's reaction.

He swiped his rag over the countertop harder. "You never know. He certainly didn't have many friends around here. A person's sins can catch up to them eventually."

Vague and noncommittal—playing it safe. He knew how things worked in Paradise Bend.

As if any of us here didn't have plenty of sins to our name. Man, if this place was any type of Paradise, it was definitely the crooked kind.

I kept my tone neutral. "Is there anyone here who he might have talked to at all? Maybe they could give me a hand with what I was going to ask him about."

"I can't think of anyone, but around here, he's more likely to have been breaking bones than hanging around to chat." He turned his back on me, conversation over. I wasn't getting anything else out of him, but I didn't think he knew any details about the murder anyway.

I looked around, wondering who to try next. The snooker guys seemed to be as good a bet as any. I slipped off my stool and sauntered over to lean against the table.

I wasn't exactly a sexpot in this hoodie, but one of them looked up after taking a shot and gave me an unrestrained leer. I forced a smile. "You play really well."

He smirked. "Thanks. I haven't seen you around here before. Looking for some... action?"

"Buddy, pay attention to the game," one of his friends said with a sigh.

"This isn't my scene usually, but I come by every now and then," I said, trying to keep him engaged. "I think I have seen you before—were you playing with Titus?"

One of the men snorted. "The Titan? He never touched a cue in his life—except maybe to break it over someone's head."

I bit my tongue. Wrong tactic. But Titus clearly had a reputation around here. No one seemed to have any specific personal animosity toward him, though.

From the corner of my eye, I noticed the man from the bar now lingering in the corner. Was he trying to listen in on our conversation? A chill washed through me. Had he realized who I was?

I was probably being paranoid, but my gut told me that I would rather be safe than sorry. This place felt like a dead end.

"Thanks for your time, gentlemen," I said and ambled off as if I wasn't in any hurry. Outside, I glanced at the reflection on the window of another storefront and saw the man follow me out. Picking up my pace, I took off toward a row of old warehouses, most of which were in terrible condition.

After walking for a few blocks, I glanced around and found the man had vanished. Crouching as if I needed to tie my shoes, I scanned the area for the space of several more heartbeats. When I didn't see any sign of him, I exhaled in relief. False alarm.

The grumble of a large vehicle brought me back onto my feet.

Slipping into the deepening shadows of a doorway, I watched an armored truck approach. What the hell was *that* doing here?

I caught a glimpse of a red bandana around the arm of the guy in the passenger seat. The Steel Knights were behind this too. The truck had to be carrying something important. Drugs? Weapons?

As it disappeared around a turn, I made a split-second decision to follow it, breaking into a sprint to catch up. I had to figure out what they were up to. We couldn't take down Colt if we didn't know everything he was preparing.

The armored truck was moving slowly as if the driver was concerned about jostling its contents too hard. That was an ominous sign. I managed to keep up with it in short dashes between bits of shelter, never letting myself get too close. When it veered into Steel Knights territory, the hairs on the back of my neck rose, but I was committed now.

After several more blocks, the truck swerved to pass through a low gateway. Behind a crumbling brick wall around a courtyard, the dingy form of another warehouse loomed. As I came up on the wall, the truck's engine cut off somewhere inside the compound and a man started shouting commands.

Itching to take a closer look, I slunk over. I hitched myself up using the few loose bricks that stuck out of the wall. It was an easy climb. Keeping my head low, I peered over the top.

Men were ferrying huge crates from the rear into the warehouse. A tall man stepped out of the back of the truck, and my blood ran cold. I didn't know his name, but his face was burned into my memory. He'd been with Colt the night of the rehearsal dinner—he was the one who'd shot my grandmother.

"Hurry up, we don't want to dawdle around all day," he hollered.

One of the men heaved his crate out faster, and it slipped from his grasp. As it crashed to the ground, its lid jolted off.

"You idiots," the man snarled. "Can't even do one thing right."

I squinted to see the crate's contents. It looked like guns, large ones nestled in straw. Lots of them, from how many I could make out and the size of the crates.

They must have been bringing in hundreds. What the fuck did they want with so many weapons all of a sudden? It almost looked like they were planning for a major assault.

Against who? Hadn't taking down the Claws been enough? How much of the Bend did they want—and what made them think they'd need an army's worth of firepower to get it?

Unless...

My stomach twisted. I dropped down the wall before I could be spotted and hurried in the opposite direction.

I needed to get back to the city, back to the mansion, and tell Wylder and his guys what I'd seen. This could be even worse than I'd thought.

I hurried past several blocks of buildings without registering much. I was so lost in my thoughts that I almost didn't notice when I bumped shoulders with somebody on the sidewalk.

"Watch it," a familiar voice snarled.

I whirled around and found myself staring at Gia, a thin jacket covering most of her skinny frame and a small duffel bag clutched against her side. My shock was mirrored in her eyes.

"What are *you* doing here?" she squawked before I could ask her the same thing. She whipped a knife out of her jacket and brandished it at me. "Are you stalking me now, you fucking bitch?"

Whoa, talk about going from zero to one hundred in an instant.

"Why the hell would I stalk a pathetic excuse for a human being like you?" I shot back. "I didn't even see you until you smacked into me."

"*You* bumped into *me*. I knew you had to be some kind of psycho. Get the fuck away from me!"

She waved the knife, but I didn't flinch. Maybe it was time Gia found out exactly what happened when you went around throwing insults at the wrong people. I didn't even bother reaching for the switchblade in my pocket—just my fists against Gia seemed like an awfully unbalanced fight.

"I have just as much right to be here as you do," I said evenly. "So why don't you scamper off and leave me to my business?"

She scoffed. "If you don't take off *right* now, I'm gonna—"

I didn't get to find out what she was going to threaten me with—and how hard I was going to laugh at the thought—because just then a cool, hard voice rang out from behind me.

"If it isn't my lovely fiancée. Come to pay me a visit?"

My body turned to ice. I spun around and came face to face with Colt Bryant.

18

Mercy

GIA SLOWLY LOWERED HER KNIFE, HER GAZE FLICKING FROM me to Colt and clearly evaluating him as a greater threat. The bulge of a gun showed clearly at his hip. "Who the hell are you?" she asked, but her bravado had gone thin.

He flashed bright, vicious teeth. "The man who owns these streets—no one you want to mess with. I'd like to speak with my fiancée *alone*."

Gia hesitated for only a second before darting away. Colt immediately returned his full focus to me. He circled me like a shark does to its prey.

As I stood face to face with him for the first time since our rehearsal dinner, conflicting impulses tore through my body. The bastard looked so fucking *smug*. Fury unfurled in my chest, urging me to hurl myself at him and rip out his throat with my bare hands if that was what it took. But the—smaller, but insistent—sensible part of me pointed out that he'd probably put a bullet in my brain before I even touched him. My chances of destroying him were way better if I lived to return with proper reinforcements.

I considered bolting after Gia—or in any direction, really—but before the thought could solidify in my head, several Steel Knights men closed in around us. I stiffened, willing back a surge of panic.

This wasn't a chance encounter—Colt had shown up prepared to overpower me. My chances had just dwindled from slim to none. No way could I take on all of them.

"So, you've finally come home," Colt said. "It took you long enough. Got bored of your shiny new friends?"

Did he know where I'd been the past few days? I balled my hands at my sides and then shoved them into my pockets, curling my fingers around the switchblade. If he was going to order my death now, I'd do everything I could to take him with me, hopeless as my chances were.

Colt tracked the movement with eyes that were too keen. He held out his hand. "Whatever you're thinking, it isn't going to work. Give it to me."

Shit. I wavered, and heard the safeties click off several guns. A prickle ran down my spine. I pulled out the folded switchblade and tossed it at him so it smacked into his chest. "Happy?"

"Getting there." He gestured to a lackey, who bent to snatch up the knife. "How have *you* been doing these days, Mercy?"

When I didn't answer, a few of his men snickered. I gritted my teeth. "Are you having fun toying with me before you gun me down? Ten to one—that's awfully stacked odds for a man who thinks he's such a hotshot."

Colt didn't rise to my bait. "Who said anything about gunning you down? I just wanted to talk."

He chuckled darkly, running his fingers through his thick golden hair. I couldn't believe I'd found him attractive once.

"Keep talking and I'll jam my fist down your throat." I took a step toward him, and immediately all his men jerked their weapons up.

"Stand down, boys," Colt said, raising his hand. "I'm sure my fiancée and I can manage to have a civil conversation."

"Don't you fucking call me that. There's nothing I want to say to you." All I wanted was to choke the life out of this asshole.

"We *will* talk," he insisted. "But this definitely isn't the best spot for it. Come along."

He motioned for me to follow him, and his men drew closer. My skin prickled with resistance, but I didn't have much of a choice. Better to stay alive a little longer and see if I could find an opportunity to escape after all.

When I didn't move right away, one of his men nudged me with his gun. "Walk."

"Don't touch her," Colt said with a warning in his voice. The hint of possession in his tone surprised me. Was he seriously making some gesture toward protecting me after what he'd done?

What did he want to talk about anyway?

With curiosity gnawing at me, I pushed myself forward. We walked for a good fifteen minutes before we reached a part of the Bend which wasn't as impoverished.

Had Colt been down in the warehouse district overseeing the weapons delivery and caught sight of me without me noticing? Or maybe that man from the bar had been some kind of narc after all, identifying me and then running off to tell his master.

Fucking Gia distracting me. I could have been back to Kaige's car by now if it wasn't for her.

Colt's men escorted me inside an old brick office building and up the stairs to the third floor. We stepped through a doorway into an airy open-concept space that smelled of raw wood.

The room was clearly being renovated, beams and chunks of tile scattered around. The breeze carried through the windows, which hadn't been fitted with fresh panes yet. My gaze latched onto one that looked out onto a narrow alley between this building and the one next door, no more than five feet away.

There was my escape route right there, one Colt and his men would never anticipate. I'd mentioned my old interest in gymnastics to Colt once, but never how that had evolved into riskier stunts after Dad had cut off my classes.

Colt motioned for his men to stand guard on the landing outside. "I'd like to talk with her alone."

I eased closer to the window I'd noticed, pretending to be examining the space. The walls at the other end looked recently painted. No furniture had been brought in yet. "What is this place?"

"Just one of my many new bases of operation within my new kingdom." Colt stalked closer to me, and I used that as an excuse to back up in the direction of the window. "Or perhaps I should say *our* kingdom?"

My jaw went slack. Colt was watching me shrewdly. "You killed my family," I spat out. My hand rose to the still healing spot on my arm where one of his men's bullets had clipped me. "You tried to kill *me*. There is no 'our.'"

For an instant, I could have sworn I saw a flash of regret before it was replaced by ruthless ice in his eyes. "I did what I had to do to protect myself," he said. "Your father was going to turn on me as soon as he had the chance."

"Bullshit. He wanted the alliance—it was *his* idea. Why would he work so hard for it only to kill you?"

Colt began to pace. "I can't tell you how your father's mind worked. I only know I've seen more than enough evidence to be sure of it. Our marriage was all part of his plan. As soon as he got a grandson as an heir, he'd have done away with me."

I thought back over all the times Dad had talked about cooperation between the Claws and the Steel Knights. I'd never heard a hint of that kind of malicious plotting. It didn't even make sense. It could have taken years, more than a decade for us to have kids, if we'd had any at all.

If he'd wanted a war with the Steel Knights, why wait around? He could have married me to some powerless man and hoped to get his heir that way.

Either Colt was making this up to justify what he'd wanted to do anyway, or he was totally delusional.

When I shook my head, Colt walked right up to me and grabbed me by the nape of my neck through my hood. There was nothing gentle about it. "You don't believe it?"

His eyes danced with a terrible light. For the first time, I began to wonder if something was seriously wrong with him.

His gaze dropped to my lips, still slightly tender from Kaige's ravaging just a couple of hours ago. His jaw clenched. Could he tell? Something inside me tightened despite myself.

Colt was an attractive man, his amber eyes like a panther about to pounce. He reminded me of Wylder in some ways—but the truth was, they couldn't be any more different. Wylder had shown me exactly who he was, no pretenses. My *ex*-fiancé had given me nothing but lies.

I shoved him away, and to my surprise, he let me go. "No, I don't," I said. "I knew my father a hell of a lot better than you did, and he was *excited* by all the possibilities of the partnership."

"I know what I've seen," Colt said quietly. "But it's become clear to me that you weren't in on his schemes. We can put the past behind us. Be my queen, and together you and I will rule all of the Bend."

I shook my head. "You're insane." Just a few weeks ago, his declaration would have woken up butterflies in my stomach, but now I felt nothing but disgust.

"I go after what I want. And *everyone* wants power. Don't lie to yourself, Mercy. You've got to see how much we could accomplish together." Colt paused. "Maybe your father knew what you'd be capable of too, and that's why he tried to break you."

I flinched. "The only person who's lied to me is *you*."

"But I now know that you had nothing to do with your father's plans," Colt said. "Your devotion wasn't false. So let's move on."

"I wasn't devoted to you," I snapped. I'd thought I'd been so calculating, but in the end I'd turned out to be a foolish, naïve girl who thought she could gain her freedom just like that. Ha.

Maybe it wasn't smart of me, but I couldn't stop my mouth from shooting off more. "You know what I think, Colt? What you're telling me is just another load of bullshit. And I'm not falling for it this time." I turned away from him and walked the last few steps to the window. The cooling evening air wafted over, beckoning me.

"What if we could rule all of Paradise Bend, not just the dregs down here?" Colt said, drawing me up short. That sounded all too close to the suspicion that had darted through my mind watching the weapons delivery.

I glanced over my shoulder at him. "What are you talking about?"

"Don't you think it's time the big men on the hill got taken down a peg? Or have you been impressed by those pompous bastards you went running to after all?"

My back went rigid. "How did you—"

Colt shook his head. "Did you really think I wouldn't realize where you'd gone? Even the Nobles can't ensure every mouth stays shut."

Fuck. This was even worse than I'd thought. Not that his stupid plan would get him very far. Wylder wasn't going to give a shit how Colt threatened me.

I raised my chin. "And there's the lie. That's why you actually brought me here—you want me as leverage."

Colt let out a short guffaw. "Hell, no. Mercy, I want you to help me take them down. Go back to them, dig up every weakness you can, trip them up with your wily ways, and lay them on a platter for me. Once the Nobles are out of the picture, we can rule the whole county. Our kingdom will stretch as far as the eyes can see." He swept his hand at the window at the front of the room.

"With the crown on your head and me under your heel?" I retorted.

"I'm not your father. You won't be a commodity; you'll rule beside me. My queen and my equal."

Sudden tears pricked at the back of my eyes. Why did he have to say this *now* after he'd screwed me over in so many ways? It was even better than I'd dared to hope for with him—but I could never trust the man in front of me again. The thought of standing beside him, of letting him lay his hands on me, made me want to vomit.

If I ever touched him again, it'd only be to ram a knife right into his heart.

But as soon as he realized I wasn't going along with his crazy plan, he'd need me out of the picture. My heart thudding, I took one final step and rested my hand on the bare window ledge.

"No thanks. Not if you were the last man on earth. Fuck you."

His face hardened. He started toward me, his hand shooting out to snatch at my arm, but I was already launching myself out into the open air.

For a few tenths of a second, everything slowed down in the whoosh of air and adrenaline. My hands and toes planted against the concrete wall of the neighboring building just as they had so many times in so many less precarious situations.

My muscles responded on what was instinct after years of practice, shoving and spinning me at the same moment. I rebounded off the wall back toward Colt's building, dropping a few feet at the same time. No looking down. Just bouncing back and forth like a rubber ball slowly ricocheting to the ground. I'd scaled three floors going up this way before. I'd just never done it letting my momentum carry me down toward the potentially deadly surface below.

Shouts echoed through the windows above. I ignored them, concentrating on the thrust of my limbs and the rhythm of my breath. Back and forth and back and—

The rough brick scraped the heel of my hand hard enough to draw blood. I sucked in a breath at the sting, my concentration wavering just for a second. But then my feet hit the asphalt of the alley.

I'd made it all the way down. I was free, completely through my own power.

Footsteps were pounding down the staircase inside so loud I could hear them through the wall next to me. Riding the rush of my success, I sprinted out of that alley and into another across the street. Turning here, swerving there, I wove through the streets toward the spot where I'd left Kaige's car, until both my lungs and my calves were burning and I was sure Colt's men hadn't tracked me.

Even if they were still on my trail, I'd be long gone by the time they got here. I leapt into the Audi and tore onto the road heading into Paradise City, clenching the steering wheel tightly to stop my hands from shaking. The one I'd scraped was bleeding a little, dappling the surface of the wheel, but all things considered, I figured Kaige would forgive me.

By the time the bright lights on the hill came into view, dusk had settled over the county. I raced up the slope and sped into the driveway, parking outside the garage since I didn't have the code to open it.

My pulse was still pounding double-time. I threw open the door, peeling off my sweaty hoodie as I went, and rushed toward the house.

Before I'd made it even halfway to the front door, five figures burst out.

"Mercy," Rowan said, oddly short for breath. "Did you go back to the Bend?"

My hackles came up automatically. "What's it to you? You're not my keeper."

Wylder pushed in front of him, Gideon, Kaige, and Anthea right behind him. One look at the fury etched on the Noble heir's face stopped me in my tracks.

"No, but at the moment, *I* am," he said. "And from what I hear, you not just went scampering home, you've been cozying up to Colt Bryant behind our backs."

19

Mercy

I froze. There wasn't any question in Wylder's statement. It was an accusation.

Anthea folded her arms in front of her chest. "Don't try to deny it. Gia told us everything."

Of course she had. I reined in my anger, holding myself cautiously. "What exactly did she tell you?"

"That you were out in Steel Knights territory and met with your 'fiancé,'" Wylder said. "Seems like a funny thing for her to make up."

My hands clenched. "She didn't make it up—but it wasn't like—"

"Don't go making excuses," Kaige snarled, shoving past Wylder. "This whole time you've been double-crossing us? After all the— I ought to—" Fury reddened his face, and veins popped from his neck and down his brawny arms. He lunged at me, only brought up short by Wylder grabbing his shoulder.

A chill rippled through me. Who the hell *was* this guy? Kaige's easy demeanor had been replaced by something I didn't even recognize, something feral and wild. If he'd gotten this enraged in his argument with Titus, I could see why Axel and the others thought he could have killed the guy.

How were Wylder and the others so sure he *hadn't*?

But despite my fear, a flicker of heat shot through the chill right down to my pussy. My God, what was wrong with me? He looked savage enough to tear me to pieces, and something about that was turning me on even as I flinched inwardly at having his hostility directed at me. An image flashed through my head of him taking me with all that brutal intensity, hate-fucking against his car in a fiercer version of this afternoon's hook-up.

I shook my head as if I could dispel my reaction. Kaige seemed to take the motion as a denial. "Don't lie to us now," he yelled, loud enough that Anthea winced. "You fucking betrayed us!"

"No, I didn't," I shouted back. "Maybe if you'd let me finish my goddamn sentence—"

"I don't want to hear anything from your stupid mouth." He jerked forward again, and it took both of Wylder's hands to haul him back. The Noble heir watched me coldly.

"We should let her talk," Rowan said quietly. "We have to know exactly what went down, what she told Colt—all of it."

Gideon nodded, his eyes sharply intense and even icier than Wylder's. "Yes. All the details, quickly." He snapped his fingers.

I drew in a breath, my skin prickling with nervous anticipation. This could go so very badly if they didn't believe me. My muscles in my calves flexed with the impulse to just make a run for it.

But now I wanted Colt and his lackeys destroyed more than ever, and I'd seen incredibly clearly that there was no way I was accomplishing that on my own.

"If *Gia* hadn't been lying, she'd have told you Colt ambushed me. She was right there—she must have been able to tell that I wasn't expecting to see him and that I wasn't happy about it. And then she took off, because all she cared about was saving her own skin."

Wylder scowled at me. "She said he's calling you his fiancée still. That's how we figured out who it was."

I barely restrained myself from rolling my eyes. "Fun fact: I don't have any control over what words that asshole uses. I'm sure as hell not calling *him* my fiancé anymore."

"Still, it's a rather friendly term," Gideon put in evenly. "And Gia got back here almost two hours ago. Where have you been all that time?"

"Colt had a bunch of his men with him. I didn't have the chance to get out of there. He took me to one of his buildings, insisted on talking to me. It took me a while to get away."

Anthea snorted. "And you just waltzed out of what I assume was a heavily guarded building with no problem at all? Sounds too convenient to be true."

Yeah, it probably did. I balked at admitting this skill to them—I preferred to keep as much as I could in my back pocket—but I had to explain my escape somehow.

"I did gymnastics as a kid," I said. "Until my dad decided it was a waste of time. But I wanted to keep practicing on my own, and while I was looking up training videos, I stumbled on parkour. It was even better—leaping and bounding all over the city, scaling buildings most people couldn't... I broke a few bones in the first couple of years, but I kept at it, and I'm pretty fucking good now, if I do say so myself."

Wylder cocked his head. "A very nice story, Kitty Cat, but it doesn't answer the question."

I glared at him. "It does if you have half a brain. I never talked to Colt about that recreational activity. So it didn't occur to him that it wasn't a good idea to let me get close to an open window. I took a flying leap and rebounded between the building and the one next door all the way to the ground. Ran off before his guys could make it down the stairs coming after me. I know the streets in the Bend pretty well, and we were close to Claws territory still."

Or what'd used to be Claws territory before the Steel Knights had pissed all over it to mark it their own.

"Bullshit," Kaige spat out, but he wasn't pulling against Wylder's grasp anymore. Maybe he'd gotten a glimpse of me using some of those techniques to get in and out of my house the other night.

I set my hands on my hips. "It's up to you whether you believe me or not. Do you need a demonstration or something?"

Rowan was studying me warily. "I never saw you do anything like that."

"Guess you didn't know me as well as you thought. Goes both ways, doesn't it?" I grimaced. "You didn't like hearing about me being in any kind of danger. I didn't think you'd want to hear about *me* putting myself in harm's way."

Anthea tapped her fingers against one elbow. "What I'd like to know is why Colt, who meant to murder you a week ago, decided to bring you around for an extended chat instead of shooting you where you stood."

It was time for the full truth, and I knew it could be an awfully bitter pill for them to swallow. "He figured I'd be more useful to him alive after all. He knows I've been staying here, and he had a proposition for me. He wanted me to join him and take the Nobles down."

Gideon stiffened while Kaige and Wylder swore in unison. "That motherfucker," Kaige said, the growl coming back into his voice. "I'm going to kill him."

"We'll get there," Wylder assured him before he turned to me. "Did you come back here to assassinate us then?"

I let sarcasm drip from my voice. "Right, that's why I just told you everything we talked about. Of course not! I wouldn't have needed to go jumping out windows if I'd agreed with him. I got back here as fast as I could because I wanted to *warn* you." *You fucking idiot*, I added silently, deciding this wasn't the right time to mouth off *quite* that much.

Wylder walked toward me and circled me like he was sizing me up. "I don't know. It's possible you're playing some kind of game. You want us to believe that you're on our side so we'll let our guard down."

I threw my hands in the air. "Why would I even *want* to side with that prick? He killed my family. He's taken everything I had. I want to see him six feet in the ground, not ruling over all of Paradise Bend."

Wylder watched me like a lion out to scent blood. He slid his fingers over the gun cradled on his hip. Beside him, Rowan shifted toward me. It was barely perceptible, but it almost felt as if he were trying to protect me from Wylder, which didn't make any sense because his loyalty lay to his boss, not to me. When I looked up, I caught a hint of pain flitting through his eyes. Then it was gone.

I fixed my gaze on Wylder again, girding myself. My father might have been a sadistic asshole, but he'd taught me a few useful things, and one of those was never to show anyone fear. *If a man sees he can't make you cower, he might hate you, but he'll respect you*, he used to say.

"You can't seriously be thinking of believing her." Kaige looked at me with pure venom. It was hard to imagine he was the same man who'd made me come harder than I had ever before just a few hours ago. Obviously *his* loyalty to the Nobles came far before any other emotion.

"It sounds to me like she's trying to double-cross us," Anthea says. "I haven't felt right about this since she first set foot in here. What's to say that she wasn't in on some scheme with Colt from the beginning?"

"He slaughtered my family in front of me without a second thought," I said. "His men put a bullet in my *grandmother*. Like you already pointed out, he tried to kill me. I've still got the stitches." I patted the bandage on my arm.

"You could simply be very committed to your role," Anthea pointed out. "He could have killed you today, but he didn't."

I swallowed a sigh of frustration. "You have to believe me, he's playing at something big here. When I was in his territory, I spotted his men ferrying weapons—enough to wage war on an entire city. They're already preparing to come for Paradise."

"Big dreams for a rat to have," Anthea said with a sneer.

I looked back at her without flinching. "My father underestimated him. Look where that got him."

Wylder eyed me silently.

"With all due respect," Gideon said. "We're not your father. He might have been a major power in the Bend, but that was the limit of it. We've got resources and manpower far beyond any small-time gang."

"Maybe," I said. "But the Steel Knights are already building their own power base, and fast. It doesn't hurt to be careful."

"Starting with you," Wylder said. "If trouble comes knocking at our door, it's chasing at your heels."

"I *declined* his offer," I said. "Even though agreeing might have saved my life if I hadn't managed to escape. Even though *you* haven't done anything for me yet. I hate Colt Bryant with everything I've got in me. I came to you because not only do I want to take him down, I want to crush him slowly and painfully until all he does is call out my name for mercy. Maybe I'll even laugh at the irony."

There was a pause following my words and I wondered if I'd said more than I should have.

"I don't trust you," Kaige said. "There's no way someone like you would have come out of an encounter with Colt unscathed unless he let you go."

Irritation raked through me. I couldn't beg or cajole them. These were hardened criminals. Once their mind was made up, they wouldn't budge.

I shrugged. "Think whatever you want. I've been completely honest."

"You know what I think?" Wylder said. "You're a pretty damn good actress, I'll give you that."

My heart stuttered. If even *he* didn't believe I was on their side, I was screwed. "Excuse me?"

"You're standing there pretending you're some kind of powerhouse when the truth is that you need us. Bad."

I couldn't even deny that. Suppressing a cringe, I lowered my head. "Yeah. And that's exactly why I wouldn't buy into some shitty plan to fuck you over. Haven't I proven I'm not that much of a moron by now?"

He was silent for a moment. Anthea stirred restlessly, probably itching to drag me to the curb—or maybe pour poison down my throat—but she let him take his time.

Finally, he rubbed his hands together. "After this little incident, I think I need to see just how badly you do want my favor. If you think I rode you hard before, you haven't seen anything yet. You want to stick around and get your revenge? Let's start by having you stay in the groupies' room tonight. No private accommodations or special treatment. If that's not good enough, you can go running back to your 'fiancé.'"

I bit back a protest. I didn't want to be anywhere near the girls like Gia who aspired no higher than hoping to get a regular ride on these guys' cocks. But my desire for revenge trumped my ego.

"Fine. Where's the groupie room?"

A smirk crossed his lips, one I longed to knock out with a punch. "You're so smart, I'm sure you'll figure it out."

20

Kaige

As we tramped into Wylder's study, my hands stayed balled at my sides.

This was what I got for letting my dick do the thinking. I'd been too distracted by a delectable ass, those sweet curves, and the eyes that always seemed to be begging me for a fucking. I still remembered how she'd looked when she'd come apart in my arms, keening and moaning. I'd given it to her good, and none of her nonchalance afterward had hidden that.

And me... I hadn't come like I had in her in years.

But none of that mattered now. I couldn't shake the waves of rage when I thought of the deception she'd hidden behind those pretty eyes. She'd told me she was going to investigate Titus's murder, to try to clear my name, and instead she'd driven straight to that jackass in my fucking car...

She was a snake in the shape of a goddess. I didn't know who I was angrier at—her or myself for falling for her act. What if I'd compromised the Nobles by giving in to her charms?

I paced from one end of the room to the other. "We should keep pushing at her until she breaks and gives away her real reasons for coming here. Then we toss her away." That was all there was to it.

Gideon gave me an analytical look that only annoyed me more. "Why are you so sure she joined forces with the Steel Knights?"

Why did he have to ask that? I couldn't pick apart all the rage whirling inside me. She'd lied to me about one thing, so why not everything else?

"If there's *any* chance she's working with them, shouldn't we assume it's true?" I shot back at him.

He started back at me with his typical cool composure. "I'm starting to think your judgment is skewed by something other than the evidence we've seen in front of us."

If he hadn't been Wylder's best friend, I'd have taken a swing at him. "You don't know—"

Wylder held up his hands, and I cut myself off, the flare of heat inside me as much embarrassment at needing the intervention as anger at the situation. He turned to Gideon. "What's your take?"

The slim guy ran his hand under his chin, a stray finger flicking over his lip ring. "Well, there are classic signs of lying: being vague about the details or laying them on thick like they planned out a huge story, delaying answering questions, touching themselves—"

I raised my eyebrows and motioned to my groin. "You mean like...?"

"No," Gideon said, frowning at me. "What is wrong with you?"

"You're the one who mentioned touching themselves."

He sighed and shook his head. "Small movements like scratching their nose and neck or even playing with their hair, anything that draws attention away from their eyes and makes them feel less self-conscious."

"So was Mercy doing all that?" I had to ask. I'd been so pissed off I could barely remember anything from the confrontation except her eyes piercing mine when I'd gone off on her.

"She seemed fairly calm to me, all things considered," Gideon said. "No excessive fidgeting. She got riled up about the accusations, but she gave her explanation clearly without going on and on about it. Based on that, I'd be inclined to believe her."

"So we're going to decide based on whether she played with her hair?"

Wylder knuckled my arm. "Let the man finish."

Gideon tipped his head in acknowledgement. "We also have to take into consideration what we know about Mercy Katz otherwise. It's clear that the Steel Knights *did* turn on her family and their associates, and family members who weren't even included in the running of the gang were murdered. She shows clear signs of anger every time she talks about Colt. She warned us about him being a threat before we had any reason to consider that. I won't discount the possibility that she could be an extremely gifted liar and master schemer, but I'd place the probability that she gave us the truth at ninety percent or better."

Trust Gideon to put a freaking number on it. But Wylder was nodding as if that all sounded reasonable to him. I glanced at Rowan, figuring I had to get support somewhere, but he was standing rigidly, his mouth in a flat line.

His voice came out flat too. "I told you from the start that I didn't think keeping her around was a good idea, but I don't believe she'd screw us over like this either."

Damn it. "So, what, we're just going to let her slink back in here like nothing's changed?"

"I've already sent her to hang with the groupies," Wylder said dryly. "Considering that Gia's the queen bee down there, I don't think they'll be very friendly. If she sticks around through that, well… We don't beat up on women, but there are plenty of other ways to determine how committed she really is—and to make her regret it if she isn't. If she has anything going on with Colt, we'll find out. We give her nothing and wait to see what we get from her."

I still didn't like it, but I had trouble arguing with his approach. The glint in his eyes said clear as anything that there'd be hell to pay if Mercy revealed any treachery. I guessed it was better having her here where we could rain down that hell if necessary, not running around doing who knew what.

"Fine," I grumbled. "We'll see if she survives the groupies first."

Anger was still thrumming through my veins as I headed out of the room. Flexing my hands, I wandered aimlessly for a few minutes and finally made my way to one of the windows that opened onto the second-floor platform of the fire escape.

The metal slats were still warm from the afternoon sun. Stretching my legs out across them, I stared up at the sky that was coming alive with stars and pulled a joint from my pocket. I knew better than to ever smoke in the house, but no one could complain about me mellowing out when I needed to out here.

My periodic vigils out here had gained me a little friend too. As if on cue, claws clicked across one of the windowsills lower down. With a little mew, the stray tabby cat who'd been keeping me company for the past few months leapt up onto the fire escape. She brushed her furry body against my arm, already purring.

"All right, all right," I muttered, but I was smiling at the same time. She was a greedy little thing. After her first couple of visits, I'd started buying packets of cat treats and keeping them on me. I fished my current one out of my other pocket and opened it while attempting not to wave the joint in her face. Then I sprinkled a bunch of the treats on the interlaced slats of the floor. "There you go. Happy?"

The escalation in purrs sounded like a resounding yes. I took another drag on the joint, letting the soothing high sweep over me, and scratched her striped back.

A creaking sound above me brought my head jerking up. When I saw a figure poised on the platform above me, my whole body tensed.

"It's just me." Mercy was staring down at me, her blue eyes darkened by the growing dusk. Through the mellow of the joint, it took me a second to figure out why she looked so cautious. Oh, right, last time I'd talked to her I'd been ready to rip her head off.

Maybe I should still be ready for that. I peered up at her. "What are you doing sneaking around up there?"

"I wanted to take another look at the crime scene. Not that it's helped much." She paused. "Got a soft spot for strays, do you?"

"She's lonely. And hungry." I glared through the bars at her, trying to summon more of my previous wariness. "And I guess I have a bit of a problem being suckered in by kittens in need, yeah."

Somehow the comment came out sounding flirtier than I'd meant it to. Mercy's lips twitched to somewhere close to a smile. She hesitated again and then moved to the ladder, easing down it until she reached the platform beside me. She stayed there, leaning against the railing a few feet away from me. At the cluck of her tongue, the cat went scampering over to her.

As she stroked the cat's back, I frowned. "She's usually skittish. I have no idea how she's okay with you doing that when she just met you."

Mercy arched her eyebrows. "How long have you been coming out here to make friends?"

"I didn't come out here specifically to— It's just a habit." I waved the joint. "She happened to come by." It'd taken me weeks to convince her to let me pet her even briefly. Probably Mercy was getting the advantage of all my past work gaining the cat's trust.

"Habit, you say." Mercy gave me a shrewd look, and I realized what that sounded like. I looked above and could still see the mangled structure through which Titus had fallen.

"I wasn't here when he died," I said tightly.

She shrugged and pet the cat some more, scratching below its neck. The animal seemed to like it, because she leaned into Mercy's fingers and pushed herself even closer. I made a mental note of that.

"What a good kitty," Mercy said to her in a coo that did something funny to my insides, and then looked up at me. "I wouldn't still be checking evidence if I thought the case was closed."

Easy for her to say. She could have been out here searching for clues that would point to me. I straightened up. "Or maybe it's an excuse not to go to the groupies' room. Afraid of what you might find there?"

We held each other's gaze for a few moments. "I'm not afraid of anybody," she said.

"Maybe you should be."

"Of you?"

"Aren't you? Most people are, for good reason." I bared my teeth in a sharp grin.

"But you're a softie under that hard body of yours, aren't you?" she said, definitely teasing now. "Taking in stray cats as your new besties. I bet you've even named her."

Shit. My expression probably gave away that she was right. She laughed—light and almost relaxed in a way I didn't think I'd ever heard before, but I immediately wanted to hear it again.

"Her name's Mittens," I admitted.

"Mittens?"

I scowled. "Is there something wrong with that? She's got those black marks over her front feet like, you know..."

"Mittens," Mercy filled in with a crooked smile. "No, it sounds like the perfect name."

The silence between us felt companionable in a way that niggled at me. I couldn't let her get under my skin all over again.

"You didn't tell me you were going to the Bend," I bit out. "You took my car."

"I didn't say I *wasn't* going to the Bend either," she pointed out. "I didn't want anyone telling me it was too dangerous or some crap like that."

"What did that have to do with investigating Titus?"

She shrugged. "I heard he enforced the Nobles' authority down there sometimes. Figured he might have made an enemy or two who'd have wanted him dead. It was the closest thing to a lead I had that Anthea hadn't already chased to the ground."

"Oh." That... actually sounded kind of reasonable. I gritted my teeth.

In my silence, she pulled a scrap of paper out and started fiddling with it. "What I can't figure out is why *Gia* was out there in Steel Knights territory. Maybe she pointed the finger at me to hide that she's made some kind of deal with them. I could tell she didn't recognize Colt, but she could have been talking to someone lower down the chain of command."

I shook my head. "There's a much simpler explanation. She grew up in the Bend. Her family's still there—her dad's got an auto shop or something. She might be annoying, but she's never given us any reason to think she has bad intentions. And she's been around a lot longer than you."

"That doesn't excuse the fact that she's a colossal bitch," Mercy muttered.

I couldn't help chuckling at that for a second before I caught myself. "Look," I said firmly. "The Nobles are *my* family—the only family I've got. I'll protect them no matter what, with everything I have. If there's any chance you're a threat..."

The paper crinkled in Mercy's fingers. She gazed down at it for a long moment. "I get that. At least, I think I do. I've never had anyone I could trust enough to be that loyal to them... No one other than myself. Colt betrayed *me*, and I'm never going to forgive him for that, just like you wouldn't forgive anyone who betrayed your people that horribly."

The softness of her voice wound around my heart. Fucking hell, this woman knew exactly how to get to me. Why did I want to believe her so badly?

Before I could say anything else, she tossed the paper to me. I caught it instinctively and opened my hand to find she'd transformed it into an origami dove. A peace offering?

My heart yanked in opposite directions. Anger was the easier route, the one I had more experience with. I knew from experience that even the people who had the most reason to look out for you wouldn't, so why the hell would she care about me when she barely knew me?

"You can go now," I said without looking at her, forcing an edge into my voice.

Mercy frowned. "What?"

I raised my head. "You want to prove you're loyal to the Nobles? Do what Wylder asked and go deal with the groupies for the night. Otherwise none of this means shit."

21

Mercy

As I climbed in through the window from the fire escape, I had trouble deciding whether to take Kaige's abrupt dismissal as a loss or the fact that he hadn't gutted me where I stood as a win. At least I'd gotten in some kitty cuddle time, no matter how standoffish the guy had been.

What awaited me in the house was more likely to be a cat fight than anything cuddly. Meandering toward the area where I'd gathered the groupies had their designated room, I spotted a set of fireplace tools by a hearth. I went over and hefted the wrought-iron poker. It might not be a standard weapon, but it could do a hell of a lot more damage than a knife if wielded well.

As I returned to the hall, Anthea appeared, her heels clacking on the hardwood floor. She looked so infuriatingly perfect with not a strand of hair out of its place. One of the Nobles' guards had barred me from entering the wing with my guest room, so I hadn't even managed to change out of my sweaty clothes from this afternoon.

Anthea stopped before she reached me. "There you are. I've been looking for you." Her eye fell to the poker on my hand, and her lips thinned. "What's that for?"

I shrugged. "Protection?" I had no idea what exactly Wylder expected to happen to me in the groupies' room, but if Gia was anything to go by, the experience wouldn't be pleasant.

Anthea gave me an odd look and then shook her head. "I think it's time you turn in for the night—if you're insisting on staying?" When I raised my chin defiantly, she sighed. "Follow me."

We headed around a bend in the hall to reach a part of the mansion that I'd never explored before. The moldings and wallpaper were equally posh, but the hall was empty of the paintings and fancy side-tables that were scattered through the other areas I'd seen.

Anthea led me to a doorway at the end of the hall. She swept her arm toward a large room. I took it in from the threshold.

Mattresses and cots were shoved against the walls, covered with tangles of blankets and discarded clothes. Dance music thumped in a staccato beat from one girl's earphones as she bobbed her head. The air stunk of cheap alcohol and pot. I guessed Gideon never ventured into this area of the house for a smoking ban to be necessary.

Seven women in total perched on various beds—including Gia. At the sight of me, her eyes widened and then narrowed into vicious slits.

"What are you doing here?" she snarled, as if this place belonged to her and not the Nobles, who could have kicked her out at any second if they'd wanted to. A few of the other groupies studied me and Anthea with interest, while the others didn't seem to care, or maybe they just hadn't registered our presence yet with their red-rimmed eyes.

"Mercy is going to stay the night," Anthea said smugly. She was enjoying my fall from grace way too much. I wouldn't be surprised if she went back and popped open a bottle of champagne to celebrate.

My grip on the poker tightened. If she thought a night in this zoo was going to scare me off, I was about to prove her wrong.

Gia smirked at me. "I guess the boys finally realized their mistake and showed you your proper place."

"Is this where mistakes end up?" I retorted. "I guess that explains why you're here."

Gia let out a hiss, but Anthea rolled her eyes at our bickering. "Make sure Mercy feels *very* welcome. Let's show her how we treat those who are caught fraternizing with the enemy."

I froze. Oh, fuck, she'd just had to rub that point in.

Gia flicked her tongue over her lips. "That's right. Poor baby went running home to her traitor fiancé, like the men here aren't good enough."

"I wasn't the one running away," I snapped. "Unlike you. Did you sprain your ass taking off so fast with your tail between your legs?"

Gia's face reddened. "What the fuck did you just say?"

I smirked in satisfaction. "It wouldn't bother you if it wasn't the truth, would it?"

Gia looked ready to strangle me, and behind her the other groupies were slowly rising, their jerky motions reminding me of zombies. No matter what they thought about Gia and her snark, they must have known that Anthea was a Noble. They'd take her word as gospel, and now they were out for my blood.

Anthea gave them a thin smile. "I know I can count on you to convince her to atone for her sins." As she turned, she practically shoved me with her shoulder. I glared at her retreating back and then turned to face the other women, who were watching me with pure hatred. If looks could kill, I'd be already dead and buried.

Drawing on the inner armor that'd gotten me through twenty-one years under my father's rule, I sauntered farther into the room, pretending I hadn't noticed the rising animosity. "So, what do you guys do for fun around here?"

Gia's gaze tracked me, but she kept her mouth shut for once. One of the other girls frowned. "What are you talking about?"

I noted a corner that held a crumpled blanket and nothing else—a good defensive position—and strolled toward it. "This is my first introduction to a cult. It's all very strange to me, but I keep an open mind. Where's the altar?"

"Are you mental?" another groupie demanded.

I shrugged. "I'm just wondering where you worship the Nobles like the loyal fanatics you are. Or am I not privy to those mysteries yet?"

One of the girls lunged at me without warning, managing to snag my ponytail. As I whipped around, she yanked at it painfully, but a swing of my poker sent her dodging farther away, her fingers slipping from my hair. A shudder ran through her skinny frame. As high as she appeared to be, she recognized me as a threat.

I aimed the poker at her and then the others. "Take one step toward me, and you'll regret it." Best to establish boundaries immediately. I had an entire night to spend with them, and if Wylder had anything to say about it, maybe even more.

Sinking into the empty corner, I braced my back against the wall and set the poker over my drawn-up knees. I could already tell it was going to be a long, sleepless night.

The women paced around me. For a little while, they took turns hurling insults like "bitch" and "cunt" at me. Gia, who'd clearly established herself as the ringleader, murmured in one girl's ear. A few minutes later, the groupie came at me by leaping onto the nearest cot and slashing her fingernails at me. I managed to smack her arm away a split-second before she dug them into my face. Gia watched with a vindictive grin.

Someone hurled an open can of soda at me, the contents splashing over my already sticky clothes. I grimaced and kicked it away. Next I got a shoe to the forehead—it would have been my eyes if I hadn't ducked quickly enough. Gia let out an approving whoop, and the other girls giggled, their eyes sharpening with a predatory gleam.

After that, they took turns spitting at me, most of them missing but a few droplets speckling my face and hair. I grimaced, swiping at myself with my sleeve as well as I could without loosening my hold on my weapon. More curses and insults battered my ears; any hard object they could lay their hands on was fair game to be chucked in my direction. A beer bottle clipped my chin so hard I was pretty sure it'd leave a bruise. I refused to wince.

They got tired eventually, of course. Someone turned out the light, and most of them got into their beds. But every time my eyelids started to droop, someone would slip off their cot with a squeak of its legs or dart toward me through the shadows. I had to snatch up the poker again and wave it at them to show I was still awake and prepared to defend myself.

My head started to swim. The stuffy smell of the room was turning suffocating, and my eyelids were heavy as lead, but I kept shifting and twitching to hold myself awake. If I drifted off, I'd be an open target.

After what felt like an eternity, sunlight finally appeared in the window. Most of the groupies were curled up on their beds, but a couple had woken up to take over the watch. As I stretched my arms, their accusing eyes followed my movements. My ass and back ached with a stiffness that had seeped into my bones.

Gia yawned and stood up. She had the bed at the front of the room, a slightly wider cot with a few neat piles of belongings stuffed under it that all of the other women seemed careful not to touch.

She sashayed over. "Poor little princess. Is Daddy coming to save you? Oh, that's right, he can't because he's dead."

I gave her a weary glower. "If that's your best shot, you need to collect better ammunition."

She sniffed. "That guy who caught you in the Bend is the one who killed him, isn't he? I'm surprised he didn't do the same to you like you deserve, the way he had you surrounded like that."

My glower turned into a glare. "So you know it wasn't a friendly chat. Why the hell did you tell Wylder I *wanted* to talk to Colt?"

As if I had to ask. She gave an innocent shrug, but her eyes gleamed with malice. "I didn't want them to go easy on you. You might have been a snitch and that whole thing was a show."

"A show I set up for who? It wasn't as if I knew I'd run into you."

"I don't know," she said. "I look out for the Nobles over some bitch who thinks she's so much better than the rest of us."

In that moment, I believed her—that however horrible she'd been to me, it was out of some misguided attempt to protect Wylder and the others. In my sleep-deprived state, a twinge of curiosity caught me. "What is it like to want someone so badly who doesn't want you at all? Don't you ever get tired of it?"

Her jaw twitched. "You have no idea what you're talking about."

Just then the sound of footsteps carried from down the hall. Gia posed herself back on her mattress just in time for Wylder to stride through the door. He was followed by Axel and another man I didn't recognize.

"Just get someone on it," Wylder was saying over his shoulder to

Axel. "The engine shouldn't be overheating like that—there's probably a problem with the radiator."

Gia leapt to her feet, her face brightening. "Do you need help with your car? I could take a look—I know a few things from helping my dad."

She reached for his arm, but Wylder batted her away. "That's not what you're here for."

He turned all his attention on me instead. At Gia's pout, Axel lifted his eyes heavenward and sighed. "I'll make sure it's handled." I couldn't tell whether he was more annoyed by Gia's antics or by having to follow Wylder's orders.

As I stood up, Wylder ambled over. "Good, you survived."

"Is that good?" I asked. "I thought you were hoping they'd beat me to a pulp."

He chuckled and stepped so close that it was either let his chest brush mine or end up pinned against the wall. I held my ground. His leather-and-brandy scent washed over me with a jolt of heat that shocked me out of my exhausted daze.

"Oh, no, Kitty Cat," he said under his breath. "I'd very much like to find out that you're up to everything I have in store. I just can't give you a pass if you skip the tests."

A weird tingle shot through me at the promise in his words, but a flicker of dread followed it. "What are you up to now?"

"Come along, and you'll find out."

I hated the sense of Gia's and Axel's eyes fixed on me as I had to decide between giving up and giving in. I huffed out a breath, but when Wylder swiveled and headed out, I followed him.

"Where are we going?" I demanded as I hurried to catch up with him.

"It's time for a very important lesson," he said in a sing-song voice that told me he was deeply enjoying this. "You're going to see just what happens when you double-cross a Noble."

22

Mercy

"THE DEAL'S STILL ON, RIGHT?" I SAID, PICKING UP MY PACE as Wylder walked faster.

He flicked his gaze toward me for just an instant. "Deal?"

A chill unfurled in my chest. "I figure out who really killed Titus, and you help me take down Colt. You swore on your fucking blood. Don't act like you forgot." Was he going to claim my supposed betrayal had voided his promise somehow?

Half a smile curled Wylder's lips. "Oh, that deal. Yes, if you can survive the next few days and you end up clearing Kaige's name, I think even he'll leap to your aid, yesterday's performance aside. But for now I think you should focus on the surviving part, Princess."

I didn't like the sound of that at all. But I couldn't imagine how he could put me through anything worse than the hell my father had. Wylder Noble had no idea just how much steel I'd built up beneath my skin.

I expected him to take me back to his section of the mansion, but instead he led me to an unmarked door and down a flight of stairs into what must have been the basement. The light dimmed as we descended.

I pressed my hand against the wall for balance, willing back the spurts of panic provoked by the vague impression of the darkness crowding in on me. Basements and I did not have a friendly relationship.

Dank air met us at the bottom of the stairs. I crinkled my nose. We took a turn into a wide room where Kaige, Rowan and Gideon were clustered just inside. Kaige was talking to Rowan while Gideon scanned something on his ever-present tablet. All three looked up simultaneously.

"Is she ready?" Gideon asked.

A shiver ran down my spine. "Ready for what?"

The set of Rowan's mouth made my stomach ball even tighter. Then the three of them stepped to the side. The sight of what lay behind them made me glad I hadn't eaten since the small dinner I'd managed to scrounge up last night before my chat with Kaige.

A huge metal table stood in the middle of the room, looking as if its legs were melded to the concrete floor. The yellowy artificial light glanced off it—and off the sallow skin of the man sprawled at one end, naked except for a pair of blood-stained briefs.

I knew at a glance that he was dead. A bluish tint was already seeping over his chest. His hairy arms lay limp at his sides, his jaw hanging slackly open. That was all I could make out of his facial features. The rest had been battered violently: eyes gouged out, nose and cheekbones caved in so shards of bone showed through the torn flesh. I had no idea what he would have looked like alive.

No doubt that was the point—no way for any cop or other person happening on the body to easily identify him.

Even empty, my stomach lurched. The cloying scent of raw meat and drying blood assaulted me, and I covered my nose with my palm. Bile rose up my throat.

I forced myself to step closer, keeping my mouth firmly shut. I'd seen dead bodies before, but none quite so destroyed. Along with his mangled face, deep lacerations marked his arms, neck, and chest. He was missing a couple of fingers. His left ankle jutted at an odd angle that suggested it'd been fractured. Even as another wave of nausea rolled through me, I recognized the signs.

He'd been tortured. Not in here—there wasn't any blood on the floor. They probably had some other room for that. Someone had sliced and diced him to see if he'd squeal.

I took a few slow breaths against my hand, gathering myself, and glanced at the guys. None of them showed a hint of sympathy for the dead man or my reaction to him. Was there a trace of contempt in Wylder's eyes? He must have been waiting for me to burst into tears and flee from the room.

I drew my spine straighter. It was about time he figured out that I *definitely* wasn't that kind of girl.

"Who is he?" I asked.

Wylder gazed steadily back at me. It occurred to me that the destruction of the man's face might have also been to prevent *me* from IDing him to anyone if I tried to pin the murder on the Nobles. They were still that suspicious of me.

The Noble heir raised his eyebrows meaningfully. "A prick who double-crossed the Nobles and got what was coming to him. He was selling information to a competitor, enough to screw us over in a deal and get someone killed."

"And that wasn't enough," Kaige added in a rough voice. "He broke into one of our guys' houses to try to steal Noble property, and the guy's daughter came home early. That fucker, he— She was only thirteen, for God's sake."

His implication was clear. Any twinge of horror I'd felt at the man's brutal death was swept away by rage. Raping a *child*? This bastard deserved every bit of violence they'd rained down on him and worse.

"How's the girl?" I had to ask.

"As well as can be expected," Wylder said. "We'll see that she gets any treatment she needs to recover." He tipped his head toward the dead man. "Her father conducted the torture to find out just how deep his betrayal ran. It was the best justice we could give him."

My hands shook at my sides. "Someone should have cut off this asshole's dick and shoved it down his throat."

Wylder blinked as if startled by my vehemence. "Well, if that's where you want to start carving, have at it."

I jerked my gaze back to him. "What?"

Kaige lifted a cleaver from a side table and offered it to me. "Here you go."

My fingers brushed his as I grasped the handle, and he pulled his hand away quickly. I balanced the heavy weight of the rectangular knife in my hand. A menacing glint reflected off its sharp edge. "You... brought me here to cut off his dick?"

Kaige muffled a snort of amusement. Gideon sighed and handed me a thin, crinkling garment that unfolded into something like a hospital gown. He made an impatient gesture toward the corpse and a large plastic sack lying on the floor by the end of the table. "Your assignment is to dismember the body for easier disposal."

"Get to work," Wylder said. "Chop, chop." He aimed a languid smile at me.

Ah. They didn't just want to show me what happened to traitors but to get me up close and personal with the corpse. My gut twisted queasily, but I tightened my fingers around the cleaver's handle.

I'd never carved up a human being before, but I'd heard Dad's men talk about it. No need to get too fancy. Lop off the legs at the knees and hips, the arms at the elbows and shoulders, and then the head... No one wanted to split an abdomen open and deal with the mess in there.

Nine cuts, that was all. Easy peasy.

I pulled the plastic gown over my clothes and picked up the cleaver again. The guy's elbow seemed like the easiest place to start.

Bracing myself and fighting a cringe at the deathly chill of the stiffening limb I held in place, I dug the cleaver into the skin just below the joint. The blade severed the muscle, sluggish blood oozing out across the metal edge, but jarred to a stop against the bone. I dug in harder, my jaw starting to ache with how tightly I was gritting my teeth.

"Your technique needs work," Gideon observed unhelpfully. The guys were all watching me with total detachment, even Rowan's face hard.

"I'm trying," I snapped. "It's not like I've done this before."

Kaige walked up beside me and made a sweeping motion with his hand. "You really have to *chop*—lift the knife and slam it down. That'll get you through the bone."

He was speaking from experience, clearly. I swallowed thickly, hesitating just for a second, and Wylder's sardonic voice rang out. "If you can stomach it, Princess. Or are you ready to give up so soon?"

"Maybe if you're so impatient to have it done, you shouldn't have used it for your stupid games." I hefted the cleaver, its weight straining my arm, and whipped it down as hard as I could at the spot where I'd already cut.

With a sickening crunch, the bone shattered. I hadn't quite struck the same spot as my first gash, and bits of vein and tendon speckled the table-top. My gut lurched again. I closed my eyes, breathing as shallowly as I could, and then gave the arm another vicious *thwack.*

The forearm split off completely. I stared at it for a moment, this horror movie scene I was bringing to life in front of me, and couldn't restrain a shudder. As quickly as I could, I snatched the wrist and tossed the forearm into the open sack.

One down, eight more to go.

"Poor Kitty Cat," Wylder taunted. "Hissing and baring your claws isn't enough to win a place with the big boys."

"You think so highly of yourself," I retorted, approaching the shoulder with trepidation.

Now that I was getting the technique down, I hacked through the rest of the arm with just two strikes of the cleaver. A little more blood sputtered over my fingers, and I outright gagged as I dragged the upper arm to the sack, but I just swiped at my mouth with a clean section of my plastic sleeve and walked around the table to deal with the other arm.

This was the grossest thing I'd ever done, but it *had* to be done. I let my mind drift apart from the details of the job, going through the motions automatically, focusing on the horrors the man I was dismembering had carried out.

He wasn't the victim. I was an angel of vengeance, packing up the trash.

"Don't get careless," Wylder said, but when I looked up at him, something in my face flattened his smirk. The others had fallen completely silent.

I glared at him. "I think I can manage." Then I got back to work.

As I finished with the corpse's other arm and moved to his knee, I kept my attention just on that limb, barely seeing the form in front of me as a person at all. The bubble of disconnection thickened around me, numbness dissolving into something harsher. All my pent-up rage from the last few days came bubbling to the surface, fueling each smack of the cleaver.

It could have been Colt I was cutting up. Strapped down and screaming while I hacked him to pieces bit by bit. Pleading as I drew out the torture, when he hadn't given any of the Claws a chance to beg. I'd just smile and slice off one more piece of him until there was nothing left but chunks of meat packed into neat little Ziploc bags that could be tossed away and lost to oblivion.

An unsettling sense of savage satisfaction gripped me. I heaved the cleaver at the corpse's throat, picturing a gurgle cutting off Colt's last pathetic words. He could choke on his own blood before I chopped his head right off. He should get to experience the slow, painful agony he'd put my grandmother through.

I wrenched the detached head up by its greasy hair and chucked it into the sack. Then I turned back to the lump of a torso. The urge shot through me to stab the knife right into this monster's heart.

A hand snatched my wrist. I lashed out with my other arm for a second before the real world around me came back into focus.

That wasn't Colt in front of me. I wasn't getting my revenge just yet. I was in Wylder's basement, and I'd just diced up a stranger's corpse. The smell of death wrapped all around me.

It was Rowan who'd caught my arm. "Enough," he said quietly. He pried the heavy weapon out of my hand and tossed it in an industrial-sized sink fixed to the wall. "You're done."

Wylder watched me with a hooded expression, but the fact that he wasn't heckling me was proof enough that I'd exceeded his expectations. Kaige's jaw had gone a bit slack, and Gideon's gaze was penetratingly avid.

I looked down at my blood-splattered hands and felt a shiver run through me.

Kaige let out a hoarse chuckle. "You've got a strong stomach."

Had he expected me to back down too?

Wylder's smirk came back. "And one hell of an appetite."

What the hell was that supposed to mean? I frowned at him and pushed myself to the sink to wash my hands. Gideon reached past me to grab a rag and a spray bottle, but he held a distance that felt weirdly respectful.

Kaige went over to heave the torso into a separate sack, and Gideon started wiping down the table. "Kitten is more blood-thirsty than any of us thought," Kaige said. His stance was softer now. Apparently seeing me cut up a man somehow put him more at ease.

I watched the congealing blood swirl away from my hands with the water gurgling down the drain. A bar of soap sat in a dish at the back of the sink—I grabbed it and rubbed it all over my skin from fingertips to wrists, digging in my fingernails, working the lather into the creases of my palms. It felt like forever until every trace of red was gone.

When I turned off the faucet and stepped back, adrenaline kept thrumming through me, leaving me dizzy. I swiped my hands across my cheeks and neck, haunted by the sense that I might have gotten the dead man's flesh on me somewhere else, although the gown I'd been wearing over my clothes looked pretty clean. Corpses didn't bleed much.

I wrenched the gown off and threw it into one of the sacks, longing for a shower. Longing to crawl out of my very skin.

This was what my father had wanted. When I was growing up, he'd never missed a chance to remind me that it was a son he longed for, an heir to carry on his legacy. Someone who'd be as strong and ruthless as he was. He'd trained me in combat while reminding me that I would never live up to *his* expectations, punishing me whenever I hesitated or fell short of the mark.

Would he have been impressed by the bloodlust I'd shown today? I wanted revenge on Colt, but the thought of reshaping myself in my father's image sent an uneasy quiver through the adrenaline dwindling inside me.

Rowan came up to me again. I didn't look over, but he spoke anyway. "You okay?"

"What do you care?"

"Rowan, Kaige," Wylder said, "prep the car for transport. Quickly. I don't want this bastard stinking up my home any longer."

Rowan looked at me for a second before he followed Kaige out.

Gideon stood off to the side, typing something on his tablet. "No missing persons reports yet."

"Won't anybody trace the murder back to you?" I asked.

Gideon smiled humorlessly. "I'd like to see them try." He glanced at Wylder. "I've got to tie up a few loose ends upstairs. The signal down here is pathetic. You don't need me for anything else right now?"

Wylder shook his head.

After Gideon was gone, I tried not to look in the general direction of the table. The smell of the disinfectant he'd rubbed over the metal surface had drowned out most of the fleshy stink already. When my gaze settled on the bags for a moment, no regret hit me, only a surge of triumph.

I'd done it. That was the important thing. I'd proved what I was made of—that I wasn't going to shy from a challenge. That anything they could face, I could too.

"You've got mettle," Wylder said as if he could read my thoughts.

I made a face at him. "Does that mean we're done with the punishments now?"

A sly smile curved his lips. "It didn't look like a punishment for you. You almost seemed to be... enjoying it."

He'd struck closer to the truth than I liked. "Maybe you're just projecting," I suggested.

He sauntered up to me and tucked his finger under my chin so I'd meet his gaze. "You're not quite how I had you figured."

"Really? And how's that?"

He teased his fingertip over the sensitive skin so delicately I couldn't ignore the tingle that shot through me. "I think under that righteous facade of yours lies something even more brutal than you let on."

I scowled at him. "You don't have the first idea about me."

"I beg to differ. I may have been wrong in my first assumptions, but that's only because I hadn't had the chance to see you for what you really are." He paused, his bright green eyes drinking in my features. "I think you liked cutting this asshole to pieces. I might even have caught a glimpse of a smile."

I shoved him away from me and tried to walk off, but Wylder caught me by my waist. With a swift heft, he settled me on the far end of the table. Not where the cadaver had been lying, thank God, but a flash of revulsion flickered through me for a second before Wylder nudged his body closer between my legs.

Abruptly, all I was aware of was how close he stood, his face less than a foot from mine, my thighs splayed around his.

"Did I say something you didn't like?" he asked. "Always stings when somebody puts up a mirror to you, doesn't it?"

"Fuck you," I spat at him, as much pissed off by the heat that had kindled in me with his closeness as by his words.

He got right in my face, his fingers tugging at my hair and loosening my ponytail so that strands of my hair fell loose against my neck. A sharper yank sent pain mixed with an undeniable spark of pleasure racing over my scalp. Leaning even closer, he brought his lips to mine, not quite closing the gap to a kiss. "Maybe you belong with us after all."

My heartbeat thundered. A distant part of my brain was urging me to recoil, but the lingering adrenaline had shifted into a wild flare of desire I couldn't fully explain.

The heat of Wylder's body and his tantalizing scent washed over me. Some crazy part of me wanted to melt right into him. I didn't let that happen, but I couldn't convince myself to pull away either.

Two of his fingers trailed along the seam of my jeans that ran up my thigh. I tracked their progress with bated breath, torn between pushing him off me and the voice in me that was screaming for him to hurry up and reach his destination.

When he paused just before the apex of my thighs, to my embarrassment, I couldn't help squirming as if to bring him the last short distance. He ducked his head next to mine, his breath vibrating over my neck with his laugh. "Steady there, Kitty Cat," he whispered in the hottest voice I'd ever heard. "I've seen you tough. Now I want to watch you come apart for me."

It felt as if every second of our interactions before now had been building to this moment, and those words in that husky tone nearly tipped me over the edge just like that. A growl escaped my throat—and turned into a stuttered gasp as he finally cupped my sex.

He trailed his hand over my scorching core, humming with satisfaction as if he could feel the wetness forming in my panties. His fingers swirled in torturous circles against my jeans over my clit before pushing harder. My lips parted with a panted breath, my own hands braced against the table for balance. He didn't sweep in to steal a kiss, just let his nose graze my temple in an almost-caress as his focus remained on my pussy.

My thighs tightened around his wrist. Fuck my best intentions. If this was what I wanted, then it didn't matter if he wanted it too, did it? And right now I wanted more of him, more of the exquisite feeling that he was making me chase. I reached for his shirt, clinging on, rocking into his touch.

With a grin I felt more than saw, he upped the tempo, rubbing two fingers up and down from clit to slit. With every stroke, he sent me careening higher, climbing to a place I wouldn't mind falling from.

"That's right, Princess of the Claws," he murmured, and just this once I didn't hate the nickname. "Let yourself explode."

He fondled me harder, faster, and I couldn't hold back a whimper at the pleasure bubbling up inside me. It swept over me in a searing wave. Another cry broke from me as I came.

My body bucked before I got a hold of myself, stiffening my spine. Wylder was already stepping away as if he was done with me, even though the throbbing between my thighs cried out for more. He gave me one of those cocky smirks, and I couldn't tell whether I'd rather fuck him senseless or chop *his* head off.

I had just orgasmed less than ten feet from a corpse I'd almost gleefully dismembered. This entire situation was messed up on so many levels. So how could it also feel so fucking right?

23

Mercy

Wylder looked so smug as he observed me that the flush of my climax cooled. Refusing to look at the bastard, I shoved myself off the table, hoping he didn't notice how my legs wobbled slightly when my feet hit the floor. The aftershock of that orgasm hadn't faded completely.

Was I fucking insane?

"You were already turned on," Wylder said, apparently reading my recovered defiance. "I just took you over the edge, exactly the way you needed it."

Before I could reply, footsteps sounded in the hall. I looked up to see Rowan and Kaige returning with purposeful expressions.

"The car's ready," Kaige said, his gaze falling on the bags of corpse pieces and a grimace twisting his lips. "This is the easy part now, right?"

Wylder laughed. "That depends on whether you prefer chopping or digging. And this room needs a thorough cleaning too."

Kaige's grimace grew. "Who's on cleaning duty? Because I call dibs on doing absolutely nothing."

"I'll get someone down here to do that," Wylder said. "Who's been on the naughty list this week?"

All three pairs of eyes settled on me. It figured. I crossed my arms in front of my chest. "If you want me to do it, you can just come out and say that."

Wylder made a show of considering. "No, I think you've handled enough housework this week."

Relief coursed through me. I just wanted to get out of here and take a good long shower and ideally scrub myself raw. Even though I had gotten used to the smell, the room still stank of death and I was sure it had settled on me. I needed to wipe away all memory of this prick's touch, too. "Can I leave?"

"Oh, no, your work here isn't *done*, Princess. Finish what you started. You need to dispose of the body."

I blinked at him. "Excuse me?"

"You heard me," Wylder said. "Our rat friend is conveniently hacked into pieces and bagged. The car is prepped. All you need to do is find a nice quiet spot in the woods to give him a final resting place. Preferably deep and dark."

That did actually sound less unnerving than doing the hacking, but — "You're sending me off in one of your cars alone with the body of a man you murdered?"

Kaige's eyes flicked to me, his expression turning dubious. "Forget that." I'd thought I'd seen a flicker of trust in his eyes before, but I'd obviously imagined it.

Rowan stepped up, looking at Wylder rather than me. "Of course not. I'll go with her. You guys have had your fun—isn't it my turn?"

Disgust roiled through me. Had Rowan really just been waiting around for his chance to add to my torment? "No fucking way," I said. "I'm not going anywhere with him."

"Who said you get a choice?" Wylder clapped his hands with a definite sound. "I don't know what kind of issues you two have with each other, but if you want anything from me, you have to learn to deal with my men. That includes Rowan." He tipped his head to Rowan, who nodded back.

What had happened between them in the five years since I'd last seen my ex to cement their bond of loyalty so deeply? The Rowan I'd known up until he was sixteen had cringed whenever I'd talked about the violence of my family life. He'd looked most natural with a pencil or a piece of sketching charcoal in his hand, not a gun. How did anyone change that quickly?

No, I reminded myself. He hadn't changed that much. He'd been an asshole when he'd strung me along and then left me in the lurch, hadn't he? I just hadn't seen it.

Wylder gave us a dismissive wave. "So, it's decided then. Off you go. Be careful of her claws, Rowan."

"I know." Without looking at me, Rowan closed one of the sacks and hefted it as if its contents hadn't been a man less than an hour ago. As if he hauled around chopped-up corpses all the time. Another twinge of confusion rippled through me.

He stood there, and I realized I was supposed to pick up the other bag. Tying it off carefully to cover its contents, I heaved it off the floor. Kaige's expression flickered. "I can—"

"I'm fine," I interrupted. "Let's get on with this."

Rowan led the way up the stairs and down a couple of isolated halls that led to a discrete back door. By the time we reached it, my arms were straining from carrying—well, mostly dragging—even half of a grown man's weight in body parts. This kind of work would keep you in shape, I'd give it that.

A dark green Ford was parked right outside. No one wanted to use a fancy ride for this job. The trunk was already open and lined with plastic sheeting. We dumped the bags in next to a shovel—just one. It looked like I was doing all the digging. Hurrah.

"Can I drive?" I asked, because it was worth a shot.

Rowan looked at me as if I were insane before getting in on the driver's side. Maybe that was for the best, because now that the weird rush of the corpse carving had tapered off, my exhaustion from my sleepless night was creeping back in. As Rowan pulled away from the mansion, I rolled down the window to let the fresh air waft over me, perking me up just a little and washing away some of the lingering smells from the basement.

I definitely wasn't going to think about the fact that Wylder had made me come with nothing but his fingers over my freaking jeans, and then had the audacity to assume that I was horny because I had cut up some dude.

"So what's your idea of torturing me?" I prodded when it was evident that Rowan wasn't going to say anything. "I guess you feel ignored that the others got their turn and you didn't?"

Rowan sighed without taking his eyes off the road. "I don't want to fight, Mer. Let's just get this over with." He said my old nickname as if it still came easily to him.

"Don't call me that," I snapped. "You've absolutely no right to call me that anymore."

He paused and then swallowed audibly. "I know."

It was only two words, but they surprised me. This was the first time that he had so much as hinted that he realized he'd messed up.

I sank into the seat. "Where are we headed?"

"That's up to you. Wylder wants you taking responsibility for this burial. Do you know any place that could work?"

The moment I started thinking about it, the image came back to me of the trees looming in the night's shadows and the rasp of a shovel through soil. The shiver that had wracked my childhood self shot through me again. "Yeah, actually I do. Get on the freeway heading north. I'll tell you when we reach the right exit."

If I remembered right, it'd be nearly an hour's drive. Given a choice, I wouldn't have wanted to spend that much time with Rowan, but the place I'd picked was discreet. I'd be even worse off if I screwed up this mission.

Rowan glanced over at me. "You sound pretty sure of yourself."

I shrugged. "Dad took me there a few times as a kid. My tenth birthday, the first time. He figured I was old enough to learn about the darker sides of our business, including the discarding of bodies."

It felt strangely freeing to admit that without hesitation. Rowan already knew just how bad my father had been; I didn't have to pussyfoot around the subject. His hands tightened on the steering wheel for a second as if hearing it bothered him. Somehow that small gesture set off another flare of annoyance.

I wasn't here to chat, definitely not with him of all people. "I need to catch up on my sleep," I announced. "It'll be a while—wake me up when you start seeing woods."

He didn't argue, just turned on the radio, finding a folksy rock station that was exactly the sort of thing he'd have listened to back in high school. Closing my eyes and tipping my head to the side against the seat, I tuned it out, letting the rumble and the vibration of the engine soothe me into a sleep not even the horrors of this morning could stave off any longer.

I woke up with a start to a hand tugging on my shoulder. Rowan released me the second my eyes popped open. "Sorry," he said. "You were really out. You didn't respond when I said your name."

I rubbed my eyes, not sure I felt any less groggy than when I'd drifted off. I stared blearily out the window, noting the thickening trees on the right side of the highway. The place where Dad liked to turn off was just a little after the forest sprang up on the other side too: an overgrown lane that ended at a long-abandoned picnic spot the forest had reclaimed.

When I looked back at Rowan, he was studying me between glances at the road. Something in his expression brought my hackles up before he even spoke. He looked… sad. Maybe even *pitying*.

As if I needed his pity.

"You shouldn't be here," he said abruptly.

I scowled and pulled my legs up in front of me on the seat. "I know, I know, I'm cramping your new gangster style. Sorry not sorry."

"That's not what I mean. Why did you even come to the Nobles? They're worse than anyone in the Bend in some ways."

I glowered at him. "At least they're loyal and they protect what's theirs rather than abandoning people."

Rowan winced. He knew exactly what I was talking about. "The past is just—it's over. You had a chance at a fresh start, a chance to leave this life behind."

"You mean with my entire family getting brutally murdered? That's your idea of a fresh start?"

"How is getting revenge going to make things any better? You're in more danger than you ever were from your father *or* Colt."

Was that true? It didn't feel that way, regardless of the tests Wylder had put me through. As much of a prick as he could be, he'd treated me with more kindness than my father, even though he owed me a hell of a lot less. Somehow I thought Rowan was letting his own feelings skew his opinion—his feelings that having me around made *his* life more difficult.

"So what should I have done?" I demanded. "Run away like a coward and hidden for the rest of my life, never knowing when Colt might track me down as the sole witness to all those murders? Well, I have some news for you. I learned the hard way that there's no point in trying to run. So I decided to stay and fight."

"And you really think you'll be better off that way?" Rowan asked.

"Please enlighten me how living in fear until the end of my days would make me happier, since you seem to know so much about me already."

His voice softened in a way that was much too familiar. "I do know you, Mercy. I know you'll deny it, but it's the truth. I probably know you better than anyone else in this world. You told me you never trusted anyone else, and I think that's true."

His tone stirred up too many memories, drawing my gaze to the curve of the lips that had kissed me so tenderly, reminding me of how he'd sigh when I'd run my fingers through the thick fall of his hair and down his body.

My shoulders tensed. "And you broke that trust when you abandoned me without any explanation. Do you have any idea how long I waited for you that night? How awful it felt when I realized you'd completely *vanished*? I—"

I cut myself off before my voice could break with the emotions swelling inside me. I'd told myself I was over it, but it was easier not to care when the perpetrator of that pain wasn't sitting right here beside me.

Rowan was silent for a moment. "I didn't have much of a choice."

I narrowed my eyes at him. "What's that even supposed to mean? You'd already made your choice. We talked about it a million times, planned every step of how we'd get out of town and make sure Dad didn't find us. I had all my stuff packed, all the money I could quickly get my hands on—I went out to the park—and all I got from you was a fucking *text message* five hours too late, just saying you couldn't do it. And that was the last I ever heard from you."

I could still remember clear as day the way he'd hugged me before we parted ways at school that Friday, his kiss branding my mouth before he'd whispered, *I'll see you at midnight. I love you, Mer. You'll never have to be scared of him again.*

We could have made it. I'd had plenty of street smarts, and Rowan had some savings from his summer job and things like that. Maybe we'd have been living in a dumpy apartment somewhere, but it would have been the two of us together, living the way we wanted, having each other's backs like I'd thought he wanted just as much as I did...

"Where did you even go?" I demanded into Rowan's silence. "I never saw you at school again. You transferred just so you didn't have to face me?"

His phone had gone out of service. I hadn't known his address, since it'd never been safe for me to visit his house anyway. Any time we'd gotten together outside of school, it'd had to be stealthy, always so careful not to draw the notice of Dad or any of his associates.

Every connection I'd had to the boy I'd loved with all my heart for years had disintegrated in the span of a few days.

Rowan's expression had tensed. "It's complicated," he said. "I think we're better off leaving it at that. I had to go, and the rest doesn't matter. It's all in the past now anyway."

The rest didn't matter to *him*. How convenient when it included any explanation of why he'd turned his back on me so suddenly. I jerked my gaze away, wrapping my arms around my legs. "Fine, then I guess there's no point in talking at all."

We drove on in uncomfortable silence until I spotted the lane, looking pretty much the way I remembered it. Rowan turned down it, slowing as he navigated the overhanging branches, and parked when that rough track came to an end.

"Now we walk until we can't see the car and find a clear spot to dig," I said brusquely. "You can carry the shovel."

The breeze wove through the leaves overhead with an eerie rustling. The forest wasn't as creepy by mid-day as during the night, but it wasn't exactly cozy either. We tramped around for about fifteen minutes before

I settled on a spot I was satisfied with. Rowan hefted the shovel as if to start digging, and I held my hand out for it. "This is my job, remember? I'll happily let you haul the bags over."

He headed back to get them without protest, and I dug the shovel into the dirt. It was dry and pliant, not too difficult to shift, although the summer heat was already making me sweat. By the time Rowan returned with the second bag, I'd scooped out a shallow grave.

It needed to be deeper. We didn't want any random animals scenting the flesh through the plastic and digging the bags up.

I stepped into the hole to get better leverage, and a chill crept over me despite the warmth in the air. Images rose up of the light snapping away overhead, the ominous click of the lock, the damp scents invading my nose...

Rowan's voice broke through the vision. "Mercy, are you okay?"

I realized I'd stopped with the shovel clenched in my hands, staring at the overturned earth. Shaking myself, I shoved the tool deeper into the dirt. "Perfectly fucking fine."

By the time I'd dug two holes I judged deep enough, blisters were forming on my hands and my head was spinning with exhaustion, but I'd refused to relinquish the shovel. At least Rowan hadn't acted as if he didn't think I could handle a little physical labor. He dumped each bag into a hole and stepped back while I filled them in again. As I patted the earth down, he scattered pine needles and twigs he'd scooped up from elsewhere in the forest in the meantime to hide the evidence of what we'd been doing here.

"Thanks," I said grudgingly.

He nodded. We didn't speak again until we'd reached the car. I tossed the shovel into the trunk, turned, and Rowan caught me by the elbow, spinning me to face him.

The feel of his bare skin against mine with him standing so close, after so many reminders of the past, made a familiar heat coil beneath my skin. This boy who was now a man—a stunning man, if I allowed myself to be honest—had been my first... everything. Those hands, that mouth, had explored every part of my body.

I shoved the sensations rising through me away and pulled away from his grasp. I'd just buried a man—and I'd gotten off with a different guy just hours ago. How could I even be thinking anything along those lines?

Maybe there *was* something wrong with me, something sick woven into my nature. But if that was the case, all I knew was I'd been brought up that way, with violence seeping right into my soul.

"Wylder isn't done testing you yet." Rowan said. "I just thought you should know."

I glared at him. "I'm not an idiot. You want to give me any tips on what he might have in store?"

His lips pursed. Of course he wouldn't betray his captain. His gaze slid away from me and then back again. "I'm not sure. All I know is that it can get even worse than this."

I shrugged. "Let him bring it on. Maybe eventually you'll *both* realize I don't break that easily."

But as I got back into the car, the chill that'd come over me while I'd been digging the grave returned to wind around my heart.

24

Mercy

When we returned to the mansion, most of the day had passed. I felt ready to collapse on my feet, but I dragged myself inside and headed to the nearest shower as fast as my weary legs would take me, leaving Rowan far behind.

I ran into Kaige on my way down the second-floor hallway. His eyes lit up for an instant at the sight of me, a glimpse of the old him showing in his expression before it was replaced by cold aloofness. "I see you're back."

"Yep," I said. Awkwardness hung around us. Well, even after our brief heart-to-heart conversation—and the intense physical intimacy we'd shared before that—I didn't really know him.

And apparently we were both going to pretend that we hadn't had hot sex on the hood of his car.

He let out a gruff sound and tipped his head toward me. "You might want to burn that shirt. Just saying." With that, he put his hands in his pockets and headed down the staircase.

I inspected the shirt carefully, but I didn't see any blood on it, only dirt which presumably a good wash could take care of. But I *was* going to need something to change into after my shower. Groaning inwardly, I took a detour toward my old guest room, which it appeared Wylder was allowing me access to again.

I pushed open the door and halted in my tracks, my jaw dropping.

The entire room had been vandalized—there was no other word for it. A bunch of my new clothes scattered the floor, drenched in some dark, viscous liquid. I picked up a shirt, pinching it between my fingers, and recognized from the smell that it had to be kitchen grease.

The same stuff was splashed all over my bed. And the origami creatures I'd been making and placing around the room were now nothing but shreds of paper scattered across the mess.

"Good, you're here," somebody said behind me. I whirled around to find Anthea standing at the door. She was barely hiding a smirk. Annoyance flared through me.

"Did you do this?" I asked. The mess was going to be hell to clean up. I wasn't even sure all the clothes would be salvageable. Grease didn't come out easily, and who knew how long it'd had to set.

Anthea looked at me with mock horror. "What are you talking about? I would never—"

My jaw twitched. I knew she had something to do with this.

"Before you go around blaming me, I'll just tell you. A few of the groupie girls took it upon themselves to redecorate."

I gazed back at her narrowly. "How convenient that no one bothered to stop them."

"Well, this is the guest bedroom, not exactly a place of interest."

Her words were clear. The room and its contents were of no consequence. Maybe she even meant me.

"If this is meant to be a threat, it's not going to work," I said. "I'm not scared of a few girls who decided to ruin my room for fun—or anyone who might have been standing on the sidelines egging them on." I touched the bracelet in my pocket that was always with me no matter where I went. At least they hadn't been able to get to it.

"Oh, but you should be scared." Anthea walked into the room, forcing me to back up. She might have been half a foot shorter than me, but she was no less intimidating for it, maybe because of the hate that radiated off her. "There are seven of them, and one of you. And as you can see they're extremely protective."

I snorted, keeping my head high. "They're junkies who want some clout. Even if you're helping them—"

Her eyes flashed. "I already told you I didn't."

"And I'm finding that very hard to believe for some reason."

Anthea raised a hand and tapped my shoulder with calm precision. "I can tell you this. If you don't take the message to heart and finally run off to wherever you belong, what I *am* going to do to you will be so much worse than this."

More threats. How passé. I mock-shivered, pretending to hug myself. "Oooh, look, I'm shaking in my boots."

"This is not a joke, Mercy Katz. The guys listen to me. And I will personally make your life a living hell, I guarantee you that."

I raised my chin. "Do it then. What's worse you can throw at me? Kill my family? Oh, that's right, they're already dead. Colt Bryant got there before you. So go ahead, take your shot."

Anthea turned on her heel, tossing her last words over her shoulder. "This is your last chance. If you don't take the hint, whatever happens is all on you."

"Pretty sure you'd blame me for it anyway," I muttered at her retreating back.

As I looked around the wreck of the room, the satisfaction of her departure fell away under a wave of dread. I'd seen enough to know Anthea was capable of making good on her promise.

But nothing she could do would drive me out of here. Giving up on getting the Nobles on my side would mean giving up on justice for my family, on getting back the only home I'd ever known... on everything.

I sighed and turned to my bed, yanking the sheets off to take them to the wash. Thankfully, a few days ago one of the cleaning women had shown me the linen closet that held the spares as well as things like towels. But, damn, all I wanted to do was flop down on that mattress and let sleep take me over.

While I was staring at it, contemplating doing just that and cleaning properly in the morning, a knock sounded on the door, which Anthea hadn't bothered to close. Gideon leaned against the frame. His eyebrows arched when he took in the state of the room. "Christ, what happened in here?"

"Ask Anthea Noble," I said. "I'm sure she'll have a great story about it. What do *you* want?"

"I'm simply informing you that based on the GPS information we got from the car and Rowan's report, you can consider today's work done."

"Halle-fucking-lujah." Seeing him, hearing him speak so matter-of-factly about the job they'd sent me on, sparked a renewed fury in me. It burned through my exhaustion enough for me to start snatching up my soiled clothes, heaping them on top of the stripped sheets. I pummeled them into a tighter ball for good measure, imagining it was one of the guys' heads I was punching. Wylder, Kaige, Rowan, the jerk in front of me—really, any of them would do at this point.

When I hefted the heap of fabric in my arms and turned to the door again, Gideon was gone. Would Wylder be stopping by next to make some of his ever-so-insightful commentary?

I didn't know who I was angrier at—them or myself. No, make it neither. It was Colt's fault I was going through all this shit, Colt's fault I had nowhere else to turn. Which only made it that much more important that I rammed his head on a pike ASAP.

The fresh wave of anger gave me the energy to march to the laundry room, rub detergent furiously into the grease stains in the hopes they'd come out, and toss everything into the massive machines that serviced the mansion. Then I stomped back to the bathroom with my one clean change of clothes that remained and let scalding water beat down on me until every particle of dirt and blood was gone.

After I'd pulled my clothes on and gone to collect clean sheets, my lack of sleep was catching up with me again. I trudged back to my room to discover a mouthwatering scent drifting out.

Someone had left a dinner plate on the bedside table. It was heaped with thick slices of pork roast and mashed potatoes, both slathered in gravy, and a pile of buttered green beans on the side.

Any sense of hunger in me had been swallowed up in my fatigue. Now it came roaring to the surface. I grabbed the fork next to the plate and started shoveling food into my mouth.

I polished off the entire meal in a matter of minutes and sat back with satisfaction warming my stomach. Okay, there might be a few minor benefits to staying under the Nobles' roof.

Ignoring the groaning of the rest of my body, I forced myself to stay on my feet long enough to tuck the sheets properly onto the bed. Then I tumbled onto it, lost to the world almost as soon as my head hit the pillow.

Wavering dreams chased me through the night, but I didn't wake up until bright sunlight was glaring through my bedroom window. I blinked, rubbing my eyes, wondering just how late I'd slept after going without the night before. My mouth tasted like ash and my head felt stuffed full of wool.

At least the room around me looked back to normal. Someone had even brought by the clothes I'd chucked in the washer, neatly folded in a pile beside the door. I'd have to figure out which of the staff was feeling friendly toward me and pass them a little of my remaining cash in thank you.

There was an odd shadow streaked across the floor, a blotch in the middle of the mid-day brightness. I looked up at the window, frowning. The glare was harsh enough that I couldn't make out more than a blurred shape pasted against the glass.

I got up, stepped toward it, and the bottom of my stomach dropped out.

It was a tail. A severed, bloody-ended cat's tail, black fur jutting all along its dangling length. Who the fuck— Why would anyone—?

My mind shot to the stray cat Kaige had talked about so fondly the other night. *Her name's Mittens.* Acid seared up my throat.

I stumbled backward, still trying to process the horrific image, and the door burst open behind me. Kaige barged inside. "Slack-off time is over," he declared, wrenching me off my feet before I could so much as take a breath and whipping me around to face my doom.

25

Rowan

I SMOOTHED OUT THE FOLDS IN MY SUIT AS I LOOKED AT MY reflection in the mirrored window. I had patiently ironed it myself, but I couldn't help noticing a couple of tiny wrinkles that'd slipped through. Maybe no one else would have spotted them, but I chided myself silently anyway.

A lot depended on this meeting going right, and even though I knew that my clothes didn't have much to do with it, every detail counted. I made an effort to always look pulled together, to project strength and competence in every possible way.

"Mr. Finlay," a voice called.

I turned around, flashing my most charming smile. I'd perfected it over the last five years when it'd become difficult to offer a genuine one. People rarely looked beyond what you wanted to show them.

"Mr. Takashi and Mr. Gordon," I said, nodding to the two men in front of me. They were flanked by two beefy men wearing sunglasses, who I assumed were their bodyguards. I shook their hands and then led them into the establishment. "The Nobles send their regards. I'm pleased to speak to you today on their behalf."

I'd chosen this hotel because I'd learned from hearsay that these men absolutely adored Italian food. The hostess came around and seated us at a table in the brunch area. Gordon's eyes lingered on her butt, and I glanced away. There were a lot of things I didn't enjoy about most of the company I kept these days, but you couldn't get the good without the bad.

All that mattered this morning was the deal. It was still in its early stages of development, and I'd been handpicked by Ezra Noble to handle this meeting after smoothing the way for a few other agreements Wylder had initiated. The old man himself was taking notice of my skills now. Maybe if I could swing a few crucial negotiations in his favor, my position within the Nobles would stop feeling so precarious.

"So, Mr. Finlay," Mr. Takashi said. "Let's get down to business."

"Why don't we have some appetizers and drinks first?" I said, flashing them another manufactured smile. "Easier to do business on a full stomach."

Sometimes when I looked at myself in the mirror, I didn't recognize myself. I felt like a puppet being pulled by strings I wasn't sure I fully controlled. But there was nobody else to blame for the life I was living. I'd chosen it all on my own.

I'd gotten here early to speak with the staff and emphasize how important it was that they give this table their very best service. Ezra had a stake in the hotel, and it'd been clear everyone was aware of how great the rewards—or punishments—for their performance could be. Soon we all had heaping plates and glasses of wine in front of us. As the other men exclaimed over the food, a satisfied warmth filled my chest.

I might still be a relative newcomer among the Nobles, and this might not have been the life I'd envisioned for myself, but I was damn good at what I did. I'd worked my ass off to ensure my value.

I swirled my wine in my glass but only took sips. As my company gorged themselves, ties loosened and their own smiles came easier. I smiled to myself. Businessmen were so fucking predictable.

I leaned forward in my chair, taking on a conversational tone. "So, about the riverfront project. Mr. Noble has taken a keen interest in real estate in that neighborhood. He's willing to invest a lot if he can take the reins."

Gordon nodded. "We've seen the bid. But I'm not aware that Ezra Noble has all that much experience with this type of development...?"

Of course the money wasn't enough to persuade them. That was where I came in.

"Mr. Noble keeps many of his pursuits discreet, as I'm sure you can understand," I said. "He's in the business of making money—for himself and everyone on board with him—not bragging about it. Did you know he's the majority owner in this chain of hotels? He handpicked the chef who cooked your brunch personally when the restaurant opened three years ago."

Takashi's eyes widened. They wouldn't have known—even *I* hadn't known until I'd done some digging to prepare for this meeting.

Gordon took in the restaurant again with renewed respect. "He has done a good job with the place."

And it made one of many excellent fronts for the Nobles' true, not-entirely-legal interests, not that I was going to mention that. These men were undoubtedly aware of Ezra's reputation. They just needed enough of an excuse to look past it. Seeing a clean-cut, sharp-looking young man with no tattoos or piercings in sight speaking up for him should set a lot of those doubts to rest all on its own.

"Everything Ezra Noble puts his mind to, he gives his all," I said. "And to show you how serious he is about this offer, he's graciously seeing to the updated landscaping in the vicinity of the project with no commitment required."

I pulled open my briefcase and extended papers to the other men, who read through the proposal. Takashi's eyes widened when he noticed the amount printed. "Are you sure your boss is fine throwing this kind of money away?"

I chuckled lightly. "He doesn't consider it throwing away. Improvements to Paradise City benefit all of us. He'd simply like you to consider this as a proof of our interest. As you can see, by giving us this project, you'll ensure a long and meaningful partnership that will be beneficial to both parties. And I'm certain your firm will thank you for it."

Takashi and Gordon conferred over the details. Then Gordon stepped aside to place a call. Hope swelled in my chest as he returned with a smile, but I kept my expression mild. Eagerness was easily read as desperation.

"I believe Mr. Noble has a deal, Mr. Finlay," he said, holding out his hand for me to shake it. "And I hope that means we get to enjoy more of his—and your—hospitality in the future. Please pass on our compliments."

I gave his hand a solid shake, holding back the sense of triumph racing through me. "I'll be sure to do that."

The joy of the victory stayed with me through the rest of the brunch and the walk out to my car. As I got in, checking my phone and confirming I had no missed messages, the urge hit me to call my dad and tell him how well the meeting had gone.

Not that he'd known I even had a meeting or had any clue what I did for work these days. Chances were he was either already three sheets to the wind or still sleeping off whatever cheap alcohol he'd drowned himself in last night.

I tossed my phone onto the passenger seat, some of my elation fading.

By the time I returned to the mansion, it was nearly noon. Ezra wouldn't be back from his business trip until tomorrow, so I couldn't inform him of the good news just yet. It was better to do that in person, to establish the personal connection of the success face-to-face.

I headed inside, fighting down the compulsion to check on Mercy again. I'd let myself peek in on her before I'd left, and she'd still been sound asleep.

Wylder had been pushing her hard, and the exhaustion must have caught up with her. Why couldn't she have just left? When I thought of her expression as she'd cut apart the corpse yesterday, first so sickened and then with growing determination, my own stomach turned.

But Mercy had never been one to back down. I'd used to think that was one of her best qualities. Now I wasn't so sure. Playing chicken with Wylder wasn't a game that tended to end well for the other person.

It turned out I didn't get much choice in finding out what state Mercy was in. As I stepped into the foyer, her voice rang out from above. My head jerked up.

Kaige had her slung over his shoulder, carrying her down the hall from her room as she thrashed in his arms. Wylder and Gideon followed close behind.

"I didn't do it!" she protested. "It wasn't me. I woke up, and it was just *there*."

What was she talking about? I hustled up the stairs and noticed the confused furrow forming on Kaige's brow. He craned his neck around, stopping in his tracks. "What are you talking about? You didn't do what?"

Mercy went still. "Isn't this about Mittens? Her tail... There was a bloody cat tail stuck to the outside of my bedroom window. I assumed she..."

"Mittens?" Gideon repeated in a puzzled tone, but Kaige's expression had shifted. He swung around without putting Mercy down and stormed back to her room. Halting in the doorway, he let out a breath of relief.

"I don't know what the hell is going on there, but that's not Mittens' tail. She's a tabby—hers is striped."

"What the hell is going on?" Wylder demanded. "We didn't come up here to talk about tabbies."

"It's a long story," Kaige told him. "I'll get back to the job." He started marching to the stairs again.

Mercy squirmed against Kaige's grasp. "What the hell are you *doing* if you're not pissed off about that?"

Wylder answered for him. "You've been asleep way too long. Lucky you, Anthea suggested the perfect way to wake you up nice and fresh."

"What?" Mercy struggled harder, beating her fists against Kaige's back, but he strode on down the stairs as if he felt nothing. Sometimes I wondered if any feeling really did penetrate that muscle-bound body.

I wanted to ask what they had planned for her now, but Wylder looked pissed about the earlier interruption and Gideon was flicking through a chart on his tablet. It seemed wiser to follow along and see for myself.

They headed down to the basement. "Remind me, Gideon," Wylder said. "How many men have managed to pass the test?"

Gideon recited the data he must have already been looking at. "Just under fifty percent of prospective recruits make it out before they faint from lack of oxygen. Of course, making it out isn't enough. The record for quickest release is three point five minutes. If they take more than ten, that's a fail no matter how you slice it."

A chill settled over me with the suspicion of where this was headed.

"Make it out of *what*?" Mercy demanded, nearly managing to elbow Kaige in the back of the head.

"Don't worry, Kitty Cat, you'll survive it." Wylder pushed open the door to the last room I'd ever have wanted to see Mercy dragged into. Oh, no.

"I'm tired of your games," Mercy snapped at him.

"This isn't a game, Princess," Wylder said. "This is the real thing—one of the trials we put any man who wants to become one of the Nobles through. We've all done it. You want to run with the big boys, you have to walk the walk. Or faint the faint, if you're going to take the route of our least impressive candidates. Kaige, get her ankles."

He strode into the dimly lit room, pulling a rope from his back pocket. As he caught Mercy's wrists and bound them together, Kaige tied her legs. Mercy cursed and jabbed at them, but she didn't get in a strong enough blow to make a difference.

She hadn't seen what was waiting for her yet. The room was bare except for a deep freezer the size of a coffin set against the opposite wall. It wasn't plugged in, but that was a small comfort.

Even though I hadn't been down here in three and a half years, I remembered it like yesterday. Being shoved into that cramped space with my wrists and ankles tied, the lid slamming shut over me, taking the light with it. The unnerving choked silence, the sense that every breath was draining away far too much of my remaining air.

The trick was kicking the lid hard enough despite your bindings to force it open again—and keeping your cool well enough to figure that out. I'd managed it in seven minutes, sweating and dizzy by the end. Mercy could have handled the physical side of it no problem—I was sure she was stronger than I'd been back then. It was her head that'd be the problem.

The guys had no idea what even a few seconds inside that thing would do to her. "Wait," I said before I could think better of it, catching up with Wylder. "We've given her plenty of tests already. We don't have to—"

Wylder gave me a shrewd look. "What's the matter, Finlay? Have you developed a soft spot for our guest? Was her pussy really that good once upon a time?"

I flinched inwardly, but the sight of Kaige carrying Mercy the last few steps to the freezer seared away all my previous hesitation. All I could think of was the moment nearly a decade ago when I'd found her in that cabinet at the museum, shaking and babbling as if her very soul was being wrenched apart.

I couldn't watch her go through that again.

"No, stop!" I shouted, lunging at Kaige, but Wylder caught my shoulder.

"Tick, tick, tick, Princess," he called to Mercy. "Every second counts, so make sure you get out fast!"

I wrenched myself from his grasp, but in the same instant, Kaige dumped Mercy into the freezer and shoved down the lid with a resounding thud.

26

Mercy

STUPID, STUPID, STUPID.

As I struggled against Kaige's hold, anger rose inside me like a cresting wave. I'd been so distracted by the cat tail I'd let Kaige capture me, let these assholes drag me into yet another ridiculous situation. His bone-crushing grip offered no give.

I couldn't even squirm away from the rope he wrapped around my ankles, and Wylder managed to trap my wrists at the same time. Shit. What the hell were they up to now?

"Wait," Rowan said, his face weirdly pale. "We've given her plenty of tests already. We don't have to—"

Wylder cut him off with another snarky remark that I barely processed. Why was Rowan arguing about *this* after everything else he'd seen his friends put me through? Was he just feeling guilty about the past after our conversation yesterday?

Kaige hefted me, striding forward again, and Rowan sprang after us. "No, stop!"

His frantic tone made my pulse hitch. Wylder simply smirked as he blocked him.

"Tick, tick, tick, Princess," the Noble heir said. "Every second counts, so make sure you get out fast!"

Then Kaige dropped me—into a huge, thick-walled box some part of me recognized as a freezer. My shoulder jarred against the smooth surface inside before my back hit the bottom.

My lungs seized. I opened my mouth to spit out a protest, but the lid was already banging shut overtop of me.

A scream caught in my throat. Total darkness enveloped me, smothering me. I flailed my bound limbs, futilely banging at the walls.

Get out. Wylder expected me to get out.

But the old panic was already rolling over me. In the darkness, this didn't feel like a freezer at all. My mind fell back through the years to the concrete pit in the basement back home.

Dad used to stuff people he had a beef with in there to torture them. He'd leave them in there for hours until they'd pissed and shit themselves, until they'd do or say anything just to end the horrible impression of being buried alive, the sense that any breath might be their last.

I knew because he'd tossed *me* in there whenever he got particularly frustrated with my failures. As the heavy cover had thudded into place, air thick with the scents of stale vomit, urine, and blood would clog my nose. The utter darkness would suffocate me. I'd scream until my throat was hoarse, scratch at the slab of cement that sealed the pit until my fingertips were scraped raw, but he'd never come. Not until *he* was ready.

The first time I'd been five. I hadn't stopped shaking for the rest of the day afterward. The nightmares had haunted me for weeks.

And each time after, it'd only gotten worse. Just the feeling of the walls around me and the closing darkness would trigger all the worst sensations of every time before.

Those sensations rolled over me now, dragging me down deeper into the pit of my mind. Another scream tore from my lungs. I flailed and gasped, sobs choking me and setting off a fresh flare of panic. I couldn't breathe.

The stench clogged my nose, the darkness squeezed tight, and my whole body turned cold. Shivers wracked my body. I was down there again, down there in that void of nothingness, and maybe this would be the time he never came at all, not until I was dead.

I couldn't manage even a shriek now. A whimper spilled out of me with a hitch of breath. Then the door above me flew open.

Light flooded in on me with a wash of gloriously fresh air. Arms descended and hauled me out of my coffin. Rowan—Rowan was holding me.

He tried to set me on my feet, but my legs gave. I slumped to the floor. Four figures stood over my quaking body, their features blurry to my tear-hazed eyes.

I had to get a hold of myself. Had to pull myself together. But no matter how much air I sucked into my lungs, I still felt as if I were drowning.

"What's wrong with her?" someone said.

Rowan knelt and started untying my limbs. The release of the pressure around my wrists soothed my nerves just a little. "She's having a panic attack. She just needs to— No, don't do *that.*"

Cold water splashed across my face. I flinched, and some dribbled into my mouth. A shudder ran through me with the vague sense that it was seeping from the coffin I'd just been dragged out of.

No, not a coffin. A freezer. I wasn't back in my family home in that awful pit. I was in the basement of the Nobles' mansion.

Rowan wrenched the rope off my ankles and gripped my shoulder. "You're okay now. Can you sit up? What do you need, Mer?"

I needed him to get away from me with his false concern. I needed to regain control and break out of this meltdown. Fuck, fuck, fuck.

Grudgingly accepting his help, I managed to push myself into a sitting position. The shaking was subsiding, but my chest still trembled with every ragged breath. Gideon knelt down in front of me and flashed a light on my eye. My hand jerked up instinctively to shield my face.

"Hey," Rowan protested.

"I was just checking to see if she had a concussion," Gideon said. "She doesn't."

"No, she's just a pathetic little girl." Wylder loomed over me. "After all your boasting, you're just a spoiled brat who can't handle a minute in the freezer without freaking out."

Now that my panic was fading, the familiar rage surged back to the surface, giving me a burst of strength. "You don't know what you're talking about."

Wylder scoffed. "Oh, I think I do. When it came down to the wire, you couldn't hide how weak you are. How the hell could we ever stand with someone who'd fall apart so easily?" He shook his head. "What happened to the girl who swore that she was going to avenge her family? Was it all for show then, huh?"

He sounded oddly angry, as if my panic attack had been an even bigger betrayal than when he'd thought I'd run off to conspire with Colt. I caught a trace of frustration under the vicious edge in his voice as if he were taking my incompetence personally. You'd think he'd be happy that he'd finally found a way to knock me down.

I met his gaze in fury, refusing to look away. I wanted to lash out at him in return, but I was afraid my voice would quaver if I tried to speak more now, and that would only make me seem weaker. Instead, I focused on taking slower breaths to regain my composure.

"There you are." Anthea walked into the room with a clack of her heels. I shifted my glare to her. Gideon had mentioned something about her being the one who'd come up with the idea, hadn't he?

She'd made those comments on the fire escape the other day, almost as if she'd recognized my fear. Had she realized the kind of trauma she might be triggering?

She barely glanced at me. "How did it go? I'm assuming not well."

"She couldn't do it," Wylder said with scorn. "In five seconds flat, she was screaming worse than an animal about to be murdered."

I winced at his description. Did this man not have a bone of sympathy in him?

Silly question. He was heir to the Noble legacy—of course he didn't. That was why I'd come to him, wasn't it? Why I'd stayed, despite all the warnings from the first to Rowan's yesterday. I'd needed a brutal ally to take on Colt.

But that brutality could be turned on me just as easily.

Anthea's lips curled in a sneer. "Well, what do you expect from the Katz princess? I'd imagine she's spent her whole life playing with dollies. I told you she wasn't worth your time."

Rowan was watching me, the intensity in his gaze making it hard for me to look at him. He was the only one who knew just how far from the truth her assessment was, and suddenly I was angry at my younger self for opening up to him. It didn't feel right that the boy who had betrayed me was the only person left in the world who really knew me.

"That's not—" I started, but Anthea cut me off.

"How did she get out?"

"You can thank Rowan for that," Wylder said. "He was feeling awfully generous toward her today."

Rowan scowled at him. "It isn't her fault. She—"

Oh, God, I couldn't sit here and listen to him defend me now, laying out the worst scraps of my history for them to mock.

"I'm not weak," I broke in, raising my voice and relieved to find it held steady. The guys thought I was a liability now, and I didn't know if I could do anything to change their minds, but I knew I had to try. I motioned to the death trap beside me. "I can take anything you throw at me as long as it doesn't involve burying me alive. Is that a scenario that comes up so often?"

Gideon snorted. "I'd hardly consider that a burial. And it isn't as if we were setting you up for a fail. Many people have managed to get free, restraints and all, including every person currently in the Nobles."

"Well, I was at a disadvantage," I said, gritting my teeth.

"What disadvantage?" Kaige asked, as if I was going to share my dark memories with him. I had decided a long time ago that I wasn't letting anybody else that far inside to give them a chance to hurt me.

"I just don't like closed spaces, okay? Ever heard of claustrophobia?"

"Those are excuses for why you failed," Wylder said. "I've already told you, we can't stand with someone we can't count on."

I raised my chin, my heart thudding. "So what are you going to do about it?"

This was it, the moment of truth. Were they going to drag me right out of the house?

My stomach bunched up as I waited for him to answer. He glowered at me. "Get out of my sight. We're done here."

"I'm not going anywhere," I said. "You saw one bad moment after I've proven myself in every other possible way. We still have a deal. You swore on your blood; you promised me you weren't going back on it. I'm not leaving until I see my side through. You don't trust me to stand with you when you come down on Colt? Fine. I'll stand back and watch. But it's going to happen." And we'd see whether he could hold me back when the chips were actually down.

Kaige and Gideon stared at me in disbelief. Even Anthea looked surprised by my refusal.

"Your stubbornness isn't going to work when you don't have the actions to match your words," Wylder said.

"I already told you, this may be my weakness but it isn't a failure, and I'm sure as hell not weak." I managed to stand up, wiping my hands on my jeans, and met each of their gazes one by one.

I saw grudging respect in Gideon's eyes, and Rowan was looking at me in a way that I didn't want to delve into further, even if he'd protected me in the end. I expected Wylder to order Kaige to knock me out and then kick me down the front steps, or worse just put a bullet in my brain and get it all over with. Well, they could try.

Wylder spun on his heel, not even bothering to look at me. "If you insist on hanging around, you can go back to the groupie room. That's the level of company you clearly fit in with. I'm sure you'll be incredibly welcome there."

Gia's face flashed through my mind and then the mess some of the women had made of my room. My teeth gritted.

"Sure," I forced myself to say. At least I was still here. I hadn't failed completely, no matter what the guys said.

"Go," Kaige said with a jerk of his chin.

I stalked out of the room, not waiting for them to change their mind. My anger was building steadily inside me, and I needed to find a way to put it to good use.

27

Mercy

I STORMED INTO THE GROUPIE ROOM IN A TEMPER. MOST OF the beds were unoccupied at this time of day, just a couple of girls in tight crop-tops and cut-off shorts giggling over some magazine.

I stopped in the middle of the room with my hands on my hips. "Did either of you pour grease all over my room last night?"

Their heads snapped up. They stared at me like deer trapped in headlights. Hell, every one of the groupies might have joined together to trash my stuff. I'd bet they'd all laughed about it afterward. Maybe Anthea had stopped by to join in the party too.

"Maybe we did, maybe we didn't," one of them said in a nasal voicc. "What are you going to do about it?"

"Oh, there's lots I can do." I stepped toward them with fists raised, and both of them flinched. "Get the hell out of here, or I'll be happy to demonstrate."

They weren't the ones I should have been the angriest at, but they were the only people in front of me, and I needed a quiet space to think. Unfortunately, I only got that for about five seconds after they scrambled out, because Gia came sauntering in right after.

"So that's how the princess gets things done?" she said, adding a heavy sneer to the word *princess*. "Going around beating up people who talk back to you?"

I scowled at her, my hands clenching. I had no patience for her snark right now. "However you want to put it. They destroyed most of my clothes and belongings, and I'm sure you had fun watching them do it."

She chuckled. "It *was* fun to watch."

"Right, because what would you know about caring about your own things? You expect men to fuck you and then pay you for it with nice clothes and a place to stay and whatever else you need."

She narrowed her eyes. "You don't know shit about me, you bitch."

"It's not nice to call other people names, didn't your mama tell you?" I shot back. "Besides, isn't that the reason you all hang around? Hoping you'll catch some gang prince's eyes long enough that he'll invite you to warm his bed?"

Gia drew her skinny frame up taller, as if she thought she'd intimidate me that way. "*Nobody* paid for my clothes. I'm here because I want to be and because I genuinely care about what happens to—" She shook her head, and I assumed she'd been going to say Wylder. "These jeans are mine. Every piece of clothing I own I bought with my own money, and I'll have you know that I can more than afford to pay it."

My eyes drifted to her jeans. They did look expensive—almost designer. "How do you manage that?"

She tossed her hair haughtily. "You have no fucking right to my business. I'm sure I can take care of myself better than *you* can now that you can't go running to your daddy."

The jab stung more than I should have let it—probably because I *didn't* have much means to pay my way through life at this particular moment. My tongue flew without consulting my brain. "Maybe you're right. But since you're so concerned about Wylder and his crew, you might want to consider just how close I've gotten to them now." I took a step toward her so I was right in her face. "So close."

She took my bait easily. "What is that supposed to mean?"

I batted my eyelashes. "Kaige likes me. Very much." Maybe not anymore, but she didn't have to know that.

She snorted. "No, he doesn't. Kaige doesn't like anyone."

"He liked me enough to fuck me," I said.

She stared at me, her jaw clenching. "You're fucking lying."

"We did it on the hood of his car in the garage. Rough and hard. He loved every second of it and was practically begging for another round. Which I didn't give him, but even then, he never gave *you* the slightest time of day, did—"

Gia lunged at me, shoving me so hard I staggered backward a few steps before toppling to the floor on my ass. My shoulders throbbed where she'd smacked her hands into them.

Holy shit, the girl had some guns on her, and not the kind that took bullets. I'd never have guessed she could hold her own in a real fight.

I sprang back to my feet, ready to have a proper go at this, but Gia's stance had gone rigid. Worry flashed across her face, and she pushed herself backward, holding up her hands.

"Forget it. You're not worth the energy."

She stalked out of the room, leaving me staring after her. She'd looked almost *scared* for a second there. Because she'd been afraid of how I'd retaliate for her shove? But she hadn't hesitated to goad me every chance she'd gotten before. I'd never gotten the impression she was worried about what I'd do to her.

So what was she nervous about now?

I rubbed my shoulder, which twinged at my touch. Damn, I was pretty sure I'd have bruises in the morning. How had Gia turned out to be such a powerhouse?

That was the one thing different about this altercation compared to all the other ones. Before, she'd only thrown words at me. Which was kind of strange if she had that kind of fighting power up her sleeves. Why had she been hiding it?

A quiver of uneasiness wove through my thoughts. Something about the situation just felt *wrong*.

Thankfully, Gia had given me the solitude I'd been searching for—but I had other things on my mind now. I scanned the room, my gaze coming to rest on Gia's bed, her possessions neatly stacked beneath it like the wall of a fortress. Driven by an itch of curiosity, I walked over and crouched by the bed.

The stacks at the front of the space were all carefully folded clothes, some of them as nice as the jeans she'd been wearing. I sifted through them, not finding anything particularly interest-worthy until my hands paused on another pair of jeans at the bottom of one stack.

The dark blue material was flecked with little white dots. Not like purposeful styling—it was only in one spot around the knee, not even on the other side. And they were so tiny I doubted anyone would see them unless they were peering this closely anyway. It looked as if she'd been doing something with bleach and gotten some stray flecks on her clothes.

Anthea's voice came back to me from our chat on the fire escape. The mixture for making rust appear—vinegar, salt... and hydrogen peroxide. That was practically the same as bleach, wasn't it?

I shook my head at myself. That line of thinking was insane. There was *no* fucking way...

But ten minutes ago, I'd have said there was no way Gia could shove me to the ground, wouldn't I?

Gnawing at my lower lip, I peered farther under the bed. There were a few more pieces of clothes she mustn't have bothered with anymore lying crumpled here and there... and something rectangular showing faintly through the slats of the cot.

Glancing around to make sure I wasn't about to be interrupted, I hefted up the mattress and reached underneath. Gia had a few magazines of her own stashed under there, right toward the back—rumpled looking as if she'd paged through them a lot.

I picked them up and eyed the glossy covers with their cover models in the latest fashions of several months ago. Why was she hanging on to these? Why go to such lengths to hide them?

I rifled through one, and the pages naturally opened to a spot near the middle. A napkin was wedged in there, with a smear of ketchup—not blood, I determined by sniffing—at one corner. Oh-kay. Why the hell would she save something like that?

In the second magazine, I found a flyer for a gym in the Bend, which maybe wasn't so odd—if her family lived down there, it could have something to do with them. Farther in, a single shoelace was lodged between the pages.

With rising trepidation, I fanned open the third magazine. The pages rippled apart, revealing a tuft of hair that looked like it'd been gathered together from a hairbrush.

Black hair, not Wylder's bright auburn. The only guy I'd seen Gia hanging around who had *black* hair was Kaige.

I rocked back on my heels. I'd noticed glimmers of jealousy in her before when Kaige was paying attention to me, but I'd figured she was just generally possessive of everyone in Wylder's vicinity. She'd certainly hung off the heir himself plenty.

But this looked like Kaige's hair. And it'd been Kaige I'd been taunting her about when she'd lunged at me with that never-before-seen show of aggression.

He obviously hadn't given her this stuff on purpose. Who offered up used napkins and stray shoelaces as gestures of affection? I'd never seen him give her even the scraps of attention Wylder sometimes did.

But she was totally hung up on him anyway. Creepily obsessed with him, even. I glanced at the tufts of hair and cringed.

Had she left that freaky drawing in my room too? Pasted that lopped-off cat tail to my window? My stomach flipped over.

The pieces were starting to pull together in my head, but the picture they were creating still didn't make sense. I rubbed the bridge of my nose, and a memory rose up.

When I'd run into her in the Steel Knights territory the other day, she'd been carrying a duffel bag. Where was that? She hadn't been carrying it when she'd left just now.

I peered under the bed again, but there was no sign of it. So she'd gone into the Bend with a bag she wasn't comfortable stashing with the rest of her things here.

I flipped to the gym flyer again, studying the name and the address. I hadn't paid that much attention to Colt's business with the MMA fights, but this place was in his domain. His voice came back to me from the rehearsal dinner, one of the last friendly remarks I'd heard him make.

We've got a new fighter who's become a real talking point—a woman who's been taking on the men, and she's good enough to topple them.

I was insane to even be considering this, right? Gia was... Gia.

Cringing, mewling Gia, who spent more time clinging to the guys than fighting her own battles.

But…

I shook my head and stood up. Sitting here speculating wasn't getting me anywhere. There was one person who could at least confirm that I didn't have the most important part totally wrong.

Leaving the magazines in their hiding place so Gia wouldn't know I'd discovered them, I slipped out of the room and made my way through the house, checking what I figured were the most likely places. The kitchen and the room with the pool table let me down, but coming out into the hall, I ran into just the man I was looking for anyway.

Kaige stopped at the sight of me with a frown, folding his massive arms over his chest. "What are you doing wandering around here? Wylder told you to stick to the groupie room."

I shrugged. "He told me to act like a groupie. Last time I checked, they have free run of this part of the house."

"Back to snark, are we?" Kaige kept his voice easy, but I could detect the tautness at the back of it.

"I got tired of sitting there," I said, watching him carefully. "Your girlfriend doesn't like me."

Kaige looked at me strangely for a second. As far as I could tell, his confusion was genuine. "Who are you talking about?"

Somehow my heart managed to lift and sink at the same time. I was ridiculously glad he wasn't serious about any of those girls, but that also meant I'd pegged Gia's obsession right.

"Gia, of course."

He snorted. "It's Wylder she has a crush on, not me. But then most of the women usually go for him, so that's no surprise. Comes with the territory of being an actual Noble in name as well as loyalty."

I gave him a wry smile. "Nope, you're definitely the one she wants. You never indulged her flirtations? She throws herself at you all the time."

He furrowed his brow as if this was news to him. "That's because of Wylder. Anyway, I don't fuck the groupies—any of them. I want nothing to do with that."

I raised my eyebrows, legitimately surprised. "Don't tell me you haven't taken the occasional interest in one or two of them? They're easy targets."

Kaige looked me up and down, his gaze leaving a trail of goosebumps. "I don't need easy targets," he said, his intention clear in his voice. Then he shook himself and stepped back.

My gaze dropped to his sneakers, the same midnight blue ones I'd seen him in most days. I'd never noticed before that the laces didn't quite match. The ones on the right shoe were a little thinner and more of a pale gray than white like the ones on the right. Thin and pale gray like the lace in Gia's magazine.

"Your shoelaces don't match," I said in a distant sort of way, the enormity of what I was slowly becoming convinced of nearly overwhelming me.

Kaige glanced down. "Yeah. Some jerk around here thought it was funny to steal the laces out of one of them. Like that was going to stop me from wearing my favorite pair." He let out a huff and then fixed his dark eyes on me again. "You don't want Wylder catching you lurking around here, kitten. Scurry on back to your room, or he'll give you much bigger things to worry about than Gia or my shoes."

As he marched off, I rubbed the tingle of attraction from my arms as well as I could. I already had bigger things to worry about than the fact that he could somehow still turn me on with just a glance.

And Gia was right in the middle of it. Her little psycho mementos must all tie back to Kaige.

I couldn't dismiss the suspicions that were crowding my head more by the minute, but I couldn't do anything else to investigate them right now. But soon... I'd do a little digging and find out whether this crazy idea of mine was actually so crazy after all.

28

Gideon

Anthea's sharp voice crackled out of the phone at my ear. "Are you sure you sent me all the files?"

I bit back a sigh, pausing in the hall. When was I *ever* less than thorough? But Wylder's aunt didn't often work alongside her nephew and the rest of us, so I supposed it was understandable that she might not be fully aware of my meticulousness.

"That's everything our contact sent to me."

She made a frustrated sound. "He's holding out on us. My brother wanted this situation settled before he got back. I'll have to take a look at the set-up with my own eyes to make the right call. Where can I find that prick?"

I could pull that information out of my head without even consulting my tablet, since I'd been delving into the matter just an hour ago. "He'll be at work now—store manager, a place with a lot of foot traffic, not good for public confrontations. But he'll be off when it closes at eleven. You could catch him then."

"Perfect," she said with an edge of malicious satisfaction that I had to admit made even me a little nervous. Anthea was definitely not someone whose bad side I'd ever like to be on.

A lesson someone else had recently learned. I slid the phone into my pocket and strode the rest of the way to the groupie room, my stance tensing the closer I got even though it'd been my idea to check on the Claws heir.

The women who hung around the mansion came on to me just as much as they did with anyone else they knew had a solid position in the gang, but it was rare that they stirred anything other than uneasiness in me. They were too desperate, too clingy. My physical needs rarely became so intense that I had any need to indulge them with a sexual encounter anyway.

But the urge to confirm that Mercy was following Wylder's orders had driven me here anyway. The girl already caused more disruption than I liked in our close-knit unit. It was my job to protect the Nobles and Wylder in particular, and my list of potential threats to our security now included her.

If there was a small, deeper impulse in me to see her just for the sake of setting my eyes on her again, I didn't have to pay attention to that.

She wasn't in the room with its rows of cots and its weed stink, though. The smell reminded me of the other reason I didn't normally come around this part of the house. Even though the few girls currently lounging on their beds weren't smoking at the moment, the traces in the air prickled into my lungs in an instant.

I drew back, frowning. Where had the girl gotten to now?

Missing information irritated me at the best of times. In this particular circumstance, it dug into me like a thorn. I marched through the house, checking every room I passed. Finally, as I approached the exercise room around back where the guys did some of their physical training, a feminine-sounding grunt reached my ears. Ah ha.

I shoved the door open, ready to tell her off for using the equipment that *definitely* wasn't for the groupies' purposes, and stopped on the threshold at the sight in front of me.

It was Mercy, all right—in the middle of a round of tumbling that had her flipping and spinning across the rubbery mats so swiftly and nimbly she barely seemed to touch them. In that first instant, I could almost have believed she was flying. Her ponytail whipped around her, she jackknifed at the waist, and her feet hit the ground, planting with only the slightest wobble.

An instant later, she launched herself forward again, somersaulting in the air and bouncing off the floor on her hands, whirling across the room as if she were made of nothing but muscular power and grace. She rebounded off the far wall, grabbing the bars mounted there to heave herself even higher, and soared a good eight feet off the ground, so high she might have touched the ceiling if she'd tried.

Even from that height, she landed with a thump but not a stumble. I mentally revised the odds I'd given to her having told the truth about her encounter with Colt Bryant. She'd said she knew parkour. Watching her now, it wasn't hard at all to believe she could have tumbled her way down three stories without breaking a bone, even with a still-healing wound. I'd seen only the slightest hint of her favoring that arm as she'd grasped the bars.

She swiveled, catching her breath, and froze when her gaze snagged on me. The mask of steady concentration that'd come over her face stuttered for a second before her expression tensed. I almost regretted seeing that focused calm leave her.

A twinge of self-consciousness traveled down my spine. If I'd tried to so much as jog across the room a few times, my lungs would have started to tighten. Even if I'd practiced my ass off, I'd never have been able to train hard enough to accomplish the moves this girl had just made appear so effortless. Anywhere near that much exertion, and my chest would seize up completely.

But even as that brief pang of mourning flitted through me, it came with a flicker of desire. I wanted to touch the strong, flexible limbs I'd just seen on exhilarating display, discover how they could move against mine—

I clenched my jaw, reining in the errant desire. I couldn't get distracted.

"What are you doing in here?" I asked, folding my arms over my chest.

She shrugged. "I got tired of hanging around the groupies and went exploring. No one was using this space. I didn't figure it'd hurt if I did. Working out helps me focus."

Her gaze dared me to complain. "You're not a guest in this house anymore," I had to remind her. "You're lucky Wylder hasn't kicked you out already."

"Lucky," she repeated with a snort, and sat down on the mat to stretch. I couldn't help studying the curve of her back, the flex of her calves and thighs... the way her breasts rose beneath the sweat-damp fabric of her tank top when she lifted her arms over her head. My hands itched with the urge to trace over those slopes.

She was curves and softness, but her body was toned enough to give her the leanness and definition of an athlete. How could that combination be so fucking alluring?

The hunger gripping me only annoyed me further. She should have been *more* than even this. Wylder had expected more. After Anthea's suggestion this morning, he'd been so energized in anticipation of putting Mercy through the freezer trial. He hadn't said it out loud, but it'd been obvious to me that he'd been sure she could conquer it like she had everything else we'd thrown at her. That he'd been looking forward to watching her crush the challenge.

I doubted he'd ever have admitted it, but he'd *wanted* her to conquer it. Maybe to have a clear point of evidence to say she'd passed every test she needed to, that we could lay off her and let her see what she could make of her place here.

And instead, somehow she'd let us down—let him down. The power I'd just seen in her had left her the moment the freezer lid had closed. She'd been as helpless as I was in the grips of an asthma attack. I might not have fully understood why that had infuriated my best friend quite so forcefully, but remembering it, I bristled on his behalf.

And possibly my own as well. I had to admit that after seeing her brave the piranhas in my tank, becoming more radiantly defiant with every passing minute, some part of me had started to bet on her success. A sinking sensation of disappointment had passed through my gut as Rowan had hauled her quaking body out of the freezer.

My next question came out harsher than I'd intended. "Why are you even here?" She'd failed; she'd faltered. She should be able to see she didn't have any real place after all. She obviously didn't enjoy the groupie life. I honestly didn't understand what she hoped to gain at this point. It made no logical sense.

She looked up to glower at me over her shoulder. "I told you, the exercise clears my head."

"No," I said. "Why are you still here at all? Things have only gotten worse for you. You should just leave."

She snorted. "So I've heard. Rowan has already given me several variations of that suggestion. Oh, and Anthea too. Guess what—it hasn't worked."

"I think it should be pretty clear by now that you don't belong with us."

She pushed back to her feet with an ease of movement I couldn't help envying. "Why, because I freaked out this morning? Are you going to tell me that you've let one moment of weakness define *you*?"

A prickle ran down my spine. How much had the other guys told her about my situation when I wasn't there? "It was more than a moment," I insisted, ignoring the discomfort that rose up at her question.

"And I've had tons more moments when I did more than any of you ever expected. I don't see why one flaw should cancel everything else out. Why do you?"

"Like Wylder said—"

"Stop with Wylder's bullshit," she snapped. "He's trying to scare me off, but it's not going to happen. That night when I was surrounded by the men who were slaughtering my family one by one, I decided that I was going to survive it and I was going to make Colt pay for what he'd done. I'm not stopping until he's dead. And the Nobles are still by far my best chance of accomplishing that. Unless Wylder has me escorted out at gunpoint, I'm not going anywhere."

Passionate determination rang through her voice. I couldn't detect any lies in her tone. Nothing mattered to her but seeing Colt destroyed—and something in that bloodthirstiness woke up a thrum of understanding in my own blood.

"You people don't trust me, and that's fine, because frankly I don't trust you either," she continued. "We don't need to be *friends*. We just need to agree to crush a common enemy. I know I can be an invaluable resource to you when it comes to the Bend. Whatever it takes, I'm going to prove I'm all in, to the point that none of you can deny it. You'll see."

The heartfelt declaration unnerved me more than I liked. I stepped back to the doorway. "Fine. You can stay."

"I don't think that's your permission to give or take away anyway," she retorted.

That was true. Her words made my lips twitch, but I wasn't going to lie. I just turned my back on her and stalked away.

Neither of us had chosen our weaknesses, but they were still weaknesses. And if I hated myself for mine, why should I forgive her for hers?

29

Mercy

I'D OVERHEARD COLT TALKING ABOUT THE MMA FIGHTS often enough to know they usually started pretty late, when the gym he held them in had closed for the night. After prowling through the mansion restlessly, avoiding the Nobles men and nabbing some leftovers from the kitchen when no one was around, I was relieved when the sky beyond the windows darkened. I pulled on my hoodie, tapped the outline of my childhood bracelet in my pocket for good luck, and headed for the door.

Unfortunately, no one had left any unattended weapons around for me to nab, so I had to make do with a paring knife from the kitchen. Luck willing, I wouldn't need anything tonight except my eyes anyway.

I was halfway across the foyer when a voice carried from behind me. "Going somewhere?"

I whirled around to find Rowan emerging from the hall. I hadn't crossed paths with him since this morning, and the sight of him made my stomach twist.

"Is that a problem?" I asked. "Haven't you been telling me to get out of here since the start?"

His gaze, far too knowing, swept over me. "You don't look like you're beaten. You look like you're on some kind of mission."

"What's it to you if I am? I promise it won't make anything more difficult for *you*."

A shadow crossed his face. "Are you okay? This morning—if I'd known what they were going to do—I was out at a meeting when they decided."

Irritation jabbed at me. I could do without yet another reminder of how I'd fallen apart during the freezer test. And when was he going to see that I wasn't some fragile girl on the verge of shattering? I hadn't been when we'd first met; I hadn't been at sixteen when he'd left me in the lurch either.

"What's it to you?" I snapped.

"I'm trying to say I'm sorry," he said, the words tumbling out roughly. "I should have stepped in sooner. You didn't deserve—"

I cut him off with a swipe of my hand. "I haven't deserved anything I've had to deal with, but that's just life. In case there's been some misunderstanding, I don't need your sympathy. The last time I needed anything from you was five years ago, and I learned my lesson then. Just let me do what I need to do."

We locked eyes for a long moment. Was he going to go running to Wylder to tattle on me? Would Wylder even care that I was going out?

But something softened in Rowan's eyes, and I saw an echo of the boy I'd loved. A quiver of electricity ran through the air between us. For just a second, a shred of that old sadness returned. I swallowed it back down.

He broke the silence first. "Wherever you're going, do you want my car?"

I frowned. "Why would you lend me it? Kaige didn't seem so happy about how that worked out for him."

Rowan lowered his gaze for a moment before meeting my eyes again. "I'd rather know you have an easy way to get back if you run into trouble again."

It felt like a peace offering—an apology I could actually use. But was it even that? Kaige had told me that Gideon had trackers in all their cars. Maybe Rowan just wanted to know he could check where I'd gone.

I didn't think any of the guys would be keen on finding out I was heading back into Steel Knights territory. I couldn't let them interrupt me until I had the proof I needed—for myself and for them.

"Thanks, but no thanks," I said, more evenly this time. "I think it's better if I get around by my own steam until you *and* your boss see me as an equal. Maybe when I get back, we can settle that for good."

Concern crossed his face. "Where *are* you going?"

I shot him a tight smile. "To find the Titan's killer. Don't wait up."

I strode out of the house, and Rowan didn't chase after me. But just in case, I sped up to a lope on my way down the hill to the busier streets where I could hail a cab.

By the time the taxi reached the area around the gym from Gia's flyer, night had fully descended over the Bend. The only lights still blazing were the streetlamps not knocked out, the windows of a few bars… and the back door of the gym, standing open as a bouncer ushered a stream of boisterous figures inside.

It didn't appear he was turning anyone away, at least. Pulling my hood up and ducking my head low, I joined the line. The guys in front of me were debating the odds for a fight and how much they should put on their favorite to win. Clearly I'd come to the right place.

The real question was whether I'd find Titus's murderer here too.

When I reached the door, the man briefly scanned my shadowed face before he waved me in. But as I passed him, he said. "You there!"

I froze where I stood, torn between the urge to run or to play innocent. A man shoved past me from behind. "Keep moving, bitch."

Glancing over my shoulder, I saw the bouncer had stepped aside to talk with some bearded biker-looking dude. He hadn't been talking to me at all. I exhaled slowly and hustled the rest of the way inside. Getting jumpy wasn't going to do me any good.

Tarp had been taped over the gym's windows to hide the light from anyone driving by. Most of the equipment must have been pushed aside to make room for the temporary aluminum bleachers set up around the boxing ring. The space was dim except the floodlights glaring off the red floor of the platform and the metal bars surrounding it. No one was likely to pick me out of the crowd now that I was in.

The smells of booze and old sweat made me grimace. I squeezed past a guy selling bottles of beer and nabbed a spot at the end of one of the upper tiers where I could see the whole platform and also jump for the floor to jet out of here if need be.

The rest of the audience was mostly men, getting rowdier as the minutes ticked by. Hip-hop music thumped from the speakers placed all over the room, heightening the sense of anticipation.

A few guys I recognized from Colt's crew walked by the edge of the ring, and my pulse stuttered. But they didn't even glance my way, circling the platform to take seats in the shadows on the other side.

I pulled my hoodie closer around me as if it could shield me. There'd been no sign of my ex-fiancé himself, but I doubted he oversaw most of the fights personally.

The music cut out. "Ladies and gentlemen," a man's voice boomed from the speakers. "I hope you have placed your bets because we're ready to begin."

Two bulky guys who looked as if they had about one brain cell between them lumbered into the ring, their hands taped and tattoos dappling their bare chests. I shifted on the hard bench, nervousness turning my saliva sour in my mouth. What if the famous female fighter wasn't going on tonight at all?

I held myself as still as I could through the first two fights, watching both pairs of men pummel each other until they were dripping sweat, spit, and blood. Just as impatience wound from my stomach up to my chest, the announcer's voice called out the third set of names. "And now, the face-off you've all been waiting for: Lady Diamond vs. The Hammerhead!"

I sat up a little straighter. The man next to me elbowed his friend. "Diamond'll take it again."

"I don't know. Hammerhead is pretty good too."

"Pfft, good my ass. Diamond's going to knock him out in seconds. The bets are mostly on how long he's going to last in there."

This was it. Two figures entered from opposite sides. The first was a man almost as broad-shouldered and tall as Kaige. I focused my attention on his opponent.

The slim woman had her long blond hair pulled up in a high ponytail. Under the glaring lights, I couldn't tell if it was the exact same straw-pale shade I was looking for. A white mask covered the upper half of her face. The rest of her was clothed in a matching white leotard with a belt of glittering stones around her waist.

The announcer gave the call for the fight to start, and the crowd went into a frenzy, screaming and shouting for them to draw first blood. The girl—Lady Diamond—was nowhere near the size of her opponent, but that didn't seem to faze her at all.

The man barreled towards her, making the first move. She ducked easily and landed an uppercut to his jaw. Spit burst from his mouth, and the crowd groaned right alongside as if feeling his pain.

I tracked Lady Diamond's movements as she circled the guy, weaving and dodging and lunging in with strikes when he gave her an opening. She was fast on her feet in a slippery way that felt increasingly familiar. Something bounced against her collarbone as she evaded her opponent again and again. I squinted, and an uneasy certainty solidified in my gut.

Those were dog tags, weren't they? Kaige had told me he'd used to carry his father's dog tags everywhere... until he'd lost them. Or they'd been stolen. After seeing the contents of Gia's magazines, I wouldn't have put it past her.

At the same moment, the woman spun toward me, her mouth twisting into a sneer I'd have known anywhere. I stiffened in my seat.

It was her. I had no doubt left. That was Gia bounding around the boxing ring. Gia the crowd was cheering on after all the duels she'd won before.

She dodged the big guy yet again, but this time instead of continuing to move away, she swung around and careened right into him. Hammerhead lost his balance and stumbled.

Gia flung herself at the bars and leapt off them to snap her legs around his neck. She heaved upward, digging her fingers into his jaw as her thighs squeezed tight.

The guy staggered, trying to buck her off. Gia smirked out at the crowd. Her stage name rang out from every side. "Diamond! Diamond! Diamond!" The entire room was rooting for her.

Hammerhead struggled to shake her off, but no matter how he twisted and snatched at her, he couldn't break her hold. His face was turning progressively blue. With just one wrench of her hips and hands, I had no doubt she could have broken his neck if she'd had killing rather than winning in mind.

Hammerhead sank to the floor, and Gia bashed his slumping head into the mat with all her strength. As he lolled there, gasping, she climbed off him and raised her hands in the air. Cheers rained down on her.

She only stayed for long enough for the announcer to acknowledge her win. As she ducked out of the ring, I slipped over the edge of the bleachers and squeezed through the latecomers who'd been left with only standing room in the aisles. I'd lost sight of her, but there was only one door people were using right now. I made a beeline for it.

I'd been closer and got there first. I ambled out into the darkness past the bouncer casually, and he didn't say a word. When I'd made it partway to the street, I heard him call out, "Great match!" to someone behind me. I darted into the shadows next to the building.

"Thanks!" Gia said, picking up her pace as she came around the side of the building. She'd left her mask on for the moment, and she had the duffel bag I'd been searching for slung over her shoulder.

I let her pass me and then slunk behind her. A short distance down the block, she tugged off the mask and shoved it into her bag. I took the moment to jog up beside her. "Hello, Gia."

Gia squeaked in shock, spinning around, clutching her bag as if she were going to use it as a weapon. When she caught sight of me, she froze in place. I readied myself to chase after her if she took off, but instead she drew herself up, the muscles in her arms flexing. Muscles I now knew could subdue a trained fighter.

Muscles that had killed a man twice my size.

I took a step back into the empty parking lot behind me, my hand going to my pocket with the paring knife. I needed answers, but I already had more than Gia might be willing to let me leave here with. So I'd just have to make sure she didn't get a chance to stop me.

Her lips curled as she watched my partial retreat. She dropped her bag on the ground to give her better mobility. "So you figured it out. You've got such a bad habit of snooping into other people's stuff."

"Is that really any worse than making up a whole secret identity?" I asked.

She barked out a laugh. "I do what I have to do to survive."

"But surviving isn't all you've done, is it?" She moved toward me, and I sidestepped. "I saw the move that you used on Hammerhead. Catching his neck like that… it reminds me of something."

An emotion closer to panic flickered in her eyes. She sprang at me, but I'd watched her moves carefully, and she was already tired from her brawl in the ring. No matter how many fights she'd won in the past several months, I'd been training to hold my own since I could walk.

I dodged and ducked, weaving back and forth as she followed me into the parking lot. I wasn't going to bring out the knife until I had to. As long as she didn't see me as too great a threat, I could hope to keep her dancing and talking a little longer. I still needed more answers.

"Is that the best you've got?" I said.

Fury flared on her face. She threw herself forward to catch me by my knees, and I managed to kick her in the shoulder before twisting away.

We circled each other. As she lunged for me again, I spun around her and snatched at the back of her neck. My fingers closed around a leather strap that snapped at my swift tug.

I darted backward, the dog tags dangling from my hands.

Gia clapped her hand to her throat. "Give those back," she snarled.

I could barely make out the letters etched in the metal by the dim light of the streetlamps, but the last name *MADDEN* was unmistakable. I raised my head.

"These don't belong to you. You stole them from Kaige."

"Whatever belongs to him belongs to me," she said.

I resisted the urge to roll my eyes. Her obsession had made her delusional.

"We don't need to play this game anymore," I said. "I know you killed Titus."

To my surprise, instead of denying it, she started giggling. "Oh, did I? And how are you going to convince anyone else of that?"

I ignored the question, focusing on my own need for answers as I kept out of range of her swings and grabs. "Why'd you do it? Don't tell me it was for Kaige. He doesn't care one bit about you."

Hurt flashed across her face before it was replaced by rage. "What do you know about that, you heartless bitch? You fucked him and then gloated to me about it. I love Kaige. I've loved him for ages. Titus was going to have him killed, so I did whatever it took to protect him."

I raised my eyebrows. "You murdered a man over an empty threat fueled by too much testosterone?"

Gia scowled. "I know what I heard. I'm not a fucking idiot. He was talking about it after—he really meant to screw Kaige over any way he could, even setting him up to take a bullet that would seem like just the wrong place, wrong time."

I didn't know if I should believe her or if she'd justified the act to herself with more delusions. It didn't really matter. "You could have just warned him instead of going all murder-happy yourself."

A maniacal glint lit in her eyes. "But my way worked, didn't it? And Kaige never even needed to worry about it. I was his avenger in the night."

What, did she figure she was Batman now? More like batshit crazy.

"Did you leave that drawing in my room? And the severed cat's tail?" I demanded. "Was it a way to scare me off?"

The confused knitting of her brow looked genuine. "What are you talking about? I wasn't threatened by you. I knew you'd never get to the truth."

"And yet here we are," I said. "Looks like you underestimated me."

"Do you think any of that matters? Wake up, I've already gotten away with it. It's the perfect crime. Titus is buried six feet underground, and he sure isn't coming back from the grave to snitch on me. Nobody believes I could be capable of it. If you manage to get back to the house alive and tell them your story, they'll laugh you out of the place."

She was probably right. I had no hard evidence, only circumstantial proof, and repeating her confession was just hearsay. The story sounded so ridiculous I hadn't even believed it myself until I'd watched her fight.

Gia drove her point home. "It doesn't matter what you say. They don't trust you. They'll never believe you."

And it'd look like I was just grasping at straws to convince Wylder I'd met his end of the deal. Damn it.

"You see," Gia continued in a taunting voice. "You're hopeless.

Really there's only one person in that house who might have figured it out eventually with all her nosing around, but I finally managed to take care of that problem too."

She had to mean Anthea. I stared at her. "What the fuck are you talking about?"

She offered a sharp little smile. "Let's just say the next drive Miss Prissy goes on will definitely be her last."

Dread climbed up my spine. She'd messed with the other woman's car somehow—and after what Gia had managed to do to Titus, I wasn't sure even Anthea could survive this insanity.

30

Mercy

As soon as the realization hit me, I spun away from Gia and took off across the parking lot. I couldn't waste precious time trying to reason with her or haul her back to Wylder. Any second I delayed could mean Anthea's death.

Maybe she'd been an ass to me, maybe there'd been times when I'd wanted to punch her face in, but I knew behind it all she'd only been looking out for the guys the best way she knew how. If I stood around and let Gia murder her, her blood would be on my hands too. Nothing about that possibility sat right with me.

Gia's voice rang out behind me, pitched to carry all the way down the block. "She's here! Mercy Katz is here!"

Fuck. I didn't risk looking back, but a sharp exclamation somewhere down the street told me that at least one of Colt's men had heard her announcement. As I pushed myself faster, Gia let out another holler, sounding almost gleeful. "That's her! That's Mercy Katz. Don't let her get away!"

I gritted my teeth and ran faster for both my sake and Anthea's, pumping my arms to keep my momentum. I couldn't let Colt haul my ass in again. Lord only knew what he'd do to me now that I'd defied him to his face.

I bolted down an alley and across the street on the other side. Veering left to mix up my path, I sprinted on. Kaige's dog tags bit into my palm where I was still clutching them. I didn't dare stop even long enough to safely stuff them in my hoodie's pocket.

Tires screeched around a corner way too close for comfort. I swerved down another narrow alley and burst out by a street that still had a decent amount of traffic at this hour. Jogging against the flow, I spotted a cab heading my way. I waved my arm, bouncing on my feet to catch the driver's attention as I hustled to meet it.

The cab had barely rolled to a halt when I yanked the door open and dove into the back seat. The driver stared back at me.

"Paradise City, top of the hill," I said, panting. "Please. Just step on it."

The engine revved as the cabbie hit the gas. Requests that tested the speed limit probably weren't unusual in this part of town. I jolted back in the seat and scrambled for my phone.

Even driving fast through the dwindling night traffic, it would take at least half an hour to make it back to the mansion. I skimmed through the profiles I'd saved in my Contacts. The Nobles kept a handy list of all the important numbers on the fridge, since I supposed they changed burners regularly and it was easier to spread the word that way. I'd entered all four of the guys on a whim I now thanked God for.

After a moment's hesitation as I debated who I'd hate speaking to the least, I tapped Rowan's name. He'd offered me some kind of help—he was the most likely to listen to me, right?

The call went through to voicemail. With a groan, I dialed Gideon, but he didn't pick up either. No way in hell was I counting on anything from Wylder after the way he'd laid into me this morning, so I jabbed the entry for Kaige instead.

Relief flooded me at the click of him answering. "Hello?"

"Kaige, it's me. Mercy." I dragged in a breath to steady my voice, but Kaige broke in before I could go on.

"Mercy? Where the fuck are you?" The angry growl in his voice chilled me.

"It doesn't matter," I said. "You just need to—"

He interrupted me again, his tone even harsher. "I think it matters. Gia just called Wylder—she's saying you followed her into the Bend and *attacked* her? She was sobbing her heart out on the phone. Is this why you were asking all those questions about her?"

Fucking hell. I wanted to wring that bitch's neck. "Of course not," I snapped. "She's lying again, just like she was about Colt. You have to listen. I—"

"I don't want to hear a word out of your mouth until you're back here and you can explain to all of us where the hell you ran off to. And you'd better get here fast, because Wylder's getting more pissed off by the second."

"Kaige!"

He'd already hung up. Dead air filled my ear. Swearing, I bit the bullet and tried calling Wylder, then each of the other guys again, but if they were seeing the calls, they were ignoring me.

They had no idea this was anything other than a spat between two supposed groupies—and who knew what other lies Gia had spun to antagonize them against me.

"Can you go any faster?" I said to the cabbie as I frantically tapped out a text message. *Anthea's in danger. Don't let her get in her car.*

I sent it and stared at the screen. The message remained unread. Why did they have to be such blockheads?

I pushed both the phone and the dog tags into my pockets and spent the rest of the drive tipped forward in my seat as if I could urge the car faster that way. Buildings whipped by outside the window. Every time we had to stop for a light, my pulse thudded at the base of my throat.

I was probably worrying over nothing, right? Why would Anthea be driving anywhere in the middle of the night? She might already be in bed, for fuck's sake.

But was Gia unstable enough to have revealed her plan to me if she hadn't been pretty sure it'd be in motion before I could get back to the mansion?

It was absurd. Wylder's aunt had been a thorn in my side from the moment she'd spoken her first words to me, but I couldn't relax until I knew I'd done everything I could to stop Gia's awful plan. Maybe I hadn't become as ruthless as my father would have wanted after all.

And actually… I was okay with that.

Finally, the taxi careened up the steep hill. The second the mansion came into sight, I spotted a car pulling out of its driveway. Not one I recognized as belonging to any of the guys, either.

"Stop!" I shouted at the cabbie, and smacked into the back of the seat when he slammed on the brakes. I tossed a handful of bills that should cover the ride at him and hurtled out of the taxi. The driver muttered some comment, but he drove off a moment later.

The car from the mansion cruised toward me, already picking up speed to take the turn and head down the hill. The light from the streetlamps reflected off the windshield, and then I caught a glimpse of Anthea's red hair and startled face behind the glass. My pulse hiccupped.

There was only one way my panicked brain could come up with to stop her. I dashed forward and threw myself into her path, my arms spread. "Stop! There's something wrong with the car!"

I couldn't tell whether she'd heard me. She honked the horn, but I didn't budge. Her eyes narrowed, and for a second I thought she was going to speed up instead and run me over.

Then the engine's growl eased. The car started to slow. I let out my breath—and all at once Anthea's expression froze.

Her body jerked as if she was stomping on the brake, but the car kept traveling forward, slower than before but fast enough that it'd still break bones if it hit me. It was gaining speed as it reached the first gradual incline before the turn. I wavered, caught in the crazy sense that if I jumped out of the way, I'd have let her down, even though I could hardly have stopped the vehicle with my bare hands.

Anthea jerked the wheel, and the car whipped to the side. It lurched up over the sidewalk and smashed straight into a telephone pole.

The hood crumpled around the pole about a foot deep, the engine sputtering. I raced over and yanked open the driver's side door.

Anthea was rubbing her chest where the seat belt must have jarred against it, her breath coming roughly. It didn't look as if she'd injured herself in any major way, but appearances could be deceiving.

"Are you okay?" I asked, every nerve in my body jittering.

She stared at me so blankly that I couldn't help worrying she'd sustained some kind of brain damage after all. Then the haze started to clear from her eyes, but she didn't look all that much less confused. With her scowl missing, she seemed much younger than her twenty-eight years.

"The brakes failed," she said. "And then the airbag failed too. You were trying to stop me. You... knew?"

"I heard that something was wrong from the person who screwed up your car," I said. "I've been *trying* to let the guys know..."

I trailed off, a shudder running through me at the thought of how Anthea would have ended up if I'd gotten here even a minute later. All the momentum from going down the hill—the car would have been flying by the time she reached the bottom, and she'd have had no way to stop it. What were the chances she'd have survived *that* crash?

Anthea was still staring. "You *saved* me. You threw yourself in front of the car..." She trailed off.

A shaky grin crossed my face. "We might not get along all that well, but you haven't *quite* pissed me off to the point of wishing you dead yet."

She didn't smile in return. Swiping her hand across her mouth, she frowned at the steering wheel and then at me again. "*Who* did this?"

Here was the hard part. "Gia," I said. "I know it sounds insane, but I wouldn't have known if she hadn't bragged about how she messed with your car. That's the whole reason I rushed back here. I guess she knows about auto mechanics from her dad."

Anthea blinked, thinking that over, but she didn't argue with me. "Why would a *groupie* want me dead?" she asked instead, shifting to pull herself out of the car.

I swallowed hard. "Because she killed Titus, and she was getting worried that you'd figure that out."

Anthea jerked to a halt. "*What?* That skinny little thing?" She looked as if she was going to make some caustic remark about my judgment, but to my surprise, she paused, and her tone came out almost respectfully. "What makes you say that?"

"I—it's a long story. We can get into it in the house. Let's just say it all started with an obsession with Kaige." I dug out the dog tags and handed them to her. "Did you hear he was missing these?"

She glanced down at them in her hand, and her lips twitched into a dazed smile. "He asked if I could keep an eye out for them while I searched for evidence. That big dolt."

Her tone was more affectionate than I'd ever heard it, in a maternal sort of way. If I hadn't realized it before, I'd have known now just how much she cared about Wylder and his crew.

"Come on," I said, stepping back to give her room. Down the street, the mansion's door banged, and I glanced over to see several figures marching toward us, with Wylder, Kaige, and Rowan in the lead. "It looks like I have a *lot* of explaining to—"

Another car came screeching around the corner. Before I could process what was happening, it'd lurched to a stop beside us, and Gia was launching herself out, straight at me.

"You little bitch!" she snapped, wrenching me toward her and nearly pulling my arm out of its socket. "You just had to screw everything up."

I tried to dodge, but she had my arm clamped too tightly in those hands that were more powerful than they looked. With an eerie chill in her eyes, she rammed her knee into my stomach hard enough that I buckled. Pain seared through my abdomen.

I regained my balance just enough to shield my face from her next blow, but my elbow throbbed from the impact, which radiated up my arm to wake up my bullet wound too. Gia swung both her fists at my side and knocked me right to the ground, my hip and shoulder smacking into the asphalt.

Scrambling to focus, I rolled away from her. I had to get distance, had to get into a position where I had room to dodge—

She came after me with the force of a Mac truck, her fists flailing. One glanced off my throat, making me choke and sputter. I snatched the paring knife out of my pocket, but an instant later she was smacking it away.

"You couldn't just let her die?" she screamed. "You didn't even like her! You just had to act like you're so much better than me."

I lashed out at her and managed to land one good kick to her calf, but then she snatched at my hair and yanked me up, my scalp crying out in pain. She clocked me in the temple and the ribs before I managed to twist around, punching her in the jaw as I did.

Gia only recoiled for a second. She whipped her leg around as I tried to retreat and toppled me onto my hands and knees this time.

Springing at me, she shoved me onto my back and slammed her forearm against my throat. My airway constricted, cutting off my breath. Her other hand grasped my jaw, her muscles flexing, ready to snap my neck. "I didn't get to kill her, so you'll have to do. Any last words, bitch?"

I couldn't speak, couldn't even gasp. One thought swam up through my desperate mind, the first tenet of parkour that the videos I'd watched had drilled into my brain: Make use of your environment to pursue your goal every way you can.

I couldn't reach anything in my environment except Gia, but why couldn't I use her?

Instead of resisting her clutching hand, I jerked my head to the side in the direction she'd been braced to twist. Her hand flew aside at the unexpected motion, and I jabbed my elbow at just the right angle to fling her arm back into her own face.

Her grip on my throat loosened for an instant, but that was all I needed. I heaved up, and we tumbled over, rolling several feet while we grappled with each other. I spotted the curb and braced my foot against it to flip myself onto her solidly enough to pin her in place.

She was already squirming with enough strength to break my hold, but as her wrist slipped from my grasp, another figure leapt in beside us. Wylder stared down at Gia, crouching with his gun pointed straight at her head.

"That's enough," he said in a cold, fathomless voice.

Gia froze for only an instant. Then she let out a shriek more animal than human. With a renewed surge of strength, she yanked her other arm free, one hand clawing at Wylder, the other closing around a chunk of concrete that'd crumbled off the sidewalk. She thrust it toward my head.

In that instant, I could already feel how my skull would crack with the impact. I recoiled, not sure yet if my reflexes would be fast enough, and in the same moment a *bang* rattled my eardrums.

The side of Gia's head burst open with a splatter of blood and brains that flecked my body from head to torso. The life went out of her eyes like a flame doused with water. Her body sagged, the concrete chunk only glancing off my shoulder instead of reaching my skull.

I shoved myself off her, my stomach flipping over. The smell of her blood clogged my nose, my shirt sticking to my skin with its dampness.

I'd been around violence and death all of my life, but I'd never seen it come for someone just inches away from me like that. A shiver ran through me from head to toe.

Wylder lowered his gun. I turned to him, lost for words. He nodded as if to say, *It's done.*

He might have just saved my life. A few minutes ago, I'd have assumed he didn't give a shit whether I made it through the day. But then, Anthea would have said the same about me and her, wouldn't she?

I stared down at Gia's ruined body, blood pooling under her and staining her pale hair, and a twisted sense of relief washed over me.

It *was* done. It was over. Titus had been avenged. Kaige's name was cleared.

Where exactly did that leave us now?

31

Wylder

MERCY LOOKED LIKE A GODDESS OF WAR, BATHED IN HER enemy's blood. Taking her in, I had to catch my breath despite the gore. The way she'd fought back, kept grasping at every hope of survival no matter how fiercely Gia had attacked her, was nothing short of spectacular.

How could I have thought this woman couldn't stand strong alongside us?

She drew herself up straight, and I had the urge to offer a supporting hand, but I could already tell from the tensing of her jaw that she'd refuse it. She wiped her fingers across her cheek, and I was jolted back to the full reality of the situation. *I* might be admiring her in her blood-drenched state, but it was doubtful she was enjoying the experience all that much.

"I can explain all of this," she said, her voice rasping. It'd looked like Gia had nearly crushed her throat.

I reined in my emotions. Some of my father's men had come out at the commotion. They were watching me now, evaluating how I handled the situation.

"I'm looking forward to hearing that explanation," I said. "But why don't we get you cleaned up first. I'd rather talk without you dripping blood all over the furniture this time."

The corner of her lips curled with what might have been the start of a smile. The sight made my cock twitch in response. Fucking hell, just like that I wanted to kiss her, blood and all.

To my surprise, Anthea stepped up beside her, nudging Mercy toward the house. "Come on. I'll walk you in."

"I'm fine," Mercy muttered, but she let herself be ushered.

"Sure you are," I heard my aunt say as they walked away. "But you'll be fine-*er* if you stop being so stubborn about letting people give you a hand now and then."

What the hell was going on there? I guessed I'd find that out when Mercy was ready to talk.

My gaze fell to the woman sprawled on the road. It was hard to see Gia as a person anymore, as anything more than a hollow shell.

There'd been a time when I'd felt a pang of guilt when I had to kill someone. Now, I could recognize it as inevitable. It'd been Gia or Mercy, and I'd seen and heard enough even without Mercy's full explanation to know I'd made the right choice.

"Let's go," I said to the guys, jerking my head toward the house. "Call the clean-up crew and have this taken care of. I need a drink before storytime starts."

By the next morning, I was beginning to think that an entire bottle of brandy wouldn't be enough to numb the ache in my head from untangling the bizarre scenario I'd been faced with. I swirled the liquid in my snifter and leaned back in my armchair as Rowan, Kaige, and Anthea trooped into my study at my summons. Gideon was already seated next to me, his fingers flicking over his tablet's screen.

Kaige looked from me to him and back again. He seemed to read my expression. "It's *true*? All of it? You're fucking kidding me."

My mouth twisted into a crooked smile. "I'm as serious as Mercy looked splattered in Gia's blood last night."

"Fuck," Rowan murmured. He hadn't raised any arguments against Mercy's convoluted tale last night, but I suspected we'd all found it difficult to accept at face value.

Anthea propped herself against my desk. "Well, we know that psychotic bitch definitely tried to kill *me*. I talked to a guy who saw her tinkering with my car yesterday afternoon—she told him I'd asked her to give it a tune-up." She rolled her eyes. "Naturally, just like the rest of us, it never occurred to him that 'some groupie chick' would have murder on the mind. What else did you manage to dig up?"

She was taking this whole situation pretty calmly considering her first point. I guessed it ran in the family.

"I excavated Gia's cot in the groupie room after the others were up this morning," I said, and motioned to the evidence on the side table by the arm of my chair. "Everything Mercy mentioned was there—the jeans with the bleach stains that could be hydrogen peroxide, the magazines with the flyer and various... tokens that appear to have come from Kaige."

Kaige's mouth pulled into a grimace. He touched the dog tags hanging around his neck where he'd kept them during every waking hour for as long as I'd known him, until they'd disappeared one night a few months ago. "Just like she stole these. Why the fuck— I barely *talked* to her."

I shrugged. "Who knows? She was clearly unhinged. I mean, anyone would have to be to fall in love with *you*, right?"

Kaige glowered at me, but the teasing remark lifted the gloom that had settled over the meeting just a bit.

Anthea picked up the jeans and studied the marked fabric. She leaned closer and sniffed. "She washed them, but there's still a trace of vinegar scent too. She must have been wearing these when she doctored the fire escape railing."

"And then she managed to ambush Titus—to overpower him?" Rowan said, not exactly disbelieving.

I nodded. "We all saw she was a lot stronger than we'd have suspected from the way she went at Mercy last night. And Gideon tracked down some footage from the fights that'd been uploaded online..."

On cue, my right-hand man turned his tablet around so we could all see the screen. It showed a man and a woman inside a boxing ring, the woman slim and blond, decked out in a shiny white bodysuit and mask.

As the video played, the two circled each other, exchanging blows, until the woman managed to get a chokehold on the guy. When she stepped forward in her victory stance, Gideon paused and zoomed in on her face. Even slightly blurred, I could see Gia beneath the mask now that I knew to look for her.

"One of our men also found the duffel bag Mercy mentioned tossed behind a dumpster at the edge of the parking lot where they initially argued," I said. "Gia mustn't have had time to stash it properly in her hurry to get back here and make sure Mercy didn't reveal too much. It had her mask in it and tape for binding her knuckles, a bunch of cash, and some flyers she must have been going to put up in town for her father's auto shop."

"Jesus Christ." Kaige raked a hand through his dark hair. "I'm just —this is all so crazy. Titus was the strongest guy here. I still don't see— getting the jump on *him*..."

"Well, we all assumed she was weak and stupid until about twelve hours ago, didn't we?" I said dryly.

Anthea nodded. "She must have tucked herself against the wall on the fire escape so he wouldn't see her as he climbed out, and then jumped on him from behind. Once she'd caught him in the right position, there wouldn't be much he could do. And she'd already set him up to fall by messing with the railing beforehand."

"Huh. I guess we should start keeping a closer eye on the groupies." Kaige let out a rough chuckle.

Rowan watched me carefully. He might have had some tie to Mercy I didn't think he'd fully shared, but he'd proven over and over that he'd do whatever it took to support and defend the Nobles. I wouldn't have welcomed him into my inner circle if I hadn't been sure of his loyalty.

As expected, his next words were an offer to be of service. "Is there anything else you need done to tie this all up?"

I shook my head. "Most of it was contained right here. We'll share the evidence with my father, and he'll ensure his people know who the real killer was. Some Steel Knights lackeys might miss their cash-cow fighter, but that's their problem, not ours."

At my gesture of dismissal, the guys, including Gideon, headed out. Anthea lingered, pushing herself off the desk. "Wylder, a word?"

I spread my hands. "Say whatever you want." Anthea could sometimes be very stubborn about particular ideas, but she had our family's best interests at heart no matter what. And from the moment I'd been designated as heir, she'd treated me as if she couldn't imagine anyone better for the position, unlike... more people than I'd prefer to consider right now.

She sank into the chair Gideon had vacated. "I want to talk about Mercy."

I raised an eyebrow. "What about her? If you're going to suggest we kick her out after all this—"

"No," she said with much more vehemence than I was prepared for. "Don't be ridiculous. I'm telling you that you'd better lay off the games and give her the respect she deserves."

I blinked at her and pretended to examine her head. "I'm not sure I heard you right. Are you sure you don't have a concussion after that accident?"

She swatted me. "I'm serious. She saved my life yesterday even though she had no reason to. She could have let it happen—I'm sure Gideon could tell you the chances of my dying if my brakes failed going down that hill are incredibly high—and after the way I've come down on her, I wouldn't have blamed her. But she threw herself in harm's way to protect me. You can't buy that kind of integrity." A hint of a smile touched her lips. "I might even call it 'nobility.'"

"It's not as if we Nobles are exactly known for living up to the name," I muttered, and threw back another gulp of brandy. As it burned down my throat, I considered her point. "I told her I'd crack down on the Steel Knights if she cleared Kaige's name. She's done that, and I'm at least noble enough to be good to my word. But it sounds like you're suggesting we don't just take up her cause until we've crushed those pricks but actually make her one of our own."

"It sounds like that because that *is* what I'm suggesting."

I studied my aunt for a long moment. She wasn't won over easily. Neither was I, and part of me had been picturing what it'd be like to have Mercy by my side for good ever since I'd seen her in all her bloody glory last night. But that didn't mean it was a wise idea. There were other considerations.

"It might be difficult for her to fit in, in the long run," I hedged.

"She doesn't have to fit perfectly," Anthea said. "She'll make her own place, just like I made mine. She's been a formidable enemy, as much as it was my fault for making her one, and I suspect she'll become an even better ally."

Mercy really had done a number on her. I'd never seen Anthea support anyone quite so emphatically—especially after being on a tear to get the same person removed from our lives just a day before.

I groped for another argument and couldn't come up with any I wanted to say out loud. Annoyingly enough, Anthea read my silence. Her voice softened. "I know why you're hesitant. But she's not Laurel."

I stiffened. "I have no idea what you're talking about. Of course she's not. Why would I be comparing them?"

"Loss changes a fundamental part of us," Anthea said, her eyes crinkling at the corners. "I don't blame you for being wary at all."

"My concerns about Mercy have nothing to do with that," I said, but even to my own ears, it sounded like feeble defense.

Maybe it didn't matter why I was hesitating but only that I could see I didn't need to. Mercy had managed to hold her own against Gia, who was a seasoned MMA fighter with brutal strength. She hadn't backed down when I'd asked her to chop up a man, not shying away once despite her obvious disgust.

I'd pushed her and pushed her again, determined to find a weak point, to bring it out into the open while I could still get her out of here in one piece. But she'd always pushed right back.

Until the freezer. I worked my jaw, remembering how Mercy had shuddered and gasped on the floor afterward. Like she was already dying. I closed my eyes.

All I'd been able to see in that moment was a frail thing I'd almost thrown into the line of fire. But it really had been just a moment, with so much strength on either side of it. How could I call her weak over that? *I* sure as hell wasn't totally invincible. Gideon could be done in by a puff of smoke.

How often would a phobia of being buried alive actually get in the way of doing what she'd need to? No one knew about it except us, and I could ensure it stayed that way.

As long as I kept a little distance, I wouldn't draw attention to her the way I had Laurel anyway.

"Fine," I said. "I'll have a chat with her."

Anthea beamed at me and ruffled my hair like I was a kid again, laughing at my scowl. She headed off to take care of whatever business she had on her plate, and I walked down the hall toward the guest bedroom that'd become Mercy's. After yesterday's horrors, I hadn't been about to toss her back into the groupie room.

I knocked on the door. "Anyone home, Kitty Cat?"

She opened the door with a jerk and eyed me as if she wasn't sure she'd actually wanted to find me on the other side. Ignoring her expression, I nudged past her to stroll into the room over to the window where the bloody present she'd been left had thankfully been cleaned up. "Huh. I didn't realize this room had such a beautiful view."

Mercy sighed in resignation. "What do you want? I was about to scrounge up some breakfast."

"Oh, nothing much. I just thought I should thank you for saving my aunt's life."

"Am I hallucinating, or did you just say thank you to me?"

I turned to face her. "Don't be so surprised. Anthea is important to me. She's family, and you saved her by putting your life on the line. That couldn't have made it clearer how far you'll go for the Nobles, so it's only fair if we extend a hand in return."

"What's that supposed to mean?" she asked cautiously.

"I already promised you that you'd have my support against the Steel Knights if you found Titus's real murderer. That's a done deal. But if you want to go at him right alongside us—and if you want to stick around after and see what other trouble we can get up to—there's a place for you here."

Her lips parted—those plump, succulent lips I'd imagined wrapping around my dick far too many times. I couldn't help taking a step closer to her, feeling the mood between us shift into something tinged with anticipation.

Mercy folded her arms in front of her, her elbows grazing my chest. From the glint in her eyes, I got the impression she was trying to provoke me on purpose. "This isn't yet another test? I've finally convinced the great Wylder Noble of my incredible prowess?"

I chuckled and let my voice drop low. "Keep calling me great, and I could be convinced of a whole lot more."

I let my hands rise to her waist, and she swayed toward me just slightly. If I leaned in to kiss her now, I was pretty sure she'd kiss me right back. Instead I held myself still, watching her.

"So you're a man of your word after all," she said, the playful lilt to her voice going straight to my cock.

"I bled for you," I reminded her, wanting nothing more than to throw her down on the bed and fuck her until she scored my skin with her claws and screamed my name in ecstasy. Only a tiny thread of self-control and the name Anthea had invoked held me back.

Mercy tilted her head to the side. "And what happens next?"

I grinned. "Now it's time to make Colt Bryant and all the assholes propping him up bleed way more than I ever did."

She matched my smile with a smirk of her own. "I'm looking forward to it."

I left Mercy's room feeling far more satisfied than any man should with a raging hard-on straining his pants. As I willed it down, the slam of a car door filtered up through the foyer. I walked toward the staircase, peering down through the windows over the front door.

A familiar gold Porsche was parked outside. A man in an impeccable slate-gray suit stood beside it, the sun catching on the silver strands that were starting to overtake the auburn in his hair.

Dad was home.

Axel had already come over to greet him. As the other man spoke, Dad's hawkish eyes roved over the mansion, darkening at whatever Axel had told him. My spine stiffened.

I needed to talk to him about Mercy before he heard too much from anyone else. The subject was going to require a certain amount of care.

Even with Anthea on her side, even with the self-control I'd managed to demonstrate so far, having the Claws princess here at all was still walking a line that was awfully dangerous—and not in a way I liked.

32

Mercy

STEPPING OUT INTO THE MANSION'S YARD, I COULDN'T HELP tipping my face to the sun and simply basking in it for a moment. Its warmth seeped right through my skin to mingle with the triumphant glow already lighting me up from the inside.

I'd been through hell and back over the past few weeks, but this was a new beginning. This morning, Wylder had all but pledged his allegiance to my crusade. It wouldn't be much longer before we had Colt on his knees and I'd see justice done for the way he'd torn apart my life and so many others.

Footsteps rustled through the grass behind me. Kaige came to a stop at my side, glancing up at the sun for a second before looking at me, his smile more relaxed than I'd seen in the past couple of days. I'd tensed up at the sight of him, but his easygoing attitude reassured me.

"I hear you've officially joined the team," he said.

"That's one way of putting it. I have the Wylder Noble stamp of approval, anyway."

"If you've got his approval, you have all of ours too."

Would Gideon and Rowan have said the same? I guessed they kind of had to. What Wylder said was the law for them, regardless of their personal feelings.

Kaige cracked his knuckles. "So, when do we get started delivering our brand of justice to that jackass ex of yours?"

I couldn't hold back a laugh. "As soon as possible, if I have anything to say about it. I noticed the man in charge got in this morning—I assume Wylder needs to run the basics by him first."

Mentioning Ezra Noble created a brief but awkward silence. Kaige seemed to struggle to figure out what to say, which was a little ominous. "I'm sure once the old man hears the whole story, he'll be on board." He rolled his shoulders and switched quickly to a different subject. "I was actually wondering if you were up for a workout. I don't know about you, but I have a lot of built-up tension after all the craziness we've dealt with lately."

I cocked my head at him, unable to stop the images of him leaning over me on the hood of his car, plunging inside me, from crowding my head. To my annoyance, my voice came out slightly breathy. "What kind of workout did you have in mind?"

Kaige's gaze seemed to linger on my lips. Then he yanked it up to meet my eyes. His tone came out sly. "Oh, just a power jog around the block. There's a path that winds around the backs of the yards up here, so we don't have to bother going up and down the hill or through downtown. Want to join me? I mean, unless you'd rather something more—"

"No, that sounds perfect," I cut in. The bastard, getting me riled up for fun. Two could play that game. "But why don't we make it competitive."

He arched an eyebrow. "How so?"

I tapped my lips, letting the movement draw his attention back to my mouth. "First one to make it three rounds wins."

"You think you can take me on, huh? And what does the winner get?"

I shrugged. "Whatever they want. Winner's choice. Wherever their... urges take them."

Heat flared in Kaige's eyes. "In that case, I'm *definitely* going to win."

"We'll see about that." I glanced down at my jeans, which were comfy but not made for running. "Give me a second to change into something more appropriate."

"But I like it when you're inappropriate," Kaige called after me as I jogged back toward the house.

I held up my hand with my middle finger raised, and his laughter brought a smile to my own lips. I already felt better, looser, than I had in days, even with the lingering twinges from the bruises I'd gotten during last night's fight.

Once I'd swapped my jeans for more flexible sweatpants, I found Kaige waiting for me in front of the house, stretching his legs. My gaze might have roved over the muscular planes of his thighs for a bit longer than was totally polite before I met his eyes again.

"Ready?" he asked with a grin.

I tossed back my ponytail. "Of course I'm ready. First one to tag in at the front steps three times wins. But you'd better prepare to lose."

"You'll have to catch me first." He took off without another word.

Cursing half-heartedly at his back, I took off after him. Kaige was strong, but a little top-heavy. His legs weren't *that* much longer than mine, and my parkour practice had given me a lot of training in speed. I followed close at his heels, trailing right behind him as he swerved at the end of the street onto the packed dirt path he'd mentioned. It looped around past the fences of the grand properties along the top of the hill, just like he'd said.

Perfect.

We tapped the front steps the first time just seconds apart, but on the second loop, Kaige started to pull farther ahead. Flat-out endurance wasn't my forte, and he'd obviously jogged this route thousands of times in the past. I loped along behind him at a steady pace, my heart thumping in an enjoyable rhythm, sweat trickling down my back. My brain shut down and let my body take over completely.

Kaige tapped in a second time several paces ahead of me and turned around with a wave and a cocky grin. Oh, I'd wipe that off his face soon enough. He'd forgotten that not all of us needed to stick to the paths.

I let him take even more of a lead, pacing myself as we started the final circuit. When I came up on the back of the Nobles' property, Kaige was already charging past the estate beyond it. I swung around and threw myself at the brick wall that surrounded the massive mansion's yard.

It only took a quick scramble and a twist of my hips to fling myself over. I landed on the grass and took off across the lawn to meet Kaige out front, tapping my toes against the front step for good measure.

When I reached the sidewalk in front of the mansion, he hadn't come around the corner yet. After bobbing on my feet impatiently, I jogged several paces back and forth. Stopping in the shade of a tree at the edge of the neighbor's lawn, I pulled out my phone, thinking I'd text a few taunts to get his ass into gear.

My thumb was just reaching for the screen when a van roared down the street and jolted to a halt right next to me. As I spun around, three guys dressed in black from their pants to their ski masks leapt out and tackled me.

My phone slipped from my fingers, but I was too busy fighting to snatch after it. I rammed my elbow onto one guy's gut, getting a grunt out of him, but when I opened my mouth to shout, another clapped his hand over my lips, snuffing out the sound. I struggled harder.

The heel of my hand smacked into a masked nose with a satisfying crunch, but three against one were shitty odds at the best of times, and they'd caught me by surprise. One wrenched my arms behind my back, another scooped up my legs, and they hauled me into the van.

I hit the thinly carpeted floor, the blood seeping from a scrape on my lip leaving a metallic flavor in my mouth. With a lurch and a rumble, the van peeled away from the curb. Before I could strike out again, someone lashed a rope around my wrists behind me. A bandana was tied across my mouth, half-choking me.

As I squirmed onto my side, glaring at the figures around me, a face loomed over me that turned my blood to ice.

Colt gazed down at me and let out a cold chuckle. "Hello there, Mercy. You didn't really think the Nobles would ever respect a cunt like you, did you? We've struck a very generous deal, and they've called me in to take out the trash."

PERILOUS LADY

Crooked Paradise #2

Mercy

As unpleasant rides went, being tied up and tossed into the back of a van by masked gangsters wasn't the worst I'd ever experienced, but it definitely made my top five. And it was rising in the ranks with every passing second.

Colt leaned forward on the bench that lined one side of the van's cargo compartment and pressed his gun into the soft spot under my chin. The cold metal bit into my throat, prodding harder with the sway of the roaring vehicle. The bandana tied across my mouth left the taste of stale sweat on my tongue. Ugh. I swallowed thickly, not daring to move.

My ex-fiancé cocked the gun and waited for my reaction. When I remained motionless, a sick smile stretched across the face I'd once thought of as handsome.

"That's a good girl," he said, leaning back in his seat. The gun stayed trained on me. "Any sudden movements, and I'll blow your brains right across the back of my van. We don't want things to get too messy now, do we?"

I searched for his weak spots. The best I could imagine was startling him enough that I could get the gun, which wasn't likely to happen with the rope lashed around my wrists behind my back. Also the three Steel Knights who sat next to him posed a slight problem.

I did take some satisfaction from watching the man whose nose I'd broken dab his balled mask against the blood streaking from his nostrils. His face was already swelling and purpling. Served him right.

It appeared that Colt didn't plan to kill me, at least not right away. A tiny bit of the tension coiled inside me faded. As surreptitiously as I could, I pulled against my restraints and found that they offered a little give. Good. I might be able to work with that.

As if reading my mind, Colt gestured to his men. "Check the ropes —and her pockets. I don't want any surprises."

One of the guys, a beefy-looking menace, dropped to my side. Before I could react, he yanked my hands farther behind me, making me wince. The man bared his teeth gleefully at my evident discomfort. Taking a second thick nylon rope, he double wrapped it around my wrists, tying it as tightly as he could.

When he was done, I could barely move my hands. He added another rope around my ankles for good measure.

The guy moved on to patting me down. His hands lingered on my chest, and he looked up and grinned at me. His eyes dared me to get his slimy fingers off me, knowing I couldn't do anything to stop him.

If Colt noticed, apparently he no longer cared how his men touched me. Disgust soured my mouth. In my head, I was already making up ways I would kill this douchebag slowly and torturously.

To my relief, he didn't reach right inside my pockets. I didn't want to know what he'd have done with my childhood bracelet if he'd noticed it. But the chain was too delicate to be noticeable through the fabric of my sweats, and he wasn't looking for something delicate anyway.

"No phone, no weapons," he reported to Colt. My fingers curled behind me, remembering my phone slipping from my grasp as I'd tried to fight off these pricks. No chance of tech wizard Gideon using that to track my location.

I was on my own here. If they would even have tried to come after me. Colt had suggested the Nobles had *wanted* me grabbed.

"Traveling light, are you?" Colt chuckled and wagged the gun at me. "How the mighty have fallen. I finally have you weak and pliant, ready to be crushed like the pest you are. But first there are some things I need to know, both for myself and my benefactors."

He'd claimed that the Nobles had made a deal with him. I found that hard to believe. Even the most powerful gang in Paradise Bend wasn't above backstabbing, but Wylder Noble had seemed totally genuine when he'd welcomed me into their ranks, and as heir apparent, his word was gold when it came to his men. Colt was just screwing with me, trying to shake me up so I'd spill something.

"Let's start with this," Colt said. "The Nobles and I are very interested in hearing everything you can tell me about your father's plans for the Bend and any other gangs he might have been associating with."

Was he still hung up on this idea that my father had betrayed *him*? I'd already told him he was delusional. I resisted the urge to roll my eyes. Those delusions had gotten everyone in my family and the upper levels of the Claws murdered at this man's orders.

Colt took the bandana out of my mouth so that I could reply. I glowered at him, unable to hold my tongue completely. "I must be pretty formidable for you to show up personally and get your hands dirty. Couldn't trust your men to catch me on their own?"

Colt slapped me hard across the cheek with his gun. Pain radiated through my cheekbone. I was going to have a hell of a bruise there, and blood was trickling through my mouth where I'd bitten my tongue.

"I'm not playing games," Colt said darkly. "This will be over a lot faster and less painfully if you cough up what you know now."

I grimaced at him. I'd allowed him to corner me again, but I wouldn't let him break me. The memory of Grandma bleeding out on the restaurant floor, of her last gurgling breaths, swam up through my mind, and my stomach lurched. No, I wasn't giving this asshole anything.

"In your dreams," I spat at him. "If you're going to kill me, just go ahead and get it over with, because I'm not telling you anything."

Colt glared back at me. "That's not how this is going to work. Make no mistake, I will not go easy on you."

"Just a week ago, you were offering me your hand. You wanted me on your side," I reminded him.

Colt's jaw ticked. "And you shot me down. It was the biggest mistake of your life."

"No, the biggest mistake was ever *considering* tying my life to yours."

Crack. He slapped me across my face again, the force of it whipping my head to the side. My ears rang, and a fresh trickle of blood dribbled down the side of my lip. I licked it before turning to him. "Is that the best you've got?"

Colt shot off the bench and grabbed my hair at the roots, pulling it back. I winced but tried not to show the pain on my face, instead turning my chin up to look at him. At this man who'd slaughtered my entire family in cold blood without blinking twice.

"You're going to tell me everything you know, bitch," he said, his dark eyes twin orbs of fury. "If you won't talk to me, I have a man waiting for us who's *very* good at digging answers out of people. By the time he's done with you, you'll be begging for a chat with me."

I gritted my teeth. My voice came out strained but steady. "Don't you know that information you get through torture is notoriously inaccurate? I might say a lot of things just so I can get the pain to stop, but what's the guarantee that I'm not lying? I could make up all kinds of ridiculous things. Then you'd look awfully ridiculous in front of your new master."

Colt looked at me as if he wanted to strangle me right then and there, but a flash of doubt crossed his face. He shoved me away, releasing my hair. "Gag her again. We'll let Billy deal with her."

As the gropey guy shoved the gross bandana back into my mouth, my ex-fiancé sat back down on the bench. I didn't like the look of concentration that'd come over his face as he stared at some distant point beyond the van wall. He played with his thumbs, paying no attention to me, as if I wasn't even in the van anymore. As if he had bigger things to worry about.

Doubt began to trickle into me. It'd been my mention of disappointing his "master" that had thrown him off. I'd thought that story was all a ploy, but maybe Colt really was answering to someone else, at least as far as this kidnapping went.

I'd dismissed Wylder as the one who had put Colt up to this, but what if I'd misjudged him? Even if it'd seemed like I could believe his promise to help me, I'd been incredibly wrong before... about the man right in front of me.

And I had to consider Wylder's father too, didn't I? Ezra Noble had just gotten home this morning. I hadn't even met the man yet, so it was hard to picture him hating me so much he'd throw me to the sharks, but Ezra hadn't established himself as the most powerful criminal in the county by playing nice. Who knew what might go on in his head?

If the leader of the Nobles really did want me gone, I was so screwed.

I shook off those doubts, trying to refocus on the here and now. Nothing mattered unless I could get away from these assholes. I'd figure out the rest later.

Colt barked at the driver to put on some music. A moment later, the screech of thrash metal reverberated through the enclosed space. My ex returned his attention to me, tapping his gun against his knee, but he didn't speak again.

The windows were tinted, so I couldn't make out more than a blur from outside. I assumed they were taking me out of Paradise City into the Bend, where Colt's power was based.

My mind whirled, trying to think of an escape plan. It seemed almost impossible right now. I'd have to see where they took me first.

The van finally pulled off the road with a rattle of gravel against the undercarriage. The door opened to reveal a yard of cracked concrete and stubby weeds—and a few more of Colt's men. Two of them dragged me out.

Several feet away stood a squat one-story building with peeling paint. The yard was so large that all the neighboring buildings stood at a distance—and from their grungy state, who knew if they were even occupied? Colt had picked this place to ensure there were no witnesses. I had no idea where in the Bend we even were.

One of the men shoved at my shoulder. "Keep moving."

They escorted me into the building. Pieces of trash and scraps of metal littered the floor. It didn't look like a place Colt did much work out of. I'd guess he didn't plan on keeping me here for too long.

Most likely, he planned on me being dead when we left.

The men marched me into a room at the back of the building and pushed me into the lone wooden chair in the middle of the space. The windows around me were so coated with dirt that barely any sunlight penetrated them, most of the room's illumination coming from the flickering bulb above me.

At Colt's gesture, his men untied my arms just long enough to bind them to the arms of the chair. "Good," he said. "I want her hands where I can see them."

I couldn't help taking a little satisfaction at his wariness of me. He'd already underestimated me once. Maybe he would again, and then I'd get my opening.

Colt's phone rang. When he saw the caller ID, he winced. Interesting. This mysterious boss of his?

He answered, and I caught the faint crackle of sound from the other end, but I couldn't make out a single word. "I'm working on it," Colt said. "We'll get everything we need."

When he'd hung up, he turned to me as if deciding what he wanted to do with me. I tested my arms, moving them slightly to check their mobility. Colt's men had secured my bonds so tightly that my flesh was going numb.

Colt's eyes roved over me for a second before he looked away. "She's ready for you, Billy."

One of the men who'd met us here stepped forward, leering at me so avidly my skin crawled. Then a jolt of recognition raced through me, turning my gut even colder.

I'd seen that face before—he was one of the guys who'd been acting as a server at the rehearsal dinner. One of the men who'd gunned down my family.

He took out a knife and turned it slowly in his hand. Anger and horror churned together inside me.

Colt gave him a sadistic smile. "You know what we want from her. Let me know when she decides to speak. I've got other business to attend to."

"With pleasure, boss," the man said.

Colt stalked out of the room with his other men trailing behind him. The door shut with an ominous thud and a click of the lock.

Billy walked around me, grinning and twirling his knife. "You and me are going to have *lots* of fun, darling."

2

Gideon

I FROWNED AT THE COFFEE I'D JUST TAKEN OUT OF THE grinder. The texture wasn't quite right. Instead of pouring the grounds into my machine, which would be a waste of its complicated mechanics, I dumped them into the garbage and reached for the bag of dark roasted beans to start over.

I'd like to think I was a simple man with a simple but fixed routine. The trouble was that if something didn't go right with that routine, it left me irritated and restless for the rest of the day. And the truth was, my current irritation had less to do with my coffee and more with the data I'd been checking.

As I turned back to my desk, my frown deepened. I'd been going over the payments various Nobles members had collected on behalf of the gang and the funds that'd been moving through our various business operations as we laundered them. The numbers in the columns wouldn't make any sense to an outsider. There was an alphanumeric code written next to each column that specified the activity and source.

Concrete figures normally appealed to me, but as usual, this list was having the opposite effect. I probably shouldn't have bothered looking it over, since it wasn't technically my job, but for Wylder's sake, I figured someone from his inner circle should be keeping an eye on things. Definitely no one else in the Nobles approached the situation with quite the same precision I did. A lot of this information was hearsay or estimates long after the fact, and the numbers never added up as neatly as I'd prefer.

Somebody knocked on the door. "Come in," I said, even though I wasn't in the best mood for company.

Rowan stepped inside. "Hey, I got that information you wanted on the Prowlers."

I only grunted in response.

"That's what I get after you've been hounding me for a week about it?" Rowan scanned my desk and must have noted the lack of steaming mug. "Ah, let me guess. You're in caffeine withdrawal."

"Something I'll fix in a moment," I muttered, spinning my chair toward my coffee setup. The grinder's current output was at least satisfactory. I added it and started the machine running. The thrum and the trickle of liquid into the waiting mug smoothed out my nerves just a tad. "So, you found out what that commotion last week was about?"

Rowan sat down on one of the chairs by the chess table. "I finally tracked down someone who was on the scene and managed to get him chatting. He said the skirmish was between two groups of dealers within the Prowlers. One of them apparently got their hands on a hot new drug, something called Glory—the others wanted in on the action, and they had... trouble reaching an agreement."

I rolled my eyes. Just like the small-time gangs to end up fighting themselves rather than getting shit done. But that information wasn't entirely unremarkable. "We've heard a few murmurs about a new drug, haven't we? Any idea what's so special about it?"

"Not yet. It doesn't seem to have spread very widely in the Bend yet, although from what I'm hearing on the street, demand is increasing quickly. There haven't been any freak deaths so far, at least. But it sounds like potent stuff."

A note of concern had come into his voice. Rowan had always been a bit softer than I liked. It bothered him that people might be snorting or shooting up stuff that might send them reeling in a dangerous way.

As far as I was concerned, anyone who took the risk knew what they were getting into. They had the freedom to be idiots if they wanted to.

I was just glad Ezra had never been all that interested in the drug trade. We ran some low-level recreational stuff like weed, but nothing that'd really fuck anyone up. Too much hassle if one batch turned out to be bad and suddenly you had the DEA sniffing around.

"Well, keep your ears peeled for any new developments," I said. "Always good to know what's going around."

As we'd talked, I'd continued to scroll through the payment records. My fingers paused over the mouse. I peered closer. "That's odd."

Rowan leaned toward me. "What?"

"Let me just…" I clicked through to the previous month, and a few more before, checking the same code. A prickle of apprehension ran down my spine. "Everything's up to date."

"And that's a problem?"

I shot Rowan a quick glower and motioned to the computer screen. "Various operations belonging to the Steel Knights pay us a tithe like every other gang in the county. Normally there are at least a few things outstanding because payments get passed on in bits and pieces or delayed while they work something out on their end. Every other organization has a few loose ends."

Rowan knit his brow. "But not the Steel Knights?"

"Not as of a few months ago. All of a sudden, they made sure to pay off all their debts. And they've paid on time—even a little early—since then." I flicked my tongue over my lip ring and reached to collect my coffee mug from the machine.

"Is that something we should be worried about?" Rowan asked.

"I'd say so." I took a sip, letting the darkly bitter liquid flood my mouth, and raised my eyebrows at him. "When do we send people in to collect more forcefully?"

Understanding dawned in his eyes. "When they get too far or too much behind. They were doing everything they could to make sure we wouldn't go nosing around in their operations."

"Exactly. No other reason for them to get so conscientious all of a sudden. They knew they were up to something we wouldn't like." I'd dismissed Mercy's original warnings about the Steel Knights' plans to overthrow the Nobles because the idea had sounded ridiculous, but there'd been evidence right here all along. And clearly it was something Colt had been planning for a while.

Before I could dwell any more on that, the door to my study burst open. Wylder marched in with Kaige at his heels.

"Ever heard of knocking?" I said mildly. Wylder's family owned this entire mansion—technically he had the right to barge in wherever he wanted.

Kaige shoved past Wylder. "Have you seen Mercy?"

His obvious agitation unnerved me more than I liked, which made me irritated all over again. "I haven't seen her since yesterday night. What's the emergency?"

"She went for a run with me," Kaige said. "We were supposed to take three laps through the path around the backyards and then meet up at the front steps. I'd pulled ahead of her by the third time around, so I got there first, but she just... never turned up."

"I assume you checked the path and obvious places like her room in case she took a detour to get back to the house a different way."

"Of course," Kaige snapped. "She isn't anywhere, and it's been nearly an hour."

The obvious conclusion hit me, bringing an unexpected twinge of disappointment with it. I wasn't sure I liked that reaction either. "She took off, then. Decided to get her revenge on her own terms."

"Why the hell would she do that?" Wylder said. He kept his voice even, but the tension running through it brought me to sharper attention. *He* was worried. "I gave her my word just this morning that she's one of us now, that we're going to crush Colt. It wouldn't make any sense for her to leave the second she got what she's been pushing so hard for."

Rowan shifted in his chair. "Maybe she decided she can't take you at your word after the ways we've jerked her around." His tone was casual, but his shoulders had stiffened. I got the impression he wasn't okay with the idea that Mercy was gone even though he'd given every indication that he never wanted her here in the first place.

Kaige shook his head. "I don't think so. It's not just what Wylder said. I found this in front of the neighbor's house. I'm sure it's hers." He smacked a phone on my desk.

"Maybe you should have led with that?" I said dryly, and picked up the phone. It was the same brand of burner as the phone I'd seen on her. Opening it, I tapped through to the recent messages. Yes, there were the urgent texts she'd sent all of us last night trying to warn us about Gia—and an unsent one to Kaige that cut off in mid-sentence as if she'd been interrupted. *Maybe hurry your ass...*

I couldn't think of many things that could have caused Mercy to drop her phone in the middle of a text and not pick it up again, and none of the ones I could think of were good.

Kaige paced to my aquarium and back again. "Check the surveillance footage. Maybe that'll show us something."

"It doesn't cover the neighbor's lawn," I said.

"Just check it!"

Wylder clapped a hand to Kaige's shoulder. "We'll figure it out. Give the man room to work." He nodded to me. "It can't hurt to take a look. We might see something useful."

The words should have sounded like a suggestion, but there was an obvious command to them. I could feel the tension in the room pulling taut like a bow. All four of us—in our different ways—were disturbed by Mercy's absence. I supposed I'd gotten used to having her around, and now our dynamic had been thrown off just slightly again. It was nothing more than that.

I pulled up the feed for the camera that gave a view of the yard and sidewalk in front of the house. "So this was about an hour ago? How long was she out of your sight while you were running?"

"I guess... about ten minutes? After I'd come around the side of the house at the end of the street, I stopped for a few minutes figuring I'd let her catch up enough to give her a fighting chance. When she didn't come around the bend, I assumed she'd pulled some kind of fast one on me. But then I couldn't find her anywhere."

Playing back the footage at ten times the speed, I studied the screen. Kaige and Mercy set off running. Several minutes later, they reappeared neck and neck. After another several minutes, they reappeared with Kaige several paces in the lead.

Just a few minutes after that, Mercy came jogging into view from the wrong angle, as if she was coming from the house rather than from the street. I slowed the recording down.

Kaige blinked, and a laugh sputtered out of him. "She *did* pull a fast one. I should have seen that coming. She must have made it over the fence with those parkour moves of hers and cut through the yard."

"That doesn't explain why she vanished afterward," Wylder muttered, stepping right up behind my chair and peering at the screen intently.

Mercy waited in front of the house for a minute, bouncing restlessly on her feet. Then she jogged out of frame toward the neighbor's. I was just reaching for the mouse to start zipping through the footage again when a white van whizzed past at breakneck speed.

Kaige froze. "What the fuck was that?"

"I don't know," I said, but I couldn't shake the apprehension that was creeping into my gut. Why would a regular delivery van be tearing away from here like a bat out of hell?

Nothing else showed in the footage except Kaige loping into sight a little later. I dismissed the window and stood up, grabbing my tablet. "I think we need to take a look at the actual scene. Show me exactly where you found her phone."

Kaige hustled along the hall and down the stairs as if Mercy's life might depend on how quickly we made it outside. I didn't like the knowledge that it very well might. As we stepped out into the warm summer sunshine, I couldn't help picturing her prancing out with a smirk to laugh at us for worrying about her. I might even have been hoping for it.

It didn't happen. Kaige strode to a spot about halfway along the neighbor's lawn and pointed to the edge of the sidewalk. "I found it right here." His hand dropped to his side, where it flexed and clenched as if just waiting for something—or someone—to punch.

The sidewalk and the neatly mown grass offered nothing. Wylder had already stalked over to the road. A breath hissed in through his teeth.

"It looks like the van took off from here in a hurry."

I joined him. Faint skid marks showed against the asphalt a couple of feet from the curb. There was no way to confirm what vehicle had made them, but the location was awfully suspicious. And—

My gaze caught on a few dark specks that gleamed wetly against the pavement right by the gutter. I knelt down and touched one. It stained my fingertip red.

My heart lurched despite my best attempt at self-control. "You fought back," I murmured.

Abruptly, I could see her in the back of my mind, striking out at her attackers with the fierceness she wore so well. Even through my concern, my cock stirred. As if this was a good time for *those* sorts of feelings. I straightened up, shaking off my imaginings, but the vise in my chest remained tight.

"What's that?" Wylder asked, coming up behind me to peer at my fingers, more urgency seeping into his tone. When I looked up at him, his eyes were stormy. He definitely wasn't unaffected by the situation either.

How had this woman managed to get so far under all our skins in a matter of days?

But that didn't matter. Right then, all I could think was that we had to get her back.

"There's blood on the pavement," I said. "The van must have sped over, and someone jumped out to grab her. In the struggle, at least one person drew blood." After seeing Mercy grapple with Gia last night, I could believe it'd been her. But even if it had been, her strength hadn't been enough.

"And then they took her!" Kaige let out an incoherent sound, his hands balling tight. Fury flushed his face. "When I get a hold of them—"

"We don't even know who 'them' is," Rowan pointed out, but I noticed his own face had paled.

I straightened up, flattening my voice but hating the dispassionate sound of it at the same time. "It's not hard to guess, is it? Who's taken her before? Who's wanted her dead this whole time?"

"Colt Bryant and his fucking Steel Knights," Wylder growled. "How the hell did they get this far into our territory without anyone noticing? They grabbed her right from our doorstep, the motherfuckers."

He was right. The move was bold and in some ways an open challenge, even though I doubted Colt would ever admit his involvement in Mercy's kidnapping unless we forced it out of him. Imagining setting Kaige loose on the prick in Kaige's current state gave me a small measure of satisfaction. The leader of the Steel Knights wouldn't survive that encounter.

Kaige swiveled around. "I think I remember seeing a van parked down at the other end of the street. I figured it was just someone making a delivery. Shit, I should have paid more attention."

Wylder smacked his knuckles against his palm. "The men we have stationed all over the city should have noticed something."

"There's no use in pointing fingers or placing blame," Rowan said quickly, ever the diplomat. "That doesn't help Mercy. We have to focus on her." His voice cracked slightly on the last word. Even he was starting to lose his composure.

Kaige shook his head, raising his hands to his temples. "What do you think they've done to her? They've had her for an hour already. Is she even...?"

He trailed off. I didn't want to complete his sentence, but the thought had occurred to me too. No doubt it'd crossed all our minds.

Mercy had been nothing but defiant to Colt. Of course he would want to get her out of his way as soon as possible.

"Bryant is a dead man walking," Wylder said in a chilling voice that made my gaze jerk to him. I couldn't remember when I'd last heard him quite that furious. I'd known Mercy appealed to him, but I hadn't thought he cared quite that much.

But then, I hadn't thought *I* cared as much as the knot in my stomach said I did either.

My best friend turned to me. "Whatever those shitheads have done, we need to find them before they can do worse. Can you get the license plate off the surveillance footage and run it?"

My mind leapt back to the recording, trying to remember how clear the back of the van had been in the split-second when it'd roared across the screen, but my practical side was already reminding me that there was no way Colt would have used any vehicle that could be traced to him or wherever his people had meant to take Mercy. I opened my mouth, dreading Wylder's reaction to that statement. Then inspiration hit like a lightning bolt.

Yes. I'd been prepared for something like this after all… even if this hadn't been quite what I was picturing when I'd made my preparations.

A smile had crossed my lips of its own accord. Kaige stared at me. "What the hell are you grinning about, Gideon? This is—"

I snapped my fingers, cutting him off. "Stop raving like a lunatic for a second and listen. We *can* find her. I've got something even better than a license plate to track her down."

3

Mercy

As Colt's henchman circled me, I tested my bonds again. They held firm, my wrists aching at the pressure.

Billy snickered. "Don't think you're getting out of this, Miss Katz. I'll get the answers the boss wants whether I have to carve them out of you or pull them out by your fingernails. But it's up to you how much fun we have. Now that you've seen what I have to offer, maybe you want to cough up a little something right away?"

I ignored him, shifting my weight on the chair just slightly. I had a little mobility. That would work in my favor.

Colt had made two mistakes that'd probably never occurred to him would cause him any problems: my ankles were tied, but not to the chair, and the chair he'd stuck me in was wooden.

He had no idea the drills my father used to run me through, tying me up one way or another and taunting me with words and blows until I managed to get free. Supposedly Dad had been training me for all the possible dangers of gang life, but I'd always known it was at least as much about punishing me for being born a girl.

Now I was glad I was a woman. These assholes just couldn't wrap their heads around the idea that I might have more skills than they did. That I might have trained harder than they'd ever imagined, even if it hadn't been my choice.

I just needed the asshole in the room to come a little closer.

Billy stopped in front of me with that ugly leer. Just looking into his face, remembering the glimpse of it I'd gotten in the midst of the carnage several days ago, made my hands itch to punch his tongue right down his throat.

Was he the one who'd shot Grandma? Or Aunt Renee? He'd been acting under Colt's orders, but somehow I didn't think he was sorry about it.

"Let's hear it," he said. "What big plans did your dear old dad have in the works? How many people had he reached out to?"

This again. I bit back a sigh and simply glared at him.

Unnervingly, Billy kept smiling, not thrown by my silence. "Or how about this—we want to know what you've spilled about the Nobles' operations to whoever you're still in contact with from your father's allies."

I hesitated, momentarily distracted. *Was* Ezra behind this kidnapping—because somehow he'd gotten it into his head that I'd been ratting out his business to competitors? I hadn't said a thing about the goings-on in the Noble mansion to anyone.

Or was this just a round-about way for Colt to try to get information about the Nobles from me, because he was still aiming to overthrow them?

I couldn't expect Billy to tell me that. He was still keeping his distance, toying with me. I needed him riled up.

"Why the fuck should I tell you anything?" I asked. "You're obviously a pathetic excuse for a man, getting off on threatening someone who's unarmed and restrained. And I guess you figure you can't do enough damage with your fists even like that—you need a knife to get the job done?"

Billy's eyes flashed, and the grin deflated. Excellent.

"Big mouth on a chick who can't move anything else," he retorted. "We'll see what you think of the knife when I'm stabbing it into you."

"Oooh, I'm so scared. As far as I can tell, all *you* know how to move is your mouth too."

His jaw clenched. I could see him reining in his anger, but I'd pissed him off enough that he walked right up to me. "If you're in such a hurry to get to the painful parts, I'm happy to start right—"

He wasn't a total idiot—he came up beside me rather than in front, where I might have had a hope of swinging my bound legs at him. But that wasn't the main part of my plan anyway.

The moment he was in range, the knife gleaming dangerously close to my cheek, I rocked forward with all the force I had in me. My weight landed on my feet. I whipped around, doubling over to lift the chair legs higher.

The solid wooden legs slammed into Billy's body, one of them clocking him right in the face. The cracking sound suggested I'd broken at least one bone.

Billy swore and stumbled backward, groping at his cheek, which I hoped ached twice as much as mine did. I flung myself toward the nearest wall, wrenching the chair toward it as I went. I rammed the chair into the concrete surface so hard the impact reverberated through my bones—and cracked the thin wooden arms.

I shook myself free of the chair, tugging at the now-loosened ropes. As I yanked them off my chafed wrists, Billy charged at me. Blood streamed down the side of his face, and his eyes were murderous.

My fingers closed around the best weapon I had—one of the broken pieces of wood, its splintered end sharp as a stake. I fumbled with the rope around my ankles at the same time. Billy swung his knife at me, and I smacked it aside with my makeshift weapon before flipping backward to slam my feet into his gut.

He plummeted to the floor with a pained grunt. I managed to heave a loop of the rope over my heel, which loosened the whole mess enough to kick it off—just in time for Billy to come at me again.

Springing to my feet, I dodged and swiped at his knife hand. My heart pounded so loud it drowned out every other sound. If I could knock the blade far enough away and he ran for it, I might have time to break one of the windows and flee that way. I didn't dare turn my back on him while he was wielding that thing.

I was not going to die here. I'd made it out of situations that'd looked even more dire before. This kitty cat was going to make full use of her nine lives.

"You cunt," Billy snarled. He slashed at me again, too fast for me to block. The blade sliced across my forearm, drawing a thin line of blood.

I jabbed at him again, weaving back and forth. He raised the knife, and then he opened his mouth, sucking in a mass of air.

Understanding hit me like a cold slap. He was going to holler for the other men, and in a second I'd be outnumbered with only a broken chair arm to defend myself.

In that instant, my mind narrowed down to one undeniable fact: I couldn't let him get out that yell, no matter what I had to do.

My body reacted without conscious thought. I hurled myself at Billy, heedless of the knife and his grasping hands, thinking only of cutting off his voice and ending that sadistic fucking smile before he killed yet another Katz.

He hadn't been expecting me to launch myself at him that boldly. We tumbled over, me on top of him, his shout coming out as a strangled yelp—and then I slammed the jagged end of the chair arm as hard as I could into his neck.

The start of his yelp turned into a gurgle. Hot blood spurted up to splash his face. A little splattered my shirt. I jerked backward, leaving the stake embedded in his throat, nausea twisting my stomach.

He gripped his neck to try to stop the flow of blood, thrashing like a wounded animal, but only for a few moments. Then his arms went limp. His body twitched and stilled on the floor, blood flowing from the wound in a steady stream. All the anger and life in his eyes glazed over.

He was dead.

I'd never actually killed anyone before. I'd imagined it plenty of times, but actually going through with the act…

I couldn't say I'd enjoyed it, but I didn't feel any particular remorse either. The only emotion gripping me other than the twinge of queasiness was the sense that the bastard had deserved it. Hell, he'd deserved worse.

I could almost hear Dad whisper in my ear: "There's the killer I trained all these years."

Before I could shudder at that thought, the door burst open. Shit. The other men had heard Billy's call for help after all.

Only two of them, though, and I'd already disposed of one opponent. They froze just inside with matching expressions of stunned disbelief, taking in me, disheveled, panting, and blood-speckled, and Billy's corpse on the floor.

I might not get another chance. Snatching a second broken piece of wood off the floor in case I needed it, I bolted for the closest window. With a quick flip, I rammed my heels into the glass with all my strength.

Pain radiated through my calves, but the pane shattered. The men shouted and hurtled after me, one of them reaching to his waist—damn it, of course he'd have a gun.

I dropped to the floor and kicked out my legs fast enough to knock his feet out from under him. As he toppled, the gun jolted from his fingers. The other guy snatched at me, and I stabbed my second stake into his upper arm. Then I leapt for the window.

A few shards of glass bit into my palms, but I didn't give a shit. I curled my body into a roll and tumbled through the narrow opening, swinging my legs down just in time to land on my feet. The second they hit the ground, I was running.

The afternoon humidity closed around me, condensing in my lungs. Shouts rang out through the window behind me. I sprinted in the opposite direction from the van, figuring more of Colt's men—even Colt himself—might be hanging around by the entrance to the yard.

Footsteps pounded out onto the cracked concrete, but I'd already reached the chain-link fence. I scrambled up it and hefted myself over in a few adrenaline-powered motions.

Up ahead lay a sea of rusty shipping containers with several low brick buildings beyond them. I wove between the big metal boxes, using them for cover. Voices hollered behind me.

"She went that way! Come on!"

"What the fuck is wrong with you people?"

I couldn't take any enjoyment from their frustration while my life still hung in the balance. I pumped my legs as hard as they'd go, only taking a tiny bit of relief when I reached the first of the actual buildings.

The whole area seemed to be abandoned. I wasn't familiar with this part of the Bend.

I clambered over another fence, dashed through a couple more yards, and found myself on an unfamiliar street. On instinct, I ran in what felt like the direction that'd take me farther from Colt and his goons. Eventually I'd have to figure out where the hell I was and how to get back to someplace I knew, but for now I just wanted to put distance between me and the guns.

The heat was baking my skin and sending up faint whiffs of a sickly meaty scent from the splatter of Billy's blood on my shirt. I grimaced, wiping at the sweat now soaking the back of my neck, and just kept running.

Five blocks, ten, twenty, veering in a new direction every few minutes just to make it harder for any pursuers to follow. Finally, when I hadn't heard any sounds from behind me in ages and I could see actual traffic on the road up ahead, I slowed down to take stock.

My lungs ached, and my cheek still stung where Colt had hit me. My palms throbbed, blood seeping from the glass cuts. Bracing myself, I plucked out a couple of shards that were still embedded in my flesh and glanced around.

I was standing next to a furniture warehouse with a foreclosure sign pasted on the window. A row of bland low-rise apartment buildings stood up ahead by the busier street. A couple of kids were chasing each other around the playground behind them, where only one of the swings was still attached to both its chains. I'd probably give children nightmares in my current state.

I was about to slink past them to where I could check the street sign when a car engine rumbled not from up ahead but behind me. My head jerked around, my body bracing to run… but the car looked way too familiar. I'd ridden in that deep blue Mustang before, hadn't I?

As I hesitated, Kaige's and Wylder's faces came into focus through the windshield.

I took a few steps back toward the furniture warehouse, but then I stood my ground and waited for them to reach me. My hands balled at my sides. I wasn't dismissing the idea of making a run for it until I'd heard what they had to say.

4

Mercy

The Mustang jerked to a halt in front of the warehouse's parking lot, and someone shoved the back door open. Rowan and Gideon were sitting there, Rowan pushing over to make room. "Get in," he said quickly.

Kaige was already rolling his window down in the front passenger seat. His expression was taut, his dark eyes fierce. "Are they close by?" he asked, sounding like he was just waiting for an excuse to crack a few skulls.

I stayed where I was. "If you're talking about the Steel Knights, not as far as I know," I said. "And I'll stay right here for now."

Wylder peered past Kaige from the driver's seat, his fingers tight around the steering wheel. "What the hell are you talking about? We're getting you out of here."

"I think I'd like to do a little more talking before I make up my mind about that."

"For fuck's—" He cut himself off with a sound of frustration.

The next thing I knew, all four of the guys were leaping out of the Mustang with an urgency that put me even more on guard. As he came around the front of the car, Wylder's gaze shot straight to my arm—to the shallow cut where a thin trickle of blood was still seeping out and then the stains on my fingers from my glass-sliced palms. Emotion flared in his bright green eyes.

Kaige barged forward, but Wylder stepped in front of him, cutting him off. The heir to the Nobles strode right up to me, picking up speed as he came.

"Hold on a second," I said, holding up my hands as if to ward him off and taking another step back.

But Wylder didn't give a shit what I wanted. What else was new? He grabbed me by the shoulder so I couldn't retreat any farther, firmly but not hard enough to hurt, which was the only reason I didn't punch him in the nose.

He scanned my face, focusing on my bruised cheek for a moment, and then down my body, tension etched all through his stance. When his attention came back to the small wound on my forearm, his jaw clenched. "Fucking bastards."

"It's fine," I said, unsettled and yet weirdly warmed by his intensity. He sure as hell wasn't *acting* like a guy pissed off because his evil plan had gone awry. No, he was practically vibrating with agitation... over the thought that I'd shed a few drops of blood?

"It's not *fine*," he snapped, examining each of my hands. "Someone grab the first aid kit from the trunk!"

Rowan hustled over with a roll of gauze. When our gazes met, his deep blue eyes searched mine, his mouth slanting at an uneasy angle. Wylder snatched the gauze from him and started wrapping it with practiced efficiency around my palms, which were barely even stinging anymore anyway. Rowan shifted his weight as if to step closer to me and then seemed to catch himself, his attention flicking to Wylder.

I couldn't blame him if he was wary of stepping in while his boss was in this mood. I wasn't totally sure what to make of it yet myself.

Wylder tied the hasty bandages off and shoved the roll of gauze back at Rowan. "We'll get Frank to have a look at them when we get back." Grasping my shoulder again, he peered into my eyes even more intently. His hand flexed and softened its hold as if he was afraid he'd accidentally wound me himself. The movement sent a tingling over my skin. "They didn't hurt you in any other way?"

"I didn't give them a chance," I said, holding myself in place against the urge to sway closer to him. All that fiery protectiveness, and something about it drew me like a moth to a flame, especially from this guy who'd made such a performance of not giving a damn about me so many times in the past.

But I had to be sure.

Kaige pushed in beside him, his face twisted with rage. "I'm going to kill those motherfuckers."

Despite myself, a smile twitched at my lips. I motioned to the cut on my arm. "I already killed the one who did this." The memory came with only a faint jab of discomfort, quickly overwhelmed by a swell of satisfaction. I'd given that prick what he'd deserved.

Kaige's mouth fell open.

Wylder blinked. "Well, fuck me. Kitty Cat doesn't mess around."

He sounded almost proud. I had to mentally stamp out the thrill of pleasure that pulsed through me.

I shook off Wylder's grasp and pulled away from him, crossing my arms over my chest and examining him for any trace of malice. "I'm perfectly all right. You weren't expecting that, were you?"

Kaige threw his hands in the air. "What were we supposed to think when you just disappeared—that fucking van—it *was* the Steel Knights, wasn't it? What the hell even happened?"

Wylder's lips had pursed when I'd drawn back, but he was still looking at me like I was some injured bird. "I'm not surprised. You've turned the tables on those pricks before. But we *should* get out of here. We're deep in Steel Knights territory. I'm looking forward to putting a lot of bullets in a lot of heads, but let's get you out of the potential crossfire first."

"I'll tear their fucking heads right off," Kaige muttered, clenching his hands.

I wasn't seeing any sign that either of them was anything other than relieved that I was okay—and furious with the people who hadn't wanted me to be. My gaze slid to the other two men.

Gideon had come up beside Rowan, his beloved tablet tucked under one arm, his smooth face as detached in its alien beauty as ever. I'd almost have thought it didn't matter to him that they'd happened to find me if he hadn't jumped out of the car as fast as the others. There was a stiffness to the way he held himself now as if he wasn't sure what to do with himself. I didn't know what to make of that, but then, I rarely knew what to make of the Nobles' tech expert.

Rowan was still standing uncertainly next to Wylder. When I looked at him, he swallowed audibly. His voice came out so gentle I'd almost think he'd transformed back into the boy I'd believed he was five years ago. "Let's go, Mercy. We can sort the rest out in the car."

There was still one part of this that didn't make sense. I fixed my gaze on Wylder again. "How did you even know where I was?" It was awfully convenient, wasn't it, that they'd shown up right after I'd given Colt's men the slip and known exactly where I'd be?

I wasn't expecting Wylder's lips to twitch with amusement. He glanced at Gideon with an arch of his eyebrows.

The other guy swung his tablet out, and I saw a map with a blinking light on the screen. "It was actually very simple," he said in his usual cool tone. "It seemed plausible that we might need to locate you at some point for one reason or another, so I attached a small tracking device to both of your bras."

Now it was my turn to gape. "You did *what*?"

He shrugged, as nonchalant as if he were saying he'd put on a load of laundry for me. "It was the most reasonable option. You only had two, so you'd nearly always be wearing one unless you were asleep, and the structure makes detection much less likely than most other clothing."

If it'd been anyone else, speaking any less practically about it, I'd have been totally creeped out. I looked down at my chest. I was still a little creeped out. "Can you de-tracker them?"

Kaige let out a rough guffaw. "I dunno—seems to me it came in pretty handy."

It had. If I *hadn't* been able to get away from Colt's people, I'd have been awfully grateful for Gideon's apparently nonexistent sense of personal boundaries. But still...

"We'll come back to that subject later." I glanced around, apprehension prickling down my spine. *I* didn't like hanging around in my ex's territory either, and my lingering worries had fallen away. For the guys to have gotten all the way here from Paradise City, they must have left before I'd gotten away from my captors—and why would they have already been heading out in search of me if getting me kidnapped had been their own plan? "All right, let's get out of here."

All four of the guys moved—but not toward the car, toward me, as if they thought I needed a full contingent of bodyguards just to walk the ten feet to the waiting Mustang. Oh-kay then. Kaige's hand hovered by my elbow as they ushered me to the curb, and then he dove into the backseat even though he'd been riding shotgun before.

Well, I wasn't against sitting next to him. As I climbed in after him, I noticed Wylder eyeing us as if he was debating claiming the other seat next to me. But it was his car. He marched back to the driver's seat with an oddly annoyed air.

Gideon got in beside him, and Rowan grabbed his previous spot in the back. He sank onto the seat, leaving a few careful inches between us. "I'm glad you're all right," he said quietly as Wylder started the engine.

Even though he'd gone out of his way to sit next to me, Kaige stayed strangely silent. His hands were balled into fists on his lap, the veins standing out in their backs, looking ready to pop.

"You wanted to know what happened," I said in an attempt to break the awkwardness of the moment. "It *was* the Steel Knights. They ambushed me on the sidewalk and dragged me into a van. Colt was there waiting for me."

In the driver's seat, Wylder stiffened. "Colt was there?" he said before I could go on.

"Apparently he wanted to oversee the operation personally."

The Noble heir's voice came out even more strained than it'd been when he first found me. "He's a walking dead man. That's an open challenge to our authority. He came right up to our gates and grabbed you—it's a fucking act of war."

"I'm sorry, Mercy," Kaige burst out, sounding so agonized that my gaze jerked to him. His hands had somehow clenched even tighter, his face flushed with more anger that he now seemed to be directing at himself. He smacked his palm. "If I'd paid enough attention to the van

—if I hadn't suggested the run to begin with—I should have been keeping a closer eye on things—"

I stared at him for a second before my voice caught up. "It's not your fault. How could you have known Colt would do something that bold?"

Kaige and I had hooked up, and he'd been flirty with me even when he was angry with *me* before, but I wouldn't have thought he'd be this affected by me being in danger. Or was it just a matter of honor for him, having failed his duty to the Nobles?

Kaige grimaced as if he couldn't accept the excuse I'd offered, but Gideon broke in, aloof as ever. "What did they want with you? Obviously not simply to kill you, or you'd be dead."

"Thanks for pointing that out," I said sarcastically, kicking the back of his seat. "Colt wanted information... About the plans my father was supposedly making against him, and about whether I'd given anyone information about the Nobles."

Rowan frowned. "Why would he ask that?"

I hesitated and decided now wasn't the best time to tell them Colt had claimed they'd put him up to it—and that I hadn't been totally sure he was lying until a few minutes ago. Their combined reaction might blow the roof off the car. Maybe *never* would be a good time to mention that.

"Probably all part of his stupid paranoia." I paused. "He did seem to be working with someone else. He took a call while I was there... He said some things about having made a deal to get what he wanted."

A deal that still could have been with Ezra Noble. My gaze settled on the back of Wylder's head and his fiery auburn hair, so like his father's. When would be a good time to bring *that* possibility up?

"It's not like anything your dad was planning matters anyway, considering—" Kaige stopped, snapping his mouth shut, but the unspoken words hung in the confined space of the car. It didn't matter now because Dad and the rest of my family were dead anyway.

"I didn't mean it that way," he added quickly.

I waved him off, settling deeper into the seat. I was bone-weary tired, and my brain was this close to shutting down, but I knew that wasn't really an option. "It's okay. It's true—my dad is gone. But Colt obviously doesn't see it that way. Anyway, the asshole he set up to torture the answers out of me didn't get anything before I broke free, and he didn't leave me with a whole lot of choice but to kill him, so it's not like they got anywhere."

We fell into a stretch of silence. We weren't quite out of the Bend yet, and even here on a busier street lined with shops, the buildings on either side of us were periodically marked with the spray-painted Steel Knights symbol.

The message was clear. Everything here now belonged to them.

Gideon held up his tablet to take a few photographs. "This didn't use to be Steel Knights territory, did it?"

My stomach knotted. "No. They're taking over every street they can."

"I didn't realize it was so bad," he murmured.

Maybe it was a good thing the situation had forced the guys to finally come down here. They could witness the changing face of the Bend firsthand.

"I told you," I couldn't help saying.

"And we should have believed you before," Wylder said, the protective note still in his voice making something inside me clench. I hadn't seen this part of him before, but I liked it. I liked it more than might be wise.

"We're going to push back," Kaige said. "We're going to push back and crush them, and that pathetic excuse of a man is going to wish he never laid a finger on you."

Rowan exhaled slowly. "He's fixated on his plan to take over, and he's convinced your dad was the one who could have screwed it up. That's why he's obsessed with getting answers out of you, I'd guess. He's afraid there's some way it could still go wrong." He shook his head. "Of course, it was always going to go wrong once he messed with the Nobles."

Wylder hit the steering wheel. "Damn straight."

The assurance in their words steadied me. We were leaving the marks of the Steel Knights behind for now anyway, passing from the Bend into the brighter, posher streets of Paradise City. As we came to a stop at a red light, Wylder yanked something out of his pocket. He twisted in his seat to hand it to me, his expression offering no room for argument. "Take this."

I reached for it automatically and found my fingers wrapping around the hilt of a knife in a thin leather sheath. I stared down at it and then back at Wylder, but he'd already turned to face the road.

"You obviously need to be armed from now on," he said. "If Colt comes for you again, I want you ready."

I wasn't going to argue with that. An almost giddy warmth bloomed in my chest at the show of trust. Wylder was arming me, giving me the means to hurt *him* if I'd wanted to—knowing I wouldn't.

And it was more than that. I drew the knife from the sheath just for a moment to test its weight in my hand and noticed the engraving on the hilt. *W.N.*

My head jerked up. "This is *yours*. I mean, obviously, but—"

"And now it's yours," he said sharply before I could protest him giving me a weapon that must have been meaningful to him in some way. Presumably he didn't go around having every knife he ever carried engraved with his initials. "I'll see that you get a gun too. There are plenty of options in the latest shipment. You're with us now, and that means whatever you need, it's taken care of."

I couldn't deny that the knife felt good in my hand. I slid it back into its sheath and held it on my lap. "Thank you."

From his profile, I saw a flicker of a smile cross his lips. "As long as you use it well."

The hill topped with its sprawl of mansions loomed ahead of us. As we drove steadily closer, I couldn't help reflecting on who was waiting for us back in the Nobles' home. My mouth went dry. But I had to say *something*.

It wasn't until we'd crested the hill and pulled into the driveway that I forced the question out. "Your father came back this morning—he knows why I'm here, right?"

The click as the engine cut off sounded ominous. Wylder's shoulders had tensed. "I assume he's heard the gist of it. I haven't had a chance to talk to him about you yet. You don't have to worry. I'll take care of that too."

"It was only—Colt made it sound as if someone had encouraged him to come after me right by your house—and those questions he had his guy ask about whether I'd spilled anything about the Nobles—"

Wylder swung around in his seat, his eyes flashing. "What are you trying to say?"

I stared right back at him, my hackles coming up. If he was going to make me spit it right out, then I would. "Maybe Ezra isn't so happy about having the princess of the Claws in his home. Maybe he already wants me gone."

Kaige sucked in a breath.

Wylder's expression went totally cold. "My father would never lower himself to making deals with scum like Colt. He'd be offended if you even mentioned the possibility. So don't."

He shoved open the door and got out without giving me a chance to respond. But I couldn't help noticing that he hadn't said his father would never turn on a guest of his son's or that he wouldn't have acted without speaking to Wylder first.

Maybe I was safe from Ezra Noble conspiring with my ex-fiancé, but that didn't mean I was actually *safe* here.

5

Wylder

I didn't even get a chance to eat breakfast before Axel waylaid me in the hall. He stopped in front of me with a cigarette butt hanging from the corner of his mouth, but since it wasn't lit, I didn't have any grounds to get on his case about it. Which he knew. The bastard looked smug as ever.

"What?" I demanded, eyeing the other man. He was nearly half a foot shorter than me, but he'd never let that faze him. My father didn't put his trust in weaklings.

"Boss wants to see you," he said. "Right now."

Of course he did. After we'd gotten back from retrieving Mercy yesterday afternoon, I'd indicated to Dad that I had some things to discuss with him, but he'd only given me a chance to briefly cover the discovery of Titus's murderer before he'd put me off to handle other business.

Naturally, he'd call me in on his own schedule without any concern for how I might be occupying myself. I was lucky I'd been up, or Axel probably would have enjoyed dragging me out of bed.

Oh, well. I'd been mentally preparing for this meeting since yesterday. Might as well get it over with already, even if I'd rather have tackled it without the pang of hunger in my stomach.

Even if there was an insistent tug in my gut trying to convince me that I needed to see Mercy, to confirm with my own eyes that she was still here, before I did a single other thing.

I squashed down that urge with significant effort. "Is he in his office?" I asked.

Axel nodded, the glee visible on his face. He was enjoying this. "Yeah. Come on, I'll go with you."

"There's no need for that."

"I insist," Axel said with a snide smile. "I have some work to go over with him anyway."

He was probably only tagging along so that he could overhear the uncomfortable conversation Dad and I were going to have. But there was no stopping him. As Dad's right-hand man, sometimes he took undue advantage of his position, which also included getting on my nerves free of charge.

Walking through the halls to Dad's study, I mostly ignored the guy, but it occurred to me I'd better ask: "What have you told him about Mercy?"

He shrugged. "Not much. I figured that was a conversation you were better off handling."

I wasn't sure whether to be grateful that I was getting to set the tone or annoyed that Axel was obviously anticipating the discussion going badly. I settled for both.

The door at the far end of the second-floor hall was closed. I knocked, steady and firm, the way Dad would see as a show of confidence.

"Come in," he called out from inside.

I walked straight in and came to a stop in front of his large oak desk. "I'm glad you have time to talk now, Dad."

My father looked up from the papers he was studying in the imposing leather chair behind his desk. Ezra Noble didn't believe in technology crowding his space. If you wanted to show him records of anything in here, you'd better have them printed out.

Other than the desk, the only furniture was a liquor cabinet stocked with vintages that plenty of people would drool over and a broad built-in book shelf. An oil-painted family portrait hung opposite the desk, showing my grandparents and Dad when he'd been a little younger than me.

We could have passed for twins if I'd traveled back in time to that moment. Now, a few streaks of silver had sprung up through his shock of auburn hair and faint lines of age marked the corners of his eyes and mouth. But none of that diminished the aura of authority that radiated off him.

"Wylder," he said softly. "I've been waiting for you." Dad never raised his voice, never showed any emotion on his blank face. You could never be prepared for what you'd get from him.

He had a way of speaking that was almost hypnotic, as if he could charm anyone he was talking to like a snake. His emerald-green eyes had a similar effect. I'd watched grown men reduced to stammers and quaking under the weight of his pointed stare. It could still send a shiver down my spine, though I was careful not to let that show.

"I came as soon as Axel told me you were ready to see me," I said, not bothering to mention that *I'd* been waiting for him since yesterday, and then added for politeness's sake, "Did you get the out-of-town business sorted out to your satisfaction?"

"It appears so, although a few of the minor pieces are still up in the air." He set the papers down on the corner of his desk and sat up straight, leaning his elbows on the desktop. "What is it you were in a hurry to report to me? Is there more going on beyond all this commotion with the groupies?"

How much had his men or Anthea filled him in on the details there? My aunt had promised she'd confirm my story, since she was the one he'd called in to investigate the murder, after all. He hadn't shown any surprise when I'd explained about Gia, even though the rest of us had found it hard to believe she'd been the culprit.

But then, maybe it didn't matter to him how far-fetched the scenario sounded as long as we were sure the matter was dealt with now. Gia definitely wasn't going to cause any more trouble.

"There is," I said, willing down my rising trepidation at this subject. "It's about Mercy Katz. She—"

He cut me off smoothly. "Ah, yes, the Claws heir under my roof. Maybe you can explain why we're still entertaining her."

"She's quite a handful," Axel put in before I could reply. "Feisty little thing. You'll like her, boss."

One of Dad's eyebrows arched. "Will I?"

I cursed Axel silently, my stomach lurching. My father's interest in Mercy was the last thing I wanted.

Reining in my temper, I groped for the clearest, most dispassionate account I could give before this meeting went completely off the rails. "As I mentioned before, she's the one who made the connection between Titus and Gia. And the Claws don't exist anymore. She came to us because Colt Bryant, the leader of the Steel Knights, murdered her family and her father's closest associates."

Dad regarded me without any visible reaction. "And how does that affect us?"

It affected *me*, more than even I was really comfortable with. Even hearing him question it set off a fresh flare of anger, spurred hotter by the memory of finding Mercy scratched up and blood-splattered in the Bend yesterday. That fucking asshole had destroyed everything she had and then come back to finish the job by tearing her apart too—

I caught my hands just before they clenched and gave away my fury. Mercy was *ours* now. It was that simple. And Colt needed to find out exactly what happened to people who messed with what belonged to the Nobles.

I just couldn't put it to Dad quite like that without putting her at even more risk.

"Bryant's move on the Claws was the beginning of a hostile takeover," I said. "He's rapidly been expanding his territory throughout the Bend, and he's made it clear that he isn't going to stop there. He has plans to take Paradise City as well."

Behind me, Axel snorted. Dad raised both eyebrows. "And you feel this is a legitimate threat?"

I had to walk carefully here. I couldn't make it sound as if I doubted his hold over Paradise Bend, but I still had to make it clear that we needed to take action.

"Bryant has proven that he's ruthless and committed, and we've gotten reports of massive weapons shipments that he's brought in. He's been adding to his manpower as well, taking on new recruits. The Steel Knights' mark is all over the Bend, with none of the other gangs out there strong enough to contest his invasion into their territory. I'm sure we can stamp out his insurrection, but there'll be less bloodshed on our side if we crush him quickly and decisively before he's gained any more ground."

While I spoke, I eyed my father carefully. Mercy's suggestion that he might have encouraged Colt to snatch her off our doorstep had made me balk instinctively, but could I say absolutely for sure Dad wasn't playing some kind of long game I didn't know about? Nothing was ever completely off the table when it came to Ezra Noble. If he felt it'd advance his plans in some way that hadn't occurred to me, it was possible.

"And?" he prompted, giving away nothing.

Frustration raked through me. "Isn't that reason enough? He's openly defying our authority. How can we let that stand?"

"Watch your tone," Dad said in a low voice, and my mouth snapped shut. I hated how quick I leapt to obey him, but I was well aware of the potential consequences of defiance. Questioning his judgment was only a short step from mutiny in his eyes, and he'd be a hell of a lot angrier about that from me than some small-time gang leader from the Bend.

"None of this explains why we're keeping this girl around," Dad said. "We're not a charity. If her father did his job right, she can fend for herself. Why shouldn't I have her escorted off the premises right now?"

I flinched inwardly. Because there were men crawling all through the Bend waiting for the chance to gut her for Colt's good favor. Because she'd proven she could stand with us, and I'd promised her my help—sworn it on my blood.

Because the thought of her vanishing from my life like she almost had yesterday set all my nerves on edge with the desire to rip apart whoever was responsible. Even if it was my father.

The strength of that reaction hit me like a cold slap, bringing me back to reality. *Nothing* could matter that much to me—definitely not some gang princess who'd turned up at our door like a lost kitten, no matter how capable she was. No matter how much space she'd somehow taken up in my head. This was just business.

It had to be, as far as Dad was concerned.

"She's had an inside view on Colt's operations, and she's eager to see him taken down after what he did to the Claws. I believe she's a valuable asset. She's proven herself loyal to us throughout the tests I've put her through. You know I wouldn't trust an outsider without good reason."

The look Dad gave me suggested he didn't actually believe he knew that for sure, even though I'd never given him any reason to doubt me. My teeth set on edge.

"Is that all there is to it?" he asked. "You have no other attachment to her?"

"No," I said, keeping my voice as firm and flat as I could. I couldn't afford for him to even consider that Mercy was more than a useful chess-piece. "I barely know her. I simply believe in making use of what we can while we can. Her father *has* trained her well. She's the one who discovered the weapons shipments. And she brought Titus's murderer to justice. Don't you think she deserves some recognition for that, not to be tossed onto the street? We wouldn't have much more honor than Bryant otherwise."

Dad rubbed his chin and glanced past me to Axel. "What do you think?"

Irritation flared through me. Why was he pulling the other man into this? Axel hadn't gotten involved in anything to do with Mercy other than to make accusations at my men and sneer at her.

Axel shrugged. "I think Colt is a fool, and sooner or later things will blow over. We've seen minor uprisings in the Bend before, and they've never come to much."

"This isn't the same as before," I said. "It's definitely not *minor*."

"What would you know?" Axel asked in a mocking voice he could only get away with because he'd been one of Dad's most trusted associates for decades. "You're just a twenty-two-year-old reckless kid."

"I'm not a kid," I snapped.

"Don't act like one, and I won't say it."

Dad shifted in his seat. "That's enough, Axel. Wylder knows the importance of keeping a cool head and evaluating a situation carefully.

He wouldn't be in any position to take over the mantle of the Noble empire otherwise."

I wished there'd been a little more warmth in that vote of confidence, rather than the sense that I was the only option for an heir he had. I drew myself up straighter.

"It's not only the situation in the Bend. Yesterday, Colt and some of the Steel Knights grabbed Mercy off the sidewalk just outside the mansion, totally disregarding the protection we've been offering her. You couldn't get a more open challenge than that. If we let him get away with it, it'll look as if we're too weak to defend our own."

"She's hardly our own," Dad said with an edge I didn't like, but for the first time he did appear slightly annoyed. My concerns that he might have been involved in the kidnapping somehow faded. I could tell he hadn't even known about it—and he didn't like the disrespect of the act, even if he didn't care about Mercy particularly. "You confronted him to get her back?"

I had to bite back a smile of pride. "We didn't need to. I told you she's proven herself capable of handling herself. She got away from his men on her own, with more information about his plans."

Dad studied me with an air that made my skin tighten. "You admire her," he said after a moment.

A denial leapt to my tongue, but if I argued too vehemently, I'd only be proving my investment. "She's stronger than many of the men we've initiated, and I appreciate her dedication to seeing Bryant fall. I think that's only natural."

"Are you sure that's all it is? I don't want to invest my resources in a fool's errand over some pretty face that's caught your eye."

And he wouldn't want me getting invested in any "pretty face" at all. A memory flickered through my head: a slumped form cowering on the floor, my father standing over her, firm hands gripping my arms when I tried to throw myself forward—

Nausea coiled around my stomach. My expression had stiffened. I spoke with perfect calm. "I have only what's best for the Nobles and our dominion over Paradise Bend in mind. I've seen what the Steel Knights are doing firsthand."

Dad didn't answer, only staring thoughtfully into space. That was actually a good sign. If he'd been sure I was wrong, he wouldn't hesitate to say it.

I pushed my advantage. "Dad, let me take care of this. I won't let it interfere with any other business you have underway. My inner circle and I will spearhead the mission to crush Bryant—we can handle it. All I need is your go-ahead and the use of some of the men when they're not occupied under your command. It'll be a chance for me to show that there's more than one Noble to fear in Paradise City."

I could tell I'd convinced him. Triumph bloomed in my chest before he even opened his mouth.

"That sounds like a reasonable proposition," he said, picking up his papers again. "I expect to see the situation dealt with quickly and efficiently. And make sure you don't bring too big a war to our doorstep. We want our enemies subdued, not multiplying."

I suppressed a grin. "Of course. You can count on me."

Dad made a gesture of dismissal. I moved to go, relief washing through me. But I hadn't quite made it to the door before he spoke again. "Oh, and Wylder?"

I glanced back, dread unfurling through my chest. "Yes?"

"I'd like to speak with the Katz girl myself. I'll send Anthea to get her when I'm done with this. Make sure she's ready."

My heart lurched. I almost blurted out a ragged *No!* Instead, I clamped my jaw shut.

Of course he'd want to talk to her himself. It was only natural. As long as I hadn't fucked up, there was nothing to be worried about. No reason at all for my gut to be churning twice as hard as it'd been a few minutes ago.

I nodded, holding my emotions in check with an iron grip. "Sure, Dad. I'll let her know."

6

Mercy

Frank finished taping the last bandage in place and gave me a quick nod. "Everything's healing well. I think you can handle them from here."

I glanced down at the thin layer of gauze wrapped around my palms and the cut on my arm and then shot him a smile. "I'll try not to show up bleeding again any time soon."

The middle-aged guy who handled the Nobles' basic medical needs let out a chuckle at that. He offered me an energy drink from his kit.

Before I could reach for it, Kaige swiped it from his hand. "I'm going to have that."

Frank frowned at him. "It's not advisable to be buzzed on those things all the time."

A cocky grin stretched Kaige's mouth. "Define 'all the time.'"

The older man sighed and left, but Anthea shook her head where she was standing by the stove. "You're going to ruin your appetite, and then what am I doing all this work for?"

"Aww, Auntie Anthea, you love cooking for us," Kaige drawled.

She skewered him with the kind of look that could penetrate steel.

"I'm not *your* aunt. You're lucky I like my actual nephew enough to put up with the rest of you. Why don't you make yourself useful and get out the plates?"

Kaige headed over to the cupboards without complaint, and I swiveled on my stool to appreciate the excellent view of his sculpted backside. Next to me, Gideon was typically occupied with his tablet. Rowan jumped up at the other end of the island to grab some knives and forks. My stomach grumbled, the mouth-watering smell of the frying bacon reminding me how much I was looking forward to this breakfast.

The five of us had gathered in the kitchen on Anthea's insistence. She'd shown up first thing this morning, apparently as soon as she'd heard about the whole kidnapping thing, and fussed over me for several minutes before insisting we all needed a good meal. I didn't know where Wylder had gotten to—Rowan had thought he'd seen him heading to Ezra's office—but he could join us when he finished whatever business he was taking care of.

Anthea glanced over her shoulder at me. She was wearing one of her typical housewife-style floral dresses, the red waves of her hair pinned back from her face with a couple of silver clips, but the domestic vibe was totally deceiving. It hid a sharp, conniving, and fierce woman I hoped never to be on the wrong side of again. I still wasn't totally sure how I'd ended up on her good side.

Presumably the fact that I'd saved her from a murder attempt by a crazy gang groupie had something to do with it. The marks from when her car had crashed into the telephone pole still dappled her forehead and arms, but she'd recovered quickly.

"How are you feeling?" she asked me with genuine concern. It was bizarre to think that just a few days ago, she'd absolutely hated my guts and been trying her best to get me kicked out of the mansion. "Are you hurting much anymore?"

I flexed my hands. The small cuts from the window glass stung but didn't throb like they had yesterday. "Just a bit. They're getting better."

"Good. Now eat up. I'm not having you get weak on my watch." She set a plate of bacon, home fries, and an omelet oozing melted cheese in front of me. My stomach just about jumped up my throat to inhale it faster.

Kaige reached for one of the home fries, but Anthea batted his hand away with her spatula. “No, that’s for only Mercy. Let her eat. She needs to get her energy back after everything that asshole ex of hers put her through. You’ll get your own plate.”

She looked at me fondly, and I found myself smiling back at her. When Anthea wasn’t trying to poison me, she could be surprisingly nice. Wylder had called her his honorary mother, and she could definitely bring out the motherly vibes when she wanted to.

Not that I’d know much about motherliness, considering mine had vanished when I was six years old. The only piece of her I had left was the little silver bracelet she’d given me back then, tucked in my pocket as always like a good luck charm.

I popped a piece of bacon into my mouth and nearly swooned. “It’s perfect,” I told Anthea, swallowing the salty, chewy-yet-crunchy strip. “If you ever want to switch callings, I’m pretty sure you could make a killing running a diner.”

Anthea snorted and turned to start dishing out the other plates. “No, thank you. I’ll stick to poisons and not-really-accidental deaths. We all need our happy place.”

As the guys returned to their seats around the island, Gideon propped his tablet next to his plate and shoveled a forkful of omelet into his mouth, barely seeming to taste it he was so absorbed in the screen. My gaze couldn’t help tracking the tempting flick of his tongue over his lip ring.

It really wasn’t fair that a guy so detached from the world outside of computers was so delicious.

“Let’s talk strategy,” he said. “Like Wylder mentioned before, we need to move in fast. Colt has been working at an astronomical speed to get his grip on the Bend. We have to cut down on his power.”

Rowan waved his fork in the air. “But how? I’m sure he’s got lots of underlings working for him. We can’t just go straight at him.”

Kaige let out an angry rumble. “Too bad. I’d *like* to punch him into a pulp.”

Gideon rolled his eyes. “I’m sure we’ll get to the part where you use your fists. But first I think we should weaken his defenses and reduce his resources."

"And how exactly are we going to do that?"

"Figuring out who his strongest allies are would probably be a good start," Rowan put in. "For him to think he's going to challenge us, he needs a large army. He's probably formed alliances with some of the smaller gangs to strengthen his position. But it might not be hard to win them back to our side."

I frowned. "That's something that bothered me. He's managed to take control over most of the Bend. I can't see most of even the small-time gangs rolling over without protest."

"It is odd," Gideon said.

Just then, Wylder stalked into the kitchen with his fists balled at his sides. He looked so grouchy he might as well have brought his own personal thundercloud with him.

I wasn't the only one who noticed. "Jeez, what's up with you?" Kaige asked before downing another mouthful of bacon.

Wylder's eyes briefly dropped to the space between Kaige and me at the island, and his gaze darkened. "I'm fine," he said brusquely, as if any of us were going to believe that when he said it that way.

His energy had seemed strange ever since they'd found me. Like something inside him had gotten wound up too tight and he hadn't figured out how to unravel it. I wasn't sure I wanted to be around if whatever it was snapped.

Of course, he'd also been oddly protective of me the whole time. The knife he'd given me—one of his personal weapons—formed a solid weight in my hip pocket. It felt weirdly intimate, as if he was touching me there through it. The thought made my insides heat.

Ignoring his boss's mood, Kaige shifted his stool a little closer to me and squeezed my shoulder while still looking at Wylder. "You'll be glad to know this one's fine too. Frank already checked her over again." Shifting his gaze to me, he leaned a little closer with a teasing arch of his eyebrows. "We wouldn't want our kitten in anything but tiptop shape, right?"

The hunger in his eyes, which had nothing to do with breakfast now, sent a deeper flare of heat through me. There was a softer edge of his flirting than there'd been before, more gently playful than aggressively seductive. After all the back and forth between us, maybe he wasn't so sure of himself. But Kaige being uncertain was actually kind of cute.

I couldn't help thinking back to the way he'd picked me up with those bulging arms and set me on the hood of his car to ravish me. I did like him fierce too.

A smile touched my lips even as I had to hold back a squirm at the memory, and Kaige's grin widened. "And smiling too. Gotta have that beautiful smile."

My stomach really shouldn't have fluttered at such a small compliment, but it did.

"We're all glad you're okay," Rowan said.

Annoyingly, something in his voice provoked another flutter. I shouldn't be getting at all mushy over the guy who'd already broken my heart once, even if he'd had my back a little in the past few days.

Wylder stalked past us to the counter without a word. My gaze flicked to Gideon, and I decided to flip it into a joke. I kicked him gently in the shin, making him finally look up from his tablet. "Maybe not all of you. Somehow I think Gideon might have been happier without me here complicating all his data."

Gideon blinked at me with those cool gray eyes of his, and a brief flicker of emotion passed through his angelic face. "Actually," he said matter-of-factly, "I'm finding your kind of complication can be gratifyingly stimulating."

That was a compliment, right? My body had certainly reacted as if it was, some of the heat from before settling between my thighs. Stimulation and gratification—I could definitely do with more of the latter to go with all of the former these guys had been supplying.

Kaige laughed and gave my ponytail an affectionate tug. "She is all that and more."

"Fucking damn it!" Wylder slammed his hands against the counter. I practically jumped out of my seat, and the tablet wobbled in Gideon's grasp. We all stared at the Noble heir, who whipped around to glare at all of us, his gaze searing. "Where is my brandy?"

"What brandy?" Rowan asked. His eyes mirrored the surprise that had shown up on everybody's face.

"*My* brandy," Wylder said in an irritated voice. "I left it in the kitchen."

"I put it back in the liquor cabinet by the bar," Anthea said.

"Well, you should have asked me before you did that," he snapped. "I could really use a drink right now."

Kaige rubbed his jaw. "It's nine in the morning, man."

Wylder spun on him. "Who the hell asked you? You know what? I can barely hear myself think around here."

"Did everything go all right with your father?" Gideon asked tentatively.

Wylder bared his teeth. "I can handle my father just fine, although it doesn't help that everyone keeps bringing him up. Why don't you all get out of here and let me have a little breakfast in peace?"

Oooh-kay then. Prince Wylder had clearly gotten up on the wrong side of the bed this morning. The other guys exchanged a glance and got up from their stools.

"Do you want me to—" Anthea started to offer, gesturing to the frying pan.

"No!" Wylder snapped. "I can figure out how to feed myself. Just go."

She made a tsking sound with her tongue, but she headed for the door with the others. I stood up too with every intention of leaving.

"Where do you think you're going, Kitty Cat?" Wylder asked in a growl of a voice when I was halfway to the door. The others had already vanished into the hall.

I turned, folding my arms over my chest, my skin pricking with an unsettling energy that wasn't exactly unpleasant. "I thought you wanted us to leave."

He prowled toward me, every bit of muscular power in his well-built body on display. "I didn't say *you*."

"You kind of made it sound like all of—"

He stopped in front of me, close enough that I could feel his breath as he fingered the hem of my T-shirt. His gaze stayed fixed on me, utterly predatory. "Why are you in such a hurry? Missing their attention already?"

I glowered at him. "What are you even talking about?"

He waved toward the open door. "I think you like having them all focused on you. Fawning over you like you really are some kind of princess."

Oh, for fuck's sake. I leaned closer, holding his gaze, every nerve alight with the electricity building between us. "I *am* a princess. The Claws Princess, as you like to remind me so much."

"And you love that too." His face tipped even closer to mine, those gorgeous green eyes flashing. "It's my attention you crave the most, isn't it? You like to pretend you don't care, but I know you better than that by now."

I snorted even though an eager shiver had rippled through me at his words. "Spoiler alert: not everything is about you."

"No, but this is."

I cocked my head, my neck straining a bit as I glared up at him. "Maybe this is about you. What are you so pissed off about anyway? Annoyed that I ruined your valiant rescue effort yesterday by rescuing myself?"

His jaw clenched. "I would have torn through every one of those assholes."

"But instead you're tearing into the rest of us. Nice." I exhaled sharply and started to turn. "Maybe I *should* just go—"

Wylder grabbed my elbow and jerked me back toward him, his fingers scorching my skin. I shoved at his chest instinctively, and he shoved right back—pushing the door closed and me up against it. "I didn't say you could leave."

"I don't answer to you, you prick."

"Then it's about time you started."

"You have some nerve," I spat out, and then his whole body was against me, pulsing with heat. It was all I could do not to melt right into him.

"You're so fucking sexy when you're furious," he said, and then his mouth crashed down on mine.

I should have pushed him off me. That would have been the sensible thing to do. But sensible wasn't exactly my specialty, and the truth was, my entire being had been craving this moment since the first time Wylder had touched me—hell, since the first time he'd *looked* at me.

It felt as inevitable as gravity or a magnetic force. We'd been bound to collide eventually. Why the hell should I deny it?

Especially when it felt this fucking good.

His mouth moved against mine, furious and urgent. I gripped his shirt and kissed him right back, refusing to back down.

His tongue traced the seam of my mouth before flicking inside. Mine tangled with it, dueling for dominance. I felt the grin on his face as our mouths mashed together. Neither of us had any plans to give up control.

So it was probably a good thing that it turned out we both wanted the same thing.

Wylder twisted the lock on the kitchen door and then swung me around to set my ass on the nearest countertop. The cool granite bit into the backs of my thighs for just a second before he heated everything up again by pushing between my legs.

I grinded against him, giddy at the feel of the hard bulge already pressing against the fly of his jeans. My hands pulled at his hair before slightly massaging his nape.

He groaned against my mouth, and that only turned me on more. I liked this version of Wylder who wasn't Mr. Cool and Cocky but lost in his lust, even if I was lost here with him.

His hot tongue delved into my mouth again and mimicked the action of a cock, doing shallow laps at first and then moving deep inside. I moaned and began to rock against him, seeking more of him. Wylder's hand skimmed down my chest and rolled my nipple between his deft fingers. I hissed encouragingly at the contact.

Panting, he broke the kiss. He brought his other hand to my cheek with startling tenderness considering the rage in his voice as he traced the bruise Colt had given me. "I'm going to kill him myself."

My own anger flared through the flames of desire. "He's mine to destroy."

Wylder held my face and looked straight into my eyes. There was something so intense and determined in his it felt like a promise. "Fine. Then we'll do it together."

His gaze broke from mine, but only so he could suck a path down the side of my neck. His fingers squeezed and kneaded my breasts as if he couldn't get enough of them. An embarrassing whimper tumbled out of me, and then another when his mouth finally descended on a nipple and sucked on it through the thin cotton of my top. My body thrummed.

It wasn't enough. I needed all of him this time.

Wylder seemed to have the same idea. He tugged at the zipper of my jeans and then pulled back to see my expression. In answer, I drew his hand to my throbbing cunt.

He squeezed tightly, making me clench with a wave of pleasure. "Fuck," he said under his breath. "You're delectable."

He tugged at my jeans so viciously I was almost afraid he'd rip the denim apart. Part of me wanted him to. He wrenched his own jeans down and freed his cock. It sprang to attention, huge and gleaming with precum and a Prince Albert piercing at the tip.

Fuck me.

My mouth watered at the sight. What would it be like to feel the metal rolling against my tongue as I took his dick in my mouth?

I reached out and rolled the ring between my fingers, spreading the slickness of his precum. Wylder's eyes closed, and he let out a grunt. But as I continued to move my hand up and down his shaft, he pushed it away with a growl. "Not right now. We're coming together this time, and I'm going to be balls deep inside you when we do."

If I'd been wet before, those words made me gush. He took a condom from his back-pocket and ripped the foil with his teeth before rolling it on. With one almost frantic thrust, he filled me to the brim.

I gasped at the fullness of his thick cock. He didn't give me a chance to get accustomed to his girth as he started to pump into me, but I was ready for him anyway. The stretch sent a delicious burn of bliss all through my torso.

As he stroked even deeper, I pushed my hips toward him. My fingers scraped his back. Our wild breaths mingled together, our bodies jerking and slapping against each other as our breaths fractured. It was savage and raw, nothing even remotely gentle about it, but somehow I felt closer to him in that moment than I had to any lover before.

Sweat trickled down my back. I arched my spine, curling one of my legs around Wylder so that he could find even deeper access. The new angle made him hit a spot so good my eyes rolled heavenward. I matched his rhythm, his thrusts plunging deeper still as he sent me careening toward my orgasm.

I looked up at him in the same instant that he looked down. There was a wild urgency in his green eyes. “You’re mine,” he snarled. “*Mine.*”

I didn’t think it was just lust in his voice. There was something more than that, something that made my heart wobble.

Before I could examine that impression too closely, Wylder bucked into me harder and faster than before, setting off a chain reaction of sensations inside me. Pleasure blazed through me and exploded in my core. I leaned in and bit him on his arm to muffle my scream.

Wylder jerked inside me, his muscles contracting. “Oh, fuck,” he muttered. With a hitch of his hips, he emptied himself inside me.

We stayed locked together for several seconds. I was still clutching his shirt, trying to catch my breath. Wylder closed his eyes as if he wasn’t ready for the moment to end.

Then he opened them again, and something hardened both in his gaze and his stance. The fire in those emerald orbs died in an instant. Something cold took its place, and a chill washed over me in turn.

He pulled out of me, yanking off the condom and heaving up his jeans in rough movements.

I pulled my panties up, watching him. “Let me just remind you that *you* were the one—"

“Don’t even go there.” He zipped himself up and then discarded the used condom in the trash. Then he jerked around to face me, his expression so emotionless it was hard to believe he’d even touched me, let alone fucked me so desperately.

“My dad wants to talk to you,” he said flatly.

That’d come out of nowhere. “About what?”

“He wants to discuss the situation with the Steel Knights and your position here. You’d better get changed so you’re ready when he calls on you.” And just like that he walked out of the kitchen, without giving me so much as a backward glance.

7

Mercy

"Jackass," I muttered as I made my way upstairs. But as much of a jackass as he'd been, Wylder was right about one thing: I couldn't very well present myself to Ezra Noble in my current ravaged state, smelling of his son.

I'd never had a problem enjoying sex as something purely physical before. Why the hell should it matter that Wylder had gone cold and distant the second our passion had flamed out?

But it was impossible to forget how he'd looked as he touched my cheek and swore to kill Colt, the intensity in his eyes as he'd pumped away inside me, his usual cool, commanding mask giving way to show something deeper inside.

But maybe I'd been mistaken about that. He hadn't even asked me if I was okay or if it was good for me. Maybe the smug bastard already knew how much I had liked it. My pussy throbbed at the memory as if it wanted more of him. Traitorous body.

Well, it was done now, and it'd been fan-fucking-tastic sex while we'd been having it. I'd just focus on that and let the Noble heir do whatever he felt like doing with himself now. *I* certainly wasn't doing him again while he was being such a prick.

Ducking into the second-floor bathroom, I checked myself in the mirror. As I'd expected, my hair was a total mess. I washed my face and then quickly hopped into the shower, hoping a quick shampoo and rubdown with soap would help me look presentable.

When I came back to the guest bedroom where I'd been staying in the mansion, I found Anthea waiting for me by my bed. She pointed at the neatly pressed pile of clothes on the covers. "My brother has summoned you," she said, somehow managing to sound both wry and serious at the same time. "I thought you might need this."

"Thanks so much," I said gratefully. I had been wondering what I was going to wear to meet Ezra. The only clothes I had now were thrift store tees and jeans that weren't going to generate much respect, and most of those had cooking oil stains on them courtesy of hostile groupies.

While Anthea waited, I quickly changed into the gray slacks and pearl-pink blouse she'd brought me. The outfit was too feminine and business-y for me to feel totally comfortable in it, but she knew her brother better than I did.

If I thought Wylder was a piece of work, his father was a whole other level of dangerous. He was the power behind the Nobles, the one who'd held them together and even expanded their reach beyond the boundaries of the county over the past couple of decades. What was he going to think of me?

I found myself staring down at the tee I'd just taken off, the fabric scrunched in my fist. My gaze lingered on the faint pattern of the oil stain that hadn't quite washed out.

Anthea must have noticed it too. Her lips thinned. For a second, she looked oddly uncomfortable.

I braced myself, half-expecting some cutting remark to come out of her after all, to discover that her sudden turn-around on me could turn back just as quickly. Instead, she shook back her hair and sighed.

"Look," she said. "About before, the things I said to you, the things I did... I was only looking out for Wylder and his boys, all right? It wasn't anything personal. I didn't know you. Most of the women who turn up here don't have anything on their minds except getting as prominent a Noble as they can on the hook. It took me a while to see that there's a lot more to you than that."

Was that... an apology, from the deadly Anthea Noble? I managed to catch myself before I outright gaped at her. A smile tugged at my lips, a strange warmth unfurling in my chest.

No matter what an ass Wylder decided to be, I did have at least one friend here now. Which was one more than I'd ever been able to count on in my life before.

"I know," I said. "I wish you'd seen it a little sooner, but—I've got bigger things to worry about than staying pissed off about that. Besides, you do make a really good breakfast. I'm happy staying on your good side and forgetting about the rest."

Anthea laughed and gave me a sly look. "I wish I'd figured it out sooner too. You are going to make life around here much more interesting—I think in a good way." She dragged in a breath. "Assuming Ezra doesn't find any fault in you. Are you ready to go? He won't like it if we keep him waiting very long."

In my newfound ease with her, I realized there was one thing I wanted to ask her, and not out in the hall where any of Ezra's underlings might overhear. "Anthea—Colt was talking as if someone had put him up to taking and torturing me. Do you think there's any chance Ezra would have done something like that?"

I cringed inwardly as I asked, worried she'd get offended, but instead she knit her brow, her gaze turning thoughtful. At least she seemed to be seriously considering it, unlike Wylder who'd given the idea a kneejerk rejection I didn't totally trust.

"I can see why you might wonder," she said after a moment, "but I honestly don't think so. If Ezra were upset with you or wanted information out of you, he'd have his own men handle it. He wouldn't trust any other gang, especially one from the Bend, to do the job to his requirements. Why would he? Colt has nothing he wants, and he certainly wouldn't feel the need to bargain with a man he considers below him."

That all made sense. Even Wylder hadn't seen Colt as a real threat for a long time, so it was hard to believe Ezra would be so frightened by him he'd make a deal rather than simply crushing him. I'd have to see how this meeting went, but a weight lifted from my chest. I swept my fingers over my hair one more time and nodded. "That's good to know. All right, let's go."

Anthea led me down the hall toward the opposite wing of the house. I willed my heart not to beat too fast. Even if Ezra hadn't been behind my kidnapping, he was still no one to be trifled with. "So, what's he like? Your brother?"

Anthea hummed to herself. "It's hard to put Ezra in a box. I can spout a whole lot of adjectives, but they really won't do him any justice. You'll see when you meet him."

That was really encouraging. I held back a grimace. I'd only seen the head of the Nobles a few times at a distance when my dad had pointed him out around town. I'd heard the stories, though—horrifying ones about what happened to people who crossed him.

Anthea glanced at me, and her expression softened with a hint of sympathy. "Look, you should be fine. You solved a very large problem we were having and protected me while you were doing it. You just have to be a little careful about what you say."

I wet my lips. "Okay. Careful how?"

"My brother is very particular, so tell him only the things that he's asked of you. He has a way of twisting your words and then holding them against you. We don't want that happening now, especially with how things stand with the Steel Knights."

Oh, great. "I'll, uh, keep that in mind," I said.

Anthea looked sheepish. "Did I come off a little intense? I swear I'm only trying to prepare you."

"No, no, this is good," I said. At least she was trying to warn me about him, which was far better than Wylder abandoning me in the kitchen. What the hell was that about anyway? If I didn't know any better, I'd think that the sex we'd had was a scenario I'd concocted in my head. If only it hadn't been so fucking good.

We passed three girls who I recognized immediately from the groupie room. One of them—one I'd sent running with a few threats the other day—glared at me.

"They don't know what really happened between Gia and you,"

Anthea said, her voice low. "But they have their ideas, none of them good."

Let them think whatever they wanted. I walked by without giving them another glance, but one of them spit right at my feet.

Anthea whirled in on them. "Do we have a problem?"

Their eyes widened. One of the girls shook her head. "No, we were just—"

"Then you'd better clean that up." Anthea pointed to the wet spot on the hardwood floor. When they all stayed frozen, she glowered at them. "Well, get on with it."

One of the girls twitched and fished a tissue out of her pocket, kneeling to dab at the spit. Anthea clearly had a reputation around here. She was still a force of fury, only thankfully it was no longer directed at me.

"Get out of here," Anthea said when the girl was done, and the three of them took off down the hallway toward the staircase.

Anthea gazed after them, frowning. "I know not to underestimate *them* now too."

Memories of Gia flashed through my mind: the fury twisting her pale face when she'd attacked me the other night, the mess of blood and brains after Wylder had shot her in the head. My stomach turned. That wasn't what I needed to be thinking about when I was about to face Ezra Noble.

"Anything else I should keep in mind about Ezra?" I asked as we started walking again.

"Well... if my brother bothers you too much, imagine him with a carrot on his head."

I stared at her. "*What*?"

"Trust me," she said as if she were confiding a secret. "It really works."

I still wasn't sure if she was being serious, but even if she was only making a joke to lighten the mood, it'd worked. I found myself chuckling thinking of the most dangerous person in all of Paradise City with a carrot balanced in his auburn hair.

We turned a corner and headed toward the back of the house. "You'll be meeting Ezra in what he calls his 'audience room,'" she said.

"He has it set up specifically for meeting with people he doesn't trust enough to bring into his study. Don't let that get you down. He can count the number of people he'll let into his actual workspace on his hands without running out of fingers."

Fair enough. Why would a man like him invite a stranger into his inner sanctum?

Anthea opened a door at the end of the hall and ushered me into a large, sparsely decorated room. A picture window looked out over the back lawn. Other than a watercolor painting hanging opposite it, the walls were bare. A buttery leather armchair stood on one side of a glass coffee table, looking every bit a throne. A matching sofa sat opposite it, with a few scattered chairs behind that.

"Have a seat," Anthea said, motioning to the sofa, and then pressed my elbow reassuringly. "Don't worry, you'll be good."

After the hurricane that'd been sex with Wylder, this situation did nothing to calm my nerves. I inhaled deeply and sank onto the sofa, which was almost disturbingly smooth and soft. Like it was meant to lull whoever was sitting on it into a false sense of security. Anthea stayed standing beside the coffee table.

The door on the other side of the room opened, and a man stepped in. At the sight of him, my pulse hiccupped.

I'd forgotten just how much Wylder resembled his father. Ezra had identical bright green eyes and auburn hair other than a few streaks of gray in it, as well as similarly sculpted features and broad shoulders. The most noticeable difference was the way he moved. I'd seen Wylder stalk and prowl across a room, but his father made his way over to his chair with the air of a watchful wolf, absolutely animalistic and feral.

I started to stand up from my seat in case he expected the gesture of respect, but Ezra just motioned me to stay put. He settled into his own chair, poised so regally it was even easier to picture it as a throne. His piercing gaze took me in. "So, here's the Katz heir in my home."

"Thank you for having me here," I said quickly.

"It's not by my choice."

The weight of his stare tangled my tongue. "I mean—thank you for taking the time to see me."

"You're here to see me," he said, arching one eyebrow.

Shit. I was saying all the wrong things already. Now I knew exactly what Anthea had meant about Ezra Noble twisting one's words. What had she said? Focus on only what he asked me, nothing else. I could do that.

"That's true," I said, and simply waited.

Ezra let the silence hang for long enough that my skin started to itch. Then he leaned slightly forward. "I hear you're the one who solved Titus's murder." I could hear the skepticism in his voice.

I drew myself up a little straighter. "Yes, I did. It was one of the groupies. She thought that—" I stopped myself. My gut told me that I shouldn't mention the fact that Gia had been convinced that Titus was trying to kill Kaige. But Ezra was still waiting for me to finish. "She thought that he was a threat to her, so she decided to take him out first."

"I see," he said. "And why did you end up here in the first place?"

That was familiar territory. I'd been expecting this question and had the answer ready. "I guess you've also heard about how Colt Bryant, my ex-fiancé, slaughtered my father and the rest of my family. I have to make him pay for that betrayal, but I knew I couldn't take him on without help. The Nobles are the most powerful family in Paradise Bend, and you have a stake in keeping the lesser gangs in line. Coming here seemed like the obvious choice."

"That's why you approached my son?" Ezra asked. Was his gaze even more penetrating than before? I fought down the urge to rub my arms as if he might be able to spot traces of my hookup with Wylder on my skin. Who knew how he'd react if he found out I'd caught that much of Wylder's attention—for however long his interest had lasted.

"Only because you weren't available," I said, keeping my voice as even as I could. "I came here looking for you right after the massacre, but I found Wylder. At first he was reluctant to help me, but I struck a bargain with him. Finding out who killed Titus and clearing Kaige's name was my way of proving I deserved his—and your—help." I assumed Wylder had already told him about our deal.

"She consistently came through on every occasion we tested her," Anthea put in, conveniently leaving out my meltdown during their freezer test. The less Ezra heard about *that* embarrassing incident, the better.

"Very impressive," Ezra said in a tone that suggested it wasn't impressive at all. He folded his hands together on his lap with a flex of his fingers. "What about your fiancé, Colt? Why do you think he went rogue? Did he give you any indication of what he was going to do?"

He had used the term fiancé—without the "ex"—for some reason. I didn't like the implication. He definitely didn't sound like someone who'd had inside dealings with the man.

"Apparently he believed that my father was out to double-cross him, so he decided to attack first," I said. "As far as I know, he's delusional. My father showed every sign of looking forward to the alliance between the Claws and the Steel Knights. And I had no idea my *ex*-fiancé was planning anything violent until it happened."

Ezra chuckled coolly in response, probably noting my emphasis. "I'm certain it's a sore topic for you."

Was he trying to ruffle me? I kept it short and sweet. "He's attempted to kill me several times. Any ties of loyalty or commitment between us are gone."

But Ezra managed to turn that around on me too. "And how can I be sure your loyalties to us will be steadier?"

I bit my tongue before a snarky remark like "How about don't try to murder me?" slipped out, but I didn't know what to say instead.

Anthea coughed, stepping in. "I've told you that Mercy saved my life. She did everything she could to warn me that Gia had messed with my car, and then she risked her own life to prevent a probably fatal accident. And I hadn't gone easy on her before then. *I* have no doubts about her sense of loyalty."

Irritation flickered across her brother's face at the interruption, but when he spoke again, his voice was even. "You can be sure I'm keeping that in mind, Anthea." His attention stayed fixed on me. "I'm curious about your position in the Claws. You're technically the heir, but I've had no reports of you working alongside your father. How much did he let you get involved?"

I winced inwardly, but I had to go with the truth. "He didn't let me. He never brought me in on anything directly related to his business dealings. But he made sure I was capable of holding my own among his men with intensive training starting from an early age."

"And yet you were only a prop," Ezra said.

I bristled. "Not by my choice. I kept myself as aware of everything that was going on as I could."

"So you went against his wishes?"

I had run myself into a wall. I shot a pleading look at Anthea, but she only offered a fleeting grimace. Ezra Noble was really good at what he did.

"Only when it was absolutely necessary," I said, trying to keep my voice level. "I did my best to meet my father's expectations, but he was never going to be happy with a girl as his heir. I wanted to be ready in case I needed to step up. He severely underestimated me and my capabilities, choosing to trust an outsider instead—and in the end, that's what killed him."

"What would you have done differently that night?" Ezra asked.

Oh, I'd thought that through hundreds of times, how I could go back and do things differently. Unfortunately, every time I came to the same conclusion. "I didn't have a chance to get the upper hand in the moment. If I'd been on more equal footing with Colt with a proper position in the Claws, maybe I'd have been able to pick up the signs of the coming betrayal ahead of time. What I *wish* I could have done is stab that bastard in his neck, gouge out his eyes, and then hang up his body in the middle of the Bend for every Claws member to spit on."

Ezra Noble might have looked faintly impressed. "As I suppose he would deserve. And you're ready to swear full loyalty to the Nobles now?"

"You've given me protection. You've given me hope when I had none. I owe you everything I can offer for that."

"Wylder has said he'll help you in your crusade against Bryant." Ezra shifted in his seat, giving me the impression of an eagle about to swoop in to his prey.

I chose my words carefully. "Those were the terms of our deal. He's a force I'll be grateful to have on my side."

Ezra considered me for a long moment. I didn't think I'd managed to get through to him as much as I'd have liked to, but hopefully it'd been enough.

"Very well then," he said finally—and maybe a little reluctantly. "I accept you as a new initiate of the Nobles. But be aware that I'll expect you to face all the same dangers my men do. Are you ready for that?"

He looked like he wanted me to say no. In this one thing, I was going to disappoint him.

"I am," I said, feeling like I had just signed my soul away with invisible ink.

8

Mercy

An energetic rapping of knuckles against my bedroom door brought me over. I opened it to find Kaige standing outside. He took in my questioning look and tipped his head toward the hall. "You're coming, aren't you?"

I blinked at him. "Coming where?"

His forehead furrowed. "Didn't— We're going into the Bend to start reminding the Steel Knights who's boss."

"What, now?" At his nod, I marched past him into the hall. "Of course I want to be there for that."

I might have believed it was a miscommunication, but when we found the other three guys around the back of the garage, examining a couple cases of pistols, the hardening of Wylder's expression told me I'd been left in the dark on purpose.

"You don't need to come along," he said shortly, already turning his attention back to the guns. "We can handle this without you."

What the hell? He'd been a jerk about our hook-up, but this was something else entirely.

I set my hands on my hips. "I'm sure you *can*. But I'm also sure this is my fight even more than it's yours, so I'm fucking well going to be part of making it happen."

"The four of us know how to work together as a team. You'd just get in the way. Go find something else to entertain yourself with, Princess."

Oh, so we were back to "Princess" again, were we? My teeth set on edge at the sting of his comments. The other guys glanced between us, tense and uncertain.

Then I registered exactly what Wylder had said. "Four? Gideon's going?" I realized how insulting the disbelief in my voice might sound a second too late and quickly backtracked, catching the tech genius's gaze. "I mean, usually you'd want to stay back here and focus on the data, right?"

"I insisted on coming along because I want to see what's going on in the Bend firsthand to supplement that data," Gideon said, cool and even. "I don't expect to be involved in much of the fighting. I know my limitations."

I spun back toward Wylder. He could lash out at me all he wanted. I'd already survived his wrath before. If it took a little more work to shut off the part of myself that cared what he thought of me now, oh well.

"If he can insist, then I can insist too," I said. "And I do. Insist. Colt is mine to crush, and I plan to be there every step of the way, whether you like it or not."

The glare Wylder shot me showed he didn't like it at all. "Wylder," Kaige said tentatively, and his boss let out a huff. Maybe he'd decided it'd be too much hassle arguing more.

"Have it your way, then. Just stay out of *our* way. And that means making sure you can defend yourself." Wylder motioned to the guns. "Take your pick."

I hesitated, taking in the array of pistols and lingering on the sleek one he'd already picked up. "You mean—"

"I promised you a gun, and I'm a man of my word. Get on with it."

Well, if he was going to be that pissy about it...

I pointed at the one in his hands. "I want that one."

Somehow his scowl got even deeper, but he shoved it toward me. "Then it's yours. Come on, everyone, let's move out."

The guys all grabbed a gun for themselves, even Gideon. I tucked mine into the back of my jeans like they did. I'd handled a gun plenty of times, but my dad had never let me keep one on me, so I wasn't used to carrying one.

He'd probably been afraid I'd get too tempted to put a bullet in his head. There'd been times when I might have.

We tramped into the garage and headed to a car that turned out to be Rowan's, which was a good choice for a mission to the Bend—unlike Wylder and Kaige, he'd gone for something low key rather than obviously expensive. The silver Toyota sedan had plenty of room for all of us and looked to be a model at least a few years old rather than shiny and new.

Rowan drove us into the Bend with ease. Of course, he'd spent much of his formative years growing up there if not as many as I had. It used to be his home too.

Wylder sat in hostile silence the whole way, only speaking up a couple of times to give an instruction. But when Rowan stopped down the street from a trio of men wearing the Steel Knights' red bandanas around their upper arms, the Noble heir straightened up with an eager expression.

The guys were circling a girl who looked barely eighteen and absolutely terrified. Their voices wafted through the open window to me with the hot summer air. "Nice tits you got there. What are you hiding under that pretty skirt of yours?"

I bristled and reached for the car door, but Wylder shook his head. "Stay inside. You don't jump in unless it's absolutely necessary."

Rowan killed the engine and got out of the car alongside Wylder and Kaige. I stayed where I was only because Wylder might have a bit of a point about my presence throwing off the guys' dynamic. I didn't want to be the reason one of them got messed up. Next to me, Gideon was snapping pictures of the buildings around us with his tablet. My hands balled on my lap.

The Steel Knights looked up and noticed the guys approaching them, frowns crossing their faces. "What the fuck do you want?" one of them called out, swinging a bat that was covered with nails.

"Ideally you, lying in several pieces on the ground," Wylder said in an easy tone, as if he were talking about nothing but the weather. "I think it's time you remembered who actually owns this county, and it's not the Steel Knights."

The girl took the distraction as an opportunity to make a run for it, but one of the Steel Knights yanked her back by her hair. As she shrieked, he looked toward Wylder and the rest with a challenge in his eyes.

I growled in anger. What an absolute shit-prick.

Kaige barreled towards the Steel Knights instantly, sending two of them flying to the ground. One of them cocked his gun at him, but before he could pull the trigger, Kaige ripped it out of the guy's hands and threw it away. He slammed his fists into the sides of the guy's head hard enough to make him yelp.

The one who'd grabbed the girl pushed her away and started to make a run for it. But Rowan was faster. He sprinted up to him and drove his heel into the back of his knee to topple him. The man reached for his gun and shot at him blindly. Rowan easily ducked and twisted the gun away from his hand while he stepped on his wrist. The man groaned in agony.

Where had my easy-going high school sweetheart learned *those* moves?

The guys didn't take out their own guns. They didn't want to kill these assholes—not today. They were sending a message, and they needed the losers to go deliver it to their idiot friends. And to Colt.

The girl dashed off. One of the men on the ground stood up shakily. He reached for his bat and brought it crashing down on Kaige's arm, but the jerk of Kaige's wrist sent the weapon smashing into its owner's face in turn. Blood gushed from his forehead. He swore and took off.

Rowan dragged what looked like the leader of the bunch over and threw him at Wylder's feet. Bending down to the battered man's level, Wylder yanked his head up by the hair and looked him straight in the eye.

"What do you fucking want from us?" the man groaned.

"You've forgotten who the boss is around here," Wylder said in a chilling voice. "This is your only *gentle* reminder. The Nobles are clearing the trash from our streets. And if anyone asks who gave us that authority, tell them you talked to Wylder Noble himself."

He picked up the nail-studded baseball bat and then drove it into the man's palm, drawing blood and a scream that echoed down the street. I had no sympathy for Wylder's victim, especially not after the way that prick had assaulted the girl. He could consider it payback.

Rowan ripped off the bandana from the man's arm and handed it to Wylder, who took something out of his pocket. At first I thought he was reaching for a gun, but then I realized that it was a lighter.

Wylder placed it under the bandana and set it on fire. He dropped it on the ground, watching as the hungry flames curled around the Steel Knight symbol, devouring it. It seemed so prophetic that goosebumps ran down my arms. This was the beginning of the end.

When the bandana was all but destroyed, Wylder stepped on it with his heel deliberately and said, "Remember this the next time we meet." He kicked the guy in the ribs for good measure and left him groaning on the pavement.

Kaige and Rowan got into the car after Wylder. We still had more work to do.

We stopped again a few streets down in front of a vandalized laundromat. Kaige stepped out first, eyeing the four Steel Knights who were hanging out on the sidewalk, probably looking to deal. None of them had any weapons in sight, but I suspected they had at least a knife or a gun on them.

Kaige casually strolled up to them. "You need something, big guy?" the closest one asked.

"I don't know. I was looking for Cunt Town and my GPS seems to tell me it's here," Kaige said with a smirk.

"You son of a bitch," the man growled and raised his fist. Wrong move. Kaige caught him easily and twisted his hand. I heard the crunch of bones breaking.

The other guys stared at Kaige in shock and fury. "You're not going to get away with this," one of them said.

Before we knew what was happening, he whistled shrilly. Kaige punched him hard, again and again, until he shut up.

The other Steel Knights tried to bolt, but Wylder and Rowan moved to intercept them. "I don't think so," Wylder said with a cruel smile that somehow electrified me even though I knew how unpleasant his viciousness could be. "No one's leaving here without paying their dues."

A couple of the guys swung at them—and the third managed to dart between them while they were occupied, dashing past the car.

Oh no, he didn't. I didn't give a fuck what Wylder had ordered me to do.

I shoved open the door and leapt out. Flinging myself after the escapee, I latched my fingers around his arm and wrenched him back toward me—and into my fist. The snap of his breaking nose was the most satisfying thing I'd heard all day. A weird, woozy exhilaration swept through me.

I stomped my heel down on the guy's shin and kneed him in the gut for good measure. When I turned around, Wylder and Rowan were striding over to me, the guys they'd been dealing with slumped on the ground. I braced myself for Wylder to berate me.

Instead, his eyes slid to the man I'd knocked down and back to my face. His jaw worked. "We got them all," he said. Not a "thank you" or a "good job," but I'd still take it over a "I told you to stay in the car."

Just as he motioned toward the Toyota, several motorcycles roared down the street, more men with red bandanas riding them. A black muscle car followed them.

I tensed, my gut lurching. I'd know that shape anywhere. I'd been *inside* it more times than I could count.

My voice came out thin. "That's my father's car."

Kaige rejoined us, and we held our ground around the Toyota. The motorcycles formed a semi-circle around us, but if we'd jumped into the car and gunned it, we could have crashed through them. I could tell from the set of Wylder's shoulders that he had no intention of running scared, though.

The car pulled up across the street from us. The windows were tinted so it was impossible to see who was inside. Then the door opened and Colt stepped out.

My blood started to boil, both at the sight of him and the fact that my murderous ex had commandeered Dad's car. I took a step forward automatically, but Kaige caught me by my elbow.

More of Colt's men leapt out of the car. I recognized one of them as one of my father's associates, Mr. Jenner. The sinewy-limbed man with graying jowls had come around the house once a month or so to report to Dad and take new orders.

I gaped openly at him. He had switched sides already? Un-fucking-believable.

Colt stayed where he was by the driver's side door. "I heard there was a major disturbance going on and thought I'd better deal with it myself. I'm going to ask that you go back to your pretty palace in the city and leave my men and my streets alone."

Wylder scoffed. "*Your* streets? All of Paradise Bend answers to the Nobles. The fact that you've forgotten that is exactly why we're here."

Colt feigned a look of surprise. "I had no idea the Nobles were even interested in the Bend. I thought you deemed all of us beneath you."

As he spoke, another car had parked behind his. A few men got out, staying a little to the side of the confrontation. More bodyguards, I assumed, but something about their stern expressions and confident poses sent an uneasy tremor through me. They weren't wearing the Steel Knights bandanas on their arms.

Who the hell were *they*?

"You are beneath us," Wylder said flippantly. "And that's where you should stay—under our heels. Do you think we don't know everything you're planning? Consider this a warning and back off *now*."

Colt's eyes flashed. The newcomers didn't stir, seemingly content just to watch. They looked almost bored.

No, they weren't bodyguards. I frowned. It was almost as if they were supervising the situation rather than participating.

My ex-fiancé crossed his arms over his chest and flicked his icy stare toward me just for a moment before turning back to Wylder. "Am I to take it that you're siding with the Claws, then?"

"We're enforcing the power of the Nobles and the respect we're due," Wylder shot back.

"The Steel Knights have been instigating violence all over the Bend," Rowan said more evenly. "That isn't good for anyone—except maybe you, for now."

Colt chuckled darkly. "When was the Bend ever free of violence?"

"There used to be a lot less," I snapped.

Beside me, Kaige flexed his substantial muscles. "And it doesn't belong to you. You don't get to make decisions like that."

"Yet," Colt said. "I'm not a ruler. I definitely do not rule these men, if they happen to take offense." He gestured to the biker gang members flanking him. The threat was clear.

"But they wear marks of loyalty to you, so we'll hold you responsible all the same," Wylder replied. "And that includes my father. But if you'd like to have Ezra Noble and his full force cracking down on you within the hour..."

Colt's smile froze on his face. "I'm sure that won't be necessary today. You're always welcome to visit the Bend as you please. I have nothing but respect for the Nobles." He shifted his gaze to me again. "Rats are a totally different thing."

He made a brisk gesture, and some of the motorcycles eased out of our way. "You're free to leave."

Wylder's jaw ticked, but he didn't say anything. Picking a fight after Colt had stood down would make us look like the bad guys in this scenario, and we'd have a hard time winning anyway when we were so grossly outnumbered.

"I appreciate your recognition of what we're owed," Wylder said, and motioned to us. He stood there with his gun in his hand, never letting his attention waver from Colt while the rest of us slid into the car.

Only when Rowan had ignited the engine did Wylder come around to his seat. We cruised through the opening between the motorcycles—not too fast so we didn't give the appearance of running away. Colt even waved at us mockingly, but I saw the way his gaze remained on me, full of venom.

"Why did he let us go?" Kaige asked.

"He's not ready to go against us yet," Wylder said. "He knows the implications if he so much as even laid his hand on any of us. Even Mercy as long as she's with us."

"Did you notice the strange men who joined him at the end?" I asked.

"Yeah." Gideon rubbed his forehead. "What the fuck was up with them?"

My gut said it was nothing good.

Wylder looked deep in thought. "He's definitely brought in more people for backup. I'm not sure who they are, but I don't think they were from around here. He's biding his time while he gathers more manpower."

"I don't like it," Rowan said.

"Me neither." Wylder grimaced. "I don't know what he thinks he's got up his sleeve, but we'd better shut him down before he pushes this power grab of his even one step farther."

9

Mercy

Of course, taking Colt down was easier said than done, especially now that we'd seen he had some kind of mysterious backup dudes. The fact that Wylder was barely acknowledging my presence even when we were all having a conversation didn't help matters. I'd thought that stepping up and holding my own with them in the Bend might shake him out of his pissy mood, but if anything, he'd gotten worse.

He set his pawn down on the chessboard in Gideon's office firmly enough to make the other pieces wobble and looked around at the guys, his gaze skimming right over the spot where I was leaning against Gideon's long computer desk. "We haven't been able to pick up any word at all about who those new assholes were?"

Rowan shifted on his feet uneasily. "The most I could gather from my connections is that there are a bunch of them, and they started showing up around Colt in the past week. And everyone seems kind of scared of them, although no one's mentioned anything they've actually done that's scary."

Wylder let out a frustrated sound and turned back to the board, just as Gideon slid his bishop over to claim one of Wylder's knights. "I checked my databases and couldn't find any matches," the tech guy said, and lifted his chin toward the board. "Give up."

"You haven't won yet," Wylder muttered. There was no sound except the burbling of the massive aquarium's filter as he appeared to consider both the chessboard and the problems in the Bend.

"They had a vibe that was a lot more pulled together than any of the smaller gangs in the Bend anyway," I said. "They're obviously not from this area."

"Thank you so much for your brilliant insight," Wylder said, still without bothering to look at me, his sarcasm razor-sharp. "Why don't you go find something else to do, Princess? We can figure this out without your 'contributions.'"

Kaige raised his head, his forehead furrowed, and touched my forearm just for a second as if in reassurance. "*I* wouldn't have known that."

I glared at Wylder for a second and then focused on Gideon, since all he ever cared about was the facts anyway. "Have the Nobles had any run-ins with organizations farther out in the state, people who might want to get back at you?"

Gideon leaned back with a swipe of his slim fingers through his ragged blue hair. "I can't think of any major conflicts since I've been keeping track of things."

"It could be based on a conflict from a while ago," Rowan said. "Before any of us were really active in the gang. The Nobles have gathered a lot of power over the past several decades—it's hard to do that without stepping on people on the way up."

"Don't you think *I* would know if one of our neighbors had a major issue with our family?" Wylder said, as cutting as before. "Stay on track, and stop getting distracted."

Distracted by me and my supposedly useless comments, he meant. I bristled, but we did need to hash out the Colt problem, and that wasn't going to happen if I called him out in front of his friends. He'd probably double-down no matter what I said, but he definitely wasn't going to let himself lose any face in front of them.

"So what do *you* think then?" I demanded, because I wasn't going to just sit and keep quiet either. I plopped into one of the cushioned revolving chairs that Gideon had by his workstation.

"I think you shouldn't even be part of this conversation," he shot back, finally meeting my gaze with eyes hard as stone. "It's Noble business."

"I'm working with the Nobles now. Your own father initiated me." And the prick in front of me had told me I was one of them now just a few days ago. How had one quick fuck changed his attitude so completely?

"Let's go over everything that we saw yesterday first," Gideon said, diverting any further argument. He pushed away from the chessboard and grabbed his tablet off the desk. "Bryant had at least one motorcycle club backing him up too. Based on the iconography I spotted, they're local, operating out of a clubhouse in the southeast part of the Bend."

"But they were wearing the Steel Knights insignia too," Kaige pointed out. "They've really thrown in their lot with that jackass."

My stomach sank as I remembered what else I'd seen. "And there was at least one guy with Colt who used to be part of the Claws. I guess some of them have joined him now that there's no leadership." Let's be real, the Claws were essentially dead. I couldn't resurrect them all on my own.

"I guess that's not surprising," Rowan said, unexpectedly gentle.

Gideon fixed his cool gaze on me. "You said that while Bryant was holding you, he got a call and acted as if he might be following someone else's orders."

I nodded. "I'm not totally sure, but he wasn't talking to them like he was in charge of the conversation. He's obviously the one directing all the local outfits we've seen joining up with him. Maybe those outsiders have something to do with a larger gang from someplace else that's supporting him."

"Some chickenshit gang that won't confront us directly." Wylder scowled. "We'll string them up like chickens, then."

Gideon frowned at his tablet. "The question is why."

None of us spoke. Without knowing who these people were, it was hard to narrow down the possibilities.

Finally, Wylder shoved himself to his feet. "Like Rowan said, the

Nobles have gained a lot of power. When you've got that, there are always people who want to take it from you for themselves simply because they see an opening. We'll just have to close that opening fast—show them, whoever they are, that betting on Colt Bryant is a bad gamble. We need to hit the Steel Knights again, but harder and where it'll really hurt."

"I'll draw on all my resources to predict his next moves so we can interrupt them," Gideon said.

"Sounds great," Wylder said. With the meeting dismissed, he strode out of the room.

I hurried after him, ignoring Kaige's questioning glance. The Noble heir was walking so fast he'd already made it halfway down the hall. I had to jog to catch him. He didn't stop until I'd planted myself right in front of him.

"What is wrong with you?" I asked.

Wylder's jaw twitched. He looked like he was ready to kill me, or maybe kiss me as furiously as he had in the kitchen the other day. The memory of that moment and the way it made my pussy tighten just pissed me off more. I didn't know if my anger was directed at him or myself.

Wylder had made things more than clear. He didn't want anything to do with me. Time for my body to get the memo too.

I glowered at him. "Answer me. I feel like I'm talking to a wall. Why are you treating me like I'm useless? I've proven myself about a million times over by now."

Wylder's gaze smoldered right back at me. "And why should I care about that?"

I barely restrained a growl. "*You* told me I was part of the Nobles now. What happened to that?"

"Just because you've wormed your way into my home doesn't mean I have to entertain you," he replied, his voice cold.

"I'm not asking you to. I just want to be a part of everything that's going down against the Steel Knights." I folded my arms over my chest. "You know I'm capable. You told me yourself. Why are you treating me like this now?"

Wylder hesitated, and for a second I thought I might get an honest answer out of him. Then his lips curled with a sneer. "It's not my fault you bought into all that bullshit. I've gotten what I wanted from you. Now I'm done with you. Deal with it."

He spoke as if I were a doll he could use and throw away. Despite my determination not to care, pain and humiliation lanced through me.

Before I could think of what to say in response, Wylder pushed past me. "And I have more important things to take care of than your hurt feelings, Princess. Bryant, for starters. We can handle him just fine without you. You're only going to end up slowing us down."

He stalked off without a backward glance, leaving me burning with an uncomfortable mix of anger and shame.

He couldn't really mean even half of what he'd just said, could he? I remembered so clearly the way he'd acted when the guys had found me after I'd escaped from Colt, how carefully he'd looked me over, how much restrained fury had radiated from him. A man like Wylder didn't get that worked up over a woman he just saw as a one-time lay to use and discard.

And the way he'd held me in the kitchen, his promise that we'd destroy Colt together...

No, I couldn't believe all that had been an act. But the words he'd just hurled at me still jabbed deep. There had to be something else going on with him, some other reason he was acting like such a jerk... but he didn't trust me enough to tell me.

So in a way, I might as well be back where I'd started. Fuck. Fuck him, fuck this whole place.

I'd still be the one to make Colt pay, no matter what Wylder Noble had to say about it.

10

Kaige

LEANING AGAINST THE METAL FRAME OF THE FIRE ESCAPE, I stretched my arms above me and contained a deep sigh. After the events of the last week, I wanted to take a nap, preferably for several days.

It didn't help that I barely slept most nights. Sometimes I never bothered going to bed, because when I did I just kept tossing and turning. The hammock in the yard was a better bet to get in a few winks, but I wasn't tired enough to resort to that yet.

I lit the joint I'd rolled before climbing out here and took a long drag. The pungent smoke immediately tingled into my lungs and loosened my muscles.

The thought of the meeting we'd just had niggled at me, but what could I contribute to our plans against the Steel Knights? I was more brawn than brains. The others would come up with an effective strategy to take down Colt.

No, it wasn't the lack of answers that bothered me most about the meeting. Why had Wylder been laying into Mercy like that? The sense that I should have spoken up for her more itched at me, but it'd made so little sense after he'd finally accepted her into our group, I hadn't been sure if I was missing something. It wouldn't be the first time.

Whatever it was, I hoped that they'd be able to sort it out, or at least that Mercy could knock some sense into the dickhead. I hadn't liked the way he was talking to her at all.

Just as the evening darkened completely into night, a faint mew reached my ears. I grinned and fished the bag of cat treats out of my pocket. When I rattled it, the stray tabby I'd gradually made friends with came scampering up onto the fire escape landing near me. I tossed her a couple of treats, and she snapped them up, purring loud enough to wake the dead.

A window slid open farther down the landing. Mittens startled but then went right back to purring when she saw who it was. Somehow she'd warmed up to Mercy in just a few minutes when it'd taken her months with me.

But then, maybe I couldn't blame the cat for that. Mercy leaned out, strands of her dark brown hair falling loose from her ponytail in a way that made me long to brush them back behind her ear. And then kiss her. And then a whole lot more than kiss her. This woman was the most perfect combination of beautiful and kickass I'd ever met.

Right now, though, she looked like she might be considering kicking *my* ass. She paused, worrying at her lip, which drew my gaze straight to that lush mouth. I yanked it back to her eyes before she caught me leering. "Hey."

"Hey." She glanced around. "I—I just wanted to get a little space. I'll leave you to it."

"No, no, there's plenty of space out here," I said before she could duck back inside. "Look at me. I barely take up any!"

I spread my arms, showing off my expansive chest and shoulders—we both knew I was actually the biggest guy around here now—and Mercy's lips twitched with a smile like I'd hoped they would. Her gaze stayed wary, though. "If you're sure...?"

I guessed we hadn't been on the best of terms lately. Which was my fault for flying off the handle at her over stupid Gia's lies. I restrained the urge to grit my teeth in frustration at myself and beckoned her out. "Absolutely. And I know Mittens could use your company too."

She looked down at the cat who'd started rubbing herself against the window ledge, still purring, and laughed. "Well, I can't turn *her* down."

As she clambered through the window, I moved to crush my blunt under the sole of my combat boots, but Mercy stopped me, reaching for it instead. "Can I have a drag of that?"

I raised my brow. "This is pretty potent stuff."

She just scowled and made a gimme gesture, so I handed it over. I expected her to cough, but she took a long, slow drag and hummed contentedly. I really should have known her better by now.

"You know, no other woman could have managed to stick with us for as long as you have," I had to say. When she raised a brow, I added, "I don't mean anything sexist by that."

"Women are much stronger than you think," she said with a faraway look.

Something about her tone made my gut twinge. "I'm sorry for how I acted before," I blurted out. "For how angry I got and how I talked to you after Gia made her accusations. And all the other stuff. You didn't deserve that. I mean, it's impressive that you were strong enough not to let it faze you too badly, but you still shouldn't have had to put up with it."

Mercy shrugged. "Your first loyalty is to Wylder, and you were following his orders, defending him when you thought you had to. I didn't enjoy it, but I'm not mad at you over it."

That was a relief. It didn't feel like I'd said enough, though. I groped for something else to say that might completely fix things between us. "I shouldn't ever have called you weak, that's for sure. Just because of that one thing with the freezer—I mean, we all have at least one weakness."

Mercy cocked her head. "Oh, yeah? What's yours?"

I gave her a crooked smile. "I can't sleep. Why do you think I down all those energy drinks? Gotta keep myself alert."

"Did you ever think it could be that all those energy drinks are what's stopping you from sleeping?"

"People might have mentioned it once or twice," I muttered, and reached to take the joint back. "But if I don't have any, then I'm sluggish and I *still* don't sleep. So I'll take what I can get."

She hummed to herself. "I don't think that's quite on the same level as melting down over small spaces."

I debated for a second before letting the question tumble out. "Have you just always had a thing about tight spaces, or did something happen...?" Rowan's reaction in the moment had given me the impression he knew more about the situation than we did—and that there was more to it than a simple phobia.

Mercy swiped her hand across her mouth, her expression darkening, and I immediately regretted the question. "Never mind. You don't have to—"

"No, it's fine," she said, but there was an artificial flatness to her even tone. She squared her shoulders. "I've told you before that my dad wasn't happy he only had a girl for an heir. When he wasn't training me, which he only did because he couldn't stand to have a total wimp as a kid, he came up with ways to take his frustrations out on me. One of his favorites was dumping me in a pit he had in the basement floor, about the size of a coffin. He'd shut me in there for hours on end."

The hairs on the back of my neck stood on end. I'd thought my parents were fucked up, but they'd never buried me alive, for Christ's sake. "That sounds horrible."

"Oh, it was. He mostly used it for torturing people who crossed him, and he never cleaned it up, so there was dried blood and piss and vomit down there. And it was totally dark once he got the concrete slab that closed it in place." She looked down at her fingertips, and I remembered the faint scars interlaced across them that were only visible in brighter light. "It was mostly when I was a kid. I'd scratch the hell out of my fingers trying to get out, crying and begging him, but he'd just laugh and leave."

"Fuck," I said, at a loss for any other words. I could imagine a younger version of Mercy being locked up in that pit, crying out for help, clawing hopelessly until her fingertips bled.

But she'd survived it. She'd survived it and come out fierce and otherwise unshakeable. She was even stronger than I'd realized.

My stomach had twisted into one huge knot. "I'm so sorry, Mercy. I know the words aren't enough, but I am."

She gave me a tight smile. "It's fine, you didn't know."

"Doing that stuff to a kid—didn't anyone ever try to stop him?" Of course, nobody had helped me either.

"He didn't do the worst stuff in front of other people," she said. "And I didn't really have anyone anyway. Well, except Grandma. She took care of me and saved me from Dad's wrath whenever she could, but she couldn't completely stop him. And that bastard Colt had her killed as if *she* was any kind of threat to him." Anguish tensed her features. She ducked her head.

I had the strongest urge to run my hands over her hair and pull her to me, as if that would comfort her.

Why shouldn't I try? If she was still too wary of me to be okay with it, she'd shake me off.

Tentatively, as if she were a wild creature I might accidentally spook, I reached for her. My fingers grazed the side of her head. When she didn't flinch at my touch, I stroked them over the silky strands.

Mercy raised her head, and I let my hand fall, but I thought she scooted a tiny bit closer to me. We sat for a moment in silence, watching as the stars came up. Then Mercy looked at me again and cleared her throat. "I had sex with Wylder."

I froze at her confession, something ugly rearing in me. For a second, all I saw was red. I wanted to smash my fist through a wall or maybe Wylder's face.

But I didn't own her. I'd thrown her away. And Wylder had clearly noticed all her assets from the moment she'd joined us just like I had. Why shouldn't she hook up with him if he'd gone for it?

He had the name—he was a hell of a lot smarter than I was, and almost as good a fighter. Not that Mercy probably cared about that part. Argh.

I rubbed my forehead, forcing my breaths to stay even and shoving away the images that tried to rise up of Mercy staring at Wylder with the same expression she'd made when she'd come with me inside her, her eyes glazed with pleasure. When I dared to look at her again, she was watching me closely, her eyes flitting over my face as if to detect any sort of emotional upheaval I might be having.

There was a fucking hurricane inside of me, but I managed to hold it in. Then I remembered how he'd been treating her lately. A scowl crossed my face. "Before or after he started laying into you left and right?"

A startled guffaw slipped out of her. "Before," she said wryly. "He's got another thing coming if he figures I'm going to go for it again after the way he's been acting. I don't know—it was a spur of the moment thing, and ever since he's been acting like I have the plague. So that's been fun. It's not like I made any promises or commitments to him or whatever. I just thought you should know. You can make whatever you want of it. *I* don't see why I should have to be tied down to one guy anyway."

Wait. Was she implying... that she'd want to hook up with *me* again?

I couldn't help noticing how luscious her lips looked as she sucked the lower one under her teeth. I wanted to grab her and plant my mouth right on her until she was moaning for my cock.

But with everything she'd revealed tonight and all the messed-up history between us, I balked in a moment of indecision. In that moment, Mercy stood up. She leaned against the railing, gazing out over the lawn.

I got up too, meaning to tug her closer to me, but then her stance abruptly stiffened. "What?" I asked, following her gaze.

She pointed. "There's something in the grass there, right across from my bedroom window. Do you see it?"

I did. In the hazy light at the edge of the security lamps' range, a dark shape showed against the green of the lawn. I couldn't tell what it was from here, but something about it set my nerves on edge. "Yeah. Should we check it out?"

I almost wished she'd say no, but Mercy was already hefting herself over the railing. She eased down the other side of the landing and then took the several-foot drop to the ground below like it was nothing.

With all my bulk, I wasn't pulling off a move that nimble. "Wait for me," I told her, hoping she'd listen, and hustled inside to take the stairs.

When I came around from the front door, Mercy was where I'd left her, thank God. We headed over to the strange shape together. An unnerving smell trickled into my nose, sour and almost meaty. My stomach turned.

Then the form in the grass came into clear enough focus for me to recognize it for what it was.

A cat's body lay on the lawn, flies buzzing around it. It'd been sliced open down the middle with its guts spilling all over the place, its skull smashed open—and its tail completely gone.

There'd been a cat's tail stuck to Mercy's window less than a week ago. I'd told myself it must have been Gia, but Gia was gone, and someone had left this here since the last security patrol. My jaw clenched with a surge of protective rage.

Whoever was targeting Mercy so gruesomely, they were still around.

11

Mercy

ANTHEA CAREFULLY PRODDED THE CAT'S MANGLED BODY with a stick. A renewed waft of the rotten flesh stink drifted up, and my stomach twisted all over again.

"It's not a fresh kill," she said. "How long ago was it that you found the tail on your window?"

I rubbed my hand over my face, trying to clear my head. The security lamps cast a faint yellow glow over this part of the lawn that only made the situation more eerie. "I found it when I woke up the same day I figured out things about Gia."

"Then I'd guess the cat was already dead or killed shortly after the perpetrator cut off the tail. They were saving the rest until now." Anthea's nose wrinkled.

Kaige was pacing back and forth on the lawn, his muscles flexing with tension I knew he must be dying to let out. "Who the hell could have done this? Why are they doing it?"

"It obviously wasn't Gia," I said. Unless her ghost had come back from the dead to haunt me.

Anthea didn't suggest that possibility. She sighed and looked around the lawn again, but after Kaige had called her out to make use of her forensics expertise, she'd already gone over the whole area thoroughly. "I haven't found any evidence pointing to the perp. They were careful about it. All I know is that from the looks of the entrails, they left the cat whole until just before they placed it here."

Kaige let out a growl. "It's obviously a threat toward Mercy. Katz—a dead cat. Even *I* can figure that one out."

"There was a creepy drawing someone shoved through my window too," I said, remembering with a jolt. "A couple of days before the tail. It was a girl with cat ears and her neck sliced open."

"I'd say it's very likely it was all the same person," Anthea said. "There are a lot of sickos out there, but they tend to indulge their inclinations alone." She tossed the gory stick aside and swiped her hands together, her voice getting that deadly tone that made me glad *she* no longer had it out for me. "It doesn't matter. We protect our own. Whoever thought it was a good idea to harass Mercy like this is going to die."

At the rustle of footsteps, I glanced up. Rowan was hurrying toward us from the house with a concerned expression. "I saw you from the window. What's going on out here?" Then he spotted the cat and stopped in his tracks. "What the hell?"

"Mercy's stalker is upping his game," Kaige said grimly, and paused. "Or her game. It couldn't have been Gia, but what about the other groupies? If one of them could have killed Titus, who knows what the others might get up to?"

"I won't discount the possibility," Anthea said. "You can be sure I'll interrogate them thoroughly." Her eyes gleamed as if she was looking forward to it. I wouldn't be surprised if she was. "Our known enemies seem like the most likely option, though."

Of course. "Colt," I said, a surge of anger racing through me. No matter where I went, he couldn't stop hounding me.

"That bastard," Kaige snapped. "I'll tear him open like he did that cat."

"Let's not do anything crazy when we don't have definite answers," Rowan said. "Shouldn't the security cameras have picked up whoever did it?" He glanced toward the house.

I frowned. We'd been too distracted the day of the cat tail to end up checking. "You'd think so, wouldn't you?" I glanced at the cat and restrained a shudder. I needed to get away from it, away from the reminder of what some insane person apparently wanted to do to me. Raising my chin, I stepped back and took on a brisk tone. "I'll go talk to Gideon. I wanted to check how things are going with his investigations into the Steel Knights anyway."

Rowan shot me a worried glance. "Are you going to be okay?"

He sounded genuinely concerned, but I wasn't about to open up to the guy who'd already crushed my heart once, no matter how much he'd eased off on me recently.

"Yeah," I said. "Nothing happened to me. It's the cat that got torn up."

Anthea gave the furry corpse a sympathetic grimace. "Poor thing."

Kaige moved as if he was going to offer to come with me, but even though I'd been feeling pretty comfortable with him on the fire escape just a half hour ago, our discovery had left my skin twitching. I needed space, and he wasn't the best at giving it.

"Why don't you make a larger sweep of the property and see if you turn anything up?" I suggested, not really thinking it'd accomplish much but aiming to keep him busy.

He perked up a little with the thought of taking action. "Good idea. I'll grab a flashlight and get right on it."

I set off for the house before anyone else could try to join me. It wasn't that late yet, and I suspected that Gideon regularly stayed up to the wee hours tapping away at his keyboard and tablet. He didn't like to leave work unfinished—that much I'd gathered.

We weren't exactly friendly, but at least he wasn't the type to play games. I could count on getting straight answers from him and a minimum of bullshit.

I knocked on his office door and got a distracted-sounding "Come in." When I pushed it open, I found him exactly where I'd expected, poised in front of his multiple monitors with his fingers racing over the keyboard and his eyes flicking from screen to screen. A fresh cup of the coffee he made so precisely was steaming away in easy reach.

His gaze darted to me just long enough to see who'd come in, then veered back to his work. "Did you need something?" he asked in his usual disinterested tone.

I kicked the door shut and sank into the wheeled chair at the end of the desk closest to me. "A couple of things, actually. First off, could you check the surveillance footage for the east side of the house?"

Gideon's hands paused over the keyboard. He gave me a longer, analytical look. "What for?"

"Someone left a dead cat on the lawn across from my bedroom window," I said. "The one that used to be connected to the tail that was stuck to my window almost a week ago, it looks like. I'm hoping the cameras will show who did it."

A hint of something more intense sparked in Gideon's eyes. He frowned and swiveled back toward his computer. "They should have. Pretty much every inch of the outside property is covered by those cameras."

He brought up a few feeds on different monitors and rewound them all at the same time. We quickly spotted Kaige, Anthea, Rowan and me gathered around the spot. The camera showed a clear view of the area all around the cat—there was no way someone could have dropped it there without coming into view.

Gideon flicked his tongue over his lip ring in a way that momentarily distracted me from our quest. "Let's see… The last patrol in that area would have been two and a half hours ago, so if we go back through that whole time frame, we should—"

He cut himself off, pausing the video. He'd rewound to the spot where one of the Noble men was clearly visible ambling along in his circuit of the grounds. I hadn't noticed anyone on the video before then.

"Is the cat already there and he just didn't notice?" I asked.

Gideon squinted at the screen and zoomed it in. "No. It's not there yet." He sounded puzzled and a little annoyed. "It didn't appear out of nowhere. They must have just been really fast. If I go forward through the footage a little more slowly…"

He fast-forwarded, and we both peered at the screen. Nothing much changed other than the leaves on the one tree in frame swaying with the breeze. Then—out of nowhere, despite what he'd said—suddenly there was a dark shape in the grass.

Gideon's mouth tightened. Without saying a word, he rewound and played the footage at that spot again, this time flipping through it what appeared to be frame by frame.

I hadn't seen wrong. One moment, the lawn was empty. The next, there was the cat. And no sign of anyone near it.

"What the fuck?" I said, leaning forward as if looking closer would change anything.

Gideon frowned and flipped back and forth through the footage there a couple of times. Then he swore.

"What?" I demanded.

He motioned to the tree. "Watch the leaves. Damn it. I never thought—fucking *damn it.*"

He sounded so frustrated I didn't dare ask anything else, just watched.

The footage played, the branches swayed in the breeze—and then they seemed to give a slight hitch as if there'd been a hiccup in the recording.

I blinked. "Someone... cut out part of the footage?"

"Something like that," Gideon said, his voice now taut. "No one could have messed with the actual footage after it'd been recorded. I have *that* system perfectly secure with multiple backups. But the cameras are digital. They send the feed to the hard drive over the network. My best guess is, whoever did it was able to briefly interrupt that signal."

"That's possible?"

"Yes. Almost impossible to avoid unless you hardwire all the cameras, which Ezra didn't want because then they can be interfered with physically." Gideon sighed. "Most people don't know how or have the tech to do it. And they must have moved fast so that no one would notice anything more than a website taking a little longer than usual to load."

His hands clenched. "I'll tell Ezra to increase the on-the-ground patrols. And that we'll need to add a few cameras with full wiring so we're covered in both ways. I should have insisted on that to begin with."

His obvious agitation sent a twinge through my chest. I'd seen how much he prided himself in his thoroughness. "It isn't your fault. I get the impression Ezra doesn't listen to much of anyone other than himself anyway."

Gideon's gaze jerked to me as if he was startled to hear anyone talk about the big boss so flippantly. Then his stance relaxed just a tad. "You might have a point there. Still, it's an oversight that obviously needs to be rectified now." He glanced at the time. "Or early tomorrow morning. Ezra won't be happy if I disturb him this late. I suppose it's unlikely this person will strike again in the same day. Maybe you should switch rooms, though. Just in case."

Was he actually... concerned for my safety? I guessed he had seemed a little relieved to find me safe and sound the other day.

"Good point," I said. "I'm not going to bed just yet, though. I did also want to ask if you've made any progress figuring out how we can strike at Colt. I'm especially enthusiastic about getting on with that now, since he's the only one I can think of who'd have much motive to be leaving me bloody presents."

A pleased gleam came into Gideon's eyes, and a small smile curled his lips. Oh, good, at least I'd given him one thing he was happy to talk about.

"I've made significant progress, actually," he said. "I'm still sifting through the data so that I have as accurate a picture as possible, but I've already seen clear evidence that the Steel Knights are going to receive a shipment that's very important to them soon."

"A shipment we could interrupt," I said with a smile of my own. "Sounds perfect."

"I think so. Just a matter of determining exactly when it's coming in and where." He shot a look at the screens that was just shy of maniacal. "While they're playing stupid pranks on the lawn, we're going to come down on them so hard they won't know what hit them. I'm keeping a close eye on all the activity around the major highways."

A prickle of memory passed through my mind. "It won't be coming on the roads."

Gideon raised an eyebrow at me. "What are you talking about?"

"Anything particularly important, Colt would have his people delivering it at the docks on the river. He's got some people there under his thumb—it's easier to avoid random checks or something."

Now it was Gideon's turn to blink at me. "How do you know that?"

I leaned back in my chair. "I *was* engaged to him for a year, you know. He didn't talk business much with me, but I was around him a lot. I listen well."

"Huh." Gideon's hand darted over his tablet. "I'll take that into account, then. We wouldn't want to ambush them right in the docks area, of course. Too easy for us to end up surrounded. But the most likely route through to the main Steel Knights holdings in the Bend from there would be..." He brought up a map on one of the larger screens and drew his finger through the air to trace a few streets.

I considered it and then shook my head. "Not quite. There's a pocket of Black Jacks territory through there, and they're one outfit that won't have thrown their lot in with the Steel Knights no matter what. There's a longstanding rivalry between them because of something Colt's dad did ages before Colt even inherited the leadership. He's tried to make peace—tried to open a conversation with them just a few months ago, but they just sent him back the head of his messenger."

Gideon eyed me for a moment with an appraising air. It was hard not to feel like I'd be coming up short under that piercing stare. But then his smile returned, a little wider this time. "It seems like it's a good thing you stopped by. I should have asked you to weigh in with your inside knowledge of the Bend to begin with."

From him, that was practically a love letter. Weirdly exhilarated by the praise, I grinned at him. "If it helps reduce Colt and his men to smithereens, I'm all in."

Something shifted in Gideon's expression that I couldn't read. He jerked his gaze away, but when he spoke, his voice didn't sound quite as cool as before. "I wonder if we could make use of the Black Jacks against Bryant then."

I hummed to myself. "I don't think there'd be much point. They're a pretty small outfit—they wouldn't add much to what the Nobles can do on their own. And they seem to prefer to stick to their own business.

They'd push back against Colt if he came into their territory, but they haven't come out of theirs to attack him. Unless he strikes against them directly, I don't think we'd get more than grudging help out of them."

"Better to rely on our own power, then." Gideon slid his thumb along his mouth, drawing my attention there again. "I just have to make sure that I can narrow down the arrival window before they actually bring the goods through."

"I'm sure you'll figure it out with plenty of time," I said. "You always seem to be one step ahead of everyone else."

He looked surprised, and then his eyes softened. "Everyone except you, it's starting to seem. But thanks for your confidence."

I never would have expected it, but the vibe between us had gotten almost… comfortable. Maybe we could be friendly after all. Me and Wylder's closest friend…

The question tumbled out before I could second-guess the impulse. "Do you know what's up with Wylder lately? He's been acting kind of… strange with me." I hesitated to use the more accurate words like "asshole" and "prick," considering Gideon's loyalty to his boss and best friend.

Gideon's smile vanished. "I have noticed that," he said after a moment. "I don't know what to tell you."

I held up my hands. "I get that you don't want to criticize him behind his back or whatever. I'm not asking you to. But you know him a lot better than I do. I was just wondering if I should push back against the attitude or ignore it or…? Whatever will mean the least amount of mind games going forward."

Gideon hesitated again, and I could tell he knew something I didn't. He sucked in a breath. "All I can say is that I'm honestly not sure what would work—or if there is anything—but you probably shouldn't take it personally."

I snorted. How was I supposed to not take it personally when Wylder personally insulted me straight to my face? But when Gideon didn't elaborate, it appeared the conversation was over.

"Okay," I said, getting up. "Thanks all the same—and for checking the footage for me. It was… actually kind of nice chatting with you."

As I reached for the doorknob, Gideon spoke. "Mercy… You should know this much. I don't believe his current attitude has anything to do with your competence or his enjoyment of your company. You haven't done anything wrong."

Somehow, hearing that from him was weirdly reassuring even if I didn't know what to make of it.

"Thanks," I repeated, meaning it, and left his office with my emotions even more jumbled up than before.

12

Mercy

Three nights later, I found myself with the guys in Rowan's car heading into the Bend again—although this time Gideon was with us only via speakerphone.

"The timing of the ships is rarely exact," he said through a faint hum of static. "You'll want to make sure to get into position within the hour."

"We're only twenty minutes away now," Wylder replied. "It shouldn't be a problem." His voice still held a bit of the edge that had crept into it when we'd had yet another argument about me coming along before we'd left.

This time, Gideon had cut it short by saying that my knowledge of the Bend made me invaluable and that Wylder would be an idiot not to have me there. It might have been funny seeing how quickly Wylder shut up at the unexpected criticism from his right-hand man if I hadn't been so annoyed that he was still acting like a jackass to begin with.

"What about the other car?" Gideon asked. Ezra had ever-so-generously allowed Wylder a contingent of Noble underlings to assist with the mission.

Rowan glanced in the rearview mirror. "Only a block behind us."

"Good, good." I could picture Gideon skimming through footage and data on his various screens with his smooth face in that perfectly focused expression of determination. "We're still not sure exactly what the shipment *contains*, so—"

"We went over this already, Gideon," Wylder said, his voice softening a little with a fond tone I didn't often hear in it. He might have wanted to toss me in the trash, but there was no denying his bond with his best friend. "All the extra details, we'll figure out once we're there."

Gideon made a disgruntled sound as if he didn't see that as a solid strategy.

As we drove on through the glow of the streetlamps outside, Kaige reached across the back seat to give my hand a quick squeeze. The affection in the gesture sent an unexpected wobble through my pulse.

When we'd talked the other night on the fire escape, he'd seemed to honestly regret his harsh behavior—and I really did understand that instantaneous aggression in defense of his people was just Kaige's default setting. And something I kind of liked about him, if *I* was being honest. The thought of him seeing me as one of his people now sent a flood of warmth down through my torso to tingle between my thighs.

Not that he was going *there* any time tonight. But... maybe later we could pick up where we'd left off. Just to blow off some steam when we needed it.

Abruptly, Gideon muttered a curse.

Wylder's posture snapped straighter. "What is it?"

"There's a cop car cruising around within a few blocks of the ambush spot. If there's gunfire, they'd hear it for sure. There must have been a call for some other reason—this isn't their typical route."

"We'll handle it," Wylder said with the smooth confidence I'd once —and, okay, still—found so goddamned sexy. He glanced back at Kaige. "Are you good to provide a diversion?"

Kaige grinned, his eyes lighting up. "My second favorite job."

That sounded a little ominous in terms of what the diversion might involve. But Wylder was already gesturing to Rowan, who pulled over to the curb. Kaige was pushing open the door before the Toyota had even rolled to a stop.

"You know where to find us after," Wylder said. "Be quick about it."

Still grinning, Kaige gave him a thumbs up and disappeared into the night. I looked at Rowan, knowing Wylder was less likely to give me a real answer. "What's he going to do?"

Rowan's mouth slanted into a crooked smile. "Create a disturbance that'll lead the cops far enough away for us to pull off the job. Knowing him, it'll probably involve at least one explosion."

Oh goodie.

As we sped down the last short distance to the ambush spot, my pulse thumped in my veins. I was so ready for this. A real strike against the Steel Knights, a chance to knock the sneer right off Colt's face. And while he was reeling, maybe I'd get the chance to eviscerate him before much longer.

The Bend's dock area was a sprawling compound arcing around a curve in the river. It had only one exit and just a few routes that made sense to take when driving away from the spot, and Gideon had picked a place for us to lie in wait that should put us right in the truck's path or at least where we could see if it took an unexpected turn before it reached us.

Rowan parked by the curb in a dark patch beneath a broken streetlamp. The other car with our extra men stopped farther down the street.

I settled deeper into my seat. We were going to have at least a bit of a wait. We'd given ourselves lots of extra time since we didn't want to miss the shipment. My fingers automatically traced over the small lump of my bracelet from my mother in the opposite pocket from my knife. I definitely wasn't anyone's *Little Angel* now. What would she have thought if she'd known I'd end up here?

Or maybe, given who my father was, this was the best she'd have ever hoped for me.

"We're in position," Wylder said to Gideon. "I'm switching to the headset now. Ping me if you see anything of concern." He ended the call and adjusted the mic in his ear.

"You can make out the edge of the wall around the docks down at the end of the street there," I said, raising my chin toward it. "The entrance is just to the right. We should see the truck carrying Colt's cargo well before it gets here."

"Assuming you were right about him avoiding the Black Jacks' area," Wylder said, his voice hard again. "You'd better hope your expert advice didn't screw this up for us, Princess."

It'd used to irritate me when he called me Kitty Cat. Now I wished he'd go back to it.

"I still contributed more to this plan than *you* did, Prince Noble," I shot back.

"I'm sure we'll have a better chance regardless if we're focused on the plan rather than jumping down each other's throats," Rowan said in the mild way he had that made any argument seem silly.

Wylder let out a faint growl, but he shut his mouth after that. I couldn't help remembering how much I'd wanted to deep-throat a certain part of him just a few days ago. A flush I didn't approve of at all swept through my body.

Even if it'd turned Wylder into an even more epic prick than before, it'd still been an amazing fuck.

A boom thundered in the distance. My head jerked toward the rearview mirror, but I couldn't see anything out there.

"That must be Kaige," Wylder said with a satisfied air.

Explosions—right. It'd definitely been audible here but far enough away that we could hope the cops would be out of hearing range of anything we got up to once they followed Kaige on his little chase.

Another boom reached my ears, this one even more distant. I strained my hearing, listening for another. A random car rumbled past us down the street. Hinges creaked somewhere nearby. I must have been braced there several minutes when a huge figure emerged from the darkness and yanked open the door across from me.

My heart just about flipped over before I recognized Kaige. He was grinning like he'd never stopped from the moment he left the car, which maybe he hadn't. "Mission accomplished," he announced, sliding into the seat.

A curiosity I couldn't deny tugged at me. "What did you blow up?"

He chuckled. "A few cars. Rich asshole types like we normally drive, so I'm sure the owners deserved it."

Wylder snorted. "How Robin Hood of you."

"Hey, gotta think of the common people."

Rowan raised his hand to catch our attention. "Movement," he said, motioning to the windshield.

A beige delivery truck rounded the corner several blocks away. We all tensed in our seats, Rowan's hands tightening around the steering wheel, Wylder getting out his gun.

"Get ready," the Noble heir told the other car over his phone. Then he swiveled to look at me. "Since you're only here to share your insights, you stay in the car unless it's absolutely necessary. I don't want you getting in the way. Understood?"

I bristled, but the truth was, he had a bit of a point. I'd never been allowed to be part of any of the operations my father had run. I didn't have anywhere near the level of experience these guys had in this kind of organized mission, even if I could hold my own in a fight.

"Fine," I bit out. "But the second it looks like you need me out there, I'm jumping in."

"Oh, don't worry. I highly doubt we'll *need* you," he drawled.

I resisted the urge to smack the back of his arrogant head, only for the sake of not screwing up the operation.

The truck drove on toward us. I braced myself for it to take an unexpected turn and for Wylder to snark at me as we course-corrected, but the vehicle stayed on the route we'd expected. As it reached us, I found myself holding my breath.

The second it passed us, the guys sprang out of the car. At the same moment, the other Noble car tore into the middle of the road, blocking the truck's path.

The driver tried to veer around them and then lurched to a halt at an angle. Wylder and the others dashed over. Shouts echoed through the street, followed by a sputter of gunfire.

I peered through the rearview window, watching the bodies fade in and out of the shadows. Had they gotten everyone in the truck? Was it already over?

A creeping sensation ran up my arms. That seemed too easy.

But it appeared that we really were done already. Wylder came into view by the back of the truck with a pleased smirk. He raised the door to the cargo area and hopped in to check out the goods.

Since the danger appeared to be over, I figured he couldn't snark too much about me joining them now. Keeping my gun in my hand out of caution, I stepped out of the car and walked over. "What were they bringing in?" I asked.

Wylder leapt back out and yanked the door shut. He was in a good enough mood with the success of the mission to forget that he was supposed to hate me now. "Some kind of drug," he said, clapping his hands together triumphantly. "We'll have to take a closer look at it when we're back on our home turf. For now, all that matters is it's in *our* hands, not—"

Tires screeched, and three cars raced around the nearest corner. Bullets thundered from their open windows.

"Take shelter!" Wylder hollered, already diving around the side of the truck. I ducked down next to him, my breath catching in my throat.

I'd been right that everything had gone too easily, but I wasn't exactly happy about that fact. Where were Rowan and Kaige? I couldn't see them anymore—they must have found something else to shield them, right?

I peeked around the rear of the truck. Men were spilling out of the cars now—at least a dozen of them with red bandanas around their arms charging up the street toward us. Almost everyone already had a gun out, pointed towards us. Fuck.

A bullet whizzed past my head as I pulled back just in time. I cocked my own gun, a tremor running through my body. I'd killed a man before, yes—but just the one, and not with a bullet. I'd never shot at anything other than paper targets and tin cans.

I could do this. I was Mercy Katz, Princess of the fucking Claws, and I was going to take down as many of the treacherous motherfuckers out there as I possibly could.

Wylder had already shouldered past me and was shooting at the incoming Steel Knights. A few of the other Nobles hustled over, returning fire at the enemy. As I watched, Wylder put a bullet right in the center of one guy's forehead as easily as if it were a target on his shooting range. He didn't show the slightest reaction to the killing.

Why should he? This was his job—and he was damn good at it.

Engines roared somewhere beyond my view. More men ran at us from a side-street in the other direction.

"Get up front," Wylder called to me. "Hold them off. We can't let them take the truck back."

The truck seemed to be less of a problem than making sure they didn't take our lives, but I followed his orders anyway. I dashed around the cab.

Rowan stepped forward. I had a moment's relief seeing that he was okay, but he wasn't looking my way. He raised his gun and took two men down with swift, clean shots, his expression intent. It was surreal to see the boy I had grown up with kill without a moment's hesitation.

He glanced over and saw me watching, but I couldn't look away. What looked like guilt flashed across his face before it was replaced with determination.

Who was I to judge him anyway? I was a killer, just like them. And if we didn't kill these assholes, they were definitely going to kill *us*.

Three more Steel Knights hurtled into sight. A jolt of recognition hit me—I knew the guy in the middle. I'd seen him hanging around with some of the other Claws lackeys by my house now and then. Jenner wasn't the only one who'd switched sides and given his loyalty to the man who'd destroyed us.

I fired a few shots and managed to catch one of the other Steel Knights in the shoulder, but my heart was beating so fast it was hard to keep my arms steady. They were everywhere. How the hell were we going to get out of this?

I glanced at the door of the truck's cab next to me, still hanging open with the dead Steel Knight guard slumped on the pavement beneath it, and something clicked in my head. They were all here to protect their shipment. If we got the shipment away from them, we'd have won.

I might not be a fantastic shot yet, but I sure as hell knew how to drive.

More shots rang out on both sides. I dove into the cab and found the driver had dropped the keys on the floor—probably as he'd been riddled with bullets. He was still sprawled halfway out the other door. I kicked his slack body the rest of the way out, reached to yank the door shut—and a Steel Knight appeared, his gun cocked and pointed at me.

"Don't move, or I'm going to blow your brains out," he said.

Oh, hell no to that. I froze as if I were complying. The second his gun hand wavered, relaxing with the thought that he had me, I kicked him right in the face as hard as I could.

He staggered backward with a violent curse and then jerked with two bullets that caught him in the chest. As he collapsed, Kaige dashed into view, his eyes wild. "You okay?"

"Yeah," I said breathlessly. "Just going to get this thing out of here."

"I'll cover you."

He ran around to the passenger side, getting in another few shots as he went. I yanked my door shut and jammed the key into the ignition. As Kaige lunged into the cab with me, a bullet punctured the window next to me, whizzing by so close I'd swear it grazed the wisps of hair along my forehead.

I should have been terrified. Any sane person would have been. But instead what swept through me then was a surge of adrenaline so potent I let out a keening battle cry. Then I rammed my foot down on the gas.

The truck heaved forward with more speed than I'd anticipated. Kaige swore and grabbed the side of the door for dear life. I whirled the truck sharply to the left and the right, clipping a couple of Steel Knights in my way. Then I aimed it toward the small gap between the Noble car and the sidewalk. "I hope Ezra thinks this shipment is worth a little damage."

Kaige fired out the window and glanced at me. "What are you—"

The wheels on one side of the cab jumped the curb. The other side smashed into the trunk of the car. I spun the steering wheel, missing a telephone pole by inches. The truck shuddered—and then we were past the whole mess, speeding down a nearly empty stretch of street so fast the wind whistled past the broken windows.

"Holy shit," Kaige said in a voice that was nothing but awe. "You're insane." He let out a delighted guffaw and leaned out the window to fire a few shots to pick off people behind us. "The Steel Knights are on the run now. The ones we didn't kill, anyway. Wylder and Rowan are heading to Rowan's car."

A giddy smile stretched across my face, the crazy thrill of the moment still reverberating through my body. "Get them on the phone, then, and find out where the hell Wylder wants me to take this thing."

But as I slowed to take a corner, not wanting to flip the truck in the process, my exhilaration faded a little. The memory of the Claws guy rose up in my mind.

How could any of our people have taken the Steel Knights' side after what Colt had done? Were they really that despicable?

Or was it possible they didn't even know what had really gone down on the night of my rehearsal dinner?

13

Mercy

By the time Kaige had directed me to a small, inconspicuous warehouse on the outskirts of Paradise City and we'd parked the truck inside, Rowan had caught up with us in his car. He and Wylder ambled into the narrow loading bay, Wylder jerking the garage-style door shut behind them.

I looked them over quickly, trying not to let him see me checking for wounds. I didn't want to show I cared, but I was relieved to see that other than a scrape on Rowan's forehead and a ruddy blotch on Wylder's arm that was on the verge of bruising, they appeared to have made it through the shoot-out uninjured.

"Did all of the Noble people get out okay?" I asked, assuming they'd been in touch with the men from the other car.

Rowan nodded. "One of them took a bullet to the thigh and another had his ear clipped, but nothing Frank can't deal with."

Kaige chuckled as he opened up the back of the truck. "We gave out a hell of a lot better than we got."

He climbed into the truck and opened up a crate that must have been one Wylder had opened earlier, its lid came off so easily. He picked up a baggie of pale gray powder and made a face. "Is this whole truck full of this stuff?"

"It looks like," Wylder said. "I'm guessing it's that new drug we've started hearing about on the streets. They're calling it Glory, right? Bryant would have been counting on getting a lot of funding for his operations out of selling this load. Not anymore." He grinned viciously.

Kaige opened the baggie with unusual care and took a quick sniff. "Holy shit, I can already tell that's strong stuff." He shook his head, his expression darkening. "So what are we doing with it? I vote that we incinerate the whole load."

Having seen his fondness for weed, I was surprised he wasn't advocating we all party with it, but maybe harder drugs weren't his thing.

Wylder motioned for him to get out of the truck and shut it again, sticking a padlock on the door for good measure. "For now, we hang on to it until we decide the best way to make use of it. No point in destroying a potential resource."

Kaige grumbled wordlessly but didn't say anything else.

"At least losing all this should slow the Steel Knights down a lot," I said. "And it showed their supporters that the Nobles are stronger." The thought of the former Claws guys who'd sold their souls to my father's murderer made my stomach roil. Every former Claws member who'd joined the Steel Knights had better be regretting their choice.

"Right," Rowan said. "This was a pretty big shipment. I wonder if the Steel Knights are the ones who've been doing most of the distributing of the stuff. If so, they'll be low on stock now."

"Well, that's even better," Kaige said, swiping his hands. "We screwed over Colt and got all this crap off the streets. That's even more of a victory than we expected. I say it calls for some celebrating."

Wylder's gaze darted to me for just a second, and I could tell his momentary hesitation was because of my presence among them. But I wasn't going to bow out because he had his head up his ass. I wanted to focus on the good things about tonight, not the parts that'd unsettled me.

"I'm in!" I said. "What are we doing?"

Kaige's face lit up. "We haven't gone to the Gilded Walls in *forever.* And there isn't much else that'll be open."

"Sounds good to me," Rowan said with a questioning look at his boss.

Wylder looked as if he'd restrained a sigh, but then he smiled. "Let's do this. Gilded Walls it is."

"It's the best place," Kaige told me excitedly as Rowan drove us there. "The husband's from India and the wife from China, so they serve both kinds of food and all this fusion stuff. I could eat a whole table of it."

I laughed, letting my gaze skim over his massive torso. "I'll bet you could, and the table too."

He caught my gaze and waggled his eyebrows suggestively. "And I know just what I'd like to eat for dessert."

I couldn't help licking my lips. I might just be up for that.

Wylder stirred in the front seat, but if he had a problem with Kaige's insinuation, he didn't say anything about it.

The restaurant was tucked away between two larger, flashier places, its sign a little faded. True to its name, a gold leaf pattern was etched on the walls. Even at a little after midnight, a couple of the tables were occupied. The rich, spicy scents that hung in the air immediately had me salivating.

A bronze-skinned man with close-cropped black hair hustled out of the back as we ambled through the cozy room, flashing a brilliant grin. I guessed this was one of the owners.

"Sir," he said to Wylder. "It's a great privilege to have you joining us again. I'll see to your service myself." Perks of being a Noble, I guessed.

Wylder clapped him on the shoulder. "Thanks, Rahul. You always take good care of us. You know our favorites."

I spoke up quickly, remembering what Kaige had said about the offerings. "Can we get tandoori chicken too?"

Rahul bobbed his head. "But of course. It's one of our specialties."

I beamed at him. "Perfect. Make it extra-spicy. And I mean by *your* standards, not your typical customer. I can handle it."

He gave me an assessing look and then a pleased smile. "As the lady wishes."

"Bring another plate of that for me," Kaige put in. "If Mercy likes it, it must be good."

I arched an eyebrow at Kaige. "I'm not sure *you* can handle it. Have you had proper Indian spicing before or only the watered down stuff?" There'd been an authentic place just down the street from my house, and as a kid I'd been determined to build up my tolerance, maybe to prove there were a few things in the Bend I could totally conquer even if I couldn't protect myself from my dad.

"Hey, I like things spicy." Kaige nudged me with his elbow. "That's why I enjoy you so much."

The owner led us to a table a little apart from the others near the back. "Will you be having any wine tonight?"

Kaige perked up even more. "Hell, yeah."

Wylder made a vague gesture. "A bottle of the best stuff you have on hand that'll go well with the food."

"And I'll have a glass of the Abree Vineyards Merlot," Rowan said.

As Rahul hurried off, Wylder shook his head at Rowan. "All your wining and dining experience, and you still go for that cheap crap when you're with us."

Rowan shrugged. "When I'm drinking for fun rather than to impress, I might as well go for what I actually like."

He glanced at me just for a second and quickly jerked his gaze away. It didn't click until Rahul came back out with a fancy-looking bottle that he set in the center of the table—and another much more modest-looking one that had a logo so familiar my heart skipped a beat.

Oh. It was the stuff we used to drink back when we were teenagers. One of the cheapest wines in the store, when Rowan could cajole someone into picking it up for us, and I'd always said I thought the flowering vine that curled around the company name was pretty.

We'd been sharing a bottle of that merlot the night we'd lost our virginity to each other in the quiet little clearing in the park that we'd made our own. It'd felt like a room all to ourselves within the ring of trees and bushes. I had a flash of memory of that younger Rowan grazing his fingers down the side of my face as he smiled at me adoringly...

I shook away all those thoughts. That might as well have happened to two different people, so much had changed since then.

Funny that he still went for the same wine, though.

The appetizers came out quickly, and we all dug in. I hadn't realized how famished I was. I could have gorged myself just on the spring rolls, dumplings, and pakoras, but I knew I had to save room for my tandoori.

When the steaming hot-plate arrived, I could tell I'd made the right choice. I took one bite of a leg, the juices of the tender chicken mixing with the perfect fiery punch of spice, and was in heaven.

"Okay," I said. "I vote that we have all our dinners here from now on. And maybe breakfasts and lunches too."

Kaige grabbed a piece and took a bigger bite than I'd have recommended when he didn't know what he was in for. He swallowed and sputtered, blowing out air over his tongue as he reached for the wine-glass and downed it entirely.

I laughed. "Are you sure you can handle *that* spicy?"

"Yes," he said with a look of determination as he eyed the next piece. "I'm not scared of meat."

"There's fear and there's knowing your limits," Rowan teased, reaching for the platter of orange chicken instead.

Wylder chuckled. "As long as you all survive the meal to fight alongside me tomorrow." Then his jaw tensed as if he'd realized that comment might sound like it included me.

I rolled my eyes at him. "Don't worry, I won't let it go to my head."

Kaige took a couple of bites. Once he got accustomed to the heat, he started to gulp everything down. I watched him in amusement.

"Do you like it?" I asked.

He nodded. "A lot actually. I told you before, I appreciate a challenge."

"Speaking of challenges..." Wylder raised his wine glass in a toast. "To putting the fear of Nobles into the Steel Knights tonight."

"To taking them down completely," Rowan added. "Tonight was only the beginning."

With a *bang* that rattled my ear drums, the glass in his hand shattered.

The world slowed down as I watched three men storm into the

restaurant, red bandanas on their upper arms. They cocked their rifles at us, and we all dove under the table on instinct. I fumbled for the gun tucked in the back of my jeans, glad I hadn't left it in the car.

The Steel Knights opened fire. Their bullets careened across the table, a few hitting the waitress who'd just walked out of the kitchen. I flinched, horror welling up inside me as the young woman hit the floor, her head lolling.

These pricks were just adding to the list of how much they had to pay for.

"When they reload," Wylder murmured, his expression grim, and the guys nodded. I flicked off the safety on my pistol, my heart thudding.

At the rasp and click of the men reloading their weapons, the guys leapt into action as if they'd always been prepared for this. I bobbed up from beneath the level of the table too, but our adversaries had already taken shelter behind the counter that held the cash register. Kaige fired a couple of shots anyway until Wylder hissed at him. No point in wasting the ammunition.

We exchanged a few shots back and forth, mostly staying below the table. My pulse was outright thundering now.

"What the fuck are they doing here in the City?" Rowan muttered.

"Has this ever happened before?" I asked.

"Never," Wylder said, obviously seething. "*Never* have any of those two-bit gangs from the Bend tried to attack us on our home turf."

Colt had gotten bolder than we'd imagined.

Wylder gritted his teeth. "We're not accomplishing anything other than blasting all Rahul's hard work to bits. We should be able to make it to the kitchen and head out the back without them getting in a good shot if we move fast enough. Ready?"

I should be after what we'd already been through tonight, but somehow I didn't feel it. We'd planned to fight during the ambush. Being attacked during a moment of relaxation had shaken me much more. But I wasn't going to admit that to Wylder. I *had* to be ready.

"Whenever the rest of you are," I said.

"You two go first." He tipped his head to Rowan and me. "Kaige and I will cover our retreat." That last word came out bitterly. He dragged in a breath. "And... *go*."

Rowan and I dashed toward the doorway to the kitchen, staying low. Kaige and Wylder hurtled after us, turned to keep their guns trained on the Steel Knights.

A bullet whizzed by over my head. The guys fired several shots, one of which struck its target from the yelp that reached my ears. Then we were bursting into the kitchen area where Rahul and a woman who must have been his wife were huddled by the fridge.

"We'll pay for whatever damages those assholes caused," Wylder called to the two of them as we sprinted toward the back entrance. "And we'll make *them* pay for intruding here."

We burst into the alley out back—just as two more Steel Knights charged at us from either side.

One of them collided with Rowan, grasping his gun hand. The other tackled me to the ground. My tailbone jarred against the cracked concrete, and pain shot up my spine.

I gasped and tried to wrench my gun around to aim it at my attacker, but he slammed my arm against the ground. It slipped from my fingers. I managed to yank my other hand free and clawed at his eyes.

When he jerked away from me, I got an opening to ram my knee straight into his crotch. He groaned and doubled over, but it wasn't quite enough. As I heaved myself away from him, he swiped at me with a knife.

I threw myself backward just in time to save myself from being gutted. The knife still slashed across my stomach, slicing through the fabric of my skirt and drawing a stinging line across my skin.

My breath hitched, but the attack reminded me of my own other weapon. I snatched the knife in my pocket, dodged my attacker's next jab, and jabbed my blade at his neck.

The knife sank in with a sickening burbling of blood and crunch of cartilage. The man toppled over to reveal Wylder just behind him, looking like he'd been on the verge of shooting him. The other Steel Knight lay bleeding in the alley, Kaige standing over him.

My eyes locked with Wylder's. In that instant, I could have sworn he was about to slam me up against the back wall of the restaurant and fuck me until I was screaming my release, spectators be damned. Then his gaze dropped to the blood seeping through my torn shirt, and his expression hardened.

"Are you okay?" he snapped, making the question sound more annoyed than concerned.

I clapped my hand to the cut. It still ached, but it wasn't deep. "Just a scratch," I said, and couldn't help adding. "This time I took care of myself."

"Yes, you did," Kaige said. "Now let's all get the hell out of here!"

We dashed around the building and dove into the car. As Rowan hit the gas and the Toyota shot down the street, I sagged into the back seat.

It'd been a close one, but we'd gotten out. Somehow I couldn't summon much sense of victory now.

Colt had crossed a line tonight, and I wasn't sure where it ended or how far he'd be willing to go next.

14

Rowan

THE TABLE TAP BAR WAS ON THE GRUNGIER SIDE AS MY typical meeting spots went. The smell of booze and sweat hung thickly in the dimly lit space. Bodies gyrated to gritty rock music on the dance floor off to the side. The gin in my gin and tonic definitely wasn't top shelf.

But I went where the people I was trying to win over wanted, and tonight Ezra had me on a very precarious assignment, so I wasn't going to raise any complaints. I'd come out to a town about an hour outside Paradise City to talk with a representative for a gang called the Demon's Wings, which operated out of a city farther west.

After hearing about the attack on Wylder right within our turf, his dad had decided we needed to bring more manpower to bear so we could crush the Steel Knights once and for all. If Colt could make new connections, so could we. But first we—or rather, *I*—had to persuade them we'd make it worth their while. My work bringing in the waterfront project seemed to have convinced Ezra that he could entrust me with that responsibility.

For both his sake and all of ours, I intended to prove him right.

I checked my watch. I always liked to be early to a meeting just so I could get a feel of the place, especially when it was one I'd never been to before. The Demon's Wings rep should be here soon, though. I scanned the figures around me in case he already was here, waiting for me to spot him, but none of the young, college-partier type clientele seemed a likely fit.

I wasn't just here to negotiate with the guy, of course. Ezra had also pointed out that since we didn't know for sure who Colt had turned to, I should first feel him out to ensure they weren't already backing the Steel Knights.

The Demon's Wings were close to the Nobles in power and influence. We'd never had any conflicts with them. I couldn't think of any reason they'd bother throwing their lot in with Colt, but there were a lot of things about this situation that didn't make much sense, so we couldn't discount the possibility entirely.

Most likely, the real problem was going to be the price. Nobody would step up in our battle unless they got something in return. I just hoped whatever they asked for, that price wasn't too steep.

I was just raising my glass to my lips again when a smashing sound made me flinch in my seat. Images flashed through my head—gunshots, the glass in my hand shattering. The two men springing at us in the alley beyond the restaurant the other night. Mercy clutching her stomach, blood seeping out from under her fingers.

With my pulse suddenly beating twice as fast, I jerked around in my seat. But it was nothing. Someone on the dance floor must have dropped their shot glass. The guy from the bar was already coming around to sweep it up. He had to shoo away some of the idiots still dancing around the area obliviously.

I turned back to the table and took a deep breath. Sweat had broken out on my brow. For a second, I closed my eyes, willing down the surge of horror that had flooded me out of nowhere.

It was *nothing*. And Mercy was fine. The wound she'd taken had been shallow, not even requiring stitches. I'd seen her just before I'd left, taking up Kaige's invitation to play a game of pool.

Remembering that didn't exactly make me feel better. I couldn't deny the twinge of jealousy that wavered through my other emotions.

I'd tried so hard to dismiss what I still felt for her, but I couldn't ignore it anymore. The thought of her in danger set off a jolt of panic, the sight of her wounded made my heart ache, and knowing she'd enjoyed at least one of the other guy's companionship in ways that used to only be reserved for me had that jealousy twisting my gut.

Nothing that had happened all those years ago had been her fault. I'd known that all along. It'd just been easier to lump her in with the rest since I couldn't have her anyway.

And now... Now it didn't matter. After the way I'd abandoned her, how could she ever look at me with the same affection? I'd lost her when I left her, and that hadn't changed.

She was never going to be mine again.

I swallowed down the pain of that knowledge and checked myself over. Shit. When I'd startled, my drink had splashed the sleeve of my dress shirt, leaving a wet blotch. So much for keeping a professional appearance.

I grabbed a napkin and pressed it to the spot, soaking up as much of the moisture as I could. Despite the mechanical whir of an air conditioning system, the air was warm, but I pulled on my suit jacket to cover the stain anyway. Better I was a little uncomfortable than look sloppy.

As I tugged the jacket sleeves straight, a burly man I placed in his early thirties—a little older than most of the crowd—strode into the bar. His polo shirt and slacks didn't stand out as much as my suit did, but he still looked more business-minded than anyone else here. And I spotted a tattoo poking from beneath the shirt's raised collar.

I stood up, and his gaze fixed on me. He sauntered over casually and confidently. I felt my back pulling straighter automatically to match his assured air.

"You must be from the Demon's Wings," I said when he was close enough that I could talk under the music, and offered my hand. "I'm Rowan Finlay, Mr. Noble's representative. It's a pleasure."

The man shook my hand firmly. "Eric Vale. I can speak for Mr. Herald as needed. Does this place work for you?"

Did he think I was going to risk the alliance by kicking up a fuss within a minute of greeting him? I pushed a mild smile onto my face. "I think it serves our purposes just fine. Let me cover the first round of drinks. What are you having?"

At the pleased gleam that entered Eric's eyes, I knew I'd already won some points with him. "A Jack and Coke would be perfect. Thanks."

I flagged the waitress. I'd given her an advance tip to make sure the service she gave us would be quick and attentive. She took my order with a bright smile and had the drinks to us before Eric had quite settled into his chair. Money greased a lot of wheels no matter what kind of establishment you were in.

I waited until Eric had sipped his drink, taking a tiny one of my own. "So," I said. "Let's get down to business."

Eric eyed me. "Yes, I'm interested to hear exactly what this business is. We were surprised when Mr. Noble reached out."

Clearly I needed to win a bunch more points before this negotiation would swing in my favor. I smiled again. "I know the Nobles and the Demon's Wings haven't had the closest of ties, but we've been aware of your presence for quite some time, and Mr. Noble has been impressed by how efficiently Mr. Herald runs his organization. When he decided to form a new alliance, the Demon's Wings were his first choice."

Not just because of what we knew of their reputation but also because we'd determined they'd had no contact on record with any gang in the Bend, but I didn't mention that part.

The other man raised his glass as if in a toast. "We appreciate the respect shown in that gesture. We've had plenty of respect ourselves for what we've heard of things in Paradise City. That doesn't explain why you're looking for an alliance now, though."

"Of course. How much do you know about the hierarchy in Paradise Bend?"

I watched him carefully as he rubbed his chin. I didn't see any sign of hidden animosity or guilt.

"Not a great deal," he admitted. "Your grip extends over the whole county, doesn't it? Collecting your tithe from the smaller-time groups that have their own bits and pieces of action here and there, like we do."

"Yes, exactly. Unfortunately, one of those groups has been creating a lot of disruption in the county."

Eric's eyebrows rose slightly, but he only looked curious, not as if he was already aware of what I was talking about. I started to relax a little, surer than ever that the Demon's Wings had no association with Colt.

"And what does that have to do with us?" he asked, swirling his drink. "Surely Ezra Noble can handle a few pissy street rats?"

"Naturally," I replied. "But there's something to be said for crushing certain sorts of rebellions as quickly and forcefully as possible. As Mr. Noble has expanded his reach to territories beyond Paradise Bend, he can't bring as large a force as he'd like down on them without leaving certain other properties vulnerable. So he has a proposition for Mr. Herald."

"I'm listening."

"All we're asking is that Mr. Herald send a contingent of his men, whoever he can spare, for one or two operations in Paradise Bend. In exchange, Mr. Noble would return the favor at whatever time Mr. Herald requires. You have our back, we have yours."

"But conveniently we have to extend ourselves first," Eric said.

I didn't let the skeptical comment faze me. "We recognize that, and so Mr. Noble is also offering a partial stake in a particularly lucrative property he's been overseeing the development of not far from your own territories. I've brought the paperwork for you to bring to Mr. Herald so he can look it over."

I retrieved the contract from my briefcase and passed it across the table. Eric studied it for a minute, unable to suppress the hint of a grin that touched his lips. I relaxed even more and allowed myself a gulp of my second gin and tonic. I just about had him.

"This is certainly generous, worthy of a man of Ezra Noble's reputation," he said, folding the papers and tucking them into his pocket.

"And our offer of manpower doesn't come with an expiration date," I said. "The Nobles never forget their debts. Rest assured that we'll be ready if you call on us."

Eric nodded. "Well, I think I've heard enough to bring this to the boss. It looks good, but it is pretty sudden. I hope you'll understand if before he commits, he'd want a more immediate, ah, contribution."

I cocked my head, ignoring the kernel of dread that was expanding in my stomach. "What sort of contribution?"

A smirk I didn't like at all curled the other man's mouth. "Oh, nothing all that substantial. Just a small token to seal the deal. I'm sure Mr. Noble has heard of Jasper Herald's taste in women."

15

Mercy

I DIDN'T KNOW THE NOBLE UNDERLING WHO STOPPED ME IN the hall, but his words set my nerves jangling in an instant. "Mercy Katz? Ezra wants to see you in the audience room."

I gave him a thumbs up, but my heart had sunk. The Noble leader hadn't bothered to speak to me since the shoot-out in the Gilded Walls. I knew he hadn't been keen on going after the Steel Knights to begin with. It'd been my crusade, and that crusade could have gotten Ezra's only heir killed the other night.

Somehow I had the feeling he wasn't super happy with me at the moment.

Kaige had mentioned that the Nobles were putting feelers out to form an alliance so they could make a definitive strike against Colt, though. Maybe then this would all be over. I had no idea what Ezra might want to speak to me about right now, though.

When I walked into the audience room Anthea had shown me what felt like a year ago, I found Ezra already in his throne-like chair. He wasn't alone. Anthea stood on the opposite side of the coffee table, her arms crossed tightly over her chest, and Wylder was poised by his father's right hand. Both of them looked way too tense.

Axel and one of Ezra's other main men lurked at the back of the room. A prickle ran down my spine. Basically, the only person in the room I could count on to be on my side was Anthea—and she also probably had the least power out of any of them, family name aside.

Ezra nodded to the sofa across from him without so much as a hello. "Sit down. We have a lot to discuss."

I sat, eyeing him carefully. "What are we discussing today?"

Ignoring my question, he shifted his attention to my waist. "How has your wound been healing?"

I touched the scabbed-over scratch from the Steel Knight's knife. "Frank says it's healing fine. It wasn't deep."

"I appreciate how energetically you participated both in that altercation and during the ambush of the truck," he said.

He did? I managed not to gape at him, but it was a near thing. "Um, thank you. I've always promised I'd hold my own. I might not have a lot of experience on the ground, but my father put me through plenty of training."

"That much is clear. And that's why I think you'd be the right fit for this job."

I glanced at Anthea and then Wylder but got no clue what he might mean from their equally grave expressions. Wylder's mouth was set in a scowl that was typical when he had to pay any attention to me these days. I resisted the urge to grimace right back at him and focused on Ezra again. "What kind of job? If there's something I can do to help take down Colt, I'm ready."

Ezra raised his eyebrows toward Anthea. "Look how enthusiastic she is. I don't think this should be any problem at all."

"You haven't told her what the job is yet," his sister replied evenly, but those words and the sense that there'd been an argument about this between them earlier set me even more on edge. What was going on?

Ezra returned his chilly gaze to me and gave me a chillier smile. "You're aware that we've reached out to another organization to add to our numbers for a more powerful offensive against the Steel Knights?

What happened last Friday was a direct call for war, and we can't leave it unanswered."

"I heard you were looking to make an alliance," I said. "Has that gone through?"

"Nearly. What do you know about the Demon's Wings or Jasper Herald?"

Both names were vaguely familiar. It took me a few moments to place them. "They're the main gang in Rallum—Jasper is the boss." My father had mentioned them once or twice. He'd kept an eye on all the major powers in the nearby counties as well as our own.

Somehow Ezra's smile got both colder and wider at the same time. "Very good. They're the organization I've reached out to. I've been able to strike a tentative deal with them to receive the reinforcements we need for the next phase of our plan. But he's asked for a minor... gift up front to seal the deal."

I still wasn't seeing how I fit in. "I guess that makes sense. Would you like me to deliver the gift?"

He let out a soft chuckle. "Miss Katz, you *are* the gift."

My back went rigid. "*What?*"

"Only temporarily," Ezra said, looking way too amused by my reaction. "He wants us to send him a woman for one evening. He'll take you to dinner, you'll entertain him and see that he's happy, and that's all there is to it."

Anthea made a strained sound. "I think the problem is the *type* of entertainment he enjoys."

That sounded ominous. I held my instant revulsion at the idea of being offered up like a choice piece of meat in check and asked calmly, "Is there a particular reason you chose me?"

"Of course," Ezra said. "Jasper Herald has very particular interests when it comes to the women he spends time with. He likes a girl who can fend for herself and put up a fight."

Even more apprehension trickled through me. Why would I need to be putting up any fights on this date?

Ezra went on as if he hadn't said anything odd. "We already know you can hold your own, so you shouldn't be intimidated by him. And you're aware enough of the situation with Bryant that you can easily talk up our cause while you're with Mr. Herald."

"It would just be dinner?" I clarified.

Ezra inclined his head. "That's all he's asked for. He'll send a car to pick you up, and it'll bring you back to this house when your date is finished."

"If there's anything to bring back," Anthea muttered. "With his reputation when it comes to women—" She cut herself off at Ezra's glare and revised her statement to simply, "He's a volatile man. I don't like this."

"I'm well aware of your feelings on the subject, but you have become rather protective of Miss Katz beyond what she appears to require. I'm sure she can make this decision for herself."

Wylder stirred, speaking up for the first time in a bored tone. "*Mercy* is the volatile one." As I bristled, he went on. "Wouldn't it make more sense to send one of the groupies? That's what they're here for anyway. They'd probably jump at the chance to fawn over this Jasper guy."

His voice stayed blasé through the entire remark, but understanding settled over me. He was trying to protect me too, without showing that he was. If he'd really hated me as much as he'd been acting like he did lately, he'd have relished the chance to send me off to what Anthea clearly thought was my potential doom.

Just how big a sicko was this dude when it came to women?

Ezra waved his hand dismissively. "They'd make a fool of themselves and put us in a bad light. Our alliance with the Demon's Wings depends on this 'date.' I've heard from multiple sources—including you—about Mercy's capabilities. It's time she put them to more use on our behalf." Ezra looked at me with a challenge in his eyes. "Unless you're rethinking your commitment to the Nobles?"

Understanding hit me. This wasn't just a job—it was a test of my loyalty to him. Ezra cared at least as much about making sure I'd follow his orders as how much Jasper would supposedly like me.

How would he react if I refused?

"I'm not rethinking anything," I said quickly. But no way in hell did I want to cater to some sleazy and potentially violent gangster—sleep with him and endure whatever else he might do to me. Anthea had implied he might even *kill* me.

And how would I really be able to defend myself without screwing up the deal and ruining the whole point of the "date"? It sounded like this asshole liked women to fight back so it was more of a challenge to finally overpower them. I suppressed a shudder of horror.

I groped for something else I could offer Ezra instead. "If you're looking for more allies, I might have an easier solution, one that won't require making any deals with people outside Paradise Bend. There are a lot of lower-level Claws members still out there in the Bend. A few of them have gone over to Colt's side, but there have to be lots that are still loyal to my father. I could reach out to them, get them to fight alongside us—"

Ezra scoffed so loudly my mouth snapped shut. "Do you think the people who rolled over for the Steel Knights while Bryant took control of the Bend will be any real help to us? Wake up, Miss Katz. If you ask for my opinion, those worthless bastards should be crushed too, right alongside the Steel Knights."

"Exactly," Axel said from behind me. "We're better off without them anywhere near us."

I didn't have any way to argue that. As I hesitated, Ezra leaned back in his chair, his gaze getting even more penetrating. "Well? Are you willing to take this job for me? Or despite all your talk and the fact that I initiated you into our ranks, should I assume you're not actually serious about your dedication to me and the Nobles?"

"I was just taking a second to think," I said.

"Actions speak louder than words," he said. I got the impression he was trying to push my buttons, waiting for me to snap. But I wasn't going to give him an excuse to dismiss me like he'd just written off everyone else left from the Claws.

For a second, I let myself picture telling Ezra Noble to fuck off and walking right out of here, out of this mess for good. In some ways, it was a satisfying image. Hell, Wylder had been encouraging me to take off and leave the Steel Knights to them for days. I could give him what he wanted and not put my neck on the line in this way that made my skin want to crawl off my body.

But I only considered it for a second. That was how long it took before the screams of my dying family echoed up from my memory. That gurgle as Grandma had slumped on the floor, gasping her last breath...

My hands clenched at my sides. Neither father nor son was going to get rid of me this easily. Colt had stolen too much from me, and I wasn't going to let any other asshole take my revenge away as well. Nothing would really be okay until I'd destroyed that bastard with my own two hands.

I lifted my chin and stared right back at Ezra. "And I'm a woman of action, so that's not a problem. If this is what you need, I'll go on a date with Jasper."

"And agree to all his conditions?" Ezra said.

More like his whims, from the sounds of things.

I shrugged as if it was nothing at all. "Yes. Just tell me when it's happening."

16

Mercy

Two hours later, Anthea showed up at my bedroom door with the dress Ezra had approved for my date, which it turned out was happening tonight. So much for having a chance to really prepare.

Anthea handed it to me, and I unfurled it in my hands. It was slinky emerald-green satin, with spaghetti straps so thin a brisk breeze might snap them and a slit from the ankle-length hem to halfway up the thigh.

Lovely. Ezra might as well be gift-wrapping me.

"I don't want you to go," Anthea said quietly. "The things I've heard about Jasper Herald..." She winced.

"If he's bad enough to freak even you out, I don't want to go either," I said. "But I gave Ezra my word. I'll... I'll figure something out if things get bad."

"You have proven very resourceful so far." She gave me a sympathetic smile. "At least let me help you get ready? Maybe if you're stunning enough, Jasper will forget he wants to do anything more than stare at you."

I snorted. Not fucking likely. But I motioned for her to stay anyway.

Having the company would distract me from the horror that might be waiting for me tonight.

I changed into the dress quickly, making a face when I saw just how low the neckline dipped. Then Anthea spent a good part of the next hour spritzing and then curling my hair and slathering my face with makeup.

At the end of it, I almost couldn't recognize the girl in the mirror. She looked like a femme-fatale, something I decidedly was not. But it was still me in the mirror.

"Wow," I said. "Are you sure you're not also a wizard?"

Anthea rolled her eyes, but her smile looked pleased. She swiveled me back toward her and gave my mouth one last touch-up with the lipstick. Then she took a little velvet box out of her purse and handed it to me. "As a final touch. In case things do get particularly bad."

I opened the box with some trepidation, but all I found inside was a gold hair pin with a gleaming pearl mounted on it. "I can stab him with it? I think the heels of the shoes I'm supposed to wear with this dress might do more damage."

Anthea laughed and plucked the pin from the box. She fixed it into the now-buoyant waves of my hair. "Stab, yes, but that's not all there is to it. You know I specialize in subtler methods. The sharp end is laced with a poison that'll slow any man down. It should give you a chance to get away from him if it comes to that, without having the murder of a crime boss hanging over your head. Just be careful while you're taking it out of your hair."

"No kidding." I touched the smooth metal surface. I wasn't supposed to take any weapons with me, but Jasper would never know the difference. Hopefully he wouldn't make me use it. "Thank you."

My gaze dropped to the jeans I'd taken off. I wasn't supposed to take any bag or purse with me, just present myself like, well, a present. Which meant I had nowhere to keep my childhood bracelet on me. After how many times my belongings had been messed with here, I didn't like just leaving it in my room either.

I fished it out of the pocket and held it out to Anthea. "Would you hold onto this for me until I get back? I want to be sure it's safe."

Anthea read the inscription and raised her eyebrows at me. I let out an awkward laugh. "It's the only thing I have left from my mother."

Her eyes widened. "Of course. I'll defend it with my life." She tucked it carefully in her purse with an air as if she'd meant that statement completely literally, which knowing her, she probably did.

Just then, the door burst open. Kaige sauntered in as if he was perfectly at home in my bedroom.

Anthea gave him a reproachful look. "You should knock."

"So I keep telling him," Gideon said, coming in after him. He was followed by Rowan. As the door thumped shut behind them, the three of them stopped in their tracks to stare at me.

Rowan recovered his voice first. "Wow, Mercy, you look..."

He didn't seem to know how to finish, which was strange for the guy who'd always been quick with his words. I abruptly noticed the hollowed quality to his eyes, as if he hadn't slept much last night. Had he known what Ezra was planning?

Would he really have been that worried about me?

"Like a siren who came out of the sea to murder us," Kaige finished for him, walking around me to take in the full view with avid eyes. "Like, seriously, I'm already dying here. I honestly wouldn't be too upset if you decided to drag me down into the sea with you."

I rolled my eyes but couldn't help the blush that crept up my face. "You don't mean that."

Kaige stepped closer. "Hell yeah, I do. I wish you were getting dressed for me, and we were the ones going out. Not that fucking asshole Jasper Herald."

With that comment, the mood in the room shifted to something more somber. "So, what are you all doing here?" I asked to try to break the gloom. "Did you just come to ogle me?"

"Not at all," Gideon said briskly. He sat on the edge of my bed and tapped on his tablet. "We thought you should go into this evening with every possible advantage. The records I've been able to dig up on him are... not ideal."

"He's a fucking lunatic," Kaige clarified, scowling.

A shiver ran down my back. "What exactly did you find?"

Gideon hesitated for a second before he spoke. That seemed like a bad sign in itself. He cleared his throat. "At least three sex workers he's hired were never heard from again. And those are just the ones where I could find enough of a paper trail, which means the actual number could be many times higher."

"I've heard of several who ended up with major injuries, even though they survived," Anthea said. "He definitely likes to play rough, and he doesn't care whether his partner is into it. He might even prefer that she isn't."

Rowan winced at those words. I tried to put them out of my mind. My goal, going in, was to avoid sleeping with Jasper by any means. Then he wouldn't get the chance to act out those urges. I just hadn't figured out how I was going to manage it yet.

"Isn't there some way we can convince Ezra to take a different tactic?" Rowan burst out. "This is sick."

Emotion rippled through his voice. Apparently my safety did mean a lot to him.

I tried not to let that shake my nerve as I squared my shoulders. "I have to go. If it means we get to crush the Steel Knights the way they deserve, it'll be worth it."

"We figured you'd say that," Kaige said with a hint of a growl in his voice. "That's why we're going to make sure you've got everything you could possibly need going in."

Oh. They'd come to help me prepare just like Anthea had. A weird warmth flooded my chest, but I couldn't help asking, "Does Wylder know about this?"

"Wylder doesn't need to know," Gideon said coolly. "It wouldn't look good for him to act as if he doesn't trust his dad's judgment anyway. But we can lend a hand... as friends." A sly gleam entered his eyes that made them hard to look away from.

Kaige touched my arm, drawing my attention back to him. "Let's go over all the self-defense techniques that might come up. Since you can't carry any weapons to your meeting, you'll have to depend on yourself and your core strength. Never turn your back on him. If you have to get him off you, use your elbows and knees since they can hit hard without risking much injury to you. And always, always, aim for the groin."

"I know all of that already," I reminded him. "I've spent my whole life learning how to defend myself."

"It can't help to get a reminder. And you'll need to be extra smart about it after the wounds you've taken recently."

I glanced down at my palms, which now showed only pink lines where I'd cut them escaping from Colt. If I could survive my ex-fiancé, I could survive Jasper too. "I haven't stopped training. I bet I've been in the gym more than you have." I hadn't had a whole lot of other things to do between missions while Wylder was shooting death glares at me every time we were in the same room.

"Well, good." Kaige rubbed his mouth. "We found some pictures of the guy. He's big—not as buff as me, but he'll have a lot of weight on you. You'll want to rely on speed and agility rather than strength."

I nodded. "Thanks for the tip."

"Just... Just come at it smart, not hard, and you'll be fine. I know you've got lots of experience putting pricks in their place."

The corner of my mouth twitched, and I managed to smile at him despite the dread coiled in my gut.

Rowan spoke up, his voice low. "From what I gathered during my meeting with Jasper's representative, Jasper is a take-no-prisoner kind of guy, like Ezra himself. His man alluded to his violent nature, so it's obviously a fact he doesn't try to hide much. In fact, I got the impression he revels in it, which means he won't be worried about shocking you or trying to keep a low profile."

"Wonderful," I said with a grimace.

"My research has turned up some more details on his recreational activities," Gideon said. "It seems he has a wide variety. He gets season tickets for the Rallum Opera House every year."

Kaige gaped. "Opera? Are you serious?"

"This doesn't seem like a good time for making jokes." Gideon skimmed through the data he'd gathered. "He has an extensive collection of classic cars, the jewel of which is a 1967 Lamborghini Miura. But what I found most interesting is this bit of info I doubt he'd like anyone knowing about."

He turned his tablet around so that we could see the screen. It showed a list of what looked like bank transactions.

"What's this supposed to mean?" Kaige asked.

"Payments he's made that I traced to a local dominatrix. One who specializes in dominating male clients. It seems Jasper enjoys receiving violence nearly as much as he likes dealing it out. From what I can tell, he's one of her regular patrons and her most well-paying."

"So our Jasper boy likes his ass spanked by a woman in tight leather, maybe even calling her his mama." Kaige chuckled. "Who would have thought?"

"It's not that uncommon for men in positions of power," Rowan said. "They have to be so in control in every area of their life that they need some kind of outlet now and then."

"Too bad it's Mercy he's looking to control tonight," Anthea muttered.

She was right. I was touched that the guys had come to pitch in however they could, especially when I doubted Ezra would have approved of me getting extra help. But so far what I'd heard hadn't told me much other than that I needed to prepare for the worst. Still, it meant a hell of a lot that the three of them were here.

"Thank you guys," I said. "Really. I couldn't be more prepared now."

I gave Rowan's shoulder a quick squeeze, yanking my hand back before the flutter that started in my chest could expand, and stepped closer to Kaige to kiss him on the cheek. He hummed in a way that suggested he'd have bent me over and explored my mouth with his tongue if Anthea hadn't nudged him away just then.

"We'd better get going. It's almost time for the car to arrive." She shot me one last fierce look. "You'll get through this. He has no idea what he's dealing with. That's always our greatest strength."

As women, she meant, and after the events of the past few weeks, I knew how right she was.

I dipped my head gratefully. She, Kaige, and Rowan filed out. Gideon got up, dismissing the app on his tablet, and then paused by the door. He turned to face me.

"If you want to just skip town and forget all this shit," he said, deadly serious, "I can arrange a car for you and the stuff to make sure no one ever tracks you down. You'd be out of here in less than ten minutes."

I blinked at him, not at all surprised that he *could* do that but startled that he'd offered it to me. Not for the first time, I had to wonder just how much was going on behind that detached, ever-logical front that I'd never guessed.

"No," I said without even needing to think about it. "I appreciate the offer, but I'm seeing this through."

An even more unexpected smile flitted across his face, amplifying his unearthly appeal. "I thought you'd say that. That's why I like you."

Did he? My body moved of its own accord. I leaned in to press a quick kiss to his lips like the one I'd given Kaige's cheek.

Only it didn't turn out that way. The second my lips brushed his, Gideon grabbed me by the waist and kissed me back hard. I found myself gripping the front of his shirt, throwing myself into the sensation, the heat of his mouth and the cool pressure of his lip ring sending all kinds of sparks over my skin.

I flicked my tongue against the ring like I'd watched him do so many times, and he made an urgent sound in the back of his throat. It was so different from the calm and collected Gideon I was used to that my insides melted into jelly.

He kissed me for a second longer and then wrenched away from me as if the separation took a massive effort. His breath held a faint rasp.

Whoa, that had really been something.

Gideon stared at me, so many emotions darting through his expression that I couldn't identify any of them and then fading away until he looked as impenetrable as marble. But when his gaze dropped to my lips, heat flared through them without the slightest contact.

"I could have smudged your lipstick," he said, as if that practical concern was all that mattered, but the unevenness of his breath told me he hadn't really been so unaffected. Hell, he'd been the one who'd grabbed *me*.

A smile twitched at the corners of my mouth. "I'll check it in the car. I can take care of a few things on my own."

"I know." He reached for the door knob, his gaze still locked with mine. "For the record, I don't think this asshole Jasper has the slightest chance of getting in your way."

Then he stepped out, leaving me alone. But only for a matter of seconds before Axel's voice called from the foyer loud enough to reach me.

"Katz, get your ass down here! Your ride's just arrived. Time to go."

Mercy

I SMOOTHED THE SKIRT OF MY DRESS AS I STEPPED OUT OF the car Jasper had sent. The black marble walls of the posh bar it'd stopped in front of gleamed, and I caught a hint of jazz seeping through the broad front window.

The man who'd driven me motioned briskly to the door. "Mr. Herald is already waiting for you. Let's not keep him waiting."

He'd already patted me down for weapons before I'd gotten in the car. He'd been brisk and efficient about that too, but his detachment hadn't comforted me. It'd given me the impression of him carefully checking over a package he was supposed to deliver for his boss's exclusive use.

He ushered me into the bar and over to a large booth at the back of the room. Everything inside had a reddish cast to it from the mood-lighting. It made the three men waiting for us at the table look even more ominous than they would have anyway.

The two who sat at the closest ends of the booth, dressed casually but with a noticeable lump of a gun at their hips, got up at our approach. Their eyes lingered on the plunging neckline of my dress before skimming over the rest of me. One prowled around me, and I could practically feel him ogling my ass. I resisted the urge to ram my elbow backward and "accidentally" clock him in the gut.

But most of my attention stayed on the man still seated at the back of the booth, his eyes roving over me just as avidly from there. This was Jasper Herald.

My first thought was that he resembled a pig. He'd slicked his graying hair close to his scalp, but no amount of gel could hide the fact that it was thinning, letting hints of the pale, pinkish skin beneath show through. The swell of his portly frame filled out an expensive-looking suit tailored to his bulk, and his wide nose was slightly upturned. He wore a thick gold chain on his neck and a Rolex watch on his wrist.

He smiled broadly at me and got up when he must have been satisfied with his men's close examination. They hadn't blinked twice at Anthea's hair pin, thank God.

"You must be Mercy Katz," he said in a jovial voice that sent a shiver over my skin. Did he think *I* was happy to be here? He held out his arms as if he expected me to give him a hug in greeting.

Uh, no, that would definitely set the wrong precedent for this "date." I lowered my head in acknowledgment instead. "That's me. Mr. Noble sends his regards. I'm looking forward to spending the evening with you."

The last bit was a lie, of course, but I was trying to keep Jasper a little placated. My attempt clearly fell short. His smile stayed in place, but a cold glint entered his eyes as he lowered his arms.

He settled for taking my hand and kissing the back of it. Cloying cologne wafted off him. I had to tense my muscles to keep from recoiling, especially after he flicked his *tongue* over my knuckle before withdrawing.

What the fuck? Was he just trying to get a reaction out of me, or did he think there was something sexy about that?

I retrieved my hand as graciously as I could manage, clenching my fingers against the impulse to wipe his saliva off on the thigh of my dress. My smile felt rigid on my face, but at least it was still there.

"I hope you enjoy this establishment," Jasper said. "It's one of the many properties I have a stake in within and around this city."

"It's very atmospheric," I said. "I like the music."

His smile managed to widen. "Excellent. I have a feeling we're going to have quite a memorable night. If you'd join me upstairs? There's a private suite reserved for my use where we can indulge in each other's company undisturbed by the other customers. It even has its own bar for our use."

And it'd mean he could have his way with me without anyone seeing. I bit my tongue against spitting out a "Hell no" that would have ruined Ezra's deal before the night had even started. "Sure, that sounds wonderful." On opposite day, maybe.

Either Jasper didn't pick up on the lack of enthusiasm in my tone or, I wouldn't be surprised, he didn't give a shit. He might even have preferred me to be unwilling. He set his pudgy hand on the small of my back and guided me toward a set of wrought-iron stairs. They led to a landing with a row of doors overlooking the rest of the bar. His hand stayed against me the whole way up the stairs, making my flesh crawl with every step.

This wasn't a man who took no for an answer. Everything Anthea and the guys had uncovered confirmed that. I just had to figure out how to divert him before he got to the point where I couldn't tolerate what he was doing.

The landing was lit with small hexagonal spots of light. I hadn't spent a lot of time in places this swanky, and I might have appreciated the interior design if not for the man next to me. I could feel his impatience coiling around me as his gaze stayed on me. He wasn't even watching where he was going.

Uneasiness churned in my stomach. I turned to him, giving me an excuse to twist out of range of his hand, and attempted the sort of practiced smile I'd seen Rowan dazzle people with. "So, Mr. Herald—"

"Call me Jasper, sweetheart," he said. "And let's save the conversation for when we've gotten comfortable."

I nodded stiffly and kept my mouth shut.

At the end of the landing, a server dressed in a tux was waiting for us. He showed us into a room with a plush divan, a low, black lacquered table in front of it, and a bar that was stocked up with all kinds of alcohol.

The server swept his arm toward the divan, "Please take your seat. I'll have your drinks ready shortly. Do you have any preferences?"

"Something strong and sweet, easy on the ice," Jasper replied, looking right at me. His gaze traveled up my body. He was almost salivating by the time he got up to my chest. Bile rose up my throat at the look on his face. "What'll you have, darling?"

I'd have him cutting out the sweet talk if I'd had a real choice about it. I settled for picking a drink—nothing too strong, since I wanted to keep my mind and my reflexes sharp. "A mojito, please, easy on the rum."

Jasper clucked his tongue chidingly. "Don't be silly. I can more than afford to treat you right." He glanced at the server. "Give her a double shot."

Well, fuck, then I'd just have to drink it very slowly. Were there any potted plants around I could toss a little into when he wasn't looking?

But when would Jasper not be looking at me? There wasn't much else in the room to draw his attention.

The vile man put his arms around my waist, his thick fingers digging into my dress as if he was trying to touch my skin through the fabric. In my head, I imagined smashing his nose into the floor and driving the stiletto heel of my shoe into the back of his skull. I'd take a million more shoot-outs and ambushes rather than end up on a mission like this again.

He sat me down on the divan beside him, his arm draped around my back. The server worked at the bar station and produced two cocktails for us.

"For you, sir, with some of our best vodka," he said with a smile.

Jasper took the drink from him, took one sip, and spit it back into the glass with a disgusted sputter. "What is this atrocity?" he roared.

The other man's expression froze with panic. Before he could reply, Jasper grabbed his wrist and twisted it. There was a sickening crack, and the man screamed. A wave of cold washed through my body.

He'd broken the man's wrist over a drink he hadn't liked.

"There," Jasper said in a cool voice. "This might be reminder enough for you to take more care when catering to important clientele. Now go and make me something better."

My heart lurched at the sudden change in his behavior. It was like watching his skin peel off slowly, revealing his true visage. The jovial front he'd put on downstairs had fallen away completely to show the gang boss beneath, a killer with no repentance. And all that portliness hid more strength than I'd assumed.

The server started back toward the small private bar, his other hand cradling his broken wrist, a faint sound of pain slipping past his tightened lips. My pulse stuttered. I couldn't sit here and watch him try to put together another drink one-handed. What would this prick do to him if he wasn't satisfied with that one either?

"Jasper," I said, restraining a cringe as I set my hand on his chest. Jasper looked down at where my fingers rested. I wondered if I'd made the wrong choice, if he had problems with other people touching him, but then his jowls quivered. His lust practically rolled off him.

"Yes, sweetheart?" he said, rubbing my shoulder in slow circles that made me want to hurl.

I batted my eyelashes at him. "Why don't *I* make a drink for you?"

He raised his eyebrows skeptically.

I patted his chest, containing my revulsion. "I'm very good at it. You'll see." Before he could stop me, I walked to the bar and dismissed the server, who left without protest. I hoped he could get medical attention quickly.

I considered the ample selection and grabbed a few different bottles. Even at my father's events, I'd rarely gotten to play with alcohol this top shelf. Too bad I was going to have to play to Jasper's preferences rather than having fun experimenting.

A splash of this and another of that. A squeeze and a sprinkle, and a small scoop of ice. "Strong and sweet, easy on the ice," I said as I went. Swaying my hips, I let the dress work the rest of its magic. Jasper's attention stayed rapt on me.

When I was satisfied with my work, I sashayed up to him, careful not to show a hint of fear. "A special blend just for you."

He raised the glass to his lips, still eyeing me. I sank into the divan, trying not to hold my breath. After the first sip, he paused. Then he sipped again. A renewed smile crept across his lips that both relieved me and tied my gut in a knot.

A happy Jasper wasn't necessarily less violent than a pissed off one, just harder to anticipate.

"Drink up," he said, nodding to my mojito. "We're only just getting started."

We'd see about that. But I picked up my glass and gave the appearance of taking a larger gulp when I'd only let a small bit of the liquid into my mouth. The extra rum gave it a sourness that turned my stomach.

Jasper shifted closer to me on the divan, moving to slide his arm around my shoulders. Impatience radiated off him. He might not even let me get through the one drink.

"That was a nice car you sent for me," I blurted out, remembering what Gideon had dug up about Jasper's love of classic vehicles. If I could get him talking about something else he was interested in, I might at least buy myself some time. "Very clean lines."

Jasper cocked his head, an eager spark lighting in his eyes. One point to me. "Oh, I have much nicer than that back home. Are you a car enthusiast?"

I shrugged demurely, forcing a giggle. "Oh, I don't know a whole lot about them, but I know when I like the look of one. They just don't make them like they used to back in the '60s and '70s anymore, do they?"

"No, they don't. Perhaps another time I'll have the chance to give you a ride in one of my beauties. Let me tell you about them, and you can pick your favorite."

As Jasper rambled about his various cars, he polished off his drink and I quickly mixed him another. I brought my glass over to the bar with me and managed to pour quite a bit of it into the ice bucket when he momentarily looked away. When I returned, though, his enthusiasm for that line of conversation was winding down.

"How did you end up with the Nobles, darling?" he asked as he took his refilled glass from me. "Ezra says your father ran some kind of operation of his own in Paradise Bend."

I plastered another smile on my face. Trust Ezra to have used that tidbit of information to rouse Jasper's interest. "Unfortunately my father was killed by another organization that betrayed him. I came to the Nobles because I knew they'd set things right."

Ezra *had* wanted me to talk up the cause a little. I strained my mind for the best way to approach it. "The Nobles always come through on their word when they give it," I added, in case Jasper had any doubts about Ezra repaying him for his help. "And the assholes responsible need to be dealt with quickly. I wouldn't be surprised if they start looking farther afield for territory to steal before long."

Jasper's eyes hardened. He'd caught my insinuation. "I'm not afraid of any street rats."

"No one was, and that became their weakness. These people benefit from being dismissed—it gives them time to shore up their power until they have a chance to turn the tables." I hoped he didn't realize that applied to *me* as well. "But the Nobles are smart enough to see the danger in leaving a supposedly minor threat to grow. They're going to crush them once and for all. If we have you on our side, it'll be done so much faster."

Jasper simply hummed to himself. Then he threw back the rest of his drink.

"Do you want another?" I asked, already reaching for the glass.

He shook his head, his gaze turning into a leer. He wrapped his hand around my bicep—just loosely for now.

"Come here, girl," he said.

I could tell I'd bought all the time I was going to get, but I couldn't help grasping for another chance to delay. "Shouldn't we talk a little more first?"

His grip tightened. "I think I've had enough talking. I know all I need to know about you."

He leaned in, his lips seeking mine, and my heart lurched. My hand formed a fist I wanted to smash into his face, but the consequences of that could ruin everything I'd worked for. Anyway, he'd probably like seeing me panicked and flailing, getting the chance to—

A lightbulb went off in my head. Thanks to Gideon, I might know everything I needed to about the man in front of me too.

I jerked back, managing to snap my arm from his hold, and looked at him sternly. I made my voice as domineering as possible. "Watch where you touch me. You didn't ask for my permission."

Jasper gaped at me, stunned. My heart thumped faster. I was taking a huge risk, but this man did apparently enjoy being dominated. Why the hell couldn't I be the one calling the shots, then?

Unless I'd gone too far, or he was only in the mood for that at particular times, or—

But he didn't lunge at me. He stayed still, waiting to see what I'd do next. A faint flush had crept into his cheeks. Was he a little turned on already?

I had to keep going before I lost the moment.

"Good boy," I said, standing up. "If you want to touch me, you have to work for it. Do you understand?"

Jasper's pupils dilated. "What kind of 'work' do you want from me, sweetheart?"

Good question. I pointed to the bar. "It's your turn to mix me a drink."

"I don't think so," he said, but his voice wasn't quite as forceful as before. I studied him carefully as he got up and walked toward me. When I circled him, always staying just out of reach as I swayed with the music, his expression became even more avid. He was enjoying the chase.

"Look but don't touch," I said, waggling my finger at him.

"Surely I can do something to be rewarded," he suggested, practically drooling. Oh, he was into it now.

I shimmied a little farther away. "Dance with me. We'll see how much you can impress me." Would I really be able to get away with turning him down?

Jasper slowly followed me, moving his hips from side to side and matching his steps to the rhythm of the music. We made a couple of circuits of the room before I could see his lust overcoming his enjoyment. Tamping down on my disgust, I continued to smile at him seductively.

It was better if he thought this dance was going to end with sex. I knew I was walking a very dangerous line. One wrong move and...

He reached to tug me to him, and I darted out of his reach, shaking my head. My nerves were jangling, but I spoke with the most commanding tone I had in me. "You're a naughty boy, Jasper. And you know what happens to naughty boys? They get punished."

Jasper's breath caught. Ugh, was that a bulge behind the fly of his slacks? Yep, he was already erect.

"Come on, girl," he said, his eyes gone dark with desire. "Don't make me wait for it."

"But the anticipation is part of the fun," I cooed. "And I need to see you've earned it."

"Oh, I can earn it, all right."

He stepped toward me, and I forced myself to keep dancing without touching him. His anticipation wrapped around me. I wasn't out of this yet. How could I—

Then he groped at my breasts, and I acted on pure instinct. Spinning around, I slammed my hand between his legs, squeezing his balls hard between my fingers. "What did I tell you about punishment?" I said with a hint of whisper.

Jasper's eyes widened, and I pressed harder. A sheen of sweat broke over his brow. He moaned, and then with a jerk of his hips, I felt him come in his pants.

Holding in a shudder, I stepped away before the wetness could slip through the fabric and onto my palm. I wanted to run to the washroom and scrub my hands until the skin was red, but instead I drew myself into a haughty posture. "Well?"

Jasper was still recovering from his orgasm, panting hard. Then he began to chuckle until he was practically roaring with laughter. I watched him warily.

"You, my dear," he said as he got a hold of himself, "are a force to be reckoned with. There aren't many who can please me in certain ways I enjoy so well. Ezra had better take care of you."

"Yes," I said, smiling thinly. "He had."

"He certainly made the right choice sending you." His eyes narrowed for a second, and his voice turned hard as steel. "You won't mention our encounter to anyone."

I could only imagine what the consequences of blabbing his secret would be, but I had no interest in gossiping about it anyway. I widened my eyes innocently. "All we did was have a few drinks and a good time."

"Good girl." Jasper smiled a cruel but pleased smile and looked down at the wet spot spreading across the crotch of his pants. "I think we're finished here. Ezra can count on the Demon's Wings' support. The deal is done."

18

Wylder

I LEANED BACK ON THE LEATHER CHAIR AND TOOK A SMALL sip of my brandy as Mozart's No 40 in G Minor played in the background. Normally, the music would have cleared my head. Tonight, I couldn't shake all the pictures my imagination kept conjuring for me.

Why did Mercy have to be so fucking stubborn? She should have taken off for someplace safe days ago. But no, she'd stuck around even with everything I'd been doing to push her away, and now she was out on a "date" with that psychotic prick Jasper Herald.

Date was a polite word for what was open sex bartering. I couldn't believe Dad had agreed to it. Why the hell had *Mercy* agreed to it? After the agony I'd put myself through, seeing the betrayal and hurt flash across her face every time I insulted her and having to hold myself back from telling her I didn't mean any of it, she'd walked straight into the lion's den anyway. Straight into the lion's *mouth*, more like it.

One thing was for sure: there was no other way the night would end except for Mercy sleeping with him. The only question was how much of her would be left afterward.

The glass cracked in my hand, a trickle of the amber liquid seeping over my fingers. I blinked down at it. I'd started gripping the glass so hard I'd fractured it. Shit.

A tiny thread of scarlet wound into the spilling brandy where the crack had nicked my skin. I watched it, remembering the time I had cut myself to promise Mercy that I was going to help her crush Colt Bryant if she cleared Kaige's name.

She'd held up her end of the deal, and I was making good on my promise. Wasn't that enough? Why did she have to get involved and put herself in the line of fire? Why couldn't she let me protect her?

Dad obviously didn't trust or respect her as much as he should have someone he'd initiated, let alone as much as she'd earned. He wouldn't have sent her on this mission otherwise. He was probably hoping she'd come back shattered so he wouldn't have to deal with her anymore.

If she survived tonight, he'd just find something worse to throw at her. We still had a battle with the Steel Knights ahead of us, and Lord knew it was going to be bloody no matter how many men we had on our side.

Unless I could come up with a way out of it. The beginnings of a plan had occurred to me after the night of the ambush, thinking of how I'd had to send Kaige to draw away the cops. Why not turn one of the biggest pains in our asses into a tool and save us all a whole lot of trouble?

I'd wanted to get the details totally solid in my head tonight, but I was too distracted. I straightened up, dropping the glass on the side table and going to wash my hands. Maybe it was never going to be perfect. I'd already delayed talking to Dad about the idea while I tried to get it there, and look what Mercy had gotten herself into in the meantime. I needed to convince him *now*, before she could find herself in an even worse mess.

And things could get a lot worse for her. I should know.

When I got to Dad's study, I found him sitting in his usual spot behind his desk, engrossed in a book. Some treatise on business strategy or politics, probably. He was dressed in his usual business clothes, an immaculate tie and shirt pressed to perfection. Sometimes I wondered if Rowan took his fashion cues from my father.

He glanced up at me, as unreadable as ever. “Wylder. I assume everything went smoothly before Mercy left for the date?”

I sat down in the armchair closest to his desk. “I wouldn’t know. I didn’t see her before she left.”

That wasn’t true. I’d watched her from the second floor as she’d gotten into the car and been driven away. She’d looked absolutely stunning in the emerald-green dress that’d hugged her in all the right places. She was all sinful curves and softness, and it should have been my hands on them, not fucking Jasper Herald—

I had to catch my fingers before they dug into my palms and bit back the question I wanted to ask. Had he heard anything from Jasper’s people yet? I couldn’t betray even that much interest.

“I’m sure she’s enjoying his company,” Dad said, setting his book down with a smile.

My jaw ticked. Mercy wouldn’t want some aging crime boss’s greasy paws all over her. But I knew Dad was trying to set me off. He wanted some reaction from me, and he wasn’t getting it.

Time to change the subject. “There was something else I wanted to talk to you about, actually. I think we can use the truck of drugs we stole from the Steel Knights to our advantage. It might be the key to taking them down for good—and in a way that won’t require tying ourselves to some other gang.”

Dad’s eyebrows arched. “Intriguing. What exactly are you suggesting we do?”

I spoke with all the confidence I had in me. “We set things up so Colt Bryant and many of the other prominent players in the Steel Knights get caught by the cops on major charges.”

I could tell at once from Dad’s expression that I was on shaky ground. His lip curled with a hint of disgust. “You want us to take help from the police?”

“Not exactly,” I said quickly. “We’d be using them like the dogs they are. Sic them on our enemies, and let them fight it out with each other while we laugh from the sidelines.”

That framing toned down his initial reaction enough that he didn’t yell at me to get out, anyway. He eyed me narrowly. “Continue.”

I didn’t have much time to convince him. I sucked in a breath. “We *have* a huge batch of the drug—a brand new drug that the cops must be aware of and eager to crack down on. I know you don't have any interest in distributing it ourselves. Rather than just toss it in the trash, we can use it as bait. We put out word on the street that we *are* going to start selling it and take over distribution from the Steel Knights."

"That would certainly piss them off," Dad said dryly.

"And that's what we want," I said, warming to the pitch. "We'll make sure just enough detail gets out for them to determine that we're storing and distributing the drug out of a building we've chosen specifically for our plan. Bryant and his men will come to take revenge for our theft and to try to show they can overpower us. But we'll also have to give a few tips to the cops that the Steel Knights are about to make a big move."

Dad's expression still hadn't budged. "This all sounds very precarious, Wylder."

"It doesn't have to be. Once they've stormed the building, we'll make sure they're trapped inside, and we'll have left nothing to incriminate the Nobles. We could even set up recording equipment that's supposedly surveillance cameras and turn them on then so there'll be video evidence of the Steel Knights with the truck. Then we send the cops in after them, they'll find the drugs and Bryant and the rest, and they all get arrested. We can leverage the dirty cops we have on the payroll to make sure the case isn't dropped or settled out of court. They go to jail, we have no more problems, and we keep our hands clean of the whole mess."

Dad started to laugh. The sound was so mocking, my stomach clenched. He always made me feel like I was still a thumb-sucking child, incapable of making decisions for myself.

"Are you done yet?" he asked.

I'd thought what I'd already said should be enough. I frowned at him. "Well—"

His tone turned outright icy. "The attack on our territory has already put a dent in our reputation. The last thing I need on top of that is to look so weak we'd turn to the police for help. It's nothing short of pathetic."

The back of my neck burned. "It wouldn't be weak—it'd be playing things *smart*. Why should we put our men at risk when we can—"

"That's enough," Dad interrupted. "I listened, and I've told you what I think of your 'plan.'" His voice dripped with derision. "Think of a better one next time, or don't bother wasting my time."

He swiveled his chair away from me, a clear dismissal. Anger and shame seared through my chest, but what else could I say to him? Maybe it'd been a losing battle trying to get him to consider *any* idea I came up with. He still only saw me as his second choice.

As I got up, Dad's phone rang. When he looked down at the caller ID, he frowned before lifting the phone to his ear. "Jasper, how nice to hear from you. I assume your evening went well?"

I stopped in my tracks, my pulse stuttering despite my best efforts at keeping my emotions under wraps.

After a pause, Dad went on. "I hope the girl met your expectations?"

I waited with bated breath, watching what I could see of my father's face carefully. All my nerves were clanging for a fight.

If the bastard had so much as laid a finger on Mercy I was going to fucking kill him. Even if that meant moving against my father and raising hell, I wasn't sure I could stop myself. Because Mercy was worth it… and that was the whole damn problem.

Jasper talked for a little longer, and Dad's lips pressed together. Definitely not a good sign. My body tensed.

"I see," Dad said. "I look forward to enjoying the results of our arrangement. Good night, my new friend."

He cut the call and turned to me. "Well, that was an interesting chat."

"And?" I said, swallowing the question I really wanted to ask. "Is the deal on?"

"It appears so. He liked Mercy very much. He seemed quite impressed with her."

I found his tone even harder to decipher than usual. Was he just keeping his delight at the news that the deal had gone as planned subdued, or had something else gone wrong that he wasn't mentioning?

"That's a good thing, right?" I said.

"Yes," he said, without a hint of enthusiasm. He paused and eyed me so shrewdly the hairs rose on the back of my neck. I did my best to mirror his impassive expression. After a moment, he looked away. "We have a powerful ally on our side. No need to rely on agents of the law. Is there a reason you're still here?"

"I just wondered whether the alliance had gone through. Good night." *You prick*, I added mentally as I pushed past the door.

He'd barely considered my plan. He'd started shooting it down from the very beginning of my explanation. When I was out of hearing range of the study, I slammed my fist against my palm in annoyance.

How the hell was I supposed to step up and prove myself the way he supposedly wanted when he decided every thought I had was worthless before he gave me a chance?

"Wylder?"

I looked up to see Gideon walking down the hall toward me. He looked almost as wound-up as I felt. What was he so on edge about?

"What's up?" I asked.

He tipped his head toward Dad's study. "I saw you coming out. You looked pretty pissed. What's going on?"

My jaw worked. If Gideon thought the plan was stupid too, then at least I'd know it wasn't just my dad dismissing me out of hand. "Let's go to my office, and I'll tell you."

In the room where I spent more waking hours than anywhere else, my eyes caught on the broken glass I'd left on the side table. Gideon's gaze slid over it too, but he made no remark. He was smart enough not to poke a dragon—at least, not unless he thought he really needed to.

I dropped into my usual chair, and he sat down across from me. As I laid out my idea the same way I'd explained it to Dad, he nodded here and there. After I finished, he set his chin in his hand, staring toward the wall with a distant expression.

It couldn't be *that* stupid if he hadn't dismissed it yet. He was actually considering the plan.

"It's high risk, of course, but whatever move we make against the Steel Knights will have to be," he said eventually. "I'd imagine that if we can control most of the parameters, it just might work. Which location were you thinking of?"

"I haven't thought it through that far yet," I said. "But it doesn't matter. Dad shot it down."

Gideon shrugged. "Why does that have to stop you? You've acted without his permission before."

"But never directly against his orders." I grimaced. "This is bigger than me. It affects all of the Nobles. I can't mess it up."

"That's true." His fingers drummed against his thigh, and I was struck again by the sense that he was agitated—in a way I'd rarely seen him unless he had some difficult problem in front of him. "Has there been any news about Mercy?" he asked abruptly. "How late are we expecting her to get back?"

I hesitated, studying him more closely. Was he worked up about the situation with her and Jasper? I mean, I was, but I had a reason to be. I'd never seen Gideon care much about what happened with the few women he'd spent time with over the years. Hell, I'd never seen him look this anxious over Kaige's or Rowan's safety, for that matter.

"Apparently she's fine," I said. "She's done with her meeting with Jasper and on her way home. It seems like she managed to please Jasper incredibly well."

Gideon's fingers twitched and his jaw tightened in a way that made me suddenly sure he was just as uncomfortable with the thought of what Jasper had expected from Mercy as I was.

How the fuck had that happened? *When* the fuck had that happened?

A flare of possessiveness shot through me, as if I should be the only one allowed to care, but at the same time... My best friend had finally found a woman who could get under his skin. Maybe I should be congratulating him. It was kind of nice to know he was human enough under his often robotic exterior to fall for someone.

"Just how bad have you got it for her?" I asked.

Gideon tensed even more than before, his gaze jerking to me. "What are you talking about?"

Was that a *blush* turning his cheeks faintly pink? I'd have laughed if I hadn't felt so heartsick at the same time. "Come on, Gideon. I've known you since we were nine years old. You think I wouldn't pick up on it when you finally had your first crush?" We'd leave aside however long it had actually taken me to notice.

Gideon sputtered. "I don't have a crush on Mercy."

I rolled my eyes. "With that reaction, I know for sure you do. Some things make more sense to me now."

He gave me a side-eye. "What?"

"Well, for starters, you've started tolerating her company, and you don't complain about her when she's not around like you do with just about everyone else." I kicked his shin lightly. "It's okay, man. It's *normal.* I was getting a little worried something in there was out of whack for you."

Gideon let out a frustrated sound. "Maybe I find her more... compelling than I'd have expected. It doesn't matter. My focus is still completely on my job, and I obviously wouldn't interfere with anything you have going on with her."

I forced myself to snort. "If you didn't get the memo, *I* don't like her much."

This time he rolled his eyes at me. "I've known you for thirteen years too, remember? I know what you're doing. I don't think she deserves it, but I'm not going to argue with you about it when you have... the reasons you have."

"Good," I said, abruptly grouchy. "Then let's stop talking about it."

Silence hung between us, but it didn't feel as comfortable as it usually did. My throat constricted. There was more I should say. More that *Gideon* deserved. If Mercy would have him, why should he have to go without just because I was forcing myself to?

"Gideon," I said finally, "just to be clear, if anything happens between you and Mercy while she's insisting on staying here, I swear to you it'll never cause a conflict between us. You're free to pursue anything you want with her."

Gideon chuckled disbelievingly. "Are you giving me your blessing?"

"Call it whatever you want. You've never liked a girl before, so it'd be very shitty of me if I cock-blocked you the one time you really wanted one."

Gideon opened his mouth, but the sound of smashing glass cut him off. Shouts rang out downstairs. We glanced at each other and leapt to our feet in unison, dashing for the door to find out what fresh hell was going on.

19

Mercy

I KNEW SOMETHING WAS WRONG THE MOMENT THE CAR pulled up at the Noble mansion. The outside security lights appeared to have been turned up to twice their usual glare. There were about a dozen men in view spread out across both sides of the lawn, fanning out as they scanned the terrain around them.

I frowned. I'd been gone for only a few hours. What the fuck had happened here?

A guy I only vaguely recognized was standing by the front steps. He wheeled his arm to direct me inside. "Go straight to your room and wait there."

I glared at him. "What? Who gave you permission to order me around?"

"I did." Wylder appeared in the doorway, his expression both fierce and so grim it made my stomach drop. Whatever was going on, it was *bad*.

I marched past him inside, annoyance prickling through me. After the night I'd just had, the last thing I needed was this new hostility of his.

More men were hustling around inside. A few of them were dumping plastic bags in a small heap in the middle of the foyer. As I watched, one hit the floor with a disturbing squelching sound that sent a twinge of nausea through me.

"What happened?" I demanded. "What's in the bags?"

"Don't worry about it, Princess," Wylder snapped. "Just go to your bedroom and stay there until someone tells you it's safe to leave."

I whirled toward him, my fancy dress rustling around my legs. "Are you fucking kidding me? There's obviously something huge going on, and I want to know what we're dealing with. So can you cut the shitty attitude for one hot minute, please? I've dealt with enough assholes for one night."

Something flashed behind his eyes, and for just a second the unfeeling mask cracked. "Why? What kind of crap did Jasper pull on you?"

I rolled my eyes. "Like you care."

To my surprise, he caught me by my shoulder, his grip unexpectedly insistent. "Tell me."

I shook him off, and he yanked his hand back as if I'd burned him. "I'm fine. He barely even touched me. Not that you'd be worried about my innocence anyway."

"Right," Wylder said, his jaw flexing. But he got over it—whatever it was—in a few seconds, his demeanor becoming frosty again. "You shouldn't be out here. Move, now, or I'll find Kaige to carry you up there."

"For fuck's sake." I turned away from him and strode over to the pile of bags to find out for myself.

Most of them were tied off, but a couple gaped open. A pungent smell that was far too familiar hit me in the nose, putrid and sour. It reminded me... of the mangled cat corpse we'd found on the lawn.

Holding back a surge of horror, I yanked open the nearest bag just as Wylder caught up with me.

The smell hit me even harder. I gagged, both at the stench and the sight of the rotting, eye-less face staring up at me from the bag.

It was a severed head, the skin patchy with gray and green, maggots squirming in the empty eye sockets and the ragged flesh at the base of its neck... and it was also somehow familiar.

As I dropped the bag, the sense of recognition clicked into place. That face had been imprinted in my memory nearly two weeks ago when *I* had severed that head from its body. After I'd already chopped the guy's limbs up for easy transport as part of one of Wylder's tests.

Rowan and I had buried the cut-up pieces in the forest hours from here. What the hell were they doing at the Noble mansion? Was this some kind of sick joke?

My head swam, bile rising in my throat. I took a step back, and Wylder clamped his hand around my elbow.

"I told you to go upstairs," he said in a taut voice.

I shook my head, but my thoughts kept spinning. It took a few seconds before I trusted myself not to vomit the moment I opened my mouth. "I've seen it now. I can't forget what's down here. You have to tell me what happened."

Wylder sighed, but I guessed I'd made a good enough point. "I can tell you recognized him. Someone must have dug up the corpse from wherever you buried him and hauled the pieces back here. About a half an hour ago, they smashed the living room window and hurled everything into the room from outside."

"Why—did anyone see who did it? Did you catch the guy?"

"No." There was enough fury in that single syllable to tell me just how pissed off that fact made Wylder. "Whoever did it was gone by the time the nearest men got to the spot. Gideon's been scanning the footage for any clue, but he hasn't reported back yet, so I'm assuming he hasn't found anything useful. We're dealing with a sick bastard and a fucking sly one."

I spun so I couldn't see the pile of bags at all, but the image of the rotting head floated behind my eyes. "It's a threat," I said. A threat meant for me. It wasn't any old corpse but the one I'd chopped up and buried. This had to have come from the same psycho who'd left me the disturbing sketch and the dead cat.

And the incidents were escalating... What would it be next?

Would Colt really have done all this just to get back at me? He'd been angry and some of his talk had made him seem kind of unhinged, but this was a totally other level. I had trouble picturing him coming up with a scheme this deranged.

Of course, I'd misjudged him before.

Another thought occurred to me with a sudden chill. "How did they even know? I cut up the guy right here in your basement—Rowan and I made sure no one was around when we buried the bags. I'm sure we didn't leave any evidence."

Wylder's mouth flattened. "Whoever it is must be watching you very closely. And your stalker is obviously well-versed in stealth. I'm starting to get the impression this is some kind of game to them."

Who else might hate my guts that much? For a second, my mind darted to Ezra, but the drawing and the cat tail had turned up before he'd even known I was in his house, let alone met me. And would he really have set things up so his own home looked so unsecured to his underlings? That didn't feel right either.

The longer I stood here with the body right behind me, the queasier I felt. But I sure as hell wasn't going to hide away in my room just to make the Noble heir happy.

"I'm going to talk to Gideon and see what's going on with the cameras," I said.

Wylder scowled, but before he could argue with me any more, I walked off. He needed to learn someday that he couldn't just order me around and expect me to jump at his command.

My legs wobbled with my first few steps, but by the time I reached the stairs, my stride had steadied. I hurried up, leaving the scene below and all the memories it'd stirred up as far behind as I could.

What a fuck-up of a night.

I didn't bother knocking, just walked right into Gideon's office. He was in almost the same pose as when I'd come to talk to him about the dead cat. His shoulders were rigid, his body tipped toward the array of screens.

He startled a bit as I swept in and spun to face me. He looked as exhausted as I felt—and almost pained.

"You're back," he said, his gaze sweeping over me. "You look okay. You handled Jasper, then?"

He sounded tense, but there wasn't a trace of doubt in his tone. *He'd* believed I could handle myself.

For just an instant, our brief but panty-meltingly hot kiss came back to me. I swallowed hard, the heat of the memory merging strangely with the much less pleasant sensations already roiling inside me.

"That's one way of putting it," I said. "He didn't take anything from me I couldn't stand to give. Of course, things don't seem much less dangerous here. You haven't found anything from the surveillance cameras?"

He winced. "You saw what happened downstairs?"

"I saw enough." I flopped into the chair next to him and frowned at the screens, which were all showing different feeds from the security system. "How could none of the cameras have caught anything? I know this asshole has that trick with disrupting the Wi-Fi, but didn't Ezra put those new hardwired cameras in?"

Gideon nodded with no shift in his uneasy expression. "He understood the problem and approved the installation as soon as I explained. But there's only one that has a view of the right part of the lawn, and your stalker appears to have found a way to disrupt that too."

He clicked a few keys, and one of the streams of footage zoomed into rewind mode. I squinted at it, wondering why it looked blurrier than the others. Men bustled about on the lawn in reverse, then vanished, and then—

A dark blotch filled the screen so suddenly I flinched. "What's *that*?"

"Oil or paint is my best guess," Gideon said. A rasp was creeping into his voice. "The men are too busy searching the grounds for me to ask anyone to take a closer look yet. It's not like it'll help us find the prick. He must have shot at it with something like a paintball gun. It dripped off after a few minutes, but that was all the time he needed."

My spirits sank. This guy was too fucking smart. He probably could have killed me already if he'd wanted to. But no, he must be enjoying terrorizing me.

It *had* to be Colt, right? Who else would revel in my distress that much?

"There *is* something," Gideon muttered, flicking through the footage. "Right—"

He nodded to the screen. Just as the liquid that had splattered the lens started to separate, I caught a flicker of movement in one of the gaps. But from the look of it, it wasn't more than someone's heel.

"If I could just pick up one identifying feature..." Gideon leaned close to the screen again, the glow reflecting off his pale face, his brow knit. He played that scrap of footage over and over, but the shape never revealed more than that dark flicker.

"Gideon," I said after a few minutes. "I don't think you're going to get anything from that. Even if we could see it clearly, the back of someone's leg isn't going to narrow things down much."

"It'd be something. Fuck!" He slammed his hand against the desk in frustration, a gesture so unexpected from the guy who was usually so coolly analytical that my skin jumped.

"It's not your fault," I said. "He obviously had it all planned out, and—"

"And I should have anticipated it," Gideon cut in, his rasp becoming more pronounced. "This fucker strolled onto our property and tossed a goddamned *corpse* through the living room window, and I can't even tell you for sure it's a *he*. What the fuck good am I if I can't even stop shit like this from happening? My one fucking job—all this fucking tech and I can't even protect you—or Wylder—or anyone here that much—"

He lowered his head and raked his fingers into his blue hair. "I can't go out there and start shoving our enemies around. I'm a liability in the field. But this, this is my kingdom. This is what I do. And I'm failing miserably."

I had no idea how to deal with a Gideon this distraught when I'd rarely seen him even mildly upset before. Tentatively, I eased my chair close enough to touch his arm. "You're doing more than anyone else could."

"But not enough. I can't afford to fail like this, not when sickos like this are lurking around just outside our doors. I can't be the weakness that allows them to come inside."

"You're not, Gideon," I said, my heart wrenching. "And there are so many ways you've helped. You're the reason we could grab the truck of drugs from Colt's territory."

But Gideon wasn't listening to me. His hands had balled on either side of his head, and his chest was hitching, the rasp filling even his breath now as if he couldn't get enough air inside him.

My pulse hiccupped. Were his lungs acting up? He was pushing himself so hard mentally, maybe he'd put his body into overload.

Like when I had my panic attacks. The fear of enclosed darkness could squeeze the breath from my lungs and turn my blood to ice in an instant.

"Gideon," I said, as soft and steady as I could manage. The way Rowan had talked to me way back when after he'd found me in the museum. "Listen to me. Just focus on my voice. Whether you want to believe it right now or not, you're the smartest person I know. Whoever is pulling this shit is just really fucking smart too. But you're figuring out his strategies, and the rest of us will do whatever we can to find clues our own way, and we'll work it out."

I squeezed his arm and then reached to rub his back with slow strokes. His breaths gradually evened out, the rasp fading. He pressed the heels of his hands over his eyes, bowing his head even more.

"Thank you," he said raggedly. "Sorry. Sometimes I can't— You must think I'm pathetic."

Every particle in my body flared in rejection of that statement. "No fucking way. You saw me freak out in the freezer the other day. I know what it's like to not be able to control your body's reactions. I'm sure as hell not going to judge someone else. You've got even more excuse than I do. There's nothing medically wrong with me."

He finally looked at me, his gray eyes clear and intense. Having all his analytical focus directed at me sent a tingle over my skin that I didn't really mind.

"What happened to you to give you a trigger like that?" he asked. "With a reaction that strong, I'm guessing it didn't just start out of the blue."

I shook my head, my throat tightening. But he'd just shown himself to me at his most vulnerable, whether he'd liked it or not. I could talk about my history if it made him feel better about that. I'd already told Kaige, after all.

"It started when I was a little kid," I said. "One of my father's favorite ways to punish me."

As I explained about the pit in the basement and the hours-long sessions I'd spend trapped in there, Gideon's eyes narrowed. "That bastard," he spat out when I was finished.

I gave him a crooked smile. "Well, he's dead now. I hope he's enjoying his stay in Hell."

"No fucking doubt." Gideon sighed and swiped his hand through his hair again. He looked at the screens for a moment before dragging his gaze back to me. "I know what it's like to have family that treats you worse than even strangers should be expected to. My lungs weren't always this bad, you know."

I hesitated and then asked quietly, "What happened to you?"

"It started out as just asthma—a pretty bad case, but I was okay as long as I had my inhaler. But the kids in the neighborhood saw me as an easy target because I couldn't defend myself that easily. I got beat up a lot, and my older brother and sister just thought it was funny. They'd even egg people on..."

He trailed off, and I thought he might stop there. But then he cleared his throat.

"One day, when I was eight, my brother stole my inhaler off me and then started shoving me around, calling over the other kids to join in. My lungs started to seize up, and I tried to grab the inhaler back from him, but I didn't stand a chance and the effort just made everything worse. I ended up collapsing on the sidewalk, and they just stood over me laughing. That's what kids do, right? Everything is a joke to them."

"Psychotic kids," I muttered. "That's awful."

"The attack got bad enough that it did permanent lung damage because I didn't get treatment soon enough. I passed out, and when I woke up, I was in the hospital. They had to perform emergency lung surgery to get me breathing again. It stabilized me, but my lungs were twice as messed up as before. Nothing's ever going to fix them." He shrugged as if it wasn't that big a deal, but I could see the anguish that passed through his eyes.

"Oh, Gideon." I didn't know what else to say. I couldn't even imagine that happening to an eight-year-old boy. His skinny body lying on the cold concrete, betrayed by his own family. "You didn't deserve that."

"It is what it is," he said, back to his usual matter-of-fact tone. "And maybe it wasn't completely a bad thing, because somehow it brought me and Wylder together. He was in my class the next year, and I saw some of the other kids hassling him in the schoolyard for some stupid reason, and it reminded me of what happened to me so much I kind of blanked with rage. Ran in there with fists flailing even though he could have defended himself just fine."

That I could imagine. My lips twitched with a smile. "Was he just as big a jackass back then?"

Gideon made a face at me. "Probably, but he also recognized loyalty just as well as he does now. I ended up wheezing in the nurse's office for my efforts, but from that day forward, he had *my* back no matter who came at me. He's supported everything I've wanted to do, taken me in when I couldn't stand to live with my family any longer. So the least I can do is make sure homicidal maniacs aren't breaking down his front door." He shot another glare at the surveillance footage.

The vulnerability he'd offered with the things he'd revealed squeezed my heart. I had the urge to lean in and steal another kiss—to keep kissing him until I'd melted all the doubt out of him. He was gorgeous and stoic and strong in ways he didn't even seem willing to admit to himself.

And he was Wylder's best friend.

Gideon probably wouldn't have kissed me earlier if I hadn't caught him by surprise. I wasn't going to throw a wrench into their long-standing friendship. It was bad enough having Wylder treating me like a second-class citizen without me making Gideon a target by association. If he'd even want to be associated with me that way.

"I have full faith in your abilities," I told him. I had to smother a yawn. "Don't beat yourself up over this. I know I don't have any authority around here, but that's an order."

There was something softer than usual in Gideon's eyes as he gazed back at me. "Thank you for listening and not treating me like something pitiful afterward. With whatever authority *I* have, I'm saying I think you should get some sleep."

"You might be right about that." Reluctantly, I got to my feet. "Make sure you get a little rest in there somewhere too."

I walked to the door, but I couldn't quite bring myself to open it without saying *something*. I turned back to look at Gideon, finding him still watching me. Something in his gaze sent a fresh flicker of heat through my chest.

"Since we're being honest," I said, "I wanted to kiss you again just now. But I can tell how important your friendship with Wylder is, and you've obviously seen how he feels about me these days, and I don't want to cause any tension between the two of you by going for it. What happened this evening won't happen again. Just—just so you know."

Gideon stared at me for the space of a few heartbeats. His silence said enough. Before I totally humiliated myself, I ducked out of the room and hurried down the hall to mine.

20

Gideon

I paced from one end of my office to the other, too keyed up to even sit down. The rhythmic hiss of the aquarium filter should have soothed my nerves, but at the moment it only sounded like an irritating thrum. What I really wanted to do was punch a hole through the wall, but I knew that chances were I'd break at least one finger in the process.

"Jesus fucking Christ, Gideon," I muttered. "Get a grip on yourself."

I was almost certainly the sharpest mind in this building, but I was also an idiot. Mercy had all but spelled out in neon lights that she wanted me. And I'd just sat there like it was nothing to me, when the truth was the total opposite.

If I was being honest, something about her had grabbed my attention from the first instant I'd met her, and she'd only become more fascinating since. The moment this evening when her lips had locked with mine—fuck, I'd never felt anything like that rush of fiery hunger in my life. But just now, I'd been out of sorts after spilling my guts, trying to pull myself back together, and then she'd tossed out that comment out of nowhere—

No, there was no excuse for gaping at her like a dimwit. She'd talked me down from the start of an attack. She'd listened to me confess the ugliest parts of my past and treated me as no less human, no less whole, than she had before. She understood the kind of darkness I faced, and she didn't shy away from it.

She was everything I could have asked for in any kind of companion, and I'd given her the absolutely wrong impression.

I stopped in front of the espresso machine, but caffeine wasn't what I needed. I needed that hot mouth under mine, that soft yet powerful body against me...

I'd just go and talk to her. Set the record straight. And she could make of it what she would. That was the only logical approach.

Of course, logical didn't mean easy. I took several deep breaths and then marched out into the hall, my whole body jittering with anticipation. Unfortunately, the second I'd locked my office door and turned around, I found myself faced with Ezra Noble.

"Gideon," he said in his typical smooth, assured voice. "Just the man I wanted to see."

Really? Oh, shit, he probably wanted to know what I'd turned up from the surveillance footage, and I'd have to spell out my failure all over again. I held myself stiffly straight, bracing for it. "What can I do for you, Mr. Noble?"

He wagged his finger at me as if I were a petulant child. "I've told you several times, Gideon, you may call me Ezra."

"Yes... Ezra," I said.

Ezra smiled at me. It wasn't a smile I trusted. He might have looked like an older version of my best friend, but Wylder had a number of qualities I appreciated that his father lacked. A willingness to think outside the box and see the strengths in those many would consider weak, for example. Ezra had only grudgingly allowed me to move into the mansion and barely acknowledged my presence until I'd worked out a solid enough setup to start delivering useful intel regularly.

This was a man who only cared about using everyone around him as thoroughly and brutally as possible. Yes, he did what had to be done, but he could also be unnecessarily cruel at times. Especially to Wylder.

He was the one person I'd never be able to protect my best friend from, not as well as I'd have liked to, and some part of me hated him for that.

But tonight he surprised me, though not in a good way. Instead of asking about the footage, he folded his arms over his chest and said, "What do you think of Mercy?"

I blinked. "I'm sorry?" Had he seen her leaving the office—did he have some idea that I'd been heading to her right now?

A flush started to creep up under my skin, but Ezra chuckled lightly and made a dismissive gesture. "Let me be more specific. What do you make of the recent activities on our property that appear to be targeting her?"

Interesting. I had the sense he was fishing for some kind of information. "I would agree that the perpetrator appears to be focused on her," I said carefully. "All of the incidents have been tied to her in some way." Did he know about the cat tail and the drawing as well as the more recent intrusions? If not, I wasn't going to be the one to inform him.

Ezra nodded. "Have you uncovered any evidence pointing to who might be responsible?"

Something in the way he spoke put me even more on the alert. "Not yet," I admitted. "But the available facts all point to Colt Bryant or someone acting under his direction. The nature of the incidents suggests someone with a deep personal vendetta."

"Agreed." Ezra tsked to himself. "She's being targeted on our property to the point that somebody breached our home to get to her. I can't help thinking that makes her a liability."

My hackles came up. If he expected me to agree with that statement, he had no idea who he was talking to. Apparently he didn't have much idea about Mercy either. But I couldn't tell him he was an idiot to his face.

"I think we'd have to weigh both sides of the equation," I said evenly. "We've faced some unpleasantness from this intruder, but no one has been harmed. On the other hand, Mercy has already provided valuable intel on multiple occasions and otherwise aided with the success of important operations. I believe her skills and experience will continue to benefit us in many ways."

"Perhaps not enough to offset the damage if this unstable party continues to escalate their hostilities."

"I don't think we have enough data to make predictions about that yet," I said, which wasn't actually true. "Besides, you sent her to meet Jasper today, and her presence helped solidify that alliance as well, didn't it?"

Something in my words made his expression harden. Wylder had told me that Jasper had called up Ezra to tell him something. Now I wondered what it was.

When he didn't speak, I continued. "It's my opinion that her value to the Nobles far exceeds any misdirection that an unknown enemy might be trying to create."

Ezra cocked his head. "So, you think the goal is misdirection?"

I shrugged. "As the former heir to the Claws, she's in a strategic position to help us greatly. Maybe someone doesn't want that to happen. Which is all the more reason we shouldn't throw away a resource before discovering its full potential."

"An interesting take, Gideon," Ezra said, his expression thoughtful. I could tell from his tone that he wasn't convinced, but he gave me a pat on the shoulder and walked off—in the opposite direction from where I'd been headed, thankfully.

I stood there for a moment, letting the conversation settle in my head. The fact that he'd insisted on sending Mercy on a date with a known predator hadn't sat right with me in the first place. It almost seemed like he hadn't wanted her to succeed. And now that she had, he was finding other excuses to question her place here... I didn't like it at all.

I might not have any clue how to protect Mercy from her unnervingly capable stalker, but I could certainly keep an eye on Ezra's reactions to her. There was something brewing in his devious mind, and it meant nothing good.

Right now, though, the only person I wanted my eyes on was Mercy herself. The interruption had rattled me, but as I strode down the hall toward the new guest bedroom Mercy had taken over, my heart fell back into a steady—if slightly accelerated—rhythm. Anticipation and anxiety twined together in my chest.

I stood in front of the bedroom door for several seconds before the fear that someone—like Ezra—would catch me there chased off the fear that she'd laugh in my face. It wasn't as if I could imagine the Mercy I knew doing that anyway. I knocked, keeping the sound quiet enough that it wouldn't travel down the hall.

For a moment, there was no response. I was on the verge of convincing myself that she was already asleep and I should walk away when there was a click, and the door opened.

Mercy looked alert enough that I didn't think I'd woken her up, but her dark brown hair was rumpled from lying down and she'd washed off the heavy makeup Anthea had painted all over her face. She'd changed from the satin gown into a thin tank top and pajama shorts.

She'd looked gorgeous all done up in her dress, but in one glance, I knew I preferred her like this: practical and straightforward and still pretty as hell.

"Hey," she said, peering out at me. "Did something else happen? Did you find something in the footage?"

Of course she'd think that's why I was here. Somehow faced with the reality of her, I lost my grip on my tongue. "I—no. I'm sorry. I didn't mean to disturb you. You're obviously headed to bed." My gaze fixed on the front of her tank top, and I noticed the faint splatter of an oil stain before I yanked my eyes away from what was also the swell of her breasts. "You should buy new clothes."

"Thanks for the advice," Mercy said dryly. "Is *that* what you came over to tell me?"

I'd obviously messed up here. Was there any chance of retrieving my foot from my mouth? "No, not that either."

She crossed her arms in front of her chest. "So, what exactly did you want to talk about, then?"

I opened my mouth and closed it again, managing to think through my next words before I said them out loud. "Can I come inside?"

The implication of inviting myself into her bedroom at night wasn't lost on me, and it probably wasn't on her either. She gave me a more evaluating look. "Sure. The hall isn't a great place for a conversation anyway."

She stepped back, and I followed her into the room. The door thumped shut behind me, and I was abruptly struck by the gravity of what I was hoping to do here.

I'd slept with women before, sure, but it'd only been for the physical release. It'd never mattered even a fraction as much as the mere expression on Mercy's face meant to me now.

She needed to know that our kiss hadn't been a mistake, that I hadn't meant to reject her just now.

I caught myself worrying at my lip ring with the tip of my tongue and shook myself. Mercy sank down on the edge of the bed. It was a basic double in an utterly basic room, like the other few guest rooms in the mansion: just a bed, a side table, and a chair in the corner. A couple of Mercy's origami figures were posed on the table. She'd only switched rooms a few nights ago, but she'd already made this one her own.

Mercy was watching me. Right. Because I was supposed to be explaining why the hell I was here. I inhaled slowly and decided that talking wasn't getting me very far. Maybe I was better off just showing her.

Ignoring the nerves jumping in my stomach, I bent down, slid my fingers along her cheek, and kissed her the way I'd been imagining since her lips had first touched mine hours ago.

A perfect little gasp slipped from her mouth, and then she was kissing me back, and every other thought swept from my mind. I felt like I was standing in the middle of a storm, and I wanted—no, *needed* more.

Before I could make good on that urge, Mercy eased back and stared up at me. Her cheeks were flushed in a way that brought out her natural beauty even more, and exhilaration flooded me at the thought that I'd made her look that happy.

"Gideon," she said, "I thought—"

I sat down on the bed next to her, tracing my hand along her cheek and down the side of her neck, reveling in the silky smoothness of her skin and in the flutter of her eyelids at the caress. Her pulse beat against my fingertips at the base of her throat.

"I gave you the wrong idea back in my office," I said. "I—I'm not used to feeling this way about someone. I want you. A lot. And you don't have to worry about affecting my friendship with Wylder. He and I already talked about it. It isn't a problem."

She blinked. "You and Wylder discussed the fact that—"

"It was a short discussion," I broke in, before she got the wrong idea all over again. "Covering only the most essential points. But it was enough. And talking isn't what I want to do now. Unless... if there's something you think we need to—"

"No," Mercy said, her voice going rough, and yanked me to her.

That kiss was even better than the first. Our breaths mingled hot between our mouths, and her tongue twined with mine. I kissed her until I felt like I'd drown in her.

Her hands traveled over my chest, and I was suddenly giddy with the thought of all the places I wanted to touch *her*, all the things I wanted to do to her—things it seemed she was just as eager for as I was. I had no idea how that had come to be, but I wasn't going to question it, not in this moment.

I tipped her down on the bed as gently as I could and then climbed atop her. Her hair fanned over the white pillowcase. As I kissed her again, I looped a strand around my finger and tugged on it. Her moan echoed into my mouth. That was all the encouragement I needed to repeat the gesture.

Her tongue came out to play against mine again. I explored the delicious cavern of her mouth, thrusting in and out with my own tongue as if I was fucking her with it. Mercy gripped me hard, her fingers digging into my shoulders like she couldn't bear to let me go. My cock that had only been half-mast went rigid, straining against my fly.

I resisted touching her entire body as I pressed more kisses along her jaw. Mercy let out little noises of encouragement with each one. She was a tempestuous being, and yet here she lay beneath me as I laid siege to her body, ready and willing to open herself up to me. It was such a fucking turn-on.

I pushed my fingers into hers as I let her feel more of my weight, her warm body cushioning me. Some part of me wanted to stay here forever.

We had all night, at least, and I wasn't going anywhere.

I continued my trail of kisses down her neck, taking in each of her reactions until I found a particularly sweet spot just above her collar bone. At the brush of my lips there, her chest hitched. Ah ha. I'd seen her touch this spot before when she was nervous.

I stopped and kissed her there again, this time using my mouth to suck softly before letting my wet tongue bring some relief to her inflamed skin. Mercy moaned, the sound deeper this time.

Oh, yes, I'd just discovered a gold mine. But I was determined to seek out every spot that could set her on fire.

I eagerly continued my explorations, this time moving up to her ears. I nibbled on her earlobe before flicking my tongue around it. Her hips pushed into me in answer with a growl that practically made me come in my pants.

I brushed her hair away from her face and looked down into her blue eyes that had darkened in lust. "I haven't even gotten to the best part yet."

Mercy grinned. Her voice came out breathless. "I think you're doing a pretty good job so far."

I teased my hand down her body and placed the heel of my hand against her sex. "Fuck," Mercy mumbled, pressing into my touch. She was so fucking wet it'd dampened the crotch of her pajama shorts. I wanted to pull them down and feel her gushing for me, let my fingers glide through the slickness. But I was enjoying this too much, charting the little pieces of her that brought her the most intense pleasure, which in turn made me hornier than I'd ever been before.

My hands brushed against her breasts. She breathed out, as if she was waiting for me to go farther. Instead, I kissed her until she was arching against me. When I let the full press of my weight meet her body, her legs rose alongside my hips as if urging me even closer to her.

I pushed against her and watched her eyes roll back as she felt my rigid cock. I did it again, this time a little urgently. A slight burn entered my lungs at the exertion, but not so much that I couldn't ignore it.

I bent down to taste one of her nipples through the fabric of her top. She wasn't wearing a bra underneath, and I felt the nub harden through the flimsy cotton. I suckled a little before biting down, making her squirm under me.

Then, all of a sudden, Mercy set her hand on my chest and nudged me back. "Wait."

My lust-hazed thoughts jumbled. Was she having second thoughts? I pulled back, braced for the rejection that might have been inevitable.

21

Mercy

The delicious press of Gideon's weight on me was turning everything around me hazy. All I could see and feel was him and his wicked, wicked tongue. He had managed to discover a few spots that made me go almost insane, and he wasn't even inside of me yet...Heck, we hadn't even taken our clothes off.

He swiped his tongue over my nipple, setting off an electric jolt through my nerves. But the intensity in his expression when he glanced up at me, a thin but pleased smile playing with his lips, made something in me twist.

I didn't know what this meant to him. I didn't know what I'd want it to mean to me beyond this moment. And there were a whole lot of things *he* didn't know that maybe he should.

He lowered his head again, and I caught him with a hand on his chest. "Wait."

He stopped, braced over me, and I regretted the loss of his touch almost immediately. Something shuttered behind his gray eyes that had gleamed with so much passion a second ago. "What's wrong?" he asked.

"Nothing," I said quickly. Gideon had said he hadn't really wanted anyone like this before, and having seen his normal behavior, it didn't surprise me to know he hadn't exactly been a ladies man in the past. I didn't want him to think I wasn't enjoying every second of this. "I just —I want to make sure we're on the same page."

He cocked an eyebrow. "How so?"

"I..." His analytical gaze made me want to look away, but I didn't let myself. "This is good. *Really* good. Just so we're clear. But—I'm not sure how much you've realized—I've been with Kaige and Wylder. And with Rowan, a long time ago. I might want one... or more... of them again. I'm not sure where we're going with this, but I'm not ready to tie myself down to anyone. I just thought I should say that before we go any further."

Maybe he'd think it was weird that I'd found myself drawn to all four of them. Maybe it *was* weird. I didn't know how I'd come to feel so connected to this tight-knit group, but I did. However weird it might seem, I didn't want to give them up. I belonged with them now, no matter what Wylder said or did to try to convince me otherwise.

Gideon blinked at me. There was a moment when I thought he might pull back and end the whole thing. But then his smile came back, curving wider this time. He brushed his fingers over my cheek in an unexpectedly tender gesture.

"That's why I like you," he said. "You say what you feel and what you mean, you don't mince words about it, but you've got your principles too. I'm not sure where we're going either. I don't think I'd want to tie you down. Well, not that way." The sly gleam that came into his eyes made me instantly twice as wet. "All I'm sure about is that I want to keep going right now."

A slightly giddy giggle tumbled out of me. "Well, full speed ahead, then."

He reached for me, and I pushed myself upward to meet him halfway with a kiss. I sucked on his lower lip, taking the metal ring in my mouth before I swirled my tongue around it.

Gideon's breath hitched. He grabbed the back of my hair urgently as he fused his lips back on mine. He might not have the overt physical power the other guys did, but he sure knew how to take what he wanted, and it was hot as hell.

He broke from the kiss to pull off my top. My nipples puckered in the air conditioned coolness of the room, stiffening more under Gideon's hungry gaze. Little thrills went down my body as he rolled one nipple between his fingers before bending down to take the other in his mouth. He sucked on my tits softly at first before biting down hard enough to provoke a gasp.

His other hand dipped inside my pajama shorts, stroking over my pussy and taking it from hot to scorching. My elbows wobbled, and Gideon took the opportunity to press me back down into the mattress. He put his legs on either side of me to hold me there firmly.

"Stop squirming," he murmured. "Let me worship you."

How could I say no when he was so good at it? He seemed to know which spots would make me keen and which ones would make me whimper.

He kissed a trail down the valley of my breasts, squeezing my tits together and offering equal attention to both sides, before continuing his path down to my belly. When he flicked his tongue inside my belly button, I almost arched right off the bed. He chuckled, his hot breath sending another flare through my torso.

His fingers slipped beneath my shorts again, and he let out a sound that was strained but approving. "You're so wet for me." His low voice and something in his expression, so awed and pleased, just made me gush even more.

He pushed his middle finger inside me, exploring me with the same certainty as when he'd been kissing me all over. "Don't move," he warned me again.

"Ummm," I said, unable to come up with anything more coherent.

As his finger curled into my sex, another wordless noise of approval tumbled out of me. He eased a second finger in and flicked his thumb against my swollen clit. While he continued to fuck me with his fingers, my body rocked against him to bring myself more relief.

Then he withdrew farther down the bed, yanking my pajama shorts off in one swift motion. He eyed my throbbing sex hungrily. His tongue flicked over his lip ring, and I quivered at the thought of it brushing against my clit.

As if sensing that thought, he dove down. In an instant, his tongue was ravaging my clit before finding its way to my slit and sucking on it. I groaned as pleasure built inside me, clutching at the bedsheets to hold myself in place.

Gideon was eager—urgent even—in his ministrations. His tongue dipped right inside my cunt. He swirled it around the top of my slit right to my bottom, almost brushing against my asshole. The slight chill of the metal lip ring against my wet pussy ignited a friction that left me gasping, heightening all the sensations in me.

The pressure was slowly rising through me, pushing me to the edge of a precipice that made my toes curl up. Gideon didn't stop—he didn't slow down one bit as his tongue continued to work on my cunt, fucking it fast before twirling around and then repeating the motion. My body buckled as the wave of pleasure crested, threatening to drown me.

I looked down hazily to see Gideon's stark blue hair bobbing as he feasted on my cunt. The sight made me moan. He looked up and met my gaze even as he continued to loll his tongue around, making little sounds of approval as he did so. Lust shone in his eyes.

I couldn't have stopped myself if I'd wanted to. Just as he dipped his tongue in again, I climaxed hard, gushing in his face. My legs shook at the force of the orgasm.

Gideon was on top of me in seconds, not leaving a moment for me to recover. His hard cock aligned at my pussy, the head pressing against my clit. Oh, fuck, I wanted that too, so badly, even though I'd just come.

I sucked in a ragged breath and noticed that Gideon was panting too, a rasp creeping into his breath. I doubted he'd want to admit it, but sex took a lot out of a person physically. It must be hard on his lungs. The final act would be even more so. He didn't look like he had any intention of slowing down, though, no matter what it did to him.

I wasn't going to remind him of his one weakness, but I could give him an excuse to recover a bit. I tugged at his shirt. When Gideon hesitated, I pouted at him. "Isn't it a little unfair that I'm completely naked while not a single piece of clothing has come off you?"

Gideon's eyes heated before he chuckled. "I like seeing you this way. You're perfect." He ran his hands along the sides of my body, which made my pussy clench again. Just his simple touch seemed to ignite every one of my nerve endings. "I, however, am not."

I tipped my head to the side against the pillow. "What are you talking about?"

He hesitated again and then put his hands under his shirt to pull it off, revealing a slim but leanly muscled chest marked with a dark tattoo that covered him from collarbone to belly.

My eyes widened as I took it in, tracing the tendrils that rose from the top of the menacing shape and the dark eyes that peered into mine from the shadowy figure's face. A few of the whirling lines followed ridges in his skin—the raised lines of scars. They blended into the strokes of the tattoo, but it didn't hide them completely.

Tension gripped Gideon's body as he watched me. I grazed my fingers down the center of his chest, avoiding the scars. "What is it?"

"The darkest god there is, ruler of death and destruction." His mouth twisted. "If the scars from the surgery were never going to go away, I figured I should do my best to turn them into something powerful."

"It's stunning," I said honestly.

A hint of a smile came back to Gideon's lips. "Hades seemed particularly appropriate. He too was shunned by his siblings and cast out of his own home. He always fascinated me with his shadowy prowess. And besides, I've looked him in the eye and survived him—several times now."

"Can I..." I trailed off, letting the question hang in the air between us. This was an important moment between him and me, and in some ways even more intimate then when he was fucking me with his tongue just moments ago.

Gideon nodded. I ran my hand farther across the expanse of his chest, admiring the taut planes of muscle that defined his slender frame. I could feel the strength running through his body, even when I gently traced the scars. I stopped, fingers splayed, right where his heart thundered in his ribcage against my palm.

"I'm not fragile," Gideon said. "I know physical strength isn't my forte, but I won't break apart under your fingers."

"I know that," I said. "You're not fragile in any way." I thought of how little Gideon had protected Wylder in school all those years ago, how he was still protecting him all these years later. "You're brave and strong—and powerful."

He gazed at me until I couldn't bear it any longer. I pulled him down to me and kissed him hard. Then I pushed us onto our sides and sat up next to him, fumbling with the button of his fly. Gideon helped, yanking off his slacks and his boxers. He grabbed a foil packet from his pocket before kicking them off the mattress onto the floor.

"You came prepared," I said, delighted and amused.

Gideon shot me a rare grin. "I try to anticipate every possible situation."

I admired his cock, my mouth watering. Thick veins ran down its substantial length, and the bob of its head practically called out to me. I snatched the condom from him and nudged him down on his back as I straddled his legs.

Gideon stared up at me. "Mercy, what—"

"No arguments," I said, tapping my finger to his lips and then rolling the condom over his length. His breath stuttered, and his cock pulsed against my fingers. Fuck, I couldn't wait to feel it inside me.

I positioned myself over him and stroked my fingers over his tattooed chest again, holding his gaze. The sultry seductress role had never felt all that natural to me, but right now, it was as if some kind of goddess had taken me over. This position would be easier on Gideon's lungs, but that didn't mean he had to give up the control he'd obviously been enjoying so much.

"I want to ride my dark god and do his bidding," I purred. "What would you have me do first?"

Desire flared in Gideon's eyes. He gripped my thighs. "Take me," he ordered. "All of me."

I was more than happy to fulfill that desire. I plunged down over him, and he thrust up to meet me. Pleasure crackled through me as my pussy stretched to accommodate him. When he was completely inside me, I gasped at the feeling of fullness. Looking down, I took in our joined bodies, licking my lips at the erotic sight.

"Ride me," Gideon commanded. "Hard and fast like I know you'll like it."

Hell, yes. The authority in his voice turned me even slicker around him.

I raised myself up and lowered myself again, gaining speed as I found my rhythm, and Gideon matched me stroke for stroke. He thrust slow and deep and then faster, with a rolling motion I realized was mimicking the strokes that had gotten me off so well with his tongue. The man was a fast learner.

Sweat rolled down my chest and glazed his. As we rocked together, I leaned down to reclaim his mouth. He kissed me back hungrily, tugging my hair in the way he'd discovered that sent sparks shivering from my scalp all the way to my sex. Then he raised his hips beneath me to press his cock against just the right spot inside me to make me shatter apart again.

Gideon wasn't done yet. He continued to guide me up and down his shaft, our motions becoming more erratic with every thrust. I set my hands on his chest to steady myself as I jerked against him, chasing one more release alongside his. My hair swayed around me with our wild bucking.

A sensation like lightning shot through my body. I ground my hips into his, he swiveled to meet me, and a curse stuttered from his lips.

His expression of pure, unadulterated lust as his release rocked his body was too much for me to handle. I came right alongside him, moaning as our orgasms simultaneously battered our bodies.

It took me a few minutes to catch my breath. Finally, I slid myself off his cock and lay down beside him on the bed. Gideon pulled me closer, his own breath rough but not concerningly so.

"Wow," I said. It seemed to be the only word I had left in my brain.

His arm tightened around me. "That was amazing."

"Maybe even godly," I said, and earned a chuckle. To my surprise, he kissed me on my cheek. Something in that sweet gesture warmed my heart.

There had been, however, nothing sweet in the way that he had fucked me. Even when I had been on the top and he had let me lead it, he'd been right there, working his hips into mine, every step of the way.

I didn't think I could give him up now either, even if I'd wanted to.

22

Mercy

"I have a mission for you," Ezra said, leaning back in his throne-chair.

I gazed steadily back at him, trying not to show the tremor of apprehension that'd run through me at his words—only a little smaller than the one that'd hit me when Axel had summoned me to the Noble leader's audience room a few minutes ago. The last mission Ezra had sent me on had nearly ended with me bloodied and raped.

But I'd survived it, and he'd see that I could survive whatever else he threw at me, just like I'd proven to his son. He hadn't said a word about my sealing the deal with Jasper in the past two days. Not that I needed the credit, but it would have shown he had a little more faith in me now.

"Great," I said. "What is it?"

"Now that we have the Demon's Wings willing to send support"—he eyed me for a second as if checking for a reaction to that vague reference to my "date" with Jasper—"it's time to proceed with the next part of our plan against Colt Bryant. We need to destroy the foothold the Steel Knights have gained in the Bend."

Well, I was a hell of a lot more for that than entertaining sleazy gang bosses. I let a little more enthusiasm enter my tone. "I'm ready to do whatever it takes. What's the plan?"

"It's come to my attention that Colt has been storing a large quantity of weapons in one of the warehouses in the industrial district of the Bend."

I nodded. "I'm aware. I saw them."

Ezra gave me a narrow look and then continued, "He hasn't been too subtle about it either. He seems to be sending a message to those who haven't joined him yet or are on the fence that they'll be able to defend themselves and no longer need our protection. We're going to show how wrong he is about that and effectively disarm him."

"Sounds good to me," I said, hoping plain old agreement would go over better.

It did get me a mild smile. "Wylder is going to run you through the details, but the primary objective is to take out the warehouse with all its weapons. Naturally, the place will be heavily guarded, so he'll be taking a large force, including both our men and some of Jasper's. But I felt it was important you joined in with your inside knowledge of the Bend and the aptitude for fighting you've already shown."

The words sounded way more generous than I expected Ezra to be. I considered him warily even as I kept a smile pasted on my face. "I appreciate that. I'll help any way I can. There's nothing I want more than to see Colt Bryant broken and bleeding and the bastards who helped him slaughter my family right there alongside him."

"Excellent." Ezra stood up and motioned to the door. "Then there's nothing further we need to discuss. Check in with Wylder, and he'll give you your marching orders."

Chances were Wylder's first orders would be to march in the opposite direction as far as I could go, but he couldn't put me off for long when his father had directly instructed me to come along. I was almost looking forward to throwing that fact in his face. Although something about the conversation with Ezra still didn't feel quite right to me.

As I left to figure out where the Noble heir was right now, I caught sight of Gideon down the hall. He stopped in his tracks, no doubt taking note of what room I'd come out of. There was something hesitant in his expression, but it didn't interfere with the new hint of warmth in his gaze.

Things had been a little awkward between us since the other night when we'd come together so passionately, but I guessed that wasn't surprising considering Gideon's lack of experience with any kind of relationship. Half the time he wasn't friendly to his own friends, other than Wylder. I actually found the tentative awkwardness combined with the undeniable signs of attraction kind of adorable in an unexpected way.

It was a heck of a lot better than how his best friend had reacted after our earlier hook-up.

"Hey," I said, walking over to him. "Did Ezra want to fill you in on the new plan too?"

His gaze flicked over my face, settling for a longer moment on my lips before returning to my eyes. But there was an odd note in his voice when he spoke. "He had a couple of files he wanted to pass on to me. What were you doing in there?"

Hadn't I basically just explained that? "He called me in to tell me he wanted me on the upcoming mission."

"Just that?"

"Yeah." I frowned. "Would you have expected something else?"

Gideon's gaze had gone distant again. Somewhere behind those cool gray eyes, a whole lot of gears were turning.

I didn't like how serious he looked, but then he shrugged it off. "No, I only wondered." He offered me a quick, tight smile. "I'd better get those files so I can watch over the rest of you properly while you're out there kicking Colt's ass."

I smiled back even though his demeanor had left me uneasy. Was something bothering him that he wasn't telling me? But we weren't exactly close enough that it seemed right to try to badger him about it. The one thing I was sure of with Gideon was that if he'd consider logically whether I was better off knowing and tell me if he determined I was.

"We'll be counting on you," I said, and set off in search of his asshole best friend.

Several hours later, I was crouched by a car down the street from the old warehouse building where Colt was storing his weapons. The summer humidity had already turned my shirt sticky against my skin even in the darkness of the early morning hour, well before dawn. The smell of gasoline and hot asphalt prickled in my nose. And Wylder was scowling at me.

Nothing so new about that. I ignored him, which I hoped just pissed him off more.

A shiny black sedan entered through the main gates of the warehouse. Could Colt be in it? I'd love for him to be inside when we blew it up. But we couldn't move from our place. We had to wait.

Finally, a man showed up a few blocks down the street in the opposite direction from the warehouse. I didn't know this guy who looked to be in his early to mid-twenties with shaggy brown hair. The sleeves of his shirt were rolled up, and I caught the tattoo of the demon skull over his right wrist.

He nodded in our direction even though I was pretty sure he couldn't make us out in the darkness.

"I still kind of feel iffy working with Jasper's men," Wylder admitted under his breath.

"Maybe you should have thought of that before I went to him," I said sarcastically.

He looked at me, his eyes narrowing. "Wouldn't want your efforts to go to waste now, would we?"

"Oh, fuck you," I muttered as I turned back to face the Demon's Wings man who was slowly making his way towards us.

"You already have," Wylder said in a matter of fact voice. I had the intense urge to hit him, but I wasn't going to compromise the mission over his dickishness.

The man stopped when he reached the car. Wylder motioned him closer. "Did you bring everything?"

He ducked down across from us and nodded. "Enough explosives to take this whole thing down twice over. Everything's in our truck. But how are you going to take it inside?"

I met Wylder's eyes before we stepped out of the darkness. I wore a sleeveless hoodie with the hood up to cover my hair and a red bandana on my arm. Wylder was dressed in a similar way.

We were going in as the Steel Knights ourselves—or at least the underlings pledged to them. We were counting on there being so many new recruits that any regulars we couldn't stealthily kill would be used to unfamiliar faces. The bandanas weren't even official Steel Knights ones, just mocked up to look that way with red fabric and black sharpie.

Wylder made a signal, and the rest of the Noble people on the job moved toward the Demon's Wings truck, slipping through the night's shadows. Then he and I parted ways.

I followed the Demon's Wings guy back to the truck, and he ushered the last few men into the back. I was bringing in very dangerous cargo tonight, but it would only be deadly to the Steel Knights. A slight smirk played across my lips at the thought.

I got into the driver's seat. A few moments later, Wylder appeared at the passenger side of the cab. "All clear."

I drove around to the side entrance, a narrow passageway that led out to the large compound around the warehouse. Wylder had disposed of the two guards he'd dispatched there. As we got out to lay down the first set of explosives, I spotted one of the bodies, which he'd dragged behind a storage container.

After we were done, we slunk toward the main building and hid behind a couple of old steel drums to observe our surroundings. A few Steel Knights men were patrolling around the building, with more no doubt inside. The black sedan was parked out in front. I wondered again who'd come inside it.

Wylder checked his watch. "Where the hell are they?" he murmured. "They were supposed to be here a minute ago."

As if on cue, the front gates to the warehouse burst open, and a shiny blue Range Rover Kaige had picked out for the mission roared inside. It crashed into the sedan, which sent the other car's tail spinning away to smash into the boundary wall.

Shouts carried from inside the building. As planned, the crash had caught the Steel Knights' attention, which meant the guards wouldn't notice the rest of us just yet.

Wylder tugged on the side of my shirt. "Come on, we don't have much time."

I nodded. We had several key strategic places we needed to plant the explosives if we were going to blow this place to the ground, all plotted out by Gideon using old blueprints of the warehouse he'd managed to dig up online.

At the end of this mission, there'd be nothing left but cinders.

Wylder sent a quick text on his phone. A swarm of people—both Nobles and Demon's Wings—poured out of the back of the truck. A handful of them ran to join us, while most came around the building to pick off the guards as they raced out to confront Kaige.

Axel was in the bunch who came to a stop beside us, his expression grim. I wouldn't be surprised if he'd insisted on being part of this group just so he could grumble to Ezra afterward about all the issues he had with Wylder.

I sent a worried glance toward the Range Rover, where Kaige was just climbing out, semi-automatic rifle in hand, ready to meet the enemy. But I had to keep moving. That was the last thing I saw before we slipped past the warehouse door.

Inside, we found ourselves in thicker darkness. Only the faintest light from the city streetlamps seeped through the grimy windows. Wylder shone a small flashlight ahead of us as we hustled past the crates between us and our destination. He motioned to the men carrying some of the homemade bombs to plant them in various nooks and crannies.

There was a dull roar outside and the sound of running footsteps. Wylder yanked me down behind one of the crates, flicking off his flashlight. His hot breath ruffled the hair on the back of my neck, and an unwelcome tingle shot through my nerves at his closeness.

It didn't last long. The hallway outside quieted, and we could hear the distant blare of guns firing. I itched to be in on the action, but this was more important. And chances were we'd be doing at least a little fighting before we were out of here.

"Clear," Wylder called out softly. We walked down the hallway as quickly as we could before it widened to lead us to a rusted staircase. We planted another bomb at the foot of the stairs before walking into the old, out of order furnace in the center of the building.

The place was rotting away with time. There were obvious signs of the Steel Knights' presence, Wylder's light catching on their mark on the blotchy walls and printed on the huge crates. I had no doubt what was inside those. I'd seen the heaps of guns mixed in with straw just a few weeks ago.

Sudden footsteps brought us whipping around. "What the fuck?" a man shouted from a nearby doorway. Shit—we'd been discovered.

In the split second that it took for Wylder to shoot the man in the forehead, he'd already raised an alarm with a shrill cry. Five more Steel Knights came racing down the metal staircase, their footsteps clanging. They rushed towards us. The sound of bullets hitting the metal pipes echoed around us.

We all leapt behind the crates for shelter. Wylder and the other guys fired off shots around the wooden edges. I peeked out, gripping my gun, trying to get a clear enough view to shoot someone I was sure was on the opposite side.

One of the Demon's Wings men with us gave a shout, and my head jerked around. More Steel Knights were coming at us from the other direction. As I whirled, the nearest one leapt right at Wylder, who was in the middle of firing at someone on the other side of the room. A knife flashed in the attacker's hand.

No. Despite all my frustration with the Noble heir, every nerve in me resisted the idea of seeing him wounded—or worse, dead. I leapt forward with a cry of warning. Instinctively, I groped for the knife Wylder had given me, knowing I could use it better in hand-to-hand combat than a pistol.

I'd thrown myself between the attacking man and Wylder, so he slammed into me instead, tackling me to the ground. He grabbed my shirt and tried to pin me. I jabbed my knife right between his ribs. With a groan, he slumped on top of me, all dead weight.

Then Wylder was there, heaving him off me. "You okay?" he asked, his face oddly pale in the eerie dimness. His flashlight had fallen somewhere. The other men were silhouettes lunging back and forth through the fractured shadows—and then there was another Steel Knight barreling straight toward Wylder as he bent to help me up.

I grabbed Wylder's hand, yanked him to the side, and slashed my knife at the incoming attacker. I wasn't quite fast enough. The guy got off a shot as I bashed his arm to the side, the bullet carving a gouge through the flesh of my shoulder. I bit back a cry and stabbed again, this time managing to plunge the knife into his throat.

He fell with a gurgle. My ear drums rattled with two shots as Wylder dispatched a couple more Steel Knights men. Then he turned to stare at me, his eyes fixing on the blood streaming down my shoulder. "He was coming for me," he said.

"No kidding, jackass," I retorted. "So was the first one. You might wish *I* was dead and buried so you didn't have to put up with me, but for some crazy reason, I happen to want you to stay alive."

He blinked, and something shifted in his expression. A dark chuckle fell from his lips. "Maybe you really are merciful."

Before I could figure out how to respond to that, Axel let out a yell from deeper in the room. "The last one's placed. We've got to get out of here and blow this place to smithereens."

Wylder's jaw clenched at his dad's right-hand man taking over the orders. "Kill anyone who stands between us and the door," he added, sweeping his arm for everyone to go.

We took off running towards the exit, the two of us bringing up the rear so we could cover the others. I clutched my gun in one hand and my now-bloody knife in the other. But we'd only made it a few paces when another yell rang out behind us.

We swung around, Wylder cocking his gun. The others were already firing. Rather than shooting, Wylder hauled me out of the way behind one of the crates. He bobbed up over the top of it and fired back. I peered around the edge of the crate, gun ready, but our attackers had taken their own shelter.

"Whatever you think you're going to do here, you're never going to get away with it," a voice called out. Did it sound a little familiar? I watched closely as one of the men rose up to take a shot at us. It was Jenner. My pulse stuttered.

He saw me too. "What the fuck are you doing here, Mercy?" he snapped.

So he was acknowledging my presence now. "I should ask you the same question," I said. "Didn't take you long to change sides, huh?"

"Everyone looks out for themselves. You ran off to find new company too, obviously."

I scoffed. "At least I didn't go running to the traitor who killed my dad and wiped out the rest of his family and inner circle in one single night. Who needs *that* kind of loyalty?"

Shock flared across Jenner's features. He ducked down again, but his voice had roughened. "What are you talking about?"

Wylder let out an incredulous laugh. "As if you don't know that Colt Bryant assassinated Tyrell Katz and his family in cold blood."

"You mean Colt killed Tyrell because Tyrell wanted to have him assassinated. Nobody but your father is responsible for the demise of the Claws."

"Is that the cock and bull story Colt's been feeding you?" I made a face at the ceiling. "Do you really think my dad would spend a year making plans for my marriage and his alliance just to assassinate his future son-in-law a day before the wedding? If Tyrell Katz had wanted Colt dead, he'd be six feet under already."

"He was biding his time," one of the others said, but I thought I caught a trace of doubt in his voice.

"Look, I was *there*. It was my rehearsal dinner, remember? Colt attacked us when we were unprepared and had given him our trust. He even tried to kill me, and I sure as hell hadn't been plotting against him. Deep down, you have to know what I'm saying is true. Unless you sold your brains along with your dignity."

"Bitch," another of the guys spat out. I caught a glimpse of him around the crate—he wasn't anyone I recognized, probably from a different gang. "Stop spewing garbage. Come on, let's take them."

Tires screeched outside, followed by a volley of angry shouts. That didn't sound good.

Axel and a few of the other men had come hurrying back to defend the Noble heir—I doubted they cared about me. "Their back-up's arrived," Axel hollered. "Let's get going, now."

Wylder tugged my shoulder. I thought of how Ezra had so easily dismissed my idea that I appeal to the former Claws members, and resolve gripped my chest.

"If my father—and the Claws—ever meant anything to you," I

called out to Jenner, "give me a little faith too. Colt should be destroyed for what he did to my family and our people. I want you to help me take him down, once and for all."

Wylder pulled me away, Axel and the others training their guns past us in case the other men showed their faces.

"Get them!" Jenner ordered in a cold voice. "Don't let any of them escape."

I flinched inwardly, but my body knew enough to start running. Wylder cursed under his breath, keeping half his attention behind us as we sprinted toward the door. He fired a few shots, and I heard a body thump. Some ridiculous part of me hoped it hadn't been the former Claws men, even after all that.

Axel and the others came charging after us, sidestepping so they could return the fire that was aimed our way. We reached the door, I rammed my shoulder into it, and just like that we were stumbling out into the humid summer night.

Fighting had broken out all across the courtyard. More cars had pulled in through the front entrance; the concrete yard was a mess of brawling bodies. Kaige and Rowan were right in the thick of it, landing punches and kicks between pulling their triggers at opponents farther away.

We had to get back to the truck so we could get out of here. There were so many men and guns between us and it. I gritted my teeth, wiped the blood off my wound, and dashed into the heart of the fight, Wylder right beside me. My pulse thrummed with a weird sort of eagerness I didn't look at too closely.

I concentrated on the attackers in front of us, kicking the legs out from under one of the Steel Knights and aiming my gun at another who was firing at one of the Demon's Wings guys. My bullets caught him in the chest, but too late—our ally was already crumpling to the ground, blood gushing from his neck and shoulder.

Damn it. I swung around at a rush of movement nearby, and found myself careening to the side as a burly form shoved past me. Before I could catch my balance, I'd collided with someone's back.

My shoulder screamed in protest at the impact against my wound. Our feet tangled, and we both tumbled over.

It was another of the Demon's Wings guys I'd stumbled into—the one with the shaggy hair who'd brought the truck. He glared at me as we scrambled to our feet. Pain seared all through my arm.

Axel reached down and yanked me the rest of the way up, ignoring the gasp of pain I couldn't hold back. "Didn't see you there," he said with a sneer. I guessed he was the one who'd bumped into me. I barely held back a glare as I steadied myself on my feet.

The Demon's Wings guy snarled at me. "Do you want me to get killed, bitch?"

My jaw twitched, but I reined in my temper. "It was an accident. I apologize."

"Stay in your lane." He pulled out another gun and started shooting at the men coming at us. Axel raised his hands as if in surrender. I didn't have time to waste my breath on him, so I hurried onward, my gun raised.

Up ahead, Kaige had already jumped into the driver's seat of the truck. It looked like I wasn't the getaway driver this time.

Wylder had made it to the truck too. "Everyone with me, get over here, away from the building," he yelled, holding up the device that would detonate the explosives.

He was going to set them off. That would definitely turn the tide in our favor—as long as we were out of the way.

I rushed toward them alongside our other allies, getting in a few more shots to help clear the path. I was just five feet from the truck when Wylder pressed the button.

The first explosion held enough power to shake the ground. I staggered, and Rowan was there, grabbing my arm to stop me from falling again.

The structure of the factory rattled, bricks shaking loose from the spire and a terrible rattling sound reverberating from inside. Debris rained down on the Steel Knights who were still closer to the warehouse.

The booms thundered louder and louder as the chain reaction sped up. Flames burst through the shattering windows, and smoke gushed up. With one final bursting sound, the roof collapsed in like it was a house of cards. The walls shuddered and toppled in on each other, the fire devouring everything in the mess of the broken warehouse.

Pandemonium had broken out across the yard. The Steel Knights who'd been too close were now just scalded bodies in the midst of the rubble. Others wove back and forth looking dazed, bleeding and dusted with soot.

The rest of the Nobles and the Demon's Wings gathered close around the truck, staring but ready with their weapons all the same. This might have been a little more destruction than we'd pictured. My eyes watered with the wafts of smoke and dust that reached us.

"Everyone into the truck," Wylder shouted.

Rowan started to guide me by the arm, but my gaze snagged on a figure swaying out of the wreckage. Jenner. He looked to be in bad shape, blood pouring from his forehead. The factory behind him burned brightly, the flames of it so hot that I could only take a few steps toward him before it became too much. But that's where I held my ground.

Rowan tugged on my arm. "Let's go, Mercy." He followed my gaze to see Jenner, whose foot caught in the rubble and tripped him to his knees. "He'd have killed you if he had the chance."

He had no idea just how true that was. But just then, the fire must have reached one of the crates of ammunition. Another explosion went off, sending a fresh burst of flames and flying rubble almost to Jenner's heels. Something in me balked at turning my back on him.

I couldn't just leave Jenner like that. He'd ordered my death moments ago, but he'd been misled by Colt... just like I'd been for nearly a year. If I could be tricked by the man for that long, if Dad could have been, did I really have any place blaming someone else for believing his lies?

I couldn't see one of our men lose his life because of one stupid mistake.

Ignoring the heat, I took off running towards him. Behind me, Rowan yelled my name. I hefted Jenner to his feet and started dragging him on his unsteady feet. He was heavier than I expected.

Both Rowan and Wylder ran over to me with tense expressions. "I'm not leaving him here," I said before they could get on my case. "Help me or get out of my way."

"For fuck's sake," Wylder muttered, blowing out his breath in frustration, but they both stepped in and pulled the guy away from me. Before I had to protest, they jogged with him over to the edge of the compound where at least there was no chance of the fire or any new explosions reaching him.

That was all I'd wanted. I dove into the back of the truck. The two guys followed me. We crouched there with the rest of the men as the engine roared. Kaige turned us toward the street, and I tossed one last look toward Jenner before we tore around the corner and away.

23

Mercy

FRANK FINISHED THE LAST OF THE STITCHES ON MY shoulder and dabbed the wound with an amber liquid. It stung enough to make me hiss through my teeth. He shook his head at me. "You're making this into a habit."

"Yes, she is." Anthea swept into the kitchen where Frank had been cleaning me up, her heels rapping on the floor. "Is she reasonably in one piece?"

"For now," Frank said dryly. He taped a bandage over the wound and patted me on the back. "No push-ups or pull-ups for at least a few days."

"And here I was so looking forward to busting open my stitches in the gym," I muttered sarcastically at his retreating back.

Anthea clucked her tongue and propped herself against the counter across from me. She looked me over. Frank had gotten my arm clean while he'd been treating the wound, but my clothes and the rest of my body were still smudged with soot and dappled with dried blood, and I stunk of smoke.

Anthea might have liked me now, but she still wrinkled her nose, which I guessed was warranted. "Come on," she said. "Clearly the boys aren't the only ones who need 'Auntie Anthea' looking after them."

She led me back to what I realized on stepping inside was her bedroom. It was twice the size of the guest rooms I'd stayed in, with a sliding glass door that led out to a small sundeck I'd noticed before from outside. The frame of her sleigh bed gleamed with dark mahogany, and I caught a peek inside a walk-in closet that held more clothes than I'd seen in one place anywhere outside of a shopping mall. The whole space smelled of the same crisply delicate perfume Anthea always wore.

"This isn't my permanent home, but Ezra makes it clear I'm always welcome here," she said in a voice that didn't sound totally happy about that fact. I hadn't pried into her relationship with her brother, but it was obviously complicated.

She shooed me toward the en-suite bathroom. "Wash yourself up, and I'll pick out something acceptable for you to wear. If you won't take me up on my offer to *buy* new clothes for you, then you can at least make sure my cast-offs go to good use."

I doubted that anything Anthea owned was in poor enough condition to be a cast-off, but when she had that many clothes, it seemed silly to argue. "Nothing too frilly or fancy," I called over my shoulder, and heard her snort.

I didn't want to get my bandage wet in the shower, so I scrubbed myself down as well as I could sitting on the edge of the jacuzzi bathtub —now *that* was a perk I could get behind—until I was sure I wasn't going to stain the ivory towels when I dried myself off. Anthea bustled in with a pair of yoga pants and a casual blouse that were still dressier than my typical wear but comfortable enough I could thank her genuinely.

When I was dressed and feeling more like a human being and not a walking dumpster, she brought me out onto the deck. The sun was just peeking over the horizon, casting a rosy golden glow over the lawn. We sank into the two lounge chairs there.

As soon as my back hit the cushions, my muscles relaxed. I hadn't slept much before we'd left for the mission. I wouldn't mind a little doze right here, but that seemed insulting to my host.

"You're putting yourself through a lot for that man," she said.

"Who?" I said, startling. The first place my mind went was Wylder—all his snark and his ordering me around, the way I'd jumped in front of him a few hours ago despite how he'd been treating me.

Anthea raised an eyebrow at me. "Your ex-fiancé. All this fighting and risking your life to get your revenge."

Oh. Of course that's what she meant. I grimaced and sagged back into the padded chair. "Someone needs to see justice done for my family. It wouldn't be the same if I let someone else handle it. I don't trust anyone else to make sure it gets done right."

"Fair enough. But I'm glad you did make it back in one piece today—and that you did from Jasper as well."

That reminded me. "Do you need your hair pin back? I didn't have to use it, but with the kind of jobs Ezra's already given me, it seems like it might come in handy again."

She waved the question off. "Please keep it. I have a few on hand, and I can always make more."

That didn't surprise me at all. But it did trigger a prickle of curiosity. "How did you get started on the whole poisons and subtle murders thing anyway? Was it just a way to pitch in with the family business?"

"Oh, no." Anthea's laugh held no humor. She tipped her face to the brightening sunlight. "My and Ezra's father didn't believe in women having *any* role in the business other than as a bargaining chip. He didn't even bother to have me trained as your father clearly did for you, although I still managed to pick up plenty by watching. It's hard to live in a house like this without absorbing some knowledge."

"I know what you mean," I said. At least half of the things I'd learned over the years had been in spite of Dad, not because of him.

"In more ways than one, I'm sure. As soon as I was eighteen, he married me off—to a man nearly three times my age, who was looking as much for a punching bag and slave as a wife."

I winced, able to picture the type of man she was talking about far too easily. A fragment of memory came back to me from an earlier conversation. "You got rid of him. As he obviously deserved."

The corner of Anthea's mouth quirked upward. "I did, and he did. There was nowhere to go when my father would have tracked me down and punished me even worse if I'd tried to run. So I kept myself sane by researching every possible way I might be able to off the bastard without it being obvious I'd done it. The internet is a wonderful thing, isn't it?"

I couldn't help grinning, thinking of all the parkour moves I'd learned that way. "It sure is."

"Well, dear old Dad took a bullet in a bad way during a deal gone sour, and my brother stepped up to lead. Ezra can be harsh and unyielding, but he'd never liked the man who'd been picked for me. He'd argued against the marriage. And at that time I'd gathered plenty of knowledge. My husband had a shocking accident that of course I had *nothing* to do with, and Ezra welcomed me back into the fold."

She shrugged. "I have my own apartment in Manhattan now and my own business connections there, but I help out the family whenever I can. I enjoy seeing justice served as well."

"Then I'm sure you can understand why I won't let this go."

"I do. That doesn't mean I like seeing you bleeding over it." She turned to look at me. "You thought I meant someone else when I first mentioned what you're putting yourself through. I find that very interesting."

I put on my most innocent face. "I just wasn't sure what you meant."

"Hmm. You're good at many things, Mercy, but you're not a skilled enough liar to get away with it around me." She considered me shrewdly. "I have picked up on some tensions, both good and bad, between you and Wylder's inner circle. Is there something going on there?"

A flush crept over my face. Would it be an appropriate time to bring up the fact that I had slept with all of them at some point? How weird would she think that was?

"I have a history with Rowan," I admitted. "And Wylder... Wylder has been acting like a dick, but I guess that's not exactly news. The others... it's complicated."

"*They're* complicated—each in their own ways. If you ask me, there's way too much testosterone around."

I grinned. "I'll agree with that."

Anthea drew in a breath. "Well, look. I'll say this. They can *all* be dicks. That's what men in this kind of life are like. If you want to make something of it with any of them, you have to be firm. Demand the answers and the actions you need from them. Hold them accountable. I've known those boys for quite a while now, and I think they've all got a lot worth admiring in them—if you insist on them showing it."

"It's not like I'm perfect either," I had to acknowledge.

"Maybe not, but we women need to have our acts more together than they do, because the second we slip up, it's suddenly a judgment on our entire existence." She grimaced. "If you can make honest men out of them, I'll be more than happy."

I looked at her suspiciously. Was she implying what it sounded like she was? Could she possibly know what was actually up with me and the guys?

"We'll see about that," I said noncommittally. "Thanks for the tip." Then I couldn't restrain a yawn.

Anthea tutted and sat up straighter. "*You* obviously need to go back to bed. Come on. I'm not going to be responsible for you ending up sleep-deprived."

After a few more hours of sleep, my stomach started grumbling too loud for my still-groggy mind to ignore it. A little more refreshed than before, I headed down to the kitchen to scrounge up some breakfast, lunch, or whatever meal it theoretically was at this time of day.

I'd just popped some bread in the toaster when Rowan walked in. He came right over to me, stopping just a couple of feet away. "Are you doing okay? How's your shoulder?"

I reached toward the bandaged spot instinctively and caught myself. "It's fine," I said shortly. "I've been through worse." *Like, oh, that time when you left me in the lurch with a broken heart.*

Rowan didn't take the hint. He kept hovering by me as I got out the peanut butter and jam. Nothing wrong with a little PB and J as a pick-me-up no matter how old you get.

"You should make sure to get plenty of fluids into you too," he said. "An intense mission like last night, it drains you more than you realize."

My old irritation flared inside me. Rowan had told me before that he wasn't going to fight about me joining forces with the Nobles or get in my way. He'd helped me during the operation last night. He was trying to look out for me now. But none of it could really matter when he still hadn't explained the horrible way he'd hurt me years ago.

My first impulse was to shut him out like I had before, but Anthea's advice came back to me. Maybe I could get the answers I wanted. Maybe I just hadn't demanded them firmly enough

I spun toward him. "Why are you acting like you care about me and my well-being anyway?"

He blinked. "I'm not just acting. I do care about what happens to you." His gaze darted to my injured shoulder as if that somehow proved his point.

"Really? How am I supposed to believe that when you completely screwed me over back when you supposedly *loved* me? You've never even bothered to explain why you totally abandoned me." I waved the knife I'd picked up to spread the peanut butter, annoyed at myself for the raw emotion that'd crept into my voice.

I shouldn't care anymore. He shouldn't have any power over me at all.

But, fuck it, he did. And he still would until I understood what he'd done five years ago.

Rowan closed his eyes, looking pained. "It wasn't like that. I swear it, Mer, I wanted to be there. I meant to be there."

"Then why the hell weren't you? If you really want to make things right, then own up to what actually happened. If we're even going to work together properly, I have to know who I'm dealing with. Unless I'm dealing with a coward."

He winced, and I knew I'd stung his pride. His jaw worked. For a second, I thought he'd refuse like he had before. But then a sigh rushed out of him.

"You're right. I just—I thought it'd be easier not to talk about it, and somehow I'd let myself be angry at you too when none of it was really your fault. At the same time, I didn't want you to have to feel guilty over it the way I have for so long..."

He rubbed his hand over his face in frustration, so much anguish showing in his expression that my heart skipped a beat. Rowan had always been so good at holding up a cheerful front. I wasn't sure I'd ever seen him look so upset.

My voice softened of its own accord. "What happened, Rowan? *What* wasn't my fault—what would I feel guilty about?"

I could tell it took an effort for him to meet my gaze. "That night... I meant to come, right up to the end. I had my bag packed, everything ready. I was just waiting the last few minutes until it was time to go, and then—then I heard the gunshot."

My heart outright stopped. "Gunshot?"

"From Carina's room."

"Someone shot your sister?" I burst out. I'd never gotten to meet any of Rowan's family, but I'd seen pictures of them. I'd heard him talk about his little sister, who was only six then and the total baby of the family. The affection had always been so clear in his voice, I'd felt almost like she was my kid sister too.

"No," Rowan said raggedly. "They tried to. She was—she was having a sleepover, and she let her friend have her bed while she took the sleeping bag on the floor. Someone shot the girl in the bed through the window—they must have assumed it was her."

Abruptly, I remembered. I'd caught a few shocked murmurs in the halls at school about some little kid who'd gotten shot in their sleep. But the name hadn't been familiar, so in my confusion over Rowan's disappearance, it hadn't even occurred to me that the two events were connected.

It still didn't make sense to me. "But—why would anyone—"

"Because of me." Rowan's hand clenched against the countertop. "Because... your father found out that I was seeing you. A week before, after we'd already finalized our plan, he stopped me in the street and warned me to stay away from you. He told me I'd regret it if I didn't stay out of your life. But I thought we were already so close to getting away, he didn't seem to know about that part, if we just hung in there..."

"And he sent one of his men to kill your sister as punishment for ignoring him." My voice sounded hollow to my ears. Oh my God. Just when I thought I'd discovered the limits of the horrors my father had been capable of, he proved me wrong. "Why didn't you tell me—about the warning, or about Carina?"

He swallowed hard. "I was a stupid, over-confident teenager who didn't really understand just how bad things could get. I knew how much of a hold he had over you. I was worried that if I told you he knew about us, you'd give up the chance we worked so hard for. You'd insist that we couldn't see each other again. I *loved* you, Mer, so much that I forgot all the other things that should have been important to me, I didn't see how much danger I was dragging my whole family into..."

His head drooped. For the first time since I'd seen him here, I recognized the weight he was carrying. "Rowan..."

"I was afraid to say anything to you afterward," he went on. "What if he came after Carina again when he realized he'd gotten the wrong girl? It killed me to know you had no idea why I hadn't shown up, but it could have literally killed her if I'd kept any contact with you. And my parents were so shaken they decided it was time to get out of the Bend. They couldn't stand to stay in the house. They let us skip a few weeks of school while they arranged a new place in the city and then moved us there. Not that the change of scenery helped all that much."

That last statement constricted my throat even more. "What happened after?"

His shoulders rose and fell in a hopeless motion. "Carina never totally got over seeing her friend murdered. My parents kept arguing, and finally they split up. Mom took Carina with her out west where her parents live, and I stayed with Dad because I'd gotten in with Wylder by then and I didn't want to start over yet again. And Dad, well... let's just say that these days he prefers vodka to me."

Tears pricked at my eyes for the man in front of me—and the boy who'd been broken so badly before becoming that man. If I'd known...

But that might have been even worse. He was right—if Dad had caught us communicating again, who knew what he might have done? Everything that'd happened to Rowan and his family and that poor little girl who'd been in the wrong place at the wrong time, it was because of me and *my* rotten family.

"I'm sorry," I said, knowing the words were too small to address the damage done.

Rowan cracked a soft, sad smile. "I might have been angry with you sometimes, but it wasn't fair of me. You never lied about what kind of man your father was or how scary he could be. I insisted on being a part of your life anyway. I fell in love with you and embraced it. None of that is on you. Besides, you're not responsible for your father's actions."

I wasn't—and neither was Rowan. All these years I'd blamed him and cursed his name over something that hadn't been his fault either. What could I say he should have done differently? Everything I'd thought about the past had been wrong.

I'd been so hard on him since I'd gotten here. Now I had no idea what to say to him. My emotions were one big jumble.

Wylder poked his head into the kitchen. He opened his mouth as his gaze fixed on me as if he meant to say something, but my expression seemed to stop him. He caught himself as if he'd thought better of it. Then his attention shifted to Rowan.

"My father wants to speak with you as soon as possible."

Rowan tensed. As I watched, he straightened up, and the anguish smoothed from his face. He'd gotten so good at burying the trauma of his past, this golden boy who'd once been mine. So good I'd never so much as suspected it.

"I'll see him now," he said, and gave me one last look. "I'm sorry it took me so long to tell you."

Then he walked out of the room at Wylder's heels, leaving me shaken to the core.

24

Kaige

I COULDN'T SLEEP, AGAIN. NO SURPRISES THERE. I stretched out in the hammock and took a big bite of the spicy taquito I'd grabbed on my late-night snack run.

The pot brownie in my pocket was going to make the perfect dessert. If I couldn't rest, I could at least have a good time.

I was just popping the last bite of the taquito into my mouth when faint voices reached me. It was three in the morning—who the hell else would be wandering around at this time? Unless one of the guys on patrol was talking to himself.

Tipping my head to the side and squinting in the thin moonlight, I made out two figures coming to a stop under a tree several feet away from me. The thicker shadows there obscured their faces, but they were close enough for me to make out their low voices clearly now, and the one who spoke next was none other than the big boss himself.

"Is everything in place as we discussed?" Ezra asked.

I froze, holding my massive body as still as I could. What was the head of the Nobles doing having a chat out here in the middle of the night? Nothing good, I had to guess. Whatever was going on, Wylder would want to know about it, since there was no guarantee his dad would fill him in.

The other man's head turned to scan the surroundings, and I stopped breathing, but he didn't pause when his gaze skimmed past the hammock. Here between the two trees that held it up, it must have looked like nothing more than a vague blob in the darkness.

When he spoke, I recognized his voice as Axel's. "I snagged the phone during the fight. The guy never had a clue. He'll definitely remember her slamming into him, though. I gave her a good shove. He was pretty pissed."

My nerves prickled. Was he talking about Mercy? I'd seen her collide with one of the Demon's Wings men in the middle of the fighting yesterday. I hadn't realized Axel had set that up, though. What the fuck was he playing at?

"And the rest?" The understated menace in Ezra's tone made my blood run cold.

"It all went smoothly. I used Jasper's contact details in the phone to arrange for him to be at a specific restaurant expecting to make a deal tonight. I just heard his men fended off the mercenary, and now he's rightfully pissed that someone tried to take him out. He's eager for blood for sure."

"Perfect," Ezra said. "Let me have the phone. I've already put out a request to speak with Jasper here this morning. I doubt he'll take much convincing. I'll say I caught her with the phone, and he'll put the rest of the pieces together from there. Easy to encourage him to believe she was acting on wounded pride after the date she was forced into."

I could hear the smirk in Axel's voice. "And then you hand her over?"

"Naturally. We wouldn't harbor some stray who'd commit an offense like that against an ally of ours."

Axel chuckled, and my hands clenched. "Two bucks says that she doesn't live past sundown."

There was a rustle as Ezra must have pocketed the phone. "That's my expectation, Axel. We get her out of the way while solidifying our alliance with a show of good faith. I look forward to seeing it through."

Every muscle in my body tensed, my vision hazing with rage. I was going to kill *them* for talking about Mercy that way—for setting her up for some kind to attempted murder—they wanted to see her *dead*. After all Ezra's talk about taking her into the Nobles—

A snarl caught in the back of my throat, and I was a split-second from flinging myself off the hammock and charging at them, fists swinging. I shifted my weight—and then closed my eyes.

No. No running in half-cocked. As satisfying as the idea was right now, pummeling Ezra Noble and his right-hand man wasn't going to fix anything, was it? They'd probably kill *me*.

And then there'd be no one left who knew and could defend Mercy from their sick scheme.

For once, I needed to think. I had to be like Gideon, sharp and strategic.

Oh, who was I kidding? Better plan—I needed to get Gideon and let him do the thinking. And Wylder and Rowan, maybe Anthea too. I didn't care how many people Ezra ruled over or how brutal he could be. We were not letting him destroy Mercy.

I waited several minutes, the thumps of my pulse almost deafening in the quiet of the night, until I was sure Ezra and Axel had gone back inside. Then I eased off the hammock and hurried to the house, all thought of anything other than protecting Mercy gone from my mind.

Everyone else was asleep, as you'd reasonably expect at this hour. I went to Wylder's room first. It was his dad—he'd have the best idea how we should handle this.

On my way down the hall, I tapped in the emergency text code we'd decided on that would provoke an obnoxious ringtone to wake him up. I could tell it'd worked because I heard him muttering swear words under his breath through the door before I even rapped lightly on it.

As Wylder opened the door, he swiped his hand over his weary face and glowered at me. "The emergency had better not be that you're out of Red Bull."

"I wouldn't use the code over something like that," I said under my breath. "This is important. Mercy's in trouble."

Wylder snapped to alertness in an instant. No matter how much of a dick he'd been toward her, he clearly didn't like the idea of anyone else causing her problems. He motioned me into his room and shut the door behind me. “Tell me everything.”

Half an hour later, we’d gathered with Gideon, Rowan, and Anthea in Wylder’s office, and I was just wrapping up explaining what I’d overheard again.

“Ezra said he’s called Jasper in for a meeting this morning,” I finished, my gaze darting to the window to check for any sign of dawning sunlight. That morning was creeping closer way too fast for comfort. “He’s going to ‘expose’ Mercy then. We’ve got to figure out some way to stop it, fast.”

Gideon rubbed his eyes, but when he dropped his hand, his face was set in an expression so coolly determined I wouldn’t have wanted to face off with him, lung condition or not. “I didn’t think he’d make a move this quickly. I might have caught on otherwise.”

I stared at him. “You *knew* Ezra was going to turn on Mercy?”

He shrugged as if anyone with half a brain cell would have known. “He talked to me briefly the other night after the... corpse incident. Whoever’s been targeting Mercy here, it’s made him see her as a liability.”

“He wasn’t convinced she was more useful to him than trouble to begin with,” Wylder grumbled. “He doesn’t think much of the gangs in the Bend or of women.” He cut his gaze toward his aunt with a slightly apologetic grimace.

Anthea just shook her head. “Oh, you’re not saying anything I don’t know. I wondered when he insisted on sending her to Jasper—whether it was really because he thought she’d handle him best and not because he was hoping she wouldn’t and it’d be an easy way to take her out of the picture.”

“He didn’t seem all that happy about her success.” Wylder sighed. “She’s a wild card. He prefers to only work with people he can fully control and anticipate. The way she handled Jasper and came back unfazed probably made her seem like not just a liability but a potential threat to his authority too.”

Silence descended on the room. We knew what happened to those who had earned the wrath of Ezra.

"Jasper *did* like Mercy, whatever happened that night," I ventured. "Would he definitely believe this story?"

"I can't imagine she won him over enough that he'd forgive a murder attempt," Anthea said. "She has a reasonable motive, and with the phone and the way Axel set her up to look as if she'd had an opportunity to steal it from his man, the circumstantial evidence is awfully convincing. And think about it—if Jasper wants to say it wasn't Mercy, he'd be accusing Ezra of lying. Whose favor do you think he cares more about?"

Even I knew the answer to that question without needing to think about it. I scowled at the wall. "There's got to be something we can do."

"Everything revolves around the phone, doesn't it?" Rowan said. "If we can get rid of the phone, then there's only a motive, no evidence of any kind."

Wylder nodded slowly. "He'd have it in his office, most likely. Possibly the audience room if he's planning on meeting Jasper there. But either way the room will be locked, and he'll have tucked it away somewhere secure inside. And he's an early riser no matter how late he was up. We can only count on an hour or two before there's a good chance of us getting caught."

Shit. My nerves jangled with apprehension and a prickle of what might have been panic. "So let's get moving, then!"

"Hold on," Gideon said evenly. "If we barge in without planning carefully, we'll only get caught. We need to take a few minutes to decide our best possible approach. Starting with, how are we going to get past those locked doors?"

A small smile curved Anthea's lips. "I think I can help with that."

After a brief, intense discussion, Wylder and I ended up being the ones to tackle Ezra's office, while Rowan and Gideon headed to the audience room. Anthea's bedroom was near her brother's, so she was playing look-out, ready to alert us the second he got up for the morning. But she'd lent us some tools.

I shifted my weight from foot to foot as Wylder fiddled with the lock picks from his aunt's personal kit. "Do you figure she's done a lot of breaking and entering before?" I whispered.

Wylder let out a low chuckle. "I'd be surprised if she hasn't done at least a little. There's a reason my dad takes good care of her, and it's not just because she's family. He protects his valuable assets." There was a trace of bitterness in his voice.

"Mercy's fucking valuable," I muttered.

"But she's too much of an unknown. And—" Wylder shut his mouth, and the door clicked open.

We slipped into the office. Not wanting to risk one of the sentries noticing the light under the door, Wylder set his phone facing away from it to cast a thin glow over the elegant room. "I'll take the desk," he said. "You check the bookshelves first."

I went to the built-in shelves and ran my hands over the rows of books there, making sure the pages moved under my fingers and that none were secret containers. Then I felt the backs of the shelves for loose spots that might have held a hidden compartment.

No such luck, and no phones just lying around either. Wylder rummaged through the desk drawers. He stepped away with a frustrated sound.

We started nudging and tugging at every other object in the room, careful not to shift anything so much that it'd be clear it'd been moved. My heart had started to sink when Wylder let out a soft cry of victory. He'd raised the top of the ottoman by Ezra's wing chair in the corner and was now lifting a phone out of the storage box inside.

I pulled the vial of clear liquid that Anthea had given us out of my pocket, some kind of concoction she'd had just lying around that would erode the metal and destroy the phone. Wylder set the device in the sturdy box she'd given us for that purpose, and I poured the stuff over it.

With a sizzling hiss, the screen melted, the metal warping, until nothing was left but a solid gray lump that could just as easily have once been a pair of fancy sunglasses or something.

A surge of relief swept through me. The phone was destroyed; there was no way Ezra could use it now. But we also needed to make sure he didn't find out who'd taken it.

We ducked out of the room, Wylder resetting the lock behind us, and hustled back to his office. Wylder texted the others on the way to let them know the first part was done. "Might as well let them get a little more sleep if they can," he said.

"What are we going to do with that?" I asked as we stepped into his office, tipping my head to the box he was still clutching.

He considered it. "I don't think we want it on our property, even if it's practically unidentifiable. You go for morning runs pretty often. Suit up when it's not too early, and chuck the phone in one of the trash cans farther down the street when you're well out of view of the house."

I glanced at the window. Just the faintest hint of light was touching the sky. "I could probably get away with going in a half hour or so."

"Perfect." He dropped into his chair and rubbed his forehead. His face looked unusually drawn, and I didn't think it was just fatigue.

"Are you okay?" I asked.

"I can't believe Dad would pull something like this on Mercy—and without even telling me. No, that's not even right. I *can*, and it pisses me off that I didn't see it coming soon enough. It pisses me off that he's such a piece of shit to begin with." He sighed. "And this won't end it. He isn't going to stop until he's gotten what he wants."

Which was Mercy gone.

"We'll think about that when we get there. At least she's safe for now." I paused. I must have been amped up from the precarious mission we'd just completed, because then I dared to say, "One of these days you're going to have to admit that she's tough enough to stand her ground."

Wylder raised his eyes. "What's that supposed to mean?"

"Oh, come on. I may not have Gideon's brains, but the tension between you two is obvious. You're crazy about her, aren't you?"

I wasn't going to tell him Mercy had outright admitted they'd had sex. He wouldn't have let himself go that far unless either he hadn't cared about her at all, which obviously wasn't true... or he was so caught up in her he hadn't been able to help himself.

He frowned. "Maybe you're talking about yourself."

I raised my hands. "Hey, *I* won't deny it. She's fucking amazing. Hell yeah, I'm crazy about her." I hesitated. "Is that going to be a problem?"

There was a pause before he spoke again. "No," he said. "Why would it? Mercy doesn't owe me anything."

"That's not what I'm asking. We're both into her. If she's going to pursue something with both of us—"

"No need to worry about that. I'm sure she hates me by now."

Having seen the way they'd interacted over the past week, I wasn't so sure about that. "I think she's just pissed off at the way you're treating her. Because you *are* being an ass. I get why you're pushing her away, but she's nothing like Laurel. She knows what she's gotten into. She's tough enough to face it."

"It doesn't matter," Wylder snapped. "The story always ends the same way. Isn't today proof of that? Dad will keep coming after her."

"And what good does constantly going off on her do when she's proven she isn't leaving no matter what you say? You're just putting yourself in a position where she won't even come to you for help if she realizes she needs it."

Wylder was silent for a long moment. He didn't appear to have an argument for that. Lowering his head, he pinched the bridge of his nose as if he had a headache. Then he said, quietly, "*She* protected me, you know. In the warehouse. A guy was coming at me, and she jumped in the way and started fighting him off. That's how she got shot. I've been a total asshole to her, and she still risked her life for mine."

"She cares about you, you dumbass." If he'd been anyone else, I might have smacked him across the head to drive the point home. "She's obviously seen enough of the not-so-asshole parts of you to think your life is worth something. Give her a chance."

"It has been harder keeping my distance after that." He sighed and glanced up at me, his eyes narrowing. "Wouldn't you mind if I went after her?"

I shrugged. "She told me straight to my face that she isn't currently a one-guy kind of girl. If she's playing the field, I'd rather she stuck to people I actually respect. And there aren't a whole lot of those."

Something strange crossed Wylder's face. Then he motioned to the door. "You'd better get ready for your run. We don't want that phone on any of us for any longer than necessary."

I didn't feel like the conversation was exactly done, but I wasn't going to push him any more than I already had. I wasn't that much of an idiot.

I tucked the phone-blob into the pocket of my sweatpants before I set off, and found a bin near the front of one of the properties at the end of the block. No one else was around that early. With a flick of my wrist, I sent it sailing into a half-open garbage bag.

Mission accomplished. There was nothing left to do but wait.

After breakfast, we purposefully decided to hang out in the sitting room that had a window overlooking the front drive and a doorway that opened to the foyer. Around ten, Jasper showed up. As one of Ezra's men ushered him to meet the boss, he glanced around with a displeased expression. One look at his porky face and those lips he must have tried to plant on Mercy made me want to kick his ass right back out the door, but I stayed where I was.

It was only a few minutes later that Jasper marched back to the front door, this time in a real huff. Whatever had happened in there had pissed him off.

As the head of the Demon's Wings drove off, Ezra emerged into the foyer, his face tight and his eyes so dark a shiver ran down my spine. When he sauntered over to our room, we acted busy with our phones, only looking up when he stopped in the doorway.

"Everything all right, Dad?" Wylder asked evenly, a picture of innocence.

Ezra smiled thinly. "I'm determining that." He scanned the room, his gaze lingering on each of us in turn, and I knew he was wondering about us. We were the only guys in the house who'd shown Mercy any support so far, after all. Of course he'd suspect us.

But if he had no proof we'd been involved, he couldn't do anything about it... right?

25

Mercy

It started at breakfast. Or rather, on my way to breakfast.

The second I stepped out of my room, Kaige was there, ambling down the hall as if he'd just happened to be coming my way at the exact same time. Which maybe he had been.

"I heard Anthea's making bacon," he said, slinging his arm around my waist. "Can't be late for that!"

The other guys were already in the kitchen when we got there, along with Anthea, a sizzling pan, and a meaty smell in the air that made my mouth water. Wylder didn't scowl or make any snarky remarks about my arrival, though. And I could have sworn some kind of look passed between all of the guys as if they were confirming something with each other.

Weird.

"Is something up?" I asked, and Kaige just laughed and guided me to the table. Then Gideon started showing me a major shopping website he'd hacked into for kicks a few months ago—"They still haven't noticed," he said, pointing out the little puke emoji icons he'd programmed into the product pages, with a gleeful chuckle I'd never heard from him before but found both disturbing and sexy—and I got distracted.

After we'd eaten, Anthea ushered me to her deck even though I'd been planning on working out—abs and legs only, of course, considering the wound on my shoulder. She kept me there for at least an hour, chatting about random things and topping up my glass of lemonade whenever it got slightly low.

Then all of a sudden Kaige was back, dressed in his work-out clothes and suddenly eager to join me in the mansion's home gym. That was when I really started getting suspicious. It all felt weirdly coordinated.

We passed Ezra in the hall, and I thought his gaze lingered on me more intently than usual. Maybe he was just making sure my injury wasn't noticeably slowing me down. But Kaige drew a little closer to me without a word, and that set warning bells jangling in my head too.

I waited to see if he'd tell me something once we were alone in the gym, but instead he challenged me to a crunch competition and then a kicking one. Once we were thoroughly sweaty, he escorted me all the way to the shower. By that point, I was surprised he didn't follow me inside, though he probably would have if I'd invited him.

I washed and changed quickly and headed out only to notice Rowan meandering along several feet behind me. He appeared to be absorbed in whatever he was looking at on his phone, but when I went into one of the lounge rooms to watch some TV, he followed me, settling into a chair on the other side of the room.

I still didn't know what to say to him after his confession the other day. He didn't seem to want to talk to me anyway, staying focused on his phone. He'd just... happened to want to be in the same room?

No, there was definitely something more than that going on.

To test that theory, I got up again after just ten minutes and marched out. Rowan stayed where he was, but lo and behold, Wylder came around the staircase, looking as if he'd hustled to make it there, just as I reached the foyer. I pretended not to see him and headed for the front door, totally at random.

"Where are you going, Princess?" Wylder asked. Okay, so he hadn't completely lost the snark.

"For a walk," I replied. "That's still allowed around here, right?"

Something flickered in his eyes. "The last time you went strolling on your own, it didn't work out so well. I could use some fresh air."

And then I'd have to endure his glowers and grumbles for the next hour? No, thank you.

I tapped my pocket and the bulge at the back of my jeans where I'd stuck my pistol. "I'm much better prepared this time. I don't need babysitting."

A crooked smile twisted his lips, one I'd used to find irritatingly gorgeous. And maybe still did, just a little. "What if I do? You can take care of me, Kitty Cat."

The smile and the fonder nickname sent a flare of heat through me that only left me uneasy. What the hell was happening here?

"What are you going to do if I say forget it?" I asked. "Chase me down?"

I stalked outside, and Wylder didn't follow. But I'd only made it to the edge of the Noble property when Gideon came trotting across the lawn with his tablet under his arm. He stopped and looked as if he was taking pictures of a couple of things near the wall, but as soon as I walked past it, he followed.

I spun on him. "What is going on with all of you today?"

Gideon blinked at me. His jaw ticked, and I knew for sure I was on to something.

"I don't know what you're talking about," he said. "I happen to find that stretching my legs now and then is an excellent way to clear—"

"Bullshit," I interrupted. "The only time I've seen you set foot outside the house before now is to go from the house straight to a car. What. Is. Going. On?"

He got a bit of a deer-in-the-headlights look, but his mouth clamped shut.

"Fine." I strode past him back to the mansion. "I know who'll have put you all up to this, so I'll just ask him."

If Wylder was involved, then he was the one giving the orders. And there he was, standing idle in the foyer as if he had nothing else to do with his time.

He cocked his head when he saw me. "That was a short walk."

"Fuck you." I marched right up to him and jabbed my finger at his chest. "Why are you all refusing to let me out of your sight? Did something happen? Was there another corpse left for me on the lawn—or right inside here?"

Wylder's gaze twitched away from me as if he was checking the room around us for anyone who might overhear his answer. That didn't bode well. "Can you keep your voice down?" he muttered.

"No," I said, deliberately raising it. "I want you to tell me—"

He caught my arm, his grip firm but not painfully so. Heat flooded my skin where he touched me. "Fine," he said under his breath. "You want to know? I'll tell you. But we're not talking about it here."

I yanked my arm back. "Then feel free to show me where we *can* talk."

He set his hand on the small of my back and escorted me up the stairs toward his area of the house, moving aggressively enough that my panties might have been soaked by the time we reached the top. Not that I'd ever have admitted that to him. He was still being a total douche. My brain knew that even if my body didn't.

Wylder stayed silent until we were in his office with the door shut. He moved away from me to the small liquor cabinet and poured himself a glass of the brandy he liked so much.

"Well?" I prodded.

He took a sip, grimaced, and turned to fully face me. "Did you hear that Jasper stopped by this morning?"

A chill washed over me. This had to do with Jasper? Had he "liked" me enough that he'd decided he wanted more? Shit.

But then, no one had told me, let alone come to get me, so maybe not.

"No," I said. "Why was he here?"

"Because my dad invited him, because he planned to frame you for Jasper's attempted murder."

For a second, I just stared at him. Most parts of that sentence didn't make sense to me even in isolation, let alone all together. "Wait—what with the who now?"

Wylder's bright green eyes bored into mine. "He set you up. Axel lifted a phone from the guy he made you crash into at the warehouse the night before last. They used it to arrange an attempted assassination. When Jasper came, my father was going to turn over the phone, saying he'd caught you with it, and then turn *you* over to the Demon's Wings for punishment."

I was still having trouble processing all of this. I sank into the nearest chair. "But—why? How did you find out? Why didn't he go through with it?"

"Thankfully, Kaige the insomniac happened to overhear my dad and Axel talking late last night," Wylder said, his tone dry yet humorless. "We took care of it before the meeting happened. The phone is long gone and irretrievable."

So I wasn't in immediate danger. But... I pressed my hand to my forehead. "I don't understand—why would Ezra set me up like that? If Jasper thought I'd tried to order a hit on him, he'd want me dead."

"Yeah. Which means my dad wants you dead." Wylder threw back a larger gulp of brandy. "He doesn't like the disturbances your presence here seems to have provoked, and he doesn't like that you were strong and smart enough to handle Jasper. You're a wild card, and a capable one, and that makes you a threat. The only way Ezra Noble deals with threats is by crushing them."

"Oh, fuck." Through my rising horror, the pieces clicked together in my head. I raised my eyes to meet Wylder's stark gaze again. "That's why you all have been on my ass no matter where I go. You don't want to leave me alone in case he tries something else."

Wylder offered a tiny shrug. "It isn't something we can sustain long-term without getting noticed, but we haven't had much time to come up with a better strategy yet."

A flicker of anger seared up through my horror at the situation. I sat up straighter. "And it never occurred to you that the most obvious part of any strategy would be *telling me* the man whose house I'm living in wants me dead?"

"I'm sure we'd have gotten to that eventually," Wylder said, but his tone wasn't exactly convincing.

I stood up, my jaw clenching. "It should have been the first thing you did. It's my life on the line. How the hell am I supposed to look out for myself if I have no idea what I'm dealing with?"

The stubborn bastard just glowered at me. "*We* were looking out for you."

"That's not good enough! What, did you think I'd give away that I knew and screw things up for you? Say the wrong thing to Ezra—as if that's *more* likely to happen when I know to be cautious, not less likely? For God's sake, Wylder, it's fine if you don't want to fuck me again, but I thought by now I'd earned a little more trust than that from all of you."

I swallowed hard, a jabbing sensation running through my chest. I wasn't just angry—I was hurt. From the second I'd walked into this house, I'd been running myself ragged proving how much I could handle, and they still thought I was safer in the dark about something like this.

As Wylder gazed back at me, something fell away in his expression. For a second, he looked almost haunted. I hesitated, expecting the rare show of emotion to vanish behind his walls as quickly as it emerged, but he didn't shake it off. He glanced at the floor and then back at me. "No matter what I say to you or how I treat you, you're not going to leave, are you?"

I folded my arms over my chest. "You only just figured that out?"

"No. Well—I don't know." He lowered himself into his own chair, looking so conflicted that my heart tugged to go to him despite everything. "I'm sorry. You *have* earned that trust, more than earned it. I just—I was trying to protect you."

The great Wylder Noble was apologizing to me? I was stunned, but not so much that I couldn't sputter a laugh at the last thing he'd said. "By treating me like dirt not even worthy of sticking to the soles of your shoes? Like I was a fucking piece of *tissue* you jerked off into and then wanted to toss in the trash?"

He actually winced. My voice might have come out pretty harsh. I'd told myself I didn't care, but I was angry about a whole lot of things from the past several days here, and it was all bubbling to the surface.

"I know it sounds stupid," he said. "But I didn't feel like I had a whole lot of choice."

"Of course you did. You had a choice not to be an asshole to me. You had a choice to let me in on the missions without fighting me every step of the way. You just didn't make those choices."

"Not because I don't trust you," he insisted. "Because I don't trust my dad. I didn't *want* to treat you like that, but I thought if I could just come down on you hard enough to force you to go before he could do even worse... I know it sounds awful, but you have no idea how far he'll go to hurt you—or me."

Hurt *him*? I found myself staring again and forced myself to sit back down. "I don't understand."

Wylder considered what was left of his brandy. Then he tossed it all down like a shot. He set the glass on a side table hard and frowned at the wall.

"When I was fifteen, I started hooking up with a girl from school. Laurel. She was... sweet and bubbly and totally separate from everything here. When I was with her, all the violence and the expectations didn't seem to matter that much. It became more than just hooking up. I fell for her. I was seeing her more and more—and then Dad found out."

A lump formed at the bottom of my throat. I knew how this kind of story ended. Rowan had told me one version of it yesterday.

"What did he do?" I asked. My voice came out quiet. Some part of me didn't really want to know.

Wylder's tone stayed flat, but he couldn't quite wring the emotion out of it. "He didn't want his heir getting distracted. Especially not by a girl. I was supposed to pump and dump them, not get attached. He saw it as a weakness and a threat to our security—if I cared too much, then our enemies could use her to manipulate me. So he decided the problem needed to be eliminated. He had her grabbed off the street, put a gun in my hand, and told me to shoot her."

I flinched. "Did you do it?"

"*No*," Wylder said savagely. "I told him he was fucking insane. He told me I was a shameful excuse for a Noble. Then he took the gun from me and did it himself. Axel and Titus were there—Titus had to hold me back from throwing myself at him, and even then I might have broken free if Axel hadn't punched me hard enough to break my nose." He rubbed the slightly uneven slant of it, the imperfection I'd noticed the first time we'd met. "And then it was already over."

My throat constricted even more. "I'm so sorry." It'd been bad enough losing Rowan and not knowing why, feeling he'd betrayed me. If I'd had to watch my father kill him in front of me...

Wylder finally looked at me again. "Ever since that day, I've been fighting my way back into his good graces. He's never forgotten that I wouldn't follow that one order. That I picked her life over his authority. If he had *any* reason to think I was at all invested in another woman now..."

Ah. It all made a bizarre kind of sense now. A humorless laugh tumbled out of me. "So what you're saying is you treated me like shit not because of how little you care about me, but because of how much you do."

Wylder's eyes narrowed. "I wouldn't put it exactly that way."

"Of course you wouldn't." God forbid he spell out anything about his feelings for me even now. But that was okay. I wasn't composing any sonnets in his honor either.

His story had doused the flames of my anger. All I had left in me was achy ashes. How could I be mad at him when he'd been trying so hard to keep me safe, even if it'd been in the most frustrating possible way?

But then he surprised me. "I *am* sorry," he said. "I meant that. You didn't deserve any of the crap I've thrown at you since we—since that morning in the kitchen. I didn't mean any of it. And I should have known it wasn't the right way. With Laurel—I kept her as far from the gang part of my life as I could. Whatever bits she did figure out, she assumed I'd protect her, because she sure as hell wasn't equipped to."

"But I can," I said. "At least if I know what I need to be on guard against."

"Yeah, you can. I don't know whether to be glad about that or pissed off that it means I can't get you away from my dad completely." He offered me a pained-looking smile. "Make no mistake, Ezra is going to keep coming after you. He doesn't react well to failure. You're not safe now even if he has no idea that I'd want you to be. But we still have to do something."

"Any suggestions?" I asked.

Wylder leaned forward. "You know, if this is the kind of crap my dad's going to pull, I don't see why I should trust his judgment in general. We can still carry out the plan *I* wanted to put in motion. If we can crush Bryant and the Steel Knights' influence all on our own, he won't be able to dismiss it. We're going to earn his respect and end this once and for all."

26

Rowan

Once Wylder set his mind to something, there really was no stopping him. That was part of the reason I admired the guy.

Just a few hours after he'd pulled us together to say we were going rogue with a plan of our own to take down the Steel Knights, we were cruising through the streets where Paradise City started to bleed into the Bend, checking out possible locations for our scheme.

"How exactly is this supposed to work again?" Mercy asked from where she was sitting in the back of my Toyota. This time she'd made Gideon take the middle, perched between her and Kaige. "How can we make sure the crime actually gets pinned on Colt and the others?"

"If the cops find them in the building with that amount of product, it shouldn't be hard to get the charges to stick," Wylder said. "With a new drug on the streets, they'll have been itching for someone to blame. And the Nobles have a few cops in their pocket to ensure everything gets filed and processed as it should."

"The trick is going to be making sure we can keep them in the building until we bring the police down on them, right?" Kaige said. "We need a place without too many potential exits."

Gideon nodded. "Anthea suggested some impressive techniques for subtly rigging the doors so we can make it very difficult for them to force their way out once we blockade them in. And I'll have the cameras set up as well so that there's footage of the Steel Knights with the truck."

Mercy's brow knit. "But how can we be sure Colt will show up?"

Wylder smiled grimly. "He came when we started kicking butt in the Bend before. I think he'll want direct payback for the theft and what we did to his warehouse."

"He'll have lost a lot of face and want to prove he can stand up for the people supporting him," I agreed. "We just have to be careful not to do anything that might raise his suspicions that it's a trap. I've already started spreading the word about the Nobles gearing up to sell this Glory stuff through a few channels. It's probably already gotten back to him."

"He just doesn't know where." Kaige glanced out the window. "Of course, neither do we."

"We're getting there." Wylder tilted his head toward the window. "What're we looking at, Gideon?"

Gideon swiped through his tablet and pointed out a few buildings we passed on the winding route he'd given me before we'd left. We all just looked and considered until we came up on a red brick building with a large, steel garage-style door that filled about half of the front of the place.

"I like that one," Kaige announced. "We could drive the truck right in there no problem."

"Assuming there isn't much garbage or equipment inside," Gideon said. "It's an abandoned auto-repair shop, went bankrupt about a decade ago, no one's ever bothered to take it over. But it does seem like a good bet on paper. Two entrances at the front and one at the back, all of them sturdy doors. The windows are barred so no one's breaking out that way. And, like you said, it *should* be easy to drive the truck in."

Wylder drummed his hands on the dashboard. "What are we waiting for, then? Let's take a closer look."

The lock on the back door turned out to be broken. We walked inside to a musty smell that made me wrinkle my nose. Wylder and Kaige turned on the flashlights on their phones and held them up.

Teenagers had clearly been partying in here—there were beer bottles gathering dust in the corners, chip bags and fast-food wrappers scattered around, and random, artless graffiti tags on the walls. I studied the spray-painted lines automatically, my fingers itching for a chance to put something more skilled up over them.

But I didn't draw pretty pictures, not anymore.

The main work bay in front of the garage door was otherwise empty. The shop equipment must have been sold off to cover the debts. I dragged in a breath, my sensitivity to the mustiness fading, and had to conclude: "This is the place."

"I agree," Wylder said. "Let's figure out where we'll set everything up."

"How soon do we want to bring the truck in?" Kaige asked.

"I'll have to spread a few more rumors, make sure we'll have some eyes in the wider area when we bring it in so word about the general location can get passed on," I said. "And we want to keep the timeline tight so they don't crash the party before we're ready."

"Makes sense."

Gideon pointed to a couple of concrete beams down the middle of the wide room. "I can mount cameras up there and there. With the angles of the shadows, I don't think anyone will notice, and it'll capture most of the activity down here."

Wylder clapped him on the back. "There we go. It's all coming together just like that."

We were all coming together. A sense of purpose—no, not just purpose, of *community*—gripped me like I didn't think it had since Mercy had walked into the mansion. When we all put our strengths to a task, we could be nearly unstoppable. I'd seen it in the past, and I could feel the same energy coming together now as we studied the room around us.

Only Mercy herself still looked doubtful. Kaige shouldered her playfully. "What's the matter, Kitty Cat? You don't like the plan?"

She swatted at him, but his teasing provoked a smile with undeniable affection. "I didn't say that. I just—" She looked around again and sighed. "Getting arrested, even getting sent off to jail for however many years, doesn't feel like enough punishment for what Colt did."

Wylder guffawed. "Bloodthirsty to the end, Kitten. Don't you worry. We'll still take care of him exactly as he deserves." He'd seemed more at ease with Mercy since yesterday, and as he spoke, his eyes focused on her with a gleam that held both amusement and admiration.

Mercy raised her eyebrows at him, still smiling. "What do you mean?"

To my surprise, Gideon returned her smile as he answered, as if he was relishing the idea of offering her revenge instead of just stating the facts. "The Nobles have plenty of contacts in the prison system, as you'd expect. It's *very* easy to arrange a painful death during a seemingly random brawl or shanking."

Mercy didn't appear to be convinced. She might have had some kind of a vibe going on with all the other guys—and it might have provoked a weird sense of jealousy mingled with pleasure inside me, wanting to keep her to myself while also enjoying seeing her become part of our harmony—but I'd known her so much longer. I could read her expression even if I'd never seen one quite like it on her face before.

"You were hoping to do it yourself," I said quietly.

She grimaced, but she didn't deny it. "He shot my father himself. I meant to return the favor—you know, just times about ten or so."

Wylder gave her ponytail a light tug. "Let me think on it, and I'll see if there's some way we can get you your moment." He turned to me. "Have you dropped the first tip to the cops yet?"

I shook my head, reaching for my phone. "I was waiting until we had our plans more solid. I can do it now."

As I walked out back where the phone wouldn't pick up the others' voices, I realized I'd grabbed the wrong one. I had my usual phone on me and a burner I'd meant to use for the tip, in case anyone tried to trace it. I was holding my regular phone. An alert for a missed message flashed on the screen. I should check that first.

I tapped through to voice mail and raised the phone to my ear. When my mother's voice carried through the speaker, my heart stuttered.

"Hi Rowan. It's been so long since we last talked, honey. Too long.

Anyway, you know your sister's birthday is coming up this weekend. Carina would love it if you could make it down here for the weekend. I know it's a long way and last-minute, and you have a lot going on, but I'd pay for the ticket. Let me know soon. And either way, give me a call when we can catch up a bit, please? I love you."

My hand kept pressing the phone to my ear after the dial tone kicked in. I closed my eyes and forced myself to end the call. A burning sensation seared through my chest.

I couldn't go. I didn't even need to think about it. There was too much happening here in Paradise Bend right now, too many people counting on me to help hold things together, too many threats looming far too close on the horizon.

I'd gotten into this life at least in part to make sure I'd be stronger, readier, deadlier if anyone ever came for my family again, especially for Carina. And now my little sister was barely in my life at all. I hadn't seen her or even spoken to her since half a year ago at Christmas. I'd already ordered a couple of birthday presents to be delivered, things I was pretty sure she'd be excited about, but it wasn't the same as being there. I knew that from the look in her eyes every time I stepped away from those rare family get-togethers.

But she *was* safe, and I'd made other commitments since then.

I stuffed my regular phone in my pocket and dug out the burner. When the cop manning the line picked up, I had my voice go a bit hoarse and let a thread of confusion creep into it, doing my best impression of a nervous bystander on the street. The guy I might have been twenty years from now if I'd never known Mercy Katz.

"Hi, yeah," I said, with a little cough. "I was just walking past Firkin Street on Carlton, and I saw a bunch of young guys who looked pretty... shady, you know? Hoodies and these red bandanas and all that. They were saying something about how they'd be moving in soon and taking over. I didn't like the sound of it at all. Anyway, it seemed like something the police might want to know about."

The officer asked me a few questions and then thanked me for my call, and I hung up with a sense of satisfaction melting a little of my regret. I'd picked an intersection far enough away that investigations there wouldn't stop us from bringing in the truck, but close enough that I could easily lay a few more breadcrumbs to bring the cops right here. And I'd also primed them to assume it'd be the Steel Knights setting up shop in this neighborhood.

I stayed out in the fresh air for a minute longer, waiting for my emotions to completely settle. As I turned to head back inside, the door swung open and Mercy stepped out.

"Are you all done?" she asked. "I was just going to grab the cameras for Gideon."

"Yeah. I made the call." I found I couldn't tear my gaze away from her. There was nothing extraordinary about her appearance today, just her typical ponytail, T-shirt, and jeans, but... she was kind of extraordinary just as herself, wasn't she? What a fucking force of nature she'd become, even more so than when I'd known her and loved her way back when.

An ache squeezed around my heart. It was no wonder the other guys were all drawn to her. I couldn't blame them for that, and I couldn't blame her for however much she wanted all of them.

But that didn't mean I had to roll over and pretend I didn't care.

She was the one part of my old life I'd somehow found my way back to. I had to hold onto her this time.

"Mercy," I said as she started to walk away.

She stopped and glanced at me. "What's up?"

I swallowed thickly and stepped toward her to grasp her hand. When I'd explained to her what'd happened the night I'd been supposed to meet her and after, I'd seen the anger fading from her eyes. It'd been obvious from her response that she'd forgiven me. She could understand the awful position I'd been in and why I'd made the decisions I had, and that was more than I'd dared to hope for. But I still had to say this.

"I don't think I ever properly apologized for what I put you through five years ago. I had my reasons, but still—you didn't know, and I abandoned you to that asshole. I made you feel like you hadn't meant anything to me after all... I wish I could have found a way to stay with you, to fight back—"

Mercy's fingers squeezed mine. "It's okay. There's no way you could have gone up against my dad. *I* could barely go up against him, and I knew him better than anyone."

"I still wish I could have." I held her gaze, willing her to recognize how much I meant this. "I'm glad you're here with us, Mer. I know I said a lot of crap when you first showed up that suggested otherwise, but I was just startled and, well, scared, and I acted like an idiot. I'm sorry about that too, and for not clearing the air sooner. Having you back in my life is the best thing I could have asked for."

Her eyes widened, and something glimmered in them—were those *tears*? Before I could wrap my head around that, she tugged me to her, reaching to grip the collar of my shirt with her other hand. Then she rose up to press her lips to mine.

I kissed her back, lost in an instant in the sensations that were both so familiar and so new. It felt like coming home after a long trip away. She smelled like she always had, like hot summer days and violets, and her lips were just as soft, but there was a confidence to the kiss beyond what she'd had before. It spoke of experience, yeah, but it also said that she was going to take what she wanted, and right now what she wanted was to be kissing me.

How could I take that as anything but a total honor?

Mercy pulled back much sooner than I was ready for. Her eyes were shining with no hint of tears now, but a bittersweet smile tugged at the corners of her mouth.

"No hard feelings," she said. "I get it, all of it. It isn't like we can pick up where we left off, but—I'm glad I'm here with you too." She dropped my hand to head toward the car. "Now let's take these fuckers down once and for all."

27

Mercy

One of the other features that'd made the derelict auto shop an ideal location for Wylder's plan was the also long-abandoned restaurant next door. After Gideon set up all his gear, he and Rowan headed off to take care of work elsewhere, leaving me, Wylder, and Kaige at the old restaurant to keep an eye on things.

There wasn't much to keep an eye on, though. It was a pretty boring stretch of town, which meant it'd make sense as a place to keep a secret stash of drugs. But I wanted to see some action *now*, and there was too much left to prepare for us to set the plan in motion until tomorrow night.

We spent a couple of hours sitting on the rooftop terrace in chairs we'd dragged up from the mess of discarded furniture below. The breeze kept the muggy evening much more bearable than in the sweltering rooms below. The laptop Gideon had left behind played footage from four different cameras inside the auto shop—footage of the vacant space with its scraps of trash and nothing else. We were keeping well back from the brick wall that surrounded the terrace, not wanting any of the neighbors to spot us, which meant I couldn't see anything below.

As the evening crept on toward night, I got so restless I couldn't sit still. Leaving Wylder and Kaige discussing the ideal time to lure the Steel Knights here, I wandered back down into the vacant restaurant. My hand slipped into my pocket to brush my fingers over my childhood bracelet, but it didn't offer much comfort.

My exploring was pretty dull until I opened a cabinet near the overturned hostess podium and discovered a bottle of whiskey had been forgotten there. I grabbed it and decided it was time to head back up to the terrace.

Wylder and Kaige had gone from strategy discussion to debating the ideal spot to hit someone if you wanted to break his jaw. They fell silent when I walked over waggling the whiskey bottle.

"Hello, boys," I said. "Look what I found."

Wylder eyed me. "Are you drunk?"

"Nope. I haven't even started yet. I should probably get on that."

Kaige made an uncertain sound as I twisted off the lid. "Do you really think it's a good idea to get drunk on the job?"

I took a small swig. The alcohol burned going down, sending a woozy rush through my veins. Oh, that was strong. But it was good. It smoothed the edges off the tension that'd been itching at me.

"Who says we're getting drunk?" I said, and allowed myself another gulp. "We're twenty-four hours or so away from shattering the Steel Knights. I think we can celebrate—in moderation, of course."

Wylder snorted, but he snatched the bottle from me and tipped it to his lips with a bob of his throat I couldn't help ogling. He glanced at the label before handing it to Kaige. "It's pretty old. Nice stuff."

Kaige took a swig and shook himself. "No kidding. That's strong shit."

"You know what they say, the older the whiskey the better," I said in a singsong voice, pulling my chair around so we were sitting in a sort-of circle. I made a grabby gesture with my hand. "Don't be greedy with it."

Kaige frowned, holding onto the bottle. "What's gotten into you?"

"Nothing," I said. Everything. *Maybe* we were going to shatter the Steel Knights tomorrow. Maybe it wouldn't actually be this easy. After all the anguish I'd been through since Colt had slaughtered my family, it was hard to believe I could be almost at the end.

Was it just like Rowan said, that I'd wanted to look Colt in the eyes while I sliced him open from throat to gut? Wouldn't it be enough to see him realize how he'd been outwitted and overcome by us?

What kind of person was I if I'd rather blow off an easy plan that didn't require much violence just for the chance to splatter his blood across a room?

I didn't want to look at any of those questions too closely. There wasn't anything else we could really do tonight anyway, so why did we have to think about it at all? Part of me did want to get drunk, to let the buzz wash everything else away.

But Kaige kept the bottle close, raising it to his lips again. A wicked impulse gripped me. There were other ways to get a buzz, ones that wouldn't give me a hangover tomorrow.

When he lowered his hand, I pushed myself out of my chair and leaned over him. "Fine, I'll just get a taste this way."

I grasped his jaw and kissed him. Kaige froze for just a second, no doubt as aware as I was of Wylder stiffening in the other chair, but then he set down the bottle with a thump and pulled me closer to him. His mouth opened, and the silk fire of the whiskey's flavor swept from him to me with the heat of the kiss. Delicious in every possible way.

Even more delicious because of my sense of Wylder watching us. I eased right down onto Kaige's lap. When I tipped my head back, Kaige couldn't resist moving his lips to my neck. I hummed encouragingly before glancing sideways, straight at Wylder.

His brows had come together, and his hands were fisted at his sides. But there was something other than anger in his expression. His eyes had darkened to the color of a sea caught in a storm, and I could see the lust written there clear as day. The sight turned me on even more.

I turned back to Kaige and kissed him even harder, giving in to the urge to grind my hips into him. His dick pressed rigid and wanting against me.

With a growl, Kaige grabbed one of my tits through my shirt and squeezed. He brought his teeth to the sensitive column of my throat, shifting under me. Even though we still had layers of clothes separating us, I could feel his pulsing cock at my core as he rubbed up and down my pussy. I hissed in pleasure.

Wylder's gaze was transfixed on us, but he was looking only at me. I opened my eyes just a fraction before I slid down over Kaige's dick again. Then I tore at his T-shirt. Kaige's muscles tensed for a second as if he objected to me taking the lead. He yanked the shirt the rest of the way off and gripped the sides of my face in a gesture of control, but then he looked at Wylder.

I followed his gaze. Wylder didn't look away, his eyes burning into mine. I was burning all over, but it could be so much more than this. If the guys could handle taking things that far.

Looking back at Kaige, I gave him one more kiss, this one softer though still passionate. In a way it was a question. The tenderness with which he kissed me back, even though I could still feel the tension running through his body, seemed like enough of an answer.

I'd make sure he didn't regret it.

I eased out of his embrace and stepped over to Wylder's chair, running my fingers along the Noble heir's shoulder. He stared up at me, not quite a glower. His jaw was tight, his hands still clenched, but he couldn't seem to look away. The humid air practically thrummed with tension and heat. Still, he didn't move.

He was pissed. I wanted him to do something about it.

The whiskey had loosened my tongue. "Are you just going to sit there and watch him fuck me?"

Something snapped in Wylder. He reached for me with a snarl and yanked me to him with his fingers tangled in my hair. The shot of pain that ran over my scalp brought a wave of pleasure with it.

Wylder kissed me furiously, his fingers knotting deeper in my hair as his hot tongue invaded my mouth. As I kissed him back, I ran my hands down the flexing muscles of his chest. Our teeth knocked against each other, our tongues dueling. Then he was pushing me down to the ground with him braced over me, careful of my bandaged shoulder.

Kaige got up, his breathing uneven as he walked over to us. My limbs tangled in Wylder's as he kissed a path down to my collarbone, his hands skimming under my top. In one swift motion, he pulled the shirt off me so all that was left was my bra.

I gazed up at them, their faces framed by the night sky with its studding of stars. The collective hunger in their eyes made my stomach lurch with anticipation. I'd never done something like this before, never been with more than one guy at once, but it felt right. Necessary. Like if we didn't fulfill the promise of this moment, we'd never get it back again.

Kaige had brought the whiskey bottle with him. He took a gulp as he sat down beside us but made no move to reach for me. Wylder's scorching mouth traveled down the valley of my breasts, stopping to swirl his tongue around my nipples through the soft cotton of my bra. As his teeth bit down on me, the feeling teetering between pain and pleasure, I moaned.

I squirmed under him as he marked a trail of kisses to the edge of my jeans and popped open the button. As he tugged them off, Kaige knelt down, his expression as hungry as a predator waiting to pounce on its prey. With a flick of his thumb, he opened the front clasp on my bra. The cups fell away, leaving me in nothing but panties.

Kaige's eyes roved my bare skin like a caress. Wylder leaned back on his heels to take me in too. As the combined heat of their attention washed over me, Kaige upturned the bottle of whiskey so that the amber fluid trickled onto my chest. The liquid warmth flowed over the curve of my tits before forming a rivulet down my bare stomach. My breath hitched in anticipation.

Wylder and Kaige glanced at each other. Even though they didn't speak, I could tell they'd communicated with each other silently.

Wylder settled over one of my breasts and slicked his tongue up the mound to the peak. Kaige descended over the other. His hot mouth sucked hungrily as if he wanted to drink in every last drop of the whiskey on my body.

I writhed under them as their solid bodies encompassed me. Their combined weight felt delicious. Our increasingly ragged breaths mixed together as they cocooned me between their muscular chests.

I looked at them with my eyelids at half-mast. My pussy convulsed at the sight of their heads bobbing up and down, lapping up every trace of whiskey and spreading heady bliss in their wake.

"Oh, fuck," I murmured.

Kaige traced his tongue down to my stomach. He poured more of the whiskey into my belly button and began to lap at it hungrily. I rubbed my legs together, my panties completely soaked now, chasing the climbing pleasure.

Wylder saw what I wanted. His fingers slipped over my throbbing pussy. He rubbed up and down the slit with the heel of his hand against my clit. My breath caught, and I let out a moan when two of his wicked fingers rose to my clit and flicked at it.

Wylder observed my face before he did it again, more urgently. "That's right, Kitten. Let's hear you mew."

"Time to get these off," Kaige announced, jerking my panties down my legs so fast a few of the threads at the seams snapped. He gazed down at my cunt, looking like his mouth was watering. "So fucking gorgeous."

Wylder hooked his fingers right inside me, making me arch off the ground. He pumped them until I was bucking against him and then held them to my lips. "Take a taste."

His gaze was so bright and avid I opened my mouth and lightly sucked on his fingers. Wylder's eyes turned hooded. He pinched my nipple as if in reward and bent down to kiss me at the same time Kaige lowered his mouth to my pussy.

I groaned against Wylder's lips. He drank up every sound I made as he ravished my mouth and Kaige licked my pussy like it was an ice cream cone in his favorite flavor. I was just climbing to the edge of the precipice when Kaige stopped and grasped my waist to flip me over.

I shifted onto my hands and knees, favoring my wounded shoulder, and squealed as Kaige pulled me back by the hips. He positioned me in front of him, and there was the sound of foil ripping open. I only ached with the lack of attention for a few seconds before his hard cock rubbed against my slit.

It slipped inside my pussy, which was so wet he met no resistance. My inner walls expanded to accommodate his girth. His dick hit an angle so deep inside me that my eyes rolled up and I nearly forgot to breathe.

Kaige drew himself out before rolling his hips right back into me, not giving me time to recover. I growled in answer as I thrust my hips back to match his rhythm. My shoulder prickled, but every other part of me felt so good I didn't give a shit.

Wylder unzipped his jeans. He freed his cock, his hand moving up and down its engorged length as he watched his friend fuck me from behind. The piercing at the tip gleamed faintly in the twilight.

I licked my lips. I'd wanted to feel that ring against my tongue since the first moment I'd seen it. "I need a taste of that too," I said, my voice coming out husky.

Wylder grinned. "Oh yes, you do." He wound his fingers into my hair again and tugged me toward him. I reached for his cock eagerly.

The shaft twitched as my lips closed around it. I swiveled my tongue around the piercing, and Wylder groaned. The force of Kaige's thrusts propelled Wylder deeper. The feeling of fullness both in my mouth and my pussy threatened to overwhelm me.

I bobbed my head up and down, sucking hard at the tip. Wylder began to grunt, his hips pumping toward me with increasing urgency. Kaige gripped my hips and pounded into me with equal vigor. Our moans mingled together as all three of us raced our way to our orgasms.

Kaige reached between my legs and flicked at my clit. I came apart around him, my pussy convulsing violently as it milked his cock. "That's right," he muttered. "Just like—*fuck*."

As he came, my mouth tightened around Wylder. The Noble heir came with a sudden spurt of hot, salty cum across my tongue. I lapped and swallowed as he rocked to a halt. His breath was harsh, but his hand was suddenly, startlingly gentle as he teased his fingers through my hair.

When he slid out of me, Wylder trailed his fingers down the side of my face to my jaw. He tipped my chin up so I'd look him in the eyes.

"You belong with us," he said vehemently, repeating the words he'd given me weeks ago that he'd seemed to go back on. "*All* of us. And if anyone tries to say there's a problem with that, we'll make it their problem instead."

Like his father. Would dealing with Ezra's disapproval really be that simple? But in that moment, my body wrung out with pleasure, I couldn't say I cared.

28

Mercy

KAIGE GAVE THE DOOR OF THE TRUCK ONE LAST SWIPE WITH his rag and turned with a big smile on his face. I wasn't sure he'd stopped smiling since our spur of the moment threesome last night. When his eyes caught mine, a tendril of heat unfurled through me despite the jangling of my nerves over the operation we were setting in motion.

"All clean," he announced.

"Good." Wylder set a somewhat possessive hand on my shoulder, but he grinned back at his friend without any noticeable animosity. "I think that's the last of it. Rowan?"

"Just finished the doors," Rowan replied, emerging from the back. "There shouldn't be any sign left that we were ever here."

A smirk curled my own lips. "But the Steel Knights will leave their fingerprints all over the place coming in. Let's see them try to explain away that." I was starting to warm to the idea of getting my revenge by siccing the cops on those bastards. Colt would hate being behind bars, losing control over his budding empire while he slowly rotted away in prison.

Wylder motioned for us to follow him. "Let's get back to our lookout spot and kick off the last few pieces."

We slipped out the back using gloved hands and headed into the restaurant next door. It was cooler today, especially now that evening was falling, a slightly damp breeze wafting against my face. We'd just driven the truck into the old auto-repair shop an hour ago and spent the rest of the time wiping the place down of any trace of our presence.

Once we were inside, I stuffed the gloves in my pocket and touched the outline of my bracelet through the fabric there, then the smooth pearl on Anthea's hair pin, which I'd worn today as another lucky charm. I'd gotten through one dangerous situation in an unusual way wearing it. Maybe as long as I had it on me, it'd somehow protect me from actually needing it.

Okay, that was silly superstition, but I liked the idea even if I didn't totally believe it.

We rejoined Gideon on the rooftop terrace. He nodded to us and tapped a few keys on the laptop balanced on his knees. "Cameras now sending their footage to the hard drive in the front office." He'd set up the surveillance system so that the cops could find the recordings we wanted them to have, but he could still keep an eye on them from his computer. I doubted he'd sever that connection until he absolutely had to.

Kaige prowled over to the narrow notch we'd carved into the terrace wall from the top edge to halfway down. It allowed us to watch the street below without anyone catching a glimpse of us. "Nothing strange going on out there right now. What do we have left to do?"

Rowan pulled out his phone. "I'll have a couple of connections drop our last rumors about the exact location of the drug shipment."

Wylder nodded. "Gideon will keep an eye on the traffic cams to see when the Steel Knights start heading our way. Mercy, Kaige, and I will head down so we're ready to spring the jams on the doors once the Steel Knights have stormed the place. Then Rowan will give the cops their final tip to bring them down here ASAP. And we get the fuck out before all hell breaks loose."

Everything was taken care of. I dragged in a breath and froze when I saw Kaige stiffen.

"Hold up," he said. Rowan lowered the phone he hadn't yet placed a call on. "There's a guy outside. He just drove up in front of the restaurant, and now he's rapping on the door like he's trying to get someone's attention."

"What the fuck?" Wylder stalked over to the wall.

I hurried after him. Once he'd gotten a look, I peered out. In the hazy evening light, the face I saw below us made my pulse hiccup.

I pulled back, speaking under my breath. "It's one of the Claws members—well, former Claws. I've seen him with Jenner helping out the Steel Knights."

Rowan frowned. "That's not good. No one should have figured out the exact location yet. But why would he come alone if he knows what's up?"

"Maybe he doesn't?" Kaige said doubtfully. "Maybe someone spotted one of us around here, but they don't know the whole thing."

"That still doesn't explain what he's up to," Wylder said, and paused. "He isn't wearing one of the bandanas."

The guy's voice reached us then, rough—almost frantic sounding. "Mercy! I know you've got to be around here. I have to talk to you."

A shiver ran down my spine. Had *I* screwed up somehow, and the Steel Knights had tracked me here?

Gideon had ambled over to take a look. He rubbed his jaw. "It doesn't make sense. He poses no threat. You could take him even with that bullet wound in your shoulder. Why would he think you'd come out?"

"Because I know him, and he isn't actually here to hurt me?" I suggested.

Wylder jerked around, giving me an incredulous look, but I was remembering the appeal I'd made to Jenner in the warehouse the other night. This guy had been there too—he'd heard me.

Had one person actually listened?

"Is there any sign of any other Steel Knights or their allies around?" I asked.

Kaige shook his head, and Gideon went back to his laptop. He flipped through several feeds of street footage. "He does appear to be alone."

I wavered for a second and then turned toward the stairs. "I'll go talk to him. Like you said, I can take him on my own if I have to."

Wylder was at my side in an instant. He grabbed my arm to stop me. "I don't think that's a good idea."

I stared back at him, matching the intensity of his gaze. "Even if he made the stupid decision to side with Colt without knowing the whole story, he's still one of my dad's people. One of *my* people. What if he knows something important?" I pulled out my gun. "I'll be careful. And if you're so concerned, you can come along for backup."

Wylder's mouth flattened, but he let me go, following close at my heels as we descended through the two floors of the restaurant. When I reached the front door, he hung back to stay out of view unless he was needed.

I eased the door open a crack. "Back up a couple of steps," I said, pitching my voice just loud enough to reach the guy outside. "I'm here. And I've got a gun on you, so keep your hands where I can see them. What do you want?"

The guy held his hands out at his sides as he followed my order. His skin looked jaundiced in the yellow light of the streetlamps, but that couldn't explain the tension and, I thought, fear etched all over his face.

"I came to warn you," he said. "Colt found out what you're planning, I don't even know how, and he's rallying the Steel Knights right now to charge over here in full force."

So our plan had just gotten off to an early start? "They're coming to recover the truck?" I said, feeling like there had to be more to it.

The guy grimaced. "No. Well, maybe that too, but he knows you're planning to ambush them. He knows you'll be staked out here, and he's planning to catch you with his own ambush. Unless you've got a whole army in there with you, you've got to take off before they get here."

A chill washed through me.

"How the fuck are we supposed to believe you?" Wylder asked, coming up beside me. He released the safety on his gun with an audible click.

The guy outside blanched. "I swear," he said, raising his hands higher, "I'm just trying to do the right thing. I shouldn't have listened to Colt—I didn't know what went down with Tyrell—but I should have realized it wasn't like him to plan to stab someone in the back. The Claws were like family to me. I'm not doing some snake's dirty work. Just hurry."

"Stay there," I told him, and yanked the door shut. I turned to face Wylder and realized the other guys had come downstairs to listen too, Gideon with his laptop balanced against his hip so he could keep an eye on the footage at the same time.

"It's got to be another of Colt's plans to fuck with us," Kaige said. "He wants us to leave so he can grab the stash without us getting in the way."

Gideon was frowning. "If he already knows that we're not actually using the truck ourselves, that it's bait and we're waiting here for them to come, then we *can't* get in the way. They're not falling for the trap in the first place—he's made us. The question is, how?"

"I'm not sure that matters right now," Rowan put in. "If that guy is telling the truth, we don't have time to figure it out. The five of us can't fight off Colt's entire force if he's decided he doesn't care about pissing off Ezra anymore."

Wylder exhaled roughly. "The Steel Knights have already tried to kill me once. I think it's safe to say that ship has sailed." He looked at me. "This was one of your father's men. Do you believe him?"

I swallowed hard. Was the decision really going to come down to my judgment? I got a little giddy knowing that he trusted me enough to ask, but I was also nervous as hell to be making the call for all of us.

All I could say was the truth. "I do. If Colt knows we're here, he'd have a much easier time killing us if he took us by surprise. I can't see how he'd benefit from getting us to run, expecting his men to arrive at any second. Rowan's right—we wouldn't stand a chance against a whole horde of them anyway."

Kaige swore. "We can't just leave the truck. I'm not letting them put that garbage on the street after all."

Gideon cleared his throat. "We might not have a choice." He jabbed at his laptop's touch pad, leaping from feed to feed. "There *are* a hell of a lot of cars heading this way in a big group—from a bunch of different directions. They're ready to box us in. We'll have a better chance getting out of here unnoticed in the smaller car."

"But the drugs—"

"Let's go!" Wylder snapped. "Run upstairs, grab anything you might have left that'd point to us being here in case the cops come after all, and let's get out of here."

I hadn't brought anything with me that I didn't already have on me. My heart thudding, I cracked open the door again. The former Claws guy was shuffling his feet nervously. He jerked to attention when I peeked out.

"Thank you," I said. "Now you get going too. If Colt finds out you tipped us off—"

He shuddered. "I know. You did a good thing for Jenner, Mercy. The Claws live on as long as you're still with us." Then he darted off into the night.

The guys were pounding up and down the stairs, shouting questions and orders at each other. I hustled to the back and peered out into the alley. We'd parked Rowan's car down by the end of it, a few buildings away. The alley was completely silent, but the air felt heavy like the hour before a storm.

"Go, go," Wylder shouted from behind me. We burst out into the alley—

And then tires screeched to a halt all around us, including at both ends of the alleyway.

Men with red bandanas around their arms poured out of their vehicles to charge down the alley toward us. I backpedaled. Wylder grabbed my elbow to spin me around, and we all raced back into the shelter of the restaurant.

Kaige slammed the deadbolt into place. I ran for the front of the building to make sure the other entrance was secure, but before I'd even made it halfway, the wide front window shattered with the bash of a baseball bat. I skidded to a halt with the guys behind me.

Cars and jeeps filled the street outside. A swarm of men had gathered on the sidewalk in front of the restaurant. I gripped my gun tightly, my palm sweating against the metal. They hadn't taken us by surprise, but we were still in an awful situation.

Wylder and Kaige fired a few shots through the window, and the men there fell back to the sides or behind the cars, but they didn't look all that scared. Someone was already battering the back door. How long would those hinges hold?

Then a familiar figure stepped out of the shadows. The light from the streetlamps glanced off Colt's golden hair. He held a semi-automatic in one hand, and its muzzle was pointed at the forehead of the Claws member who'd warned us. He shivered in Colt's grasp, his eyes wide and panicked, as the asshole used him as a human shield.

"Too late," he sneered at us. "Your stupid little trick failed, and now it's all over."

"Get out of here before you regret it," Wylder said, as if he were in any position to make threats. "This is Noble territory."

"I wouldn't be so sure about that, Mr. Noble. If my friend is right that there are only the five of you working this operation, I have twenty men for each of you. You're at my mercy."

His friend?

Before I could wonder more about that, Colt's gaze fixed on me. "Speaking of which—did you miss me, Mercy? This time there won't be any crazy stunts and quick escapes. Every avenue is cut off to you. And soon I'll be cutting you down."

"Not if I get to you first." I spat on the ground in front of me.

A couple of the Steel Knights laughed. Colt simply wrenched back the head of the guy he was clutching. "Why don't you all come out peacefully, and at least a few of you can survive. I'll even promise that Mercy and the Noble heir will get much less painful deaths than if I have to send my men in there after you."

"I'd rather shoot myself in the head," Wylder said.

Colt's face turned grim. "You chose this."

He made a motion with his hand, and a hail of gunfire shattered the last chunks of glass clinging to the window frame. Kaige and I dove behind the hostess podium, the other guys ducking behind overturned tables. The furnishings rattled with the impact of the bullets, but at least they were solid enough to catch them.

When the men outside moved toward the window again, we all shot at them. My wounded shoulder was already aching from the tension in my stance. Wylder managed to hit one guy in the forehead, Rowan one in the chest.

They pulled back again, but two out of a hundred hardly evened the odds. And the back door was still thumping and groaning. We couldn't defend ourselves from both sides.

"What now?" Gideon asked in a low voice from where he was hunched over his laptop. "We could put a call out for back-up."

"It'll take anyone we can reach too long to get here to really help. And then my dad will curse my memory even more than he will anyway." Wylder reloaded his gun and cocked it. He caught my eye across the shadowy space. "No, we're doing this ourselves, and we're going to take down as many of those fuckers as we possibly can. We won't let Bryant win. Forget clever plans. It's time to go at them guns blazing, just like he came at Mercy's family."

29

Mercy

MORE BULLETS CAREENED THROUGH THE BROKEN restaurant window. We fired back, trying to pick off anyone who showed a vulnerable area, but the best I managed was a hit to one guy's arm. There were too many of them, moving too quickly in the dark.

And the banging on the back door was getting louder. I thought I heard the wood of the frame starting to splinter.

"Careful with your shots," Gideon said, his voice low but urgent. "We don't want to run out of ammo too soon."

Oh, shit, I hadn't even thought of that. I only had one spare clip on me. The other guys might have been carrying a few more, but I'd already seen each of them reload at least once. Did we have enough between us to take out every one of our enemies out there even if they'd lined up for clear shots?

My stomach sank, dread filling me despite Wylder's determined words. We were going to go at them guns blazing, sure, but it was becoming more and more obvious that we'd just be mowing down as many of them as we could before they took us out.

I just hoped I could put Colt in a lot of pain before I kicked the bucket. That wasn't too much to ask, was it?

As that question passed through my mind, someone flung an object like a large can through the window. It hit the floor a few feet inside with a clatter, and thick smoke burst out of it.

Oh, no. "Smoke bomb!" I yelled, scrambling farther backward.

The smoke followed us toward the kitchen, forming a giant impenetrable haze. It moved faster than we could. In seconds, the guys disappeared somewhere within the blanket of smog. My eyes watered. I ducked low, coughing as I tried to squint through the worst of it.

Footsteps thundered toward us. The Steel Knights had used the cover of the smoke to storm the building through the window. I fired at the blurred figures that came into view through the gray fog, praying that the guys were still beside and behind me, not out there in that mess.

The shots blaring on either side of me seemed to confirm that. Several of the figures dropped. But more kept coming. I pulled the trigger on my gun and realized I'd emptied my second clip. The gun was useless now.

The smoke was clearing now, revealing dozens of men barging toward us amid the toppled furniture, using it for cover just like we had minutes before. I dropped my gun just as three Steel Knights converged on me. Throwing myself backward, I banged my ass against the wall. I'd been cornered.

One of the guys leered, brandishing a gun in one hand and an axe in the other. "Colt wants to be the one to kill her, but that doesn't mean we can't carve her up a little first."

Adrenaline blared through my veins. They expected me to cringe in the corner while they descended on me. Yet another bunch of assholes assuming I was a pussy just because I had one.

"You can try," I retorted, and launched myself at them, whipping out my knife at the same time.

Shoving between two of the men, I jabbed the blade into one's side. As he screamed in pain, I yanked it out and swung it in the other direction. It sliced across another attacker's chest just as he snatched at me. I kicked him hard, sending him stumbling backward into the third guy. A searing pain spread from my wounded shoulder, but I focused on the thudding of my heartbeat instead.

More men were crowding in on us. Kaige shot one point blank in the head and then ducked down next to me. He yanked me toward the kitchen, and I dashed there with him, staying low.

He got off a couple more shots at guys who came too close, but one managed to slam a baseball bat across his back. He staggered, groaning, but swung his powerful fist to clock the prick in the temple. As the other guy reeled backward, Kaige shot him too.

We were seconds from the kitchen door when I heard the back door finally give out with a crackling of broken wood. Kaige jerked me in another direction. I spotted the other three guys crouched behind a long banquet table that'd once stood at the back of the room. Our last bit of shelter in the chaos.

As we ran toward it, a man lunged at me and hauled on my knife hand. Another two guys tackled Kaige. At the twist of my wrist, my fingers spasmed and the knife fell from my grasp.

Wylder let out a shout, and both he and Rowan threw themselves toward me to help. Rowan's shot caught my attacker in the throat. The guy sagged with a gush of blood, but more shots rattled my eardrums from farther away.

Wylder stumbled as a bullet clipped his thigh. Another caught Rowan in the side of his chest. He staggered into me, a red blotch spreading across his shirt just below his armpit.

"No!" The word burst from my lips, and I was dropping with him, trying to cushion his fall. He twisted with a grimace of pain and pointed his gun at the men closing in on us, but nothing happened when he pulled the trigger. He'd used his last bullet defending me.

Wylder got off two more shots, and then there was nothing but a hollow clicking sound from his pistol too. He sank down next to us, his other hand pressed to the bleeding wound on his thigh.

Gideon stared at us from behind the table, his jaw tight, his hands empty. Either he'd run out of ammo earlier or he'd given his to the other guys who were more practiced fighters.

Kaige was now flailing under the combined weight of three guys trying to wrestle his gun away from him. When he shot one, another leapt in to take that guy's place, stomping on Kaige's elbow. A groan reverberated past Kaige's clenched teeth.

"Hold them for Colt," someone said, and understanding hit me like a punch to the gut. We were done. It was over.

But as the men loomed on us, yells rose up from farther away. Gunfire blasted outside, which didn't make much sense considering the Steel Knights had no one to shoot at but us, and we were way back here.

Several figures burst through the crowd. "Claws!" one of them shouted, punching his fist in the air. It was Jenner.

Even as I gaped at him, he and the men he was leading opened fire on the Steel Knights around us. Dozens of the men with red bandanas crumpled, too startled to shoot back in time.

My appeal had worked. Not just on the one guy who'd warned us, but on Jenner and whoever else he'd spoken to as well.

Just for a second, my spirits soared. We could get out of this—get Rowan to a hospital, get Wylder patched up—

Then someone behind me grasped my hair and wrenched me away from the guys. Pain exploded through my scalp. When I lashed out with my fists, the muzzle of a gun jammed against my temple.

On my knees, I stared up to see Colt standing over me, one hand still clutching my hair, the other pressing the gun to my face. He sneered down at me before raising his gaze toward Jenner and the others, who'd stopped in their tracks at the sight.

"Drop your weapons," Colt said in a voice so vicious it was almost a hiss. "Or your princess dies right here."

Their gun hands wobbled, and panic shot up my throat. I might not be able to make it out of this alive, but the guys would still have a chance. If the Claws gave up, we were all dead.

"Don't listen to him!" I said, my gaze darting around me for anything I could use as a weapon. "He's going to kill me either way."

"Bitch." Colt wrenched my head back and forth so violently I saw stars. "I'm going to have my men shoot yours now, and you can watch them die in front of you, knowing you brought this on them."

No. Wylder had refused to give up, and I wouldn't stop either. I swung my hand toward my hair where Colt was gripping me, clawing at the strands—and my fingers brushed against something small and cool that came loose at their touch. Something I'd almost forgotten.

"No more surprises," Colt said with a cold smile, and slammed my head against the wall.

Agony spiked through my skull. I fought against the wave of pain and caught his wrist with my other hand. As he twisted to the side to dodge the blow, probably thinking I was aiming to strike at his chest or gut, I stabbed Anthea's pearl hair pin straight into his forearm where his artery would be.

Colt swore and kneed me in my belly, knocking the breath right out of me. I collapsed to the floor. His gun still trained on me, he glared down at the pin lodged in his arm. "Did you really think that would hurt me? Surely you—"

His voice cut out with a sway of his legs. His whole body lurched as he tried to regain control and failed. His knees gave, and he fell forward onto his hands, his gun smacking the floor.

Anthea's poison had worked its magic.

"What the fuck did you do to me?" Colt rasped, but he was shaking all over, unable to catch his balance enough to spin on me. Anthea had said the stuff wouldn't kill a man, just slow him down a lot. And that was all I needed.

"Get them!" Colt snapped out, but Jenner and his men were no longer so worried for my safety. The second any of the Steel Knights moved, they shot them, walking toward me and the guys to form a protective barrier around us.

Us and Colt. I heaved myself to my feet, ignoring the pain in my head and the spinning of my thoughts. I could still focus enough to finish the job I'd been waiting to carry out for so long.

"You, Colt Bryant, are a dead man walking." I slammed my heel into his ribs, and he sagged to the floor. His fingers twitched around the gun before Gideon stepped in, kicking it away.

Gideon knelt beside Wylder and Rowan, pressing his hands to their wounds. "I figured it was reasonable to call for back-up *now,*" he murmured. "Your father's men will be here within twenty minutes. Try not to bleed too much before then."

As Wylder muttered something about disobedient underlings, I crouched with my knees on Colt's back to hold him in place and then jerked down, slamming his head against the tiled floor with my elbow. I punched him once, twice, three times for good measure, until his nose crunched against the tiles and his eye was purpling.

And still he laughed, sputtering blood from his mouth. "You don't get to win, Mercy. You've already lost everything."

Rage unlike anything I had ever felt before turned my vision red. My hand found my fallen knife on the floor and raised it. The smile vanished from Colt's face.

"No," I said. "You tried, but I found everything I really needed. And now you're *never* going to have the chance to take another person from me."

I shoved him onto his back and slammed the blade into his chest. Blood welled up around the wound, and Colt's expression stuttered.

I yanked out the knife and stabbed him again and again—for Grandma, for Aunt Renee, for every person in my family that he'd slaughtered. For Wylder and Rowan and Kaige and Gideon, who he'd tried to do the same to. More blood spurted up, hot against my skin, but I kept going, tears burning behind my eyes.

When my hand finally fell to my side, the handle slick against my palm, solid arms wrapped around me. They brought Kaige's musky scent.

"You're done, Mercy," he said in a low voice. "He's dead. Colt is dead."

I blinked and stared down at the body before me. Colt's head had lolled to the side, splattered with blood from the multiple wounds in his chest. His unblinking eyes shone glassily. Not a hint of life remained in his pallid skin.

He was dead. I'd killed him. It was over.

A broken laugh spilled from my lips. As I grasped Kaige's arm, hugging him back as well as I could in that moment, the remaining Steel Knights fell back and fled the building. They had no fight left in them faced with the Claws members' guns and the dead body of their leader.

"Thank you," I said to Jenner when he glanced back at me.

He dipped his head. "I should thank you for reminding me of my proper priorities. We'll stay with you until the Nobles arrive. And when you're ready to raise up the Claws again, we'll be waiting."

I couldn't wrap my head around those words right now. I turned toward the guys, groping for Rowan. His face had paled, and half of his shirt was stained red, but he met my gaze steadily enough to reassure me that he wasn't on the verge of death himself. "Don't worry about me," he said raggedly. "I can hang in there."

"He'd better," Wylder muttered, wincing when Gideon balled a new rag against his thigh to replace the blood-soaked one. "Knowing my father, if I lose even *one* man in this goddamned fight against ridiculous odds, he'll still call it a loss."

Kaige let out a raw, wild laugh, and then the others laughed too, and I knew that as bloody and damaged as we were, we were going to be all right.

30

Mercy

THE GATHERING CONSISTED SOLELY OF EZRA, THREE MEN from his inner circle, Wylder and his closest associates, Anthea, and me. I had to assume the only reason the head Noble was holding it in his audience room instead of his office was my presence. Apparently I still hadn't earned enough clout with him to be trusted in that space, which I suspected meant he was also still plotting my doom.

I didn't let that vague threat dim too much of my enjoyment of the wine and hors d'oeuvres he'd offered up, though. There was a celebratory vibe in the air. Colt was six feet under, along with a substantial number of the Steel Knights. His other lackeys had backed off from the corners they'd previously claimed. And after a week to recover from their wounds, Wylder and Rowan were both on their feet, standing near me.

Ezra held up his wine glass. "To my son, for eliminating the greatest threat we've faced in years on his own initiative and with no lives lost on our side. And to a Paradise free from any challenges to our authority!"

"To Mercy too," Kaige piped up with a rebellious glint in his eyes, "for being the one to put that bastard Colt Bryant in the ground."

Ezra's lips thinned slightly, but he still drank with the rest of us. His gaze slid over me, pausing to offer only the palest of smiles.

Yeah, the guy definitely wasn't ready to exchange friendship bracelets just yet.

Axel brushed past me to the side table, not quite touching me but making my body tense at how close he'd come. I hadn't forgotten the role *he'd* played in framing me. The less time I spent in his presence, the better.

"Now that the Steel Knights have been crushed, we have new questions to consider," Ezra said. "I hope we can all put our minds together. While we rule over all of Paradise Bend, we've always managed the areas outside the city proper through our associations with and dominance over the lesser gangs there. The destruction of both the Claws and the Steel Knights will create a power vacuum there."

Anthea nodded. "Which means we need to keep an eye on who steps in to fill it."

I kept my mouth carefully shut. The guys and I had decided not to mention the assistance we'd gotten from Jenner and the other former Claws members during the last fight. Knowing there were men loyal to me in the Bend, even if it was only a handful, would only increase any worries Ezra had about me. And understandably, Wylder had also preferred not to mention that we'd have been slaughtered without the sudden arrival of help we couldn't have counted on.

There were all the smaller gangs that Colt had caught up in his push for power... and the mysterious group we'd never been able to find out any details about. The memory of the strange, silent men standing behind Colt that one time sent a prickle down my spine.

Maybe they'd gone back to wherever they'd come from now that he was gone, and that was that. But I'd have liked to know for sure.

"Exactly," Ezra said, picking up from Anthea's remark. "Over the next few days, we'll reach out to the small bases of power in the Bend and feel out what their intentions are and how much loyalty we can count on from them. We may need to dole out some... consequences to those who aligned themselves with Bryant. But the greatest challenge is behind us."

His men drew closer to him, and they fell into a quieter

conversation between sips of their wine. I watched them from the corner of my eye, wishing I could step close enough to listen in without Ezra taking me for a spy.

A hand squeezed my shoulder—gently, still careful of the gunshot wound that now barely twinged even during my push-ups. I looked up to see Kaige beaming down at me. "What are you thinking?" he asked. "You shouldn't look so serious right now."

I tucked a strand of hair behind my ear. "Oh, it's nothing much," I said, and then decided to just be honest. Kaige would understand. "I can't shake the feeling that I'm missing something."

"Maybe you're missing six-foot three inches of pure muscle," he said, pointing a thumb at himself.

I laughed and swatted at him with my hand. When his eyes heated, I immediately found myself thinking back to the last time his cock had been inside me.

On the other side of the room, Wylder was watching us. When I swallowed, I could still feel *his* cock filling my mouth. We'd definitely have to do that again sometime.

"But really, what is it?" Kaige prodded.

"What is what?" Gideon asked. He'd ambled over to us, nibbling on a crab cake.

"Nothing specific," I said. "You still haven't turned up anything about where Colt was getting the drugs, have you?"

Gideon shook his head. "Unfortunately, no. And there's no sign of his mysterious associates either. They seem to have disappeared off the face of the Earth."

"That's good, right?" Kaige said.

I frowned. "I'd like to think it is, but nothing about this has been that simple before."

"It's possible they wanted something from him and he was unable to deliver," Gideon said. "I wouldn't let it worry you."

He was right. We were supposed to be celebrating. I shook off my uneasiness as well as I could. It was second nature after all those years under Dad's thumb, but he was gone too. I could make a fresh start for real now.

Anthea walked up to us carrying a plate full of pastries, and we each took one. As the sweetness exploded in my mouth, my worries seemed even farther away.

"So how's everybody feeling?" Anthea asked.

"Good as new," Rowan said, walking up to us. He gave me a small smile before taking a bite of a pastry. Only Wylder remained at a distance, almost as if he was unwilling to join our group. I wondered if it was because of Ezra's presence, and he didn't want to accidentally tip him off to how close the two of us had become.

"What do you think—" I started to ask, and one of the Noble initiates burst in from the hall.

"Mr. Noble, there's something you need to see."

Ezra gave the young guy a look that could have seared through steel, obviously pissed off about the interruption. "Not now," he said flatly. "We're occupied."

"I'm sorry—it's just there's someone outside. He says he has to see you, that it's a matter of life and death."

Ezra frowned but put his glass down.

A matter of life and death? What the hell was going on now?

When Ezra left the room, the rest of us followed without any discussion. Nervous tension wound around my gut again.

Ezra marched out the front door, Axel and his other men right behind him, their guns now in their hands. The guys and I slipped out behind them, staying on the landing while they went partway down the front steps.

A college-aged guy I'd never seen before was standing in the middle of the front walk, surrounded by four Noble men who all had their guns aimed at him. His clothes and hair were rumpled, and his forehead shone with droplets of sweat. He held a large tablet in his shaking hands.

"Here I am," Ezra said in a darkly cool voice. "What do you want?"

"You're Ezra Noble?" the man asked. His eyes darted from side to side before coming back to focus on the Noble boss.

Ezra nodded. "Who are you?"

A tremor ran through the guy's body. "I've been sent with a message for you." He tapped the tablet's screen.

An image appeared there: a man wearing a dark dress shirt posed in front of a white background. His wiry salt-and-pepper hair was pulled back in a short ponytail at the base of his neck, but several strands had sprung free around his square-jawed face. Even standing still, his wide-shouldered, barrel-chested body radiated strength.

But that wasn't what really caught my attention. Twin scars, identical Xs, marked his cheeks. And his fierce eyes, fixed on us through the recording, gave me a sense of chaotic energy powerful enough to make me shiver.

He spoke with a voice so deep it was chilling, as if it was echoing from a pit the sun never reached the bottom of. "Hello, Ezra Noble. My name is Xavier. I look forward to meeting you face to face in the near future, but for now we'll stick with this. I wanted to thank you personally for running the rats off the streets of the Bend. The mess you've cleaned up will make it easier for me and my people to sweep in and take what we've decided to make ours."

Ezra bristled, but he couldn't exactly talk back.

The man in the recording kept going, unaware of the reactions he was provoking. "I have to say, I like what I've seen of your style. You'll be entertaining opponents. I can't wait to tackle the challenge of removing all of Paradise from your grasp."

My heart sank. The war wasn't over after all.

But just when I thought I'd heard the worst I could have, Xavier raised his voice again. "Is my lost pussy cat still with you? She's made a lot of trouble for all of us since she came running your way, hasn't she." His gaze crept across the screen as if he was looking for someone.

For me, I realized, restraining a flinch. A lost cat that came running to the Nobles? Who else could he mean?

The guys were looking at me now, their stances tensing as if they could defend me from an image on a tablet.

A cruel grin stretched across the man's face. "I hope she liked the presents I left her. I put much thought and effort into each one. And don't worry, there's more to come."

Presents? My stomach flipped over. The drawing, the dead cat, the unearthed corpse—that had all been *him*.

But why? I'd never seen him before in my life.

"Until next time, Nobles," Xavier said, still grinning, and vanished into a hiss of static before the screen went black again.

Ezra was just opening his mouth to speak when the guy clutching the tablet exploded with an audible *boom*, splattering blood and flesh in every direction.

RUTHLESS QUEEN

Crooked Paradise #3

1

Mercy

IT TURNED OUT HUMAN REMAINS WERE DIFFICULT TO GET off of grass, especially remains that had recently exploded.

At least I wasn't right out in the middle of the mess anymore. From the living room window, I could see the Noble lackeys who were hosing down the front lawn. The blood that had painted the grass looked thinner now, but the blades shone faintly red under the morning sun.

When I breathed, a metallic taint remained in the back of my throat. I'd rinsed my mouth out in the shower several times, but I couldn't quite get rid of it.

An hour had passed since the unknown man had burst apart all over the lawn outside the Noble mansion. Even now, the visceral violence of the moment replayed in the back of my mind over and over. That and the moments leading up to it. The video he'd played for us... That creepy-ass dude who'd claimed he was going to take over Paradise Bend now that Colt and the Steel Knights were destroyed...

It all left me with a clammy sensation wrapped around my gut.

Wylder and his inner circle were lounging on the sofa and armchairs around the room, but none of them looked remotely relaxed.

"Do we have any idea who this Xavier guy is?" Rowan asked the room at large, as if he knew exactly what I was thinking. "Did any of you recognize him?"

Wylder shook his head. "No, never seen that fucker. I think I would have remembered him."

Anybody would. The X shaped scars on his cheeks, raised and pinkened with age, had shown clearly even on the small tablet screen. And the way he'd spoken, so chilling and impassive, was burned into my memory. The man had to be a psychopath, maybe even a worse one than Colt.

I tore my gaze away from the window and started pacing. "I've got no idea either. What the hell does he want with us?"

With *me*. He'd addressed me directly in the video. A shudder ran down my spine.

Kaige got up and caught my shoulders in his hands. "Mercy, come sit down."

I almost argued, but his expression was so concerned I gave in. I didn't think I could feel any worse on my ass than on my feet anyway. And Kaige didn't show emotions other than flirtiness and rage very often, so when you got something else from him, you knew it was a big deal.

I sank onto the sofa between him and Wylder, and he slung his arm around my back. I let myself lean against the hard planes of his brawny chest. When I looked up at Rowan, I thought I saw a flicker of something in his bright eyes, but he looked away.

Wylder had a nonchalant air, but I knew that was only a front. I wondered if he and Kaige had discussed the threesome we'd had the other night on the terrace. Not that now was a great time to be thinking about that interlude, as spectacular as it'd been.

Gideon seemed oblivious to the rest of us, clicking furiously at his tablet with one hand as he raked the other through his jagged blue hair. Then he let out a short exclamation of victory. "Here it is."

"Here's what?" Wylder asked, leaning forward.

"I was checking the CCTV footage in the area. I figured a guy wouldn't walk up here with a bomb in his stomach unless he had a reason to believe *not* following orders would be worse."

"And?" Rowan asked.

"See for yourself." Gideon held up the tablet to us.

I squinted at the grainy image from a traffic cam. It only took a moment to recognize the row of shops in the background, just a couple of blocks away from the hill in Paradise City where the Noble mansion stood. And then another moment to notice the beefy figure at the corner of the screen, whose frame and salt-and-pepper hair in its short ponytail immediately triggered a sense of recognition.

That was Xavier.

He was standing by a car parked at the curb. With a motion that looked almost careless, he shoved another figure—the young man who'd appeared at the mansion's doorstep—away from him, down the street. The man hesitated for a second and then passed out of view.

Xavier lingered, glancing down at what I assumed was his phone from time to time. Gideon sped up the footage. Finally, Xavier got into the car and drove off.

A chill ran down my spine. "He was so close. He must have been monitoring things to make sure the guy went through with it." And then triggered the explosion when he was done. What had Xavier threatened to do to the guy if he'd chickened out?

"He's been here before, much closer," Wylder said, his voice grim. "He confessed on the video that he was the one leaving those grisly things around the house—first the dead cat and its tail and then the dug-up corpse."

I didn't want to focus on those gruesome memories. I finally had my answers about who'd been leaving me the horrible "gifts," but I couldn't say I was at all comforted. The realization that this psycho had been right outside my bedroom, just inches from the place where I'd been sleeping, made my skin crawl.

"In what part of his fucked-up brain did he think those were gifts?" Kaige growled. His body curled tighter around me as if he could somehow shield me from the rest of the world.

I placed a hand on his thigh. "I don't think he expects us to see them that way. He wanted to scare me. I just don't know why."

"That is the strangest thing," Gideon agreed, shutting off the video feed.

Wylder scowled. "Why does he want anything from any of us? The video was meant for Dad to see. It was a warning. This Xavier asshole wants to establish something here. He's coming for us, and he wants us to know it."

Wylder was right about that. Xavier had practically called for war on the streets of Paradise Bend.

Not that we hadn't been fighting already, with Colt and all the other gangs he'd brought in...

I paused, a startling thought emerging from the confused haze in my head. "Do you think Xavier is the mastermind behind Colt's takeover of the Bend? I mean, we knew Colt had help from outside in the form of drugs and weapons. There were those strange men who just stood back and watched when he confronted us, and whoever he was taking orders from on the phone. We assumed the people backing him just left, but that never made much sense to me. What if it was Xavier?"

Rowan knit his brow. "That's a good point. We never figured out who his biggest backer was, did we? It'd make more sense than Xavier coming out of nowhere, completely unconnected."

Kaige frowned. "But he seemed happy that Colt's gone."

"Typical kingpin strategy," Wylder said with an edge in his voice. "Use whoever you can to clear the way and then kick them aside when you don't need them anymore. Xavier let the locals go into the line of fire to take down the Claws and whoever else was going to stand up against an invasion, and now he's ready to step up himself. Which'll be easier if Colt isn't there complaining about how *he* was the one who was supposed to take the throne."

Gideon rubbed his mouth, shifting his silver lip ring. "It's odd that Xavier would decide to reveal himself to us, though. What did he gain from that?"

"More fear and intimidation, or at least that's what he's probably hoping for," I said. "The guy's obviously psychotic, and he likes a spectacle. Who else would throw rotting body parts around?"

Rowan nodded. "He wants us to panic and make mistakes that'll play into his hands. But that's the last thing we should do. We don't know how powerful he is or how far his reach extends. Whatever moves we make, we need to be careful."

"And protect Mercy," Kaige spoke up. "Obviously the motherfucker has something against her."

I nudged him gently with my elbow. "I think I've proven enough times that I can take care of myself."

Kaige huffed. "Of course you can. You're the most resilient woman I know, but we're not leaving anything to chance. I think you should stay inside until we catch that piece of shit."

I rolled my eyes. "Are you suggesting that I lock myself in my room?"

"If it comes to that, I'll do it myself." A sly grin twitched at his lips. "And maybe even give you some company."

Even in the middle of this mess, he just couldn't help himself, could he? I had to laugh, the tension in my chest easing just slightly. The reprieve didn't last long before the uneasy ache returned, though.

I eased out of Kaige's embrace, running my hands back over my hair. "I feel like even with Colt gone, nothing has changed. It's almost as if we're back to square one." And somehow this situation felt far more dangerous than before. There were crazier people than my ex-fiancé out there. People who were willing to go to some very extreme lengths to make a point.

"Don't think like that," Rowan said.

"I can't help it." I smacked my fist against my knee. "I don't care how powerful or insane this guy is; we can't let him win. I don't want an outsider to swoop in and take control of my home."

"That won't happen," Wylder said firmly. "We're going to protect Paradise City *and* the Bend, and send this prick packing. No matter what he throws at us, we're fighting back by whatever means necessary. We'll be smart about it, sure, but this isn't the time to cower in a corner."

Just as I was about to agree, Axel sauntered into the room. The bald, tattooed man didn't look particularly pleased with any of us. "Boss wants to see you," he said curtly, fixing his gaze on me. "Now."

I raised my eyebrows. Why would Ezra Noble want to see *me*? Shouldn't he be strategizing with Wylder and the rest of the top Nobles members?

"What does he want?" I asked, getting up.

Axel shrugged. "Beats me." Something told me he knew the reason but couldn't be bothered to divulge it. He might be one of Ezra's most trusted men, but he always seemed to go out of his way to antagonize his boss's son and anyone associated with Wylder.

Of course, Wylder and his inner circle had plenty of reasons to be wary of any interest Ezra showed toward me regardless. The man had tried to set me up to be murdered not too long ago.

Wylder stood up too. "I'll go with you."

"We'll all go," Rowan said. Gideon turned off his tablet, and Kaige sprang to his feet beside me.

Axel folded his arms over his broad chest. "Boss wants to see *her*. Alone."

"We're going," Kaige insisted.

"Since when are you a package deal?" Axel asked, irritation creeping into his voice.

I looked at the guys. His question set something off in me. Axel might not have meant it that way, but we *were* a package now. We were a team. Our near-death stand-off against the Steel Knights last week had cemented an invisible bond between us. I could feel that in my gut... and possibly a few other places too.

Wylder ignored Axel and ambled out of the room. Axel grumbled under his breath as we all followed.

Since I wasn't a trusted member of the upper echelon, Axel directed us to Ezra's audience room rather than his official office. "It's your funeral," he muttered, pushing open the door, but he hadn't put up that much of a fight against the guys coming along. He probably liked the idea of Ezra getting pissed off at them.

I glanced around and found all four of the guys' faces were set in similarly determined expressions. Kaige squeezed my shoulder.

Whatever Ezra had in store for me, I wasn't going to face it by myself. I'd faced every problem I had alone for most of my life, so I'd have survived on my own—but I couldn't say I wasn't glad that I didn't have to.

When we entered, I was surprised to see Anthea standing beside the sofa. I'd expected Ezra to be alone, but a few men from his own inner circle were also there, flanking him where he sat in the leather armchair that could have passed for a throne.

All eyes focused on me when I walked in.

Ezra cocked his head at Axel. "I only asked for the girl."

"They insisted," Axel said.

Ezra's eyes narrowed as he turned his gaze toward me. Not a good sign. "Very well. They'll need to be informed soon enough anyway. Take a seat, Mercy."

The cheerful daylight streaming through the nearby window did nothing to ease the knot in my stomach. Just like during our previous meetings here, I sat down on the sofa opposite Ezra. His chiseled features were just as difficult to read as usual, but I thought I picked up a hint of strain he wouldn't normally have betrayed.

For everything the head Noble had been through, somehow I suspected this was the first time he'd had a man explode on his front lawn.

I looked from him to Wylder, who moved to join his aunt near the window. Father and son were strikingly similar in features, and no matter how many times I saw them together, the resemblance was jarring. Not least of all because Ezra's deep green eyes held none of the warmth I'd found in Wylder's.

"So, we finally know who's been targeting you," Ezra said.

I took a deep breath. "It looks that way. I've never seen that guy before, though, and I—"

Ezra held up a hand to stop me. He turned his head to look at Wylder. "Clearly the conflict we're dealing with goes far beyond Colt Bryant and the Steel Knights. You and your men spearheaded that problem. How could you have failed to notice that a larger power was involved?"

Wylder took a few steps forward. "We didn't fail to notice it. We were aware almost from the start that there was some outside presence. But we had no reason until now to believe that they were interested in the Bend—or Paradise City—for themselves rather than acting based on some deal they'd made with Bryant."

"Or you chose to ignore the signs," Ezra said coldly. "And thanks to your recklessness, we have a bigger problem than the Steel Knights. A problem that seems in part to have something to do with our guest." His gaze flicked back to me.

I stiffened in my seat, but Wylder spoke first. "I don't believe we were reckless. If this Xavier was in the picture all along, then we'd have had to deal with him either way. We got rid of Bryant, which means now we can focus all of our attention on this newcomer and whoever he's brought with him. We'll simply track him down and put things in order."

"Will you?" Ezra's eyes swept over to Kaige, Rowan, and Gideon, who'd stopped just inside the door. "I have left things up to you so far, and look where that got us."

Anthea stepped up beside Wylder, her chin raised defiantly. "He did take care of Colt. I'm sure he'll be able to neutralize the new threat too."

Ezra flat out ignored his sister. He liked using Anthea for her skills with poison and other surreptitious killings when it suited him, but from what I'd seen, he didn't have much more respect for women than any other man I'd met in this life.

"Whoever this Xavier is, the most disturbing fact is that he managed to trespass on our property several times and was able to get away with it. That puts my life along with yours and Anthea's and everybody else under my authority in danger."

Wylder's jaw ticked. As if Ezra really cared about anything other than himself and maintaining his image of power.

"The disturbing things he talked about were objects he left behind specifically for you," Ezra said, turning back to me. "And that suggests that he has some kind of personal vendetta against you."

I gritted my teeth. "I have no idea who this guy even is. I've never seen him before today."

"Your assurances, unfortunately, don't do much to ease my mind. The man is obviously deranged. He blew up a human being on our lawn—God knows what he'll do next. As long as you're staying in our home, I can't help but think he'll continue to target you here and therefore us. That makes your presence a liability that eclipses any help you could possibly offer us."

My gut tightened in anticipation of what he would say next.

"Dad," Wylder said, his jaw clenching. "She's the one who took down Colt in the end. She was instrumental in our plans every step of the way."

"Do you think I haven't considered that?" Ezra said sharply. He pointed at me. "I'm not being unreasonable. I won't bargain with a terrorist, so I have no intention of handing you over to him. But you can't expect me to harbor you and offer my protection any longer. Consider all ties between us severed. I want you out of the mansion within the hour."

My heart lurched. Shit. I should have seen this coming.

"It isn't just me he's after," I had to say. "His message was mostly aimed at you. I don't think me leaving will actually solve your problems. And I've been nothing but loyal to the Nobles the entire time I've been here."

"She's right," Kaige jumped in. He pushed forward and might have barged right in front of me if Rowan hadn't grabbed his arm. "You can't just throw Mercy away after everything she's done for us. She could be the key to taking this bastard down."

"When she may be the entire reason he's set his sights on us in the first place, that's hardly reassuring," Ezra said in an acidic tone. "And loyalty means very little when it comes with so much chaos. We hadn't had any problems with Bryant until you turned up here, and now yet another menace has come at his heels. I can't consider that a coincidence."

"Dad," Wylder started, his voice rough. I knew how hard he was trying not to show that I mattered to him for any reason other than business—because the last time he'd cared about a girl for other reasons, his father had murdered her in front of him—but it was obviously taking all of his self-control to hold back.

Ezra didn't even let him get out his protest. "I've made my decision. It's not open for negotiation. Miss Katz, go pack whatever things you have here and be out the front door before noon—that's an order."

"This is ridiculous!" Kaige said. "Mercy's one of us now."

Wylder's hands balled at his side. I could sense the tension in him pulling tight like a bow about to let loose an arrow. How much would he damage his own standing with his father if he spoke up too much for me?

I pushed myself to my feet even though my insides felt like lead. I didn't know where I was going to go or who I'd be able to turn to outside these walls, but I couldn't stand here and watch the Nobles tear into each other when they needed to be focused on the problem that threatened us all.

Ezra wasn't going to change his mind. As touching as it was to hear the guys speaking up for me, I knew that. What happened to me didn't really matter as long as this psycho didn't lay claim to the streets where I'd grown up.

"Fine," I said, the single syllable making my stomach turn. "Fine, I'll leave."

2

Mercy

ALL FOUR OF THE GUYS GAVE ME MATCHING LOOKS OF MUTED horror. Their gazes burned into me, but I tuned them out, focusing only on the man who held the power of life and death over everyone in this room.

"Thank you for everything the Nobles have done for me," I said, nodding to Ezra. Not that *he'd* done all that much for me—but he'd like to think I believed he had.

Without another word, I strode out of the room. I only had an hour to figure out where the hell I was going from here, and I suspected the clock was already ticking.

Kaige caught up to me in the hall. He grabbed me by my elbow and whirled me around so I was facing him. "What were you thinking?"

"Ezra was going to kick me out anyway," I said, meeting his furious gaze head on. "Might as well leave with my dignity."

Gideon stalked up behind the bigger guy. "Is that what it was about? We wouldn't have let him run you off."

"Really?" I said, keeping my voice low. "And how would you have stopped the head of all the Nobles?"

Rowan joined us just as I finished speaking. He grimaced. "We could have tried to speak up for you more. There's a psychopath on the loose out there, and he's already made you a target. We don't want you adrift on the streets."

"I know." I didn't want to be out there either. But— "Ezra had made up his mind. I could see it. The only thing arguing about it would have done is cause more tensions between all of you and him when everyone in the Nobles should be tackling the Xavier problem. If you deal with him, then you won't need to worry about me, right?"

Rowan gave me a look that seemed to say he'd worry about me regardless. I didn't know what to make of it. There was so much history between us, good and bad, and even now that I knew and understood why he'd taken off on me years ago, I still couldn't say exactly where we stood.

But it was Kaige who spoke first. "I'll come with you."

I raised my eyebrows at him. "Don't be ridiculous. This is your home. You belong here with these guys and Wylder." Who was conspicuously absent from this conversation. Probably trying to keep the heat off of me by hiding how much he cared, but somehow it stung a little anyway.

"And so do you," Kaige said fiercely.

"Yes, you do," Rowan added. "Even if my behavior at first suggested otherwise."

"We were wrong," Gideon said matter-of-factly. "And after what we went through with Colt, you're undeniably one of us."

Unexpected tears pricked at the back of my eyes. Just weeks ago, I'd lost my entire family. Somehow I'd found another one in the last place I'd ever thought I would.

But to make sure I didn't lose them too… I had to leave them.

"Thank you," I said. "Maybe when Xavier is taken care of, we can convince Ezra of that too. For now, I'd better get packing."

"Wylder will find a way to fix this," Kaige insisted, but I could see from the flicker of doubt in his eyes that he didn't totally believe it either.

When I reached my room, I was reminded all over again of how little I had here *other* than the guys. A few changes of clothes, bought used and roughed up over my time here. A handful of origami figures I'd made out of scraps of paper that weren't important enough to bring with me anyway. Some basic toiletries.

I touched my pocket, tracing the outline of the bracelet my mom had given me for my sixth birthday—just a few months before she'd disappeared from my life. I still had that. I was alive; I'd gotten my revenge on the man who'd taken so much else from me. Things could be worse.

I was stuffing my clothes into a backpack when the door swung open. Wylder strode inside and kicked it shut behind him. One look at his stormy expression told me that if he'd tried to talk his father down, it definitely hadn't worked.

It was easier to make light of the situation than admit how twisted up I felt inside. "Well, you must be happy," I said breezily. "You've been trying to terrorize me out of your house for ages, and now you're finally getting rid of me."

Wylder's green eyes darkened even more. He walked right up to me, hooking his fingers into the belt loops of my jeans and pulling me towards him. The musky smell of him, laced with a hint of the aged whiskey he liked so much, washed over me, and my pussy clenched. I had to hold myself back from swaying even closer.

"You know that's not true," he said.

An eager shiver traveled down my spine. "Isn't it?" I challenged.

"We've talked about why I pushed you away before. And it sure as hell wasn't ever because I didn't *want* you." He dipped his head, letting his breath spill hot down the side of my face. "You belong here with me and my men. You're one of us now."

His words weren't a request but a demand. One I wished I could give in to, especially when he was touching me like this. Wylder Noble was addictive any way you sliced it, but never more than when he got this possessive.

When he slid his hands down over my ass, I swallowed the sound that tried to slip from my throat and forced my voice to stay steady. "Are you really ready to fight your father over this?"

He grimaced, the fire in his eyes dimming for a few seconds. "I will. You can count on it. But I know that's not a battle I can win when we're in the middle of a bigger one. When we've crushed that psychotic jackass..."

I rested my hand on his chest. "I know. That's exactly why *I* didn't fight."

Wylder held my gaze for a moment, a sense of shared understanding passing between us that somehow affected me even more than his touch.

"I'm not letting you set off into the jungle out there completely on your own," he said. "My dad doesn't need to know everything. I'm going to do whatever I can to keep you safe even if you're not inside these walls."

I cocked my head. "What do you mean?"

He lifted his chin toward the backpack. "You look ready to go. Do you know where you're heading?"

The question sent an uneasy twinge through me. I hadn't let myself think that far ahead in much detail yet. Maybe because I knew there were no easy answers. "I'll figure it out. I'm not leaving Paradise Bend, that's for sure. But I know my way around."

"Of course you do. But that doesn't mean we can't lend you a hand." Wylder motioned toward the door. "Gideon's checking the properties the Nobles own in the county to see which are currently vacant. There's got to be one where we could set you up surreptitiously. At least then you'll have some kind of safe space until the rest is sorted out. When we know where you're going, Rowan and Kaige will follow your cab and make sure no one's tailing you there."

I found myself choking up a bit. It was a team effort, like always, and like always, Wylder was the one calling the shots. He might not be much of one for mushy declarations, but he couldn't have made it more obvious how much I did mean to him now. He was defying Ezra with every gesture he made in my defense.

"You don't have to stick your neck out like that," I had to say. "I'll survive this, like I've survived a hell of a lot before."

"I know you will," he said, moving closer again so his body was pressed right against mine. "I just don't want to take any chances."

"You're beginning to sound like Kaige," I teased.

A faint smile crossed his lips before falling away. "I don't want to see you get hurt. Again." His expression turned pained, and I wondered if he was thinking about Laurel—the high school girlfriend his father had ordered murdered in front of him.

I didn't want that. I didn't want him to be reminded of her when he looked at me.

I cupped his jaw and stroked the edge with my thumb. He gazed down at me unblinking.

"Nothing is going to happen to me," I said. "It'll take a lot more than Ezra Noble and this Xavier psycho to put Mercy Katz in the ground."

Wylder's lips twitched with an approving smile, and then he was pulling me right to him. I met him halfway. His mouth captured mine, hot and demanding, as he tangled his fingers in my ponytail with a teasing yank that walked the perfect line between pleasure and pain. When a gasp escaped me, he took the opportunity to slip his tongue past my lips.

I kissed him back just as hard, gripping his shirt with one hand and his thick auburn hair with the other. He tilted his head, fusing us together even more closely as if he couldn't get enough of me. His tongue curled while it explored my searing mouth.

He shoved me back against the wall, squeezing my ass and lifting me at the same time. The hard bulge in his jeans pressed against my cunt. I gripped him even harder, arching into him instinctively, and a groan spilled from his mouth into mine.

With obvious reluctance, he eased back. He bit my lower lip softly, and when I hissed, flicked his tongue over the spot, bringing another rush of pleasure. Then he drew away completely, gazing down at me with so much hunger in his gaze I almost melted.

"Fuck," he said in a raw voice. "You have no idea how much I want to bend you over that bed and take you right now, without giving one shit who hears us."

I wet my swollen lips, and his eyes tracked the movement. My pussy was doing more of the thinking than my brain right now, because I was seriously considering encouraging that course of action. But before either of us could do anything momentously stupid, Wylder's phone buzzed in his pocket.

He pulled it out and checked the message. "Gideon. He's found you a perfect spot in the Bend."

Somehow I was both relieved by the news and disappointed to have the moment interrupted. "Are you sure this is a good idea? The property belongs to Ezra, doesn't it? I don't think he'll like it much if I leave the mansion only to start living in one of his apartments."

Wylder gave me a cocky grin. "That's why I'm glad to have Gideon on my side. He can conjure up a rental agreement in the database so it appears the place is already occupied, so no one'll try to show it to prospective renters. Dad doesn't keep very close track of everything he owns around here. Just don't make your presence too obvious."

"I can handle that. Do you have the keys?"

"There's a lock with a code. I'll text it to you. Which reminds me." He held up the phone. "This is a new burner I grabbed that I'm going to use only for communicating with or about you. I'll keep it hidden so my dad doesn't find out. I'll text you the number—if you need to reach out before we check in on you, that's the only one you should use. Got it?"

I arched my eyebrows at his authoritarian tone. "This isn't my first time on the run."

His smile turned a bit sheepish. "You'll go to the apartment?" he asked insistently.

"It sure beats crashing in an abandoned warehouse somewhere."

"Good. You'll need to buy food and whatever else until we can come see you—take this." He dug out his wallet and handed me a wad of cash. Something in me balked at accepting the charity, but I knew he didn't mean it that way. It was a matter of honor for him to make sure I was taken care of.

And grocery store food sure beat dumpster-diving.

After I'd pocketed it, he paused and then ducked down to kiss me again. His hands came to rest on either side of me, trapping me against the wardrobe. Our scorching breaths mingled with each other.

When he pulled back the second time, he rested his forehead against mine. "I'm going to miss having you around, Kitty Cat," he said. He hadn't called me by the nickname for so long that the mention of it almost startled me.

While I stood there cocooned in his heat and scent, a part of me didn't want to leave. But I didn't have much choice.

I nudged him away from me. "I think my hour is just about up. I'd better get going before I end up with Axel dumping me on the front lawn."

Wylder lingered by the door as I swung the backpack over my shoulder. "Listen," he said abruptly. "I'm not going to tell you to hide away in the apartment all day and night. I know you wouldn't listen to me if I tried to order you to anyway."

I laughed. "I'm glad we've gotten a few things straight."

He shot a half-hearted glower at me. "Just... when you *do* go out into the Bend, be careful about it, all right?"

There was so much concern in those words, I softened. I reached for his hand and squeezed it. "I will be. I'd like to keep breathing too, you know."

We couldn't have more of a send-off than that. I walked down to the foyer alone. A few Noble men were gathered around. Patrolling had been doubled since the incident. All eyes turned to me as I sauntered past them.

Axel was with a few others out on the lawn, smoking a cigarette. He looked almost gleeful to see me leave. The grass glistened wetly, the traces of red finally gone, but a hint of the meaty smell lingered in the air. A sense of foreboding crawled down my spine.

I had one enemy behind me and another in front of me. Was Xavier still lurking nearby, watching me even now?

As I headed down the hill, I called for an Uber. If Kaige and Rowan were following me as Wylder had promised, they were doing a good job of staying discreet. As far as I could tell, I was on my own.

I dragged in a breath and touched my three lucky charms: the bracelet in my pocket, the knife at my other hip, and the pistol tucked in the back of my jeans. Two of those I could thank Wylder for.

Why did I have to be torn away from my guys right after I'd started discovering such a strong connection between us?

When the car finally arrived, I got in and threw one last look at the hill where the Noble mansion stood. Then I glanced down at the backpack on my lap. I'd come to Paradise City's rulers with so little, and in some ways I was leaving with even less... but in other ways, I had so much more.

Of course, that just meant that now I had a lot more to lose.

Mercy

THE BREEZE FLICKED THROUGH MY HAIR, THE SUMMER AIR cooler now that it was evening. I leaned forward on my rooftop perch, watching passersby come and go on the street of shops below me. With the sky darkening and the streetlamps blinking on, no one would have been able to make out my form where I'd used my parkour skills to clamber onto the top of the bank on the corner.

I'd been roaming around the Bend for the past couple of days since I'd left the Noble mansion—being careful like I'd promised Wylder I would be, but needing to see for myself what was happening out here in the aftermath of Colt's fall. So far I hadn't run into Xavier, which I couldn't say I minded. My explorations had left me unsettled, though.

This was my home. I'd lived here since I was born, but it didn't feel like the same place anymore. There was more tension in the atmosphere than I ever remembered feeling before, a nervousness to the way people moved. Most of these stores would normally have been open until well past dinnertime, but now they were locking their doors at six or seven. By now, coming up on eight, nearly everyone had vanished.

A pang ran through my chest at the thought of how much the ongoing battles for territory had affected the Bend.

Not *quite* everyone had gone home for the night, though. Raucous guitar music echoed through the streets. It grew louder until a car came around a bend, windows down, radio blasting a heavy metal song. The driver swerved back and forth a little as if he was distracted or drunk.

The car jerked to a halt in front of a bar partway down the street, and the music cut out. I frowned, narrowing my eyes.

That bar was the main reason I'd chosen this spot tonight. It was closed, the windows already gathering dust from disuse. The place had used to be one of the Steel Knights' main business fronts, but it didn't look as if anyone had been operating out of it since Colt's death. I'd wanted to keep an eye on it just in case some of his former underlings were still in action.

The five guys who pushed out of the car and swaggered across the sidewalk to the bar weren't Steel Knights though, at least as far as I could tell. It was hard to make out their features in the deepening shadows, but none of them had the typical red bandana wrapped around their upper arms. Three of them carried axes, the other two baseball bats studded with spikes.

Even though they hadn't seemed to be keeping their arrival quiet, they glanced around shiftily as if they were worried about getting caught at whatever they were about to do. One guy flexed his shoulders, and I got the impression he was putting on his swagger to hide his nerves.

"Come on! Let's tear it all down!" he shouted.

He and the other guys went at the bar with their weapons like they wanted to demolish the place. The bats smashed through the front windows, sending broken glass spilling into the bar's interior. A guy with an axe hacked through the door. They barged inside, and more smashing and thwacking sounds reached my ears as they plowed through the furnishings inside. Every now and then, one of them let out a little cheer.

What the hell was going on? Who were these guys? One of the smaller gangs Colt had allied with who'd decided to give him the middle finger after his death? But I couldn't figure out what he'd done that would have pissed them off that much, or what the point would be now that he was gone anyway.

The growl of incoming engines reached me. A few motorcycles and a car roared up the street from the opposite direction. Peering through the dim light, I thought I recognized a mustached man on one of the motorcycles from Colt's crew.

But at the sight of the four men who got out of the car, pulling out guns as they did, a chill ran down my spine. Unlike the bikers, who were wearing tees and jeans, that bunch had on collared shirts and slacks. The air around them reminded me of the mysterious men who'd been hanging around watching Colt's confrontation with the Nobles before —the ones we'd never been able to identify.

Now I had to wonder if they were Xavier's people. If he'd been egging on Colt's quest for power, planning to steal that power for himself once the Steel Knights had done his dirty work, that would fit.

The guys who'd been trashing the bar had emerged at the sound of the new arrivals, their original weapons discarded and their own guns in their hands. They hung back by the broken window, using the walls for cover. "What the fuck do you want?" one snarled.

"Your blood all over that floor," said one of the posher guys, and opened fire.

Guns blasted on both sides, one group taking shelter in the bar and the other around their car. There were grunts and shouts, and I thought at least one guy must have been hit.

Now I was even more confused than before. Why was the first group going up against whatever remained of the Steel Knights and what I assumed to be Xavier's people? I definitely hadn't seen any of them around the Noble mansion. Who else would have dared to take on the guys who'd nearly conquered all of Paradise Bend?

I kept my ears pricked, barely breathing so I could pick up as much of the conversation below as I could. In between shots and muttered curses, the two groups were yelling at each other.

"The Storm has claimed this territory," hollered a guy I thought was with Xavier's group. "Anyone who crosses us will pay for it."

One of the men inside the bar let out a rough laugh. "I don't think so. The Red Shark is going to take it all. Death to the Storm!"

More gunfire thundered between them. I furrowed my brow. Who the fuck were the Storm and the Red Shark? I'd never heard either of those names before. None of this made any sense.

The Storm side—which seemed to be made up of Xavier's men and former Steel Knights—had the benefit of numbers. There was a thump as another of the men inside the bar fell. The remaining guys on the side that'd talked about the Red Shark made a break for it, running to their car.

Two of them managed to dive inside. The third, trailing behind with a limp from a shot he'd already taken, caught a bullet in the chest. He collapsed on the sidewalk, and his associates didn't even try to help him. Their car peeled away from the curb at top speed, tires screeching.

The Storm people fired a few more shots after them, but then one of the posher men held up his hand, and the others stopped. They took in the wreckage of the bar with grim expressions.

"Fucking Red Shark," one said. "What the hell is that asshole thinking, sending his people in here now?"

So the Red Shark was a person—a he? Did that mean the Storm was too?

I didn't get any more answers. The Storm men took a quick look inside the bar, shaking their heads as they came out, and then drove off without another word.

I stayed in my crouched position for another few minutes, my heart thumping so hard I didn't trust myself to scramble down just yet. No one else turned up. No one ventured into the street at all, the windows in the store-top apartments along the street staying dark, their curtains drawn. The dead body lay there on the sidewalk in a puddle of blood.

My stomach churned. I'd hoped that after Colt's death, most of the violence in the Bend would peter out. It might actually have gotten worse.

The faces had changed, but the cycle remained the same. More groups fighting over the same piece of territory. Why did everyone want Paradise Bend so much?

For the same reason Ezra Noble intended to keep his hold over it, I guessed. I might not like the man, but he'd better hurry up and kick all these assholes back to wherever they'd come from. I'd cheer him on.

There was nothing I could do about the problem on my own. Finally, I peeled myself off the roof and made my way back to the apartment the guys had arranged for me, leaping between buildings and slinking through shadowed alleys.

I hadn't wandered far. I was back at the place in under ten minutes. While I'd memorized the key code for when I needed to use the apartment door, tonight I scrambled up the back of the building with the help of a couple of ridges in the wall and a drain pipe. I'd left the bedroom window just a smidge open so I could squeeze my fingers under the pane and shove it up to slip inside.

Why get myself seen in the building's hallways if I didn't need to?

The apartment was plain but clean and pre-furnished, a modern two-bedroom with tiny bedrooms and an open concept living room/dining room/kitchen about the same size as just the kitchen back in the Noble mansion. I didn't need even that much space, though. I was happy enough still having an actual bed to lay my head down on.

As I reached the bedroom doorway, my instincts prickled. I hesitated, struck by the sense that I wasn't alone here after all. But before I could even pull out my knife or my gun, a wryly amused voice carried from the room outside.

"I should have known you'd come in through a window rather than a door."

I rolled my eyes and stepped out to find Anthea standing by the narrow kitchen island. "And I should have known you'd just let yourself in if you came to visit." Even if she didn't know the code, I didn't imagine there were many locks in the world Anthea Noble couldn't get past.

She hadn't bothered to turn on the lights, so I checked that the blinds were drawn and flicked the switch myself. The stark glow of the pot lights blazed off her bright red hair. She raised a mug of tea she'd made in the dark to her lips, smiling at me over it. "Sorry if I startled you."

"I don't think you really are sorry," I grumbled, flopping onto the linen sofa that faced her. "What are you doing here?" My pulse hiccupped despite my casual tone. Had something happened to one of the guys?

Anthea didn't look distressed, though. She waved her hand dismissively. "Of course I'd come to check up on a friend. Just because my brother is being even more idiotic than usual, that doesn't mean I've got to follow in his footsteps."

I couldn't help smiling at her breezily insulting description of Ezra. There'd once been a time when Anthea had regularly insulted *me*. I definitely preferred being on her good side. She actually had become a pretty good friend… which wasn't something I'd ever really had before.

A bittersweet twinge passed through my gut. Ezra wouldn't be happy if he found out she was *still* friendly with me. He was doing his best to take that newfound happiness from me too.

"How are the guys doing?" I asked, with an odd surge of urgency. I wasn't used to caring this much about any of the men in my life either.

"They're keeping it together and mostly avoiding trouble." Anthea studied me with those piercing eyes of hers. "How have *you* been getting by, Mercy?"

I shoved my uncomfortable feelings aside and shrugged. I wasn't going to complain, not when I was benefitting from the Nobles' hospitality even now. "I'm fine. Just been taking a look at what's going on in the Bend, but keeping my head low."

"Good. I definitely don't want that Xavier menace sniffing around here." She grimaced. "We can't get rid of him soon enough. I don't know why Ezra can't see that it isn't at all fair to blame you for the havoc some psychotic prick has decided to wreak." She let out a huff and shook her head. "Well, I'll keep working on him. Whatever I can do to get things sorted out so you can stand with the Nobles like you deserve, I'm on it."

My throat constricted. I hadn't really expected her to keep caring that much about what happened to me. "Thank you. I appreciate it a lot. But you don't need to risk pissing off Ezra on my behalf. I really will be okay."

"It's not about whether you'll make it through or not. I already know you will. Women like us always do." She shot me another confident smile. "But you should have a life that's more than just getting by. And I think we'll tackle this new problem faster if we have you working alongside us. I don't like the look of things down here."

That comment had me immediately on the alert. "What do you mean?"

She glanced toward the window. "I know I haven't spent a lot of time in the Bend, but there's much less activity on the streets than I'd expect this early in the night from what I recall. I saw several of the Steel Knights marks that they put up around this neighborhood defaced—scratched up or partly sprayed over. There was a hostile vibe to it that I didn't like."

Trust Anthea to have already picked up on nearly as much as I had. I nodded. "I think it might have something to do with the new guys in town."

Her eyebrows arched. "New guys?" She beckoned me over, reaching for the kettle to pour me some tea too.

"Yeah," I said as I walked up to the island. I rested my elbows on it, thinking back over the shoot-out I'd just witnessed. "It seems like there's a new gang in town, one I'm not at all familiar with. They broke into one of the old Steel Knights' businesses tonight and started bashing it up. Then some guys I think are with Xavier and former men of Colt's came by, and a fight broke out... They were talking about somebody who goes by 'the Red Shark' and 'the Storm.' I don't know if those are their leaders or what."

Anthea frowned, stirring a little sugar into my tea. "That doesn't ring any bells for me yet. The last thing we need is even more troublemakers in town." She slid the mug across the island to me. "Tell me everything you saw."

4

Wylder

We pulled up outside the apartment complex where we'd set up Mercy to live, and I peered out at the gray concrete walls. This was one of the nicer parts of the Bend, but it was still pretty grungy looking. Amateur graffiti marked the side wall, and rust was creeping around some of the window frames.

It was only a few blocks from the official border of Paradise City, but the two places might as well have been worlds apart.

"It was the nicest property I felt we could get away with confiscating unnoticed," Gideon said, taking in my reaction.

Kaige looked out the window and shrugged. "It isn't so bad. I've lived in a lot worse."

So had Gideon. From what I'd gathered, Rowan's family had been comfortably middle-class, but I was the only one here who'd grown up in a mansion.

I shouldn't let that turn me into some kind of snob, but I couldn't help wrinkling my nose as I stepped out of the car. I didn't like the idea of Mercy living here alone. It didn't matter that I knew that she could take care of herself. She deserved better. She should be treated like a fucking princess.

"Do we have everything we need?" I asked.

Rowan nodded to the large rucksack that he then hoisted over his shoulder. "Yep."

I motioned to the side alley. "You know what to do."

Gideon had scoped out strategic places where we could set up surveillance so that we could keep an eye on the building, just in case trouble came calling. It made me feel slightly better when we couldn't be here to personally protect her 24-7.

"If we all stick to the plan, we should be done within the hour," Gideon said, giving Rowan and Kaige a critical glance.

I clapped him on the shoulder. "I'm sure you can keep them in line. I'll go in and see how Mercy's doing. Meet me in the apartment when you're done."

As the three of them scattered, I climbed up the dingy staircase to the third-floor apartment. The low-rise building was five stories total but no elevator. It figured.

I knocked on the door and waited. A minute passed, and there was no sound on the other side. I knocked again, frowning, and then checked the handle, but the door didn't budge. I didn't remember the code off the top of my head.

"Wylder?" said a voice from behind me. I whirled around to find Mercy just tucking the knife I'd given her back into the pocket of her jeans.

A smile tugged at my lips. God, it was good to see her, cheeks flushed and dark hair in its typical ponytail, looking like her usual impervious self. I had the urge to grab her in a hug, but something in me balked. Just because I was glad to see her didn't mean I was going to go all mushy.

Instead, I turned it into a joke. "Thinking about slicing and dicing me?"

She laughed and nudged me aside to reach for the door. "You did tell me to be careful. Come on, unless you want to shimmy around the building to go in a window."

So that's how she'd snuck up on me. Pride coursed through me. Damn, she was good.

The inside of the apartment was about as drab as the outside, but at least it'd come with all the basics: sofa, table, kitchen appliances. Nothing hung on the walls, but Mercy had added a couple little touches that made the place already feel like it was hers. A few of her silly origami figures stood on the coffee table, and she'd placed a bowl on the kitchen island with some fruit she must have bought with the money I'd given her.

She flopped onto one end of the sofa, totally at home. Well, she'd had five days to get settled in. Which she obviously hadn't forgotten either. She shot me a narrow look. "It took you long enough to come by."

"Things haven't been so smooth back home with Dad," I said. "I didn't want to risk coming here until I was sure we wouldn't be bringing trouble with us."

"I don't suppose the Grand High Noble has changed his opinion of me."

I grimaced. "No, but he's gotten distracted by other things."

"Mostly Xavier, I hope." Mercy straightened up again, her expression instantly alert. "Things are a mess down here. He'd better be ready to step in."

That sounded ominous. I sat down next to her. "What's going on? He's mostly been focused on figuring out where Xavier came from and how big an operation we're up against, not what's going on down here."

"I haven't had a whole lot to do other than keep an eye on things around here," Mercy said. "Carefully, of course," she added dryly when I started to protest. "I haven't figured everything out, but from what I can tell, there are two groups going up against each other right now."

"What? I thought Xavier was out to get *us*, and there haven't been any clashes between him and the Nobles yet."

"I'm a little confused too." She glanced toward the window, maybe thinking about whatever she'd witnessed out there. "There's one group that says they support 'the Storm,' which seems to be a code word for their leader. Maybe that's Xavier. I've seen guys who look like the ones we figured were his in that group as well as some former Steel Knights.

I'd guess the remaining Steel Knights threw in their lot with the guy who was backing Colt after Colt died. It'd make sense."

I nodded. "Nowhere else to go. We sure as hell wouldn't welcome them if they knocked on our door."

Mercy smirked and then went on. "Then there's a bunch I haven't recognized at all that are working for someone they call 'the Red Shark.' Another code name, I'm guessing."

"The Storm and the Red Shark," I repeated. "Never heard of either of them."

Mercy sighed. "It's very weird. Anyway, the Storm people I've seen so far look more confident and experienced, but the Red Shark people have been hitting them hard and quick wherever they can. There've been a few run-ins already with bodies dropped on both sides."

I raised my eyebrows, impressed all over again. "You've really been putting the puzzle together." But then, I shouldn't be surprised. This was the woman who'd exposed a murderer none of us had even suspected. When Mercy put her mind to something, she got it done.

That was one of the reasons I liked her so much.

"It's important to me," she said. "There are people here, families who are afraid to step outside after dark. The violence that Colt sparked isn't over yet. I want to see it finished." She paused, giving me a pointed look. "While the Storm people and the Red Shark guys are busy fighting with each other, it seems like it'd be a good time for the Nobles to sweep in and take care of both."

I held up my hands. "Hey, I agree with you. But you know it's not up to me. Dad is pretty pissed off that we didn't realize this Xavier psycho was a factor beforehand. Now he wants to be sure of exactly what and who we're dealing with before he takes any major action. He won't admit it, but I think that whole exploding lackey thing unnerved even him." My own stomach still turned, remembering that bloody scene.

"How long is he going to procrastinate?" Mercy muttered. "What if things take a turn for the worse?"

Seeing the worry etched all over her gorgeous face, something in me softened. "You care about these people."

"This is my home. Of course I care about them."

Caring could be dangerous, though. I knew that, and I made a point of caring about as few people as possible because of it. The fact that Mercy had worked her way into becoming one of that small number still kind of amazed me.

"Do they care about *you*?" I asked.

"They don't know me. Not yet," Mercy said more to herself than me. "But I don't need them to. I just want all of them to have more choice about their lives than I did."

She got up, stepping toward the window. The afternoon sunlight glinted off her dark hair in a sort of halo, and right then, I couldn't tear my eyes off of her. My determined, vengeful princess. She sure hadn't lost *her* spark with Colt's death. If anything, her fire was burning even hotter.

And damn, did I want to burn right with her in all the best ways.

We couldn't get anything else done for the Bend right now, but there were plenty of other things I'd like to do when she looked like that. When it'd been five days since I'd so much as touched her.

I got up and walked over to her, setting my hands on her waist and bowing my head close to hers. "So tell me, Kitty Cat, in between all this prowling, did you ever get lonely here all by yourself?"

Mercy didn't step away. The mood in the air changed, almost crackling with anticipation. I could see the shift as her eyes darkened and her tongue came out to flick across her lower lip.

"I wasn't *totally* alone," she retorted in a teasing tone. "Anthea managed to come by and keep me company."

I dropped my voice lower. "I certainly hope you didn't do with her all the things I'd like to do with you."

Mercy cocked her head. "I guess you're lucky I don't swing that way then, because otherwise she could totally get some."

I let out a little growl and tugged her closer so her breasts brushed my chest. Even with the layers of fabric between us, the sensation sent a flare of heat straight to my groin. "Keep talking like that, and I'll have to find some way to remind you how good you have it with me." I guided her around and eased her backward toward the bedroom door.

Mercy let me direct her steps, but she gazed up at me with mischief as well as desire in her eyes. "*Was* it good? It's been so long, I can't quite—"

I'd been kind of hoping she'd make the first move, but one of us had greater patience, and it sure as hell wasn't me. I grasped her ponytail and yanked her toward me, and our mouths crashed together. It was all heat and teeth and tongues, some kind of battle for dominance I wasn't sure I wanted to win.

I tugged her hips against mine, letting her feel the hard press of my cock. Her breath hitched against my lips. I kissed her harder, walking her farther backward at the same time, pausing on the threshold of the bedroom when I couldn't resist grinding into her. She curled her fingers into my shirt and arched against me. Her needy gasp mingled with my groan.

The bedroom was bare except for a queen-sized bed and a narrow dresser next to it. I lifted her and tossed her onto the bed, climbing over her as she settled onto the covers. Then we were kissing again. Her fingers dug into my hair, tugging gently and then insistently enough to send a prickle of pain through my scalp. I chuckled. "Easy, Kitten."

When she grumbled impatiently, I kissed a trail down her jaw to her collarbone, swirling my tongue around it, tracing the shape of the bone under her warm sun-kissed skin.

She hooked her thighs around my hips and pulled me to her. I had no choice but to oblige. I pinned her hands above her and brought my mouth back to hers, thrusting my hard cock against her pussy through our jeans at the same time.

I was so hungry for her I could have come just like that, but something in me held back. Yes, it would feel fantastic to plunge into her like I had before—but that first and last time we'd fully fucked, I'd made her feel like I'd only been hooking up with her for my own gratification.

I was man enough to rein in my horniness and make this time all about her, wasn't I?

"I'm going to give you loads to remember the next time you're all on your own," I promised darkly, pressing a kiss to her throat and then her sternum, all the way down to her belly over the thin fabric of her shirt. With one flick of my thumb, I opened the fly of her jeans.

Mercy moved to sit up to get closer to me, but I pushed her back on the bed with a firm look she accepted just this once. Maybe because she could sense that what was coming was going to go in her favor anyway. When I gripped the waist of her jeans, she lifted her hips to help me pull them off her. Then I bowed my head to lap my tongue over her cunt through her panties.

They were already damp, the musky flavor of her seeping through. Mercy's breath stuttered, her hips rocking as if to urge me on, and I was more than happy to meet that wordless demand.

I peeled off her panties, almost ripping them off in the process, and nudged her thighs apart so that I could look at her swollen pussy. I leaned closer and took a sniff of her arousal and almost came in my pants. She smelled abso-fucking-lutely incredible.

"Who needs dinner when I've got this," I murmured against her thigh, nipping the soft, warm skin with my teeth. I knelt beside the bed and pulled her to me so that her legs were draped over my shoulders, her pussy right at the edge of the mattress for the taking. "I can't wait to taste you properly."

I lowered my head, swiping my tongue from clit to slit. Mercy moaned, grasping my hair again. Her musk was sweet like honey with just a hint of saltiness to it. Delicious. Grinning at her reaction, I lapped at her slit greedily, all the way to the pucker of her asshole. As I licked, Mercy squirmed so much she almost arched off the bed.

Holding her down, I buried my mouth in her wet, hot cunt before seeking out her engorged clit with the tip of my tongue. I pulled at it slightly with my teeth, teasing the line between pleasure and pain. With a keen, she tensed her thighs on either side of my face to keep me in place, not that I had any intention of stopping.

I devoured her hot pussy, working my fingers inside so that I could simultaneously eat her out while pumping in and out of her. Mercy outright mewled like a kitten, the sound turning me on even more.

I liked doing this to her. I was in absolute control. She didn't owe anything to me, but in this moment I owned her body and owned my own lust. I wanted to see how many times I could possibly get her off without once giving in to my more selfish desires.

I reached up and grabbed one of her breasts, squeezing the nipple while I continued my onslaught on her pussy. Her channel squeezed around my tongue and her legs clamped around my neck, almost shutting off my air supply. And then she came with a scream.

That wasn't enough to satisfy me. I swirled my tongue faster and delved my fingers deeper, seeking out the most sensitive spot inside her. Mercy's legs shook as I propelled her straight into a second orgasm that had her shuddering.

Her head sagged back against the covers. As she panted there, I eased away for a moment. I licked the pussy juice off my lips before giving her a sly grin. "Enjoy yourself?"

"Fuck, yes," she murmured, her eyes at half-mast. She started to sit up, her legs still splayed in front of me with my early dinner on display, and the bedroom door swung open.

"Rowan and Kaige are just finishing up the last installations downstairs, but I wanted to—"

Gideon glanced up from his damned tablet and stopped in his tracks, his eyes widening. He blinked rapidly, otherwise stock-still, his eyes darting as if he wasn't sure where to look. It must have been pretty fucking obvious what we'd been doing.

"I—er—clearly you're busy," he said. "This can wait. Nothing urgent."

He spun to leave, but I hadn't missed the way his gaze had been drawn to Mercy's partial nakedness, the heat that had flushed his cheeks—or the quick adjustment of the crotch of his khakis. My best friend could be so detached sometimes you'd mistake him for a robot, but there was no denying that right now he was turned on.

Mercy sat up, her T-shirt drifting down to partly cover her, but she didn't look bothered that he'd seen her. If anything, *her* eyes had lit up too.

Then it hit me. She didn't look concerned because he'd seen her before. I'd given Gideon my blessing to go after her, and sometime in the past couple of weeks he had.

Jealousy reared its ugly head inside me. I clamped down on it, resisting its ragged claws. I'd told Gideon it wouldn't change our friendship if he pursued something with Mercy, and I wasn't going to make myself a liar.

It hadn't been so bad working with Kaige to get her off the other night. Why would it be horrible to see her with a guy I trusted even more?

I stood up as Gideon reached for the door, a renewed sense of authority rising inside me. "Who said you have to leave?"

Gideon glanced back at me, hesitant but not unwilling. I looked from him to Mercy, who arched an eyebrow at me, waiting to see what I'd do next. Oh, *she* was game, all right.

I focused on my best friend. "I think you liked what you just saw. You like *her*, don't you?"

Gideon's tongue skimmed over his lips, making the ring there quiver. He considered Mercy in a way that was weirdly analytical and lustful at the same time. Gideon was an intense guy, but I wasn't sure I'd ever seen him quite this intent on anything. The observation only strengthened my resolve.

"She's an impressive woman," he said finally, as if we were talking about a new model of car, but the rasp in his voice hinted at much more emotion than his words.

"No denying that." I dropped my gaze to Mercy and teased my fingers down the side of her face. "Why don't you repay the favor I just did for you by passing it on to my best friend?"

I said it like a suggestion, but my tone made it a command. Mercy let out a little laugh, and I half expected her to tell me off for daring to give her an order like that.

Instead, she got up and walked right past me to Gideon, her luscious hips swaying from side to side. Gideon's gaze stayed locked with hers the entire time, his Adam's apple bobbing in his throat and desire hazing his eyes. He set the tablet down on top of the dresser.

Mercy trailed her fingers down Gideon's chest and glanced over her shoulder at me. I got the impression she was actually enjoying having an audience. Once her fingers reached his pants, she slid down the zipper as she kneeled in front of him. Gideon sucked in a breath, transfixed.

When she delved into his boxers, his cock sprang free, already erect. As Mercy stroked her fingers over it, I focused on my best friend's face. His expression had gone slack, nothing but pleasure written there now. She had him in the palm of her hand, quite literally.

Then she leaned in and wrapped her mouth around his cock.

Gideon's head fell back. He tried to balance himself by putting a hand on Mercy's shoulder as she bobbed up and down over him. She cupped his balls, and he let out a noise from the back of his throat, his eyes rolling back.

Holy shit. I'd thought it would be difficult to watch this, but somehow it was one of the hottest things I'd ever seen: my tightly-laced best friend unraveled by the bold, confident woman we both wanted. My own cock had begun to throb. I rested my hand over the crotch of my jeans, rubbing it lightly to release a little pressure.

Gideon's hands splayed in Mercy's hair, guiding her motions as he fucked her mouth with his dick. His motions were growing erratic. Mercy hummed so eagerly my cock got even harder.

Fuck it. I unzipped my jeans and released my rigid erection. Precum was oozing out of its tip. I smeared it down the length, imagining Mercy taking my cock instead of my best-friend's. But did I even want that? The sight of them going at it hot and heavy set off a fire in me I'd never expected.

My movements didn't go unnoticed. Mercy glanced up, swiveling her tongue around Gideon's dick as she pulled back, the act and the mumbled curse he let out electrifying me even more. She took in my stance with a slow grin and curled her fingers to beckon me over.

Hell, yes. Without a second thought, I walked up to her, feeling as if I were in a trance. This woman could work some kind of magic, that was for sure.

She stroked her hand up and down my cock, slicking more of the pre-cum around and then sucking the head between her lips.

I'd forgotten just how good the wet heat of her mouth could feel, the jolts of pleasure when she worked her tongue over my Prince Albert piercing. A strangled noise escaped me. My balls clenched with the need to unload.

With a hungry but sly glint in her eyes, Mercy eased back, keeping one hand running up and down my length, and downed Gideon's cock again. She looked like she was having the time of her fucking life.

Something about her taking charge of the situation that I'd begun made it even more erotic. She squeezed my balls, making me growl, and then turned from Gideon to me again, teasing him with her fingers this time. Her tongue circled my piercing and tugged on one of the metal balls. Then she took me all the way down so avidly I almost lost it right there. I clutched at her, pushing my hips toward her so that I could fuck her face faster.

Her tongue slid all the way down to the base of my cock as she kept pumping away at Gideon's with her hand. She drew back, the shaft springing out with an audible pop, and switched between us. Back and forth she went, bringing me right to the brink of release and then stretching out the moment a little longer.

Finally, Gideon's hips started to jerk, his breath stuttering. Mercy didn't torment him any longer. She sucked him down hard, and he exhaled raggedly as he came. He slumped back against the wall next to the door with a nearly delirious smile.

Mercy swallowed and was on me a second later, bringing all her tricks to bear. She sucked and lapped her tongue over me and teased the piercing with the edges of her teeth. After all that build-up, it took less than a minute before I careened right to the edge of that blissful precipice. With one more swirl of her tongue, I lost it, exploding into the heaven of her mouth.

"Damn, you're incredible," I said, dropping down on the edge of the bed.

A faint blush colored Mercy's cheeks, but she smirked at me and grabbed her jeans. "I think I've made my repayment in full."

"And then some."

How had a woman this badass walked into my life out of nowhere and turned everything I'd wanted on its head? I'd never felt anywhere near this strongly about another girl, not even Laurel. Every cell in my body screamed to possess her, body and soul.

And maybe that wasn't a good thing.

How could I possibly keep her when I knew that if Dad found out, I'd have signed her death warrant?

5

Rowan

THE APARTMENT WE'D ARRANGED FOR MERCY WASN'T anything amazing, but I was glad to see the door looked solid and the interior was clean, none of the furnishings too shabby. The most unusual sight in the place was Wylder at the kitchen counter, prepping sandwiches.

Coming in behind me, Kaige let out a teasing whistle. "Wylder, you really cooking, bro?"

"It's just sandwiches," Wylder said with a roll of his eyes. "Pretty sure even you could manage that."

"Not if you're already making them." Kaige flopped onto the sofa across from Gideon, who was fixated on his tablet as usual.

"Where's Mercy?" I asked.

"In the bathroom," Gideon said abruptly. "She wanted to take a quick shower."

He didn't even glance up, but something about his tone made me study him for a moment. I had the feeling I was missing something, but then, it was hard to tell what was going on in Gideon's head at the best of times.

"Tell her to hurry up," Wylder ordered. "Can't leave a man waiting when he's gone to the trouble of making lunch."

Kaige snorted, and my lips twitched with a smile. I walked to the doorway Wylder had motioned to. The door stood ajar.

It was a bedroom, pretty spartan, the bedcovers a little rumpled. The door to the en-suite bathroom was closed, rustling sounds filtering through it. Mercy must have already finished her shower.

I'd only just thought that when she walked out, dressed and rubbing a towel over her long hair. She stopped in her tracks when she saw me.

Awkwardly, I took a step back. "Hey."

"Hey," she said, lowering the towel and offering a small smile. "I didn't know you were here."

"Kaige too," I said, and then couldn't figure out how to follow that up.

I was supposed to be the smooth-talker, ready to handle any situation, but my mouth never seemed to work quite right when Mercy was around. We hadn't talked all that much in general since the night of the confrontation with the Steel Knights, when I'd apologized for so many things and she'd granted me her forgiveness with a kiss.

I wanted so much more than that. Even standing before me in her typical T-shirt and jeans, she took my breath away. We'd been so close before, and now...

Now I had no idea what *she* wanted or how to even bring up the subject. Especially when it was obvious she'd caught the attention of all three of my brothers-at-arms—and welcomed it too.

As if on cue, Kaige poked his head into the room. Mercy's eyes lit up at the sight of him, and a pang of longing ran through my chest. She hadn't reacted that happily to me.

"Come on, before I eat all of Wylder's hard work," he said, grinning.

"As if I'd let you," Wylder retorted from behind him.

Mercy rolled her eyes, still smiling, and I walked with her into the main room. Wylder had set out plates for all of us on the narrow kitchen island. Mercy grabbed the nearest sandwich and took a big bite. Then she raised her eyebrows at Wylder. "Wow, this is pretty good."

He picked up his own. "Of course it is. I might not be up to

Anthea's standards in the kitchen, but a real man knows how to make a proper sandwich."

"Just as long as you don't expect me to make you any," she teased. "My place is definitely not in the kitchen."

He smirked back at her. "Oh, I'm perfectly happy with what you have to offer elsewhere."

Her only response was to aim a playful kick at his shin. The electricity between them crackled in the air, and my skin itched with it. I didn't know just how much had happened between them over the past few weeks, but I was pretty sure it'd gone well beyond one quick kiss.

I swallowed down my jealousy and took one of the other sandwiches. "So what's the plan for the rest of the day?"

As Gideon came over to join us, grabbing a sandwich with one hand while still holding his tablet with the other, Wylder chewed thoughtfully. "Mercy's made some interesting observations about a new power struggle in the Bend. My dad doesn't want to launch a full offensive yet, but I don't think he can object to us cracking a few heads to get some answers."

I nodded, a different sort of electricity prickling through me. The anticipation hyped me up, but it wasn't all a good sensation. With the way the situation in the Bend had escalated, I knew talking wasn't going to get us anywhere. I'd be calling on the other skills I'd built up so that I could stand alongside Wylder Noble. It wasn't how I'd prefer to contribute, but I hadn't earned my place here if I wasn't at his side every time he needed me.

"I'm in," Mercy declared.

Wylder frowned. "You've stuck your neck out investigating these guys enough already."

"I haven't done enough until the Bend is back to the almost-peaceful existence it had before."

"We don't want to paint a target on your back."

Mercy rolled her eyes. "As if I don't already have one? No one's managed to hassle me yet, and I've been out every night."

"You have?" I asked automatically with a twinge of worry.

Mercy looked at me briefly before turning back to Wylder without answering me. I guessed it had been kind of a stupid question. Had I really expected Mercy Katz to stay cooped up in this place for five days?

"Exactly," Wylder said to her. "You've done your part; now hang back and relax."

Mercy let out a huff of breath. "Wylder Noble, how many times have we had this conversation before? You'd think you'd know better by now."

"She's right, Wylder," Gideon said matter-of-factly. "She's going to come no matter what you say."

"Exactly." Mercy folded her arms over her chest with a triumphant expression.

Wylder sighed. "Fine. But at least let us take the lead. We still have a lot more experience with actual brawls than you do."

My stomach knotted. Mercy had seen me in action before, but I hadn't enjoyed knowing she was witnessing the violence I'd become capable of. Today might be even worse. But I couldn't exactly tell her she shouldn't come for fear it might ruin her impression of me.

I wasn't the same guy she'd dated—the guy she'd loved—five years ago. We both knew that.

We chucked the plates in the sink for later and headed down to the unobtrusive car we'd picked for this trip, not wanting anyone down here to realize who was in it. The hot summer sun blazed over us, but even in the middle of the day, the streets were quieter than I remembered. Only a couple of people ambled by on the sidewalks, their eyes darting nervously when they saw us.

"It's eerie out here," Gideon said.

"Everyone's sticking close to home or work," Mercy said. "Trying to avoid getting caught in any crossfire."

She frowned, but in a way that was better for us. I slid into the driver's seat. "That'll make it easier to find our targets. Who are we looking for exactly?"

Mercy got in the back and stretched out her legs. "We're probably better off looking for the Storm people. The Red Shark guys seem to lay pretty low except when they're on the attack."

Kaige rubbed his forehead as he sat next to her. "Hold on. I feel like

I've missed a whole movie. What the hell are you talking about? Shark, Storm, is this the fucking National Geographic Channel?"

Mercy guffawed and explained about the two groups she'd noticed clashing in the Bend over the past week. From Wylder's expression as he got into the front passenger seat, I could tell she'd already filled him in.

"Same cycle, different faces," he said. "Let's look for some of Colt's former men, the ones who seem to have thrown in with the Storm and probably Xavier. I'm very interested to hear what they have to say about all this."

I started the engine and pulled out into the street. I hadn't lived in the Bend for years, but I still had a decent idea of where the tough guys might hang out during the day. We cruised by various bars that hadn't opened yet and other businesses. We were just coming up on one of the smaller parks with a rusted slide-and-swings set when a chemical burning smell reached my nose.

A second later, a plume of smoke came into view farther across the patchy field. Several guys were standing around a big metal trash can that was spouting flames. It looked like they'd set up a grill over the top and were roasting burger patties on it, like some kind of trailer park picnic. A few of them were gulping from beers, and others were smoking what looked like joints—blatantly, as if they didn't care who saw them.

Mercy leaned forward, her eyes narrowing. "At least a couple of them were with the Steel Knights. I recognize that guy with the blond buzz cut and the one with the snake tattoo around his neck. That's got to be a Storm group."

"Perfect," Wylder said, even though we were outnumbered close to two to one. "Park the car. We'll crack some heads until they're down or running, but hold on to those two you're sure were Steel Knights so we can ask them a few questions after."

They weren't expecting a fight, definitely not one as brutal as I knew Wylder wanted to deliver. We could take them. I stopped the car by the curb, and we all got out except Gideon, who hung back with a tense expression.

Instinctively, I tapped my knife in my pocket and my gun at my back, checking the position of my weapons. It was better if it didn't come to blades or guns when we were just trying to send a message, but we had to be ready for anything.

Wylder sauntered right up to the group around the trash can. The humid late-summer air stunk of strong weed and cheap beer. The men looked up at him, a few of them taking on defensive postures.

"Who the fuck are you?" snarled a block-headed guy near the front, but I could tell a few of them, including the two Mercy had pointed out, recognized the Noble heir. They stiffened more than the others, their fingers tightening around their beer bottles.

Wylder didn't speak. Instead, he nodded to Kaige, who punched the nearest man so hard he went sprawling on the grass.

"What the fuck?" someone shouted. The men leapt in, but in their semi-inebriated state, their reflexes let them down. We tore through them like a bowling ball through a set of pins.

Wylder held one of them by the back of his collar and slammed his face against the makeshift grill with a sizzle of burning flesh. As that guy screamed, a man to my side smashed his beer bottle and lunged at Mercy. I caught his arm first.

With muscle memory trained by years of martial arts classes, I used his own momentum to swing her attacker around and jab the jagged glass right back at him. The shards sank right into his chest through his shirt, blood welling around the spot. He stumbled away, swearing, and ran.

But we still had more to deal with. Kaige was throwing his fists every which way, and Wylder was slamming one guy's head into his knee, breaking his nose. I wasn't as wild as one or as vicious as the other, but I held my own.

I ducked as one of the men swung a plank they'd been using for firewood at me. I gripped the edge of the board and heaved it back at the perp. It hit him square on his forehead and nose, drawing blood. But he came at me again. I pummeled him from one direction and another, dodging around him, until he buckled over, and then I kicked him in the side of the head so hard he slumped on the ground unconscious.

Somewhere to my left, Mercy was ramming her elbow into another guy's temple. I was vaguely aware of her glancing my way, and my stomach balled tighter, but I couldn't let any thought of her judgment distract me.

This was the new Rowan Finlay. I was in control, and I wasn't going to let anybody fuck with my crew.

Kaige sent one more guy reeling to the ground. The only ones left were the two Steel Knights Mercy had pointed out.

The blond man tried to make a break for it, but I snatched the back of his shirt and clocked him in the throat hard enough that he gagged. As I pinned him to the ground, Kaige dropped the guy with the snake tattoo. He hunkered down on the guy's back, and his prisoner groaned.

A couple of their associates lay bleeding and unconscious. The others had taken off. Wylder stalked over, cracking his knuckles, which were flecked with blood. Now that the worst was over, Gideon emerged from the car, carrying his tablet and watching the scene with an analytical glint in his eyes.

"Let's get this over with quickly," Wylder said to our captives. "I'm sure you'd like to go back to your partying and not, say, have your ribs crushed and your skulls bashed in. Answer our questions, and you're free to go."

The guy I was holding swore and tried to squirm out of my grasp, but I gripped him firmly and smacked him across the temple. Mercy knelt by his head with her knife drawn.

"I remember you from the last big fight," she said with a sharp note in her voice that made my pulse skip a beat. "You have no idea how much I'd like to use this. But if you play nice with the Nobles, I'll play nice with you."

She wasn't the same Mercy Katz I'd known either. But I'd always been aware there was a fierceness inside her, always liked it. I just hadn't realized how deep it ran.

Wylder crouched next to the tattooed guy, cocking his gun. "What the lady said goes for me too. The Nobles can show mercy." He winked at her. "We've just run out of patience for upstarts who think they can take over our territory. What's this I hear about someone named the Storm? Is that your new boss?"

"What are you talking about?" the guy under me sputtered. "We don't know anything about him."

Mercy arched an eyebrow. "Who said it's a him?"

He winced, knowing his lie was exposed. Wylder shifted his attention. "We know a lot more than you seem to realize. You were already working with Xavier alongside Colt, weren't you?"

When both men remained silent, he jabbed his pistol against the tattooed guy's temple.

"I don't know," the blond guy said in a panicked tone. "My loyalty was to the Steel Knights. Some other pricks showed up and started talking to Colt like they had an equal say in things, and then after he died that Xavier fuck showed up and said we were his now. He claims Colt made an agreement with him and he's holding us to it."

"And you just went along with that?" Mercy asked, her lip curling with a sneer.

"He shot anyone who argued about it. He's a fucking psycho. I wanted to stay alive... and hell, why wouldn't I want to be on the winning side? It was pretty much the same guys we were working with under Colt."

We'd guessed right about Xavier's involvement with Colt, then. But there was still a lot I didn't understand. "And does Xavier want people to call him the Storm?"

The guy I was holding let out a ragged laugh. "No, he talks about 'the Storm' like it's someone even bigger than him. All I know is, I don't want to ever meet the asshole who's keeping that menace on a leash."

I exchanged a glance with the others, a chill tickling down my spine. Xavier wasn't the leader—he was working for someone even more powerful than him? That wasn't a good sign.

Wylder tapped his gun against the tattooed guy's head again. "What else do you know about the Storm? Has he come into town?"

"Not as far as I know. It's Xavier we've dealt with. I don't think anyone except Xavier's guys has any clue, and maybe not even all of them."

Gideon frowned. "You've got to have at least some idea what Xavier and the Storm want, don't you?"

"Isn't it obvious?" the guy said. "Look around. He wants all of Paradise Bend. Now that Colt's gone, he's going to take everything for himself."

"Not just the Bend but Paradise City too," Wylder said.

"Yeah. The way the Storm's guys talk, they figure once they've got the whole county, it will make the perfect jumping off point to secure the rest of the state. It seems like he wants everything the Nobles have and then some."

Wylder leaned back on his heels. I could see the wheels turning in his head. Xavier might be obsessed with Mercy, but it was clear his interests —or those of his boss—went far beyond her. "And the Red Shark?" he asked after a moment.

"I'd never heard of him—or them, or whatever they are—until a week ago," the blond guy said. "They turned up out of nowhere and started messing with our properties, taking potshots at them. But Xavier's determined to crush them. I definitely wouldn't want to be on *that* side."

Kaige jabbed the tattooed man with his elbow. "What about the drugs?" he demanded. "Where'd that Glory stuff come from?"

Why was he worrying about that? But I guessed it was a reasonable question. The new drug people were calling Glory had only turned up in the city alongside Colt's bid for power.

"Colt was using it to fund our new operations," the man said, with a hiss of pain as Kaige jabbed him again. "Xavier brought more with him, so maybe he was supplying it the whole time. Colt never liked talking about where it came from."

"So basically you don't know a hell of a lot, do you?" Kaige growled.

"Look, the Storm's guys don't like us asking questions. And no one wants to cross Xavier. We just want to stay alive."

"Well, you've accomplished that much. For now, anyway." Wylder motioned for Kaige and I to get up. We released the two former Steel Knights men, easing back with our guns out in case they made any sudden moves. But the guys picked themselves up gingerly, the tattooed one favoring his left shoulder, which looked like it might be dislocated, and the blond one rubbing his hip. They studied Wylder warily.

"Get the fuck out of here," Wylder said, waving his gun. "Storm, Red Sharks, it doesn't matter—you picked the wrong side. The only winners around here are the Nobles, as we just proved. Go tell your friends all about it—and if you know what's good for you, after that you'll get the hell out of the Bend."

Mercy

It was late enough that the night air was getting a bit of a bite to it. I pulled on a thin black hoodie over my tank top and leggings and slipped out the apartment window. The wind nipped at my ponytail as I jumped to land on the roof of the two-story building next door.

Once I was on my feet, I took off running, leaping gaps and climbing trellises and even pipes but not letting my feet touch the ground below. It was safer up here where I could easily melt into the shadows of the city.

Wylder had told me to lay low for a few days after our discovery that Xavier was working under somebody else, somebody who was potentially more powerful than him. And also crazier? I didn't even want to think about that. But I couldn't just wait around doing nothing.

I landed on the terrace of a squat brick building deeper within the heart of the Bend and scrambled over the bars to drop into the alley below. As I checked my watch, a wry voice carried from farther down the alley. "You're late."

Anthea sauntered over. She'd traded her usual housewife-y dresses for sleek, dark-washed jeans and a black blouse, but even though we'd gone for similar colors, she still looked ten times more professional than me. Well, we each played to our strengths.

I grinned at her. "Only by three minutes."

She harrumphed. "Well, you can't tell me you got stuck in traffic."

"Hey, the pigeons around here can get pretty vicious."

A soft laugh tumbled out of her. She peered past me onto the quiet street. "So, what's the plan?"

"We're going to have a chat with the former Claws members."

Anthea raised her eyebrows at me. "Haven't they all gone into hiding since they turned against the Steel Knights and basically lost that battle for them?"

I shrugged. "I haven't seen them around, no. But I know the usual spots where they'd get together. I'm pretty sure at least a few of them are doing a little business out of a pawn shop a couple of blocks from here."

"Sounds like you've got the situation under control. What do you need me for?"

I tapped her with my elbow. "You're the best person I know at reading people and picking up on subtle clues. I'm going to be asking them some questions they might not really want to answer, about what they found out after they switched sides to join up with the Steel Knights. You can tell me if you think they're being less than truthful. And if I can't convince them to talk, maybe next time we'll come back with some of that truth serum of yours."

Anthea smirked and followed me down the street. We stuck close to the fronts of the buildings, out of the glow of the streetlamps, though half of those were broken or burned out anyway.

The pawn shop's windows were dark and streaked with grime. A very sad looking guitar lay across the display ledge next to a china doll with a chipped nose. The sign on the door was flipped to CLOSED, but I ignored that and headed around to the back.

The back door's paint had mostly flaked off, but the lock held well enough when I tested it. I glanced at Anthea. "This is the other reason I asked you to come. You brought your lock picks?"

She brandished a fabric case. "I'm going to give you a few lessons and my spare set next time I visit so you don't need me for this part."

All it took was a jiggle and a flick of her wrist, and the lock disengaged. As she put her tools away, I took out my gun and eased the door open.

I couldn't be sure exactly how friendly these guys would be. Some of the former Claws men had stood up for me and the Nobles during the shoot-out with Colt, but some of those same men had shot at *us* just a few days before that. And tensions were clearly running high in the Bend these days.

When the door shut behind us, the storage room we'd stepped into was almost totally dark. A faint glow emanated from down a set of concrete stairs that led to the basement.

"Hello?" I called out, not too loudly since I didn't want my voice to carry outside. "Whoever's here, I just want to talk."

The air shifted next to me, and my instincts kicked in before any thought had a chance to. I ducked and punched the body that'd come at me square in the ribcage, sweeping my attacker's legs out from under him at the same time. He went down with an *oof*.

As I turned my gun on my attacker, Anthea illuminated him with the flashlight on her phone. The guy stared up at me, going still as he blinked in shock, and I let my gun hand lower just a little.

It was the man who'd come to warn us about Steel Knights' impending arrival when we'd been setting our trap—who'd stopped us from getting caught in *Colt's* trap. His face had paled beneath his sprinkling of mouse-brown hair.

"Mercy Katz," he said. "What are you doing here?"

"I had a few questions that I thought my father's former associates could help me out with," I said with a crooked smile. "I'm guessing there are at least a few more of the old Claws downstairs."

The man nodded warily, but got up and beckoned to me. "Come on. They won't mind seeing you. I'm sorry—we can't be too careful with the way things have been going. After Jenner and a bunch of the others stood up to the Steel Knights, all of them that are left have been gunning for us."

Funny about that, when their new leader had said he was glad we'd taken down Colt. But then, Xavier wouldn't want the former Claws messing up his plans either. It probably suited him just fine to have some of his new men eager to take down anyone who'd ever challenged their side.

"I never caught your name," I said to the guy as he led us down the stairs.

"Roy," he said, and then called down the stairs, "Everything's okay. Mercy Katz came by to talk to us."

We came around the bend at the bottom of the stairs into a wide, concrete-walled room lit by a couple of bare bulbs. There were four other guys there, all of whom looked at least vaguely familiar, though I didn't know any of their names either.

They were standing in a semi-circle around the doorway, one with a knife in his hand and another just tucking his gun back into his jeans, but the card table in the middle of the room with a pile of chips in the middle suggested I'd interrupted a poker game. I spotted sleeping bags and blankets bunched against the walls. These guys must have been living down here, not just working out of the place.

A pang of guilt hit me. I wasn't the only one who'd lost things in this unexpected war.

"Mercy," said the guy with the gun, giving me a respectful bob of his head. He looked about forty, with a hint of gray just starting to creep through his short moustache, and he held himself with an air of subdued authority. "I'm sorry about your dad. Colt deserved everything you gave him." His gaze slid past me to Anthea. "Who'd you bring with you?"

I touched Anthea's arm. "This is Anthea Noble, a good friend. I couldn't have taken down Colt without her—or without plenty of help from others in the Nobles too. For now, I'm allied with them."

The men eyed both of us but didn't raise any complaints. The Nobles had been standing up to the chaos that Colt—and Xavier—had been instigating, at least as much as Ezra had allowed. Even if these guys had chafed under the Nobles' rule from time to time, we all knew we were on the same side.

"So you came by just to chat?" one of the other guys said, folding his arms over his chest. "What about?"

Roy snorted. "Don't be like that with her, Wheeler. She was the boss's daughter."

Wheeler grimaced at him. "The boss is dead. She's just some chick."

"Shut it," the guy who seemed to be the leader snapped. "If we'd done our job better, maybe he wouldn't be."

"You know *I* didn't have any part in that shit, Kervos," Wheeler retorted, holding up his hands. "I never even knew she was getting married—that's how much anyone bothered to tell me."

Kervos rolled his eyes and turned back to me. "What do you need, Mercy?"

Anthea spoke up. "Why don't you go back to your game while we talk? We don't want to keep you away from it."

The men gave her an odd look, but I assumed she had a good reason for suggesting that. And hey, maybe it'd give me a chance to prove I was more than just some "chick" too. I tipped my head toward the table. "I see there's an extra chair. You want to deal me in next round?"

Wheeler started to make a disgruntled noise, but Kervos swatted him across the head and motioned me over.

The men threw down their last bets, and it turned out Kervos had won. As he scooped up the chips, one of the other guys shuffled the cards and dealt them around the table, including me this time. Roy hung back behind Kervos, and Anthea stood behind me like some kind of guardian angel.

I examined my initial hand and held back a wince. Not looking so great so far. But the key to winning wasn't always in the cards but how you presented yourself. I'd gotten pretty far in this life by acting like the boldest person in the room.

I let a smile creep across my lips and tucked my cards close as if treasuring them, my gaze daring any of the men around the table to challenge me.

"What can you tell me about everything that's going on in the Bend now that Colt's fallen?" I asked. "We've gathered that he started working with this Xavier guy and a group led by the Storm—any idea how that went down?"

The dealer laid down a card that didn't help me at all, but I let my smile widen anyway. "The Steel Knights never told us much even when we joined up with them," he said.

Kervos nodded. "They'd just say things like that they'd made some new connections, brought more power on board. And that they needed the backup after Tyrell had been scheming to take *them* down." He sighed. "I should have pushed harder about that and not bought into their stupid lies."

"Hey, standing up to them put targets on all our backs," Wheeler said. "We might have been dead men if we'd challenged them back then."

"Still," Roy said tightly, "we owed Tyrell more than that."

I glanced at the faces around me. "So none of you saw any actual evidence that my dad meant to betray the alliance with the Steel Knights?"

The next card gave me no favors either, but I tossed a handful of the chips Kervos had offered me at the start into the middle anyway. The men studied the growing pile, Wheeler frowning. "I wasn't around enough to see anything," he said, and set down his cards. "Fold."

The other guys shook their heads. Kervos swiped his thumb across his lips. "Tyrell wanted that alliance more than anything I'd ever seen."

Anthea leaned forward. "I think you saw something. What is it you don't want to tell us?"

God, she was like a wolf about to go for the throat. Yet again, I was glad I could call her a friend now instead of having her as an enemy.

Kervos stared at her, his eyes twitching in a way that definitely seemed sketchy. "I don't know what you're talking about."

I waggled my hand of cards at him. "I think you do. Whatever it is, just spit it out. Dad's gone, and that means I'm the closest thing you've got to a boss now."

Wheeler snorted at that comment, but I ignored him, totally focused on Kervos. The older man grimaced. "It could be nothing. It was just something that seemed strange to me. And it didn't have anything to do with Colt or the Steel Knights, so I wouldn't have mentioned it."

"Well, I'm asking you to now," I said. "What'll it hurt to tell me? Maybe it could help."

"All right, all right. It was just that a few months ago, before all this went down, Tyrell asked me to bring him a bunch of records and other info on how much money the side-business I'd been handling was taking in and from what sources. He wanted it laid out all organized and shit. I know he made similar requests to some of the other guys."

Anthea chuckled. "And it seemed strange to you that he wanted proper accounting?"

Kervos glowered at her defensively. "Well, yeah. He said he wanted to be more on top of things so everything could be streamlined when the deal with the Steel Knights was fully settled, but that never totally made sense to me. It wasn't how he normally operated, that's all."

"It's true," I said slowly. "That is kind of strange. Dad was never much of one for getting things written down." He'd thought it'd be too easy for someone to find out things he didn't want them to and take advantage of the information.

In my mind's eye, I could see Dad tapping the side of his head with an almost manic gleam in his eyes. *That's why I'm the one on top. Because I can keep track of everything anyone needs to know in here. They all depend on me.*

A sudden desire for concrete data didn't point to any sort of betrayal, though. I mulled it over a little longer and set the knowledge aside in case it meant more to me later. "What about this Red Shark person who's sending his guys into town now? Have you had any run-ins with them?"

Roy barked a laugh. "We've been avoiding running into anyone at all since the Steel Knights started gunning for us."

Kervos took the card dealt to him and considered his hand before adding, "I've never heard of them before. Seems like they came out of nowhere. My best guess is they have some long-standing grudge against Xavier and whoever-all stands with him, and they tracked him down here. Fuck Colt Bryant for dragging us all into this mess."

"You can say that again," I muttered. Suddenly I wished I could stab my ex-fiancé another dozen times. "Well, thank you for telling me what you could, even if it wasn't much."

I accepted a card. My hand was still shit. I cocked my head, sitting up a little straighter, and tossed another handful of chips into the center of the table with a smug smirk.

The other men contemplated me. One folded. I met Kervos's gaze. "How much of your winnings am I going to put in my pocket?"

He muttered a curse and threw his cards aside too. "I'm sure you've got a better hand than I do. Take what you've already gotten."

I couldn't help cackling as I spread out my cards on the table. I didn't even have a pair.

The men all stared as I scooped up the chips. Then Roy started to chuckle. Kervos slapped the table with a loud guffaw. "Holy hell, Katz, you do have some balls on you. More than a lot of my men. I'll give you that."

"I think what you mean to say is that she has a sizable pair of *ovaries*," Anthea said archly, but she was smiling too.

"Look," I said in a more serious tone when I had my little heap in front of me. "I have a lot to thank you for. You stuck out your necks for me and the Nobles, and the people who matter won't forget that. It's getting crazy out there, and I don't like what's happening to the Bend. We're going to take action... but we might not be able to tackle all of these pricks on our own. Can we count on you to stand with us if that's what it takes to get these assholes gone?"

The men exchanged a glance. Wheeler winced, but Kervos squared his shoulders. "It's hard to give a promise when we're not fully sure what's going on out there. All these powerful new groups in play..."

I held up my hands. "I'm not going to force you. Unlike *some* people, I don't want loyalty that only comes under threat."

"If anyone can set things back the way they should be, it's her," Roy piped up, looking a bit nervous. "You saw the way she took on the Steel Knights all on her own."

"She did have a little backing," Kervos said dryly, but his expression was warmer when he turned to me again. "I can see you're not the type to back down easily. Maybe your father should have let you step up more while he was still alive. It's impressive how much you've accomplished in just the past few weeks. If the time comes when we could turn the tide, call on us, and we'll have your back. Just get our home back for us."

I summoned all the conviction I had in me. "You'd better believe I will."

Kaige

I WAS COMING OUT OF THE GYM WHEN I RAN INTO GIDEON—almost literally, since the guy never looked where he was going when he was staring at one of his tech devices. One of these days he'd walk right into a wall.

"Any update about who this Storm prick is?" I asked automatically.

Gideon tore his gaze away from his phone's screen for long enough to raise an eyebrow at me. "Believe me, as soon as I've got anything, you'll be among the first to know. How many times have you asked me in the past twenty-four hours already?"

"I want a go at him," I said with a grumble.

An uncharacteristic smile tugged at Gideon's lips. "I'm sure Wylder will let you at him first."

Electronics aside, I had to admit that in the past couple of weeks, he'd been a little more... relaxed, or cheerful, or some other word I didn't normally associate with the computer guru. I couldn't help suspecting it had something to do with Mercy. She'd had a pretty major effect on all of us, it seemed like.

All the more reason I should get to pummel that X-scarred asshole's head in for threatening her. And killing that cat. Who the hell went around carving up innocent animals just to send a message?

When we reached the foyer, Wylder and Rowan were standing by the door, their heads bent together in conversation. My spirits lifted with the thought that they might be planning another excursion to see Mercy, even though we'd just checked in on her two days ago and we did have to keep a low profile about it. Waiting two days seemed like ages to me.

As we ambled over to join them, Hector stalked past us. A massive bruise was blooming over his right eye, another coloring his left cheek. Damn.

When he'd headed outside, I tipped my head in the direction he'd gone and asked Wylder, "What the hell happened to Hector?"

Wylder sucked a breath through his teeth. "Dad lost his shit on him. He just heard from Jasper Herald that the Demon's Wings don't want to get involved in this shit, which is apparently deeper than Jasper expected, so he's withdrawing from our alliance. It works in our favor, really, since he contributed men already and we haven't done anything for him, but Dad wasn't happy. And he took out his unhappiness on the nearest available face."

I couldn't say hearing that surprised me. Ezra Noble wasn't exactly known for gentleness. At least Wylder could be glad his dad didn't turn his fists on him... not that Ezra hadn't been plenty hard on Wylder in other ways.

None of our dads were winning Father of the Year awards, to put it mildly.

"News about the Storm is spreading fast, huh?" I said. "We don't even know who he is or why he wants Paradise Bend so bad."

Rowan shrugged. "I don't think it's that complicated. We heard from the Steel Knight guys that he sees the county as a good jumping off point to make more power grabs, and it *is* prime territory. Ezra's been increasing his empire for years. If someone could just grab all of the Nobles' operations and make them their own, they'd be making a lot of profit out of that war."

"It wouldn't be that simple," Gideon said.

"Of course not. But it'd probably be simpler than building the same connections and businesses up on their own from scratch."

"We haven't lost the war yet," Wylder said. "Paradise Bend is and will always be our turf."

I nodded, feeling adrenaline pump through me. Whatever was coming, we were ready for it.

"What are you guys talking about?" a voice said from behind me. I spun around to find Axel there, a cigarette dangling from his lips.

"Have you forgotten the no smoking in the house rule already?" Wylder said with an edge in his voice.

Axel took out the cig with a smirk. "It's not lit, so technically not a crime. Are you going to answer my question?" He gave us a pointed look.

"Like most people around here, we're talking about the guy who thinks he's going to take the county from us," Rowan said mildly.

Axel made a skeptical sound. "You kids have been busy lately. Always coming and going. I don't remember Ezra giving you any missions."

Wylder grimaced at him. "My dad gives me leeway to make some of my own decisions, you know. We have work to do. We can't sit around while our enemies are already moving against us."

"So you've been going down into the Bend, then?"

"That *is* where this Xavier and his men appear to be operating from," Gideon replied, his voice flat.

"Funny. I'd imagine that's where Mercy scampered off to also. I don't suppose you've run into her at all."

I had to fight the urge to bristle. Who the fuck was he to talk about Mercy when he'd probably egged on Ezra's decision to kick her out? But he obviously suspected we'd stayed in contact with her against Ezra's direct orders. I had to keep my cool.

Which meant keeping my mouth shut and letting the other guys do the talking. I wasn't much good with my words, and I didn't think using my fists to shut Axel up would win us any points with the big boss, as much as I might have enjoyed doing it.

"If she's around, she's been staying out of sight," Wylder said without betraying any emotion. "We obviously haven't gone looking for her, considering my dad's feelings on the subject. Why? Are you worried about her safety, Axel?"

Axel snorted. "Somehow I think you must be."

Wylder gave him a bored look. "As far as I've been able to tell, Mercy's very good at taking care of herself."

Axel eyed the four of us for a moment longer, looking like he was hoping his gaze could dig right into our skulls and read our minds. My hands itched at my sides. I wished so much that punching him on his stupid, smug face was a good alternative to answering his questions. Imagining doing it calmed me down a little.

"Whatever you get up to, I hope you're keeping your loyalties in mind," Axel said finally, and sauntered off.

Gideon waited until he was out of sight and then muttered, "We definitely have to stay careful. I've noticed a couple of the men who report to Axel watching us around the mansion. They're probably keeping track of when we come and go."

I stiffened as an awful thought hit me. "They couldn't track us with one of those fancy thingamajigs you use, could they?"

He rolled his eyes. "I doubt they have enough brain cells to even think of it, but I check our vehicles over carefully before we leave. And the new van I'm having custom-made is almost ready. We won't keep that here at the mansion."

"That fucker, spying on his own people," Wylder muttered. "If he spent half as much energy tracking down Xavier and his boss as trying to screw *me* over..."

His phone rang before he bothered to finish that sentence. He checked the caller ID and brought it to his ear. "What?"

Whatever the guy on the other end said, it made Wylder's expression darken. "Seriously?" he said, scowling. "The balls on those assholes."

As he hung up and turned back to us, my pulse hiccupped. "Is it Mercy?" I whispered, remembering to keep my voice quiet.

Wylder shook his head, his mouth set in a grim line. "No, a contact of mine in the Bend was calling. He says the Storm's people are handing out free samples of Glory—from *our* waterfront property."

"What the fuck?" I said. No wonder he'd been pissed.

"Exactly. Come on, let's deal with this before my dad has yet another reason to be bashing faces. Maybe Axel will keep his trap shut if we prove we're handling more problems than he's managed to."

It was only a half hour later, as we cruised along the highway toward the condo development Ezra had recently bought into that was right near the border of Paradise City and the Bend, that an obvious question occurred to me. "Why the fuck are they giving out free drug samples?"

"Glory is one of the main ways the Storm's people have been funding their operations here," Rowan said from where he was sitting next to me in the back. "They must have brought a new shipment in, and they want to get as many people hooked as possible so they can sell the rest and bring in the cash quick."

Wylder had insisted on driving this time, his knuckles standing out stark white because of how tightly he was gripping the steering wheel. "And they're doing it out of prime Noble territory just in case they can get us in trouble with the cops as a bonus."

"But the project isn't completed yet," I said. "Anyone could have broken in. Even I know it'd be stupid for us to deal right out of a property that's in our name. Who's to say the Nobles are involved?"

"The cops don't care about logic," Gideon said in his know-it-all way. "They like easy targets. If they can pin the blame on us that easily, they'll go for it whether it makes sense or not. We can deal with the attention, but having the cops sniffing around will distract us from the bigger issues."

"So we'll just make sure that doesn't happen," Wylder said, gunning the engine so the car roared along even faster.

"We should take the lay of the land first, see exactly who's there and what they're doing and saying, before we go at them," Rowan put in. "We need to find out everything we can about these guys."

Wylder nodded. "They don't know we're onto them. We go in, scope things out, and then lay down our kind of law."

When the tall, half-finished building came into view up ahead, Wylder pulled off onto a quiet street a few blocks away and parked the car. Gideon stayed there, monitoring whatever traffic cam feeds he could tap into in case he needed to send us a warning, and the rest of us set off on foot.

The waterfront property was being built right on the bank of the river that cut its way through the heart of the Bend before skirting around the city. Work was progressing fast, and the steel frame gleamed against the sky. The lower part of the site was hidden away by a temporary wall of steel and plastic panels.

As we approached, I saw a stream of people ducking in where one of the panels had been wrenched to the side. These must have been the people coming to get the drug, not already high, but I could tell that a lot of them weren't any strangers to the experience. Most had a jittery look to them, their gazes twitching around as they made their way in. The sight made my skin crawl.

The weed I smoked to help me relax and brief highs from party drugs were one thing. You could indulge in those and not fuck yourself up. But these people looked like they'd been into the serious shit, the kind of crap that took over your life and turned everything good in it rotten. If they thought Glory would help them fill that hole, it wasn't anything I wanted a part in.

We joined the line and hung back by the wall after we'd slipped in. I had to reel in my jaw from gaping as I took in the scene.

The Storm's people had gotten the word out pretty widely, and quite a crowd had turned up to take advantage of their offer. A few guys were standing around a couple of crates in the middle of the wide cement slab at the base of the building's frame. As newcomers came over to them, they handed out little squares of white paper. There were a couple dozen people making their way over now, and nearly a hundred meandering around the slab and across the beat-up dirt of the rest of the site.

A few of those who'd just left the distributors were urgently snorting the drugs off the slips of paper in their hands. One guy staggered and then tipped his head back to gaze up at the sky with a loopy smile. Others were stumbling around in various states of chemical euphoria, their eyes glazed. Here and there I spotted some sitting on the ground rocking while they hummed to themselves.

I'd known that crap was strong when I first caught a whiff of it, and the confirmation was right here in front of me.

A man stumbled into me as if he couldn't even see I was there. My arms shot out instinctively, pushing him away from me and recoiling. It was like a fucking zombie apocalypse in here.

"Kaige," Wylder said quietly. "We're trying not to attract attention yet, remember?"

Right. I dragged in a deep breath and stuck close to his side. We circled around the steel frame, gradually getting closer to the guys handing out the drugs. The three of them started chuckling to themselves as if this was some kind of elaborate joke. My stomach churned.

A guy who'd obviously already had a good snort swayed back over to them, making grasping gestures with his hands. "Come on, man. Another hit—you've got lots there."

"One each," the closest dealer said with a sneer. "You got your sample. You want more, you pay up. Unless you don't want it that bad."

"I do. I do." The guy patted his pockets and winced. "I'll be back. That stuff is fucking amazing."

I gritted my teeth and wrenched my gaze away, only to find myself staring at a couple lying together by a stack of lumber. The woman's shirt was gaping open far enough to expose one of her breasts, but she didn't seem to care, even though a kid who couldn't have been more than eight was standing there next to them, tugging at her shoulder. "Mom, Dad, please, I want to go home."

Neither parent responded to his pleas. My spine went rigid, images I'd buried welling up behind my eyes. My hands clenched at my sides.

That wasn't the only kid here. A man was just going up to the dealers now with a little girl not much more than a toddler clinging to his pant leg. When he held out his hand for his sample, the girl started to cry. He shoved at her with his leg as if she was just an annoyance. "Shut up, Jess. Daddy needs this."

She continued to wail. One of the dealers glared at her and then her father. "Get her the hell out of here. We don't want to have to listen to tantrums."

As if it wasn't their fucking fault she was so upset. They were the ones luring the parents in—they were the ones doping them up so they didn't give a shit about their own kids.

Rage shuddered through my body. My heart pounded in my ears, and my vision flared with red. Suddenly I was marching up to the dealers with only the faintest awareness of Wylder snapping my name from behind me.

When the closest guy turned toward me, my fist was already swinging. My knuckles connected with his cheek, knocking him right off his feet. As he sprawled on his ass, clutching the side of his face, his associates fumbled for their guns.

I slammed one of those guns right into its owner's face hard enough to split his lip. At the sight of the streak of blood, savage satisfaction coursed through me. I whirled to face the last guy, who had his pistol pointed right at me, but I was too keyed up to care. I was going to crush him too.

Two more guns cocked behind me as Wylder and Rowan came up to flank me. The first guy I'd punched staggered to his feet and drew his own gun. "Who the hell are you and what the fuck do you think you're doing?" he demanded.

"I know what *you* are: little pieces of shit," I said. "These people have kids with them, and you're dealing drugs to them?"

"How's that any of your business?" the third one growled.

"I'll show you how exactly." I flung myself at him, trusting Wylder and Rowan to handle the other two.

I punched the man square on his gut before he could pull the trigger, heaved him over my shoulder, and whipped him toward the ground. He hit the concrete with a cracking sound and a groan. I dove onto his chest and punched him across the jaw. "You. Little. Piece. Of. Shit."

My haze of anger was broken by the distant wail of a siren. "Kaige," Wylder called out. "Come on, we need to get the fuck out of here."

My gaze landed on the little girl still standing just a few feet away. Her father was gaping at me, but she was just staring, her eyes round with terror. Terrified of *me*, even though the assholes I'd been smacking down were the real bad guys here.

"Kaige, come on!" Wylder yanked at my arm. The police cars were close—too close. We heard the sound of slamming doors.

"Fuck." At least the dealers would have to make a run for it now too. I might not have done much for the kids, but I couldn't let Wylder down too.

We sprinted to the opening in the wall. Some of the people who hadn't gotten their hit yet were pushing out ahead of us. Others were too high to really register what was happening, the babble of their confused voices carrying through the construction site.

We leapt through the opening and raced across the street, ducking into the alley there just as footsteps pounded around the corner. "Stop!" a voice hollered. "Police!"

Not a fucking chance. We dashed through the alley, my breaths rough in my throat, and burst out onto the next street over. The car was just up ahead. Another siren blared in the distance. I hurtled forward with all the strength I had in me and dove into the backseat behind Gideon.

"I tried to warn you as soon as I saw them coming," he said as Wylder dropped into the driver's seat, Rowan scrambling in beside me. The engine roared.

"I know," Wylder said. "Kaige flew off the handle, and we had to rein him in before we could get out of there."

His voice was flat, but I could hear the anger coursing through it. As he yanked the steering wheel and sped off toward home, my stomach sank.

We'd almost been caught by the fucking cops, and it was my fault.

8

Mercy

SOMEHOW I WAS STANDING AT THE BANQUET TABLE FOR MY rehearsal dinner all over again. Gunshots thundered all around me.

Grandma fell, blood gushing down her dress. One bullet and another caught my father in the chest—but it wasn't Colt firing them. His face had been replaced by Xavier's, while an even larger shadowy figure loomed behind the scarred giant.

Another bang—and I jolted out of sleep, the sheets tangling around my limbs. My heart was thumping hard. It took me a second to realize that I really was awake in the bedroom of the Nobles' apartment, but for some reason the banging sound hadn't stopped.

It was coming from the apartment's front door: an insistent heavy knocking.

"Open up!" a muffled voice hollered. "Police!"

Shit. My heart practically lurched right out of my chest. I vaguely registered the glowing numbers on the clock perched on the dresser: 2:06 a.m. What the fuck were the cops doing here in the middle of the night?

What were they doing here, period?

Another bellow cut through my confusion. "If the door isn't open within thirty seconds, we're busting it down. This is your final warning."

I scrambled off the bed and grabbed a hoodie off the floor. I'd gone to bed in just a tank-top and pajama shorts, no bra. Tugging the hoodie on, I checked that I hadn't left anything incriminating lying in view. My gun was on the mattress lying next to my pillow—I shoved it between the headboard and the wall, grabbed my knife, and shoved that into the pocket of my hoodie on the way to the door.

After fumbling with the lock and yanking the door open, I found two cops standing in the hall outside. They gave me a once-over, their eyes lingering on my bare legs. I had the urge to see if they wanted an even closer look, like if I slammed my knee into their smug faces, but I wasn't quite annoyed enough to be that suicidal despite my interrupted sleep.

I hadn't seen much of the police in the two decades that I'd lived in the Bend. They mostly focused on civil disputes and personal crimes, looking the other way when it came to all the gang activity in the area. Most of them were getting payoffs from one organization or another.

"Are you alone in here, ma'am?" the shorter cop asked, saying the last word with a bit of a sneer. The suspicion in his eyes convinced me that he knew who I was—or more importantly, who my father had been.

I didn't like to admit to being on my own, but if I said someone else was here, they'd probably demand I bring them out. "Yep, just lil ol' me," I drawled. "Is there some reason you woke me up at two in the morning, officers?"

The tall one glowered at me and barged right past me into the living room. "We got a complaint about a disturbance, some sort of ruckus that had people concerned. We'll need to check the place out and make sure everything's in order here."

That was total bullshit. If there'd been a "ruckus" in or around the apartment, *that* would have woken me up instead of these bozos. It was just an excuse to get them inside without a warrant.

So what did they actually want?

The tall cop started prowling through the apartment. A prickle of apprehension ran down my spine, but it was hard to keep an eye on both him and the short dude who stepped inside and planted himself in front of me.

Shortie narrowed his eyes. "Miss Katz, isn't it? You've been a difficult woman to find."

I folded my arms over my chest. "Who's been looking for me?"

"An awful lot of people, I suspect, after the massacre we found in that restaurant downtown. Whoever was responsible took out your whole family... but somehow missed you. Very interesting."

My stomach tightened. "'Interesting' isn't the word I'd use."

"You couldn't be that torn up about it," Tall Guy tossed out from where he was opening and closing the kitchen cupboards. Did he think the "ruckus" had been started by a cereal box and a stack of plates? "Isn't it strange that nobody came forward to receive the bodies, especially the last remaining member of the family?"

"I didn't have much choice about that," I snapped, and then clamped my mouth shut. I'd had to steer clear to save my own life. No way would Colt have stood back and just let me claim the bodies, arrange funerals—I'd have been lucky to make it through the doorway of the coroner's office alive. But what did these assholes care about that?

Guilt twisted through my gut anyway. I'd assumed that by now it was too late to do anything for my family, but maybe I'd dismissed the possibility too quickly. "Are the bodies still in... custody, or whatever?"

Shortie snorted. "They were cremated a couple of weeks back. We don't have room to hold onto a pile of corpses for ages, especially with how many of 'em have been turning up lately." He shot me another narrow look. "I believe the coroner holds onto the ashes for a while, if it actually matters to you."

"That's good to know," I said, stiffly grateful. I could still do something for them then. There were a few places Grandma and my aunts might like their ashes scattered. Dad... He'd be lucky if I didn't drop his down a sewer drain.

But right now I had nowhere safe to keep the ashes. Even this apartment didn't really belong to me. I couldn't take a stash of urns with me while I was on the run.

"And what exactly are you doing *here* right now?" Shortie asked, raising an eyebrow.

I glanced around. "In the Bend? This is my home."

"No, I mean in this apartment."

The prickle of apprehension came back. "Is there some reason I shouldn't be?"

He gave a disbelieving cough. "It's also interesting that we find the sole survivor of the Katz family in a place owned by Ezra Noble."

I kept my expression carefully blank. "Should that mean something to me?"

Tall Guy let out a scoffing sound as he bent to check under the sink. What the fuck did he expect to find anyway?

Shortie kept glowering at me. "I can't imagine your dear old dad kept you that much out of the loop about how things work in the Bend. What are you doing for the Nobles, Miss Katz? Why have they set you up in this nice place? They must have you on the payroll."

I shook my head, ignoring the growing knot in my stomach. "I have no idea what you're talking about."

"I guess we'll see about that," Tall Guy remarked, coming around the kitchen island and glancing under the stools.

I frowned, stepping to the side as if I could block him from coming any farther into the apartment. "You're not supposed to just randomly search people's homes, are you?"

He sneered at me. "We told you, we got a report. If someone was hurt in here or there was a violent incident, we need to check to make sure you're not covering it up."

In the kitchen cupboards? I bit back the urge to let loose my snark out loud. Instead, I turned slowly on my heel, letting my eyes dart around the room.

They were here for a reason. They expected to find something... because someone must have pointed them my way. Someone who was confident that the cops wouldn't leave with empty hands.

Nothing in the living room looked out of place to me... Except the little pillow on the sofa. I hadn't paid much attention to it when I'd come in last night, but I had a distinct memory of eating my breakfast yesterday morning with the TV on and my feet propped on top of that pillow. It was straightened up against the arm of the sofa now.

If it hadn't been for the cops' presence, I'd have assumed Anthea had stopped by and instinctively done some tidying up. But suddenly the discrepancy seemed much more ominous.

As casually as I could, I ambled over to the sofa and plopped myself down on it as if I were bored with the proceedings. Then I slid my hand past my hip as if to scratch my back. Instead, I tucked it behind the pillow, feeling quickly for anything other than the fabric of the cushions.

My fingertips brushed the corner of what felt like a plastic baggie wedged next to the seat cushion. At the same moment, Short glanced over at me. My pulse hiccupped. I raised my hand and scratched the back of my neck next.

Tall Guy had gone into the bathroom. Shortie was stalking through the living room, examining the bookcase around the TV. Any second now, he'd want to check over the couch.

When he glanced my way again, I stared up at the top shelf and frowned as if I'd just noticed something there I wouldn't want him seeing. His gaze jerked away from me in an instant. I restrained a smirk.

The second his attention was back on the shelves, I dipped my fingers behind the cushion again, snagged the baggie, and tugged it out. I managed to stuff it in the back of my hoodie and set my hand back on my lap just as Shortie shot me another suspicious look. I leaned back on the couch and muffled a yawn, kicking my foot impatiently in the air.

What the hell was in that baggie? I couldn't check it in front of him. At least the bottom of the hoodie was fitted enough that the bag should stay in there as long as I kept it zipped up.

Shortie left the bookcase and started toward me, just as Tall Guy came out of the bathroom. There was my opportunity.

I leapt up before Shortie had to insist and pressed my thighs together as if I were about to wet myself.

"Sorry," I said. "I've got to dash to the bathroom."

"Wait a second," Shortie said, scowling.

I bobbed on my feet. "Please. I had to run to answer the door when you woke me up—I didn't have a chance then."

Tall Guy looked me over, and I smiled innocently at him while continuing to jitter on my feet. He sighed and motioned for me to get on with it.

I wasn't going to get much time before they figured out something was up. I hustled into the bathroom, shut the door firmly, and sat down on the toilet to actually pee in case the jerks decided to listen in. While I did my business, I pulled out the baggie and examined it.

It held maybe a quarter of a pound of a fine gray powder that looked very familiar. I took a quick sniff and grimaced.

Yep. This was the same drug we'd stolen a huge shipment of from Colt—the stuff they were calling Glory.

I sure as hell hadn't brought it into the apartment. So who had? How had they even gotten in here? And why had they wanted to get me arrested?

The apartment had never really felt like a home, but now the walls around me didn't offer the slightest sense of security. An enemy had breached them, and I hadn't even realized until it was almost too late.

If I lingered any longer in the bathroom, the cops would get suspicious. I emptied the drugs into the toilet and flushed them away along with my piss. Then I folded the baggie as small as it'd go and squeezed it behind the window frame. Even if they checked the bathroom again after I came out, they weren't going to find anything.

I washed my hands and walked back out to find Tall Guy shaking his head at Shortie. "—a bad tip," he was just saying. He shut his mouth at the sight of me.

Shortie glared at me as if blaming me for wasting their time, when they were the ones who'd gotten me up at two in the morning. "It seems everything's in order here after all, Miss Katz. If you have any reason for concern, I'm sure you'll notify the PBPD."

"Absolutely," I said with forced brightness that I doubted they believed.

They marched out, and I shut the door firmly behind them, pushing the deadbolt into place. But the thunk of the heavy metal lock didn't reassure me as much as it used to. Someone had gotten past it once already.

At least once. How many times had the intruder come in here before? Planting the drugs might not have been the first time.

The thought made my skin crawl. I glanced toward the bedroom, but my nerves were too jittery for me to get back to sleep. Something was very, very wrong here.

And if they'd come for me, who else might they be coming for?

I grabbed my phone, taking a small bit of satisfaction in knowing that now I wouldn't be alone in getting woken up to bad news in the middle of the night.

Wylder picked up his new burner phone after a few rings, his voice tired but tense. "What's going on?" he asked without preamble.

I swallowed thickly, resisting the urge to hug myself even though he couldn't see me anyway. "We've got another problem."

9

Gideon

I CONTAINED MY THIRD YAWN AS I TAPPED AWAY ON MY tablet. Wylder had woken me up way too early in the morning with three simple words that had effectively dissipated any annoyance I might have felt: "Mercy's in trouble."

The swaying of the van made me hit the wrong digital key. I muttered a curse to myself and bit back a sharp comment toward Kaige, who was driving the van I'd just finished setting up to my satisfaction yesterday. I didn't actually want him to slow down when who knew what might be happening to Mercy while we rushed into the Bend, and hurrying never made for a smooth ride.

Beside me on the padded bench that lined one side of the van's large cargo area, Rowan stared at the flat-screen monitors I'd mounted all along the opposite wall. Various surveillance feeds from the cameras we'd set up around Mercy's apartment and footage from traffic cams I was in the process of hacking into flickered across their glowing surfaces. He let out a low whistle. "You really outdid yourself."

"And yet some bastard managed to get into Mercy's apartment anyway," I said, unable to keep the edge out of my voice even though it wasn't Rowan's fault. If anyone was to blame for a flaw in the security system, it was clearly the guy who'd set it up, a.k.a., me. I gritted my teeth and frowned at the footage before me.

As far as I could tell, no one except the cops and Mercy herself had gone into Mercy's apartment tonight. Now I was scanning back through the earlier footage. I'd been skimming through it regularly since we'd set it up, but I could only keep so close an eye on it without Ezra or one of his men noticing that I was even more glued to my devices than usual. I must have missed something.

Damn it. I knew exactly who'd been able to circumvent my security efforts before, and it was the last person I wanted anywhere near Mercy. The image of Xavier's X-scarred face and ominous grin flashed through my memory.

Wylder swiveled in the passenger seat to peer back at us. "Anything?"

"I'll tell you as soon as I find something," I said, my stance tensing even more. I hadn't been able to defend the Noble mansion effectively, and now I'd fucked up somehow when Mercy needed me more than ever. What good were all the skills I'd built up if they didn't fucking *work* when they were supposed to?

Kaige swung around another turn. Through the small, tinted windows on the van's back doors, which allowed us to see out but no one else to see in, the darkened streets looked just as deserted as they did on my screens. The rumble of the van's engine sounded almost blaring in the stillness. I hoped that was just my nerves talking and that we weren't drawing every creep in a ten mile radius to our meeting spot.

The van jerked to a halt. To give Kaige a little credit, the tires only screeched a tiny bit. Almost immediately, there was a knock on the back door.

Rowan leapt up to pull it open and stepped back so Mercy could scramble inside.

She was wearing an oversized hoodie and sweatpants, and her hair was pulled into a messier ponytail than usual, several stray strands falling around her face. She flashed a smile at us as if this were an ordinary get-together, but her gaze darted behind her before she yanked the door closed.

As soon as she did, Kaige hit the gas again. The van lurched away from the curb.

"Thank you for coming so early in the morning," Mercy said, swiping her hand over eyes that looked slightly bleary. Of course, she'd gotten even less sleep than the rest of us. Her gaze twitched to the back windows and the view behind us again, and I could tell that as nonchalant as she was trying to be about this situation, she was nervous.

Who the hell wouldn't be? We'd promised her a safe haven, and it'd been violated by a total psycho.

I flicked my fingers across my tablet to switch the focus of a few of the screens to the cameras mounted on the outside of the van and footage from the streets around us. "I'll make sure no one's following us. So far we haven't seen anything."

She took in the array of screens and let out an awed laugh. "You've obviously got every possible angle covered."

"That was the idea. Doesn't seem like it worked out so well after all."

Mercy sat down on the carpeted floor and leaned against the bench next to me. She reached up to give my knee a quick but affectionate squeeze that sent a flare of heat straight to my cock despite my distraction.

"Hey, I'm fine," she said. "We'll figure it out like we always do."

She might not have been fine, though. The jackass had decided he wanted to frame her rather than kill her—this time. For all we knew, he *could* have killed her any time in the past week and just hadn't bothered to. I jabbed at the tablet with more force, as if that would change anything.

"Here," Wylder said to Kaige. There was a rattle of gravel against the undercarriage as the van pulled off the road.

When the engine cut out, the two guys squeezed past the front seats into the cargo area with the rest of us. The space was big enough to fit us all fairly comfortably, but I wouldn't have wanted to hold a party in here.

Wylder crouched down across from Mercy while Kaige hovered next to him, looking like he wished he'd gotten there first. Wylder's gaze took her in, and he met her eyes with an intensity I didn't often see from my best friend. "You're sure you're okay?"

"Tired and irritated, but I've been a lot worse," she said, offering another smile. I couldn't help thinking it looked a bit stiff around the edges. This woman knew how to hold herself together, but even she had limits.

"What exactly happened?" Kaige demanded. "These cops showed up—they were looking for drugs someone had planted?" Wylder had given us a hurried secondhand explanation as we'd hustled to the van, but no doubt it'd been missing some details.

"A little more than an hour ago, a couple of cops started banging on my door," Mercy said. "As an excuse to search the apartment, they claimed there'd been a call about a disturbance. I had a bad feeling about it, obviously, so I looked around too, and managed to find a baggie of what I'm pretty sure was Glory tucked in the couch cushions."

Kaige let out a growl. "Fucking Glory."

"You got rid of it?" Rowan asked.

Mercy nodded. "I got a chance to flush it down the toilet. The cops left empty-handed. But I have no idea how the baggie got there in the first place... I'm pretty sure it must have been during the afternoon when I was out of the apartment yesterday, but maybe I'm wrong. And why set me up like that?"

The rest of us exchanged a glance. We hadn't had a chance to fill her in about the incident at the waterfront property yet.

"It seems to be Xavier's new strategy of choice," Wylder said tightly. "Get drugs on our property and then sic the police on us. A few of the Storm's people had a whole Glory party at the new waterfront property yesterday. The cops got there before we could break it up. They almost caught *us*."

"What?" Mercy's eyes widened. "Why didn't you tell me anything?"

"It just happened, and it didn't seem like something you needed to know about urgently. I figured I'd bring it up the next time we dropped in." He ran his hand through his auburn hair and grimaced. "Those Storm assholes. Using our own fucking strategy against us. *We* were going to sic the cops on *them* with the truck we stole, and now they've stolen our plan and spun it around on us." He smacked his fist against the floor.

I'd have pointed out that we had bigger problems than copyrighting our schemes, except just then I caught a blurred shape on one of the screens. Sucking a breath through my teeth, I tapped the controls to pause that one and cycled back through the frames to the right spot.

Mercy caught my reaction, looking from me to the screens. "Did you see something?" Her whole posture had gone rigid.

"Not anything happening right now," I assured her, and her shoulders relaxed just a bit. "It's footage from one of the cameras around the apartment building—from yesterday afternoon, like you thought..."

There. He was only on the screen for half a second, but I recognized Xavier's burly form. He hadn't come right up to Mercy's building, though. He was heading into the run-down office building next door.

Everyone around me had fallen silent, clearly recognizing him too. Wylder swore a few times. "How'd he get from there into Mercy's apartment? There's no sign of him going to her building?"

I shook my head, my stomach twisting. "He must have used similar tricks to what she has in the past—gone from a window or the rooftops to one of her windows." I had a camera in the hall outside her front door, so he definitely hadn't gotten in that way. None of the feeds had been covered or cut out even briefly—I'd come up with a way to program the system to alert me if either happened.

But he'd found a way around it anyway. My hands clenched on my lap. "I'm sorry," I said, my strained voice rasping in my throat. I couldn't hold my own in a fight, couldn't physically protect her, so I was supposed to manage it this way. And this prick had shown me up yet again.

Mercy looked up at me with concern in her dark eyes—concern for *me,* when she was the one who'd been in danger—which knotted me up inside even more. She reached for me again, grabbing my hand this time. "It's not your fault. He's beyond anything any of us have had to deal with before. But we're not going to let them win."

I had to figure out how to stop him from winning before we could be sure of our victory.

"I get why they came at us through the waterfront property," Kaige said. "But why target Mercy?"

Mercy's brow knit. "Yeah, it's not as if I'm such a huge threat."

"You're selling yourself short," Wylder said. "I'm sure Xavier found out how big a role you played in taking down Colt. He might be happy with the result, but that doesn't mean he wouldn't realize you could cause problems for him too."

"And he's seemed to have some vendetta against you for a while now," Rowan pointed out. "Leaving that crap at the mansion for you to find... For whatever reason, he's fixated on you."

But he was still playing with her, terrorizing her without following through—yet. It probably amused him to know he could get under her skin. Like a game of chess he was playing with us, and he kept catching us off-guard no matter how many moves ahead I tried to see.

"He was obviously in your apartment," I said abruptly. "You can't go back there. It's compromised."

Wylder nodded. "We'll find another safe location to move you to."

But what location would actually be safe? What place could I *keep* safe for her? I stared down at my tablet, and a wave of anger and despair washed over me.

If I didn't step away from this conversation, I might hurl the device at the screens I'd put so much work into setting up, and that wouldn't help anyone.

I pushed to my feet. "I need fresh air to think properly. Give me a minute."

The other guys blinked at me, but I walked right past them and hopped out of the van into the cool early morning air.

A hazy greenish glow was just touching the distant sky as dawn crept closer. The narrow alley we'd pulled into stank of urine, but I didn't dare walk farther than the end of it several paces away. What if I screwed us over again by letting someone catch a glimpse of me?

The van door thumped behind me. Mercy walked over. "Hey, are you okay?"

"I just... have a lot to think about," I said. The last thing she needed was to be burdened with my worries along with her own.

She nudged her shoulder against mine. "Nowhere to get acceptable coffee around here. It's definitely too early to go without caffeine."

I cracked a smile despite myself. It'd only been a couple of months since she'd barged into our lives like a whirlwind, and she already knew me so well. Better than anyone except maybe Wylder, really. She was the first person I'd willingly shown my scars to. The first person I'd *wanted* to open up to.

I didn't know how it'd happened. I barely knew what to do with the emotions that rushed through me whenever she was near. They were exhilarating but also unsettling.

I grappled with my words. "I don't like how he keeps upping the ante. I feel like they're backing us into a corner."

"You always get us out of any corners we end up in." She touched my cheek to turn my face so I'd meet her eyes. "You're beating yourself up like you did over the shit Xavier pulled before, I can tell. But did you ever think that you did *more* than anyone else here managed? You're the one who got him on camera to confirm it was him. You're the one who figured out which apartment I should stay in so I wasn't out on the streets where he'd have gotten to me that much easier."

Whether it was her touch or her words, warmth flowed through me, melting a little of my sense of failure. She wasn't wrong. It just didn't seem like enough.

"I hadn't looked at it that way," I admitted.

"Well, I'm not going to forget it."

She bobbed up to plant a gentle kiss on my lips, fleeting but sweet. Somehow the simple gesture squeezed my heart more than when that mouth had been wrapped around my cock. Not that I hadn't enjoyed the latter a whole lot too.

When she drew back, she flashed me a conspiratorial smile—like we'd already figured out the answer together.

Resolve solidified in my chest. Mercy saw me, right through to my core, without pity or judgment. So what if I wasn't sure how to handle the emotions she stirred in me? All that mattered was that I wanted to kill anyone who messed with her, preferably slowly and painfully. If Xavier had been in front of me, I'd have gotten started on it right now.

But he wasn't. It was just me, empty-handed.

Maybe that was the problem. I'd spent all my time trying to be prepared for him to come to us instead of aiming to take him down before he even had a chance.

"Okay," I said. "Let's go back and get on with the planning."

Wylder and the others were in the middle of a conversation when we climbed into the van. "We're going to have to deal with the cop problem before we can focus on getting the Bend back," Wylder said, and nodded to me. "We can't fight a war with them breathing down our necks."

"How are we going to do that?" Kaige asked.

"We could lay low for a few days and let them make the next move," Rowan said. "See what they're planning next."

"No," I said. Every eye turned to me. I drew myself up into as firm a posture as I could manage. "I'm tired of waiting around for them to make their moves. They're too unpredictable for us to learn much like that anyway—and they're getting too close to making major damage. We need to squash Xavier and everyone who stands with him as quickly as we can."

Mercy cocked her head. "What exactly are you suggesting, Gideon?"

"We take the fight to them," I said. "If the Storm is going to set us up, we can just as easily do the same damn thing to them."

10

Mercy

When we pulled up around the back of the apartment building where I'd been staying, Gideon was deeply immersed in the real estate listings he'd pulled up on his laptop. "By the time you finish checking the place over, I'll have a new spot picked out," he said without looking up. "More secure this time."

Part of me was a little worried there wasn't any place that'd be totally secure from the psycho stalker I seemed to have picked up, but I didn't want to say that out loud. I curled my fingers around my childhood bracelet in my pocket.

The other guys escorted me to the building's back door and up the stairs to the apartment. The thought of stepping back into that space now that I knew my privacy there had been violated made my skin crawl, but Wylder had understandably wanted to take a look around just in case the intruder had messed with something I hadn't noticed. I'd already packed up my meager belongings before I'd gone to meet the guys.

"Never liked cops," Kaige muttered as we climbed the stairs. "They're never on the right side."

He made it sound somehow personal. "Wasn't your Dad in the army?" I asked, remembering his dog tags. Their chain gleamed around Kaige's neck. Like my bracelet, he always kept them on him.

Kaige touched them self-consciously. "Yeah," he said, and then fell silent. I was about to push him to go on when we came out into the hall near my apartment. I stopped in my tracks.

The door to the apartment was slightly ajar. Wylder glanced at me. "Didn't you lock it when you left?"

"Of course."

The hairs on the back of my neck stood on end. Was *he* in there now, behind the door, waiting for us to show up? Xavier. The image of him from the video recording flashed through my mind, and dread curdled in my stomach. I reached for the knife at my hip.

Wylder and Rowan both drew their guns. Kaige's hands squeezed into fists. He stepped forward first, storming up to the door and kicking it open as if he figured he'd just pummel whoever was on the other side.

He barged right in with no sounds of struggle. The rest of us hurried after him. As we stepped inside, I noticed the curtains billowing around the living room window. The window that'd been closed when I'd left the apartment. I ran to it.

"Mercy, wait!" Kaige called from behind me, but I ignored him. I leaned over the narrow ledge into the dim dawn light to look below.

I couldn't make out anyone or anything moving in the shadows below. My heart thumping, I pulled back inside just as Rowan reached my bedroom doorway. His hand whipped to his mouth, muffling a curse.

"What now?" Wylder snapped. He marched over, reaching the doorway just as I did.

Rowan stepped inside and over to make room for us, careful to avoid the walls. For good reason, I realized as soon as I peered inside.

A cloying, metallic smell filled my nose—not rancid like when Xavier had tossed a chopped up corpse into the Noble mansion, but equally unnerving. Even more unnerving were the dark red streaks that had been smeared across the walls all around the bed where I'd been sleeping just a few hours ago. A pool of it was soaking into the blanket.

Some of the streaks were just random splatter, but others formed letters. *The cat's running scared now*, one wall said. And beside the door, *Next time I'll paint with yours.*

Kaige had come up behind us. He stared at the mess, his jaw dropping. "Is that blood?"

My nose had wrinkled. "Sure smells like it," I said, trying to keep a jaunty tone despite the horror swelling inside me.

"Probably from some kind of animal," Rowan said, his mouth twisted at a queasy angle. "We know he has no problem killing random innocent creatures."

Like the cat he'd slaughtered and left gutted on the lawn outside my window. I closed my eyes for a moment, gathering myself.

Wylder gripped my shoulders and forced me to back out of the room—but to be fair, I didn't really fight him. I'd seen enough.

"He came back," I said. "He must have been here less than an hour ago." But then he'd left again before we got here. He could have stayed and attacked us.

But that'd never been his goal before. "He's toying with me," I went on, opening my eyes again to glare at the window. "He wants to scare me. Well, fuck him."

Okay, so I was scared. But that didn't mean I was going to run off with my tail between my legs.

Wylder let out a growl. "The bastard is taunting all of us."

Kaige paced the living room, his fists clenched so tight the veins stood out in his forearms. "Let me get my hands on him, and we'll see who's laughing then. He's a fucking coward."

"Let's move quickly," Rowan said. "We don't want to hang around here any longer than we have to." He shot a worried glance at me, and I knew he mostly wanted to get me away from the threats painted in blood all around my bedroom. Despite my efforts, a shiver crept down my spine at the memory.

"He's not putting one finger on you," Wylder assured me, his eyes blazing with unrestrained fury.

They stalked through the apartment, checking around all the furniture. Wylder grabbed the baggie that'd held the drugs from where I'd stashed it in the bathroom when I pointed it out. None of them turned up anything that concerned them—as if the bloody walls weren't a big enough problem.

"I'll figure out someone we can call on to clean the mess up who won't mention it to my dad," Wylder said as we headed back to the van. "Worst comes to worst, we'll wash it off and repaint ourselves." He clambered into the back of the van, where Gideon was still hunched over his tablet. "Got anything yet?"

Gideon's tongue flicked over his lip ring the way he often did when he was deep in thought. "I think so. It's not the best spot but not awful. It takes a key rather than a lock code, though. It'll take me a little while to get a copy of that."

"What do we do until then?" Kaige asked.

"We could take her back into the city," Wylder said stubbornly, as if it'd be easier to hide me from his dad there.

"Guys, I'm right here," I said. "You can't decide for me. I say I stay in the Bend. Xavier's come right to the Noble mansion before—it's not like he stays away from the city. It'll be easier to hide where people are used to looking the other way and questionable stuff is going down all the time."

"She does have a point," Rowan said, and turned to Gideon. "I'd like to know how Xavier found out about this place to begin with. You were really careful, weren't you?"

"I've gone over the records I set up," Gideon said. "There's nothing in them that should have tipped anyone off—and they'd have needed to get into the Nobles' servers to look in the first place. I haven't seen any breaches."

I grimaced. "It's probably my fault. I've been going out so much. The Storm's people have probably been able to get access to the traffic cams like Gideon can. All it'd take is catching one glimpse of me and they could have pieced together the footage to get an idea of where I was staying."

"That means we have to be even more careful this time," Wylder said.

The tension on his face made something clench inside me, but as much as I appreciated his concern for me, I couldn't simply accept it. "I don't know if that's possible. I can't stay cooped up in some apartment day in and day out while the Bend is falling apart around me. If Gideon can point out all the cameras to me, I'll avoid them as much as possible, but... this guy is good, and he has a lot of men on the streets. I've just got to make sure he never catches me unprepared again."

"So do we." Wylder motioned to the other guys. "I say one of us needs to be with Mercy at all times." I opened my mouth to protest, and he cut me off with a glare. "You'll be safer that way than on your own. This isn't up for discussion."

"I don't need a babysitter," I huffed, not knowing whether I wanted to kill him for his over-protectiveness or kiss him. I didn't like him bossing me around, but when it was because he couldn't stand the thought of anything happening to me, it was kind of a turn-on at the same time. Fucking hell.

"Of course you don't," Gideon said matter-of-factly. "Safety in numbers is just a logical strategy."

I found it harder to argue with that. As I sighed, Kaige perked up. "I volunteer for the first shift!"

Wylder rolled his eyes at him. "Big surprise there. Fine, you can stay with Mercy in the van while Gideon gets her new apartment sorted out. I'd imagine she'd like to get some more sleep."

Kaige waggled his eyebrows at me. "And I'm sure I'll enjoy getting you ready for that sleep."

I swatted him, but my lips twitched into a smile. "All right. It's a plan."

We cruised along several streets until Wylder found a discreet place to park. It was a small lot around the back of a pawn shop that was boarded up, not big enough to fit more than five cars and with a high picket fence surrounding it. Kaige got out and used a stray board to smash a rusty-looking security camera mounted on the fence.

"Was it even still working?" I asked when he came back.

He shrugged. "Better safe than sorry."

Gideon had pulled a couple of sleeping bags out from under the seats up front. "I thought it was best to be prepared for a longer stint in here, even if I wasn't prepared specifically for this situation," he said, setting them on the floor. "There's a storage box with various snacks when you're ready for breakfast."

"Jackpot," Kaige declared, and started unrolling the first sleeping bag.

Rowan had sat down on the bench, the pen in his hand flying over a scrap of paper.

Wylder took one last glance around. "We'll come back to switch off and hopefully get you to a proper home as soon as we can. Don't call us unless it's absolutely necessary. We don't know who else is tracking us."

I nodded, shaking off a fresh shiver.

Wylder walked right up to me. He grasped my shoulders, holding my gaze, and the heat of his body washed over mine. "For once in your life, be fucking careful, Kitten. The Bend isn't going to burn down in the next seven hours. Stay in the van until we get back."

"Fine," I said, swaying toward him instinctively. I was probably going to be sleeping most of that time anyway. After the late-night waking and all the shocks of the night, I was exhausted.

He kissed me fast but hard and kept his hand on my arm as he looked at Kaige. "Keep your head on straight and make sure she stays safe, or I'll take that head right off you."

Kaige just grinned, unoffended by his friend's domineering act. "Got it, boss. I'll keep her way too busy to even think of setting foot outside these doors."

Wylder's grip tightened just a smidgeon, but whatever jealousy he might still have over my connection with the other guys, it wasn't much. He released me and motioned to the others.

Gideon grasped my hand and squeezed just for a second, a show of affection that was unusual enough coming from him to startle me. "I'll get everything worked out—better this time."

"It wasn't your fault," I said, but he didn't reply to that.

Rowan stopped in front of me, holding out the piece of paper he'd been doodling on. "Just... a reminder that there were better days before, and there'll be better days again," he said awkwardly. The second I took the paper, he hurried out after the other guys, shutting the van's back doors behind him.

I unfolded the paper, and a softer smile crossed my face. It was a cartoon drawing of a sun and a cute little kitten lying on its belly under its rays. Yeah, someday, maybe I could be that relaxed.

I turned to Kaige and noticed he'd laid out the sleeping bags not beside each other but fully unzipped with one on top of the other, like a single mattress topped by a blanket. I raised my eyebrows at him. "You just assumed we're sharing a bed?"

He aimed one of his cocky grins at me, as if nothing in the world could be all that wrong. "Don't go telling me I was wrong now. You'll break my heart."

I snorted, but I didn't actually mind anyway. Being in this small space so close to him, feeling the heat of his gaze on me, a little of my tiredness fell away behind a flare of desire. Maybe a little of his bedroom skill was just what I'd need to put all the craziness of the night behind me.

I slipped under the top sleeping bag, and Kaige scooted over beside me. He slipped his arm behind my head. His fingers stroked over my shoulder, but his voice softened. "You know, it's okay to be scared once in a while. *I'm* fucking scared of this Xavier dude every now and then. It keeps us humble."

I tipped my head toward him, letting my forehead rest against his cheek. "Since when are you humble?"

"Oh, all the time. I'm just very quiet about it," he teased.

His other hand drifted over my thigh, drawing more heat over my skin through my jeans. But I couldn't quite settle into the moment. Too many worries were niggling at me.

"How big of a problem do you think the whole thing with the waterfront property is going to be?" I asked.

Kaige shrugged, but I felt his body tense beside me. "Beats me." The casualness of his tone sounded forced.

I turned over so that I was lying on my side, my gaze focused on him. Kaige looked down at me. Though adorable was not a word I'd normally associate with Kaige, that's exactly how he looked tucked beside me in the van's cramped space.

"Something about what happened there bothers you," I said. "And don't you dare say I'm wrong. I can tell."

He made a dismissive sound, but his gaze flicked away from me. "It's nothing."

"Kaige," I said warningly.

"Fine," he grumbled. "It's all in the past anyway. I just don't like being around druggies or the people who turn them into druggies. My parents were... deep into some pretty hard stuff, and I saw how it changed them. I hate seeing other people pissing their lives away like that."

My throat constricted. "I'm sorry."

"That's why I didn't want to tell you. Why're you sorry? You didn't do anything."

But it obviously affected him a lot. "I know," I said, struggling to find the right words. "But I'm sorry you had to deal with that. Tell me more about them. You know you can talk to me about anything."

His voice turned teasing again. "Why would I want to talk when I can just do this?"

His fingers trailed downwards to my pussy. My breath caught at the sudden contact. I knew he was trying to distract me, but it was awfully hard to remember why I should mind when he was stroking all kinds of sparks through my nerves with his fingers running over my slit through my jeans. I wanted those fingers inside me.

He obviously wasn't ready to talk. I could respect that. I'd get him to open up to me eventually.

I nudged my head up to kiss him and he met me halfway, pulling my body on top of his. He moved my hips up and down so that his crotch was lined up to mine, taking charge like he always did, and just like that I had no interest in talking anymore either.

11

Mercy

As the engine idled, Kaige drummed his fingers on the steering wheel. "Are you sure this is a good idea?"

"Definitely," I said, scanning the street through the windshield. The mid-day sun blazed over the row of run-down shops, making me grateful for the blast of air conditioning washing over us. "Wylder said I shouldn't leave the van, and I won't. He didn't say anything about the *van* going places."

Kaige snorted and glanced at me sideways. "Somehow I don't think that's because he wanted you driving all over town."

"Well, I'm not driving. You are." I sank back in my seat and checked my phone for any new texts from the people we were supposed to meet. "If Xavier is closing in on me, then it's even more important we find out everything we can about his operations as soon as possible. These guys helped me before—trust me on this."

To my relief, Kaige nodded. It'd taken some coaxing to get him behind the wheel in the first place, but he was committed to my little side-mission now.

Thankfully, his patience didn't need to be tested any longer. Two figures sauntered out of the shadows of an alleyway and headed straight for the van. They climbed in through the back door I'd left unlocked. I twisted in my seat.

"Hey, Kervos," I said, nodding to the bigger guy and then the slimmer one. "Hey, Roy. Thanks for coming out."

The two former Claws members I'd played cards with the other night came over to lean against the back of our seats. "You remembered my name," Roy said with a little laugh. "I got introduced to your dad at least half a dozen times, and he always acted like it was the first."

"Tyrell had a lot more people to keep track of," Kervos grumbled, but he gave me a nod that seemed approving before taking a closer look at the space behind him with its wall of screens and other tech. "Quite the setup you've got here."

"It's not really my van," I admitted. "I don't know how to use all that stuff. We're just relying on our eyes today. You said you know a few businesses the Steel Knights were operating that might still be active?"

"Even in hiding, we hear things," Kervos said.

Roy rubbed his angular chin, darkened with a few days' old scruff. "What do you want to check those out for anyway?"

"If we're going to strike back at the Storm's people most of the Steel Knights seem to have joined up with, we've got to hit them where it'll hurt," I said. "Whatever they're doing to make money, wherever they're stashing supplies."

"Makes sense." Kervos pointed down the street. "The nearest place we can try is a few blocks south and then take a right on Maple Avenue."

Kaige pulled away from the curb and headed south.

Most of the businesses we passed looked like normal stores and restaurants, but that didn't mean they weren't fronts to hide gang activity. Even in the middle of the day, barely anyone was out walking the streets. It was so quiet it made my stomach ache.

How long was it going to take for the Bend to recover, even if we crushed these Storm assholes tomorrow?

A moment after we'd turned the corner, Kervos motioned to a building just down the street. "There. That salon. The Steel Knights had some hookers using the rooms overtop, and they sold stolen merch out of the back sometimes."

Kaige slowed as we cruised by. I spotted the remains of a Steel Knights symbol spray painted in red beside the door, but someone had scrubbed most of it off.

We parked down the street and watched for several minutes. A woman went in through the front doors who was probably just a regular client. Then a couple of guys who didn't look as if they'd had a haircut in at least a year ambled out from the alley that led around back, one of them with a duffel bag slung over his shoulder. The bulge at the back of the other's jeans told me he was carrying a gun.

"There you go," Kervos said, following my gaze.

"They're not wearing the Steel Knights bandanas on their arms," Kaige pointed out.

"Neither were the ones I've seen with the Storm's people before." I frowned. "I guess that makes it even more likely the ones using the salon have gone over to the Storm. Drive around the block so I can get a closer look at it."

Kaige did as I asked, and I jotted some notes about potential access points and the activity we'd seen. I wasn't sure the salon was seeing enough action that cracking down on it would make much impact, but we had to keep our options open.

Next Kervos directed us to a convenience store that turned out to be closed. We watched it for a half an hour without anyone coming or going. That didn't guarantee they were no longer using it, but it obviously wasn't a happening spot.

The butcher shop we checked out next was similarly deserted. Finally, we ended up parked near an old arcade that I remembered had gotten popular with my high school peers a few years back when retro gaming had become cool again.

We'd only been there for a couple of minutes when a truck stopped outside and some men hauled several boxes in through the front door. None of them were wearing bandanas either, but I expected as much now. They had an air about them that told me whatever was in those boxes, it had nothing to do with video games. I caught a flash of a pistol when one guy lifted his arms to close the back of the truck.

"I think any Steel Knight who didn't want to stick around with the

Storm's people got shot for their trouble," Roy said. "They're all or nothing, those guys."

We'd just have to show them what we were capable of when we put all our might into this war.

A few more guys went in and out of the arcade, and I saw movement by one of the upper windows. This place was definitely the most active out of the bunch, which made it the most promising target.

"We'll see what else Gideon can dig up on that spot," I told Kaige as I jotted down a few more notes. "Let's get out of here before they notice us."

"You're really going after these pricks?" Roy asked.

"Somebody's got to. The Bend doesn't belong to them." I shot him a look. "Do you want to stay in hiding for the rest of your life?"

He grimaced. "Okay, I get your point. Well, I hope we helped."

"It's a start. Any news about the Storm himself?" I asked. "Has anyone seen him—or someone they think is him—in the Bend?"

Kervos shook his head. "No sign of him. He seems to operate his entire business through that crazy one, Xavier."

"Keep your eyes and ears peeled for any news about him. He's the one calling the shots. Him and this Red Shark dude."

"Haven't gotten any reports about him either," Kervos said. "They obviously like to hang back while their lackeys do the work."

"There's one more place which we haven't checked out yet," Roy said suddenly.

Kervos glared at him. "We're not going there."

"Going where?" I asked curiously.

"The Storm's people are rumored to have set up their headquarters close to the factory that you blew up a few weeks ago," Roy explained, ignoring Kervos's scowl. There was an awkward pause following his words. Back then, the former Claws members had been fighting for Colt, actively trying to kill me and the Nobles.

"They have their own headquarters here now?" Kaige asked. "The fucker's moving fast."

I gritted my teeth against the sudden wave of anger. Xavier was trying to take the Bend over, hook, line and sinker. "Where is this place?"

"I haven't looked into it myself, but from what I heard, not too far from here," Roy said. "There'll be a lot of Storm people around, though."

Maybe even Xavier himself. I sucked my lower lip under my teeth to worry at it and glanced at Kaige. He caught my expression and glowered at me. "I don't think this is a good idea."

He might be right. But if the Storm's people had established themselves that deeply, I wanted to know what we were up against.

"We'll drive carefully in that general direction," I told Kaige. "If we see too many people on the streets, we can always turn around."

Kaige let out a wordless mutter of protest, but he started the engine. But we'd only made it a few blocks when my gaze caught on a figure on a corner up ahead, and I grabbed Kaige's shoulder. "Stop!"

He swerved over to the curb and parked with a jolt. Kervos and Roy swore where they must have jostled on the bench.

"What's wrong?" Kaige asked, staring at me wide-eyed.

I leaned toward my window, squinting. I definitely hadn't seen wrong. "Axel's up there. A couple of guys are coming over to him. It looks like they're talking."

"Axel?" Kaige bared his teeth and bobbed up in his seat to peer over the parked car in front of us. "What's he doing skulking around here?"

"Who's Axel?" Roy asked from the back.

"One of Ezra Noble's top guys," I said. "He... doesn't like me very much. Maybe he's doing some business for Ezra in the Bend." We couldn't let him see me and Kaige together, that was for sure.

"He might be keeping an eye out for us," Kaige said as if he'd had the same thought. "Or just for you, Mercy. He was asking a lot of questions about whether we'd seen you since you left the mansion."

I watched Axel for a minute longer. He nodded at something one of the guys had said and clapped another on the back. I thought I'd seen those two around the Noble mansion before—lower underlings. One of them had a lightning bolt shaved into his buzz cut on the back of his head.

The three of them definitely weren't a big enough force to be taking on the other gangs. Kaige might be right about his reasons for being here. Axel could have assigned a few of the lesser Noble guys to lurk around hoping to catch us out. Asshole.

"Let's get out of here," I said. "We should probably let Gideon do his magic to find out more about the possible Storm headquarters before we go barging in there anyway."

Kaige gave a relieved sigh and gunned the engine to pull back into the road. But he was distracted enough by Axel that he didn't notice he nearly cut off another driver zipping past us right then.

The other car's horn blared. Kaige hit the gas, and the car swerved around us, but Axel and his two companions had all jerked around to stare in our direction.

Shit. "Go, go, go!" I said, sliding down in my seat so I wouldn't be visible through the windshield.

Kaige jammed on the gas pedal again and spun the wheel. The van lurched forward and spun around. We roared off down the street in the opposite direction.

"Do you think they saw you?" I asked Kaige.

"With all the special stuff Gideon got on these windows, I don't think they'd be able to make out much of anything, and they were still pretty far away," Kaige said. Then he glanced at the rearview mirror. "Fuck, he's jumped into a car to come after us."

"He must have figured anyone who took off like that is up to something," Roy remarked.

My pulse hiccupped. If Axel caught me and Kaige together, all our lives were going to get a hell of a lot harder. "Can you lose him?" I asked Kaige.

"I'll do my best. Hang on!"

Kaige rammed his foot down, and the van roared, throwing me back in my seat. I grabbed the door to steady myself.

The van wasn't built for racing. The engine groaned in protest as we tore down the streets, turning corner after corner. But the white sedan we'd seen Axel get into was matching us turn for turn.

As we sped toward the next turn, a low, grassy embankment came into view ahead of us. A narrow road below it ran parallel with the adjacent street. The embankment was steep, but Kaige made no sign of slowing down or turning. Instead, he pushed the engine even harder, staring straight ahead.

"Kaige," I said. "What are you doing?"

He flashed me a grin. "Losing him. Just trust me and brace yourself."

"Man, you're crazy," Roy said from behind us, but he sounded at least as impressed as he was worried.

"I know," Kaige said just as we hit the curb of the embankment.

The van jerked forward violently. For one instant, we were suspended in the air. I closed my eyes, bracing for the impact.

When it came, the sudden jolt wasn't half as bad as I'd been expecting. My eyes popped open to check the rearview mirror. We were speeding away, leaving all sign of Axel's white sedan in our dust.

Relief coursed through me. Kaige gave a triumphant cheer, and I grinned back at him. Sometimes, a little bit of crazy was good.

After a couple more turns, I realized we'd ended up in a particularly familiar neighborhood. "We're near my old house," I said. "The Steel Knights might still be hanging around there."

Kaige's expression darkened. "Maybe we should give them a run for their money, then."

"Hey, we're not here to get into any fights, remember? Wylder definitely wouldn't forgive me for that."

Something flickered across Kaige's face and vanished. He nodded.

As we cruised by the house, I couldn't help peering out the window at it. I didn't see any men standing guard on the sidewalk nearby, but a couple of guys were standing on the porch. As we passed, two more came out, swaggering like they owned the place.

My teeth gritted. "I guess the Storm's people have totally taken it over now."

Kervos shifted on the bench to get a better view out the back windows. "I don't think those are Storm men. Look at the graffiti outside."

I jerked around in my seat, craning my neck to stare through the tinted glass as the view of my father's house dwindled behind me.

Someone had marked a different red logo on the telephone pole outside the house—a gaping mouth full of pointed teeth.

"Pretty sure that's the Red Shark's guys," Kervos added.

One of the men had looked kind of familiar, hadn't he? Was he one of the Red Shark's people I'd watched fighting with the Storm's forces?

"What would the Red Shark's men be doing at your house?" Kaige asked, his forehead furrowing.

As I settled back into my seat, my stomach sank. "I don't know. Maybe it's one of their wins over the Steel Knights?" But I was pretty sure the Steel Knights had only been watching the house because Colt had hoped to catch me coming there. What possible value could it have to these newcomers?

I wasn't totally sure I wanted to find out the answer to that question.

12

Mercy

WYLDER WAS SCOWLING AT ME, BUT BY NOW I'D PERFECTED the art of ignoring his bad moods. "Going off like that was totally reckless," he said. "I told you to stay put."

"Oh, get over it already," I said, and Anthea tried to muffle a snicker. I motioned to the supplies on the floor of the van by our feet. "We wouldn't have been able to pull off this plan if I hadn't done some scouting."

Anthea fanned herself. "Why don't we go over the last stages of that plan before I melt in here?" We'd turned off the air conditioning while the van was parked so we didn't run down the battery, and it was already getting sweltering inside.

Kaige rolled his shoulders, his expression momentarily tensing as he looked at the bags of Glory that were among our other equipment. "Right. We go in, leave the drugs, get out, and sic the cops on the Storm's people. No big deal."

"It's a little more complicated than that," Gideon said, glancing up from his tablet. We'd already gone over a blueprint of the arcade building, figuring out the best room to target and how we'd enter.

Kaige waved him off. "Details, details."

"We also need to plant the drugs carefully," Rowan said. "It won't do us any good if the Storm's people find the baggies like Mercy did in her apartment and dispose of them before the cops get there. But we don't want them so well-hidden that even the cops can't find them."

Anthea nodded. "I was just getting to that." She motioned to the smallest of the bags. "You want to leave a trail. Just a very light dusting, nothing you can even see. The cops will bring K9 units, and they don't need much to sniff it out. Stash the larger bags somewhere really out of the way, where no human is likely to spot it, and lay down the trail to ensure the dogs will find it. Even better, put the larger bags in different places, each with their own trail, so even if one gets found, you still have a chance."

I clapped my hands. "That's fucking brilliant."

Anthea grinned. "That's what you brought me in on this operation for, isn't it?"

"All right," Gideon said, setting his tablet aside. "We've covered everything. I should get on with my part before the next shift change."

He stood up, his expression typically cool and unfazed, but the flick of his tongue over his lip ring made me suspect he was more nervous than he was letting on. He didn't normally go out to face our enemies so close up.

And he obviously wasn't the only one concerned. Wylder got up too, frowning. "Are you absolutely sure you need to do this on foot? We could park closer to the building—"

Gideon shook his head. "I've taken a careful look at their security system. The device I can use to hack into the alarms only works at a very close range." He cracked a rare smile. "Let's just be glad I don't have to go right inside. Through the wall should work just fine."

It still put him awfully close to all the Storm's men on the other side of that wall. A twinge of my own worry ran through my gut. "You've got your gun?"

He patted the back of his jeans. "I'll be fine. It's about time that I stepped up more and took one for the team like the rest of you do on a regular basis." Determination hardened his voice.

Wylder folded his arms over his chest. "You've done plenty for the team already. You do all kinds of shit we don't know how to."

"You're definitely the brains of this group," Kaige said with a chuckle.

"Well, I'm going to use those brains in closer proximity than usual, that's all." Gideon stepped toward the back doors.

Wylder didn't stop him, even though he still looked tense. He nodded to his best friend. "Give us the signal when you're done and get the hell back here as fast as you can. We'll take care of the rest."

Gideon hopped out into the back alley where we'd stashed the van. It led all the way to the other end of the block and the back of the arcade building. With luck, we wouldn't have to set foot on the street where we could be spotted at all.

As Wylder pulled the door shut, Kaige turned to me. "I'm more worried about Mercy. You're the one who's going to be leaping off of buildings."

I rolled my eyes at him, adding an affectionate nudge of my shoulder. "I've done it a gazillion times. You've *watched* me do it plenty of times. I'll be fine." I'd been using my parkour skills since I was ten, and at this point, I could make the necessary leap with my eyes closed. I checked the knife at my hip and the gun at my back, and refastened the laces of my shoes to make sure they were secure, finally adding a pat of my childhood bracelet for luck.

"*You* need to actually stay put this time," Wylder reminded Kaige. "No charging into the fray unless we get into a real fight. Otherwise, you're just keeping watch."

Kaige brought his fist to his chest in a salute. "Got it."

We popped the buds into our ears so we'd be able to hear any warning Kaige gave us, and he put on the inobtrusive mic Gideon had fixed to look like a wristwatch. Just as I was tightening my ponytail, a message flashed across the screen in the center of the array of displays. ALL CLEAR.

Rowan reached for the door. "That's our cue."

The four of us other than Anthea spilled out into the evening shadows and set off in different directions, other than Wylder and Rowan heading down the alley toward the back of the arcade together.

Kaige ambled over to where he could see down the street from the mouth of one lane, and I scrambled up onto a dumpster that put me in jumping reach of a fire escape. I clambered up the metal rungs onto the rooftop of a building on the opposite side of the alley.

Most of the stores were right next to each other with no gap in between, giving me an easy jog across the roof tiles and shingles. I had to make a couple of sprints to hurl myself over laneways, but I landed easily both times, the impact radiating through my legs and exhilarating me. Parkour was the closest I'd ever get to flying.

As I came up parallel with the arcade building, the warm breeze played with my ponytail. I eyed the open window we'd already spotted and the ridges on the wall around it, and rubbed my hands together. The room on the other side was dark, which meant it was probably empty. No problem.

I took a running start and launched myself off the roof toward the window. The air whipped past me, and I heard a faint sound below me that was probably one of my guys, watching. My fingers caught on the top of the protruding window frame, and I automatically shifted my position so my feet hit the window ledge with more of a light thump than a heavy smack.

I held myself there for several seconds, listening for any disturbance inside. When nothing reached my ears, I bent down and slipped through the opening. My sneakers made only a faint scuffling sound on the floor inside.

I'd come into a room some of the men must have been crashing in overnight. Sleeping bags and a few cots stood around the space, and the smell of sweat in the air made me wrinkle my nose. There was no sign of any of the Storm's people around right now.

I crept to the door and eased it open. Voices carried faintly from a room at the other end of the second floor, but no one was in the hall. The stairs we'd seen on the blueprint stood just to my right. I slunk down them as quickly as I could.

At the base of the stairs, I had to pause, flattening myself against the wall with my heart thudding, as footsteps traveled by in a nearby hall. When they'd faded away, I darted to the storage room we'd identified and ducked inside.

It was dark too, but I didn't want to risk discovery by turning on the main lights. I got out my phone and flicked on its flashlight to cast a thin illumination over the space.

Several dusty defunct arcade machines stood in a couple of rows against one wall. The others held shelves stuffed with boxes, and a few large crates had been pushed up against the arcade machines. I'd be willing to bet at least some of them held stolen property. Maybe we'd get the Storm's people on charges other than drug possession.

I made my way to the back door and unlocked it. Wylder and Rowan hustled inside. Wylder gave my arm a quick squeeze. "You're a fucking superhero, Kitty Cat," he whispered.

"How many men are inside?" Rowan asked, pulling the baggies of Glory out of the rucksack he was carrying.

"At least a few upstairs and several down here," I said. "I managed to avoid all of them. Hard to be sure when there's a bit of a racket from the actual arcade too."

"Well, let's stash this stuff." Wylder glanced around in the dimness. "I'll wedge one behind those machines over there. They don't look like they've been touched in years."

I grabbed a baggie from Rowan. "I'll do one of the crates."

Rowan hefted his own. "Under the shelves seems out of the way enough."

We split up again to put our contraband in place. Then Rowan opened up the smaller baggie and we each took a small handful. I smeared the powder on the concrete floor so it disappeared into the rough surface in a line leading to the crate I'd picked and up the wooden side. We brought our trails together in the middle of the room and left a wider trail leading to the back door. Wylder wiped traces around the door frame for good measure.

"No dog's going to miss that unless it's lost its nose."

Just then, Kaige's voice crackled through my earphones. "A car just pulled up out front—a bunch of guys are getting out, carrying some stuff. They might be heading back to where you are."

"Good thing we're already done," Wylder murmured. We hustled out the door and shut it firmly behind us. If the Storm's guys noticed it was unlocked, hopefully they'd blame each other's carelessness. They had no reason to assume anyone had been inside.

At least, they wouldn't have had any. We'd only just stepped away from the door when a couple of figures appeared from a laneway a few buildings away. In the light of a security lamp over them, I immediately recognized one of them from the Steel Knights.

Unfortunately, he recognized us too. "It's the Katz girl!" he snapped, yanking at his partner. "And the Noble heir. They were fucking with our stuff!"

I glanced wildly at Wylder and Rowan and knew we'd all come to the same conclusion in an instant. There was no way we could let these guys live, or they'd give away our plan. We had to take them down before they alerted the Storm's people inside the building.

"What the hell were you doing in there?" the Steel Knight guy demanded, raising his gun as he marched toward us.

None of us bothered to answer. We threw ourselves at them, aiming to get all the advantage we could out of a little bit of surprise.

I drew my knife as I charged, more comfortable with the blade than my gun in close combat. Wylder pulled one of his own out of his pocket. "No shots fired," he hissed—the sound might bring their colleagues running. Then he slammed his knife straight at the guy with the gun.

He only managed to slash the guy's wrist, but deep enough that the Steel Knight dropped his gun. I kicked it away and then aimed a roundhouse at his partner, who'd grabbed at me. My kick to his gut sent him stumbling backward into Rowan, who clocked him in the temple with a swift fist.

Wylder tried to knock the first guy to the ground, but the Steel Knight fought back savagely. He landed a punch to Wylder's face that split the Noble heir's lip and clipped his shoulder when Wylder ducked. I threw myself in behind him, knocking the legs out from under the Steel Knight. As he stumbled, Wylder was on him, plunging his knife straight into the guy's heart.

Rowan had been facing off with the other guy. I turned to see him aiming several quick, vicious strikes at his opponent's head. His eyes were bright with a sort of wildness I'd never seen in him before.

It distracted me for just a moment, so I wasn't totally ready when the guy he was fighting flung himself away from Rowan and straight into me. His fist rammed into my ribs, and his greater weight sent me tumbling to the ground with him on top.

He groped for his own gun. I squirmed against him, flinging elbows and knees, and he slammed my head back so hard that stars of pain exploded behind my eyes.

My attacker wrenched his gun around, aiming it right at my face—and then his head jerked to the side with a gush of hot blood all over me.

I gasped and gagged, whipping my head away even as the metallic taste seeped into my mouth. The man slumped over me. The ragged end of a broken plywood board dug halfway through his neck, practically decapitating him. What the—

My gaze focused on the figure standing over us. Rowan was breathing hard, his mouth set in a grim smile. As I watched, he jabbed the board even deeper into the guy's neck. Any lingering struggle went out of the body as it collapsed completely. On me.

Wylder yanked at the guy's arm, and I scrambled out from under the body. The Noble heir gave the scene a softly approving whistle and nodded at Rowan. "Make use of whatever you can get your hands on. Very creative. I like it."

A glint of triumph lit in Rowan's eyes for just a second before they caught mine. His gaze darted away, his expression turning suddenly uncomfortable.

I swiped at my face with my hands. My fingers were already sticky with blood. My shirt wasn't going to be much help either, since it was practically drenched with the stuff. I restrained a shudder.

"You okay?" Rowan asked, his voice oddly stiff.

"Yeah. Just... bloody." I pulled my soaked shirt away from my torso and grimaced. "At least none of it's mine."

We looked down at the two bodies sprawled in the alley.

"We can't leave this mess behind," Wylder said. "We'll drag them to the dumpster and get them out of the way until my contacts can dispose of them completely."

He clapped Rowan on the shoulder. "Nice work. I've always been able to count on you to do whatever it takes." Wylder shot a grin at me. "You should have seen him when a bunch of assholes thought they'd get one over on me back in high school. Finlay here practically tore them apart, didn't stop even when they'd nearly gutted him. That's why I took him on."

"You know I've got your back," Rowan said, but he was still avoiding my gaze. This obviously wasn't the time to find out what was bothering him, though. We had a couple of dead jerks to take care of.

I bent down and grabbed the thinner one's wrists. "Let's get moving before anyone else shows up to join the party."

13

Mercy

THE VAN PULLED UP JUST AS WE REACHED THE END OF THE laneway where Wylder had texted the others to meet us. The back door swung open to reveal Anthea's grim smile. "Need a ride?"

We clambered in to meet her and Gideon. Kaige craned his neck from where he'd taken the driver's seat, and his jaw dropped. "What the hell happened to you, Mercy?"

I glanced down at my blood-drenched clothes, feeling the tacky sensation of the smeared splatters drying on my face, and grimaced. "We ran into a little trouble. Somehow that seems to end with me covered in blood a whole lot more often than I'd prefer."

"Me too," Kaige muttered darkly. "You took care of the bastards?"

"It's all under control." Wylder waved him back toward the wheel. "Now let's get out of here."

Rowan turned to Gideon, who was taking me in with a tight expression. "Has there been any sign that the guys in the arcade realized something was up?"

Gideon's gaze jerked back to his tablet and then the screens on the van's wall, some of which were showing traffic and security cam feeds. "No unusual activity. I think we're good."

I let out my breath in a huff. "I guess we'll find out when we sic the police on them."

"Let's just take a look with our own eyes," Kaige said, turning the van toward the arcade.

"Kaige!" Wylder protested.

The other guy shot him a defiant look. "I'll cruise by quickly. We should be sure this isn't going to backfire on us, right?"

Our attempts to trick our enemies had gone sideways before. Wylder scowled, but he made a gesture for his friend to keep going.

The van turned the corner and headed along the street with the arcade. Kaige slowed just a tad as we approached the building. Gideon held up his tablet to record the scene. All of us held our breaths, but to my relief, everything seemed quiet, no noticeable activity.

"I imagine there would be quite a ruckus if they found the drugs or any of us meddling with their business," Anthea murmured.

Just as we passed by, three men came out of the arcade. Two of them I recognized as Storm men from my past observations, but the other one—

"That's one of Axel's guys," I said, frowning as we left them behind.

Wylder's head jerked around. "What?"

"You remember Kaige and I told you that we crossed paths with Axel and a couple of his men yesterday. One of those guys was with the Storm's people at the arcade." The young dude with the lightning bolt in his buzz cut—it wasn't exactly a common hairstyle.

"What would he be doing with those assholes?" Kaige demanded.

"Keep driving," Wylder told him. "To the new apartment. We'll sort it out." He beckoned Gideon over to the bench and sat down on it hard. "You got them on camera, right?"

Gideon nodded. I sank down at his other side as he brought up the footage. The three guys ambled out, and I pointed to the one I'd seen with Axel. When he turned his head, the shaved lightning bolt was clearly visible at the back of his head. "Him."

Wylder paused the video and studied the screen. "I have seen him around the mansion at least a few times. He must be one of the newer recruits mostly working under Axel."

"Why would he be hanging out with the Storm's people, then?" I asked.

Anthea rubbed her mouth. "I suppose there are a few different explanations."

"My father vets people pretty carefully," Wylder said. "This is probably part of one of his operations—send the guy in undercover to dig up information on the Storm's resources before the Nobles launch a full attack."

That did make sense, but my sense of uneasiness didn't leave me. "Well... keep a close eye on him if you see him around again, just in case."

Wylder tugged on my ponytail, which had managed to escape the bloody spray. "We'll take care of anything that needs taking care of, Kitty Cat. Now let's get you to your new apartment so you can get cleaned up."

Kaige drove us deeper into the Bend. The three-story building he pulled around back of was more run-down than the first place they'd stashed me, but I didn't need anything posh.

"Sorry," Wylder said, wrinkling his nose as we tramped up the steps in a stairwell that smelled like stale beer.

"It's fine," I said. "If it wasn't for you guys, I'd be sleeping in an abandoned warehouse or something."

"It was the best I could find where I was sure no one would notice the sudden occupation," Gideon said, scanning the hall we came out into.

The apartment itself was a bachelor, the whole thing about the same size as just the living room and kitchen in the other place. A plain bed stood at one end—"I changed the sheets for you," Anthea murmured to me. A shabby love seat squatted in the middle, and a table that'd only seat two stood in front of a short stretch of counter, fridge, and stove that looked like they'd been transported out of the '70s.

I glanced into the bathroom and found that it held only a cramped shower stall squeezed next to the toilet. At least the showerhead emitted decently warm water. I grabbed soap and shampoo out of my bag and headed in. "Time to get all traces of this dead asshole off me."

Rowan took out his phone. "I'll leave the anonymous tip to the cops about the arcade. If we're lucky, they'll get it taken care of tonight."

As I scrubbed myself off in the shower stall, scarlet swirled into the water around my feet. I worked shampoo through my thick hair two times and even gargled with soapy water a few times. The I rubbed more soap all over me again and again until the water ran totally clear. I stepped out to grab a fresh change of clothes in a much better mood that wasn't at all dampened by the mildew creeping along the grout between the tiles.

When I came back out, Anthea was just finishing unloading a couple of bags of groceries into the kitchen cupboards. Gideon glanced at me over the top of his tablet. "I've got the new cameras up and running. I'm trying an experimental program that will hopefully alert me if a form similar to Xavier's moves past them. I'll probably get a lot of false alarms, but better that than missing him."

I went over and gave him a quick kiss on the cheek. "I already feel better knowing you'll be watching over me."

Rowan ran his hand through his hair, meeting my gaze and then jerking his away. "Everything's set up with the cops," he said.

Something was definitely bugging him. I didn't think he was likely to tell me in front of the other guys, though. Rowan had worked very hard to present a certain kind of image in his new role. I wasn't going to try to undermine that, not when I understood where he was coming from so well now.

Gideon cleared his throat. "Are we going to continue having someone with Mercy at all times? I could take this shift."

I grinned at him. "As much fun as I'm sure we'd have, I think it's actually Rowan's turn."

Rowan startled, but he quickly caught himself. "All right," he said, looking solemn. "I didn't have anything to take care of back at the mansion tonight."

Wylder looked from him to me with a speculative expression, but thankfully he didn't let his possessive prick do the talking. "Sounds like everything's settled. The rest of us had better move out before anyone starts wondering too much about where we've been." He leaned in to claim a quick but demanding kiss. "We'll be seeing you soon."

"I'm counting on it," I said, swatting him.

As she headed out with the guys, Anthea squeezed my shoulder. "Rest up. You need it after today."

No kidding. All the running around from the last couple of days was beginning to catch up with me. My body ached from being constantly on the alert.

Anthea had left a bottle of what looked like nice wine along with the food, I couldn't help noticing. When everyone had left, I grabbed that and a glass out of the cupboard. I was going to need a little help relaxing.

"Do you want anything?" I called over my shoulder to Rowan.

"No," he said, his voice oddly tight. "I'm fine."

When I looked over at him, he was pacing the room, his gaze averted. I took a sip of the wine I'd poured and went over to join him. He stopped when I reached him, but his posture stayed tensed.

Whatever was bothering him, it'd started with the fight in the alley. I cocked my head, waiting until he met my eyes. "You know, you were pretty impressive out there tonight."

He raised his eyebrows. "You think so?"

"Yeah. I mean, it's not how I'd have pictured you when I knew you before, but that's understandable. You've changed a lot since then."

Rowan's mouth twisted. "I have. More than you've even seen yet. You know as well as anyone that you can't get into this kind of life—can't survive it—without a certain amount of ruthlessness."

"Well, maybe that's not totally different," I said. "You let the ruthless side of you come out to protect me. I know you'd have done whatever you could to defend me back when we were teenagers too."

A new intensity came into his deep blue eyes. "I'd have done anything for you, Mercy. You're right. That one thing hasn't changed."

Something in his tone sent an eager quiver right down to my pussy, but I didn't think we'd gotten to the heart of the matter yet.

"Not just that," I said, and went to my bag to dig out the little sketch of the kitten he'd drawn for me. "There's a lot of the Rowan I fell in love with in this too."

But when I held it up, he shook his head, tearing his gaze away from me again. "You can't go by that. Everything went to hell the night Carina's friend was murdered in our house. I brought the threat to our family. I knew I had to do something—make myself into someone—who could protect them too." He let out a rough laugh. "But my family fell apart anyway, and the guy you knew might as well be dead."

I grasped his arm. "I don't think that's true, Rowan. Going through shit like that hardens you, but it doesn't have to take you over completely—and I can tell that it hasn't. I know I was harsh on you when I first came to the Nobles, but that was only because I didn't understand why you vanished on me. There's nothing *wrong* with who you are now. And that guy can still make me smile with some pen on paper." I waggled the sketch.

Rowan winced. "That's the most I've really drawn in years," he admitted. "I still get the urge, but… It doesn't feel like it fits with the life I'm living now. How can I even deserve to enjoy trying to make something… something beautiful or whatever when I'm also the kind of person who'll destroy a person's life by hacking his neck in half with a piece of plywood?"

Now we were getting somewhere. "You did what you had to do," I said. "You can't blame yourself for that."

"I know. I don't. That's the point. They were the enemy, and we needed to take them down by whatever means necessary. I can't apologize for it, because I'd do it over again if I had to."

I ran my thumb up and down his forearm. "I'm not asking you to apologize."

"But maybe you should." He raised his head, his eyes somehow fierce and sad at the same time. "The guy you loved is gone. Something… something's broken in me. I thought I was protecting my little sister by joining up with the Nobles, but I've become someone I don't even trust around her anymore in case I scare her somehow. That's just how it is, but that doesn't mean—" He cut himself off and exhaled sharply. "That doesn't mean I like you seeing it."

A sudden rush of affection hit me. That was the most Rowan-like sentiment I'd ever heard, even if he didn't recognize it.

I tugged him closer to me, gazing up at him. "You know what?

Seeing you like that doesn't make me like you any less. Maybe I even like you more. I'm sure I'm broken in all kinds of ways most people wouldn't understand. But you can now. I don't have to hide anything from you—and you don't have to hide anything from me."

"Mercy," Rowan said roughly. Heat lit in his eyes, but he held himself still as if he was afraid of what would happen if he let himself move.

I reached up to touch his cheek. "You were a total badass out there tonight, as brutal as you needed to be. But I think—I *know*—you can still be tender. If you can still find beauty in things, then of course you deserve to let your other talents shine. You can be more than one thing, and I'll enjoy all of them."

I eased up on my toes, giving him enough time to move away if he didn't want this after all. My body was already burning with just a few inches between us. Rowan let out a strangled sound and dropped his head to meet my kiss.

Despite everything he'd been telling me, our kiss was pure honey, sweet but intoxicating. His hands came up to cradle my face. His tongue traced the seam of my lips and coaxed them apart, and I melted into him.

I tugged him over to the loveseat. Rowan moved with me without breaking the kiss, lowering himself with me and lining his body above me as if we were picking up exactly where we'd left off five years ago.

I liked his weight on me. I ran my fingers over his short-cropped hair, enjoying the softness of the tufts. Rowan grazed his teeth over my bottom lip before sucking on it. I groaned, and he slipped his hot tongue back into my mouth.

Making out with him was so familiar but at the same time a rush of a new experience. I could sense the new confidence and fierceness in him.

But like I'd assured him, that ferocity didn't take away his capacity for gentleness. He left my mouth to kiss a slow trail down the side of my neck, soft and reverent, as if he were worshipping my body. I found myself flashing back to the first time we'd slept together, when he'd worked over my cunt with his mouth until I'd come and then entered me when I was so slick and eager I didn't feel more than a pinch of pain.

In the present, I yanked his collared shirt, impatient for the feel of his newly hardened muscles against me. Why the hell had we waited so long to get back to this?

When I traced my hands over Rowan's bare chest, he groaned. "I missed you so much. No one else could ever compare to you. It feels like a miracle to have you back."

"I missed you too," I murmured, my throat tightening as I realized just how much I had. He'd been the only gentle thing I'd had in my life, and maybe I'd needed that. Needed someone *I* could be tender with, not always putting on a tough front. Rowan had given me room to discover a side of myself that wasn't always on the defensive.

He drew my T-shirt over my head and gazed down at me. The bra I was wearing was plain, but he looked at me as if I was the most amazing sight he'd ever seen.

"You're so beautiful," he whispered. "You always were, but somehow you've gotten even more gorgeous."

Emotion swept through me. I pulled him close again, tucking my legs around his hips so he had no choice but to lean into me. He rocked against me with a rhythm that brought a moan to my lips that he caught with a kiss. His deft artist's hands removed my bra with a few tugs and closed over my breasts.

He caressed them until pleasure was flowing all across my chest and then dipped his head to catch one of the peaks between his lips. He twisted the other nipple, provoking a sharper jolt of bliss. I gasped, arching into him.

"Fuck," Rowan muttered. His hand dropped to the fly of my jeans. We squirmed against each other as he peeled those off and I undid his. When he pulled back to kick them off completely, I made a disgruntled sound at the loss of contact.

Rowan chuckled and lowered himself back over me, but not before I noted the outline of his rigid cock straining against his boxers. My mouth watered. I wanted him so bad.

I sat up, meaning to devour him in the best possible way, but Rowan shook his head and eased me back down with a sweetly sly smile. "I don't know if I can make up for the five years I left you on your own, but I'm going to give it my best shot. Tonight is all about you, Mercy."

He tugged my panties down. Before I could argue, he'd curled his finger inside me. My head tipped back with a moan. He pumped the finger in and out of me slowly at first before adding another and another, gradually filling me, stroking my clit with his thumb.

Did I deserve this kind of sweet devotion? It was kind of hard to believe it, but I couldn't see stopping him either. If Rowan thought I deserved it, if it made him this happy to cherish me like this, it couldn't be *wrong*, could it?

"So wet for me," Rowan said, his voice rough. He brought his fingers, now coated in my pussy juices, to his lips and licked them off one by one. "I've missed your taste too, Mer."

At his words, something unraveled in me. I was hungry for him, the kind of hunger I had buried deep inside me for years. But no longer.

I pulled him down, and our mouths met again, open with teeth and tongues. Reaching beneath the waist of his boxers, I curled my fingers around his swollen cock. With a guttural sound, he grabbed at his pants and retrieved a condom from his wallet. As he stared down at me, his eyes growing hooded with lust, something shifted in his pose and his expression.

"Put it on me," he said, his voice quiet but commanding at the same time, so passionate it sent a giddy jolt straight to my pussy.

I peered at him through my eyelashes and gave his dick a few more forceful strokes. I did love the darker side of him too, just as much as his sweetness. "Let me have it then," I murmured, holding out my hand.

I tore open the packet and rolled the condom over him. Rowan's eyes closed for a moment at the sensation, and then he nudged my thighs apart to settle his hips between them. There was barely space for the both of us on the loveseat, but neither of us cared.

He gave me a finger to suck on which I did obediently. When I was done, he slid that inside me. I gasped quietly, my hips rising as his fingers explored my wet pussy. He watched me carefully, his eyes transfixed by my reactions.

As Rowan brought me close to my peak, he hesitated for just an instant with a hint of a question in his gaze. I gave him the smallest of nods, and just like that he withdrew his fingers and thrust his cock into me all the way to the hilt. Pleasure rushed through my body.

I clutched him, rocking my hips to meet his powerful rhythm. Our sexual exploits before had never felt quite this intense. My pussy clenched around his dick as he continued to stroke in and out of me. Every nerve in my body seemed to be quaking, ready to embrace my release alongside him.

He put his arms around my head as if to cocoon me in his embrace. "You have me, and I have you," he said, breathless but determined. "I'm never leaving you again, Mercy."

The words, both possessive and loving, sent me spiraling closer to the edge. I wrapped my legs around his waist to pull him even closer, needing all of him that I could get.

Rowan circled his hips to hit a sweet spot inside of me that made me gasp in turn. Sensing that I was close to exploding, he increased his pace, his thrusts becoming erratic as he pumped in and out of me. A groan reverberated from deep in his lungs.

The feel of it where our chests met made us jerk against each other harder, our naked bodies slapping together, and a blazing orgasm tore through me. Rowan followed me right after, bucking into his release, and his last thrust tipped me over the edge once more.

Our bodies collided and melded together. We lay panting in each other's arms, his weight almost crushing me, but I didn't want to move. I wanted to stay like this for weeks on end, tucked in the heat of his embrace.

Maybe this moment had been inevitable. I was totally tangled up with all four of my guys now. And they *were* mine. I couldn't imagine ever giving this up, no matter what Ezra Noble had to say about it.

14

Mercy

Wylder came into the apartment with a scowl I was starting to think had become permanently plastered to his face. "Hey," he said gruffly, tugging me to him for a quick kiss, so I didn't think his bad mood was anything to do with me this time. But as he flopped down on the loveseat, his expression didn't lighten.

I glanced toward Kaige and Gideon, who'd come in after him. "What's up with him?"

Gideon sat down at the little table, setting his laptop on it. "Wylder's convinced Axel saw us leave."

"He's getting too hard to avoid, the way he's keeping an eye on us," Wylder grumbled. "Like he hasn't got better things to do."

"Even if he did notice us heading out, he can't know where we've gone," Gideon said in a matter-of-fact voice. "I checked carefully across our entire—very roundabout—route. There's no way he could have followed us all the way without me noticing."

"Right," Kaige said, slinging his brawny arm around my waist. "And Axel's being Axel. He's all talk, no action."

"I'm not so sure this time," Wylder said. Agitation was clear on his face. He sprang off the loveseat again to peer out the window, but I already knew it offered nothing but an up-close view of the brick wall of the office building next door.

Rowan came out of the shower, rubbing a towel over his hair, which was even spikier when damp. I smiled at him, resisting the urge to go over and run my fingers through it, and he grinned back. Whatever tension that'd remained between us had completely vanished. A flare of heat shot through me at the memory of his cock buried deep inside me.

But I wasn't going to be led around by my pussy when we had bigger issues at hand. "What happened with the arcade? Did the cops crack down on the Storm's people?"

Gideon grimaced. "There's good news and bad news. Police followed up on the tip and raided the business. They confiscated the drugs and took the men on site in."

"And the bad news?"

"The Storm's overall drug operation doesn't seem to have been significantly affected. They're still dealing it out on the streets—we saw people on a few corners when we were driving in today, blatant as ever."

Kaige grunted. "At least it should get the cops off *our* backs about Glory now that they've got clear proof of these other guys dealing."

"And we weren't going to topple the Storm overnight." I rubbed my hand over my mouth. "What about the Red Shark's people? Have they been up to anything new?" The image floated up in the back of my mind of the gaping jaws spray-painted on the telephone pole outside my old house.

"I actually wanted to talk to you about that," Gideon said, his fingers flying over the laptop's keyboard. "A few days ago, I was able to place bugs near a couple of places where we've seen the Red Shark's people getting together. I've recorded several conversations since then. None of them have revealed anything we could use against them, but I did hear something that gave me pause. Since you know the Bend best, I'd like to hear what you make of it."

I squeezed Kaige's arm and stepped away from him to sit down at the table across from Gideon. He ramped up the volume and hit play.

There was a faint scratching noise, followed by static. Then a man's voice filtered through the tiny speakers. "Quiet night, huh?"

"Color me relieved. Maybe we won't have to risk our guts being blown out for once," said a second guy. They obviously had no idea anyone was recording them.

"Damn right, man. This place...it's not as quiet as it looks. I definitely didn't expect us to get this kind of pushback."

"Neither did the boss, I think," another one said. "He would have thought twice before coming in."

"Hell, yeah. The invitation we got might as well have been torn to pieces before we even showed up. I don't know why we even bothered coming when the people who sent it have been taken out of the picture. What's the point in sticking around? Especially when we're dealing with that psycho the Storm has on his payroll."

The other guy made a derisive sound, but I could hear the nervousness in his voice. "Yeah, his own fucking men are afraid of him."

"I say we should get the hell out of here before things get worse, but who the hell will listen to me?"

Gideon paused the recording and glanced at me. "What do you think?"

I shook my head, reeling from what I'd just heard. "Someone invited the Red Shark into the Bend? Why would anyone do that?"

"Colt invited the Storm, as far as we can tell," Wylder pointed out from where he was still staked out by the window. "Maybe someone didn't like how much he was taking over and wanted to balance the scales."

By turning this place into a full-out bloodbath? I winced. "I'm not sure I agree with their strategy."

"But whoever called them in, they're gone now," Rowan said, frowning. "Who's been 'taken out' who was a major player here other than Colt and your father?"

"No one I can think of." It couldn't have been Dad, right? He hadn't even known what Colt was planning before he'd died, or he'd never have walked into that restaurant for the rehearsal dinner in the first place. "Maybe... Maybe Colt brought them in too? He figured he and Xavier would have crushed the Nobles by now, and he could get the Red Shark's people to clash with the Storm and they'd destroy each other, leaving everything for him?"

Gideon ran his thumb over his lip ring. "It's possible, but I'm not sure I can see him planning anything that risky and complex."

Me neither. But then, Colt had gotten pretty crazed in the last few weeks before his death. Who knew what all had been going on in his head?

"Or could it have been someone lower down in the Steel Knights—or the Claws?" Kaige asked. "Someone who was pissed off about what Colt was doing?"

"They wouldn't have had much authority to orchestrate some kind of invasion," Wylder said.

Rowan cocked his head. "They wouldn't necessarily have needed it if they put on a good enough front. They might even have pretended to be someone else, and they're not dead after all."

"Yeah." A shiver ran down my back. If people had been working behind the scenes to bring in not just one but two different gangs we'd never heard of, who else might turn up next? "I guess it doesn't matter all that much now."

"That's what I said." Wylder marched back toward us and slapped his hand on the back of the loveseat. "It sounds like the Red Shark's people are already considering leaving. The Storm is obviously the bigger threat. I figure we should go out and mess with them some more today."

Yes. At the thought of taking some kind of action, as vague as it was right now, my back straightened and my resolve steadied me. It didn't matter where these assholes had come from or why—we were going to kick their butts right back to where they belonged. "Sounds good to me. Where are we headed?"

He tossed his car key in his hand. "Like Gideon said, we spotted a few of them out on the streets on our way in. Let's drive around a bit, find the biggest fish, and see if they can lead us to someone even bigger. We want to hit them where it'll hurt even more next time."

We tramped down the steps and into the fresh evening air. Wylder got into the driver's seat of the van. Kaige followed him, and Gideon sat down on the bench to scan the video feeds, Rowan joining him. I stood behind the front seats, peering through the windshield as Wylder pulled out of the alley where he'd parked.

"There's a skatepark about ten blocks that way," I said, pointing. "It's always been a popular spot for dealing."

"We'll check that out first, then," Wylder said.

We cruised by the concrete ramps and stopped where we had a decent view of the park. The streetlamps had flickered on to cut through the deepening shadows with a yellow glow.

A couple of guys were standing at the edge of one of those pools of light, their hands in their pockets, looking shifty. No skateboards, either. I peered around and spotted the edge of a duffle bag poking from where they'd tucked it away behind a nearby bench.

"That's probably where their stash is," I said, motioning to it. "Looks like they brought a lot. They must be planning on doing a lot of business tonight."

"We should keep an eye on things," Wylder said. "Once they start bringing in a decent amount of cash, they'll be handing it off to someone. When that happens, we follow those guys to wherever the money's going. Get closer to the heart of their operations."

"Right," Kaige said, leaning forward in his seat, his gaze intent on the dealers.

Wylder nudged him. "We're *only* watching. Not engaging. At least not until I give the word."

Kaige nodded, but it was hard to tell how much he was really listening.

Wylder tuned the radio to a rock station, and wailing guitars filled the van's interior. As Gideon tapped away on his laptop, the screens mounted around us wavered to show views from traffic and surveillance cameras from around the neighborhood. "I'll give you a shout if I see anyone who looks likely heading this way."

But the only people who turned up during the next half hour were customers. As I'd suspected, the dealers knew they'd picked a good spot. Several people on their own or in pairs wandered by as if they just happened to be taking a walk that way, but stopped briefly to chat with the sketchy-looking men. Cash and baggies of pale gray powder changed hands.

"It's definitely Glory," Kaige muttered. "Fucking Xavier."

"I've been hearing more and more reports from people I know on the streets," Rowan said. "It's getting increasingly popular. Unfortunately, I think their stunt at the waterfront property paid off."

Kaige just growled at that.

I was just rolling the tension out of my shoulders when a few kids who looked around eleven or twelve showed up with skateboards at the far end of the park. They pushed off, the wheels of their boards rattling loud enough that I could hear it through the walls of the van when the next song petered out. The kids laughed and cheered each other on as one and then another hurtled across the curved surface, turning a few tricks that weren't too far off from my parkour skills.

"They're pretty good," I said, just as Kaige snarled, "What the fuck?"

The dealers were sauntering closer to where the kids were riding. When one of the boys stepped off to the side to catch his breath, the men sidled even closer and started speaking to him. The kid looked a bit taken aback, his shoulders coming up, but he raised his chin, putting on a tough front like everyone learned to pretty early on in the Bend.

His friends came over to see what was going on. One of the dealers fished a small baggie out of his pocket and dangled it briefly before closing his fingers to hide it against his palm. My stomach twisted.

Wylder had tensed in his seat. "Pricks," he hissed, but he stayed in his seat. "When we're ready, they're going to regret coming into our city so fucking much."

"What do you mean, 'when we're ready'?" Kaige demanded. The veins on his neck looked ready to pop. "Don't you see what they're doing? Those monsters are trying to give drugs to literal babies."

"The kids don't look all that impressed," Rowan said reasonably. "They'll probably turn it down."

Kaige smacked the dashboard. "How smart were you at that age, huh?"

He had a point. Curiosity might get the better of them, and who knew what other bad choices that could lead to. That was exactly what the dealers were counting on. Get them hooked before they had enough experience to know better. My fingers tightened around the back of the seat, my knuckles whitening.

"It's not our problem," Wylder said in a strained voice.

Then one of the kids stretched out his arm, and the dealer moved to put the baggie in his hand.

"Fuck this!" Kaige shouted, and threw the door open. Before any of us could stop him, he was charging into the skate park.

"Shit," Wylder mumbled, fumbling for his own door.

"Kaige!" I yelled after him, but he didn't even slow down.

Rowan and I scrambled out the back. Kaige was bearing down on the drug dealers, who'd jerked apart from each other, staring at him.

"Fucking cowards, what do you think you're doing giving drugs to kids?" Kaige yelled. "I'm going to break every bone in your bodies one by one."

The men must have been able to tell they didn't stand a chance against Kaige's hulking form, even two against one. Their eyes widened, and they took off in opposite directions. The preteens gaped as Kaige barged through their midst, chasing down the guy who'd offered the baggie to the kids.

"Get back here, you fucking animal," he hollered. "You're a big enough man to ruin people's lives, but not to get what you deserve?"

We raced after him. "Kaige!" Wylder snapped. "Let him go. You're going to ruin what we're trying to do here. This isn't how we stop them."

Kaige just pounded on across the park in pursuit of the dealer. I sucked in a ragged breath, pushing my legs harder, and added my own voice. "Kaige, please, listen to me. It's over. The kids are okay. Just—stop. Please."

My final plea penetrated whatever haze of rage was gripping him. Kaige slowed and came to a stop. He stared after the dealer, who'd vanished around the side of one of the ramps, and then back at us, his expression almost bewildered.

I caught up with him and grabbed his arm. "Thank you. It's okay. It's over."

He peered down at me, and his voice came out choked up. "He was going to—"

"I know," I said. "But he didn't, and he's gone now."

"And now we've got to get out of here before he brings a ton of his friends down on us," Wylder added from beside me.

I tugged Kaige's arm, and he came with us back to the van. The kids had fled, leaving us alone. Kaige's jaw worked, but Wylder raised his hand. "Don't say anything. You fucked up our whole plan."

"I couldn't just sit there and do nothing!"

"Yes, you fucking could. For once in your life—"

Wylder cut himself off, stopping in his tracks. As Kaige and I followed his gaze, Kaige froze too. My heart stuttered.

We'd almost reached the sidewalk, but down the street, half a block from the van, an all-too-familiar car had just come to a stop. I recognized Axel's tattooed scalp through the windshield before he climbed out.

"Hello, boys," he sneered, his gaze fixing on me. "What do we have here?"

Wylder grasped my elbow and yanked me close. "Mercy," he said, low and more urgent than I'd ever heard him. "Get the fuck out of here. *Now.*"

I stared at him, every particle of my body protesting the idea of leaving them to face the music alone. "But—"

"*Go!*" he repeated as Axel strode toward us. A couple more guys were getting out of the car behind him. "I don't know what will happen if Axel manages to take you back to Dad."

I couldn't mistake the fear in his voice. He knew his father and Axel way better than I did. Maybe it should be his call.

My hands clenched at my sides, but *I* was afraid of what Wylder might do if I stayed and he felt he had to defend me right here and now. Shit.

I gave him and Kaige one last, apologetic glance, and just this once, followed Wylder's orders. Spinning around, I took off in the opposite direction as fast as my feet would carry me, regret burning a hole in my gut.

15

Wylder

Axel was glowering at me as if I'd gone against *his* authority somehow. As if he had any real authority over me.

"I thought the instructions couldn't be any clearer," he said. "No contact with the Katz girl after she leaves the mansion."

Instead of answering, I glared back at him. We'd arrived back at the mansion half an hour ago, and Axel had insisted on marching me straight to my father's office after barking at one of the lower lackeys to find the man in charge. Dad hadn't shown up yet.

"What do you think you're going to get out of tattling on us?" I asked. "No one likes a rat, Axel."

"I was doing my job, unlike you," Axel retorted. "Maybe you've forgotten who you owe your loyalty to."

"Don't fucking talk to me about loyalty. Everything I've done so far, every difficult decision I've made, and every bullet I've nearly taken has been for this family."

My father's cold voice carried from the doorway. "And yet you're willing to throw all of that away for the princess of the Claws."

He strode inside, his face an impenetrable mask, but I could tell he was angry. The chilliness of his tone was a dead giveaway.

He closed the door behind him and walked to his desk. I got up from the leather sofa and approached him. "Dad, you have to hear me on this."

"Hear what exactly?" he said. "You went behind my back and met with Mercy Katz. Several times, I'm guessing, since I highly doubt Axel just happened to catch you on the first occasion. He's said he's noticed you and your inner circle vanishing on unexplained missions quite often."

"I have every reason to believe that they've been helping her from the moment she left the mansion," Axel jumped in, like the brownnosing prick he was. "I wouldn't be surprised if they've been using Noble resources to help her get by."

What a fucking dickhead. He *wanted* that to be true so he could look even better to Dad for having caught us, as if spying on me and my men was what our resources should be focused on instead. No one had been using those apartments anyway.

My fingers itched to close into a fist, one I longed to drive into the wall—or, even better, Axel's self-satisfied face next to me. Hell, I wanted to punch Dad too, just to see some reaction, to catch him off-guard enough that he might think beyond the box he'd already put my disobedience into.

But I knew that wouldn't actually work. My father believed in self-control. I had to play this situation strategically. God knew what would happen if I really pissed him off and he took it out on Mercy.

"What do you have to say about that, Wylder?" he asked, his gaze boring into me.

"I haven't touched the Noble accounts or anything earmarked for other purposes," I said stiffly. I wasn't sure I could say the same for Anthea, but I wasn't going to drag my aunt into this after everything she'd done to help us. "What I do with my personal money and time shouldn't be relevant."

Dad made a scoffing sound. "I think it is if you've been focused on that girl rather than the real problems we're facing here. We sent her away for a reason. She's no longer a part of our organization. Why are you and your inner circle still associating with her?"

I took a deep breath before I finally answered, the sense prickling over me that more than one life might hang in the balance here. "With all due respect, Dad, I didn't agree with cutting ties with her in the first place. She left the mansion as you ordered. She hasn't been involved in any larger operations the Nobles have been working on. But she's been instrumental in my own continued efforts to get these intruding gangs out of Paradise Bend."

His tone turned even icier. "Are you suggesting I made a mistake?"

There was no good answer to that question. I squared my shoulders. "No, only that we had a minor difference of opinion. Mercy knows the Bend better than any of us do—she's given us intel that my men and I have been able to use to strike at this Storm guy's operations. You wanted her to leave because Xavier was targeting her, didn't you? Now that she's gone, he hasn't come near the mansion. Why shouldn't I take what she can offer while she's someplace else?"

"And just how much of what she's 'offering' are you taking?"

The insinuation in his voice was clear. My stomach knotted, but I kept my tone even. "Anything we could use to tackle Xavier and the rest of the assholes trying to usurp us. That's all. And we've made a lot of headway into disrupting their presence here thanks to her."

Axel snorted in disbelief, but I kept my attention focused on Dad. He skimmed his hands over the top of his desk and then folded them in his lap.

"Xavier appears to have gotten distracted by the other new presence in the Bend," he said. "I don't think we can judge how much of a thorn in our side he'll be until they've settled that conflict—at which point, it seems likely he'll focus his attention back on us. And who drew that attention to us in the first place?"

It took all my willpower not to snap at him. My voice came out rough despite my best efforts. "Not Mercy. The whole reason he and the rest of the Storm's people came here was obviously to take over Paradise Bend. We'd have been in their way regardless of what happened with Mercy. It doesn't make any sense to blame her."

Dad's eyes narrowed. "So now you're questioning my mental faculties."

Shit. "No," I said, scrambling for another argument, but Dad leaned back in his chair with an air of finality.

"It's clear to me that this girl has warped your priorities in dangerous ways, Wylder. You've gotten too close to her to see the full problem she presents."

"What's that supposed to mean?" I demanded.

"Your interest in her clearly goes far beyond ensuring the success of our organization. I think it's personal now. Perhaps it has been all along." He pinned me with his stare, as if he thought he could read the truth from my mind straight through my skull.

I did my best imitation of his hardened expression, shoving down my apprehension. The last thing we needed was him realizing just how much Mercy meant to me—and not just me but my friends as well.

"That's not true," I insisted. "All I care about is getting the Nobles through this unexpected war. I'll use whatever I can, and she's nothing but a means to an end."

"That's not how it looked to me when you told her to take off on us," Axel muttered, and turned to my father. "He got awfully up close and personal with her, murmuring in her ear. Protecting her from us mattered more to him than facing up to how he went against your orders."

My jaw set on edge. "No one asked your opinion."

"But I'm glad to hear it, especially considering it supports my suspicions." Dad pushed back his chair and stood up, bringing the full impact of his height to bear. We stood equally tall, but he had a little more heft to his shoulders and a weight to his presence that always made me feel smaller.

I remembered abruptly Mercy's comments outside the arcade the other night—how she'd noticed one of Axel's men there. I hadn't really figured he was acting outside of Axel's orders, but if I could use it to deflect even a little attention from this line of conversation, I'd take it.

"Maybe you should be aiming some of those suspicions at your right-hand man," I said to Dad, motioning toward Axel. "He doesn't seem to be keeping very good track of *his* people."

Axel's head jerked around. "What the fuck are you talking about?"

I met his gaze with my own accusing one. "We've seen one of the guys who reports to you in deep with the Storm's people, acting all chummy with them. What's *that* all about?"

To my surprise, rather than shooting back a quick retort, Axel's expression twitched with what looked like surprise. Had he not actually known about his underling's activities? But a second later, he was glowering at me again. "I've told my men to take the lay of the land and find out what we're up against. They're following *their* orders."

"And what have they managed to uncover so far?" I asked.

"Enough with the interrogation," Dad snapped. "I brought you here to get an explanation for your behavior, not put one of my most trusted men on trial."

I spun back to face him. "This is what you've been training me for, isn't it? To develop my judgment and trust my instincts. I'm telling you that Mercy is doing a lot more good than harm to our interests—yours and mine—and I wouldn't have anything to do with her if that wasn't true."

"That's not what I see," Dad said, staring me down. "I see a child taking on decisions bigger than himself and putting us all in harm's way just to satisfy his own ego and urges."

How the hell did I get through to him? "You have to trust me on this," I started, knowing I was losing the argument but refusing to give up.

Before I could go on, Dad stepped around the desk to loom right over me. "And why the fuck would I do that when you went behind my back and did the exact thing I asked you not to?"

"He's still a boy," Axel sneered. "Me and my men will clean up the mess in the Bend a lot faster than they've managed with all their running around with the girl."

"Yes. I think if Wylder wants to prove what he's really made of, he'll need to start by cleaning up *his* mess." Dad turned to Axel. "Where did Mercy go?"

"She took off running—I didn't want to go after her when I knew it was more important we deal with our own." Axel shot an accusing look at me. "I'd bet he knows."

I didn't, though. Mercy was smart enough not to go back to the new apartment, one that was in the Nobles' name. I had no idea where she'd have fled to, and that realization made my heart sink.

Of course, it wouldn't be that hard to find out. She'd still have her phone. I could reach out to her in an instant. No way in hell was I telling the men in front of me that.

"How should I know?" I said. "We met up at agreed spots. I have no clue what she was up to the rest of the time."

"We'll track her down quickly enough," Axel said.

Dad made a dismissive gesture. "No need for that. Like I said, my son needs to clean up his own mess." He lifted his chin toward me. "I want *you* to track her down."

If my heart had sunk before, now it dropped all the way to my shoes. "What for? I thought you didn't want me to have anything to do with her."

Dad gave me a sardonic smile. "Oh, there's one thing I'd like you to do with her, just to ensure that we're still clear that family comes first. The girl has served her purpose. We can no longer allow her to undermine our standing in Paradise Bend. The sooner she's out of the way, the less our association with her will injure us in the long run. Before she can become any more of a threat than she already is, you're going to get rid of her."

My throat constricted. "You want me to kill Mercy," I repeated, with the faint hope that I'd somehow misunderstood his meaning.

No such luck.

"You heard me," Ezra said. "Your defiance has put you on thin ice. Do this, and you'll have *started* to earn my trust back. I need my heir to be ruthless and focused. I need to know that when the time comes for you to lead the Nobles, you won't be taken off course by petty little distractions."

He spoke as if Mercy's life meant nothing at all. I couldn't help arguing, even as a wave of hopelessness crashed over me. Once Ezra Noble set down a decree, his mind wasn't going to be changed. "But if you just—"

He held up his hand to stop me, his expression as foreboding as I'd ever seen it. "I don't want to hear another word about it. You say she's just a means to an end to you? Then make her a means to getting back into my good graces. Kill her, and bring me the proof. You have five days."

16

Mercy

FROM A SAFE DISTANCE, I OBSERVED THE FRONT LAWN OF MY old house. A couple of guys were standing at the edge by the sidewalk just beyond a streetlamp's glow, sipping beers. No lights shone in the windows, and in the hour I'd been watching, I hadn't seen anyone moving inside or going in or out.

Now or never. With Wylder and the other guys dealing with whatever the fallout was with his dad, I couldn't just sit around twiddling my thumbs. I needed to know why these Red Shark jackasses had set up shop in the house. Had Dad been keeping more secrets than I'd guessed?

My heart skipped a beat at the thought of how I'd run off on the guys, but I'd only done it because Wylder had insisted. I just hoped he found a way to get through to his own dad—or to stand up to him in a way that wouldn't get him hurt for his trouble.

I forced myself to push those thoughts aside and crept through the night's shadows to the back of the house. After ducking through the neighbor's yard, I scaled the sturdy fence between our properties with a leap and a quick scramble, and sprang from there into the oak tree in my old back yard.

The leaves rustled. I crouched on the branch in the darkness for the space of a few breaths, listening hard. When no sound of alarm was raised, I clambered across the tree and made my way through one of the second floor windows, just like I had when I'd gone to retrieve my bracelet weeks ago.

Inside the house, I stood completely still for another minute, confirming there were no sounds of movement around me. My fingers drifted over the outline of the *Little Angel* bracelet in my pocket. When no noise reached me except faint laughter from the men outside, I slipped down the darkened hall.

Maybe it was a risk coming here right now. But something had been niggling at me ever since Gideon had played that recording of the Red Sharks guys talking. If I was going to find any answers to the questions I couldn't get out of my head, it'd be here.

Back when everything was... well, as normal as my life had ever been, Dad's home office had always been locked, even when he was inside. He hadn't allowed me to set foot in there since I'd been around seven or eight, but I'd understood more than he'd realized when I'd been a little kid.

I'd come equipped with the lock picks that Anthea had given me a brief tutorial on during one of her recent visits, but it turned out I didn't even need them. The door was standing ajar, the knob completely removed. One of the past intruders had broken in. I picked up my pace, setting my feet quickly but silently on the floor as I hurried over.

At the doorway, I scanned the room quickly. The intruders had gone through the contents on Dad's desk. Papers were strewn all over the room. Chairs had been overturned, books had been pulled off the bookcase, small trinkets that Dad had collected over the years as mementos of particularly big jobs lay smashed on the floor. Whoever had gone through the place, they'd been thorough.

Had they figured out his secret stash?

My heart thumping wildly in my chest, I walked to the corner of the room and knelt. The thick curtain over the window gave me the confidence to get out my phone and use it for a light. I felt along the baseboard with my other hand. There. I pressed down on the wobbly spot and pried open the loose section before flashing the beam of light inside.

A sigh of relief rushed out of me. It didn't look like anything in Dad's favorite hiding place had been discovered.

I pulled out a wad of cash first and pocketed it. That could come in handy now that I was relying completely on myself for housing and food. Next I found a couple of notebooks, a phone, and a United States passport.

I shook the last item open. The picture was Dad's, but the name was fake. He'd never used this one—none of the pages were stamped.

Sitting down on the floor, I turned to the notebooks next. He must have written some pretty important stuff in them if he'd kept them in there. By the dim glow of my phone, I flipped through the pages.

Unfortunately, whatever illicit business Dad had written about, he'd been more careful than just hiding it behind the baseboard. The notebooks were full of a mix of recognizable words and what looked like random strings of jumbled letters and numbers. He'd written it in partial code. I'd known he'd used one sometimes, but he'd never shared it with me. Or anyone else, as far as I knew. He'd meant the information in here to be for his eyes only.

I snapped pictures of the pages in case I lost the notebooks. Maybe Gideon would be able to crack the code and make something of the information. Then I stuffed them into my bag and picked up the phone. It was my last chance of figuring anything out myself tonight.

The screen was smudged and a crack ran across one corner. I was afraid it might have died with all that time in storage. But Dad had obviously charged it regularly, and he'd shut it off completely between uses so that it kept some power. It turned on when I pressed the button, the screen flashing to show 15% power remaining.

It asked for a passcode, but I'd been able to pick up Dad's typical one from careful observations over the years. There were a few benefits to being constantly underestimated. I tapped it in.

There were no apps on the phone other than the standard ones that came with installation. I checked the text messages. The most recent conversation was with a contact Dad had labeled "Teeth."

I frowned at the screen. I couldn't think of any of the business associates I knew of who'd gone by that nickname.

The moment I tapped through to the conversation, a chill washed over me. I skimmed back through the messages to make sure I wasn't missing anything.

The text conversation had started about five months ago and gone on for several weeks after that—pretty much right up until Dad's death. Here and there, messages had been deleted as if they'd contained particularly sensitive information, but what remained told a clear story.

I think this alliance could benefit both of us, Dad said at one point. *You'll take over some of my territory here, and share some of yours with the Claws, and we'll expand our reach together.*

We definitely see the reasoning behind your proposal, the contact he'd named Teeth had answered. *We're just working out the logistics. This isn't the kind of thing we'd want to move quickly on.*

And later, from Dad, *Is everything going forward as you hoped? If you need more specifics on my businesses here, I can give you that.*

The response: *Everything looks good. I believe we can get started within the next few months. You're ready for our arrival?*

You'll be welcomed with open arms. We're going to do great things together.

The more I read, the more my dread grew, until my eyes started to blur. I swiped at them and forced myself to read all the way to the end.

It wasn't hard to guess who Dad would have given a code name like "Teeth" to. I'd seen the shark-jaws logo on the post outside, and the content of the messages brought all the other pieces together.

Dad had been talking to someone from the Red Shark's organization for months. *Dad* had invited them into the Bend, offered them an alliance and territory to expand his own power. That must have been why he'd asked Kervos and others for documentation on their business activities—so he could show these guys how profitable associating with him would be.

My father was the reason the Red Shark's people were here, causing so much more violence than the Bend had already faced.

I slumped back against the wall, dropping the phone to my side. An ache spread through my chest. I didn't want to believe it, but how could I deny what I'd just seen?

Dad hadn't said anything in the texts about taking out Colt or about needing to go up against the Steel Knights. I had to assume he'd meant to bring Colt in on the arrangement once we were married. Obviously he hadn't discussed the newcomers he was encouraging to take a stake in our territory with my former fiancé beforehand, though.

But somehow Colt had caught wind of the negotiations and assumed Dad meant to betray him with the new alliance. He'd lashed out first… and now here we were, a whole lot of pain and blood later. Most of it from innocent people who'd had no idea about any of this mess.

"For fuck's sake, Dad," I murmured in a choked voice. It figured he'd set a complete catastrophe in motion and manage to get taken out of the picture before he had to deal with any of the consequences.

No, that fell on *me*.

What the hell was I supposed to do? How could I look anyone in the Bend in the eye, all these people who'd had their homes, businesses, and loved ones destroyed because of Dad's stupid decision…?

I stayed crouched there in his office for longer than I'd meant to, my head spinning. I just couldn't get a grip on myself.

I needed to hear someone else's voice, to talk it through with someone who could help me see where the fuck I went from here. And I only had one person I could reach out to, risky as it might be.

Desperately hoping that Ezra hadn't discovered Wylder's extra phone, I got out my own and tapped out a text to him with shaky fingers. *I need to see you. ASAP. Please tell me you're okay.*

My chest constricted more with every passing minute while I waited for a response. Then a new text appeared. *All important parts still intact. What's going on?*

I just need to talk to you face to face, if you can manage it. Is there somewhere safe we can meet?

The next answer came much faster. *The picnic table near the fountain in Calliver Park. I've got something to talk to you about too. Give me an hour.*

Thank God. I dragged in a breath and managed to push myself off the floor now that I had a destination in mind.

I left the house the same way I'd come in, feeling like a zombie. Each beat of my heart drove the knowledge I'd just discovered in deeper like a knife in my gut.

It was Dad's fault I'd lost my entire family. Dad's fault my whole life had been ruined—not that I regretted missing out on marrying Colt, but everything else... Dad's fault the Bend was in chaos, ordinary people afraid to even walk down the street. Dad's fault those streets were being painted with blood.

And with Dad gone, who could anyone point the finger at but his heir?

I slunk across rooftops and through alleys, making my way to the park, which lay near the border where the Bend turned into Paradise City proper. It was surrounded by a wrought-iron fence with a gate that was locked at night, but a few metal bars weren't enough to keep me out. I climbed inside, wove through the trees until I spotted the picnic bench by the limestone fountain with its sculpture of a trio of leaping dolphins, and melted into the shadows to wait.

It didn't take long before the soft rasp of careful footsteps reached my ears. Wylder stopped right by the tree I'd hidden behind. "You can come out now, Mercy."

I stepped out, raising an eyebrow at him. "How did you know I was here?"

"Intuition?" Wylder said.

I smiled. "Or just pure luck."

"It's weird, but I can always tell where you are," Wylder said, taking a step towards me. He looked me over. "Are you all right, Kitty Cat?"

My heart raced at the concern in his words. "Kind of. Not really. Everything's..." I made a vague gesture, unsure of how to put all the turmoil inside me into words. All I wanted to do was run my fingers through his soft auburn hair and pull him closer for a kiss.

But even though he smiled back at me, it didn't quite reach his eyes. My own smile faltered. "Are *you* all right? What happened with your dad? You said there was something you had to talk to me about."

Wylder stiffened a tiny bit, but only for a moment. Then he shook his head. "We can get to that later. Something's obviously wrong. What's going on, Mercy?"

I swallowed hard. "Are you sure? Your dad must have been furious. Are the other guys okay?"

"He was mostly angry with me, and I handled it." Something in his tone made me think that hadn't been too easy. "Don't try to dodge the subject. You said you needed me here. Tell me what happened."

He gazed into my eyes so intently that I found I couldn't hold his gaze. My head drooped. "I went back to my old house. I knew—my dad kept some secret documents and things in a hidey hole in his office. I just wanted to make sure there wasn't anything I was missing. But there was."

Wylder gripped my shoulder. "You went back there? Aren't the Red Shark's people using it in their operations?"

"Yes, but I was careful. No one saw me. That's not what matters." There was no point in putting it off. I had to just spit it out. "They're using the house because my dad's the one who invited them into the Bend. That's what the guys Gideon caught in his recording meant."

Shock rippled across Wylder's face. "Are you serious? How do you know?"

I explained everything I'd found out from the text conversation with the contact named Teeth. "They were talking about joining forces. Dad wanted to expand his territory, and he figured an alliance with a bigger power was the way to do it. Expanding by sharing their territories or something... I don't know what was going on in his head."

"Why the fuck would he want to do that? He had plenty already without bringing a bunch of strangers into it."

"I know!" I threw my hands into the air. "But he did, for whatever stupid reason, and now— I've been defending myself and him all along, refusing to believe Colt's claims about Dad, saying the Steel Knights were the real problem, but— Maybe *your* dad is right. My family is the biggest threat Paradise Bend has faced. We're where we are now because of the Claws."

"But not because of you," Wylder said. "Are you even listening to yourself? Your father didn't make you a part of his plan. You didn't know about any of this until just now. *You're* not responsible."

"I was right there. Maybe he thought he was doing it for me, so Colt and I would inherit more— It doesn't make any difference. I'm the leader of the Claws now, and there's no one else who can take responsibility. Everything—the violence on the streets, and the deaths—it might as well be my fault."

My vision blurred with a sudden welling of tears. "Fuck," I muttered, pressing my palms to my face. I didn't want him to see me crying.

"Mercy." Wylder's grasp on my shoulder tightened. He gave me a little shake. "Get a grip on yourself. You're in shock."

Despite my best efforts, tears rolled down my cheeks. "If I'd found out sooner—if I'd managed to stop him—if I'd been able to say something before the Red Shark's people showed up—"

Wylder's voice hardened. He sounded almost angry. "Listen to me. You're not to blame for your Dad's shitty actions—or Colt's either, for that matter. From what you said, the real problem was Colt making assumptions instead of talking to your dad to find out what was going on like a sane person would have. All he had to do was mention what he'd heard, and it would have all been sorted out. He's the one who flew off the handle instead."

His forceful tone brought up my hackles, pissing me off enough that my tears dried up. "If my father hadn't gone after more power in the first place—"

"You're not him, something I'm very glad for. Why the hell do you think you owe him anything?"

"I don't," I snapped back. "It's about what I owe the Bend."

"There," Wylder said, jabbing his finger at me. "There's a little of the Mercy I thought I knew. Are you really going to run away because of what you wish you'd done, Princess? Or are you going to stay and fight? Where's the cat with the claws, with enough fire to burn down the world around you? You're not going to let this one thing break your spirit, are you?"

His fingers dug into my shoulder painfully. I pushed his hand off me and shoved him back.

"No," I said, my voice almost echoing in the thick foliage of trees around us. I was more than this. I was more than my father's actions, more than the men who had tried to put me under their thumbs.

Wylder nodded in appreciation, his stance starting to relax. "I didn't think so. The woman I know always fights back."

I glared at him, my emotions even more jumbled up than before—but he'd stirred up a defiance in me that seared away the most hopeless parts. "You wanted me gone not too long ago," I couldn't help reminding him. "I never did then, did I?"

Something in his face softened. "No, you didn't. And I never really *wanted* you out of my life. I thought I was protecting you. Obviously that didn't work out very well for either of us."

"You don't think so?"

Wylder stepped up to me again and put his hand under my chin, slowly stroking it with his thumb. I relaxed into his touch automatically. Even with all the history behind us, he was the first person I'd turned to when I was in trouble. And he had come for me in more ways than one.

"I don't want you to go even though I know you'll be safer that way," he murmured. "You're stuck with me now, Kitty Cat."

He didn't kiss me. Instead he touched his forehead to mine. We stayed there for a few moments as my mind cleared and the last of the helplessness I'd been feeling dissipated.

I wasn't alone. I had Wylder and Kaige and Rowan and Gideon. And I had the Bend. No matter what had led us here, I couldn't back down now.

"I'm not going anywhere," I said, easing back so that I could meet Wylder's gaze. "The Bend is still my home. It's broken, but I'll do everything I can to fix it. I'll rebuild it better than it ever was, and at the same time I'll rebuild my family's legacy. The Katz name doesn't end with my dad."

Wylder nodded, affection shining in his eyes. "So what comes next?"

I raised my chin. "I *am* the head of the Claws now. That means it's time to take some responsibility and see if I can undo what the leader before me set in motion. Let's find out if I can convince the Red Shark that his invitation's been revoked."

17

Mercy

It felt weird to be standing in front of my house again, this time in daylight and facing the front door, as if I hadn't snuck inside just last night. In the guise of darkness, I'd been able to pretend that I was in a different reality, one in which my house belonged to me. Now I had armed strangers eyeing me from what was technically *my* porch.

I dragged in a breath and fidgeted with the collar of the button-up shirt Anthea had lent me so I looked more professional than I felt. Then I marched up the front walk.

The men on the porch straightened up, but they didn't draw the guns I could see at the waists of their jeans. They were expecting me. I'd called this meeting with the Red Shark's people as the current leader of the Claws and the daughter of the man who'd called them into my world.

A couple of the men—younger ones—shifted restlessly on their feet. I didn't think they liked my arrival. Well, too bad for them.

As I climbed up the steps, refusing to let my nerves show, the front door opened. A man in a polo shirt motioned me in. “Mercy Katz. You came.”

I fixed him with my best Claws Princess look. “I said I would.”

He gave me a tight, sharp-edged smile. “Some of us thought it was a prank. But we made sure we were prepared anyway. Come in.”

As if it was his house and not mine. I bit back the snarky remarks I wanted to make and stepped over the threshold.

The family pictures that had been hung in the foyer were missing, leaving pale marks on the striped wallpaper where they’d been. The only one left was of Dad alone, and it’d been disfigured with streaks of red and black paint. Had these pricks defaced it, or had that been the Steel Knights who’d staked a claim on this house before?

The man saw me watching the picture. “Like that?”

I ignored his bait. “I’d like to get on with our meeting. Are you in charge of the Red Shark’s presence in Paradise Bend?”

Several men had come down the stairs and stepped into the hall to watch, a couple of them with guns in hand. More than one gaze lingered on my chest. I restrained a shudder of disgust.

“Don’t go by appearances, boys,” said the man who’d greeted me. “This one bites. Hard.” He nodded to me. “Your reputation precedes you. We’ve heard that you took on the Steel Knights and killed their leader yourself. We’d just like to make sure you don’t get any of the same ideas here. My boss is this way.”

He led me into the dining room. Someone had smashed the crystal chandelier that hung over the broad oak table. My teeth set on edge as I took in the man sitting at the head of the table.

He was middle aged, with a creased forehead and a graying goatee, dressed in a suit I could tell was expensive. He glanced up from his newspaper with a bored look as if I’d disturbed his reading, but I didn’t let that faze me. I knew the Red Shark’s contingent was on the losing side of the battle with the Storm so far. I’d seen the edginess of his men. They wouldn’t be so worried about little old me if they’d been sure of their foothold here.

“So you’re Mercy Katz,” he said, setting the newspaper aside. “You have ten minutes to tell me exactly why you’re here, or my men will put a bullet in your head." He smiled thinly as if he hadn't just threatened my life.

I echoed his expression. He wasn't going to intimidate me. I'd faced much worse. "I don't even need ten minutes. It's very simple. I know that my father's the one who suggested you come here and take a stake in Paradise Bend. He never told me about that deal or why he made it, but he's dead now, so I don't see how it matters. What matters is you don't have any deal at all with anyone alive here."

"Are you looking to make a new one, Miss Katz?"

I folded my arms over my chest. "No. I'm telling you I think you should leave. You don't have any alliances here. You've lost men to the Storm's forces, and they're obviously not letting up their attacks. What's the point in staying?"

He cocked his head. "Why do you care? Just want us to make things easier for you when you try to reclaim your territory."

"No," I said. "I want to stop seeing blood all over the streets and the people I grew up with living in terror. But I'll point out that this territory was never really my father's to bargain away anyway. The whole county belongs to the Nobles, and they're not interested in giving it up."

The man snorted as if I'd said something ridiculous. Then he tapped the tabletop. "Yes, your father is gone—and thanks to you, I understand, so is Colt Bryant and the Steel Knights. The two most powerful gangs in this part of the county. That leaves quite the power vacuum. You can't expect us to walk away and leave it all to the Storm."

"So you're willing to kill whoever stands in your way out of greed?" I asked.

His eyes glittered coldly. "We've already killed plenty, and we have no shortage of weapons coming in to take down more. And the one good thing the Storm's troops have done is prove just what an avid customer base exists here for certain types of products. We have our own merchandise we'll be moving in."

Nausea gripped my stomach. "More drugs?"

"Among other things. So if you don't have any better argument than you've already presented..." He raised his eyebrows.

I resisted the urge to punch him right in his haughty face. "If the

Storm's people don't crush you, then the Nobles will. You're fighting a losing battle here."

His shoulders stiffened, but he waved me off. "We'll see about that. I think we're done here." He pointed at the guy who'd escorted me in. "Send her off."

The guy stepped toward me, but I jerked away before he could touch my arm. There obviously wasn't any way these men would listen to reason. They were too caught up in their egos and greed.

"This is my house," I couldn't help reminding them. "I can get out on my own. Thank you very much for your hospitality."

I strode down the hall and out the door. I could barely breathe until I was halfway down the block. Sweat had broken out on my forehead. I stopped to swipe at it, and a van rolled to a halt next to me. Kaige leaned his elbow out the driver's side window and grinned. "You look like you could use a ride."

Rowan and Gideon were waiting in the back. As I dropped onto the bench next to them, Wylder pushed past the seats from the passenger-side one to join us. Kaige started driving again, taking us farther from the Red Shark's men and that uncomfortable conversation.

"It didn't go so well, huh," Wylder said, nodding to the screen where our voices were being recorded in erratic wave patterns.

I reached inside my shirt and pulled out the bug that had been pinned against my collarbone. "I don't think they even considered my suggestion."

"Well, it was worth a try," Rowan said.

I gave him a crooked smile and turned to Gideon. "Do you think the bug picked up anything in the conversation that we could use against them?"

"We got a few tidbits we might be able to spin the right way to get the cops focused on them, if we want to go that route," Gideon said. "He confessed to bringing weapons into the Bend and to multiple killings, if in a vague way. And intending to get in on the drug trade."

"Okay." I sagged back against the wall of the van. We hadn't figured there was all that much hope of convincing the Red Shark to back off, but we'd at least hoped to get some ammunition we could use as leverage to force them out.

"The Storm's people are still the bigger problem," Rowan pointed out.

Wylder nodded. "We'll sit on this recording for now. We'll have it in our back pocket when we really need it. Mercy did good."

He tugged my ponytail in his usual affectionate way, but his expression stayed tense, and his gaze only held mine for a second. Uneasiness prickled over my skin.

He'd said last night that he needed to talk to *me*, but he'd never gotten around to telling me what that was about. Something was obviously bothering him.

But it was something he didn't want to discuss in front of the other guys, I had to assume. He wasn't likely to tell me much if I undermined his authority by badgering him about it with them around. The next time we were alone, though, I'd have to drag it out of him.

Gideon had gone back to tapping on his tablet. "Hey," he called over to Kaige, "take a right up here and then stop at the end of the block."

As Kaige followed his instructions, Wylder gave his best friend a curious look. "Where are you leading us now, oh tech genius?"

A sparkle came into Gideon's eyes at the compliment, but his jaw tensed too. "I've got plans for a few more ways we can screw with both the Storm's and the Red Shark's guys, but I need to pick up supplies. There's a store near here where I can pick up a few... unusual items."

The building he had Kaige park outside looked practically abandoned, the windows dim and the sign over the doorway cracked. Spray-painted graffiti marked the outer walls. But Gideon sauntered inside with more confidence than he usually showed when we were out on a mission, enough that I enjoyed admiring the view of his ass before he vanished through the doorway.

The rest of us got out too, stretching our legs and scanning the rest of the street. We ambled to the corner and glanced around, but there was no sign of any activity in the area. Both nothing dangerous and nothing simply normal. It was only just coming up on the evening, and the Bend was way too quiet.

But the Red Shark, the Storm, and all their lackeys didn't give a shit about how their war was killing this place, did they?

Kaige's stomach let out an audible growl.

Rowan shook his head. "Are you hungry already? We had dinner before we left."

"All the running around makes me super hungry," Kaige said. "And I'm not going to apologize for my appetite. It's how I got these guns." He flexed his massive biceps, and all three of us laughed.

"Guys." Wylder hadn't been taking part in our banter. When I glanced at him, he was gazing intently down the street. A black SUV was cruising toward us.

Beside me, Kaige stiffened. "That isn't Axel again, is it? That fucker—"

Before he could finish his sentence, the SUV jerked to a stop and four men poured out. The three in front had guns at the ready. In their wake, the fourth stomped out onto the sidewalk in heavy combat boots, his form looming over the others, and I got my first in-person look at the man who'd been haunting me for weeks.

Xavier was a hulking figure, towering no less than six-five, with corded shoulders. He might even be wider than Kaige, if that was possible. The angry scars on his cheeks must have become less pronounced with age, but it was still unnerving seeing how the ominous Xs drilled into his skin took over most of his face.

But that wasn't even the worst part. His eyes had a manic glint in them, and his toothy smile widened when he saw us. Every nerve in my body clanged in warning: this man was unhinged. An involuntary shiver passed down my spine.

"Hello, my cat," he said, addressing me directly. "We finally meet."

Wylder pushed in front of me, his stance rigid, his hand leaping to his gun. Xavier's gaze fixed on him, and he let out a low, rolling laugh. "Do you think that little toy is going to stop me? Do you really think a bitch like her is worth protecting?"

"I think I didn't fucking ask you," Wylder said. "Back off."

"Oh, no." Xavier strolled toward us, his men flanking him. He didn't bother to draw his own weapon, as if he thought he was bulletproof. "But if you want to make me toss you aside to get to her, that'll just make it more fun."

I didn't have any weapons of my own on me—I'd left them behind to go into the parlay with the Red Shark's men. My hands balled into fists. I wasn't going down easy anyway. "I've never done anything to you. I don't even *know* you. Leave me alone, asshole."

Xavier clucked his tongue. "Sorry, but it's time to collar the cat. I've given you free run for too long."

Just then the door to the shop opened, and Gideon strode out. "I couldn't—"

His words died when he saw Xavier, his feet skidding to a halt.

Xavier cocked his head at Gideon, and an expression came over his face that turned it even uglier. "And you must be the kid who's been messing with my people's security systems."

Gideon didn't speak, standing rigidly still. I wasn't sure he had a weapon on him either, and Xavier was closer to him than we were.

Xavier sneered. "You know what happens when you piss off the lion? I will tear you limb from limb until you beg for death. It's payment time." He nodded to his men.

The three guys charged at Gideon. Xavier barreled toward me, his teeth bared.

Kaige threw himself into the fray, tackling one of the men before they'd even reached Gideon. Rowan took a shot at one of the others, who slowed, ducking. Wylder stayed between me and Xavier, firing his own gun, but Xavier dove to the side at the last second.

We spun around, Wylder shooting again and hitting Xavier in the chest—but the impact barely seemed to shake the beast of a man. He thumped his stomach, and I heard a thud that told me he was wearing a Kevlar vest under his shirt.

Before Wylder could take aim at Xavier's head, the other man launched himself at us with a roar. He managed to knock the gun right out of Wylder's hand, his shot going wild. Wylder whipped out a knife and slashed it across Xavier's arm, and I aimed a kick at his gut that from the looks of things hurt my foot more than it did our attacker.

Xavier cracked his knuckles, circling us for a second, considering Wylder's knife. From the corner of my eye, I saw Rowan and Kaige shielding Gideon as they wrestled with Xavier's other two men.

One of the lackeys punched Rowan hard enough that blood flew from his mouth. He landed with a thump on the ground and rolled back onto his feet. The guy was already swinging his gun hand up to shoot Kaige while the last attacker had him distracted.

Rowan sprang in the way so fast he was almost a blur. He wrenched at the man's arm with a snap of breaking bone and pulled the trigger right at the guy's face for good measure. The front of the attacker's skull burst apart.

Kaige threw the last guy to the ground so hard that he lay there, stunned. As they hurried Gideon to the van, Xavier made another grab at me. At the same time, he slammed his elbow into Wylder's ribs to force him to the side. Wylder let out a pained huff of breath, staggering. Xavier's meaty hand snagged on my wrist.

Acting purely on instinct, I karate-chopped his forearm with all the desperate strength I had in me. Xavier just yanked me closer to him, his other hand reaching for my throat—

And then Wylder rammed his knife into the monster's shoulder.

Xavier's grip shook, and I pulled free.

"Come on!" Rowan yelled from the van. Another car was just screeching to a halt behind the one that had brought Xavier, and the guy Kaige had toppled was starting to push himself upright.

I hated turning tail and running, but sometimes that was what you had to do to survive.

Wylder and I dashed for the van. The second we'd thrown ourselves past the back doors, Kaige hit the gas as hard as he could. The tires screamed in protest, leaving marks on the pavement. Shots boomed after us as we heaved the doors shut.

Then the gunfire stopped. I looked through the back windows to see Xavier staring at us, several men around him, his smile back in place. Even with the tint on the windows hiding my face, it felt like he could see right into my eyes. Then he threw back his head. The last thing I heard before we raced around a corner was a cold laugh spilling out into the dusk.

The sound chilled the blood in my veins. I rubbed my bruised wrist. "He wasn't even trying that hard. He's still toying with us."

What the hell were we going to do when he decided to really get serious?

18

Rowan

My hand moved rapidly over the paper. With every stroke of my pencil, the harsh lines of the man's face became pronounced. His X-like scars took over both of his cheeks, extending all the way to his jaw.

A shudder ran through me, but I couldn't stop myself. After yesterday's run-in with Xavier, I hadn't been able to get the image of him, of the savagery in his eyes, out of my head. This seemed like the only way to get it out.

"What are you doing?" said a voice from behind me.

I snapped back to attention at the kitchen island, flipping over the paper automatically as my head jerked around. Ezra Noble had come up behind me so quietly I hadn't realized I was no longer alone.

He studied me from where he'd come to a halt a few feet away. "What do you have there, son?"

"Er, it's nothing important," I said. "I was just sketching a little."

"All the same, I'd like to see it." Before I could protest, if I'd even have thought that was wise, he stepped up to the island and lifted the paper. As he studied my rendition of our greatest known enemy's face, his expression revealed nothing. "That's quite an interesting drawing."

"We had a run in with him yesterday. It was... unnerving. Drawing him felt like a way of taking control, even if that sounds silly."

"It's not silly at all if it works." Ezra pushed the paper back to me. "You've got talent. I didn't know you liked to draw."

"I haven't much lately," I admitted, wondering why the big boss was in here making casual conversation with me. Other than our relatively brief discussions about the few projects he'd taken me on directly for, like the negotiations for the waterfront property, we'd rarely talked. He definitely hadn't ever expressed interest in my hobbies. "Is there something you needed me for, sir?"

Ezra leaned against the counter, offering me a mild smile. "You can call me Ezra. I think you've earned it."

Even stranger. I kept my stance looking relaxed on the outside, but inside every part of me went on the alert. "Thank you."

"You haven't had quite the amount of support you deserve in our ranks lately, have you, Rowan," he said.

I had no idea where he was going with this. "I'm not sure what you mean," I said cautiously.

"Well, my son was your original supporter, but it's hard to say where his mind is lately, isn't it? So focused on that Katz girl, and making odd decisions on the fly. He hasn't always been quite so erratic."

Apprehension wrapped around my stomach. I didn't think Wylder had been behaving all that oddly, but that obviously wasn't what his father wanted to hear. I settled for a noncommittal response. "I think a certain amount of unpredictability is expected given the unpredictable situation we've found ourselves in."

Ezra nodded. "Very generous of you. That's the kind of loyalty we should be rewarding. But he still sees you as less than those other two of his, the computer fanatic and the meathead, just because he's known them longer. That's not how *his* loyalties should work."

I still wasn't sure what his goal was here, but he was obviously trying to drive a wedge between me and Wylder. Did he think I'd agree with his assessment of the other guys, that I was bitter about my place in

Wylder's inner circle? Maybe he was hoping for that—that I'd be easier to manipulate because *I* had less history with his son.

An eerie calm settled over me. I needed to know what Ezra had up his sleeve, and I was just the man to figure it out, wasn't I? In the past week, I'd mostly been called on to use my combat skills and the viciousness I only let out when I had to. It was nice to have a chance to put my preferred talents to use, working with my words rather than my fists.

I'd rather I didn't have to use them against the man who held all our livelihoods—and our lives—in his hands, but beggars couldn't be choosers. If my position in the Nobles was at stake here, I intended to hold onto it every way I could.

"I guess he is a little closer with the other guys," I said, keeping the same unconcerned tone and watching Ezra's body language carefully. "That's understandable too."

"Not in a man who's meant to become a true leader. I have no idea what's going through his head these days. How will any of the men respect him if he's willing to be led around by his dick by some girl?"

Ezra shook his head, and I resisted the urge to clench my jaw in anger. He clearly had no idea about my and Mercy's shared history or about how those feelings had been reignited. He was probably hoping I'd let something slip about her relationship with Wylder.

But then Ezra went on in a different direction. "While he's busy chasing a piece of ass, you could enjoy much more authority if you reported directly to me. You've done good work for me in the past. I'd like to see that rewarded."

Report directly to him? He wanted to take me into *his* inner circle, alongside Axel and the few others Ezra totally trusted? Technically that'd put me on almost equal footing with Wylder rather than beneath him.

A little thrill shot through me. Even though I couldn't say I had any interest in the offer, I still recognized it as an honor.

If it was even about me and not about undermining Wylder, that was.

"What exactly would that look like?" I hedged, fiddling with the corner of my paper. In what other ways was he planning to disrupt Wylder's operations?

Ezra gave a casual shrug as if it was no big deal. "You would no longer be answerable to Wylder. Consider it a promotion. You'd come to me for your marching orders, and I'd assign men who'd report to you and follow your own orders in turn. You'd essentially be on the same level as Wylder himself."

"But not quite, because he's your son," I had to say, nudging him just a little.

"Blood isn't everything," Ezra said. "Power should be earned. I wouldn't consider the position of heir certain just yet."

Was he really saying what I thought he was? My pulse stuttered, but I made myself look awed instead. "You can't really mean you think I could fill those shoes..."

He patted my shoulder, leaving my skin crawling. "You sell yourself short, Rowan. If you play your cards right, who knows, the rulership of the Nobles might be up for grabs. Think my proposition over and let me know when you're ready to start."

He ambled out of the kitchen without any indication that he'd even considered I might refuse. I stayed frozen on the stool by the island, chilled through to the bone, with that fake smile still plastered on my face.

He wanted to replace Wylder—to wrench everything Wylder had worked for away from him over a few disagreements that frankly I thought Ezra had the wrong idea on. And he was trying to lure me away with that promise. Not that I'd have trusted anything the snake said after he'd revealed how little respect he had for the son he'd raised.

What was he going to think if I turned him down, though? Fuck.

"I need a drink," I muttered to myself, and headed over to the lounge room with the home bar.

I poured myself a double shot of vodka and downed most of it in one go. It burned down my throat. The sour taste made me grimace, but I threw back the rest to chase it.

"What's gotten into you?" Wylder said from the doorway. "I thought day-drinking was my domain."

He grinned at me as he came over to the bar. I motioned to the bottle. "You could have some too if you're feeling left out. I'll pour."

Wylder shook his head. "I'm not much for vodka, and I've already been hitting the brandy as much as I think is wise." He rubbed his temple. "It's been a shitty couple of days, hasn't it?"

"You can say that again." I eyed the bottle of vodka, debating whether I could stomach another shot. Whether I might say something stupid if I did.

"Thanks for looking out for Gideon when we were up against Xavier and his pricks," Wylder said. "All the power in that brain of his, but he definitely isn't going to take down three thugs in a fist fight. I'd have jumped in there, but..." He grimaced.

He'd had to protect Mercy from Xavier himself. I'd have liked to take a few swings at that prick too.

But even as my frustration with her psycho stalker flared up, most of my nerves settled, the uneasiness in my gut fading. Wylder *did* appreciate how I contributed to the team, and he wasn't afraid to say so. I'd sure as hell rather be working under him than a treacherous bastard like Ezra.

Which meant I knew exactly what I had to do now with my loyalties.

"Of course," I said. "Gideon's practically family. And so are you. And speaking of family... Your dad and I just had a very unusual conversation."

Wylder frowned. "About what?"

"About you, actually."

"Ugh, I'm not surprised. What did he say?"

I hesitated for a moment, not because I had any doubts about telling Wylder, but because I didn't want to make the revelation more painful than it had to be. But who was I kidding? Hearing it was going to suck no matter what.

"He was feeling me out, trying to see if I've been unhappy working under you," I said. "Making comments about your competence. He's encouraging me to come over and answer directly to him." I paused and swallowed thickly. "And he hinted that you might not inherit the Noble empire after all."

To my surprise, Wylder started laughing. Then I heard the harshness of the sound. There was no humor in it.

"It figures," he said with unconcealed bitterness. "He lays down the law and doesn't even wait to see if I'll step in line. Gee, thanks, Dad."

I could tell I was missing something. "Step in line about what? Did something else happen between you two after Axel caught us with Mercy?"

Wylder's face turned serious, and his green eyes cut to mine. The silent anger in them was unmistakable. "He... He ordered me to kill Mercy. And he gave me five days—three now—to actually execute that order." The glass in his hand cracked. Wylder looked down at it but didn't even flinch.

A rush of panic and rage nearly overwhelmed me. I grappled with my emotions, fighting for control. "Excuse me?"

"There's nothing more to it. He wants Mercy out of the way, and he wants me to prove I'll fall in line by being the one to do it."

A sudden chill broke through every other feeling in me. "Why didn't you say anything? You aren't really—?"

Wylder's eyes flashed before I could finish the question. "Of course not," he snapped. "And—I was going to talk to Mercy about it, but then the whole thing with her dad and the Red Shark came up—I couldn't figure out how..." He grimaced. "And I didn't want to tell anyone else until I'd talked it through with her. I can't do it, but I'm not sure what I should do instead."

"Fuck," I muttered to myself. "Damn it." I'd had no idea that our attempt to protect Mercy would come to this. "What have you thought of doing? We're running out of time here."

"If I knew, do you think I'd be sitting here not doing it?" He exhaled harshly and then pinned me with a sharper look. "You weren't happy having her around at first, but you two seem to have worked out your issues. I take it you'll stand with me on this."

I didn't see any point in lying to him about it. "She's the only woman I've ever really cared about." The memories of our naked bodies twining, Mercy's gasp as I brought her to the peak of pleasure, flickered through my mind.

Wylder hummed to himself. "I guess she's made an impact on all of us." He paused. "You know, I didn't see this coming—how close all four of us have gotten with her. Heck, I never expected to have the same taste in women as Kaige. And it isn't easy sharing her when she's gotten under my skin like this..."

He trailed off, but I didn't know what to say. That was the first time Wylder had openly acknowledged our shared interest in Mercy—not just his and mine but Kaige's and Gideon's as well. I knew something had happened between her and the others, but his words were that much more confirmation.

I pictured her fierce eyes, the protective stance of her curvaceous body when she got ready to fight. I wasn't surprised the other guys liked her so much.

Jealousy gripped my chest, but only for a moment before it started to fade. Mercy had found a kind of home—a kind of *family*—with the four of us just as we had in each other. I wanted that for her even more than I wanted her all to myself. After everything her real family had put her through, she deserved it.

And Wylder obviously felt the same way. "Who the hell am I to say no to a woman like that?" he said with a shake of his head.

"She is one hell of a woman," I agreed.

"And you." Wylder clapped his hand to my back firmly. "My dad can go fuck himself if he thinks he's coming between us. If I haven't said it enough, let me make it totally clear now—I see you as a brother. I know how loyal you've been, how hard you've worked for me, and I value every bit of that. Maybe you joined the party late, but that doesn't make you any less than the others. You have my trust and I'll always have your back."

Pride more potent than anything Ezra's words had provoked swelled inside me. I smiled at Wylder despite all the anxiety still gnawing at me after his admission. "Right back at you. Since you value my input... can I make a suggestion?"

"Go right ahead," Wylder said, his tone going serious again.

I pushed my glass aside and fully faced him, my gaze intent. "You *have* to tell Mercy and the other guys what's going on with your dad. We'll have a much better chance of coming up with a good solution if we can put our heads together."

Wylder bristled for a second, his lips flattening. "I can't just—" Then he sighed, his shoulders coming down. "No, you're probably right. I just hate thinking about how Mercy will look at me when I tell her."

"As long as you're not trying to carry out your dad's orders when you do, I think it'll be just fine," I said dryly.

He rolled his eyes at me, and somehow everything seemed totally normal again. Like there was nothing unsurmountable in front of us—like we'd tackle this problem like we had every one before and come out on top.

"You're not alone, no matter what we're up against," I reminded him.

He raised an empty glass to me in a silent toast, a grin playing with the corners of his mouth. And just like that, I felt totally at home as well.

This life might not have been the one I'd have pictured myself living, but there was a lot of good in it too, in ways that mattered to me now. And not least of those was this brotherhood we'd forged.

19

Mercy

WHEN WYLDER FINISHED LAYING OUT WHAT HIS FATHER HAD ordered him to do, for a moment my head just spun. My mind was foggy from interrupted sleep. I hadn't wanted to stick around any one place for even a whole night now that I was on the run, since I had no idea how easily Xavier might find me. I hadn't gotten enough rest in days.

Maybe I was hallucinating due to sleep deprivation, or this was all a bad dream.

"Your dad... wants you to kill me," I repeated. It didn't sound any better coming from my lips.

"He says that's the only way I can prove I'm loyal to him," Wylder said with a grimace. "Obviously I'm not going to do it."

He looked straight at me, his green eyes shining with the truth of that statement. Tendrils of warmth wrapped around my chest and squeezed me. I nodded at him, hoping he could tell how much I appreciated what he was doing for me no matter what it might cost him in the future.

I looked around at the other guys and Anthea, who I'd met in the back of Gideon's van just ten minutes ago. They all looked as shocked and upset as I felt. I wasn't at all worried about Wylder's intentions, because he'd never have admitted any of this if he was even considering going through with it. But still...

This was Ezra Noble's twisted revenge for crashing into his life and supposedly leading his son astray. As the initial surprise wore off, I found I was almost numb. It wasn't really that much of a surprise, was it? He'd gotten to be the head of the Nobles by knowing how to hit where it hurt.

Kaige swore and smacked the bench with his fist. "So what happens if—*when*—you don't do it?"

"I don't know," Wylder said, and grinned in a humorless way that made me wince. "Maybe he'll kill *me*."

Anthea's head snapped up. "Don't talk that way. He values you more than that. We've simply got to find a way around the problem." She rubbed her mouth and glanced at me. "What if you just took off? I could give you enough cash to get you a hundred miles away from here and set you up in a hotel for a while. You lay low, Wylder can say he couldn't find you, and hopefully it all blows over."

Gideon raised his eyebrows. "Since when does Ezra let things just 'blow over'?" His tone was typically cool, but his hands had tensed around his tablet.

Anthea let out a huff of frustration.

Even with my life on the line, I couldn't suppress a yawn. Kaige's anger faded in the wake of concern. He passed me a packet of M&Ms from the bag of food they'd brought for me. "Here. Sugar plus caffeine is a great combination."

"Thanks," I said, but after I ripped open the package, I just stared at the brightly covered candies. My stomach had balled tight.

I looked at Anthea. "I'm not leaving my home anyway. Even if that home is pretty crappy right now." I held back yet another yawn and scowled at the thought of the early morning rain shower that'd soaked the hell out of me on the terrace where I'd spent the second half of last night.

"It wouldn't necessarily be for that long," Rowan started.

"No," I said firmly. "The Bend needs me—it needs all of us. The way Xavier came at us the other day just proves that. He knows we're the best chance the city has of stopping him and the Storm's people. I'm not cutting out on them."

When I rustled the candies in the bag without taking any out, Gideon held out a steel thermos to me. "Would coffee go down better? This is my own blend."

I blinked at him and accepted it. "Don't you need it?"

He shrugged, but there was a fondness to the gleam in his eyes that warmed me more than the thermos in my hands. "I already drank some, and I think you need it more."

"Thank you." I unscrewed the cap and sipped some of the still-hot liquid. The bitterness seared down my throat—clearly an acquired taste—but it did jolt me into a higher state of alertness. Mission accomplished.

Kaige cocked his head. "In all the years that I've known you, why haven't you ever offered your special coffee to me?"

"You never asked for it," Gideon said simply.

Kaige grumbled something half-heartedly about inconsiderate friends, and I laughed. I'd missed their presence and their banter. Heck, I even missed watching Wylder lose against Gideon in their stupid continuing games of chess. I missed the whole stupid Noble mansion, not because of the huge rooms and fancy furnishings, but because it was where I'd been able to live with them.

Too bad Ezra lived there too.

"We can't do nothing," Anthea said, getting us back on topic. "There are other ways, if I pitch in. A little messy, but... we could find a corpse that's the right stature and age to pass for Mercy. I have contacts who could help with that. Then we disfigure it beyond recognizability and tell Ezra it's her."

Kaige made a gagging sound.

Wylder just shook his head. "No."

"I could come up with a similar approach that's not quite as gruesome," his aunt started.

He cut her off with a sharp motion. "*No.* Nothing that means faking that I really did kill Mercy. I don't want to pretend I'm the kind of guy who would. It's a coward's way out. Besides, Mercy would still have to stay in hiding then, or things would get even worse for both of us."

Anthea frowned. "Think about it very carefully. You're walking a thin line. I've known my brother even longer than you have, and he doesn't take kindly to having his orders outright ignored."

"We only have a couple more days before the time he gave Wylder runs out," Rowan said. "What are our other options? Is there any chance of convincing Ezra that Mercy's a useful asset after all?"

"Yeah, right," I muttered. "If he hasn't figured that out yet..."

Gideon recovered himself enough to poke at his tablet. The surveillance feeds on the screens flickered and shifted. "None of this talk does us any good if we get slaughtered by the Storm's people or the Red Shark's in the meantime," he said in explanation.

"If we knew how to get rid of them and could prove Mercy played a big role in making that happen, maybe Ezra would have to admit she's all right," Kaige suggested. "I know we kind of tried that with Colt, but this Xavier asshole did turn up right afterward... Ezra was happy for a little while before that."

"Then we just have to figure out how to crush all our enemies in two days," Wylder said. "Got any brilliant brainstorms?"

Kaige pointed at Gideon. "That's his area."

"And mine." Anthea tapped her lips. "Give me some time to make some calls, and maybe I'll have another idea by the end of the day."

"Nothing that means Mercy plays dead," Wylder told her. "I'll figure something out one way or another—something that doesn't mess up her life any more than it already is."

He spoke confidently, but the corners of his mouth had pulled tight with worry. My throat constricted. I didn't want his life getting messed up over me either.

Before I could say that, Gideon's head jerked up. He motioned to one of the screens. "Well, look at that."

We all glanced over at the feed he'd indicated. A few guys had gathered on a street corner in the grainy footage that must have been from a street cam. I immediately recognized one of them from the confrontation with Xavier the other day.

"Storm people," I said. "That one guy, at least, is pretty high up. What do you think they're doing?"

"I saw them stash a duffel bag right before they got into position," Gideon said. "Looks like they're planning on doing some major dealing. They're outside some apartment buildings, lots of foot traffic, people coming and going."

As if on cue, a couple of kids darted by, waving at each other. They didn't even glance at the Storm's people, but Kaige stiffened next to me. His jaw clenched. "We should shut them down. We can call the cops on them—they'll have no idea we spotted them, right?"

Gideon turned to Wylder. "We were looking to trace some of the key players to the Storm's local center of operations. One of these guys might lead us there if we keep an eye on them undisturbed. It's up to you."

Before Wylder could answer, Kaige spoke up again. "You've already been narrowing down the locations watching their activity with all this." He waved to the screens. "We don't need these pricks."

"We might," Wylder cut in with a bit of an edge in his voice.

Just then, another car pulled up at the edge of the screen we were watching. I leaned forward, studying the figure who got out. A chill trickled through my stomach. "Gideon, can you zoom in on the feed?"

"Sure." His fingers skimmed over the controls on the tablet.

As the view closed in on the men and the new guy who'd joined them, my eyes narrowed. "I thought so. It's that guy who works for Axel—he's hanging around the Storm's people again."

"What?" Wylder's head whipped around. "That's the same guy we saw with them at the arcade."

"Damn right," I said. "There's no mistaking that hair. But what the hell is he doing with the dealers now?"

"He's supposed to be investigating the Storm, isn't he?" Rowan said. "At least that's what Axel said."

"Yeah," Wylder said, but he knit his brow.

"He seems to be hanging out with them an awful lot," I said. "Look at how friendly they're being with him. I don't know."

"Axel didn't seem totally sure about what the guy was doing," Wylder admitted. "He's been so busy keeping an eye on us, I'm not sure how closely he's been watching his people. I wouldn't expect him to make a mistake *that* big, though."

Gideon tapped the screen. "Either way, I'm recording this. We'll have proof if he's up to no good."

"Fuck." Kaige swore so loud I startled on the bench. He leapt up and smacked his fist into the doors, making them shudder.

"Hey!" Gideon protested. "A lot of money and work went into this vehicle."

"And we don't want to be drawing attention to it," Rowan added, looking at the bigger guy with concern.

Kaige spun around. "Don't you see? Maybe Axel's guy is doing exactly what he's been ordered to. Ezra's heard about how popular Glory's getting. What if he wants to get in on the drug trade now?" The fury in his voice showed just how much that idea disturbed him.

Wylder stood up too. "Calm down. There's no point in jumping to conclusions like that. My dad's never been interested in dealing drugs before now."

"But now there's Glory. And we never thought he'd order you to kill Mercy either, did we?" Kaige stomped from one side of the van to the other, his face flushing. "Where's that intersection? I should head right over there and pummel that fucker and every other piece of shit involved in this into pieces." He slammed his fist into his open palm.

"Kaige," Wylder said with a warning note, "get yourself together and sit the fuck down."

Kaige swung toward him. "And do nothing? While they're poisoning the whole goddamned city?"

Wylder grabbed his arm and held his gaze steadily. "And how is charging in there going to help anyone, huh? How well did that work out for us last time? Your hotheadedness got us caught with Mercy, and the time before we were nearly nabbed by the cops. So chill the fuck out *now*."

Kaige stared at him. He'd gone still, but his whole body was rigid, his face still red.

Wylder dropped Kaige's arm but kept his gaze fixed on his friend. His tone hardened even more. "I know you've got shit from your past to deal with, but I can't tolerate you flying off the handle constantly. Going off the rails only hurts the rest of us. If you want to be part of this team, you need to get yourself under control."

"Maybe I should just leave, then, since all I do is screw things up," Kaige yelled abruptly. He shot a fierce but guilty look at me. Then, without another word, he shoved open the back doors and leapt out of the van.

"Kaige!" I said, but he'd already slammed the doors behind him. By the time I got them open again, he'd stormed out of sight. I turned back to the others, my heart heavy. What Wylder had said wasn't untrue, but I'd never seen Kaige so upset he'd leave us behind. "Is he going to be okay?"

Wylder sighed and dropped down on the van's floor, rubbing his forehead. "I'm sure he'll be fine. It's better if he clears his head instead of raining all that thunder down on us."

"But what if he runs into the Storm's people—what if he really does try to take them on all by himself?"

"I wouldn't worry about that." Wylder gave me a crooked smile. "Knowing him, he's headed for the train station. There's one place he always goes when he gets too close to the edge. I just hope this time he leaves a lot more there before he comes back."

20

Kaige

THE AMTRAK JERKED TO A HALT, ALMOST THROWING ME OUT of my seat. I caught my balance, rubbing my eyes blearily. The conductor's voice carried robotically over the speakers. "Last stop, Festival Beach. All passengers must now leave the train."

I'd reached my destination. And in the two-hour ride, it felt like I'd slept a lifetime. In fact, it was the deepest sleep I've had in a while. The buzzing haze that usually filled my head, fueled by insomnia and too many energy drinks, had cleared, leaving me shockingly refreshed.

Wouldn't it be nice if I could feel this way without shelling out for a fucking train ticket?

I was in too good a mood from the rest to feel that sour about it. All the stress that had propelled me to the station had faded away. I yawned and grinned, and then noticed the kid from the family in the seats opposite me staring. He was coming out to the beach with Mom and Dad like I'd used to—about the same age too, four or five.

I aimed my smile at him, but he looked away to his mother, who was taking down the luggage from the overhead rack. "Mommy," he hissed, as if he thought I wouldn't hear him, "what's on that man's arms?"

He meant the vine tattoos that encircled my biceps, disappearing under the sleeves of my T-shirt. He didn't know they wrapped around my chest as well. They'd just felt right when I'd had them designed. I wasn't totally sure whether they reflected the trapped sensation that I was all too familiar with or an attempt at reining myself in for my own reasons.

The mother glanced at me and made a face. She dropped her voice lower than his. "Let's go, sweetie. And remember, you don't speak to men like him."

Men like him. As if I'd been so different from her son when I'd started out. As if it was strangers who'd mess you up and not the people who should have been taking care of you.

"Kid," I said. The boy startled but turned his wide eyes on me. "Monsters don't always look so monstrous. Don't go by appearances."

The mother's lips pressed flat, and the father urged the boy down the aisle away from me. Fine. I didn't want to hear any more of their shit anyway. I heaved myself out of the seat and headed down the aisle in the opposite direction toward the car's other doors.

As soon as I stepped out onto the platform, the humid air condensed against my skin. The train ride had only taken two hours, sure, but I might as well have come to another continent. The smells of sand and salty ocean water wafted over me with the heat, and the sun beamed down from a smog-free sky. I fucking loved Festival Beach.

I navigated the crowd heading out of the station. Most people around me were tourists, judging by their dorky sun-hats and Hawaiian shirts or sarongs. No one wanted to waste the last few weeks of summer.

The beach lay just across the street from the station. I walked straight across the road and the boardwalk, kicked off my shoes, and sank my feet into the sand. Hot on the top and cool down beneath, just like I remembered. The perfect combination.

The sun glinted off the deep blue water up ahead. Memories rose up as if tossed by the ocean's waves: running across the sand so fast it sprayed out around me in my wake, spreading my arms as if I were an airplane about to take off into the air. Mom and Dad laughing as they watched, their arms hooked together. Dad coming down to the edge of the surf with me and helping me sculpt a sandcastle.

I could still picture every detail of the last one we'd made, complete with four turrets and a ring of little pearly shells along the outer walls. Mom had applauded and snapped pictures. Then she'd swept me up into her arms and carried me right into the water, where we'd paddled around until my skin was sticky with salt and my fingers pruned. My eyes had started stinging, but I'd never cared about that.

I opened my eyes now to the squawk of seagulls flying above me, and those flashes of the past disintegrated. Despite my train sleep, tension was starting to creep back into my chest.

As if I could outrun it, I walked down to the water and then half a mile along the ocean, rolling up my jeans and letting the foam tickle against my bare calves. The Atlantic water was chilly even this late in the season, but it kept my mind on the present. Plenty of people were splashing around in the ocean, enjoying the relief from the muggy weather.

Right near the train station, couples and families had crowded the beach with a patchwork of towels and umbrellas. Gradually, I left the babble of their happy voices behind me. That atmosphere didn't fit who I was now anyway.

I walked on until the beach got rockier, dark crags of stone jutting from the sand here and there after the boardwalk had ended. No one was venturing this far today—except me.

I wandered on even further just to be sure I wouldn't be disturbed, and then I hunkered down on the other side of one of the boulders. Folding my arms behind my head and stretching out my legs, I closed my eyes and just listened to that rhythmic hiss.

I didn't realize I'd fallen asleep again, but all of a sudden I was jolting awake to the sound of my name. A figure was standing over me, framed by the pink tones coloring the sky that was now shifting toward evening. Her ponytail tossed in the wind.

"Kaige?" Mercy said, crouching down next to me. "Are you okay?"

My pulse lurched, and I shoved myself upright. "Mercy?" It couldn't really be her, could it? I was still dreaming, or she was a hallucination. Frank would be so happy to know he'd been right and all those energy drinks had finally fried my brain.

But then her tanned, solid hands came down on my arm. Electricity buzzed through me as I registered her touch.

She was here. She was real.

The last of the sleep left my eyes, and I stared at her, horrified. Of all the places... "What are you doing here?" I asked.

She looked at me sheepishly. "Wylder told me about this place. You... seemed pretty upset when you left. I wanted to make sure you were okay."

I shook my head to make sure I was hearing her correctly. "Wylder told you?"

He had absolutely no right to. Irritation flared in my chest, followed by a jab of guilt. They'd both probably been worried about me doing something stupid—more stupid than the crap I'd already put them through.

Mercy looked at me with concern I couldn't quite believe I deserved. "Is that a problem? He isn't really angry with you, you know. He was just frustrated."

"*You* should be frustrated," I muttered, rubbing my forehead. "Because of me, you've got a bounty on your head. And you still came looking for me."

Mercy cocked her head at me as if I was being ridiculous. "I'm sure Ezra would have found a way to screw me over no matter what you did. And I was worried about you. In case you haven't noticed, I kind of like you a little bit."

Her wry tone brought a smile to my mouth even as my heart squeezed at her words. "Just a little bit?" I couldn't help teasing.

She socked me in the shoulder in answer and sat down on the sand next to me, close enough that I could tuck my arm around her waist. I watched her from the corner of my eyes, still having a little trouble believing she was real.

No one had ever cared this much about me before. No one had ever bothered to follow me here. It was partly that the guys figured I knew what I needed and could sort myself out on my own, but... it was kind of nice having someone track me down just so I wouldn't be alone.

Mercy drank in the sea air and gazed around us. With the nearby boulders sheltering us, the beach looked empty. I couldn't hear a single voice or laugh in the distance. Most of the families farther down had probably left for the day.

The cooling evening breeze played with a few stray strands of Mercy's hair. She tipped her face toward it. "So, why this place?"

I hesitated. Even Wylder didn't know the whole story.

Mercy glanced over at me. "You don't have to talk about it if you don't want to."

A stronger impulse rose up in me—to show her I could be just as real with her as she'd been with me. I wasn't sure I wanted her knowing all the fucked up stuff, but there were some things it wouldn't be too bad to share.

I motioned behind me. "When I was a little kid, my parents were friends with another family who had a beach house out here. They'd have us come out to stay for a week every summer. Best times I had in my whole childhood."

My throat had started to tighten. Mercy ran her fingers over my hand. "You don't sound so happy talking about it."

I shrugged, my other hand coming up to wrap around my dad's dog tags where they dangled from the chain around my neck. All kinds of uncomfortable emotions were swelling up inside me. I wanted to run away from them, away from Mercy's questions—but how would that be fair to her?

She deserved to know what kind of guy she was letting herself get tangled up with, didn't she?

I dragged in a breath and looked down at my knees. Something inside me hummed in tune to the waves, helping me gather my words.

"My dad never totally got over the stuff he went through when he was enlisted, before I was born," I said. "He'd have nightmares, wake up screaming. One time he punched Mom so hard in his sleep that he gave her a black eye. He didn't believe in shrinks, though, thought they just messed you up more. At first it was only now and then, but it started getting worse. He'd get edgy even when he was awake... I think that's why he ended up turning to the drugs."

Mercy squeezed my hand. "You told me both of your parents were addicts. I didn't realize that's why."

I nodded, my head feeling heavy with the weight of the story and all the awfulness that came with it. "At first it was only a hit here and there, and he encouraged Mom to give it a try—I think so he wouldn't feel alone, to convince himself it was okay. But they got hooked fast. We had one last good summer here when I was five. Then everything went to hell over the next winter. Dad lost his job. Mom's barely paid enough to cover the bills. They cared more about getting their next high than making sure we had anything in the house to eat."

"I'm so sorry," Mercy said, resting her head against my shoulder.

Would she still want to be this close to me when she heard the whole thing? I forced myself to keep talking. "The next summer, they brought me out here again. I was so happy, thinking maybe it was a sign that things would get better again. I was a naïve kid. I didn't realize my mom had just lost her job too. My parents showed up at the beach house and begged their friends for money. That was the only reason we'd come. And they tried to use me for pity points."

Mercy sucked air through her teeth. "Kaige—"

I shook my head. Now that I'd begun, I couldn't stop the truth from pouring out of me. Even the parts that hurt coming out.

"Things only went from bad to worse from there. Their friends obviously turned them down. Back in the city, I started grabbing whatever food I could out of park garbage cans when people would toss sandwich crusts or whatever. The electricity and then the water got shut off. My parents didn't seem to care about that or me. The only time they noticed I was even there was when they came down from a high and got angry. They would beat the shit out of me, saying they'd have it so much easier if they didn't have to take care of me. As if they even were."

"That's horrible," Mercy said in a choked voice.

And it wasn't even the worst of it. I inhaled shakily as darkness began to consume me, the same darkness that haunted the edges of my mind every time I started to relax back in the Bend. Drugs had ruined my parents and infected me with the ugly rages that I would have to carry for the rest of my life.

"Then they decided I was the solution to their problems," I went on. "They—They started hiring me out when I was eight. Letting men come and do what they wanted with me, as long as they paid. The first time, I didn't even understand what was happening till I felt the pain..."

The blaze of that pain had almost made me pass out. I'd begged the man to stop, but he didn't care, and neither did the one after him or the next one.

"They'd always come after I'd gone to sleep for the night," I said, staring at the ocean because I couldn't bear to see Mercy's expression. "When I got into bed, I never knew whether I'd make it through the night alone. I'd lie there, braced for another one to come... It fucked me up. Not just the sleep, but all kinds of ways. I can't stand letting anyone else be in control of me in any way now. I always have to be in charge when I'm hooking up with someone, and I don't even know how to take control of myself when my anger explodes."

"Kaige," Mercy said, her voice quieter now. Her hand squeezed tight around mine. I still didn't dare look at her.

Do you see me now? I wanted to ask her. Do you see how much ugly and monstrous stuff there is in me? Maybe that kid on the train and his parents had been right about me after all. They'd known what I was because I never could get rid of it.

"I wear Dad's tags hoping they'll be a good enough reminder," I said out loud. "Even someone who went through all that army training, all that discipline, can still totally fuck up his life and everyone's around him. I might have a temper and I might get into a rage sometimes, but I *never* want to let myself be so weak I'd hurt someone who didn't deserve it for my own gain. And maybe it's fitting too, because in the end Dad died a death worse than a dog's."

"What do you mean?" Mercy asked.

I grimaced, taking in the crash of the waves. "Eventually my parents' appetites got so big nothing was enough to keep them satisfied. They were getting their drugs from some small-time gang in the Bend. They ended up stealing some, and a guy came to collect. My dad lunged at him, trying to fight him over it—the guy shot him right in the head. Mom ran off. I never saw her again after that. But I didn't mind. I wasn't even upset at that point. I *admired* the guy who stood up for himself and blew Dad away."

My mouth twisted into a hard smile. "That was what led me to the

Nobles. I wanted to be like my own dad's murderer—to join a gang so I could learn how to be that strong and defend myself. I was only ten, so it wasn't like I could just sign up or something, but out on the streets, I heard pretty quick that the Nobles were the badass-est gang there was. I found ways to start doing little jobs for them when I could. Wylder noticed me and spoke up for me... and I finally had a life I didn't hate."

I swallowed hard and finally forced myself to turn toward Mercy. "There you go. That's my whole fucked-up life." I didn't think I wanted to hear what she'd say about all that, but it was too late to turn back now.

21

Mercy

I STARED AT KAIGE IN SHOCK, STILL REELING FROM everything he'd revealed. The abuse he'd suffered at his parents' hands… the way they'd let others do things even worse to him… I couldn't begin to fathom his pain.

He looked so miserable, so unlike his usual cheerfully flirty self, that it made my heart ache. He was tensed as if he thought at any second I was going to tell him to get the hell away from me.

I entwined his fingers in mine and gripped them tightly, sending all the assurance and strength I could to him. He had to know his past wasn't going to change how I saw him.

"It isn't your fault," I said. "You were betrayed by the people who were supposed to love you. That pain shaped you into the man you are today, but it doesn't mean something's wrong with you."

"But it is," Kaige whispered. "I feel the rage and—and the fear inside of me almost like it's alive. I've tried putting it behind me so many times but it just takes over at the worst possible moments." He pressed his hand to his temple. "Maybe coming here was a bad idea."

I shook my head. "No. You faced up to your past and opened up to me. I think that means you're healing, Kaige. You just don't know it yet."

I rubbed his shoulder with my other hand. His unpredictable and erratic behavior made so much sense now. Kaige had been dealing with his trauma, not letting anybody in, not wanting to give anyone any power over him after how much his parents had taken away. "I'm glad you told me," I added.

He scoffed. "And how does it make you feel about me?"

"Nothing's changed," I said simply as I stroked my fingers across his back. It was ironic how I felt like I needed to be so gentle with this big man who was at least twice my size. But in this vulnerable state, I could almost see the younger Kaige, the six-year-old whose parents had led him out here one last time only to use him as a prop to try to fuel their addiction.

Kaige looked over at me. For the first time, I caught a hint of hope in his dark eyes. Affection swelled in my chest. Without thinking, I leaned forward and pressed a kiss to his lips.

He kissed me back only tentatively, as if he still wasn't sure he could believe that I was for real. I moved my lips to his cheek, then to the rough scuff of stubble on his jaw. A breath shuddered out of him, followed by an eager growl that sounded more like the man I knew.

I walked my fingers teasingly up his chest. "You know, I've had a lot of fun while you were in charge. But maybe it's time you learned how to let someone else share that role with you."

Desire still shone in Kaige's eyes, but I could see him debating my suggestion. It was probably incredibly hard for him to even consider it.

"You don't have to give up complete control," I said, and pressed another kiss to the side of his neck. "It'd just be a little back and forth. If it bothers you too much, you just have to say so."

Kaige let out a groan. "It's too hard to say no to you. You're a fucking enchantress, I swear. Come here."

He leaned forward, but only close enough that his mouth barely grazed mine. When he opened his mouth, the hot air of his breath played on my lips. I made an impatient sound, my panties dampening in anticipation of the passion I knew he could unleash.

"Why don't you demonstrate what you're thinking?" he murmured, his deep baritone so sexy I was instantly twice as wet.

I wasn't going to wait for a second invitation. My whole body was humming with hunger for him now. I glanced around, making sure we were well out of sight from the rest of the beach, and climbed onto his lap.

He adjusted me so my legs straddled his muscular thighs, then met my eyes as if to say, *Your turn*. I smiled and shifted forward, letting my legs ride up to his hips. My pussy settled against the bulge of his erection through our jeans. I wet my lips, holding back a moan at that first bit of giddy friction and the bolt of pleasure that shot up from my core.

I nudged his chest, and he tensed for a second before lying back on the sand. Splaying my fingers against the planes of muscle, I ran my hands down to his six pack and up again to tease along his jaw. "Is this okay?"

His hands came around to circle my waist. "More than okay."

I didn't want him just lying there, though. Maybe it was time he took a few orders from someone other than Wylder. "Kiss me," I said.

He cocked an eyebrow. "Where?"

I pressed a finger to my lips. Kaige eased back up on his elbows, meeting me when I lowered myself toward him. He gave the corner of my mouth a quick peck before sliding his lips right across mine with a flick of his tongue. I shivered eagerly and moved my head so that I could kiss him harder.

"Don't be impatient," Kaige chided. "I think it's my turn to call the shots."

I huffed my disappointment, and he chuckled. "I like this way too, wildcat," he said before gently pressing a kiss to my lips.

I sighed just as his tongue slipped into my mouth, gently playing against my own as he tilted his head to kiss me deeper. We made out like that, switching the tempo between shallow kisses and deeper ones, trading control back and forth.

My hips began to move against his, seeking out more of that delicious pressure. Kaige growled and gripped my hips, but he didn't stop me. I sank down against him, putting my arms around his shoulders. The solid planes of his chest almost crushed my boobs. I liked the feel of them, the hardness against the soft curves of my body.

He squeezed my breasts as he kissed me harder and then let me go, resting his lips on mine so that when he spoke I felt the vibration of the words on my own. "What next, Kitty Cat?"

"I think you've neglected some places." I pointed at my jaw and trailed down to the valley of my breasts.

Kaige's gaze followed, hot and dark. He kissed down my neck, nipping and sucking at his whim, setting my skin on fire. My head fell back to give him better access.

He kissed across the path that I had shown him, lingering at the neckline of my shirt. I pulled it up without him asking and then tugged at the hem of his. He didn't hesitate. The second his shirt was off, he unhooked my bra.

Our clothes ended up in a bunch on the sand, but I was past caring. I ran my hands down his powerful corded muscles, tracing the vine tattoos that trailed across them.

"These are beautiful," I said.

"You think so?" Kaige glanced down at himself. "I keep changing my mind about whether I love them or hate them."

"Hmm. Let me worship them a little, and we'll see what you think then."

I slid down his body and dappled kisses along one line and another, following the tattoos across his shoulders, pecs, and abs. When I traced the tip of one vine right beside his bellybutton with my tongue, he groaned and dug his fingers into my hair.

"See," I said. "It isn't so bad when you share control."

"No, it isn't," he said. "But I know where I want you right now." He hauled me up over him so that I could feel the hard press of his cock lined against my cunt again. I gasped at the sensation of it and then smiled. Yeah, he was definitely enjoying this.

Kaige tugged me even higher, cupping my breasts with his huge hands before bringing them to his mouth. When his hot lips wrapped around my nipple, the rush of pleasure made me moan. His tongue laved the hardened nub before swirling tenderly around it.

He tested the weight of my other breast in his hand, pinching the tip between his thumb and forefinger. I could feel his own impatience growing in the shifting of his body beneath me, the urgency of his movements. He sucked on my nipple hard, and before I could recover from the onslaught of his tongue, he rolled us so I was pinned under him.

"Okay?" he asked.

Oh, fucking, yes. I grinned up at him with a nod. "Fuck me. Fuck me with everything you've got. Everything you are. I want all of it."

With a strangled noise, he wrenched down my jeans and panties. As he nudged my legs apart, I reached for the buttons on his jeans and unzipped him. His cock sprang out, hard and wanting against my thighs. I rubbed the head, slicking the precum around, and then helped him into the condom he dug out of his pocket.

I had no idea if anybody on the beach was close enough to overhear us, and honestly at this point I didn't care. Kaige slowly eased into me. I gasped as my inner walls adjusted around his girth.

For a few seconds, he stopped above me, as deep as he could possibly get inside. Our past two encounters had been hard and fast, as if all that mattered was getting to the point of release. As if he was running away from things he'd rather not think about. But tonight he was taking it slower, like he was making the most of every second. Somehow that turned me on even more.

Kaige started to move inside me, stroking in and out. I rocked to meet him, humming encouragingly as his unhurried movements drove me toward my peak. He stretched my arms on either side, leaving me spread eagle beneath him. Sand clung to my skin, warm and grainy. It tickled against my skin as he increased his strokes.

His hips worked between mine as he picked up his pace, steady and sure, hitting a spot deep inside me. At the same time, his fingers went to work between us, rubbing my clit. A heady swell of pleasure was building inside me. When I moaned, he leaned down to capture the sound in his mouth.

Then all at once he pumped into me even faster, his motions becoming almost erratic. I clung to him, letting the first wave of ecstasy sweep through me. He continued to fondle my clit and didn't let his pace falter as my pussy began to quake, milking him. The second the aftershock of my orgasm subsided, he pounded into me again, kissing me at the same time. His hips rotated in a circle and drove him even deeper inside me, and I toppled over the edge again.

Kaige followed me with a loud moan of his own. Our mouths swallowed each other's cries as we came together this time.

Afterwards, we stayed wrapped around each other, listening to the sound of the waves. The cool, salty air from the sea teased across my naked back as Kaige played with my hair. The moon had risen above us. It was well and truly night now. I didn't know just how many hours we had spent together here.

I drew circles on his chest and heard his breath even out.

"Did you like that?" Kaige asked gruffly.

I raised my head to look at him. "It's never been better."

Something lit up in his dark eyes, so pleased and even joyful that my heart squeezed. An emotion I wasn't ready to name coursed through me from head to toe.

Was I falling for Kaige—was I falling for all four of these guys? I had a deep emotional connection with them, but I knew the bond that was growing between us was more than just friendship or loyalty.

How far would it go?

"Mercy," Kaige said. I heard the catch in his voice when he said my name. Did he know what I was thinking?

I leaned forward to brush my lips against his. "Yes?"

"I like this," he said. "Just—just lying here with you. Maybe as much as I liked making you come, if that doesn't sound totally insane."

A light laugh spilled out of me. "It doesn't. I like it too. Well, both things." I winked at him and then nestled my head against his chest again.

All I wanted to do was fall asleep and remain that way for the next few hours, but I knew we couldn't ignore the problems waiting for us back in Paradise Bend for much longer. I sighed. "We should probably head home soon."

Kaige nodded. "Yeah. But the trains run pretty late. Let's just give it a few more minutes."

I couldn't argue with that. We lay in our little cocoon of contentment, and I tried not to think about the hell that'd be waiting for us when we returned.

22

Mercy

"Look at that," I said, peering through the windshield of the plain Ford that Wylder had chosen for this drive.

Wylder's gaze jerked to follow mine. "Look at what?"

"Exactly." I motioned to the street ahead of us. "More nothing, just like we've seen all night. We haven't seen any sign of the Storm's people or the Red Shark's guys."

It was past eleven at night, and we hadn't even driven past any drug dealers selling Glory. I hadn't seen this little gang activity in the Bend in… maybe as long as I'd been old enough to notice.

"I guess we can hope that means our tactics have been working," Wylder said with a grin. "They got tired of fending off the police as well as each other and decided to cool it for a bit."

"Now we just have to get them to head right out of town," I muttered.

Wylder nudged me with his elbow. "Don't be so pessimistic. One step at a time. I, for one, would like to celebrate this victory."

He drove back toward Paradise City until we passed into the outskirts and pulled off onto a secluded side street. Then he dug a couple of wine coolers out from under the seat. He passed one to me, popped open his, and held it out to me. Shaking my head in amusement, I clinked the bottles together. "Cheers."

Wylder threw back a gulp of the stuff and grimaced. "Maybe I should have brought my brandy. Oh well." He sank into his seat, stretching out his legs, and glanced over at me. "Kaige has been much chiller since you went out to collect him at Festival Beach yesterday. What exactly happened out there?"

I shrugged. "We talked."

"Just talked?" Wylder said with an arch of his eyebrows, but I didn't think his interest was totally casual.

I wasn't going to feed his competitive side. "Yep. Talking helps, you know. Sometimes much more than you think."

"Well, all that *talking* seems to have helped Kaige a lot."

I rolled my eyes. "There's no euphemism to it, Wylder." Even if Kaige and I had gotten in some pretty spectacular not-just-talking afterward.

"Look, it doesn't have to be a thing." Wylder dragged in a breath and barreled onward with a rush of words I got the impression he'd rehearsed in his head. "You're into him, and you're into me—and Gideon and Rowan too. Well, I guess things never totally ended between you two, huh?"

Where was he going with this? I settled for answering the easiest question. "Rowan and I had a pretty complicated relationship."

"But you've figured it out, at least mostly." His fingers tightened around the neck of the bottle. "You have no idea how much I want to keep you all to myself. To know no one except me gets to touch you. The things I've imagined doing to you, *with* you..."

The vehemence in his voice sent a rush of heat through me. "Me being with the other guys doesn't stop us from doing all kinds of things too," I had to point out, holding myself back from squirming in my seat.

Wylder sighed. "It doesn't. And, even though part of me wants to make you only mine—I can also see that isn't fair to you. You're too much woman to be constrained to just one guy. As long as you're *only* with us, I can see the benefits to enjoying the extra help keeping you satisfied." He shot me a sly grin. "In all kinds of ways."

Okay, my panties were definitely soaked now. But I felt the need to clarify: "What exactly are you saying?"

"I'm not going to make you pick," he said with his usual air of assurance, as if the decision was totally up to him. "In case you were still wondering about that. I figure there's nothing wrong with you being 'our' woman. As long as you're willing to put up with all of us."

I cocked my head as if considering. "You *have* been a jackass for a pretty significant amount of the time I've known you."

Wylder snorted. "But it's been fun, hasn't it? Neither of us are easy people. I like when your claws come out, Kitty Cat." He rested his hand on my thigh and squeezed. "You spent a long time under your father's thumb in a shitty situation. Maybe between the four of us we can make up for all the time when no one in your life valued you anywhere near enough."

My stomach clenched, both at his words and his touch.

"That's definitely something to think about," I said as a strange but exhilarating emotion rose up through my chest.

Wylder glanced at me sideways with one of those cocky grins. "So, out of the four of us, who's your favorite?"

I gave him an incredulous look. "Do you really want to know that?"

"Of course. I love hearing my name from your mouth. Especially when it's accompanied by moans."

I smacked his arm. "That's a lot of confidence."

"It's called self-assurance," he said, wagging a finger at me.

"I still have your knife on me. Be careful what you say."

"A little blood never hurt anybody. Besides, you know I like it kinky." Wylder's grin only grew.

I laughed. It was good to know that no matter what happened, Wylder was never going soft on me. And I did like it that way. "Well, for the record, the position of favorite is still up for grabs. But I will make you work for it."

An eager glint came into Wylder's eyes as if he was going to start on that "work" right now, but before he could do more than stroke his hand up my thigh, his phone buzzed in his pocket. With a grumble, he drew back and pulled it out, hitting the speaker phone button when he saw the caller ID. "Hey, Gideon, what's up?"

Gideon's voice crackled through the line. "There's a problem."

Wylder frowned. "What are you talking about? We didn't have any operations planned tonight."

"*We* didn't," Gideon said. "But your dad had that deal going on tonight—the shipment coming in."

I glanced at Wylder. "I didn't know about this."

He waved his hand dismissively. "It didn't really have anything to do with you. Just typical business—some of our people bringing in stolen merch. There's a small cargo plane that's supposed to land at the private airstrip just outside of the Bend right around now."

"Yeah, that," Gideon said. "The cops seem to have found out about it."

"What?" Wylder said, sounding incredulous. "How the hell would they know anything?"

"I don't know, but they're closing in on the place. They'll be there and have it surrounded in five minutes or less."

Wylder swore and started tapping texts into his phone. "I'll warn the guys. What the fuck could have gone wrong? Axel was handling this one personally. He's a prick, but he knows how to keep his mouth shut about Dad's business."

"This is a particularly important shipment too, isn't it?" Gideon said.

"Yeah," Wylder muttered, still tapping away furiously. "It's one of the main reasons Dad was out of town so long last month. Fuck. If the first deal with his new associate goes sideways, the entire deal could fall apart." He stared at the messages he was getting back and banged his hand against the car door. "I'm not getting any responses. It's too far for us to get there in time to warn them in person. Who all would be out there with Axel?"

Gideon hummed thoughtfully. "All the usuals, I'd guess. Let me see..." His end of the conversation went abruptly quiet. Then he muttered, "Shit."

My pulse stuttered. "What?"

"I've been paying a little extra attention to that guy of Axel's we've seen hanging out with the Storm's people," Gideon said. "Put a tracker on his car a couple days ago. Right now it's out in that part of the warehouse district where we've heard the Storm's people probably have their headquarters."

"Why would he be out there when his boss has a major deal going on?" I turned to Wylder, a chill washing over me. "Unless he tipped the Storm's people off, and they sicced the cops on us this time."

"Fucking hell." Wylder sent off one last text message and glared at the screen. "I'm just going to call. Gideon, I'll have to get off the line."

"I'll keep monitoring the situation on my end."

Wylder hung up and clicked to dial Axel's number. He left the phone on speaker mode, the ringing carrying through the car. It took three before Axel picked up with an annoyed, "What the fuck are you harassing me about, kid? I'm dealing with enough problems already."

Yells and screeching tires carried through the phone line. Axel swore a few times as the sounds started to fade. The cops had already arrived, I realized, and he was heading away from the scene. He must have had lookouts who'd spotted them in time for at least some of them to flee.

"Cops are there, right?" Wylder said quickly. "Did you manage to get the goods?"

"No. Had to get the fuck out of there before— They managed to nab a few people even as it was... How the hell do you know what's going on here?"

"Gideon spotted it," Wylder said. "I tried to contact you and your men earlier. Of course, it looks like one of those men is the one who sold us out, so..."

Axel had started barking orders to whoever was driving, his voice muffled, probably with his palm over the speaker. At those last words, he came back on the line. "What's that supposed to mean?"

"That guy of yours you said was investigating the Storm," Wylder said, his jaw clenching. "Was he supposed to be there at the airstrip tonight? Did he know about the deal?"

"Who the fuck cares? I have a disaster to deal with."

"Was he meant to be there?" Wylder repeated with deadly firmness.

Axel paused, and in the momentary quiet, I sensed the

understanding hitting him. "He didn't show. The cops must have grabbed him early."

"Then it's awfully funny that Gideon can trace his car to one of the Storm's people's main hideouts right now, isn't it?"

More silence. Then Axel switched over from shock to defensive anger like the flick of a switch. "How the fuck do you know about any of this? Seems like you've been awfully involved right when things went sideways."

Wylder let out a sputtered guffaw. "Are you accusing *me* of sabotaging things just so you don't have to admit you picked a rat for your team?"

"You're the one who said it," Axel snapped back. "Someone has to pay for this mess. I guess we'll just have to find out what Ezra says about it. I expect to see you back at the house when I get there. Have you even finished the last job he gave you?"

The job that was murdering me. We hadn't wanted to talk about it, but Wylder's time was up tomorrow. He looked at me, determined but with a question in his eyes.

He'd made a hell of a commitment to me just minutes ago. Certainty gripped me that I needed to show him I was just as all-in as he was. That I'd be here with him no matter what shit his dad rained down on us.

I reached to grab his hand and squeezed it. Then I took the knife he'd given me out of my pocket. Holding his gaze, I slid the blade across my palm like he'd done to his thumb when he'd sworn to help me take down Colt if I cleared Kaige of the murder suspicions on him. A blood promise.

Wylder's eyes tracked the movement of the knife, the blood that welled up from the shallow cut. I held up my hand so he could see it clearly. "I'm in this with you," I whispered, holding his gaze when it lifted to my face. "All the way to the end."

Wylder gave me a tight little smile, but his eyes shone brightly. He turned back to the phone.

Axel was yammering again. "Did I hear someone there with you, kid? What kind of—"

"Axel," Wylder said brusquely, "shut up. You're not seeing me tonight. Possibly not for a few days. I have my own business to take care of, and maybe it's time both you and Dad realize just how much you need *me* after all."

He hung up before Axel could do more than start to sputter and tossed the phone on the dashboard. In one swift movement, he captured my wrist with his strong fingers. I kept my hand steady, ignoring the stinging in my palm.

"Blood for blood," I said, my voice still quiet. "We're in this together."

"Yes, we are," he murmured. Then he slowly leaned in and licked the blood clean from the small wound.

As his tongue made contact with my sensitive skin, I sucked in a breath, but I didn't flinch or pull back. He wiped a tiny smear of blood from his lips and smiled at me with the warmth of the sun. "I couldn't ask for anyone better to have by my side."

I smiled back and brandished the knife, the tip of the blade still bloody. "Maybe it's time for the prince and princess of the Paradise Bend to become king and queen and reclaim what both of us really deserve."

Wylder's eyes heated. I saw lust in them, and resolve, and something else—just for me. "Damn right."

I didn't know how the hell we were going to deal with Ezra or the invading gangs or anything else we were up against, but in that moment, everything felt totally right.

Until Wylder's phone buzzed again.

Wylder let go of my arm with obvious reluctance and snatched the phone off the dashboard. He frowned at the screen before answering. "They've gotten out of there, Gideon. We were too late to salvage the deal."

"That's not what I'm calling about this time," Gideon said in an unexpectedly panicky tone. "Something's been set off in the Bend. The Storm's people came out of nowhere—they're all over the video feeds—they're attacking everyone they can get their hands on. It's a fucking massacre."

23

Mercy

THE EARLY MORNING SUN SHOULD HAVE LIT UP THE STREETS of the Bend with a cheerful glow. Instead it caught on splatters of blood staining the roads and sidewalks—and here and there the wall of a building. The legs of a corpse that hadn't yet been found protruded from one alley we drove past in the van. Several of the worst streets were cordoned off with police tape, cops swarming the place and hauling away bodies.

Other than a few other cars we passed, the police were the only people we saw out and about. All the businesses were closed; none of the regular civilians dared to leave their homes.

As we cruised by a house that had its door bashed in and pools of blood drying on the front walk, my stomach flipped over. "How many people did they kill?"

"It's still not clear," Gideon said, peering at his laptop. He had his full arsenal out today, the screens mounted in the back of the van all flicking from feed to feed, his tablet on the bench beside him. "I couldn't keep track of them last night. The Storm's people burst out of vehicles all over the place, broke into all kinds of buildings, shot the people inside or mowed them down as they tried to run. I'm not sure how many were even their actual targets vs. bystanders in the wrong place at the wrong time."

That possibility made me feel even more sick. That psychotic asshole Xavier had taken things even further, gone on some fucking rampage through my city, and now look at it. Who the fuck did the Storm's pricks think they were, anyway? My hands clenched into fists.

Then my gaze caught on a familiar store up ahead. I stood up abruptly. "Hey, stop for a second?"

Rowan pulled over. He glanced at the street ahead and then back at me. "Isn't that...?"

A man was carrying sagging boxes from a convenience shop on the corner to the back of a pick-up truck, where a few suitcases and pieces of furniture were already stacked. A woman and a little girl stood huddled off to the side of the door, watching him work, their gazes darting around nervously.

"Mercy?" Wylder prompted from the passenger seat.

I swallowed hard. "I used to come here with my Grandma. The owner was the son of one of her friends."

Mr. Phillips looked as if he'd aged a decade in only a few months. I remembered him a smiling man at the counter who always used to give me a lollipop even when I was too old for it. When he turned back toward the store now, I only saw exhaustion and fear in the lines on his face.

Another man poked his head out from an apartment window over the neighboring store. "Phillips, are you closing up permanently?"

"Yes, son," Mr. Phillips said, pausing by the door. "It's time to move on for good. Might be better for you to do the same if you can."

I stood transfixed as he grabbed one more box from the store and then locked the door. A FOR LEASE sign hung in the now-dingy window. As he put a hand on the small of his wife's back to lead her and his daughter to the truck, his gaze passed over the van as if he didn't see it at all. Maybe he couldn't see anything except the new horizons he was fleeing toward.

The urge gripped me to run after him and yell at him for abandoning his home to these monsters. But Mr. Phillips was doing the best thing he could, wasn't he? He was protecting his family the only way he knew how, taking them away from this hell before it was too late.

Anger flared through my queasiness. The Storm had changed my home for the worse, first by manipulating Colt into bringing chaos to the streets and then swooping in to claim territory. They had turned this place into a literal horror show, the streets red with blood. And what had *I* been able to do about it?

As much as I hated my father, I almost wished he was alive. He would see what his mistake had done to his home, and maybe he'd have done something to fix it. He'd been cruel, but he'd known these streets.

I couldn't bear to watch any longer. The guys were studying me, uncertain of my reaction. "Let's just keep going," I said, dropping back onto the bench and taking a few deep breaths. The combined scents of my four men wrapped around me, settling my nerves just a little.

As Rowan pulled away from the curb, Gideon looked at me, an expression I couldn't read on his normally impassive face. His mouth tensed as if he was about to say something but couldn't quite decide whether he should.

Before he could, Wylder motioned to him. "It was mostly Red Shark people the attackers were after, as far as you can tell?"

Gideon nodded. "They hit several locations where I'd already noticed Red Shark activity. My best guess would be that this was a concentrated effort to end the threat they posed completely." He frowned at the laptop's screen. "And it seems to have worked. There were at least a couple of Red Shark hideouts they mustn't have known about, and I have footage of several people packing up and driving off from those, right out of town."

Kaige turned from where he'd been standing with his hand on the back of Rowan's seat. "The Red Shark's guys took off?"

"What was left of them. The offensive worked."

The jolt of the van's wheels over a pothole made my gut lurch harder. "Then the Storm won that battle."

"And that means they're now in a perfect position to focus all their attention on crushing the Nobles," Wylder said grimly.

"Not if we have anything to say about it!" Kaige declared, smacking his balled hand into his palm.

"Right," I agreed, wishing I had something—or better, some*one*—to punch right now. "We're not letting those bastards get away with this."

I didn't need my father. We'd beaten Colt, and we'd destroy these assholes too. The Storm and his men were going to pay for what they'd done to this place. If I had my way, by the end of this they'd wish they'd never even heard of Paradise Bend.

Wylder's green eyes were fixed on me. "You look like you're scheming something, Queen Katz."

My lips twitched into a ghost of a smile at his callback to our conversation last night. "I'm getting started on it. But I think we're going to need some help, and obviously we can't go to your father or anyone working for him for that." I paused. "Let's see what the rest of the Claws are up to."

Finding the former Claws members wasn't as simple as just showing up. We swung by the shop where I'd met with Kervos and his small crew earlier, but the basement was abandoned, pretty hastily from the looks of things. A half-full mug of coffee was sitting on the card table. Gideon glanced at it and wrinkled his nose as if he could already tell it didn't meet his stringent criteria.

Rowan turned to me. "Any idea where else they might have gone?"

I worried at my lower lip. "I can think of a few places we can try, but if they're trying to avoid being found after that massacre, they might not go anywhere that's ever been associated with the Claws. I did get Kervos's number. Let's see if he'll answer a text."

If he didn't, it might be because he was dead. I didn't want to say that out loud.

"Are there traffic cams in this neighborhood?" Wylder asked Gideon as we tramped back upstairs. "Maybe you can see which direction they took off in."

Gideon dipped his head in a jerky motion. He seemed more tense than usual. "I'll do whatever I can."

But we'd just piled back into the van when my phone pinged with a response to my text. *We're in the back of the pub your dad sold. Make sure no one sees you.*

My heart leapt. "Never mind about the cams. I know where to go."

My dad had owned the pub down on Morton St. until I was twelve years old. He'd used to hold meetings there, letting me play behind the counter as long as I didn't touch any of the bottles. Then the guy who was managing the place double-crossed him somehow or other, and even though he'd taken care of the traitor, the betrayal had soured the place for him. He'd sold it off and moved his activities elsewhere.

Business mustn't have gone much better for the later owners, because we arrived to find the windows boarded up. Rowan parked around the corner, and he and Kaige hung back to keep an eye on the street while Wylder and Gideon joined me. We made our way over through the alley to the back rather than tramping along the sidewalk out front.

The lock on the back door was broken. As I eased it aside, a groan reached my ears. I pushed past it into the shadowy room.

Kervos was slumped on the floor amid the empty boxes that'd once held bottles of vodka and gin. Roy leaned over him, wrapping a bandage around his mid-section. My pulse stuttered.

I hurried over. "Is he okay? What happened?"

"'He' can speak for himself, and he'll be just fine," Kervos muttered in a strained voice. "Although I'll admit I've been in better shape."

"It looks like it's healing okay so far," Roy told him, and turned to us. His face had gone wan. "You've seen what the Bend looks like. Those Storm jackasses went crazy."

"They attacked you too?" I glanced around and realized it was just the two of them. "Where are the others—Wheeler and...?" I'd never gotten the other two guys' names. Another jolt of panic hit me. "What about Jenner and the other Claws people you were still in touch with?"

Kervos sat up carefully, favoring his injured side. "We've heard from Jenner. He and a few people made it out. He's the one who warned us the pricks were coming."

"We just weren't fast enough," Roy added. "We only got a little way down the street when they were everywhere, shooting like mad—I'm surprised they didn't kill *each other* the way they were going at it." He let out a rough chuckle, but his voice was taut with fear. "That guy with the scarred cheeks was in the middle of it all, fucking *applauding* them in between firing his own shots. He's insane."

Wylder frowned. "Why would he come after you? I understand them wanting to take out the Red Sharks, but all you were doing was laying low."

Kervos shrugged. "Like Roy said, the guy's clearly absolutely fucking nuts." I thought I saw his muscular frame contain a shudder. It said something about Xavier that he'd unnerved even this experienced gangster. "I think he wanted to clear out anyone who'd ever had any loyalty that wasn't to him or Colt. He even—"

He grimaced and swiped his hand across his mouth before continuing. "He had a few of the Claws guys who'd stayed on with the Steel Knights contingent with him. They must have told the Storm's people where to look for us. But I saw, when Roy was dragging me out of there after I got shot—they died too. The Storm's men turned on them as soon as they thought they were done with us and blasted their skulls open."

"It was a fucking bloodbath," Roy said, looking away.

Gideon had been standing rigidly next to me during the conversation so far. Now, he started to pace the room, one arm tucked tight around his tablet, a wild light in his normally cool eyes.

"This isn't good," he said. "It's too close to spiraling out of our ability to control the situation. We need to hit back—hard and fast, before they can get any more of the upper hand."

Wylder shot him a puzzled look. "Don't forget smart. Hard and fast on its own is only going to get us killed too."

"Smart goes without saying," Gideon retorted. I'd never heard him speak to Wylder that sharply.

Wylder looked taken aback too, but Roy cut in before either of them could say anything more. "You've got to be crazy to want to take them on."

"What else can we do?" I demanded. "Look what they're doing to the Bend. Look what they've done to you! We can't let them take over everything."

Roy opened his mouth and closed it again before answering. "I'm not sure we have a lot of choice."

I set my hands on my hips, summoning all the determination I had in me. "We always have a choice. This is my home, and I'm not letting some psycho chase me out of it. Kervos, you said we could call on you if we needed you. Is that still true?"

Roy and Kervos exchanged a glance. Maybe they were thinking *I* was insane. Things had gotten a lot worse since Kervos had made that offer. But the thought of running away and abandoning the place where I'd grown up made my chest ache.

People like Mr. Phillips didn't have the skills or the resources to fight back, but we did. If we didn't stand up to Xavier and the Storm, who the hell would?

"I have a plan," Gideon said abruptly into the silence that followed. "We can do it on our own, but it'd be easier with a little help. It will be dangerous, though. I'm not going to let that stop me."

Kervos shook his head in disbelief. "You could be talking about a suicide mission."

"Hey," Wylder said. "If Gideon says something should work, it'll work."

I looked at both of the men who'd once served my father. "This is your home too. We could take it back. Put the fear into them instead of living with it ourselves. If I go down, I'm going to go down fighting. I obviously can't force you, but it'd mean a lot to have your help."

Roy sprang to his feet. "You know what? You're right. Those fuckers killed our friends, they're destroying the Bend. If you've got a way to take them down, I want in." Anxiety still glinted in the whites of his eyes, but I saw the same courage radiating from him that had brought him to warn us the night of Colt's ambush.

Kervos sighed. "Well, I can't let this kid show me up. Let's at least hear the plan."

A slightly manic smile curled Gideon's lips. "Xavier thinks he's terrified everyone in the Bend now, right? He'll never expect us to target him right in the heart of his operations the very next day. I've figured out exactly where the Storm's headquarters in the Bend are located." He raised his chin. "It's time to invade."

24

Mercy

As the van eased to a halt a couple of blocks away from the building he'd identified as the Storm's local headquarters, Gideon slicked his dark hair away from his forehead. With his normally blue locks turned jet-black with spray dye, his lip ring taken out, and bronzer rubbed on his face and arms to give his pale skin more of a tan, he looked like a different person altogether. It was kind of disturbing.

"Who are you, and what have you done with our tech nerd?" Kaige joked.

Gideon flicked his tongue over his lip where the ring should have been, the only sign he showed that he was nervous. "The tech nerd part of me is alive and well under the disguise. At least I *can* disguise myself. No one would fail to recognize you unless we invent a shrink ray."

As Kaige chuckled, Wylder squeezed past the seats and put his hand on Gideon's shoulder. The discomfort in his gaze echoed the tightness in my chest. "Are you sure you want to do this?" he asked.

"Positive," Gideon said without hesitation. "I'm the only one who *can*. Believe it or not, my job is the easiest part of the plan. Let me pull my weight while you guys give them the hell they deserve."

Wylder turned to face Roy, who was sitting on a bench near the back door. "And you?"

Roy gave him a tense grin. "A little late to back out now, isn't it? It's all part of making these pricks pay. I'm glad to do my bit."

I peered down the street. It was a rundown commercial strip on the edge of the warehouse district, so nondescript and out of the way it'd have been easy for the Storm's activities here to go unnoticed. We'd parked around a corner so we weren't in view of the building, but I'd seen the exact area in photos Gideon had pulled up. They were using a small, three-story building that'd been a budget hotel until it'd gone out of business years back, wedged between a dive bar and a shoe outlet store. Classiness obviously hadn't been a consideration.

Rowan had come around to the back and picked up Gideon's laptop. Gideon moved to join him. "You've got it?"

"Everything's ready to receive the data you're going to send, right?" Rowan said, studying the screen. "All I've got to do is confirm that it's come in."

Gideon nodded. "It doesn't really need monitoring. I'd just like to know someone's keeping an eye on things."

"Of course."

"All right." Gideon squared his shoulders and turned to Roy, grabbing a length of nylon rope we'd picked up on the way here. "Let's get on with this."

Roy stood up and let Gideon tie his hands behind his back. He tested the bindings and exhaled roughly. "Not too tight. They'll hold, but I should be able to shake them off fast if I need to."

"Perfect." Gideon tucked a USB drive and a few devices I couldn't have recognized into the pockets of the baggy cargo pants he'd put on and gave us one last glance. I couldn't help reaching for him and planting a kiss on his cheek. "For luck."

He met my gaze, his eyes momentarily flashing brighter. "Is that all the luck I get?"

I grinned despite my concerns and gave him another kiss, this one on the mouth and hard enough that Kaige let out a low whistle. "Are you sure we can't trade places?" he said with a laugh as I let Gideon go.

Gideon shot him a mock-glare, but a little smile played with his lips.

He smoothed it out, took the gun Wylder handed him, and saluted his boss. "I'm just going to go in, get the goods, and head back out. I'll see you soon."

"I'm counting on it," Wylder said, looking like he was restraining a grimace.

Gideon clicked on the mic hidden behind the collar of his shirt and nudged Roy out of the car. As he ushered the former Claws member down the street, he held the gun to Roy's back. His voice carried through the van's speakers. "Have to make it look convincing."

They disappeared around the corner. Then all we could hear was the faint rasp of Gideon's breath and the rustle of his clothes.

Wylder stalked from one end of the van to the other. "Fuck. He had to insist." He shook his head as if shedding his worries and reached for the stash of weapons we'd gathered.

Kaige and I joined in, each strapping a couple of holsters over our shoulders and hefting another gun each. I settled on a pistol I could easily wield. With a fierce grin, Kaige grabbed a semi-automatic rifle. Wylder hefted the bag with the explosives.

We finished our prep just in time. A voice I didn't recognize carried through Gideon's mic. "What the hell is this?"

"Found another one of those Claws idiots poking around the neighborhood," Gideon said, putting on a tough, careless tone. The Storm's people had taken on so many new recruits from the Steel Knights and who knew where else lately that we figured they'd accept him as long as he acted like he belonged. "He didn't want to open up. I thought the boss might want to talk to him about any friends he's still got hanging around."

"Shit," muttered another one of the Storm's guys. "I thought we got all of them."

"Apparently not," the first guard replied. "Xavier isn't here. You really think this guy knows anything useful? We could just shoot him."

I tensed, but Gideon laughed with impressive confidence. My heart squeezed with affection at how well he was holding his own. "Yeah, I'm sure Xavier would just *love* us making that call without his say so. I'll stash him in one of the rooms and get back to work."

"Who are you again?" the second guy said all of a sudden.

"Terence," Gideon said, and snorted. "Come on, man. We did a drug run together on Ridge Street." Gideon must have recognized him from the feeds and known there'd been a lot of Storm people around that night.

"Yeah, yeah," the man said, sounding chagrined. "Take him inside and stick him in one of the rooms upstairs. He's dead meat anyway."

"I didn't do anything to you," Roy protested, playing up the prisoner act.

"You picked the wrong side," the first Storm guy retorted.

"Well, fuck you," Roy said. We heard a soft thud followed by a grunt from Roy.

One of the Storm's men must have punched him.

"Keep your mouth shut, dickhead," the guard warned. "The boss will deal with you once he gets back."

There was a sound of a slamming door and then muffled chatter. Stairs creaked. We stood braced, hanging on every sound. Gideon's breath was rasping harder now.

Another door thumped. He let out a sigh of what sounded like relief. "Good to go," he said as if to himself.

That was our cue. "Be careful," I murmured to him, even though I knew he couldn't hear me. Wylder motioned to me and Kaige, and we hustled out of the van.

We ran along a side street at a sprint and burst out across from the old hotel. As the men in front of the door shouted an alarm and raised their guns, Wylder hurled two grenades one right after the other.

The guards dodged to the side just as one grenade blasted the door right off its hinges. The other landed on the hood of the car parked outside the hotel, where it exploded with a force that shattered all the vehicle's windows and blackened the frame.

The car's alarm began to wail. We dove down behind the vehicles along the opposite curb to wait for the Storm's people's response, guns at the ready.

It didn't take long. Yells were already carrying through the air. Kaige popped his head over the trunk of the car next to ours and took the first shot. Wylder took aim over the roof. I peered around the front bumper.

Storm men were charging out of the building, guns jerking in every direction, searching for their attackers. They didn't expect someone to make such a bold opening move and then retreat. Which meant they left themselves way too open in their hurry to defend their base.

Kaige and Wylder let loose a hail of bullets. I pulled the trigger on my own gun, aiming as well as I could at the men whose expression shifted from furious to startled in an instant.

They were responsible for destroying my home, every single one of them. I had absolutely no qualms about taking them down when they'd have happily killed me a hundred times over.

I managed to catch one in the thigh, another in the stomach, and a third in the chest. All of them collapsed. More fell with sprays of blood from Wylder and Kaige's shots. By the time they'd figured out that we weren't right on their doorstep but firing at them from fifteen feet away, more were slumped on the ground than still standing.

The few who remained ducked behind the smoking remains of the car. Another couple appeared by the front door. Wylder managed to pick one off before the other jerked out of view. We could hear the ones behind the car swearing.

Wylder shot me a devilish grin and grabbed another grenade from his bag. With a yank of the pin, he flung it toward the already burnt-out car.

At the clang of it hitting the car's roof, the men cursed again and bolted back toward the hotel. Kaige plowed them down with a frenetic series of bangs and a whoop of victory.

Then the street was silent, other than the ringing in my ears after all that gunfire. Wylder reloaded his revolver and pointed it at the blasted doorway, watching for movement.

My heart thudded wildly. The whole idea had been to distract—and destroy—as many of the Storm's people on site as we could while Gideon was at work, to make sure no one stumbled on his efforts. And to make it easier for him and Roy to get back out again when he was done. Had we bought him enough time?

That wasn't our only goal, though. "Do you think that's it for them?" I hissed at Wylder.

"Come on," he said. "Kaige, you stay ready to take down anyone who shows their face in the doorway."

Staying low, Wylder and I dashed forward to the bodies sprawled closest to us on the sidewalk and the edge of the road. I felt one guy's pockets and then another's, yanking out their phones. Wylder grabbed three more. I tossed the ones I'd gotten to him, and he stuffed them into his bag.

"Between these and whatever Gideon nabs for us, we should come out of this mission with info on every part of the Storm's operations here," he said under his breath with a triumphant grin. "Maybe we'll even find out where these assholes came from."

There was a stomping sound from inside, and Kaige took a shot over our heads. After he fired a few more times, I heard a body thump against the floor.

"I don't see any more coming," he said.

Wylder swung his arm. "We got what we came for. Let's go!"

We took off toward the side street we'd come up from. The plan was to meet Gideon and Roy back at the van. If he came out and joined us in full view, it was too likely the Storm's people would realize the full extent of our assault—not just on their men but on their computer systems. The longer they went without realizing what Gideon had stolen from them, the more use we'd get out of that information.

Hopefully our friends would be on their way out any second now.

The second we reached the van, we threw ourselves inside. Kaige leapt into the driver's seat and started the engine so we could tear away as soon as the others reached us.

Rowan was still sitting braced on the bench with the laptop on his knees. "I don't know half as much about this stuff as Gideon does," he reported, "but it looks to me like he's already sent a crapload of stuff. I think—"

A sharp voice crackled through the van's interior. "What the hell do you think you're doing?"

I flinched before I realized the sound had come from the speakers—from Gideon's mic. Then my heart hiccupped all over again.

"We were just—" Gideon's voice replied.

"Don't let him get away!" someone else hollered.

There were two ear-splitting bangs, followed by a thud. Bile shot up my throat. I clapped my hand to my mouth just as Gideon's voice carried through the speakers with a soft "Fuck."

Was he still okay? He hadn't been shot?

Another new voice reverberated from the speakers, but this one I recognized. "Who the fuck was that? And who's this prick?"

A chill swept through me. It was Xavier. The boss had returned.

"Some Claws guy," another man answered. "Better off dead anyway. This one acted like he was with us—he said he was bringing him in for questioning."

"And you bought that lame-ass story?" Xavier demanded. There was a fleshy smack of knuckles meeting the side of a head and a pained groan.

I dropped my face into my hands. Roy must be dead—he was the one they'd shot. And they had Gideon cornered.

"I was only trying to—" Gideon started again, his voice rough. Something cut him off, the sound warbling. I realized Xavier must have grabbed him by the front of his shirt near the microphone.

"You're not acting alone, are you? The fucking Nobles or the Katz girl sent you? Ha!" Fabric tore, and Xavier chuckled darkly. "Can you hear me, Mercy? Or maybe it's Wylder Noble on the other end. Either way, listen up. I've got your man. What are you going to do about it?"

Then, with a sputtered crackling, the line went completely dead.

"Shit," Wylder said, spinning toward the doors. "Shit, shit, shit." He looked ready to rip right through the steel. I jumped up, wanting to race out there with him, all the way back to the hotel. What was that psychotic bastard going to do to Gideon?

Why had we ever let him go in there?

"Stop!" Rowan said, standing up, his voice harder than I'd ever heard it. When I looked at him, he was shaking, but his gaze stayed firm. "We can't get him out right now. You *know* you'd be running right to your deaths. If we want to get Gideon back, we have to pull back and regroup so we can figure out some way of beating them."

Wylder swore again and punched the wall of the van. Kaige had turned in the driver's seat, watching his friend with a taut and uncertain expression. I glanced toward the doors, but I knew Rowan was right.

Running off to be slaughtered wouldn't save Gideon—it'd end any chance we had of rescuing him.

But the thought of leaving just about killed me too.

"We *are* coming back," I said, a tremor running through my voice. I had to say it out loud. "We figure out how to get the better of those assholes as fast as we can, and then we're getting him back."

"You'd better fucking believe it," Wylder snapped. He raked his fingers through his fiery hair, but he must have seen the truth as clearly as I had. With a haunted look in his eyes, he nodded to Kaige. "Let's get out of here before that psycho's goons come looking. We'll be back soon."

Kaige grimaced, but he hit the gas and swung the van around.

With every block we put between us and the old hotel, it felt as if another piece tore off my heart.

25

Gideon

THE PUNCH KNOCKED OUT MY BREATH AND LEFT ME PANTING on the floor. The two Storm men who'd dragged me across the hall kicked at me a few more times.

"Look at this weakling," one of them sneered. "Some bait. Who would bother coming for him?"

They stalked out of the room, slamming the door behind them. A deadbolt clicked over.

I tried to move my arms, but my lungs were burning. My breath was coming in strangled gasps now. When Xavier had ordered them to grab me, I'd tried to fight, tried to make a run for it—anything would have been better than ending up tied up and imprisoned like this. Better that they'd shot me than using me as a lure so they could kill everyone else too.

But I hadn't made it, and the effort had left me straining just to draw enough oxygen not to black out.

As I wheezed and coughed, my vision swam. Dark dots speckled it.

The image of Roy's slack face, his eyes staring glassy and unseeing, rose up. Blood staining his shirt and seeping over the floor. His dead body limp where the Storm's people had shot him. My stomach clenched almost as tight as my chest.

Fuck. Fuck. I'd been so close, but I hadn't made it, and one of our allies had died over my risky plan. It'd been my idea—I'd convinced Wylder. I'd convinced them all, and now look where I'd gotten myself.

I might die before Wylder even tried to get me out of here if I couldn't manage to drag more air into my lungs.

Each labored inhalation filled my nose and mouth with a stink like rotten cheese, which only made me feel sicker. *Just breathe*, I told myself. *Just fucking breathe, Gideon.*

If only it were so fucking easy. My lungs were shuddering as if threatening to collapse on themselves, and my pulse was going haywire. Sweat beaded on my forehead. The darkness crept in on my sight.

I had to snap out of this. I had to get my stupid, broken body under control.

I'd managed it before. A different memory wavered through my mind: Mercy, talking me down from an attack in my office just a few weeks ago. The unexpected softening of her tone, the assurance with which she'd spoken. The words came back to me, washing through my nerves.

Listen to me. Just focus on my voice. You're the smartest person I know. We'll work this out.

She wasn't here for me to really listen to her, but I took her advice as well as I could in my addled state. I thought of the kiss she'd given me before I'd left the van and the smile she'd offered afterward. Of her vehemence when she'd insisted she wasn't leaving her home to the Storm. Of the other kinds of passion she'd shown me.

I want to ride my dark god and do his bidding.

I'd felt so powerful in that moment with her in my bed, powerful and capable and wanting to do whatever I could to please her at the same time... She brought out something in me I didn't recognize, something no one else ever had. But it was good.

Abruptly I realized that the burning in my chest was subsiding. My breaths still snagged in my lungs, but it wasn't quite as hard to pull in enough air to stay alert. My vision had cleared. I wasn't outright wheezing anymore.

I lay still for several more minutes until my breathing evened out completely and my thoughts had unjumbled. A pang of affection shot through me.

Mercy had managed to be here for me even when she was nowhere nearby.

That was only my most immediate problem solved. A searing mix of guilt and panic trickled through my veins. I was still being held captive by our worst enemies. I'd still brought Roy to his death. I'd managed to send all the data I could scrape off the laptop I'd found back to my own computer, but I hadn't been quite fast or careful enough. They'd caught us before we could get out of there, and because of that I'd become an epic liability.

Because I knew my best friend. It might have been easier to leave me for dead—they had to realize that coming for me would be walking into a trap—but Wylder would never accept that. He'd come. And no doubt Mercy, Kaige, and Rowan would be right by his side ready to fight for me too.

Why the fuck had I ever thought I should step away from my devices and my screens to venture right into the lion's den? Total madness.

But I was here now. I was still alive. If there was any way I could turn this situation around, I had to find it, not lie here moping about my failure. Otherwise I really would be less than worthless.

With my hands tied behind my back, it took a little effort just to roll onto my side so I could take stock of the room. The space was small and dingy, with a matted carpet and thick curtains blotting out most of the light from the window at the other end. The only furniture was a bed with a stripped mattress and a boxy end table next to it. It didn't look like it'd been the nicest place even when the hotel had been open.

I couldn't hear a peep of sound from outside. Whatever Xavier and his goons were doing now, they didn't seem to be worried about me.

But maybe they should have been. As I squirmed and sat up, it occurred to me that I still had a couple of my devices on me. The goons hadn't patted me down all that carefully, only looking for anything large enough to be a weapon.

I'd shoved a couple of my tiniest trackers in my hip pocket in case I saw something good to stick them on, and those hadn't been found. Maybe I could do something useful with the trackers and get even more information to help the Nobles crush these pricks.

Of course, that meant I had to get the damned things out of my pocket. With my hands tied behind my back.

At least, since these were cargo pants, the hip pocket was on the side rather than in front where it'd have been even harder to reach. It took a hell of a lot of contorting to get my hands anywhere near it, though. I knelt on the ground, twisting at the waist and yanking at the fabric as hard as I could to pull the pocket closer, stopping now and then when my breath started to rasp again, hunching and leaning every which way until I found the right angle.

I ended up arching over on my back in some kind of demented yoga pose, tugging the flap on the pocket open, and shaking my legs until gravity pulled the little metal circles out to patter on the floor. With a sigh of relief, I sat back up and scooped them into my restrained hands.

Once I had them in my grasp, it wasn't hard to peel off the protective plastic on the adhesive side. I gripped them by the non-sticky edges and contemplated the room, debating the best spot to put them.

Nothing in the room right now was likely to go anywhere, so there was no point in tracking the furniture. I'd have stuck one on myself, but Wylder knew exactly where I was already. What might be useful is if I could get them stuck on one of the Storm's people's clothes without them noticing... Maybe they'd lead us to a secret supply building or even their home base outside of Paradise Bend.

The bottom of a shoe would be my best chance. I stepped closer to the door and carefully dropped one and then the other tracker on the floor a couple of feet from the entrance, where anyone coming in would be most likely to step. In the dim light, the thin metal circles, barely wider than the tip of my finger, just looked like a couple more stains on the carpet.

I'd only just had time to think that when footsteps thumped on the other side of the door. The lock clicked.

I scrambled backward, my heart lurching. I couldn't let them realize what I'd been doing. And once the light from the hall spilled into the room, I'd need to do my best to ensure they didn't look at the floor.

The door burst open to reveal Xavier's scarred face and broad-shouldered frame. He lumbered into the room with a maniacal glint in his eyes. "I thought it was time to check up on our guest. I hope my boys treated you well."

I couldn't hold back my urge for sarcasm. "Excellent. I got the VIP treatment." My gaze flicked across the floor as surreptitiously as I could manage. Fuck, he'd stepped right past the trackers, missing them both. Maybe if I could get him to move around some more... but it was hard to concentrate on that with the psychotic monster looming over me.

He was carrying a knife which he flipped from one hand to the other. "So...Gideon, is it?"

"You know my name," I said.

Xavier's eyes narrowed, and for the first time I got a sense of the bubbling anger in him. The veins bulged in his thick arms. "I do," he growled. "I know a lot of things. You and your little friends have become very annoying."

"I'm going to take that as a compliment," I said, not knowing where this sudden burst of confidence was coming from, only that it was either let it loose or end up huddled on the floor in terror.

"You shouldn't," Xavier snarled. "I'm not impressed by this stunt your friends pulled out there today. I gave you all too much rope, clearly, but don't worry. Now I'm going to reel them all in, with you dangling on my line."

He poked me in the chest, forcing me to stagger backward, and stalked past me to pace the room. Which took him farther from the trackers. So much for that.

All at once, he spun on me again with another jab of his finger. "I don't like the mess you made of my men," he snapped. "And that little bitch and her dad stole the fucking world from me. I'm not even close to finished putting her through all the pain she deserves. And you're going to help me make them pay. The games are over. The Katz and the Noble heirs think they can pull one over me, but I'm going to crush them like the pathetic children they are."

Mercy and her dad had stolen *what* from him? Was he so deranged he thought the Bend should have been his to begin with—or he blamed her for fighting back and him for bringing in the Red Sharks?

Or maybe he really did mean the whole world. With the crazed look on his face, I wouldn't be surprised.

As if on cue, a cockroach scurried out from under the bed. Before it could go very far, Xavier smashed it under his boot. He didn't bother looking at the floor. "Crush them," he repeated. "Just like that."

I didn't want to fuel his fire by telling him he was wrong, but I had to point out, "This was our territory first. It's a little bizarre to blame us for defending against your attack."

Xavier snatched me by the collar and jerked his hand up to my throat. "Is that what *you* were doing here, little boy?" he said, hot rancid breath spilling over my face. "Defending yourself? What did you think you were going to accomplish poking around on my turf?"

Holy fuck. He didn't actually know what I'd come for—which meant he hadn't figured out what I'd done. I blinked, holding in my surprise as well as I could, and managed not to laugh, even though the whole situation suddenly seemed hysterical.

I must have shut down the laptop quickly enough when I'd heard the men coming that it'd looked like I'd never gotten it on in the first place. I'd been heading for the door with Roy when they'd caught us.

I sure as hell wasn't going to tell Xavier how much of his operational data was now in Wylder's and Mercy's hands. I raised my chin as defiantly as I could with his knuckles nearly crushing my windpipe. If my voice shook, it was only because my heart was hammering so hard against my ribs. "I was supposed to assassinate you."

Xavier stared at me for a few beats. Then he threw back his head with a laugh so loud it rattled my ear drums. "And they thought *you* were the right one for the job? They're even bigger idiots than I thought. How've they managed to stay alive this long?"

He shoved me away from him, letting me go so my back banged into the wall. I gritted my teeth. "They picked me exactly because you wouldn't expect it. Here I am, and you still don't believe it. I'd say that's pretty smart."

"Hmm. Somehow I think there's more to it."

"Well, getting rid of a bunch of your men in the meantime wasn't exactly a loss."

"It was to me," Xavier snapped, and spun toward the door again.

My pulse stuttered with the fear that he'd notice the trackers if he looked down.

"Maybe not," I said quickly. "We know you've got a traitor from the Nobles on your side. Anyone who'll double-cross for you will double-cross *you* as well."

Xavier swiveled back toward me with a fierce expression, his boot coming down just an inch shy of the nearest tracker. So fucking close. "What are you talking about? No one would dare bullshit me."

I was bullshitting him right now, wasn't I?

"How do you know?" I shot back, letting whatever popped into my head spill out of my mouth. "I'm sure Ezra has heard all kinds of interesting things from his guy."

"Good thing I know not to trust a rat with anything important, unlike Ezra, isn't it?" Xavier waved me off and turned back toward the doorway. "It doesn't matter. I'm going to destroy the boy and the cat, and enjoy doing it."

His head started to dip, his gaze veering toward the carpet and the trackers, and panic blanked my mind. I spat the next thought that crossed my mind. "And that won't matter anyway. You won't even have gotten the real heir."

Xavier's head jerked up. "What the hell are you talking about?"

I opened my mouth and closed it again. But it couldn't hurt to say this, could it? It was mostly a lie anyway. It'd distract Xavier, confuse him, and maybe give us an opening. "Wylder's the younger brother. He's just a decoy. It's his older brother Roland who's the real heir."

"Really?" Xavier loomed on me again. "Then where is this real heir?"

"Oh, you know, he's got all his training to get through," I said, making things up as I went. "Ezra wants him totally prepared when it's time to take his rightful place. He moves around a lot, learning from all the best people."

"Liar," Xavier said.

I shrugged as if I couldn't care less. "There are these things called birth certificates. It wouldn't be hard to confirm that Wylder isn't Ezra's oldest kid." As for the rest, well… I'd either be dead or long gone before Xavier had any clue what was real there.

Xavier considered me for a few more seconds before he stepped even closer and raised his fist. I tried not to shrink away. He punched the wall right behind me, taking a good chunk of plaster off. "Whether it's true or not, your friends have been thorns in my side for too long," he sneered. "I'll enjoy slaughtering all of them."

He marched away from me toward the door. He was looking ahead, not down—but I could tell he was going to miss the trackers again with his feet as well as his eyes.

With a sudden burst of defiance and determination, I made as if to charge at him.

It was ridiculous—I didn't stand a chance even with all my faculties, let alone with my arms tied up. Xavier heard my footsteps and whipped to the side. He slammed his fist into my gut just before I reached him. I smacked into the wall and crumpled, agony exploding through my torso.

"Nice try," Xavier sneered, and stomped out of the room—with his boot landing right on the second tracker. It stuck on, vanishing underneath when he strode away. As the door closed in his wake, I let myself smile around the metallic taste of blood seeping from where I'd bitten the inside of my lip at his punch.

It was worth it. I'd accomplished one useful thing here. When I got out of this place, who knew where Xavier might lead us when he thought he was going unseen?

If I got out of this place. My stomach sank all over again. Xavier had talked about killing Wylder and Mercy with pure delight. What would that menace have waiting for my friends and my woman when they came for me?

26

Mercy

ANTHEA SIGHED AND LEANED BACK IN HER CHAIR, PINCHING the bridge of her nose. She'd spent hours sorting through the folders Gideon had managed to transfer from whatever computer he'd found in the Storm's local headquarters. Meanwhile, the rest of us had been pacing the abandoned pub my father had once owned. It'd seemed like a good a place as any to hold a meeting.

We were all too restless to stay cramped in the van. Of course, the stale boozy smell that permeated the air didn't exactly make for a comforting atmosphere either.

Nowhere in Paradise Bend would be comforting right now.

"What did you find?" Wylder demanded, coming over.

"Plenty of information about their past operations," Anthea said. "Businesses they've set up deals with in the Bend, ideal locations for distributing the drugs, that kind of thing. Even some observations about the Red Shark's activities, which seems to be a moot point now. But I'm not seeing anything that exposes any weaknesses that'll help us get Gideon out of there."

"Keep digging," Kaige insisted.

Anthea shook her head. "I've gone through everything. They haven't kept any information that was all that vital in general on here—nothing about definite future plans, nothing about their activities outside of Paradise Bend."

The ache that'd been sitting in my stomach since the moment we'd driven away without Gideon intensified. "And we still have no idea who the Storm is or where his people came from?"

"Not a hint about that either."

"I guess it's not surprising they wouldn't have that stuff on a computer," Rowan said, though he looked just as worried as the rest of us. "Gideon's put us several steps above a typical gang in terms of tech, and even Ezra doesn't like to leave a digital paper trail whenever he can help it."

"Fucking damn it!" Wylder punched the bar counter and then shook his fist with a hiss.

"Hey, beating up on the furniture is my job," Kaige said, but he couldn't work any real humor into the joke.

"We're running out of time." I reached past Anthea to bring up the recording of the message Xavier had sent through Gideon's mic about an hour after his capture. The psycho's gruff voice carried through the speakers. "You have twenty-four hours to come retrieve your boy, or you'll be picking his corpse off the street." He followed the warning up with a chuckle that sent a shiver down my spine.

That'd been twelve hours ago. We'd gone right through the night without landing on a way to get Gideon back, and now hazy dawn light was starting to creep through the dirty front window. My hand clenched, but I knew punching the laptop would be the opposite of helpful.

"You know this is a trap, right?" Anthea said gently. "They're obviously going to be waiting for you to show up."

"What's the alternative?" Wylder asked, his voice strained. "We can't just leave him there for them to kill!"

"I'm just saying that we have to come up with a solid plan. Rushing right in there will only let them kill all of you."

"Well, we can't just sit here and do nothing. He's in there with that fucking monster." Wylder shuddered. "God knows what state we'll find him in."

The comment echoed my own thoughts, but I couldn't let hopelessness fill my head. "Gideon is stronger than we think."

"We only need one thing that would give us an advantage," Rowan said. He frowned at the computer. We'd been counting on finding that advantage in the files it held.

My gaze fell on the phones we'd grabbed off the fallen Storm men. I motioned to them. "Maybe there's something else on those. They'd need to be using their phones for more immediate communication—they might not have been as careful about what they said in texts." That was the whole reason Gideon had wanted us to take the phones while we had the chance.

Unfortunately, he'd also been the one who could have hacked past their lock codes. Anthea grimaced and rubbed her forehead. "I know my way around a computer for the basics and a little more, but I can't break into a locked phone."

We glanced around at each other, but we all knew the rest of us wouldn't stand a chance. We'd already confirmed that all five of them were locked. Shit.

"The Nobles have other contacts," Anthea pointed out. "I'm sure there's someone on the payroll who could—"

"No," Wylder cut in firmly. "I told you what happened after the deal at the airstrip went sour. Dad knows I've sided with Mercy over him. I'll be lucky if he doesn't put a bullet in my head the next time he sees me. He's never going to offer up any of the Noble resources. So unless *you* know a specific person we can go to who'll support us over him..."

She sighed. "No. Most of my contacts are back in New York. I *might* be able to get ahold of one long distance, but they're not generally the type to want to discuss illegal methods in ways that can be recorded." Anthea paused, tapping her lips. "But we could still get what we need from your father. All you have to do is put on a show of having turned against Mercy after all—"

"*No*," Wylder said, even more vehemently than before.

"It wouldn't have to be as extreme as faking her death. We could always—"

He slammed his hand down on the table hard enough to make the laptop jump. "No. I'm done with Dad thinking I'm his marionette, dancing when he pulls my strings. It's time I stood up for what I believe in like the man who's one day going to be ruling the Nobles should."

He sounded like a leader then, so much that a glow of pride lit up inside me. Maybe I'd taken an unconventional route when it came to my current relationships, but I had found myself some awfully impressive men, hadn't I?

Now I just had to figure out how to retrieve one of those men before I lost him completely.

Anthea gazed steadily back at Wylder for a moment and then inclined her head. "I see your point. I don't entirely agree with it, but I accept it. So, what now?"

Wylder turned to Rowan. "You've handled a lot of the negotiations with the outlying gangs we associate with. Can you think of anyone who could handle the phones?"

Rowan rubbed his mouth. "With the current state of things in the Bend, I'm not sure how easy it'd be to get anyone to come out of the woodwork, especially when they can't be someone whose ties are mainly to Ezra. Let me think."

Watching Wylder step up as a leader sent my thoughts in a different direction, toward the men *I* was theoretically meant to inherit. One of whom had died for our cause yesterday afternoon.

I swallowed thickly. We hadn't told Kervos about Roy's fate yet. Before we'd set off for the Storm's headquarters, he'd managed to get in touch with Jenner, and we'd dropped him off with him and several other Claws members who'd survived the purge. In his injured state, he wouldn't have been able to pitch in with the attack anyway.

An idea tickled up through the twinge of guilt. "Maybe there's someone good with tech stuff still with the Claws," I said. "That's easier than tracking down someone who's got no stake in this war at all. We can go ask them now, before we lose any more time."

Wylder gave me a tense but grateful smile. "Lead the way, Queen Katz."

Jenner and the rest of the remaining Claws had holed up in an abandoned house in one of the more derelict neighborhoods in the Bend. Even .with newspapers plastered over the windows, they were sticking to the large but unfinished basement to avoid any chance of being spotted from outside.

As we tramped down the steps to meet with them, the hushed conversations fell totally silent. A steady dripping echoed from a pipe at the other end of the dim space.

My shoes scraped against the cracked concrete floor as I came to a stop. Jenner and a couple of the others got up to greet us. The dozen or so other guys stayed on the blankets and sleeping bags they'd probably recently been sleeping on. Kervos stirred, just waking up where he'd been dozing in a corner. He sat up quickly and winced, clutching his side.

"Where's Roy?" he asked before we could say anything.

My pained expression must have given away the answer. Before I even spoke, he swore.

"The Storm's people shot him," I said, forcing my voice to stay steady. "They've captured our man who went in with him and are threatening to kill him too. That's one of the reasons we came to talk with you. But first—it's just about breakfast time. We figured you could use some food."

Rowan and Anthea held out the bags of groceries we'd stopped to buy on the way over. I wasn't going to show up and demand favors from my father's former people while offering nothing in return. Seeing the state they'd been reduced to living in, I couldn't help feeling I should have brought more. At the same time, my hope dwindled.

How much help were we going to get out of people who'd fallen so far?

As if to prove me right, one of the other guys muttered a curse and shook his head. "Why are we even staying here? These pricks are going to slaughter us all."

"No," I said. "We're not going to let that happen."

Someone else snorted. "What are you going to do about it?"

Wylder stepped forward, his eyes flashing, but I put out my arm to hold him back, even though I'd bristled too. Maybe there *was* something more I could offer them. Maybe I needed to show them we didn't have to be this beaten.

"I can understand why you'd ask that," I said, drawing myself up straighter and pitching my voice so my words filled the whole room. "You haven't seen much of me before today. My father didn't let me get very involved in the Claws' business. But I can tell you that I was always watching and listening, paying attention to everything I could. I *wanted* to take control over my destiny. I'm here today as your leader and the true heir of the Claws. I'm here as Mercy Katz."

"Mercy," Jenner said, as if he was going to stop me. He moved to put a hand on my shoulder, but I shook him off.

"My father let you down. I can't put all the blame on him, but he reached out to the Red Shark, he didn't tell Colt what he was doing, and that set this whole catastrophe in motion. He let me down too by never trusting me enough to give me a chance to be a real part of the Claws. But I'm going to change all that now."

"What can you do that he couldn't?" one of the guys muttered.

"Well, for starters I didn't get myself killed," I retorted. "I'm here, standing with you, ready to listen to you. But right now, I want you to listen to me—really listen. The Bend is *our* home. I don't want to see some assholes barge in and ruin everything. I'm stepping up as the head of the Claws, and I intend to put everything back the way it should be, without bringing in outsiders who'll terrorize everyone.

"Xavier and his men thought they could break you, but yet here you stand, a testimony to the strength of the Claws. We can rebuild our home, take back the streets, and kick out the pricks who tried to destroy them. We can avenge all our friends and loved ones who already died in the fighting, every drop of blood that was shed. I'll do it on my own if I have to, but I'd rather have all of you on my side. I think you deserve the chance to show what you're made of too."

There was a momentary silence. My stomach twisted. Then Kervos spoke up in a hesitant but not hostile voice, glancing at Anthea and the guys around me. "Would that mean joining the Nobles?"

Wylder folded his arms over his chest. "Mercy is her own woman.

I'm glad to have her as an ally, but I sure as hell don't expect her to bow down to me. We'll work together, but the Claws belong to her. You answer to her, not me."

A few murmurs passed between the assembled men. I held my breath. Would the things I'd said be enough? I didn't know how else to convince them, but I didn't know how much hope we had of winning this war without whatever help they could give us.

Jenner stepped in front of me and dipped his head. When he raised it, his eyes glinted with a wild sort of hope. "I'll recognize you as the new head of the Claws. I'll fight with you—for all our fallen brothers, but also for *you*."

When my lips parted in surprise, he gave me a small smile. "Your father could be a great leader at times, but he was ruled by his ego. Every time you've reached out to us, you've given us a choice and treated us with respect and humility—even when we'd turned our backs on you. It would be my absolute honor to show the same loyalty in return."

"And mine," Kervos said. "I've seen what you're capable of. So did Roy. We can't let those fuckers get away with this, and you're the woman to take them down. I'll pledge myself to you."

A bittersweet smile stretched across my face. One by one, the other Claws members began to nod. "And me." "And me." The words echoed in the room.

I could feel their spirits lifting as hope lit their faces again. Goosebumps erupted down the back of my neck. Momentary tears pricked at the backs of my eyes. Here they were, battered and driven underground, but they were still willing to rise against their enemy one more time.

I pumped my fist in the air. "For the Claws."

"For the Claws," they echoed back. In that moment, I was one of them more than I'd ever been before.

"For the Claws," Jenner said, clapping me on the shoulder. "Let's take back the Bend."

"Thank you," I said quietly.

"You earned it. Now, what do you think we can do about your man they're holding hostage?"

I inhaled deeply and held up the bag with the stolen phones. "These belong to some of the Storm's men. We think there might be information on one or more of them that'd give us key information into how they work, something we could use to get the upper hand. Is there anyone here who knows how to crack the lock codes on them?"

A young guy near the back of the room held up his hand. "Toss them over here. I should be able to handle that."

I handed the bag to another guy who passed it on. As our volunteer got to work on the first phone, the other men dug into the food we'd brought. It was obvious they were starving.

I stepped back by the door with Anthea, Wylder, Kaige, and Rowan. Looking around the room at the Claws men—*my* men now—sent a weird quiver through my chest that was both anxious and excited.

"We're really doing this," I murmured. "*I'm* really doing this." I was going to lead the Claws. Dad would be rolling in his grave if he knew.

"You looked like a goddess telling them how it was going to be," Kaige said with a grin. "A goddess of blood and vengeance. The Storm's people aren't going to know what hit them."

"You were made for this life," Rowan put in. "I didn't always believe that was a good thing, but now I know you can turn it into something great."

I glanced at Wylder, who was frowning. "You don't look so happy."

He shook himself and tucked a finger through the beltloop of my jeans. "Not because of anything that happened here, Kitty Cat. I could watch you make declarations all day. You really are becoming a queen now."

A warm glow of affection sparked in my chest. I squeezed his hand. "And we'll rule together." I knew why that wasn't enough. The heaviness of our loss was weighing on my spirits too. "It won't feel right without Gideon here. We've got to get him back."

"We will," Wylder said fiercely, and Kaige and Rowan nodded.

Anthea let out a huff of breath. "I'll just be glad when this is all over and I can get back to killing people so discreetly no one can even tell it's murder, like everyone civilized should."

An unexpected laugh burst out of me. Kaige snorted, and Rowan took my other hand. I'd never been so glad to have all of them with me.

Just then, the man at the back stood up with one of the phones in his hand. "I might have found something. Come take a look."

My heart leapt. I tugged Wylder's hand, and he came with me. It was time to get Gideon back.

27

Mercy

Rowan, Wylder, and I crouched by a building a block away from the Storm's headquarters. We watched as another Wylder, flanked by Kaige and several of the Claws members, walked up the street toward the old hotel. The Wylder on the street rolled his shoulders as if working tension out of them.

"That's the tenth time he's done that," the Wylder beside me—the real one—muttered.

"He's probably just nervous," I said.

"Maybe he should be. Does he really look that much like me?"

The three of us considered Sam, the Claws guy who was acting as Wylder, for a moment. A few of the Claws had volunteered to take on the role, but he'd been the one whose build was closest to Wylder's, and his blond hair had taken the auburn dye easily. We'd even gotten Anthea to trim it so it was the same style. He'd put on sunglasses so the differences in his features weren't so obvious.

I doubted many of the Storm's people had noticed much about the real Wylder other than his bright hair and his overall shape anyway. And having Kaige next to him helped sell the illusion. Sam had even spent a couple of hours observing Wylder back by the house, getting him to pace and move his arms so he could get a sense of his usual energy.

"I don't know," I said. "I think he's pretty good."

"That's not how I walk," Wylder insisted.

"Well actually—" Rowan began.

Wylder glared at him. "There's only one of me."

I rolled my eyes. "Of course there is, and thank God for that. It doesn't matter if he's not perfect. They've just got to believe it's you for long enough to stay distracted while we sneak inside."

Go in, take down as many of the Storm's people as we could—ideally including Xavier—and grab Gideon on the way out. Other than the show happening on the street, it was a pretty simple plan. I just hoped it stayed simple.

Fake Wylder, Kaige, and their entourage of Claws men came to a stop across the street from the headquarters. We'd warned them to keep a good distance from the old hotel so that none of the Storm's people would get a good look at Sam. He nodded to Kaige and shouted toward the building in a voice that was a decent imitation of Wylder's usual cocky tone. "Here we are, assholes. Now where's my man?"

"Is that how I sound?" Wylder asked.

"Yep," Rowan and I said at the same time. When Wylder narrowed his eyes at me, I had to smother a snicker.

I craned my neck to see if any of the Storm's men were coming out onto the street. It looked like they'd learned their lesson after our last attack. They stayed behind the walls of the hotel, where they'd hastily fixed the door, but we clearly had their attention. Faces appeared by the windows.

"So you're not a total chickenshit after all," one of the Storm's guys hollered back. "Good for you."

"Hand over our man now, and we'll leave peacefully," Sam demanded. "You're *all* chickenshits if you keep trying to win through pathetic tactics like this."

"Says the man at a disadvantage," called someone from inside the building. "Come inside and get him if you want him that badly."

"Okay, they're focused on them for now," Rowan said. "Let's get moving."

I nodded, and we ducked around the building to the alley that would take us close to the back of the hotel. It was empty except for the thick stink of garbage wafting to my nose.

We zigzagged around the dumpsters and reached the red brick building of the bar next to the old hotel. There, we stayed in the shadows and peered up at the back windows of Storm headquarters until we were sure no one was watching us. Then we made for the back door of the bar.

As I reached for the keypad by the door and tapped in the code we'd managed to find in the files Gideon had sent us, my heart thumped faster. It beeped, and the deadbolt flipped over. Relief rushing through me, I pushed the door open.

Cool but musty air washed over us. We slipped inside, closed the door, and spotted the stairs to the basement just a few steps away.

Wylder walked partway down first, his gun in one hand, his phone offering a little illumination in the other. "Looks clear. No one around this early in the day."

"The bar doesn't open until three," Rowan said.

I smiled. "Perfect for us."

As we descended into the stuffy basement storage room, Wylder wrinkled his nose. "I wonder how many deliveries Xavier's already taken through this route. Did the Steel Knights use this place before? We weren't aware of any activity around here."

"They might have kept it quiet," I said.

We'd only found out about the bar's secret thanks to the text chain the Claws techie had managed to dig up. One of the Storm's guys had told someone passing on goods to them to come through the bar and down here so it wouldn't be obvious where they were going.

"Ah ha." Wylder shoved aside a stack of crates to reveal a narrow door in the wall that faced the hotel. This door was older than the one in the alley, with a keyhole and nowhere to input codes. But that was fine. I'd done a little practicing of my own this morning—with Anthea, to warm up my lock picking skills.

Drawing out the picks, I took a deep breath to steady myself. Then I knelt down and fit them into the keyhole. Anthea's advice rolled through my mind as I adjusted them. *Take it slow and easy. Feel your way to the right spot...*

With a click, the lock disengaged. Grinning triumphantly, I straightened up and twisted the knob.

The passage on the other side was just as narrow, with crumbling brick walls that'd obviously seen better days. We slunk along it to the door at the other end, which should lead into the hotel's basement.

We stood still for a minute, listening, but no sound came from the other side. We'd figured it was unlikely they'd have guards down here when they didn't expect anyone to know about the secret entrance. I did my trick with the lock picks again, and in the space of several heartbeats, I had that door open too.

We closed it behind us as we came out into a larger storage room. A distinct chemical smell hung in the air. Wylder narrowed his eyes at the plastic boxes stacked along the far wall. "Glory?"

"No doubt." I had the urge to toss over one of the explosives from the bag slung across my back, but blowing up their stash here would only ruin our real plan. We didn't want the Storm's people to have any clue we were coming until we were destroying them.

They'd all be focused on the fake Wylder and the other men outside for now. Using the element of surprise should be easy.

It was getting out again that'd be the hard part.

Wylder tucked his gun into the holster under his arm and took out his knife. Rowan and I brandished our own blades. We crept down the hall that led into the storage room and found a set of stairs that would take us up to the first floor. A couple of voices carried down to us.

Rowan tapped his finger to his lips. We eased up the steps, feeling them out carefully to avoid any creaks. A couple of men came into view in what appeared to be a large kitchen, leaning against one of the counters with guns at their hips, just chatting.

Wylder pulled into the lead. He braced himself stock still on a step a few down from the top, where the shadows still hid him. Then he launched himself into the room so fast I lost my breath.

"What the—" one of the guys exclaimed. That was all he got out before Wylder had plunged the knife into his neck. As the first guy slumped with a deathly gurgle, the Noble heir was already lunging at the second guy.

The Storm's man had reached for his gun, but Wylder caught him with a knee to the gut and slashed his throat when he doubled over. That body thumped to the ground too. We froze, glancing around the room and through the doorway.

No one came running. More voices were carrying from the front of the building, along with mocking laughter and occasional gunfire. We'd told our guys to take a few shots here and there to keep the Storm's people occupied until we were in place. From the sounds of things, they were doing their job well.

A door at the other end of the kitchen showed the gleam of sunlight through its window. I added that exit to my mental map of the place.

We'd just started down the hall toward the front of the hotel when a guy stepped out of a room closer by. Rowan acted immediately, springing at him and twisting his neck with a grunt and a snap of bones. The guy crumpled to the floor, his body slack. Rowan stared down at him, panting.

"I wasn't sure that would even work," he admitted in a whisper.

"Good thing it did." Wylder drew his gun again and nodded toward the rooms up front. "Sounds like most of them are gathered up there. We aren't going to get much farther without someone raising the alarm. Let's take out as many as we can before they realize we're here."

That was the strategy we'd discussed before. I readied my own gun, and we eased down the hall until it opened up into a larger foyer.

A broad staircase led up to the second floor. Straight ahead was the front door, where a few Storm men were staked out, peering through the panes of the small window. I could see several other men in each of the front rooms on either side of it, watching the street, a couple of them taking shots at the fake Wylder outside.

Wylder smiled thinly. Without a word, he caught my eyes and pointed to the door. Then he looked at Rowan and motioned to the room on the left. So he was going to take the right. I tensed, waiting for his signal to move.

He swung his hand and leapt toward the room he'd picked in the same instant. Rowan dashed to the left, and I stepped forward, raising my gun.

This was for Roy, and my family, and every other person who'd died because of the Storm's arrival in the Bend.

We all opened fire at the same time. I squeezed the trigger again and again, braced against the recoil. The thunder of the shots made my ears ache, but I didn't give a shit.

One bullet and another hit the three men by the door. Before they'd managed to turn all the way around, I'd delivered at least one fatal shot to each of them. They toppled together in a heap in the front hall.

I grabbed another clip from my pocket and reloaded quickly. Wylder and Rowan were still shooting. I darted to Rowan's side in time to see him taking down the last of the guys in his room, planting a bullet in the man's skull just before the other guy could raise his own gun. The bodies lay in a row along the windows.

As Wylder fired his last shot, another sound reached my ringing ears. Footsteps thundered across the floor above us. Some of the Storm's people had been watching from upstairs, of course. We just hadn't known how many.

We ran back toward the staircase. Wylder and Rowan took shelter at the edges of the doorways, shooting at the figures charging down the stairs. Wylder aimed a worried but determined look at me and jerked his chin toward the kitchen.

We'd known Gideon would probably be farther up, and also that we couldn't take out more than one floor of Storm men before they caught on. Wylder and Rowan were going to hold off the pricks as well as they could on the bottleneck of the stairs while I made my way to Gideon around back.

I sprinted down the hall the way we'd come, fumbled with the lock on the back door, and shoved it open. My pulse pounded with the seconds ticking away. The faster I could get up there, the better.

I spotted a small dumpster heaped with garbage bags outside the shoe outlet store on the other side of the hotel, ran over, and shoved it toward the hotel with all my might. It scraped against the ground, but it moved. As soon as it was close enough, I flipped up onto it. It got me just high enough to jump up and hook my fingers around the ledge of a closed second-floor window.

The cracked stone bit into my fingertips. I scrambled upward and swung my body around, smashing the glass with my heels and diving through the frame in the same motion.

The shouts and the blaring of gunfire covered the sound of my entrance. I landed in a small room with a couple of twin beds, the covers rumpled. Empty beer bottles, cigarette butts, and fast food wrappers were strewn across the floor. The Storm's people didn't exactly live in style.

I stopped only long enough to smack my foot along the window frame, clearing the remaining shards of glass, since it might be my escape route too. Then I stalked to the doorway and peeked out into the hall.

I couldn't see the staircase from here. The shots echoed from around a bend in the hall. But as I stepped out, a couple of guys burst from a nearby room. They spotted me as my gun arm swung up.

My first shot hit one in the head, but the second went wide. The other man lunged at me, snatching at his own weapon. With a lurch of my heart, I whipped out my knife and heaved myself forward to meet him. The blade sank into his chest just before he could pull the trigger.

Wylder and Rowan weren't going to be able to hold off the men on the stairs forever. I hurried along the hall, trying each door I passed. The first three opened no problem to rooms a lot like the one I'd smashed my way into, all of them empty. The fourth doorknob jarred in my grasp—and then flew open to reveal a man with his lips pulled back in a snarl.

I wasn't sure what he'd been expecting, but he startled at the sight of me—just long enough for me to pump three bullets into his chest. He teetered and collapsed on the floor. I glanced past him to confirm Gideon wasn't in the room behind him and moved on.

Where the hell was our tech genius? They hadn't moved him to a whole different building, had they? Fear started to wrap a chill around my gut—and then I heard it.

Someone was singing an off-key version of "Hotel California" in a thin, raspy voice that sounded an awful lot like the guy I was looking for. Despite the odds we were up against and the blood already spilled, my lips twitched with a smile.

I raced down the hall, following the singing, which grew louder with every frantic step. There. I stopped at the door it was filtering through and fumbled for the lock picks. As soon as the pins clicked over inside, I heaved the door open.

Gideon lurched to his feet. His hands were tied behind his back, his cheek purpling with a bruise, but he was there in front of me and essentially all right. "Mercy?" he croaked.

I was so relieved I could have cried, but there really wasn't time. From the volume of the voices and thumping footsteps outside, some of the men from the stairwell were heading this way. I didn't even have time to untie him.

"Come on," I said, grabbing Gideon's elbow. "Nice singing, by the way."

As we hustled out into the hall, he sputtered a laugh. Even though I hadn't gotten him to safety yet, his face had lit up just like I was beaming inside with the joy of having found him. "I could tell something was going down," he said. "Figured it'd help you guys find me if you were looking, and at least annoy these jackasses if not."

A roar of pure rage split the air and shattered my good mood. I knew in an instant it was Xavier—and he was coming for us.

I kept looking over my shoulder as we dashed for the room I'd entered through. A couple of men charged around the corner of the hall, and I shot at them. I couldn't tell if I'd hit either, but they pulled back for shelter. The shots they fired thudded into the walls just inches from us.

I shoved Gideon into the bedroom ahead of me and yanked the door shut just as several more shots rang out behind us. Bullets smacked into the wood, one of them piercing nearly all the way through. Shit.

When we made it to the window, Gideon froze up. "It's fine," I said urgently. "Just aim for the dumpster—it's full of shoe boxes. You'll survive. I'll be right behind you."

Gideon braced himself and jumped. He hit the garbage bags below with a *whoomph.* I was just about to climb after him when Xavier's voice broke through the shouts swelling in the hall outside.

"I'm going to skin that fucking cat!"

Oh, he thought so, did he? My pulse hammered through my veins, and I lifted my gun, sitting on the ledge and digging into my bag at the same time. If I could get in a good shot right before I jumped, if I could take out the menace who'd been terrorizing me before I'd even known he existed...

"Mercy," Gideon called from below, sounding worried. I swallowed hard. I'd give it one shot—

But I didn't get the chance. The door blew off its hinges, a swarm of men outside—but none of those at the front of the pack was Xavier. I caught a glimpse of his dark hair farther back, but I knew even as my finger itched on the trigger that I'd never hit him with so many people in the way.

I'd made it this far. I might have been willing to die to take that monster down with me, but Gideon wouldn't be safe until I got him farther away.

My teeth clenching with regret, I hurled the grenade I'd taken out of my bag instead.

When it exploded in the doorway, I was already jackknifing through the window frame. I landed on my feet next to Gideon, sinking into the bags with a groan of tearing cardboard. The bang of the explosion sent a puff of smoke into the air above us.

It wouldn't hold off whoever had survived for long. I helped Gideon clamber out of the dumpster, and we ran down the alley. I sent the quick text I'd had at the ready to Wylder—the special alert sound he'd programmed would tell him I'd gotten Gideon out.

We veered down a smaller driveway and hustled along a side-street, slowing when Gideon's breath turned ragged. Just as we turned the corner to double back toward the van, it roared around the corner to meet us, Rowan at the wheel.

As it screeched to a halt, the back doors flew open. Wylder and Kaige waved to us from inside. They grabbed us to help us in, and we sped away from the headquarters as fast as those tires could take us.

28

Mercy

I SLUMPED AGAINST THE BENCH, MY ENTIRE BODY ACHING from the workout I'd just put it through. My lungs were burning, so I could only imagine how Gideon felt. He sagged next to me, his breaths labored but starting to even out.

The van's tires screeched as Rowan took a sharp turn, following the zigzag route we'd decided on to make it harder for any Storm people to give chase. As we swayed with its movements, Wylder crouched next to Gideon and cut through the ropes binding his wrists.

"You're okay?" he asked, his voice gruff with obvious concern.

"Fine," Gideon said, though he couldn't stop himself from rasping a little more than usual. He took another gulp of air and managed a shaky smile. "Those fuckers had no idea who they were dealing with, did they?"

Kaige cracked his knuckles. "Hell, yeah. We painted that hotel red."

I pushed myself up straighter, my pulse still thrumming away with adrenaline. "What about the Claws guys? Did they all make it out?"

Kaige nodded. "As soon as Wylder and Rowan burst out, we knew to take off. Their cars were even closer than the van, so they must have made it to them no problem. The whole time we were there, the pricks shooting from the windows didn't manage to do more than clip one guy in the arm. He'll survive."

I should have felt relieved hearing that, but I was still keyed up. My body seemed to think the battle wasn't over yet.

I turned to Gideon, checking him over to make sure he hadn't taken any injuries worse than the bruise on his cheek. He had a little cut at the corner of his jaw too, and the ropes had rubbed the skin on his wrists raw. I frowned, inspecting them, and grabbed the first aid kit stashed under the bench.

"They're no big deal," Gideon insisted as I dabbed at the marks with an antiseptic wipe.

I elbowed him lightly. "It can't hurt to be careful, tough guy."

Gideon turned to Wylder. "I'm sorry. It was my fucking plan, and I—"

Wylder held up his hand before his best friend could go on, his gaze firm. "It was a great plan, and we got a ton of information out of it. Hopefully information we can use for more than just staging your rescue. You made it out, and you gave us an excuse to take down a whole lot more Storm men in the process. I'll call that a win."

The growl of the motor sputtered out. Rowan had parked outside the desolate strip mall where we'd decided we'd regroup, far from any of the Storm's holdings and anywhere they'd think Claws or Nobles might go. He squeezed between the seats to join us. "We accomplished a lot today. We took out a big chunk of the Storm's manpower in the Bend and showed we're a force to be reckoned with."

Gideon chuckled. "Whatever the hell you did to pull that off, it was pretty fucking spectacular." He aimed a shy grin at me. "Especially your part."

What felt most spectacular to me was having him here with us again, all in one piece, okay enough to even joke about what he'd been through. I squeezed his arm, a swell of urgent emotion rising up over me. "I'm just glad you're safe."

I didn't just want to tell him, though. The frenetic beat of my pulse urged me to *show* him just how happy I was to have him back. I cupped Gideon's face in my hands and kissed him.

I'd meant it to be a short peck, but as soon as our lips touched, something in me unraveled. Gideon tilted his head to deepen the kiss, his hand rising to grip my shirt with a similar urgency. Our tongues tangled, our breaths rushing together, and just like that we were outright devouring each other as if we'd starve if we couldn't absorb every possible bit of passion from the melding of our lips.

Gideon ran his fingers into my hair with enough force to loosen my ponytail. He pulled me even closer, tugging me to straddle him. I kissed him harder, knowing the other guys were watching us and finding that not a single part of me cared.

Gideon eased back just enough to press a trail of kisses down my neck, tilting my head to the side for better access. He didn't seem to mind the audience either, at least not in this moment after the rush of our escape. He lowered his head to suck on the sensitive spot at the crook of my shoulder.

As I moaned, my eyes opened a fraction. Wylder, Kaige, and Rowan were standing over us, their eyes locked on us. A thrill shot up my spine. They were mine—all of them. And I was their woman.

I didn't just want them watching—I wanted every one of their hands touching my body.

I gazed up at them with a lick of my lips in invitation, my eyelids fluttering when Gideon bit my skin lightly. A whimper slipped out of me.

Kaige broke from the ring around us first. He sank down beside us, caressing my leg from my knee up to my thigh. Gideon froze for just an instant before shifting slightly to the side to give Kaige better access to my body. A giddy warmth flowed through my body, not just desire but the delight at seeing them accept each other.

As Gideon nibbled his way along my shoulder, Kaige teased his fingers into my hair at the back of my scalp. He leaned in to kiss me on the lips. One of my hands ran down Gideon's lean chest while the other slipped around the back of Kaige's neck.

Gideon nipped the lobe of my ear, and I moaned against Kaige's mouth. He pressed the advantage, dipping his hot tongue inside my mouth. Our tongues caught together in a frenzied dance, with each trying to gain control over the other. The stroking sensation made my pussy walls squeeze with a gush of arousal soaking my panties.

As Kaige's kisses became even more eager, another set of hands skimmed over the side of my hips. They were confident, knowing just where to touch me. I peeked from the corner of my eyes and saw Rowan kneeling at my other side. His eyes reflected the same awe as I felt. A breathless giggle escaped me, the sound vibrating against Kaige's mouth.

Rowan's hands climbed up to my breasts and fondled them, tracing my curves, teasing my nipples. Bliss rushed through me from every direction. When Kaige dropped his head to test my other earlobe between his teeth, Rowan claimed my mouth. Gideon gave my hair a little tug and kissed his way down to the neckline of my shirt. The three of them seemed to find a rhythm as they played with my body.

I tugged the hem of Kaige's shirt and pulled it off him, then ran my hands down the massive tattooed landscape of his torso. His muscles flexed as I circled a finger around his nipple. Gideon unbuttoned his own shirt, keeping his eyes on me. I kissed Rowan on the lips more urgently while my fingers skimmed to the crotch of his pants. He was hard, his cock straining against his fly. Kaige and Gideon sported similar bulges.

I stroked all three of them, moving from one to the next while their hands ran all over my body. My skin felt as if it'd caught fire. Rowan pulled back so Gideon could yank my shirt off of me, and then Kaige ripped my bra open to lick down my spine.

I arched my back at the slick of his demanding tongue, gripping both Rowan's and Gideon's shoulder. Our combined groans reverberated through the van.

"Enough," Wylder said roughly, snapping me out of my trance. The guys glanced around to look at their leader where he was standing stiffly by the van's back door, but none of them moved away from me. I was surrounded entirely by their delicious heat and weight. Wylder had better not fucking ruin this moment.

The Noble heir stepped forward, forcing Rowan to move behind me to make room. When I saw the look in Wylder's bright green eyes, I bit my lip.

All at once, he caught me around my waist and lifted me right off

Gideon. I squeaked as he whipped me around and slammed me against the wall over the bench, our heads just below the roof. Before I could recover, his lips were on mine.

The hard press of metal at my naked back made the experience even more raw. The heat of his kiss shot right to my core, which gushed as soon as his tongue came out to play against mine.

Wylder ground his cock into my stomach, and I growled against his lips. The wall of the van shook behind us at the force of our kiss. It was savage and take-no-prisoner, the force of it sweeping me away in the storm of Wylder's passion. I kissed him back hard, tilting my head so I could have deeper access to his sinful mouth.

Then he pulled me away from the wall and laid me down in the middle of the dense carpet. His gaze roved over my body, lingering on the swell of my naked breasts. I jutted my chest forward and looked at him with a challenge in my eyes.

A wicked smile curled his mouth. As he reached to flick open the button on my jeans, he glanced around at the other guys, who'd drawn back to give us space and see what would happen next.

"I think the new queen deserves a full celebration," he said in a low voice full of promise.

Answering smiles sprang onto the other men's faces—and my own. A quiver of anticipation ran straight to my cunt. Then my lovers closed in on me, discarding their shoes and kicking off their jeans as Wylder stripped me of mine. The avid lust in all their eyes made me dizzy. It was all for me.

They sat on their haunches around me. Four pairs of practiced hands roamed over my skin, touching me everywhere and sending tingles down my body. From that moment onward, we were all in this together. We were making something bigger than any passion we could have shared with only two or three of us.

We'd won against the Storm today, and we won a victory for our hearts right now.

Rowan kissed me again, his deft tongue tracing the seam of my lips. A mouth latched on to my left tit and sucked hard. A few moments later, another devoured my right nipple.

I closed my eyes against the onslaught of sensation. Fingers skimmed impatiently over my inner thighs before hooking around my panties and pulling them down to my knees, ripping the lace in the process.

My eyelids fluttered open at half-mast to see Gideon as he knelt between my thighs. He inhaled my cunt deeply before he lapped the center, his eyes staying fixed on me. As his tongue nudged inside my hot, wet slit, my eyes rolled back. Molten pleasure washed up from my core.

Rowan traced his fingers along my chin to tip my head so he could kiss me again. Kaige circled the mound of my breast with his tongue, while Wylder worked the hard nub of my nipple between his teeth. The pain and the pleasure made a heady mix.

Gideon continued to lap at my cunt greedily, as if he couldn't get enough of me. I writhed against the floor, the friction of the carpet tingling through my nerve endings.

Rowan pulled back just a few inches, his hand dropping to rub his erection through his boxers. "Condoms," he said, his voice coming out a little strangled. "I hate to break up the party, but before this goes any further—"

Gideon looked up from between my thighs, his lips shiny with my pussy juices. "The container next to the first aid kit."

Rowan gave him a quizzical look and reached under the bench. I tried not to whimper at the abrupt stillness around me. The other guys watched as Rowan retrieved a plastic container.

"I wondered what that was," Kaige said.

Gideon offered a satisfied smile. "Everything we might need is in there."

Wylder raised his eyebrows. "Even lube?" His gaze dropped back to me, nearly scorching.

"I said everything, didn't I?"

Kaige let out a guffaw. "Gideon had a sex kit in his van the whole time. Who would have thought?"

Gideon shot him a narrow look, but he was still smiling. "You know I like to be prepared for every possible contingency."

"And thank God for that," Wylder muttered, but his eyes hadn't left me.

The heat in the van seemed to have increased by about ten degrees. Rowan pulled out a condom, and the other guys moved as if agreeing that because he'd been the one to suggest this step, he should make use of them first. I couldn't say I had a problem with that.

As he rolled it over his jutting shaft, he nudged my legs apart and knelt between them. I slid my fingers into his ash-blond hair and pulled him to me. Our mouths collided, and in the same moment he pushed himself into my slick pussy.

He fucked me thoroughly, his strokes slow and deep at first before he switched to shallow but faster thrusts. Our bodies clung together, my legs circling his hips as he drove me towards my peak. Gideon's skillful tongue had already brought me to the verge. I clutched Rowan's shoulders as he bucked into me hard and fast. There was nothing sweet or gentle about this encounter.

The other three joined in every way they could, their fingers trailing over the sensitive spots in my body. Rowan grunted, his strokes more and more erratic. I squeezed my legs around him, pushing him deep inside me just as he came with a loud groan. A wave of an orgasm tore through me. My pussy walls convulsed around his cock.

"Oh, fuck," Rowan murmured as he almost collapsed on top of me, his dick still throbbing inside of me, sending delicious aftershocks through my core. He panted as he rolled to the side.

Before I could catch my breath, Gideon was on top of me, kissing me. The nerves in my body came back to life in an instant. He pulled me up to a sitting position, my legs around his hips as I straddled his lap like I had before, but with no clothes separating us now. He rolled my nipples between his fingers as he kissed me and then rubbed the curved length of his dick along my slit where his tongue had traveled before. I wrapped my arms around his neck to hold him tighter.

Our eyes met, reflecting lust at each other, just before I lifted myself on my knees and impaled myself on his cock. My pussy was already sensitive from the first orgasm, and something about the angle of my current position hit a spot so deep and sweet inside of me I practically came again right then and there.

Gideon's breath stuttered out of him. Before I could worry that it was too much for his lungs, he gripped my waist and guided me up before slamming me down on his dick again.

Both of us let out a loud sigh, my mouth hovering over his.

I gripped his shoulder blades hard before we repeated the motion. My tits bounced as I began to ride his dick earnestly, my body catching onto a rhythm. Gideon's eyes were half-closed as he watched me. I circled my hips around his, and his hands slipped to my ass where he squeezed.

We kissed each other sloppily as I continued rocking over his dick, our moans mingling. Then impatient hands cupped my breasts from behind. I glanced back to see Wylder crouching behind me. The head of his cock slicked precum down my spine to the curve of my ass.

"How'd you like to have even more fun, Kitten?" he said in a voice so heated I nearly spontaneously combusted. One of his hands trailed down my side to my ass cheeks and dipped between them to circle the pucker of my other hole. He held my gaze with a question in his eyes.

His touch sent lustful shivers through me. I'd only tried anal once before and hadn't enjoyed it all that much, but this was Wylder, looking at me like I really was a queen. He wouldn't offer if he didn't know he could make it good for me.

I dipped my head in the slightest nod. A grin stretched across Wylder's face. He flicked open the lube and spread some over his fingers.

I continued to ride Gideon at a slightly more subdued pace as Wylder massaged my other opening. Gideon's eyes shone brightly as if he was nearly as excited to see us pull this off as I was. Finally, Wylder worked in a finger and then two, massaging me and stretching me to prepare me for his cock.

A low keening spilled from my lips. "Fuck, that feels good."

"Nothing but the best for Queen Katz," Wylder murmured.

I was momentarily distracted by Kaige lurching to his feet in front of me. He gazed down at us, stroking his cock at the sight. Taking in its huge, rigid girth, my mouth watered.

I reached out and curled one of my fingers around the head. Kaige hissed. I took that as encouragement to draw him toward my mouth. Why stop with two delicious cocks when I could have three at the same time?

I was Mercy Katz, and I took what I wanted.

Wylder eased out his fingers. He shifted me at an angle that let Gideon's dick hit a spot inside me that made me gasp. The tip of

Wylder's cock nudged my asshole. I almost stopped breathing in anticipation as my lips wrapped around Kaige.

Wylder took it slowly. He pushed inside my ass bit by bit, letting the rocking of Gideon's thrusts draw him deeper. My eyes flew opened at the overwhelming sensation of fullness. He'd primed me well. There was a hint of pain and tightness, and then my body relaxed around him with a wave of sharper pleasure.

Wylder started to buck alongside me and Gideon, driving deeper every time I dropped to meet their cocks. For several seconds, I just floated on the incredible feelings rushing through me. But I couldn't forget Kaige.

I took him into my mouth again and sucked hard. Kaige's fingers dug into my hair. A moan reverberated through my whole body as I bobbed my head up and down on his cock while riding his two closest friends at the same time.

Gideon reached down and swiveled his thumb over my clit. Wylder put his hands on my hips and fucked my ass harder, while Kaige swayed his hips to fuck my mouth. I grazed his sensitive skin with my teeth until he swore helplessly. Then Rowan was there with us too, finding the space to fondle my breast, propelling me toward the most epic release of my life with the rest of my lovers.

Gideon flicked my clit at the same time that Wylder drove into me and Rowan squeezed my nipple. Another orgasm tore through me, shattering my vision and throbbing through my body. My pussy walls clenched to milk Gideon's dick.

"Mercy, ah," Gideon groaned as he lost himself in me, pushing me towards the peak again. Everything around me turned white with a blaze of ecstasy.

Wylder came with an animalistic groan while Kaige emptied himself half in my mouth and half on my breasts. They caught me as I sagged between them.

We settled onto the floor of the van together, tangled in the spent bodies of the four men who'd come to mean more to me than I'd ever expected. Their combined heat and weight lulled me. I stroked Gideon's hair softly and clasped my finger around Rowan's. My toe teased along

Kaige's calf, and my heel nestled against Wylder's thigh. We all panted in unison as we caught our breaths.

"How was that for a victory party?" Wylder asked, pressing one last kiss to my hip bone.

A giddy laugh tumbled out of me. "That was the best fuck of my entire fucking life."

The others chuckled in agreement and nestled even closer to me. What I'd said was entirely true. Tucked there between them, I couldn't imagine ever letting them—or this—go.

If only there weren't still so many jackasses out there determined to rip us apart.

29

Wylder

As the van climbed up the hill to the Noble mansion, I glanced at Mercy. She had a speck of mud on her cheek that I instinctively reached out to flick off. Mercy looked at me, a wicked smile crossing her lips, and for a moment I almost forgot about where we were and the fact that we were about to confront my Dad.

Almost, but not quite.

Just hours ago, I'd had my cock balls-deep in her tight asshole as she writhed between me and the only guys I trusted in this world. It'd been some kind of heaven watching her come apart for us. But I didn't deserve any kind of heaven if I couldn't also make sure she was safe from my own family.

Rowan parked in front of the mansion. Immediately, the atmosphere in the van turned somber. Tight lipped, Mercy got up and shoved her gun in the back of her jeans. She touched her pocket where I knew she kept the little bracelet she always carried on her.

The rest of us kept our weapons in our hands. We weren't going to go in instigating a fight, but we'd be ready to defend her the second we needed to.

Anthea's favorite Mercedes was parked in the circular drive already. She got out when we did, moving to join us. I'd texted her letting her know we'd be coming, and she'd wanted to show her support.

We fell into a ring around Mercy, me in the front, Rowan and Gideon on either side, and Kaige behind her. Anthea stayed beside me. We marched through the crisp evening air up the stairs and into the stark light of the mansion's foyer.

Axel was already standing there, a cigarette dangling from his mouth. This time it was lit. A few other guys were hanging back closer to the wall.

"So the kid's come back," he said around the cig. "Your dad'll want to see you in his office." Then his gaze caught on Mercy, and his eyes narrowed. "What the fuck is *she* doing here?"

"She's with me," I said, firm but even. "And how many times have I talked to you about smoking in the house?"

Axel snorted. "What are you going to do about it?"

I walked up to him, snatched the cigarette from his lips, and crushed it under my heel. As I stepped back to rejoin the others, Axel scowled at me. "He's not going to want her getting any farther into the house."

"Then I guess we'll just have to talk here," I said. "It's up to him. Are you going to tell him I'm back, or should we all go see what he has to say for himself?"

Before Axel could answer, Dad appeared at the top of the staircase. "I'm more interested in hearing what you have to say for *yourself*," he said in a cold voice that carried through the high-ceilinged room.

Apprehension prickled over me, but I held my ground. Dad strolled down the stairs as if there was nothing all that urgent about this confrontation, but I saw him take note of Mercy and watched his gaze harden even more.

It really was up to him whether we hashed this out here or in the greater privacy of his office, but I wasn't walking away from her, that was for sure.

"I had business to take care of," I said. "Protecting our interests. And that included making sure we have Mercy Katz on our side, no matter what you say about it."

Dad came to a stop at the bottom of the stairs. He made no move to usher us elsewhere. His hands were empty, but I knew he'd have at least one gun on him somewhere. I wasn't going to give him a single clear shot at Mercy.

"*I* decide what protects the Nobles' interests," he said in an icy tone. "You don't have that authority yet, as you've apparently forgotten. Or have you simply chosen this whore over your other loyalties? She opened her legs to you, and you forgot about family, just like that?"

Mercy shifted her weight behind me but stayed silent. I'd asked her to let me handle my dad, but I had to imagine that promise was burning her up inside now.

I raised my chin. "I haven't forgotten my place. I'm here, aren't I? We've been in the Bend fighting against the Storm's forces, and Mercy's been with us every step of the way."

Ezra snorted. "How honorable of her, considering the fact that she's the one who brought that psychotic man of his to our door in the first place."

"Her leaving hasn't stopped the Storm's people from targeting us," I pointed out. "We've been able to weaken their resources and steal valuable intel on their operations with her help. Help we're lucky she's willing to give, considering that you've been trying to get her killed one way or another for weeks now. She's shown more loyalty to the Nobles than practically anyone around here even with you treating her like crap."

"I don't owe anything to a stray who came begging for charity," Dad said even more coldly than before. "Besides, you haven't made all that much progress, have you? Xavier isn't dead, is he? And we're no closer to finding out the reason he and his people are here."

"Maybe not," I said. "But we've weakened them and we showed them we aren't going to go down easy. We're already putting together a plan to get them out of here for good."

"None of that matters. I gave you an order, Wylder. You went against my wishes and continued to align yourself with her. You have one last opportunity to rectify that now."

"No," I snapped. "*You* have the chance to get your head out of your ass and start treating her like the valuable ally she is."

"Or what?" Dad demanded. "You'll run off again like the spoiled brat you apparently are? I raised you better than this."

"Maybe Wylder should run," Axel sneered, and glared at me. "All your running around playing hero ended up with five of our men getting arrested and a major deal going sour. How're you going to make up for losing *that* ally?"

I blinked at him in honest disbelief. "Are you fucking kidding me? *You* were in charge of that deal at the airstrip, and it was one of your men who sold us out. Which we wouldn't even know to make sure the rat doesn't come back into the fold if Mercy hadn't noticed how suspicious he was acting."

"You have no proof it was—"

"Actually, we do," Gideon piped up. "And not just circumstantial anymore. There were records of him on the Storm's payroll in the data I was able to grab from their headquarters."

Axel spluttered for a second before recovering himself. "And he'll be taken care of, because I know how to do my job, unlike you." He cut his gaze toward Mercy.

"You don't get to tell me what my job is," I shot back, and turned to Dad again. "You might not want to see it, but we've accomplished a lot, and Mercy's been a part of it the entire way. We've gotten the cops off our back with their drug trafficking suspicions, we've gotten several of the Storm's men arrested and killed dozens, and now we've compromised their headquarters. Trust me, this once. It won't take much more to—"

Axel broke in with a rough guffaw. "Did you snort some Glory on the way here? You don't get to make those kinds of decisions. You've gone fucking rogue, and you come in here accusing *me* of shit?"

"Oh, shut the fuck up," I told him. "This is between me and Dad. You've never cared about the Nobles beyond pumping up your own ego."

The vein in Axel's temple bulged. "You're just a stupid kid," he spat out. "Waltzing in here like you can magically solve all the problems I've had to clean up after your crazy plans—"

"The only one who's made any mess around here is you with *your* stupidity."

"Maybe I haven't made enough of a mess, then," Axel growled with a flare of his nostrils. He whipped his gun from the waist of his jeans, clicking off the safety as he raised it.

My body reacted automatically. I couldn't tell whether he was aiming it at me or Mercy, but my response would have been the same either way. With a hitch of my pulse, I jerked up my own gun and pulled the trigger.

The bullet hit Axel right in the middle of the forehead. Blood sputtered from the wound, flecks of it landing on my shirt. My father's right-hand man collapsed to the floor in a heap, his glassy eyes wide open, his face caught in shock. Blood pooled beneath his head and seeped across the pristine marble floor. I lowered my hand with a weird rush of adrenaline and relief, but not a hint of regret.

"What the hell do you think you're doing?" Dad said, raising his voice just a tad for the first time. His face was a mask of tension.

I met his gaze steadily. "What I had to do. Isn't this who you wanted me to be, Dad? A leader who's focused and ruthless? You wouldn't accept any member of the Nobles making accusations and trying to undermine you—and Axel's been doing that to me for *years*. This is my home too, and anyone working for the Nobles needs to be loyal to both of us. Or do you only have a problem with me getting fucked when it's not by one of your men?"

Dad stared at me as if he'd never seen me before. His jaw worked, but he couldn't seem to find his words. That was fine. Let it sink in.

I wasn't totally sure what I'd do if he told me to get the fuck out, but I was done cowering. I was done blaming myself for the shit *he'd* thrown at me. It was time to write my own story.

Before Dad could get around to speaking, someone pounded on the door. One of the lackeys poised around the room ran to answer it.

"Delivery for Ezra Noble," a man's voice said. "Do you need any help bringing it in?"

"We'll manage," the guy said brusquely, but he motioned over another lackey. We stepped back as they dragged a large crate, waist high and equally long and wide, into the foyer.

What the hell was that? The last time we'd gotten a surprise on our doorstep, it'd ended with a man's guts exploding all over our front lawn. A sense of foreboding washed over me.

Dad obviously hadn't been expecting this package either. Snapping out of his shock, he marched over. "What the hell is this?"

"I don't know," the first lackey said. "The delivery guy didn't say."

We kept a few steps back as they looked it over. There was no identifying information on the outside of the wooden slats, and when they tugged on the lid, it didn't budge.

"You'll need a crowbar," Kaige said.

One of the guys glanced at Dad, who nodded, his expression grim. The lackey dashed out of the house to the garage and returned quickly with a curved length of wrought-iron.

He looked at the crate with a nervous expression and then at me and Dad. "Maybe you should keep your distance."

Right. Who knew what opening the lid might trigger? We moved to the sides of the staircase for shelter, the other lackeys pulling back too. The guy with the crowbar winced when he must have realized he'd volunteered for the dangerous job, but then he wedged the flat end under the lid and started heaving at it.

After a couple good tries, a few nails popped out. He moved to the next corner. When he heaved up the third, the whole lid flipped off and crashed to the floor.

No explosions. No monsters springing out.

"What's inside?" Dad asked, reemerging.

"I don't know," the lackey said. "All I can see on top is packing peanuts."

As Dad walked right up to the crate, the rest of us followed. He brushed aside the foam peanuts with a few brisk sweeps of his hand and then jerked it back as if he'd been bitten. All the color drained from his face.

"What?" I sprang the rest of the way forward.

My gaze caught on the bloody stump of an arm first. *He's sent us another dismembered corpse*, I thought distantly, remembering the rotting limbs Xavier had tossed through one of the mansion windows not that long ago. But this one was fresh, the only odor a sickening meaty one with no hint of rot yet, and—

My eyes slid over the arm and a protruding foot and landed on the face still half-buried in packing peanuts. My stomach lurched, and my legs wobbled under me.

It was Roland.

My older brother. How the hell— Why would Xavier— None of this made any sense.

I squeezed my eyes shut, but the image of my brother's decapitated head swam behind my eyelids. Nausea crawled up from my stomach, and a different burn caught in the back of my throat.

I'd always thought— I'd never gotten the chance— How could he be *dead*? I wanted to scream bloody murder, to punch someone, and part of me also wanted to cry.

But I couldn't. Not in front of Dad and all the men watching this spectacle. Not in front of *my* men. Even Dad was standing rigid, his hand over his mouth but no sound coming out, holding all his emotions in.

Cold and ruthless. It wasn't the kind of leader I wanted to be all of the time, but right now, it was who I had to be. The fucker who'd done this was going to pay in blood.

Anthea's face had paled, her mouth pressed tight, but she plucked a note out of the corner of the crate. *I hope you like my gift, Ezra*, it said in a hasty scrawl, followed by a signature that was simply *X*. As if we'd have any doubt about who this had come from.

"This is what we're up against," I said, pointing at the crate, relieved that my voice only shook a little bit. "This is what that psycho's capable of, and we need every asset we can get to take him down. I'm the only heir you've got now. From here forward, you'll respect that and me. We have to stand up against this asshole together and with everyone who's willing to stand with us, which includes Mercy and the Claws who'll follow her, or we're going to destroy ourselves before the Storm's people even have the chance."

Dad was silent for another long moment, though he lowered his hand from his face. My stomach kept churning. He looked as if he'd aged ten years in that instant. His face was blank, as if he was in a place far away, his grief locked inside of him.

All this time, he'd still been hoping Roland would walk back through that door properly and reclaim the throne that'd originally been meant for him. I'd always suspected it, but I could see it written all over Dad's face now.

He drew himself up to his full height and met my eyes. "Yes. This menace needs to be wiped right off our streets, right out of the county. Whatever it takes."

I nodded back at him, but my spirits didn't feel any lighter. Dad didn't like being backed into a corner. I'd have to keep watching my back and Mercy's. The second the Storm's people were out of the picture, I had no idea how pissed off he'd be with me, but I didn't for one second believe he'd just forgive my defiance.

30

Mercy

I FLICKED ON THE BASEMENT LIGHT BUT THEN STOPPED there at the top of the stairs, my legs refusing to move.

"You okay?" Rowan asked from behind me.

"Yeah." I dragged in a breath. We'd been going through my old house, checking whether Dad or the Red Sharks who'd recently vacated it might have left behind anything useful. So far nothing. All that was left was the basement.

Nothing down there could hurt me anymore.

"This place just brings up a lot of bad memories," I added, and pushed myself to tramp down the stairs.

With nothing else left to do, all four of the guys followed me. Weirdly, I felt both comforted and unnerved by their presence. I wanted them with me, but I wasn't sure I liked them seeing the place that was the root of so much trauma—of the most fragile parts of me.

The small fixture in the ceiling lit the long, wide room with a yellow glow. Dust tickled my nose, the dank scents of old cement and long-dried bodily fluids traveling with it.

Kaige stepped past me and prodded a long metal pole mounted on one wall. "Was your dad a secret ballet dancer or something?"

My mouth twitched even as my gut twisted, looking at the thing. "He'd handcuff people to that to hold them up while he interrogated them," I explained. "It annoyed him if they collapsed on the ground where he couldn't hit quite as many sensitive places."

Avoiding looking at the floor at the other side of the room, I walked over to the locker in the corner. When I opened it, I found nothing but a few cobwebs. Either Dad hadn't stashed anything in there recently, or one of the gangs that'd come through since had cleared it out.

I turned around to find that Wylder had wandered over to the rectangular concrete slab fitted into the floor, the one I'd been trying to ignore. He nudged it with the toe of his shoe. "What's this?"

My heart was already thumping faster. I debated walking over to join him, but decided I was happier right here. "Open it up if you want."

"Mercy," Rowan started.

I shook my head before he could go on. "It's okay. They all might as well see it." I'd already told Kaige and Gideon about the pit, but somehow it'd never come up with Wylder in any detail before now.

Wylder heaved the concrete lid to the side and peered into the coffin-sized hollow underneath. "I don't get it."

I swallowed hard. "He'd dump people he was pissed off at in there so they'd be more... malleable when they came out. Or just to torture them until they bled out and died. When it's closed, there's no light at all, and the lid's way too heavy to shift from underneath." My thumb ran over my scarred fingertips of its own accord.

Wylder glanced at me, a flicker of understanding and then horror crossing his face. It must have been obvious I'd spoken from experience.

Gideon was studying the pit with an analytical expression, but a furious glint had sparked in his eyes. Kaige's muscles flexed as if he thought he could beat up my past for me if he took out his own fury on the source of my torment.

"It's where I learned to be afraid of closed spaces," I finished. "A long time ago."

Wylder sucked in a breath through his teeth, his own hands clenching. "Just when I thought I couldn't hate that prick more." He kicked at the lid, which didn't budge it, and then shoved it back into place with his hands. When he looked at me again, I could tell he was remembering the time he'd prompted my fear. "I'm sorry. I had no idea."

I shrugged. "How could you have? I didn't tell you."

"I didn't give you a chance to. I was such a shit about it." He let out a little growl and stalked over to me, clasping my hand in his, his thumb meeting my palm where they held identical scars. The cuts where we'd drawn blood might have healed, but our bond remained in place. "I am *never* letting anyone torture you like that again."

Gideon's jaw twitched as he caught my gaze. "What your father did was unforgivable."

"I wouldn't agree with throwing a grown man in there, let alone a little kid," Rowan said, his voice soft. "But you made it through. You didn't let him break you."

"You made yourself a total badass, in spite of that asshole," Kaige put in. He cracked his knuckles. "It's a good thing for him he's already dead, or I'd make him regret every fucked-up decision of his life, starting with that."

They closed in around me, but their nearness didn't make me feel at all claustrophobic. Instead, I was cocooned in the warmth of their bodies. They knew my weakness... and by now, I knew theirs too. Somehow we'd all become something more than we were before. It was thrilling even if it scared me how much I liked it.

Gideon's phone buzzed, breaking the moment. He dug it out of his pocket and grinned.

"What's up?" Wylder asked.

"Looks like the cops found the trail of evidence we left them," Gideon announced. "Very handy that the Red Shark's people fled town so they're not around to speak up for themselves—the perfect scapegoats. The Nobles have been cleared of all charges relating to the drug activity at the waterfront property."

Rowan breathed a sigh of relief. "Then we'll be able to resume construction."

"Too bad we couldn't pin it all on the Storm's pricks," Kaige grumbled.

Gideon frowned at his phone. "I'm still waiting to see if that tracking device I managed to get on Xavier's boot takes us anywhere interesting. It seems active, but he's only been going around the places we already know the Storm's people are active so far."

"One thing at a time," Wylder said, clapping Kaige on the back and then glancing at me. "Let's get the hell out of this place."

I smiled. "Yeah."

We climbed back to the first floor, and I stopped there to look around the kitchen and into the dining room beyond. "I'm thinking I might take this place back over for myself. Make it the new Claws headquarters. I'll need to set up security, obviously... I'll have to talk to Jenner and the others and see how they want to go forward from here."

"You're their queen," Wylder said, nudging me. "They've got to listen to you. And I'm sure it'll be more comfortable for you to have your own place without my dad lurking around."

He paused, a shadow crossing his face. A question had been itching at me ever since the night when that mysterious package had been delivered to the Noble mansion, and now it rose up again. It'd clearly shaken up both Wylder and his father. I hadn't totally understood the comments Wylder had made about heirs. But it'd seemed so painful that I hadn't wanted to bring it up, giving him room to do so.

But it'd been two days, and he hadn't said a peep to me. I hadn't heard anything other than a few comments between the Nobles about a funeral being set up late this afternoon. Maybe Wylder was waiting for me to show I *wanted* to know.

"Wylder," I said carefully, "who was it Xavier sent to your father? I know you might not want to talk about it, but you don't have to shut me out."

Wylder's mouth twisted. He ran his hand over his face and seemed to gather himself. The other guys stood around us silently, and I got the sense from their awkwardness that they already knew what he was going to say.

"That was my older brother," he said finally, his voice gone a little raw.

"Roland. *He* was meant to take over the Nobles from my father. Dad trained him for it since he was a little kid. But when I was thirteen—Roland was eighteen—he decided he didn't want this life. He took a bunch of money out of the Noble accounts and ran for it. I haven't even known where he's been."

My heart sank. That was even worse than I'd imagined. To lose his only brother, without even having had the chance to talk to him in so long. "I'm sorry," I murmured.

Wylder grimaced. "You don't need to feel sorry for me. I don't even know... He's basically a stranger now. And—all these years, I kept waiting for him to show up and say he wanted to rule the Nobles after all, and my father would have shoved me aside for him in an instant, even after everything..." He shook himself. "I gave in to more of Dad's demands than I should have trying to prove myself. I let him get away with what he did to Laurel. Never again."

I squeezed his hand. "You did the best you could."

"Maybe. Funny that when I finally got the guts to really stand up to him, Roland was already dead and gone, I just didn't know it yet." He raised his head, his tone darkening. "And no matter how I felt about Roland then or now, he didn't deserve to die like that. Xavier's added one more item to the list of things he needs to pay for."

"And we're going to make him regret every one," Kaige promised, baring his teeth.

"So let's get on with that." Wylder swung his arm to the door. "Pack up. We're grabbing an early lunch for a massive planning session."

We stepped out into the morning sunlight. I locked the door behind me, and I turned back around just in time to see something small and glinting whip through the air and sink into Kaige's neck.

"Kaige!" I yelped. It was some kind of dart. What the hell?

Kaige staggered, snatching at the thing. I was springing to help him when my ears caught several faint popping sounds in the distance. The next instant, pain jabbed into my own neck.

A rush of dizziness swept over me. I pawed at the dart, spinning around and nearly tripping over my feet. The other guys were stumbling too. My vision rippled and dimmed, and then the entire world faded to black.

LETHAL EMPRESS

Crooked Paradise #4

Mercy

I WOKE UP GASPING, IMAGES OF MY MEN DROPPING LIKE FLIES around me flashing through my mind. Someone had attacked us—we'd been hit by darts—and then everything had gone dark.

My eyes popped open, and the world swam for a moment. My head was throbbing, and there was a pinch of pain on the side of my neck where the needle had hit me. My body burned to move, to defend myself and the guys if they were still with me, but I was too dizzy to orient myself... Where the hell *was* I?

As my vision cleared, everything around me came into sharper focus. I was lying on my back in a large room. The air was warm, and a soft glow washed over me from a crystalline fixture encased in an elaborate molding on the high ceiling. My head rested on a silky pillow. I managed to sit up and found that the rest of me had been lying on a thick Persian carpet.

Whoever had brought me here had taken a whole lot more care in my comfort than I'd have expected. I'd have assumed it'd been Xavier or someone else with the Storm behind the attack, but they'd never treated me anywhere near this gently before.

Not just me—us. My men were spread out on the rug around me, each with their own pillow under their heads. If I hadn't known better, I'd have thought they were having a good night's sleep.

I scooted toward Rowan, who was nearest to me, and gripped his shoulder. "Rowan," I said urgently, giving him a shake. "Wake up." When he didn't respond, I slapped him lightly on his cheeks.

His eyes opened, and he blinked up at me as if trying to place me. His voice came out creaky. "Mercy?" Then all at once, he tried to sit up—too fast. His body swayed with what I guessed was the same dizziness I'd been hit with when I first woke up.

"Careful," I said. "Somebody sedated us. It takes its time wearing off."

Rowan tensed, his gaze flicking around the room as he ran his hand over his short blond hair. "Who grabbed us? What the hell is going on?"

"I don't know. I didn't see anyone when it happened, and no one's been around since I woke up."

At my other side, Wylder groaned and rubbed his forehead, swiping away the auburn strands that had fallen rumpled across it. Gideon and Kaige were stirring as well. At least they all appeared to be *alive*. These days, with everything we'd been through, I'd count that as a blessing.

Wylder looked at me, concern darkening his bright green eyes. "Are you okay?"

I stretched my arms and rolled my head experimentally. The dizziness was gone, and the pain in my neck had already faded. "I'm fine," I said. "For now."

With a jolt of fear, my hands dropped to my sides. I was still wearing the same clothes as I remembered, but my weapons—my gun and my knife—were gone. So was my phone. Shit. It wasn't surprising, but the loss still made me feel uncomfortably naked.

Kaige was frowning as he checked himself over. His massive brawn flexed beneath his fitted tee. "My gun's been taken too. Who the fuck is messing with us?"

Gideon winced when he came up with nothing as well. I wouldn't be surprised if he was more bothered by his missing phone than his lack of weaponry. With his tongue flicking over his lip ring, he peered around the posh room with its old-fashioned stylings and knit his brow. "This is very strange. They obviously could have killed us, but they didn't. So they must want something from us other than our lives."

Wylder arched an eyebrow. "Which means we can assume it wasn't Xavier, right? That fucker *definitely* wanted to mount all of our heads on pikes."

"Yeah," I said, pushing myself to my feet taking in the rest of the space. A long, polished oak table stood at the other end of the room with five matching chairs on either side. A few pieces of what looked like expensive artwork hung on the walls. "But who else would have wanted to take us captive? And why leave us here like this? They haven't even restrained us."

"They figure we don't stand a chance of escaping even without tying us up," Wylder muttered, looking offended by the implication.

Kaige focused on the door. He got up, wobbling for a second, and marched over to try the curved handle. It jarred in his hand, locked. He growled at it. "We need to get the fuck out of here."

"Easier said than done," Rowan murmured as he stood.

There was a huge bay window, but it was locked too, with iron bars running over the panes so even breaking the glass wouldn't get us far. Wylder walked past it along the length of the room. I peered at the daylight showing through the window. It was impossible to tell how many hours had passed since we'd been taken or even whether it was still the same day, and I found it jarring to not have any sense of the actual time.

"How *long* have we been here?" Wylder said abruptly. "Did I miss Roland's funeral? If these assholes stopped me from being there for my brother... Damn it!" He slammed his fist into the wall.

"Wylder," I said, going to him and placing a hand on his shoulder.

He stiffened, guilt etched all over his face. "It was the least I could do for him, Mercy. His last send-off. He deserved it."

"He does, and you'll be there when it happens." I didn't know if that was true, but I had no idea how else to console him. I hadn't gotten to have a last send-off for my family either. At some point, when I didn't have a psycho breathing down my neck, I could go pick up the ashes from the coroner... Maybe I could have some kind of ceremony then.

As that thought passed through my mind, a key clicked in the lock on the other side of the door. We all froze.

Before we had a chance to come up with any kind of plan, the door flew open and two men and a woman strode into the room. They were dressed in collared shirts and dress pants as if they were here for a business meeting and not a kidnapping, but I could make out the outline of a holster at each of their hips. They were armed. One of the men rested his hand on his weapon without taking it out—just a reminder that he could if he needed to.

We all eyed them warily, but the woman simply gave us a mild smile. "We'd appreciate it if you'd please sit down at the table. Our boss will be with you shortly."

"Your boss?" Wylder demanded. "Who the fuck is that, and where the hell are we?"

The woman didn't flinch at his hostile tone. She motioned toward the table. "Please, just sit, and he'll explain everything."

I exchanged a glance with the guys. This was all very weird, but we *did* want an explanation, and it didn't look like we were getting out of here easily anyway. We were probably better off finding out what we were up against.

We nodded in mutual understanding and turned toward the table, but Wylder hesitated. "What time is it?" he asked the woman. "How long have we been here?

"It's just past noon," she said without needing to check. "You arrived about an hour ago."

His shoulders came down an inch. The funeral had been scheduled for four o'clock, if I remembered right. He'd still have a chance to get there… if this "boss" had any intention of letting us leave after he'd given his explanation.

We walked over to the table and by unspoken agreement sat in the chairs facing the door. I'd rather have a wall at my back, and I'd bet the guys felt the same way. The three figures who'd ordered us to sit there sauntered over but stayed standing at the edges of the room.

I shifted on my seat, itching for answers. Thankfully, I didn't have to wait long. The door opened again, and a silver-haired man stepped into the room, flanked by two other men who looked like bodyguards.

The man in the middle was obviously the guy in charge. He wasn't all that tall, but his broad shoulders filled out his expensive suit, and he gave off an aura of power that quivered over my skin even from across the room. His slate gray hair was slicked close to his knobby skull, which made his thick eyebrows stand out even more over his penetrating eyes. As he walked over to the table with even but unhurried strides, I placed him in his mid to late fifties.

He was a total stranger. I'd have remembered that face if I'd seen it before. The guys' expressions showed the same confusion I felt.

The man sat in the seat in the center, opposite Wylder. His bodyguards stayed standing behind the chairs on either side of him. He considered Wylder, then me, then the other guys, his gaze returning to the Noble heir after a moment.

"Wylder Noble," he said in a smooth conversational tone, and tipped his head to me as well. "And Mercy Katz. The heirs to two of the most powerful gangs in Paradise Bend, even if that's not saying much."

I bristled automatically. "Who the hell are *you*?"

He showed no sign that my tone affected him. "I'm the man who really owns everything you believe is yours."

Wylder's hands clenched where they were resting on the tabletop. "I thought you were going to explain why you dragged us here. All I'm hearing so far is cryptic bullshit."

A hint of a smile tugged at the corners of the man's lips over his narrow, jutting chin. "Cryptic, maybe, but not bullshit at all. There's a lot you don't know about how the world works, Mr. Noble. But I know a lot about all of you already." His gaze flicked along the table. "Kaige Maddon, the enforcer with an anger problem. Rowan Finlay, the negotiator and peacekeeper. And Gideon Whitlock, the brains locked in a body that betrays him."

Gideon's back went rigid. "Anyone could have known that," he said in a low voice as cool as his dyed blue hair.

"I'm only scraping the surface." The man folded his hands in front of him and gave us a real smile, and just like that, I was sure he meant everything he said. A chill ran down my back.

"I'd still like your explanation," I said.

"Of course you would. It'll just be difficult for you to wrap your heads around it." He drew in a breath. "Let me start by apologizing for the abrupt way I had you brought to me. Time was of the essence, and I didn't want to risk any complications in securing your cooperation. I've done you no harm, and I'll let you go once you've heard my proposal. I've been watching the situation in Paradise Bend for some time now, and it's become clear that you could be valuable allies there."

"Allies in what?" Wylder said. "What proposal? Why should we listen to a damn thing you say?"

The man fixed his gaze on the Noble heir. "Because I really do own every inch of ground and every brick on every property you consider your own. Did you honestly believe that the Nobles were the highest level of power a criminal organization could reach? You have lesser gangs paying tribute to you, and in turn those above you take their cut."

Wylder frowned. "We don't pay tithe to anyone."

"Oh, but you do. Those of us higher up simply have more subtle ways of collecting our dues." The man cocked his head. "Haven't you wondered about the recent surge in conflict in your county? Where all these unexpected intruders are coming from and why?"

"Are you responsible for that?" Kaige burst out, looking ready to jump over the table and throttle the guy if he said yes.

The man chuckled darkly. "No, I'm trying to put a stop to it. It's actually very simple. I'm part of a group of thirteen who call ourselves the Devil's Dozen. We each have a code name: I go by 'the Long Night.' Between us, we control all the illicit and underground businesses throughout the world. Each of us has holdings on various continents, our own territories that we rule over from behind the scenes and benefit from. Every criminal who rises at all above the level of petty pickpocket answers to us, whether they know it or not. And Paradise Bend is part of my domain."

"I've never heard anyone mention the Long Night or the Devil's Dozen," Gideon said.

"Which speaks to our expertise in secrecy." The man who called himself the Long Night smiled thinly. "Most who get far enough to find out that much about us are either working directly for us or don't live to tell the tale elsewhere. You can consider yourselves a lucky exception—for now."

I wasn't sure if I bought his story, but *he* sure seemed to believe it. Another shiver ran down my back. "Are you going to tell us why you're making an exception?"

The Long Night gave a vague wave of his hand. "There's always jockeying for power between the Devil's Dozen members. It's hard to avoid it among master criminals, as I'm sure you can imagine. I've been distracted by other concerns recently, and the Nobles' continuing expansion throughout the state—with excellent financial results—caught the eye of a couple of my rivals. They set their sights on Paradise Bend and decided they'd grab it and everything associated with the organizations there out from under me before I realized what was happening."

He shook his head, apparently at the folly of those rivals, and something clicked in my head. This tall tale suddenly made a sickening sort of sense.

"The Storm," I said, my voice coming out in a hush. "And the Red Shark. That's who you're talking about—they're in the Devil's Dozen too, with the same kind of crazy code names."

And this was why we'd never heard of them before, hadn't had any idea where they'd come from. We'd been caught in the middle of a territory war involving gangs bigger than any of us could have dreamed existed before this meeting.

"Aren't you a clever little thing?" the Long Night said with apparent amusement. I hated the patronizing note in his tone. Maybe this superiority complex came automatically with the knowledge that you reigned supreme over vast territories and millions of people, but that didn't mean I had to like it.

"What is up with the weird names anyway?" Kaige asked, looking bewildered.

"They're connected to traditional labels for the full moons, which are important to us for reasons you don't need to know," the Long Night said, and turned his attention back to me and Wylder. "Let's focus on where you come in."

Wylder's jaw had hardened. "Yeah, I'm still waiting to hear about that. If you're so all-powerful, why don't you get rid of the idiots who're trashing our home? Why're you sitting back and letting us take all the blows?"

"At this moment, I have other, rather pressing responsibilities," the Long Night said. "I've seen what you can do even with your meager resources, and it's rather impressive. The Red Shark has backed off, but the Storm's forces remain. Before I expend energy and manpower I'd prefer stayed elsewhere, I'd like to give you a chance to clean up the mess for me."

"You want us to do your dirty work, possibly because you see us as expendable," Rowan said evenly. "Why would we help you?"

The Long Night leaned forward on the table, his hands clasped in front of him. "I intend to protect what's mine and keep my reputation intact. I need this conflict to end soon if I'm going to ensure that none of the others in the Devil's Dozen get ideas about my territories being vulnerable."

"That doesn't answer his question," Gideon said evenly.

The older man gave him a baleful look. "I was getting to that. I'll offer you support in the form of information about the Storm's operations and a certain amount of supplies. If you can run the Storm's people out of Paradise Bend for good within a week, I'll support both Mr. Noble and Miss Katz in running your respective organizations as you see fit. Besides that, I have other business opportunities to offer you in the long run once you're done with the Storm."

"Within a week?" I repeated. "That hardly gives us any time at all."

The Long Night looked at me with his hollowed eyes. "That's all I can afford before the risk to my status becomes too great. You're lucky I'm offering you any opportunity at all. If you don't come through, I'll have to crack down on the fighting with everything I have—and that'll mean a total clearing of the board. There won't be anything left for you to call home, and none of you will be around to mourn that loss. I'll knock down the Nobles and the Claws and everyone else with a stake in the underground businesses of the county and set up people who answer directly to me to run things."

The Long Night's gaze slid across us as we all took in that statement. His smile turned grim. "So, what do you say? Will you take the deal, or would you rather die?"

2

Mercy

WITH THE LONG NIGHT'S LAST WORDS RINGING IN MY EARS, I blanched. "You're not serious. You'd slaughter *everyone* in all the gangs—?"

The Long Night raised an eyebrow. "I wouldn't say it if I wasn't serious. I need it to be clear to everyone watching that I'm in control. It's up to you whether the law is laid down by you two in my stead or whether I have to rain down hellfire myself to get it done. If you aren't an asset to me, then you're a liability I can't afford to keep around."

Beside me, Wylder shook his head vehemently. "I don't understand. All we need is more time—"

"My colleagues have left me no choice," the older man said. "If things continue the way they are, extreme measures will be necessary. I can't have my authority challenged elsewhere over this squabble here." He spoke as if this was nothing more than business to him, as if he wasn't talking about destroying hundreds of lives. And maybe he *didn't* care.

I glanced at Wylder, whose jaw was clenched, his fists bunched at his sides. The stakes were so high, and if we failed, we'd lose everything.

Gideon gave the Long Night a narrow look. "I wonder if you're setting us up for failure. Using us to thin your enemy's ranks so there's less for you to clean up when you do have to sweep in."

"I trust your capabilities." The Long Night studied Gideon and then Wylder. "Maybe you don't feel the same."

I couldn't keep quiet. "The Storm has a massive presence in the Bend already. If you actually want to give us a chance, make it a real one."

"Unfortunately, Miss Katz, not everything is about you. Time is slipping away from us, and every moment you waste here arguing with me about it is another precious second lost that threatens my empire. And if you think that what you've seen so far is even a quarter of the actual size of Storm's army, you're very, very wrong."

Fear coiled in my gut. He didn't seem like it on the surface, but the Long Night was just as terrible as the Storm or the Red Shark. There was clearly a reason this group that called themselves the Devil's Dozen had been able to maintain control from the shadows over the decades. They were ruthless.

I knew without a doubt that the Long Night would make good on his promise to sweep through the county and kill anyone who stood in the way of his power. In my mind's eyes, I already saw the destruction. My ears echoed with the imagined screams as a massacre of everyone who'd ever associated with any of the gangs in Paradise Bend—Nobles, Claws, Steel Knights, or the many other smaller outfits—raged through the streets.

I cleared my throat and glanced at Wylder before turning back to the Long Night. We couldn't make a decision this huge and horrible with the man insisting on it breathing down our necks. "If you don't mind," I said, "I think we should take a few minutes to discuss this in private, just between the five of us."

"Very well," the Long Night said. "I respect that you want to take your time before making any commitments. Just remember that the clock starts ticking soon. I hope to hear a positive response from your side."

He rose from his chair and signaled to his people. Both the

bodyguards who'd arrived with him and the three figures who'd entered ahead of him pulled in around him and walked with him out of the room. They closed the door behind them until it was only the five of us.

The second we were alone, Gideon's gaze darted along the molded details of the ceiling. "I'm not sure how 'private' this conversation really is. I find it hard to believe that a man in his position wouldn't have cameras on us."

Rowan sighed. "Well, there's nothing we can do about *that*. He's going to find out what we decide anyway."

Wylder pulled his chair back and to the side so he could face me better. "Did you have specific thoughts you wanted to share?"

I rubbed my temple. "I don't know. It's so much to take in. But I was having a hard time even *thinking* with him sitting there staring at us."

"Are we really considering tying ourselves to this guy?" Kaige asked, grimacing.

"If what he said is true, then we've been tied to him all along," Wylder pointed out. "He's apparently been skimming money from the Noble businesses for years. Dad's never mentioned anything—maybe this Devil's Dozen organization really does have methods to take their tithe that can go unnoticed. I guess it wouldn't be impossible with all the stages of money laundering and the rest. There's a lot of cash changing hands all the time."

Kaige shook his head, the chain with his father's dog tags sliding against his neck with the movement. "It's wild, though. A shadowy organization created by creepy old men with an obsession with the full moon, and they run all the criminal business in the world? It feels like I've tripped into some crazy movie."

"It might sound strange, but I've always had the impression there might be a higher force above us," Gideon said. "Certain things happen too smoothly or conveniently."

Kaige snorted. "I think you're confusing Jesus with code-named gangsters."

Gideon rolled his eyes at the bigger guy before turning to us. "I definitely don't see any reason to doubt the Long Night's version of what's happened in the Bend. Think about it: the Storm's and the Red Shark's people showed up seemingly out of nowhere, and we'd never heard about them before. That's because they aren't just regular street gangs fighting for territories. They're the true kings of the underworld."

"And if we hope to win against one of them, we probably need the inside knowledge this guy can give us," I said. "The Storm has too much power over us right now, at least if we want to end things quickly."

"Can we trust the Long Night to keep his word?" Rowan said.

"I sure as hell don't," Kaige muttered, swiping his hand over his dark buzzcut. "He calls himself the Long Night, for fuck's sake. He's fucking looney tunes."

Gideon nodded. "I don't know about his sanity, but he could be playing at something he's not telling us about, manipulating us." He paused. "Although this is a very elaborate ruse, if so."

"Any deal with him is a deal with the devil," Wylder said with a growl in his voice. "He admitted it himself—he's one of them, which means he's equally or even more dangerous than either the Storm or the Red Shark. Look at what he's already threatened to do."

I sucked in my breath, my thoughts finally settling into some kind of order. "I totally agree that he's dangerous and that we can't really trust him. But how can we say no? The alternative is to let him come in and steamroll over not just the Storm's people but all the rest of us. From the way he's talking, he doesn't care if he has to paint the whole county in blood just to clean the slate—people from all the gangs, innocents caught in the crossfire. It'll be awful."

Wylder frowned, but I could see the wheels turning in his head.

"He gave us one week," Kaige said. "We can't do shit in that."

"It's still better than the no time at all we'd have if we refuse to even try," I said. "The Long Night is going to give us information and resources—that help might be enough for us to get the upper hand quickly."

Rowan tipped his head toward me. "I agree with Mercy. This way at least we get a chance to do things our way and survive. Lord knows what will happen if he sends his own men in."

"Chaos," I said, thinking back to my vision. "Utter, bloody chaos."

The Long Night's words echoed in my head, *There won't be anything left for you to call home.*

Wylder let out a rough breath. "I see what you're saying, and I know you're right. No way in hell am I giving up and rolling over. Winning this war is going to be hard for more reasons than just the Storm, though."

I looked at him with a tug of my heart. "What do you mean?"

"This guy came to me instead of my dad. Dad won't be happy about that, which is just going to add to the friction that's already there between us." He closed his eyes for a second, his expression tightening, and I knew he'd made a decision. My heart thumped faster.

I couldn't fight for the Bend on my own, and the other guys would follow Wylder's lead. I needed him by my side.

Wylder opened his eyes to gaze at the closed door for a long moment. Then he said, "There's nothing we can do about Dad's hurt feelings now. We have to make the best of what we have. And that means fighting as hard as we fucking can. It's still our territory too, and we're not going to let any asshole crash in and take it from us, no matter what special secret group he's part of."

My body began to thrum with anticipation. Now that we were agreed, I didn't want to wait to get started. I could feel the seconds passing us by.

"They'll never own Paradise Bend, not really," Wylder finished.

I sat up straighter in my chair and looked at the other guys. "Everyone's on board?"

Rowan and Gideon nodded despite their solemn expressions.

Kaige sighed. "I still think this is insane, but I don't think it's going to stop being insane no matter what I do. I'll always have your backs."

"I guess we'd better let him know, then," I said.

Gideon scanned the room again. "Is there a button somewhere we can press, or...?"

We examined our surroundings for a few minutes, and finally Rowan went over to the door and knocked on it loudly. One of the men in the collared shirts opened it and peered inside. Behind him, I could see the long stretch of a corridor with big bay windows at the end, the green of foliage showing through the glass.

The building must be huge. I couldn't think of any place like this in Paradise Bend. Where exactly were we?

"We're ready," Rowan said. "We'd like to give the Long Night our answer."

The man's lips thinned. "I hope for your sake that it's the right one."

Rowan returned to the table, and we sat there in silence. A few moments later, the door swung open, and the Long Night walked in. This time he was alone.

The dull thud of his loafers on the plush carpet was the only sound in the room. Instead of sitting down, he stopped behind one of the chairs, his hand clasped over the top. "So, what have you decided?"

"We'll take your deal," Wylder said. "We get one week. You don't make a move on any of us until then. And you fill us in on anything useful you know about the Storm."

A triumphant smile came over the Long Night's face, and his silver-blue eyes almost glistened. "I'm glad to know you've decided to take my help after all. I must admit, I was starting to have my doubts. Stubbornness could become one of your fatal flaws, Mr. Noble."

"I like to see it as a virtue," Wylder retorted.

My throat had constricted now that we were setting this deal in motion. "What exactly are your conditions?" I said abruptly. "We don't have to take down the Storm himself, do we?"

The Long Night let out a low, humorless laugh. "Of course not, girl. You'd never get close enough to him. I doubt he'll even set foot in your little county himself. I'm not going to ask for the impossible. I only want his men out of Paradise Bend—permanently. You need to beat them and beat them well enough that they'll have no interest in returning." He gave us all a narrow look. "Do you accept those terms?"

For a second, I couldn't breathe. Beat them that definitively—in a week. It was hard to imagine. But like I'd said earlier, what choice did we have but to try?

"I'm in," I said.

"We all are," Wylder put in, speaking for his inner circle as well. The other guys tipped their heads.

"Excellent." The Long Night rubbed his hands together. "I'll have you driven home and see that you receive the resources I promised immediately. I'll even give you a small reprieve—your week will start tonight rather than right at this moment. Seven nights from today, I want all trace of the Storm gone from Paradise Bend. Good luck."

3

Wylder

I TUGGED AT THE BLACK TIE AROUND MY NECK. IT FELT LIKE a noose, slowly choking off the air to my lungs. I loosened the knot, but that didn't do much.

The tie wasn't the problem—I was. I'd been on edge since the moment the lid on that crate had popped open to reveal my brother's mutilated body, sent by Xavier.

I gazed at the freshly dug grave and the casket that'd just been lowered into it. It was made of polished mahogany with embellishments along the edges. Nothing but the finest for my brother.

We'd only just made it back to the city in time to change our clothes into something more fitting and get to the ceremony before it started. Dad had been eyeing me from the moment I'd gotten here, with an expression like he wanted to lay into me but wouldn't in this kind of company.

Or maybe it was Mercy, standing next to me, that he was shooting his periodic death glare at. He probably didn't want her here after he'd done so much to drive her out of our lives, but she was back, and she was staying. Dad would have a fight on his hands if he tried to challenge me on that subject again.

I couldn't stop my mind from tripping back a few hours ago to the immense mansion where the man who called himself the Long Night had held his impromptu meeting with us and made his demands. Did Dad have any idea that he'd been working under someone else all his life, while he made such a show of being the head honcho? How the hell was I going to tell him what I'd learned? I could only imagine how pissed off he'd be... if he even believed me.

Now, at the priest's direction, he dropped a handful of dirt onto the coffin. Anthea stepped forward too, her expression tight. I wondered how she felt about all this. She'd never talked much about my brother, but I knew she'd grown up alongside him, much closer to his age than mine, more like siblings than aunt and nephew. But then she'd been sent into that horrible marriage and Roland had taken off... The opening of the crate was the first time she'd seen him since his disappearance, just like it was for me.

Like usual, she kept her emotions close to her chest. But as she stepped back, she quickly swiped at her eyes.

Then it was my turn. The sun-warmed soil was gritty against my fingers, and it fell onto the polished surface with a faint patter.

As I stepped back, a fresh wave of guilt surged over me. A part of me had always thought Roland would come back. There'd been times early on when I'd wished he would so Dad would lay off on me. But after everything that'd happened with Laurel, I'd lived in horror of the idea all the same. I hadn't wanted my brother to swoop in and take what was mine after I'd sacrificed so much for it.

And now he was gone. There was no way he'd ever return to us for any reason. No way I could have my brother back and see if we could fix our broken relationship.

The priest said his prayer. The Nobles who'd gathered for the ceremony listened in silence, a few of them poised farther back from our circle to stand guard. When the prayers were over, Dad took his spot to speak.

He cleared his throat, revealing more emotion in that sound than he usually showed in an entire month. "He was my son, my blood. I wanted so much more than this for him. He was born to be exceptional, and we'll never see how much of that promise he might have fulfilled if he'd come back to us another way." His voice caught. He lowered his head for a moment to gather himself. "You will never be replaced or forgotten."

I didn't want to take his words personally, but they felt like a jab directed at me, a reminder of the fact that he didn't consider my performance as his heir to be particularly promising.

As Dad stepped back, he made a motion for the grave to be filled in. My pulse stuttered.

"Wait," I said. "I want to say something for my brother."

All eyes turned to me. Dad's face hardened a fraction, and his lips thinned. Ignoring him, I took his place at the head of the grave.

The words started slowly and then tumbled out. "I can't talk about Roland the way I'd want to because we weren't really all that close. He was five years older than me, and always committed to helping Dad manage the family business." Until he hadn't been, I didn't mention. "But the times he did spare to hang out with me always stuck in my mind. I wanted to be just like him. And then, when he left, I realized he'd been doing even more than I'd ever noticed, never letting the stresses or challenges of the work affect how he treated me."

I took a deep breath as memories rushed up inside me. The relief that'd been mixed in with my horror at seeing Roland's body had been nothing to do with him. It'd been Dad's fault, like so much else. He was the one who'd pitted me against my brother by bringing out the threat of his possible return whenever he felt I'd screwed up, comparing me to him at every turn.

I peered down at the coffin, wishing I totally believed that my brother's spirit might be around to hear this. "Roland, there are a lot of things I wish I could go back and change—one of them being trying harder to bring you home and fix our relationship. I let us both down. But I won't now." I raised my hand, clenched into a fist. "I will avenge you."

Soft murmurs spread through the small crowd at my declaration. Dad was looking at me with an unreadable expression. Only the pit of the grave separated us.

The priest murmured another prayer before a few men took up spades to fill in the grave. I went back to Mercy, who slipped her hand around mine and gave me a gentle squeeze of reassurance. Dad's cool gaze lingered on us. The rest of my inner circle must have noticed, because the three guys drew a little closer around us as if they thought we needed protection.

Which, given how Dad had acted over the past several weeks, might not be wrong.

But it turned out it wasn't him we needed to defend against. Just as we were about to walk back to the cars, several sharp *bangs* crackled through the air.

Gunshots.

The guards shouted in alarm, as if we needed a warning to realize we were under attack. I ducked instinctively, pulling Mercy toward the ground with me and reaching for the gun at my waist.

The priest who'd performed the ceremony toppled over onto the freshly churned soil, blood gushing from multiple bullet wounds. A few of the underlings at the edges of the gathering were crumpling among those rushing for cover.

A bunch of men with rifles hurtled toward us over the rise of a nearby hill, taking more shots seemingly indiscriminately. I aimed to shoot back at them, but there were too many of our own people milling around. None of us had been prepared for an assault on this scale, not here during a fucking funeral. There was nothing but gravestones to take shelter behind, and our attackers had the high ground.

"Get to the cars and get out of here," Dad hollered with a wave of his arm, and for once I agreed with his order. Several underlings closed tight around him to shield him. They took off for his car.

Staying low with Mercy and my men around me, I hustled backward toward the other vehicles parked along the graveyard's driveway as quickly as I could. But that didn't mean I was going to stop fighting. I managed to take a few shots when I got an opening. One caught a charging guy in the jaw, but the attackers were moving too quickly for any of us to get a good aim.

"The Storm rules here and everywhere!" one of the other pricks yelled, and Mercy tensed even more than she'd already been beside me.

"Xavier," she muttered, as if there'd been much doubt about who would orchestrate an attack like this.

"Let's just get the fuck out of here," I said through gritted teeth.

I'd come in my car, and Rowan had brought his as well so we weren't packed in like sardines. We dove behind the statue of an angel for extra cover and then bolted for the vehicles. Mercy ended up at mine with me, the three guys at Rowan's.

Kaige moved to rejoin me, but I motioned him to stay where he was. More Nobles were racing around us, Dad scrambling into the back seat of his own car with bodyguards around him, shots echoing over the grassy hills. I just wanted us gone, fast and uninjured.

I tossed the keys to Mercy. While she unlocked the car, I got in a couple more shots, including one to the shoulder of an asshole who'd thought he could blast away my woman. The second she yanked the door open, I shoved her inside toward the passenger seat and dove in after her.

The wheels screeched as I careened along the driveway and onto the street beyond the gates. My heartbeat thumped in my ears so hard my bones seemed to rattle with it.

"Fuck, fuck, *fuck*," I spat out. "The fuckers didn't let us have one day of peace. My brother didn't get a proper good-bye even in his death."

Mercy looked over at me, her own expression taut with anger. "They're all jackasses, and I wish we could have taken them all down. But—" Her shoulders stiffened as I jammed on the accelerator. "We'll deal with them. We've got the Long Night backing us up against the Storm and Xavier now."

I couldn't shake the anger coursing through me. The buildings beyond the windshield were unfamiliar. I had no idea where in the city we were now, and I didn't care. I slammed my fist against the steering wheel.

"He killed my brother, mutilated him almost beyond recognition, and now this." I shook my head, all the horrible thoughts from the last few days washing over me. "But Xavier isn't the only monster here."

Mercy frowned. "What do you mean?"

"You know what I felt first when I realized it was Roland in that crate? Not horror or pain or grief that my brother was gone. I was *relieved*. Because I knew he wasn't coming back to take my life away from me and that automatically cemented me as the Noble heir, regardless of Dad's intentions."

"Wylder—"

I glanced at her, my grip on the wheel tightening. "I'm fucked up."

She shook her head. "No, you're not."

"I am. My first reaction was to see my brother's death as a personal gain."

"It isn't like that at all," Mercy said. "Your father drilled it into your head that you had to be perfect if you wanted to be his heir. He used your brother to get to you, to mold you into what he wanted you to be."

I laughed shakily. "And he's got that now."

Mercy spoke with total certainty. "Wylder, you're nothing like your father."

There was no pity in her light blue eyes, only concern for me. The heat of my anger started to simmer down. My foot eased up on the gas, and she tipped her head toward a vacant lot we were just coming up on, the cracked cement dotted with sprouting weeds. "I don't think anyone's following us at this point. Maybe you should stop and take a few breaths."

She was right. Like she was so often. I exhaled raggedly and twisted the wheel to bring us into the lot, parking close to the shabby building next door so we wouldn't be easily visible from the road. Then I cut the engine and pressed the heels of my hands against my forehead.

"How can you be like this?" I asked.

Mercy blinked. "Like what?"

"You're so fierce, and you take no prisoners, but somehow you can be so understanding when it comes to me and my fuckups."

"I'm not any more perfect than you are," she said. "But I think that's okay. You and I are both human, and at the end of the day, we're simply trying our best. Neither of us had parents who made it easy for us."

I brought my hand to her cheek and caressed it. My rage was simmering deep inside me, but I was no longer directing it at myself. I was still wound up from the encounter with the Storm earlier, and all I could think about now was finding some way to release that energy.

There was one way we'd both enjoy.

I tugged Mercy toward me, and she met me halfway. Our mouths caught together like a snare. We kissed deep and fast, our tongues tangling with each other.

My fingers sank into her hair, loose from its usual ponytail for this formal occasion, and a growl reverberated from my throat. The fire inside me was raging hotter now, but it wasn't all anger anymore. In an instant, I'd gone achingly hard.

This wasn't enough. I unbuckled my seat belt before reaching for Mercy. I caught her by the waist and lifted her on top of me, loving the little gasp of surprise that spilled out of her. She sank onto my lap, already diving in for another kiss.

As our mouths melded together, I shoved the seat as far back and down as it would go. My fingers leapt to the back of her dress. I yanked the zipper all the way to her ass and dragged the straps over her arms. Mercy fumbled with my suit jacket and then the buttons of my dress shirt at the same time. She tossed my tie to the side.

The second her naked breasts brushed my chest, I groaned. When I nipped Mercy's bottom lip with my teeth and flicked my tongue over the spot, she moaned in turn. We were burning up together, our skin scorching everywhere we touched.

She ran her hands over the plane of my chest, and my muscles flexed under her eager fingers. I ground my hips up into her. The feel of her against my rigid cock made me want to explode right there.

She made a rough sound against my lips, and I bent down to take one of her nipples into my mouth. As I sucked and nipped, the impatient noise changed into a whimper that got me even harder. I switched from one breast to the other, and Mercy swayed back toward the steering wheel, her eyes at half-mast and her lip bit beneath her teeth ever so temptingly.

When I released her nipple with a loud, wet *pop*, she leaned toward me again. She put her hands against the headrest and pressed her hips toward me, rubbing against my erection. When she lifted up to free me from my slacks, her ass bumped the middle of the steering wheel.

We both flinched at the sudden honk. Mercy's hands froze on my belt buckle. "Do you think someone heard us?" she asked.

I raised my eyebrows at her, practically panting in need. "Do you care?"

A naughty look came over her face. "No."

She jerked at my pants, and my dick sprang from its confines. Mercy wrapped her fingers around its length, sending pulses of pleasure through my veins. She stroked me from base to tip, swiveling her thumb over my piercing with a more potent jolt of pleasure. I leaned back against the seat, unable to hold back a grunt.

When I was aching and wanting, she stopped, but only to grab a condom out of her purse. I helped her roll it over my cock. She set her palm on the roof to balance herself as she slowly sank down on my dick until I was completely sheathed inside of her. I could feel her pussy tremble around my cock. The sensation drove me nuts.

I put my hands around her waist and pulled her up, only to slam her down on my dick. Her greedy cunt easily swallowed my cock to the hilt. She circled her arms around my neck, the heat of her body coiling against mine. As she rode me hard and fast, her perky breasts bounced up and down, the nipples brushing against my chest.

The sounds of our pants and moans filled the car as we moved urgently against each other. Gripping her hips, I swiveled them just as I buried my dick inside her again. Her eyes rolled back with a piercing keening. Her brown hair fanned wildly across her shoulders, sweat streaking down her neck.

I swept the strands back from her face, wanting to see her clearly. A storm of emotions coursed through my body, almost overwhelming me. I was a walking inferno, and I would probably have burned myself down by now if it weren't for her. She burned just as brightly, but the fire in her made my own burn hotter and clearer in all the right ways, showing a path through the chaos.

The realization crashed into me hard and fast: I never wanted to lose her. And she deserved to know what she meant to me after all the crap I'd put her through.

I rolled my hips beneath her again and felt her pussy start to clench around me. She was so close. I grasped her face so her eyes met mine and said with all the truth I had in me, "I love you, Mercy. So fucking much. I love you."

At the same moment, I bucked even deeper into her. Mercy's legs shook, and a cry tumbled out of her as her pussy walls convulsed around my cock.

The sensation set off my own release. I came with a shout, the force of the orgasm making me clench my teeth.

We slowed together, our breaths coming ragged, her body going slack over me as we eased down from the peak together. Mercy's heart thundered where her chest came to rest against mine, echoing my own frenetic pulse. My dick was still buried inside of her.

Before more than the slightest twinge of worry could hit me that she hadn't said anything back yet, she raised her head and planted another kiss on me, long and lingering and more tender than anything we'd shared in the past several minutes. Then she drew back just a few inches. An emotion I'd never seen before shimmered in her bright eyes.

"I love you too," she said, her voice rough. "I just hope—you *are* okay if I feel the same way about certain other people too?"

A bubble of exhilarating happiness exploded inside of me. I laughed. I couldn't help myself.

"Mercy," I said, cupping her face in my hands. "You might not believe it, but I've decided I actually prefer it this way. You're not just my girl; you belong to all of us. Together. I'm lucky that I get to be a part of this amazing thing we've found."

A smile curled her lips, and I knew I would do anything to preserve it. "Do *you* really believe that?" she checked.

I nodded. "You're our woman, and we're yours." Images from our collective romp in the van came to my mind. It'd been the most erotic experience of my life, and seeing how much pleasure Mercy had gotten out of it...

Nothing would make me walk away from this. I trusted the three men of my inner circle more than family, and she belonged with us. That was all there was to it.

And that wasn't all we were going to do together. I hugged her tighter and then gave her my fiercest grin. "You got my head on straight. Now it's time to crush the Storm and Xavier, just like they deserve."

4

Mercy

It felt strange, being back in the Katz house with the remainder of the Claws forces sitting at the long dining table and standing by the walls around me. Like I'd stepped right into my father's shoes with them barely cooled from his death. But there wasn't any time to ease into my role as Queen of the Claws. We had a hell of a lot of work ahead of us.

Despite the invaders who'd come through my childhood home, it still smelled the same, wisps of old cigar smoke and gin hanging in the air. Someone had rigged up a chandelier over the table that wasn't quite as nice as our old crystal one but did the trick, its warm glow spilling over the assembled crowd.

I'd summoned them as soon as I'd gotten back from Wylder's brother's funeral, and they'd arrived in the falling dusk. It was full night now, the yard dark beyond the window. Our one week had begun.

"All right," I said, resting my hands on the table from where I was standing at its head. "You're all here because you're willing to go up against the Storm and do whatever we can to stop him—or any other outsiders—from taking over our home. We've got a limited amount of time to make that happen before someone who might be even worse crashes the party. So I want to figure out what we have to work with. I want to hear what you're particularly good at, any strengths or expertise you've got that might help us win this war."

The men around the table shifted in their seats. I was only starting to learn their names, other than Kervos at my right hand, who'd already pitched in plenty, and Sam next to him, the red dye not yet totally washed out of his hair from when he'd played the role of a substitute Wylder in an earlier gambit. A pang formed in my chest at the thought of Roy, who'd come to warn us about Colt's ambush weeks ago and maybe saved my life… and then lost his own life at Xavier's hands.

Jenner, the most senior member of the Claws who'd stuck around, hadn't shown up yet. I hoped that wasn't a bad sign.

After a moment, Kervos spoke up. "I've handled a lot of stolen car operations." He motioned to a younger guy with spiky black hair across the table from him. "Quinn and I can hotwire any vehicles we need for getting around or transporting supplies. And I'm not bad with a gun, if I do say so myself."

Quinn nodded, and several others around the room chuckled. "I'm a good shot!" someone piped up, and another voice added, "Yeah, me too," and in a few seconds it sounded like I had a whole house full of desperados.

"Okay," I said with a small smile, holding up my hands for the chatter to die down again. "That's good to hear, because I wouldn't be surprised if we need to do a lot of shooting."

"That means we're going to need lots of guns," Sam pointed out. "Me and a couple of the other guys have some connections there, and I know where your dad had a stash that I don't think Colt or Xavier ever touched."

"Perfect." I pointed at him. "I'm assigning you and whoever you want to take with you to get those weapons and bring them back here to distribute. None of us should be going out on the streets unarmed, and I'm going to need a few of you stationed around this house, our base of operations, on a rotating guard. The Storm's people have proven that they're ruthless—we can't give them any vulnerable moments to take advantage of. Is there anyone who's particularly good at other kinds of fighting, or at things like climbing and breaking into places if we need to?"

One by one, different men raised their voices. I made mental notes, studying their faces and picturing them carrying out the skills they mentioned. It felt natural, much easier than I'd expected, as if I'd been preparing for this all along without realizing it. But then, maybe I had. I'd committed a lot of details to memory over the years watching Dad from the sidelines, wanting to be ready for whatever trouble might be coming for him—or for me, from his hands.

I glanced at my notes on my phone. During the ride back to Paradise Bend in the Long Night's posh car, the resources he'd promised had started arriving, including reports on several business ventures the Storm was involved in. We might need to mess with those to get the upper hand.

"Does anyone have experience with or at least knowledge about sports gambling?" I asked. "Organizing bets on games and that sort of thing?"

A couple of guys lifted their hands. I got their names and committed those to memory too. "Good, I might need you for a special mission at some point. And how about property management? I know my dad owned a bunch of buildings in the Bend."

There was a momentary silence. "Meso handled a lot of that," Sam put in. "He— The Steel Knights took him out. He refused to go over to Colt's side when everything first went down."

Kervos nodded with a grim expression. "I haven't seen anyone who worked with him on that side of things around lately either."

I let out a breath. Well, I couldn't expect to have everything handed right to me. And Rowan had done some negotiations involving property for Ezra, so that might be all we needed.

"How about—" I started, and paused at the creak of footsteps.

"How about you all wait a few minutes before getting started without your elders," Jenner grumbled in a good-humored way, coming in to join us. He limped a little with an injury he'd taken during Xavier's attempt to wipe the last of the Claws out of existence, and shadows darkened the skin under his eyes, but he stood steadily enough. And he wasn't alone.

A girl who looked about ten years old, with her blond hair in two braids and wearing a sparkly unicorn T-shirt, kept close to Jenner's side. He rested his hand on her shoulder.

My eyebrows rose. "Who's this?"

The kid's mouth stayed shut tight, her eyes widening as she took in the crowded room.

Quinn frowned at Jenner. "Why'd you bring Sarah over here?"

"I couldn't exactly get a babysitter with how everything's been lately," Jenner said. He turned to me. "This is my daughter. She won't get in the way."

I couldn't blame him for not wanting to leave her alone with the rampages the Storm's people had been going on. I hadn't even known he *had* a kid... There was so much catching up I had to do with the Claws men.

My Claws.

I nodded. "It's fine. Sarah, is it? I like your name. Mine's Mercy."

"Won't you say hello to her?" Jenner asked patiently.

Sarah pulled a little away from her father, gripping his arm. "Hi, Mercy. It looks like you're really busy."

Beside me, Kervos chuckled. "This is why I like kids. They tell it how it is."

"We were actually just finishing up the most important part," I said. "Why don't I show you where you can hang out for a bit, and catch your dad up." I glanced around at the others. "The rest of you can take a break. There's beer in the fridge—just don't go crazy. We've still got a lot of planning to do."

Sam let out a little whoop, and half of the group tramped over to the kitchen. I led Jenner and Sarah over to the living room and turned on the iPod one of the guys had mounted on a portable speaker. "Do you like listening to music?" I asked her.

She smiled shyly. "I love Billie Eilish."

"Let's see... You're in luck." I started the album playing and patted the sofa. "You can hang out here, even sing along if you'd like."

She hopped up and started swaying with the tune. I stepped off to the side with Jenner and cocked my head at him. "I'm assuming there's a good reason she's here? This is the first time I've seen her."

Jenner sighed. "I need a drink first."

We walked over to the kitchen, and he squeezed past the other guys to the fridge to grab a beer. With it in hand, he came back to the entrance to the living room and looked across it toward his daughter. He tipped the bottle to his lips and chugged half of it without stopping.

"So...?" I prodded as he lowered the beer.

Jenner made a face. "She mostly lives with her mom. Mostly *lived* with her mom. That woman took off two days ago. She got scared with all the violence going on around here, which I can't blame her for, but she skipped town alone, leaving Sarah behind. I guess she didn't want to have a kid with her, slowing her down. I got a text message from her and by the time I showed up at the house, she was already gone and Sarah was waiting without even a suitcase."

My heart tugged at the picture he'd painted. My hand brushed over my pocket where I had my bracelet from my own mother on me like usual. Had my mom left for the same reasons Sarah's had—thinking it was easier to make a run for it without me by her side?

A lump filled my throat. "I'm sorry."

Jenner took another swig of the beer. "I didn't make the best choices in partners when I was younger, obviously. And maybe it's my fault too that I haven't been around to pitch in as much as would be ideal. I don't know. But I don't want anything to happen to Sarah. I've always tried to be there for her as much as I can even with the kind of life I live." He paused. "I haven't got a clue how to keep her safe, Mercy. It's hell out there right now."

It was. And for some of us girls growing up in the gang life, it'd been hell all the way through, since way before the Storm had ever shown up on our doorstep.

I watched Sarah bob with the melody, and resolve coiled tight around my chest. I wasn't my father, not one bit, and I was going to see that no other girls in the Bend grew up the way I had if I had anything to say about it. Things could be better for them than they'd been for me.

"You two can stay here," I said abruptly.

Jenner blinked at me. "What?"

"Until the mess with the Storm is cleaned up, Sarah can stay here and so can you, so she'll have you with her. There are too many rooms in here, and the silence practically echoes. God knows I need company. Since I'm running the Claws out of here again, people will be coming and going all the time anyway, and it'll be the best protected building we've got. I don't want her out on the streets in harm's way."

Jenner's voice roughened. "Mercy, I—"

I held up a hand. "You don't have to say anything. It's the only answer that makes sense." I lifted my chin toward where Sam and Kervos had gone over to join the girl, Kervos offering her a chocolate bar he must have grabbed from the stash on the kitchen counter. "Besides, she already seems to enjoy the company of our men."

Jenner cracked a small smile. "She does, crazy as it sounds. They're good to her."

"Now that we've gotten that settled..." I elbowed him lightly. "Let me fill you in on what we already discussed, and then we'll get everyone back to business."

I filled him in on the basics of the Long Night's deal and what we'd learned from him. Jenner's expression turned more serious by the second.

"If you need anyone else on the betting side of things, I was involved in a little of that when I was starting out too," he said. "And I know most of the guys here fairly well if you want advice on who to give what job to, who *shouldn't* be working together, that kind of thing."

"Thanks," I said. "That'll be a huge help."

He tipped his head to me. "I can already tell you're going to be a very different kind of leader than your father was, Mercy—and I'm thinking that's a good thing."

His vote of confidence warmed me for the five seconds it took before I noticed that Sarah had wandered away from the sofa. She crept over to the doorway that led to the basement stairs, and my pulse hiccupped.

I hurried over, forcing myself to slow as I reached her so I didn't freak her out too much. Flashes of the horrors I'd experienced in that dark space flitted behind my eyes, sending another chill through me.

I tugged Sarah gently back, shut the door, and fished out my keys so I could lock it.

"There's nothing down there you'd want to see," I said, keeping my voice carefully even. "Nothing good at all. Promise me you won't go down there even if someone leaves it open, all right?"

"I promise," she said in a soft voice.

"Perfect." I gave her arm a quick pat. "Now do you want to keep chilling out with the music, or do you want to hear what we're discussing? I think you're big enough that you've got a right to know what's going on if you're interested."

Jenner's mouth tightened, but after a moment's contemplation, Sarah just said, "I'll go back to the music." But her "Thank you" as she headed back to the sofa sent a sharper twang of foreboding through me.

If we couldn't get the Storm's people out of the Bend in the next seven days and the Long Night made good on his promise to clean the slate, it wouldn't be just the men in the next room who'd suffer. Every kid with any ties to the local powers would pay for our failure too, including Sarah.

The clock on the mantel seemed to tick louder, each second inching us toward our possible doom.

5

Gideon

Wylder paced by the chess table as I delved deeper into the files the Long Night had sent us this afternoon. A lot of the information I hadn't been able to examine thoroughly via my phone on the trip back, and we'd hurried to Roland's funeral right after. This was my first real deep dive, but Wylder wasn't exactly patient. Especially after the attack we'd just faced.

"We have to strike back," he muttered. "Hit them where it hurts, give them no time to recover. Just keep hitting them again and again, until they're forced to leave."

Kaige looked up from where he'd been watching the fish cruise by in my aquarium. "Well, obviously. But we don't know how, do we?"

"I'm working on it," I said shortly. "There's a lot to sort through here. Information on the Storm's business activities, his strongholds, the drug trade... And I have to cross-reference it with what's actually happening around the county right now. Finding out about some arrangement they've got in Timbuktu isn't going to help us."

I grabbed a company name and fed it into my usual search app. The results turned up nothing remotely inspiring. I sighed and went back to the files.

"Has the Long Night said anything about manpower?" Rowan asked. "I got the impression we're on our own as far as putting people on the streets."

I nodded. "It sounded like the whole reason he brought us on is to avoid putting his own men in the line of fire. We have Mercy and the Claws who've stuck around, and at least some of the Nobles..."

I glanced at Wylder sideways, but he just kept pacing without saying a word. He hadn't talked to his dad about the Long Night's proposal and the deal we'd made with him yet. I didn't see how we had a hope in hell of pulling off a victory without the full power of the Noble forces behind us, and we weren't getting that without Ezra's go-ahead, but I wasn't going to question my best friend right now. Not when he'd just watched our enemies tear apart his brother's funeral.

Not when I was at least partly to blame for that funeral being necessary in the first place.

I ran another search, and my spirits lifted slightly. My fingers sped over the keys as I homed in on the bit of data that'd shown a little promise. After a few minutes, a smile stretched across my face.

"What?" Wylder asked, coming over to lean against the desk. He'd picked up on my good mood.

"I think I've got something. The Long Night has this company listed as the Storm's main weapons supplier in the States. I'm seeing evidence that they've got a major shipment headed toward Paradise Bend—it should arrive around late evening tomorrow."

"More weapons," Kaige grumbled. "Perfect."

I searched through the records I'd dug up, and my heart started to sink again. "Maybe not just that. The truck they're using is outfitted with seating as well. From the looks of it, the Storm is bringing in a contingent of new men too."

Wylder spat out a curse. "Over my dead body."

I very much hoped it didn't come to that.

"We won't let them get far," I said, checking my maps for possible routes. "I think we can hit them on their way into the county. They won't expect us to have figured out the shipment is coming, considering we only realized thanks to the Long Night's inside information. We'll take them by surprise, mow down all their new soldiers, and confiscate the weapons for ourselves."

Rowan hummed. "The first step to pushing them out of the Bend is not letting them get any more of a foothold than they already have."

"I like it," Kaige said with a jerk of a nod. He cracked his knuckles. "I just wish we didn't have to wait until tomorrow."

"We work with what we've got," Wylder said. "It's a good plan. You can figure out where we'd need to ambush them, Gideon?"

"I think so. It should be easy to track the truck through street cams and other footage now that I know what to look for. We'll stay ready to course-correct if they deviate from the most obvious route. And I'll..."

I hesitated, trailing off. I'd been going to say that I'd be right there with the others, directing them on the ground. But the image had flashed through my head of Xavier looming over me, a knife flashing in his hand and a cruel grin stretched across his scarred face. Even though I wasn't facing the slightest bit of exertion, my lungs started to constrict.

"You can give us instructions from here just fine," Wylder said. "That's what you've always done before. Or you can come along—it was your idea. Whatever you think would work best."

The fact that he was letting me decide what I was most comfortable with only made me feel more guilty.

I couldn't say I'd been wrong to get more involved in the hands-on fight against the Storm and his men, but my last major plan had backfired on us. I'd gotten a good ally killed, I'd nearly been killed by Xavier, and my friends and my woman had needed to risk their lives to rescue me. The one victory I'd scored during my capture, the tracker I'd managed to stick to one of Xavier's boots, hadn't turned up any useful intel yet.

Some good had come out of the initial plan, at least. I'd been able to pass on all kinds of data from the computer I'd hacked in the Storm's local headquarters, some of which had helped me put together the pieces for our current plan alongside the Long Night's data. But ultimately, I'd been a liability. I wanted to destroy Xavier and the Storm any way I could, with bullets and fists as well as my computers if need be, but what if I only screwed things up again?

I set the question of whether I'd join the ambush in person aside and focused on another matter we could no longer ignore. "We'll need a lot of people. The Storm could be bringing in as many as twenty, maybe even thirty men on this truck. They'll be well-armed. We want to outnumber them enough that we can deal with them easily without many—if any—casualties on our side."

Rowan frowned. "Between the Claws and us, we'd only have a small advantage in numbers."

"We shouldn't have to rely only on ourselves and Mercy's people," I said, and looked at Wylder. "We have the Nobles too. At least, we should have them when your father understands what we're really up against here."

Wylder let out a huff of breath. "Or he'll kick me to the curb for making up stories that sound crazy to him."

I could tell that even though he was balking, he knew I was right. His mouth twisted as he grappled with the idea.

A sudden resolve gripped me, a flicker of anticipation coursing through me alongside it. I might not be a whole lot of use in the middle of a battle, but I had plenty of other strengths. The largest was that I knew my data. Wylder's current problem was one I could actually tackle.

"We should go talk to him now," I said. "Give him time to wrap his head around it before we need to get into the thick of preparing. I'll come with you—I'll bring my tablet, show him all the evidence, and lay out a case for why his cooperation is necessary to *his* survival as well as everyone else's."

"He's not going to like hearing that either," Wylder said, but then he sighed and offered me a smaller smile. "But I'm not leading us into a slaughter just because I hate talking to him. Let's go take him on together." He glanced at Rowan and Kaige. "You two, get some sleep. I want you totally fresh tomorrow."

He marched toward the door, and I hurried after him. As he strode down the hall, his gaze snagged on one closed door, and his steps slowed for just a second.

My gut knotted. That room had been Roland's back before the guy had run off.

A surge of emotions, more than I was used to dealing with, swept through me. I bit my tongue, and a metallic trickle of blood seeped through my mouth.

I couldn't keep quiet about this. Wylder deserved to know.

I stopped completely, and Wylder immediately turned to me with a quizzical look.

"I need to tell you something," I said. "But first you should know how incredibly sorry I am that I fucked things up so badly."

Wylder's forehead furrowed. "What the hell are you talking about?"

My throat tightened, but I forced myself to keep talking. "It's my fault. That Xavier targeted Roland. I—when he was questioning me, and I was doing whatever I could to distract him so that maybe I could get the tracker on him, I babbled a bunch of random things, and one of them was that you had an older brother. Most of it was bullshit. I claimed that Roland was off training to eventually come back and take over, that you were some kind of decoy..."

I winced inwardly at the memory, knowing how close that idea came to the fears that had driven Wylder to pull out all the stops to live up to his older brother's legacy in Ezra's eyes.

"I was just shooting my mouth off, saying the first things that popped into my head that I thought would catch his attention," I went on. "I had no idea—I mean, none of us knew where Roland even was. It never occurred to me that Xavier would manage to track him down and do something like that. But I shouldn't have brought him up at all—I should have realized what a mistake that was—"

Wylder was staring at me. The vice-like sensation crept around my lungs again, until I could barely breathe.

"I'm sorry," I added again, hating how weak my voice sounded. "I should have told you sooner."

My best friend dragged in a breath, ragged with emotion. Then he let it out in a rush and stepped forward to clasp my shoulder. "I know you were only trying to help every way you could. And you really *couldn't* have known that Xavier had the kind of resources to track Roland down when not even my dad has been able to. And—hell, I can't imagine what it was like, being captured by that guy. I'm impressed by how well you did keep your head together."

What, that I hadn't completely fallen apart? "Any of the other guys —" I started.

Wylder shook his head. "It would have been hard for any of us. But yeah, it was probably harder for you because you're not usually out there fighting people face to face. I recognize that. I'm not going to blame you for what that sicko did." He squeezed my shoulder. "Roland might have been my brother by blood, but you're my brother in every other way that matters. I know you would never purposefully betray me or the Nobles."

Relief I still wasn't totally sure I'd earned trickled through me. I ducked my head. "Thank you." Maybe there was more I should have said, but I couldn't find the words. And besides, we had another possible villain to tackle that needed to take priority over my self-doubt. The seconds were ticking away before the Long Night swept into Paradise Bend.

We walked around the landing to the opposite wing and down the hall to Ezra's office. Wylder knocked on the door. There was no response. We waited a minute, Wylder trying again. Then he checked the handle and found it unlocked. We glanced at each other.

Ezra never left his office unlocked unless he was in it.

Wylder turned the knob and pushed the door open so we could enter.

Ezra was sitting at his desk, a glass in his hand. He took a long swig of whiskey before he turned to us with a glare. "I'm not entertaining anybody."

Wylder's jaw locked. "It's important."

"Go away," Ezra muttered before he poured some of the fire-colored liquid into his glass.

"Dad," Wylder said, his tone stiff. "It's important. The lives of every man working under us are on the line. So please put the fucking whiskey away and let us talk to you."

Instead of answering, Ezra hurled the glass at us. Wylder ducked, and it shattered on the wall behind us. Wylder turned to Ezra with a glare that his dad returned with a tight smirk. He was more out of it than I'd realized.

"Ran off with your whore today while I had to fight for my life at the cemetery," he sneered.

"You got out of there before we did," Wylder answered calmly. "I saw you driving away before I'd even gotten into my car. I'm not sure what you expected me to do after that. And you don't call Mercy a whore."

Ezra's lip curled with a sneer. "I'll call whoever I want whatever I want."

"No. Not with her." Wylder took a few steps until he was standing right in front of Ezra's desk. Something had changed in him. I could feel that, and maybe Ezra felt that too. He fell silent, staring up at his son.

Wylder seemed to take his silence as an opening. He sat down in one of the chairs opposite his dad, and I took the one next to him.

"I had an interesting meeting earlier today," Wylder said. "Have you ever heard of the Long Night?"

I studied Ezra's expression carefully. He knit his brow, looking only puzzled. It didn't appear to be a show. Maybe he really hadn't had any idea that there were powers calling the shots over his head.

"The long night?" he repeated. "What's that?"

"It's a who," Wylder said. "That's the name he goes by."

"And who is this 'he'?"

"A very powerful man who brought me, my men, and Mercy in to talk to us about the war in Paradise Bend."

Ezra considered his son for a long moment. "Go on."

Wylder quickly recounted the story of the darts and how we'd woken up in the immense mansion, the explanation the Long Night had given us about the organization he and the Storm were part of, and the proposal he'd given us.

"But he's only given us a week, starting tonight," he finished. "He wants this dealt with quickly, or he's threatened that he'll put all his own men to the job and wipe the whole county clean so there's no one left who answers to anyone but himself."

Ezra's jaw worked as if he were chewing on the idea. "I'm supposed to believe that some lunatic who named himself after a full moon has been manipulating our business pursuits without me having the slightest idea—"

"You don't need to believe it," I broke in, with a hitch of my pulse that I ignored. Arguing with Ezra Noble rarely went well for those who dared to. "You know I deal only in facts, Mr. Noble. The fact is that what we saw out there was clearly the domain of a man with far more resources than even you possess. He's given us some of those resources as they relate to the Storm, information we had no hope of getting on our own." I held up my tablet. "I can show—"

Ezra cut me off just like I'd done to him, his gaze snapping back to Wylder. "And *you're* the one he offered this deal to?" His tone had gone icy cold.

Wylder's expression hardened. Apparently he'd given up on trying to be tactful after his dad's earlier reception. "Maybe that isn't so surprising considering that Mercy and I have been the ones out there in the Bend trying to fix this problem while you've spent most of the past couple of months denying there even is one."

Ezra stiffened in his seat. "I still rule the Nobles, as you'd better remember."

"Of course you do," Wylder retorted. "But who the hell cares who's sitting on the throne if in a week there'll be no Nobles at all. Can you set that crap aside for long enough to save our hides, for fuck's sake?"

Ezra's eyes flared. Before he could speak, I jumped in, keeping my tone carefully even. "We have plenty of intel, and we're already making plans. But we need all of the Nobles on our side, fighting with us, if we're going to have any hope of reclaiming Paradise Bend in the timeline we've been given. With enough manpower and the information the Storm can't imagine that we have, we can strike quickly and decisively and maybe have a real chance."

"Or else we'll all end up like Roland in a week's time," Wylder added.

Ezra scoffed lightly. "Maybe you should have thought twice before agreeing to a devil's deal. The Nobles won't be taken down that easily." But I saw the way his knuckles had whitened where he'd clasped his hands together. Between the two of us, we were managing to convince him of the gravity of the situation.

"He didn't give us much of a choice," Wylder said. "It was either this or have him start the slaughter immediately if we said no. And I'd rather not take my chances against twice as many enemies. We need the Storm's people gone from Paradise Bend anyway. You know what a menace they've been."

"You have the Claws on your side courtesy of your plaything, don't you?"

Wylder took a few deep breaths to calm himself, but I could feel the anger radiating off him. "Think about it, Dad. If the Long Night makes good on his promise, it's game over for all of us. Is it really worth risking that on the assumption that there couldn't be anyone more powerful than you? Let's clean up the Bend once and for all—you, me, and the rest of the Nobles, together."

Ezra was silent for a few beats. Then, with a long suffering sigh, he said, "Fine. The deal's been made without my input, and there's nothing I can do about that now. And we do need the Storm's forces cleared out. But anything that happens, it's on you. You can call on any of the Nobles when you need to, but I want to be kept informed if and when that happens."

"Shall I send you a file or would you like notes over dinner?" Wylder said dryly. There it was again, that edge in his voice. My relief was quickly swallowed by the tension stretching taut between them.

"That's alright," I said hastily. "I can fill Ezra in."

Both father and son turned to look at me. I swallowed hard. "I mean I can act as the go-between, keep you both appraised of what's going on and any new developments. It's better this way since my job is staying behind the scenes anyway." Anything to reduce the chances of a blow up between the two reigning Nobles. My efforts might not be enough, but at least I was contributing something.

And it terrified me less than the thought of confronting Xavier face to face another time. I'd take Ezra Noble over that monster any day.

"I find that satisfactory," Ezra said. "Now get out of my office. You got what you came for."

Wylder stood stiffly, and I followed him out the door. Taking in his rigid posture, I couldn't help thinking that Ezra had been totally wrong. Wylder hadn't gotten what he really wanted out of his father at all.

But I wasn't sure he'd ever get the respect I knew he craved, not while Ezra could still dangle it over his head like a carrot on a stick.

6

Mercy

I shielded my eyes against the sun on the horizon. Evening was falling quickly, casting an ominous shade of orange across the scattered clouds as if foretelling horrible things to come.

Our first day out of the seven we had to drive the Storm's people out of the Bend was almost over. I just had to hope it'd finish with a strong step in the right direction.

I took a deep breath as I looked below the steel railing that ran the length of the old Bailey Bridge. The river churned beneath our feet, and the wind made the girders groan. Next to me, Wylder checked the bullets in his gun and rubbed his fingers over the smooth metal surface of the muzzle. Rowan and Kaige stood nearby, and a huge force of Claws and Noble men was assembled around us.

We were staked out on either side of the bridge that led into the Bend, not the most popular route into the county but a shortcut to the interstate lines—one Gideon had discovered that the Storm's transport company had frequently used before. He'd confirmed just a few minutes ago that the new truck was headed straight toward us.

As I watched the occasional car or truck zoom past us, I shifted from foot to foot restlessly. Anytime I spotted a vehicle approaching that looked remotely larger than a standard car, my pulse sped up. But unless the transport truck broke several rules of physics, it wouldn't be here for about ten more minutes.

Rowan had turned to talk to the nearest Noble men. I watched him direct them to different strategic positions along the sides of the bridge where they could duck down out of sight behind the beams, ready to leap out the second we had the truck cornered. We had a truck of our own, albeit a smaller one, waiting for our signal at the other side of the bridge. The plan was all coming together.

"The anticipation is killing me," Kaige muttered.

"I know it's not your strong suit, but be patient," Wylder said. "It'll be better for us the darker it is once they get here."

He was right. We'd have more shadows to hide us, more of a false sense of security for the Storm's people. But I shared Kaige's sentiment. I wanted to get this done.

Wylder clicked the pistol's chamber into place and took aim at the distance. The dark water of the river looked almost ominous as it flowed past us below. A faintly fishy scent drifted up on the breeze. I wrinkled my nose.

"At least your dad came through," I said, glancing back at the forces gathered behind us and offering my own people a nod. "We'll overwhelm these assholes for sure."

"He didn't have much choice once we explained the situation to him well enough," Wylder said, his voice going terse. "After everything that's already gone down, it took hearing that we'd all be dead in seven days for him to finally get off his ass. I can't believe that for all this time I thought he ruled things around here."

"In a lot of ways, he did," Rowan said as he rejoined us. "It's not as if he knew the Long Night was siphoning off profits from his successful ventures."

Wylder let out a disgruntled sound. "Either way, my dad is directly responsible for the mess we've got here now."

"So is mine," I said. I didn't like acknowledging the role my father had played in the conflict, but I couldn't deny it.

Wylder's eyes flashed. "Maybe so. But tonight we begin our first step toward getting us back on the path we should be on."

The headset he was wearing crackled. I faintly made out Gideon's voice speaking into Wylder's ear.

"Got it," Wylder said, and swiveled to face the men, both those we could easily see and those disguised in the shadows. "The truck will be here in just a few minutes. Everyone's in position, so just do the job you were given, and we'll come out of this on top. The Storm fuckers don't stand a chance. We want to destroy every man in that truck if we possibly can. They all die here."

A low cheer passed through the assembled force. A shiver traveled down my back at the same time. I knew why that was the plan—any man left alive was one who might kill us in the future. But at the same time, my stomach clenched.

The people I'd killed before had already been attacking the Bend. The men arriving tonight had never set foot here before. We knew why they were coming—it wasn't any mystery—and anyone working under the Storm was obviously a threat. But still, the thought of a full-out massacre reminded me a little too much of Colt and his men mowing down my family at our rehearsal dinner.

Wylder must have caught something in my expression. "You okay?" he asked me.

"Yeah," I said nonchalantly. The shadows were rapidly gaining on us. The moon peeked out of the clouds overhead, its glowing face staring down at us. "We have to do what we have to do."

"We wouldn't need to go to these extremes if they hadn't torn through the Bend first."

"I know." I let out my breath. "I'd better get into *my* position."

Because I wasn't as practiced with a gun as most of the men, my job was to hang back by the end of the bridge and pick off anyone who broke away from the pack and headed this way. I walked over to one of our cars that was parked a short distance away, which I was going to use for cover, and took out my gun. Leaning my elbows against the hood, I waited.

It barely seemed like a minute before the headlights of a huge truck appeared in the distance. Anticipation coiled in the pit of my stomach.

The last of the regular cars drove off the bridge. Two pickup trucks driven by Nobles roared onto the road, cutting off both lanes and blocking the transport truck's route into the county.

The truck started to slow, and snipers, one of them from the Claws, popped up on either side of the girders. With silenced shots that were still loud enough to echo through the night, they blew out the tires on each side.

The truck screeched, careening to the side and then jerking to a halt as the driver must have slammed on the brakes. As the other truck of Nobles roared toward it from the far end of the bridge, men sprang out of the cab and the back of the cargo hold. Guns gleamed in their hands.

We were ready for them.

Wylder and the rest of the Nobles and Claws leapt out of hiding all around the truck. More bangs thundered through the air.

The Storm's driver tumbled to the ground by his open door, blood blooming on his forehead. Several figures who'd been charging out of the back crumpled in a tangle of bodies. More bullets pinged off the metal sides of the truck.

The Noble and Claws forces swarmed the doorway before many more of the Storm's men had a chance to burst out. Shouts and groans carried through the darkness as our people mowed down those too packed inside to have much chance of defending themselves. A fresh trickle of queasiness wrapped around my gut.

But I had to stay focused. A few of the Storm's people had managed to scramble away from our onslaught. A couple of them hefted themselves up onto the steel beams to try to use them for shelter and a higher vantage point to pick off our men.

And a couple dashed for the larger shelter of the city buildings, straight toward me.

One of them was already bleeding pretty badly, staggering with his steps. Steeling myself, I aimed and got a clear shot at his head when he paused to catch his balance against a lamppost.

Really, he looked half-dead already. I was just putting him out of his misery.

Bam.

The pistol jerked in my hands, and the man fell, blood and brain splattered across the side of his face. I didn't have time to feel anything about it, because another man was running past me, this one much faster than the first.

I took a hasty shot at him, but he was moving too quickly. The bullet thudded into the brick side of a building instead. He was past me now, dashing toward the streetlights farther down the road.

Swearing under my breath, I shoved away from the car and sprinted after him. I took another shot, but he ducked, and it probably would've have gone wide anyway. I had hardly any experience with shooting while running.

This was my one job—I couldn't let my men down. If I could get close enough to use my knife...

My feet pounded against the asphalt, my lungs already starting to burn from the extreme exertion. I was starting to gain on the runaway. Just another ten seconds, and I might—

I was just raising my hand to fire at much closer range when a sedan roared up the road, its headlights blinding me. As I whipped up my hand to shade my eyes, the car veered right in front of me with a screech of its tires.

Even as I backpedaled, the door swung open, and a massive figure stepped out into the hazy light. Xavier sneered at me. "Hello, Mercy."

The headlights behind him made his profile even harsher, the X-shaped scars on his cheeks turned absolutely grotesque. A few of his men spilled out of the car behind him. He took out his gun.

My heart lurched. I lunged for the closest shelter: a mailbox at the edge of the sidewalk.

Bullets spewed in my wake, several thumping into the side of the mailbox. I sent a quick mental apology to the people whose letters had just gotten blasted in my defense and sprang for an alley several feet away. Heavy footsteps thumped after me.

"You thought you could pull a stunt like this and I wouldn't find out immediately?" Xavier hollered after me. "Where are your boyfriends now, Mercy? Not around to keep their kitten safe anymore, it looks like."

I didn't waste my breath replying. I didn't need anyone but myself to keep me safe.

As I hurtled into the alley, I leaned into my momentum and threw myself at the wall on one side. The second my feet and reaching hand smacked into the concrete surface, I shoved myself toward the opposite wall as hard as I could.

Back and forth, I ricocheted up the walls, gaining a few feet in height with every leap. As Xavier and his men charged through the mouth of the alley, I heaved myself onto the roof of one of the buildings.

I crouched there by the eavestrough, panting to catch my breath. Xavier motioned to his men to fan out around the building. "I'm going to catch you one of these days, little kitty," he called, peering up at me. I couldn't tell whether he could actually see me in the darkness or was just guessing at my position.

My gaze darted around. I'd inadvertently run myself into a dead end. This building was the last one of the block before the corner, where I didn't have a hope in hell of leaping the entire street. The only way off it was to jump to the building on the other side of the alley—right over Xavier's head.

If he sent his men up here, I might be screwed.

Sweat beaded on the back of my neck. I inched along the rooftop slowly, aiming to get a little distance from Xavier, but he prowled further into the alley at the same time. "Mercy," he said in a sing-song voice. "Come out, come out."

Then he whipped up his hand. I'd only just yanked myself back from the edge when a bullet clipped the corner of the roof just inches from where I'd been watching him. I chomped on my tongue and winced.

"Hiding away like a scaredy cat," Xavier taunted. Something far darker than a sneer came into his voice. "Josey gave up her life for you just so you could become a total chickenshit? What a fucking waste."

I froze in place. How the fuck could he know that name?

Xavier kept going. "I'm looking forward to flaying the skin right off you. Riddling your bones with bullets. Grinding you into a pulp."

He shot at the roof again, but a few feet farther along. He assumed I was still moving. I dragged in a breath, forcing myself to focus through my shock.

It didn't matter what he'd said. I couldn't worry about that now. If I wanted to stay alive, I had to get moving.

I eased a couple of steps back so that I could straighten up and eyeballed the opposite roof. The flattest spot was right across from me. As long as Xavier didn't double back right away, I should be fine.

Should being the operative word. I was staking my life on that hope.

I swallowed hard and backed up a little more to give myself a running start. Xavier had stopped talking, so I had no idea where he was, but as soon as I peeked over the edge, he'd know where *I* was. I had to go in blind.

I braced myself and then hurtled forward with all the strength I could push into my legs.

My feet practically flew across the hardened tar. If Xavier heard me coming, I didn't stop to worry about that. All my attention narrowed down to the need to propel my body across the six-foot gap between the buildings.

I hit the edge of the roof and sprang. The air whipped over my clothes and through my hair. A shot rang out, and I half expected to feel pain searing through one of my limbs—but I hit the shingles of the opposite roof with a quick roll, planting my hands to steady myself.

A tug in my gut called for me to stay, to see what else Xavier might say. Whether he'd mention something that would explain the taunt he'd made. But I couldn't trust a single word that came out of his mouth. I had to get somewhere safe and make sure the rest of my men had stayed safe too. I had to warn them that Xavier and others had arrived.

I took off across the roof, running over that building and onto the next where there wasn't any gap between them. As I fled, I yanked my phone out of my pocket and tapped out a hasty text to Wylder. When I felt safe enough to stop, I'd give him my location and ask someone to pick me up.

My heart was still hammering away in my chest. I made another, smaller leap and spotted a telephone wire arcing across the street that I could use like a zipline to get across.

As I reached it, I couldn't help glancing up toward the stars twinkling into view overhead. Those words Xavier had said replayed in my mind again. *Josey gave up her life.*

How the hell did he know my mother's name—and how was he so sure she was dead?

7

Mercy

Ezra did not look pleased with our victory. He kept stalking around the sitting room where the guys, Anthea, and I had gathered to discuss the results of yesterday's ambush and our next steps, his mouth set in a rigid line. About a dozen Noble men were staked out in the yard around the mansion. I wondered if he was getting paranoid. Maybe the news that he wasn't really the top dog around here had gotten to him.

"So, Xavier showed up?" Anthea was saying. "How did he find out?"

Gideon looked up from his tablet. "I'd imagine he was tracking the shipment. He must have been able to tell the truck had stopped for longer than made sense and immediately rushed over."

"Thankfully all our people got out of there in time—with the truck and all the weapons," Wylder said with a tight smile. "The prick got distracted by his obsession with Mercy."

"Seems to be a common problem," Ezra muttered without stopping his pacing. Wylder shot him a brief glare, and then everyone pretended he hadn't spoken.

I rubbed my hands over my knees, which were scraped under the fabric of my jeans from my leap across the rooftops. The faint sting barely penetrated my thoughts. My fingers drifted up to trace the line of my *Little Angel* bracelet in my pocket.

The way Xavier had said Mom's name: *Josey*. The familiarity in his tone. His certainty that she was gone. I hadn't mentioned it to the guys because I knew we had much more important things to focus on—like, oh, the fact that the Long Night was counting the hours until he'd send his people in to slaughter us all—but my nerves were still rattled.

I'd never known what'd happened to my mother. She'd just vanished one day—all her things gone from the house when I'd gotten home from school. Dad had refused to say more than that she'd "left." I hadn't known whether to believe him, knowing how he was... but how could Xavier know anything about her fate?

It didn't make any sense at all, and I didn't like that.

I pushed those thoughts aside. "All's well that ends well. We struck a good blow, and now we have more weapons and the Storm has fewer people here. How do we hit them next?"

"Yeah!" Kaige smacked his hands together. "I'll punch as many of those assholes as we need to."

As I gave him an affectionate kick from my seat next to him on the couch, Ezra scowled. But my gaze was drawn to Gideon, whose face had darkened as he peered at his tablet's screen.

"We definitely hit them hard," he said, "but the Storm is stepping up his game too."

"One of our properties was attacked this morning," Ezra snapped. "Let's not beat around the bush."

"We had to expect some kind of retaliation," Rowan said. "It didn't go that badly. The men at the factory were able to defend it, so the Storm didn't take anything from us. There was one casualty, but that's it, right?"

Ezra's scowl didn't shift. "One too many."

I bit my tongue against pointing out that if he'd pitched in more from the start of the conflict, it might never have gotten this far.

Gideon cleared his throat and raised his head. "There's actually another thing, one I've only just confirmed. The truck last night was the biggest consolidated influx of Storm troops to come into the city in the past day, but it wasn't the only one. At least three other smaller trucks arrived. From what I can tell from the footage I've been able to dig up, they've still added a couple dozen men to their ranks."

Wylder muttered a curse. "And there are probably more coming. Can we catch them before they get here like we did with the transport truck?"

Gideon grimaced. "I haven't been able to find a pattern yet that would allow me to predict which trucks are associated with the Storm and when they'll be arriving. These were much more low key than the big one. I'm working on it, though."

Ezra let out a snort but said nothing.

"Fucking hell," Kaige said, running his fingers through his short, dark hair. "So yesterday was for nothing?"

"Not exactly," Anthea pointed out. "You took their weapons and at least half of the manpower they hoped to add to their forces. If the strike hadn't hurt, the Storm wouldn't have pushed back at us right away. Xavier's pissed off."

"Anthea's right," I said, grateful for her logical thinking. "We can't give up. We still made *some* progress, and we're only just getting started with the new intel we got from the Long Night."

"Right." Kaige perked back up again. "So, when are we going to go shoot them all down? That'd be a quick way to deal with the pricks."

Wylder shook his head with a crooked grin. "While I appreciate the sentiment, going head to head against the Storm's people without surprise on our side is only going to mean a bloodbath for all of us—and I don't know that we'll come out on top even then. We have to play this strong but smart."

"But we have to do something."

"And we will," Wylder promised. "Thankfully they can't know that we've secured the alliance of the Long Night. That's our wild card."

"I'm with Wylder on this one," Gideon said. "And with the new information we've gotten, I have been able to identify a few locations where the Storm may be storing vital equipment. It's not clear what exactly is in each place, but we're talking weapons, vehicles, possibly stashes of Glory."

Kaige growled at the mention of the drug. Gideon brought up a map on his tablet and pointed out four buildings he'd marked with a red X. Two of them were deep in the Bend and two others near the border of Paradise City.

"I'm not sure yet which one is most active, since I've only just narrowed my search down to those," Gideon went on. "But I'm keeping a close eye on them, and hopefully by tonight we'll have a solid idea of which would make the best target. That seems like a reasonable direction for our next attack."

"So, I'll get to punch or shoot *someone* then?" Kaige asked. "Just to be clear?"

Wylder gave him a baleful look. "You didn't spill enough blood last night? Yes, I'm sure there'll be guards, and someone will need to dispatch them."

Ezra had remained silent for this part of the conversation. He turned abruptly toward the doorway. "My advice to you? Don't get killed." He strode out of the room, muttering under his breath something about needing a drink.

Anthea sighed. "Should I go talk to my brother?"

"Don't bother," Wylder said. I could tell from his tone that his patience with his father was at an all-time low. "The longer he wallows, the less he can interfere in what we do."

Anthea nodded reluctantly. Things had gone so wrong between Wylder and his Dad that I couldn't help but feel a little responsible, knowing it was in part because Ezra disapproved of his son's relationship with me. But I had to admire the change in the Noble heir at the same time. He finally had enough leeway to take charge for himself, and he was making good use of the opportunity.

He clapped his hands. "All right. I'll send out a few small teams on foot to investigate those buildings and the activities around them—from a distance, without alerting the Storm's people. Gideon, you keep crunching the data, including the reports those teams send in, to figure out our best target. Kaige, maybe you and I could—"

Gideon cut him off with a sudden exclamation and a loud ping of his tablet. We all jerked toward him. "Is something wrong?" Rowan asked.

"No." Gideon's gray eyes had lit up with an eager gleam. "We've finally got something—from the tracker stuck on Xavier's boot. He's left the county, going somewhere new. He's got to be doing something to prepare for *his* next attack against us. Maybe he'll lead us to an even better target."

We all gathered close around to peer at the tablet's screen. Gideon had switched to a different app with a map view. A little blinking dot moved across the road at a quick pace.

"He's in a car, obviously," Gideon said. "Driving fast. Taking a lot of sudden turns like he wants to be sure he isn't being followed." He chuckled to himself almost gleefully. "Little does he know."

Rowan leaned on the back of the sofa to watch. His hand drifted over my shoulder, and I raised mine to squeeze his fingers in return.

"That's a good sign," he said. "He wouldn't care about being followed unless he was going somewhere important."

"Exactly." Gideon watched the screen avidly. "No sign of slowing down yet. I think we should see where this leads before we make any decisions. But it could take a little while. I doubt he'd go *too* far from the county while we're on the offensive, but it could still be hours."

Anthea stood up with a brisk swipe of her hands. "Well, it's just about lunchtime. I'll whip something up so we'll all be well-fueled in every possible way."

My mouth immediately started watering at the thought of one of Anthea's meals. "Count me in."

We ended up gathering around the island in the kitchen, Gideon leaving his tablet propped up in the middle so we could all follow Xavier's movements. Wylder sat close enough to me that our knees touched, and a quiver of warmth ran up my leg remembering our passionate interlude in the car after the funeral. And more than that, the words he'd said to me.

Love wasn't something that came up all that often in our kind of life. My dad sure as hell hadn't been in love with my mom or any of the other women he'd brought around. I wasn't sure I'd have said it to Wylder if he hadn't said it first so I knew it was something he'd have wanted to hear. But damn, was I glad it was.

These were good men, all of them—the four I'd found myself

tangled up with. I leaned against Kaige's shoulder for a moment, and he pressed a quick kiss to my temple. Anthea clucked her tongue at us, murmured something about "young love," and got to work over the stove.

Xavier's dot didn't stop until we'd all polished off the juiciest hamburgers I'd ever eaten along with a heap of Anthea's famous fries—or at least, they should have been famous. I was just licking ketchup from the corner of my mouth when Gideon leaned forward.

"He's stopped." He cocked his head to the side, giving the screen a puzzled frown. "There's nothing on the map there. It's way out from any town—no buildings even showing up."

"I guess it makes sense that the Storm would have some kind of secret bases set up," I said, studying the image. "These people are obviously very good at staying under the radar."

"And he's got to realize how easily someone with the right skills can use traffic cams and so on to spy on his movements, like Gideon already has," Anthea pointed out. "Somewhere way off the beaten track would be hard for anyone to trace."

"Right," Rowan said, shooting a smile at Gideon. "We'd never have known about this if you hadn't managed to get the tracker on Xavier."

Gideon's laugh sounded a little raw. "I'm glad something good came out of that SNAFU after all."

"The Storm has got to have some pretty important stuff stashed there if he keeps it so carefully hidden," Wylder said. "Especially if Xavier's going there now while he's gearing up to get his revenge for the bridge ambush. I say that's our target. We hit it tonight."

All of us around the island nodded. I hopped off my stool. "I want in, but I should check with my men back in the Bend and see how many Claws are up for another mission. Let me know when you've worked out our best approach."

I'd only just turned toward the door when a couple of Noble men hustled inside. They were ushering a boy who looked to be in his mid-teens ahead of them. I paused, frowning. The kid couldn't have been out of high school, with sandy blond hair a few shades darker than Rowan's and a sharply regal nose that didn't quite fit the boyishness of the rest of his face. I'd never seen him before.

It appeared that Wylder hadn't either. He got to his feet, casting a critical glance over the boy. "What's going on?"

"This kid turned up outside saying he wanted to talk to the leader of the Nobles," one of the guards said. "I wasn't sure if we should bother Ezra with it."

Wylder hesitated, and I knew he was debating whether he could claim that leadership himself. How would Ezra react to this new arrival in his increasingly hostile state? On the other hand, how would he react to Wylder going over his head again?

Before he made his decision, I stepped forward and pointed toward the Noble heir. "Wylder speaks for the Nobles. Anything you need, you can talk to him about it."

Wylder's gaze snapped to me, but he didn't argue. The guard shrugged, and the boy eased away from them. His eyes flicked nervously from side to side, but then he drew his chin up with obvious determination. "Thank you for hearing me out."

Rowan's voice took on the gentle note it always did when he was putting someone at ease. "Why don't you start by telling us who you are?"

The boy took a deep breath. "My name is Beckett. You don't know me, but I know about you. I'm the son of the man you call the Storm."

8

Rowan

I NARROWED MY EYES AT THE KID. SOMETHING ABOUT HIS appearance had heightened my instincts. I kept my attention on him, my gaze skimming over him carefully.

There was no way of telling if his story was true. We'd never met the Storm, so I couldn't check for family resemblances. Why would the son of the man we'd been fighting against want to talk to *us*?

Beckett opened his mouth to go on, but Wylder raised a hand to stop him. The Noble heir looked around as if he expected his dad to appear around the corner any second. If Ezra did find out who'd supposedly walked into our midst, I could only imagine the scene he'd make. The kid would be lucky to live a minute longer.

"Not here," Wylder said gruffly.

Beckett frowned. "What's wrong?" The kid looked spooked, as if he was expecting somebody to charge him from the door. I was still having a hard time wrapping my head around the idea that the Storm had children—or any family really.

But I guessed he was a person like the rest of us—like the Long

Night, who might have had kids and even grandkids for all we knew—no matter how much power he held.

"Let's take this to the back sitting room," Anthea said briskly, and I was immediately grateful. Both Wylder's office and Gideon's would hold too much information relating to our plans. The back sitting room had a door that locked, but it was small enough that no one used it for anything official often.

Wylder nodded and motioned for Beckett to head out of the kitchen ahead of him. The Noble men started to follow us, but Wylder shook his head at them. "I'll handle him."

I half expected them to argue, but apparently the Noble heir was making strides in winning over his father's men. They stepped back with respectful dips of their heads. It probably helped that Axel wasn't around anymore, spewing his venom.

In the hall, Wylder took the lead, Kaige and I falling into step on either side of the kid and Mercy, Gideon, and Anthea bringing up the rear. He wouldn't be able to get away with much. We tramped into the cozy space with its antique sofa and chairs set and heavy velvet curtains, which Wylder jerked shut over the window. I locked the door behind us.

Wylder gestured to me. "Rowan, pat him down."

Beckett's eyes twitched even more nervously as I stepped toward him, but I kept my expression mild. "Stand with your legs a foot apart and your arms raised," I instructed, and he moved right away.

I briskly checked him over, paying particular attention to obvious pockets and typical places to conceal a holster. When I turned up nothing, I backed up and crossed my arms over my chest, considering him. "It was a big risk coming in here totally unarmed."

The kid shrugged, but the flick of his tongue over his lips showed he wasn't really all that nonchalant. "Would you have trusted me otherwise?"

"We still don't," I had to point out.

"Well, I was hoping to talk, not get into a fight. I'm counting on you wanting information about my father more than you want to shoot up some teenager who's put himself at your mercy."

Wylder pointed Beckett to a chair. He sat down, taking a quick swipe at his forehead, where sweat was starting to shine. Anthea pulled out a water bottle from a mini fridge and handed it to him.

Beckett eyed it suspiciously before snatching it from her hand. I raised an eyebrow at her as she walked toward me. Anthea shook her head to indicate that she hadn't put anything in it, as adept as she was with chemical effects. I guessed a kind overture couldn't hurt anything.

Wylder dropped into a chair across from the kid. "So, you're really the Storm's son?"

"That's what I said, didn't I?" Beckett replied.

"Are you having second thoughts about coming here?" Wylder asked.

Beckett froze, his jaw tightening before he seemed to come to a decision. "No, but I'll admit I'm still not sure this wasn't a stupid idea. I just... I didn't know what else to do."

"You said you have some information about the Storm," I put in. "How can we know whether you're actually who you say you are and whether you're telling the truth rather than trying to throw us off?"

The kid gave me a look that seemed to imply I was being an idiot. For all his nerves, he had a lot of bravado too. That did line up with him being a child of privilege. I could tell his clothes were custom tailored and good materials too.

"I don't know how I could prove it to you," he said, a little haughtily, "since you don't know enough about who my father is to recognize whether I'm telling you something only his son would be aware of. But the fact that I came here at all should show that I'm putting *my* trust in you. And if you use the information I can give you, then you'll see pretty quickly that I'm being honest."

"Your father has been making things very difficult for us," Mercy said. "His people have hurt this county way more than anyone else in the entire time I've been alive. That doesn't exactly make us want to welcome anyone associated with him."

Beckett's mouth twisted. "I can believe it. And if I had any say in it, he and his shadow would be far away from here. Things were bad enough before—" He cut himself off with a sharp breath. "I want the war here to be over too. That's why I came, and why I'll help you."

"Where did you say you're from again?" Gideon prompted, obviously trying to prod him for more details about the Storm that he might not have meant to give away.

"That's not important," Beckett said, dodging the question easily. "If Dad and the rest of his men leave Paradise Bend, they won't bother you anymore, no matter where they go from here. That's all you really care about, isn't it?"

Abruptly, Kaige loomed over the kid's chair. "I still don't see why we should listen to you at all. Maybe this is one of your asshole dad's twisted plans, huh? Why would you come here wanting to *hurt* him?"

Beckett's voice tightened. "I don't want to hurt him. I want to save him from the mess he's created."

"Oh, and we're supposed to feel sorry for *him* now?"

"Can you please back off?" Beckett said, looking straight at Kaige. I had to give it to him: the kid had balls. "I'll explain if you give me the chance."

"Kaige, stand down," Wylder said, quiet but firm. Kaige grumbled under his breath and sat down on one of the chairs, which creaked in protest under his brawn.

"How old are you?" I asked Beckett.

"Sixteen," Beckett said. "But I've been on the sidelines of my father's business since I was twelve, and I knew about it for much longer than that."

Just like Ezra had drawn in Roland from the start, from what I understood, and then started shaping Wylder into his vision of an heir as soon as he'd lost his older son. Despite myself, I felt a trickle of sympathy I quickly tamped down on. Maybe that reaction was exactly what he—and the Storm—wanted.

Beckett was non-threatening. Even though he was almost as tall as us, he still had his boyish features, barely on the cusp of adulthood. But looks could be deceiving.

"Growing up like that must have been tough," Mercy said evenly, but I thought I caught some pity in her tone. She knew what it was like being dragged into this kind of world as a child better than any of us in this room.

"I guess, but it was the education I needed," Beckett said. "It's a brutal world out there, especially for a family like mine, constantly surrounded by people who'd like to take a grab at our empire, but we still have to play nice with them. You should know that without my help, you're unlikely to win this war in the long run. The Storm is far more powerful than you think. He has the resources to keep going and going until everyone who stands against him in this city is wiped out."

"And why would you want to stop him from doing that?" Gideon asked, with a cock of his head as if he were genuinely curious rather than looking for proof. Knowing him, he probably was.

Beckett took a deep breath. "Over the last few years, Dad has become increasingly hungry for power. He's been taking over any territories he can by whatever means necessary. He saw a power vacuum in the Bend, and decided to make a move, but the resistance you've been giving him has only made the change I saw before more extreme. He's pushing our men harder than ever, giving more control than ever to that loose cannon Xavier, and neglecting our usual businesses."

"Xavier isn't the only one to be blamed," Mercy said. "Your father sent him here."

Beckett sighed. "I know. Dad would never have given him this much authority in the past. He's... He's insane. The things I've seen him do just around us..." He swallowed hard. "But he gets the job done, and these days that's all Dad seems to care about. Unfortunately, that means that Xavier has gained considerable power, more power than I'm comfortable him having."

"And now you're feeling sorry for us here in Paradise Bend?" Anthea said.

Beckett shook his head. "I won't pretend or lie to you. What happens to this place isn't my concern. It's my father I'm worried about. This new aggressive approach is earning us all kinds of enemies and setting a standard for the people who work for us that I hate. I'm afraid we'll be dealing with the fallout for decades, long after his empire becomes mine. I want to inherit something more stable and even peaceful, not an organization built out of violence."

Wylder raised his eyebrows. "Well, I hope you didn't come to us thinking *we* care what happens to the bastard or your family's 'empire'."

Beckett glanced around the room, his posture stiff. "I know, and I don't expect that. You just have to understand that I love my dad despite the path he's been going down, and despite our differences I don't want to see him hurt. I want to see this crusade of his over with, and I also want it to happen without him ending up dead or with much more bloodshed on either side. I can give you information on his operations that will help you tackle him quickly, more effectively—and without the slaughter getting even worse."

"Too bad," Kaige growled. "Because I'd like nothing better than to get my hands on that cunt and rip him apart for bringing war to our doorstep."

Beckett swallowed visibly. "You've got to understand. I know he's done terrible things to you. But he's still my dad, and he hasn't been a bad father most of the time... He's all the family I really have."

A pang radiated through my chest. Every sign I could pick up on said he really was worried about his father, and I hadn't noticed any holes in his story. I could usually spot a lie once someone really got talking. And something about his explanation and the anguish on his face resonated with my own past, bringing out a surge of emotion from deep inside me.

I'd always wanted to save *my* family, to protect them from the crap I'd inadvertently brought into their lives and then my dad's poor decisions. I'd failed. How could I tell this kid he deserved to fail too?

Whatever he could tell us might be useful. We'd gotten extra intel from the Long Night, but he wouldn't know his opponent's secrets as well as that opponent's own family.

"Kaige, enough," Wylder said. He turned back to Beckett. "Why are you here *now*? The Storm has been tearing through the Bend for weeks now."

"I heard about the ambush and the massacre of Storm men last night," Beckett said, his voice rough. "My father was upset to the point of stomping around ranting about it. He gave Xavier more freedom to do whatever he feels he needs to do, which I know is only going to make things worse... I felt like I had to do *something*, and if I waited any longer, it might be too late for everyone."

Could Xavier really get worse than he already was? Had his previous actions actually been *restrained*? I shuddered inwardly at the thought.

"You've put a lot of faith in us," I said, watching him carefully. "Aren't you worried that we'll hurt *you* or use you against your father somehow?"

Beckett gave me a pained smile. "That's a risk I'm willing to take. Anyway, taking me hostage will only make the situation worse for you, not better. Dad'll go totally berserk. You don't want that any more than I do."

I believed he was telling the truth about that too. I paused and glanced at Wylder. "I think we should give him a chance. See what information he can give us and how we can use it."

Wylder gave me an assessing look. "Are you sure?"

He might not trust the kid, but he trusted my judgment. I studied Beckett again, wanting to be sure I didn't misuse that trust. But every instinct in my body told me I was looking at a kid who was terrified of the situation he'd been watching unfold and desperate to turn it around.

I nodded, my gaze darting to Mercy. "I can recognize what he's going through to some extent. I gave up a lot to try to protect my family. If he's willing to offer anything that'll benefit all of us, we should let him. Lord knows we need it right now."

Wylder appeared to contemplate my words for a few moments. Then he focused on Beckett with a lift of his chin. "Can you tell us anything about a facility belonging to your father that's about an hour north of the city, several miles off any major road? Someplace Xavier might have had a reason to go."

Beckett's face twitched with surprise. "How did you—?" He shook his head as if he'd decided the question didn't matter. "That could actually be a good place to start. My dad has a base out there that he's been using to funnel resources and men into the Bend and other operations in this state. If you could destroy that, it'd strike a real blow against his efforts here and show he's up against even more opposition than he was ready for. Maybe that'd be enough for him to rethink continuing his campaign."

"If this place is that important, I assume it'll be heavily guarded," Mercy prompted. "How do you see us managing to take it down?"

Beckett gave her a small smile, and I caught the hint of ruthlessness in his eyes—no doubt cultivated by his father without the Storm ever realizing that one day his son might turn it against him.

"What if I told you there's a way to destroy it without anyone ever knowing you were even there?" he said.

Wylder leaned toward him, his interest piqued. "Tell me more."

Mercy

We tramped through the forest, our flashlights set on the lowest brightness so they only lit up the underbrush a few feet in front of us. We had to be sure we wouldn't be seen from a distance. Around us, thick branches of trees tangled together with a thick canopy of leaves that all but blotted out the moonlight. It'd rained briefly in the afternoon, and the smell of damp soil filled my nose.

Something snapped a few feet away. Wylder and Rowan whirled around. There was a flash of bright eyes and a reddish-brown body as a small fox scurried away.

"There used to be some of them in the city around the parks," Rowan murmured as we walked on. "I haven't seen one in ages."

"Well, at least there aren't any snakes," Kaige said, and then looked to the others for confirmation. "Right?"

Wylder gave him a reassuring swat and motioned for him to get a move on.

We were about half a mile away from the Storm's secret facility and drawing closer with every step that we took. Beckett had informed us that the buildings were surrounded by a high chain-link fence that was electrified, and armed guards patrolled the property. But he'd given us a way in that would avoid all of the security measures.

A metallic glint caught my flashlight. It was the jaws of a hunting trap with a rabbit caught inside it. It looked like the trapper hadn't come around in a while, because the fur was eaten away by maggots. Its empty eye sockets stared at me as I walked past it.

"Still think this is a good idea?" Kaige asked.

I took a deep breath. "Rowan's a good judge of character. If he thinks the kid was being genuine, I'm okay trusting him with this. It's not like we won't be careful."

"It'd be an awfully convoluted plan for screwing us over," Rowan pointed out. "And I think we all know a thing or two about growing up quickly and wishing we could change the course our parents set us on." His dark blue eyes scanned our little group.

He was right about that. There was one thing we all had in common —our parents had thoroughly fucked us up.

Wylder nodded. "We had to do something. We're already through the second day of our week. I don't totally trust the kid, but that's why we're here—to find out whether we *should* trust him. At least we're taking the risk ourselves. My dad would probably have sent his least favorite underlings out to take on the danger." He grimaced.

"I think anyone who sends us stumbling around in a forest in the middle of the night has bad intentions," Kaige grumbled, before turning to me. "Mercy?"

I peered off into the darkness, and my stomach twisted. "So many people have already died. If Beckett can give us a way to win this war without tons more death and collateral damage, I think we should take it. Maybe this and a couple more definitive strikes will be what it takes to end this once and for all." I paused, ducking my head. "I'll fight as long as it takes, but I've got to admit I'm getting tired of it."

Kaige grunted. "I never get tired of fighting. But I *am* tired of seeing assholes trying to gun you down, so if this means that part's over, I guess I'm okay with it."

"Glad to have your support," Wylder said dryly, and then held up his hand, bringing us all to a halt.

Unless we'd deviated from the directions Beckett had given us without realizing it, the faint pinpricks of light that showed between the trees from up ahead were the distant security lights of the Storm's facility. There was another short stretch of forest and then an expansive field between us and the compound, but the "doorway" we were looking for should be right around here.

Wylder cast his flashlight around, veering to the right as he scanned the ground. After several seconds, he let out a triumphant sound and pointed his beam at a tree with a subtle marking on the bark. We hurried over and helped him pull over a layer of moss that covered a circular metal hatch in the ground.

The four of us eyed it cautiously. Wylder rubbed his jaw. "Let's take the lay of the land up here first, make sure everything looks the way the kid led us to expect." He reached into the pack he was carrying and pulled out a pair of binoculars. "Want to do the honors, Kitty Cat? You're the best climber between us."

I smiled and accepted the binoculars. Glancing around, I picked out the nearest tall tree with branches spaced decently well. With a running start, I leapt up to grab a lower branch and hoisted myself onto it. It took less than a minute for me to clamber above the thicker canopy to a spot where I could see more easily between the thinning treetops.

I raised the binoculars to my eyes, my other arm pressed against the rough bark of the tree trunk, and peered toward the security lights. With a couple of flicks of the dials, the building came into focus.

The place looked like some kind of storage facility. Beyond the metal fence, I spotted a few men going about their usual patrol. A narrow dirt road snaked away from the facility and probably led back to the main road. Two huge trucks were parked just inside the gate. Beckett had told us that his father moved shipments of supplies through this place, sometimes stashing things there for later use, and that some of his underlings went through additional training inside the building.

I climbed down and reported everything to Wylder. The Noble heir cocked his head. "That all matches up with what the kid told us." He turned to the hatch. "Now for the real question: is this a brilliant plan or a devious trap?"

We all knelt down around the hatch. I swept a few stray bits of soil away from a small electronic keypad off to the side. Rowan tapped in the code Beckett had passed on.

Immediately, a faint sound of air whooshing reached our ears. Wylder snagged his fingers around a small latch and pulled it up with little effort. He shone his flashlight into the opening, where the steel rungs of a ladder fell away into the thicker darkness of a tunnel that supposedly led under the ground to the Storm's facility—a secret escape route for the inhabitants. Now it'd become a secret entrance for us—although we weren't even going all the way into the building.

Some of us weren't even going into the tunnel itself. I wished I could have joined the guys, but I'd anticipated the effect the sight would have on me. Taking in the tight space and the darkness pooled inside it, my skin crawled with an eerie chill. My heart started to thump faster.

I closed my eyes against the prickles of panic, focusing on the hoot of a nearby owl and the brush of the breeze over my bare arms.

"It's okay," Rowan said gently. "None of us can do everything. Wylder and I will manage just fine."

"Anyway," Kaige said, "*someone* needs to stand guard."

"And from the looks of things, you'd block up the whole tunnel if we tried to squeeze *you* down there," Wylder teased. He hefted his bag. "Let's go."

Rowan attached his flashlight to the pocket on his shirt and scrambled down the ladder. There was a faint thud as his feet hit the ground. We all gazed down at him. Seeing him in the dark, narrow space made my chest clench up all over again. I forced myself to keep looking.

He was taking on this danger when I couldn't because I was too weak to get over my stupid claustrophobia. The least I could do was see him off. My brain had to figure out that I wasn't going to be suffocated or buried alive when I wasn't even *in* the damn tunnel.

Rowan ducked deeper into the narrow space to make room for Wylder's descent. When the Noble heir reached the bottom, Kaige leaned farther over, frowning. "This place doesn't look too stable to me. Just don't get trapped in here."

"We won't," Wylder said. "Send us an alert if you see any movement nearby, and don't get seen yourselves. If this all goes according to plan, we'll be back in less than half an hour."

They vanished into the darkness, and I finally let myself look away. Kaige wrapped his muscular arms around me and nipped my earlobe, offering a welcome distraction with the heat of his body. “Guess it’s just us now. I can think of a few interesting activities to keep us busy.”

As much as I enjoyed having him this close, I pushed him away with a playful shove and an arch of my eyebrows. “We’re *supposed* to be standing guard. There might be Storm men around. We should keep a close watch.”

Now that I was no longer looking into the dark passage, my panic was easing, leaving only a leaden feeling in my arms and stomach. Even just standing next to him, Kaige’s massive, solid presence bought me comfort.

“What do you think they’ll find down there?” Kaige asked as he stepped back from the hatch, his gaze scanning the woods around us.

“The underground entrance to the compound,” I said. “So far everything else has gone the way Beckett said.”

He shook his head doubtfully. “I just hope it’s not a trap. It would be too easy to get us in there together and then bury us.”

I shivered at the thought. Kaige’s brows came together. “I’m sorry. I shouldn’t be talking like that. Don’t think about it—there are a hell of a lot of easier ways to trap us if they really wanted to, right?”

“Probably.” I rubbed my arms, willing away the renewed chill. “I just wish my fear didn’t hold me back in situations like this.”

“How often does it even come up? Like Rowan said, none of us can do everything.” Kaige stepped closer to me again, putting an arm around my shoulder. I couldn’t help leaning into him. He looked down at the hatch, and his expression turned momentarily serious. “I couldn’t have come up with a plan like this. My brain just doesn’t work in all these fiddly sneaky ways. I know that tackling our enemies like this is better for us in the long run, especially when we’re up against people as powerful as the Storm, but the only way that ever occurs to me is to crack some heads.”

I lifted myself on the balls of my feet to give his cheek a quick peck. “You’ve got more than muscle to offer.”

He shrugged without meeting my eyes. “Gideon and Rowan, they’re smart and quick on their feet. Wylder and you—you’re natural leaders, and I've seen the way you coordinate with each other and the people under you during fights. What am I except a couple of fists? Very powerful fists, sure, but I'm nothing without my body."

The doubt in his tone squeezed at my heart. "You don't really believe that, do you? Because I don't."

"I know what people see when they look at me—I know what I am." Kaige seemed to shake off his momentary pensiveness. "But hey, there are some benefits to being a guy who's all about the body. Think of all the amazing ways I've been able to handle this one." He traced his fingers down my side to my hip.

I elbowed him lightly. "Focus on keeping watch. You can show me more of those bodily talents later."

Kaige gave me a flirty grin, though I thought I saw a hint of his earlier uneasiness lingering in his deep brown eyes. "Is that a promise?"

I wagged a finger at him. "If you promise to keep your eyes on the woods instead of me until we're done here."

"Aww, you're no fun." He pinched my hip.

I rolled my eyes as I returned my own gaze to the darkened forest around us. "I think I've proven that's not true at all."

Kaige snickered, but he fell into a companionable silence, watching for any movement between the trees. My pulse kept pounding, not from claustrophobia now but the basic uncertainty of what Wylder and Rowan would have found at the end of that tunnel. Beckett had seemed sincere, sure, but how could we trust *anyone* in this kind of life?

On the other hand, look at how many great things had happened because my men and I had found a way to trust each other.

At a rustling near our feet, my gaze jerked down. Rowan was just climbing up the ladder. Dirt speckled his hair and clothes, and he had a smudge on his temple, but otherwise he looked no worse for wear. He panted a little as if he'd run the whole way, though.

"Are you okay?" I asked as Wylder clambered out of the tunnel after him.

"Perfect," the Noble heir said with a grin. "The explosives were exactly where Beckett said they'd be, just waiting to cut off the escape route and destroy all the evidence inside if the Storm's people were making a run for it. Of course, with our way, they'll be the ones getting destroyed."

Rowan matched his smile. "We laid the fuse all the way out here. There's nothing left to do but light it."

Wylder held up the end of the thick rope we were using as a fuse. We'd soaked it in kerosene before bringing it out here, and the chemical tang wafting off it itched in my nose. He snapped his fingers. "Lighter?"

I held out the one I'd been carrying for this purpose. All four of us stood around the mouth of the tunnel as Wylder flicked on the flame. He held it to the end of the fuse and dropped the rope the second it lit up.

It fell to the floor of the tunnel, the flames already streaking along its length out of view like a serpent made of fire. Kaige grabbed the hatch and slammed it down. "Let's get the hell out of here before the place blows!"

We turned and jogged through the forest as fast as we could in the darkness, not daring to even turn on our flashlights now. I didn't think it'd been more than a minute before an earth-shaking *boom* split the air and rattled the branches around us.

I spun around. Orange light danced and flashed in the distance in the tiny gaps between the trees. The initial explosion was followed by a thundering crash of thick walls collapsing. In my mind's eye, I pictured the hail of concrete and mortar—and the bodies engulfed in the blaze.

I leaned against a trunk to catch my balance. The breeze licked over me, carrying a trace of acrid smoke. My throat constricted around it.

We'd mostly wanted to obliterate this resource of the Storm's, to show him we could tackle him on his own turf. But at least some of the men in and around that facility would have died in the explosion—some of them men who might have had nothing to do with Paradise Bend.

But that was what this war had come to. How many innocent people had fallen in the Bend because of the Storm's reign of terror?

My people were safer now because we'd managed to strike a major blow against our enemies.

Kaige raised his hand to request a high five from Wylder. Wylder smacked his hand, but his expression was somber. He wasn't unaffected by the lengths we'd gone to for this victory either.

"It looks like Beckett set us on the right path," Rowan said. "He didn't know we'd found out about this place until he showed up at the mansion, and he hasn't had a chance to leave or do anything unmonitored since he arrived. I don't see any way this could have been a ploy to convince us."

Wylder nodded. "The kid's legit. Now let's get home and find out what other ways he's willing to help us rain havoc down on his dear ol' dad."

I gave the flickers of the flames one last look and hustled with the others through the forest toward our car.

10

Mercy

THE GUYS DROPPED ME BACK AT MY HOUSE WITH A PROMISE to pick me up early next morning to regroup and strategize. I waved goodbye to them and watched them drive down the darkened street. It was past midnight, and all but a couple of the lights in the house were off. I hoped Sarah was sleeping okay in her new room. I'd managed to find an old bedspread from my childhood with pink and purple clouds printed on it that she'd squealed over on sight.

A few of the Claws men had come to a stop on the lawn near me, braced to leap to my protection, but the street around us was dead. I nodded to them with a smile of thanks and headed up the front walk to the house.

Sam was hanging out in the living room with a couple of the other guys, passing a joint around as they discussed some new job they were putting together to increase our income. "Everything good?" I called to them.

Sam grinned at me. "Yep."

I'd noticed a change in their morale ever since we'd successfully carried out the ambush on the weapons truck. While it hadn't been as all-encompassing a blow as I'd hoped, it seemed to have had a positive effect on the Claws men in general.

I picked up a target practice board that'd been knocked to the ground. It was splintered with knife gouges. When I passed through to the dining room, I found the table laid out with an assortment of weapons from the ambush—guns of all sizes, from pistols that would easily fit into one of my hands to semi-automatic rifles.

We were definitely well-armed now. Jenner figured we could sell a bunch of the extras to help fund our continuing operations.

I sighed deeply. My body still buzzed with the adrenaline of our forest mission, and I knew sleep wouldn't come easily.

Instead of making my way upstairs, I walked through the house and opened the door to the backyard. Maybe the cool air would help soothe the growing restlessness in me. It almost felt like I was holding in a breath and waiting for something, but I didn't know what.

The sky was clear, stars twinkling through the thin haze of city smog. It was so silent out here that I could hear the crunch of a few fallen leaves under my feet. The grass was overgrown, in desperate need of trimming, not that landscaping was a big priority at the moment. Wild tufts of weeds knotted along the edges of the white picket fence that towered a good seven feet off the ground. Dad had always liked to keep the neighbors out of our business.

I'd have to clean this place up better... when I had time. It was hard to wrap my head around the idea of doing anything that wasn't directly toward our fight against the Storm. Who cared if my backyard looked a bit ratty when we might all be dead in less than a week?

I sucked in the cool night air and tipped back my head, letting the breeze lick over my skin. Of its own accord, my hand dropped to my pocket, where I was carrying my childhood bracelet like usual. The one that'd been my mother's last gift to me.

A sudden urge came over me. I tucked my fingers into my pocket and pulled out the thin silver chain. It gleamed in the faint light. I ran my thumb over the words engraved in the narrow panel: *Little Angel*.

We'd played out here all the time. Flashes of memory passed through my head: Mom swinging me around over the grass. Us tumbling onto the lawn together and rolling all the way to the flower bed, giggling. Her boosting me up so I could perch on the lowest branch of the tree. I'd always demanded to get up there, and she'd gone along with it, even though she'd hovered nervously beneath me in case I'd fall.

I never had. What would she think of my climbing abilities now?

I glanced back toward the house. The memory of the last morning I'd had with her was fragmented too. I'd only been six, and I hadn't known it was going to be my final glimpse of her. I could picture her willowy figure swaying through the kitchen, humming a tune under her breath as she prepared pancakes for me with sweet maple syrup on top.

She'd always been there. It'd never occurred to me that she might leave. She'd given me the bracelet on my sixth birthday, kissed my nose, and told me I'd always be her angel, no matter how old I got.

And then less than a month later, she'd disappeared.

She and Dad hadn't been married—I knew that much. And they'd argued sometimes. I had shaky memories of those moments too: of cringing in a corner when he'd lay into her for some small oversight. She'd been the only woman who'd ever given him a kid, and he'd blamed her for not managing to produce a son for him. I wished I'd had the guts to point out to him that if he couldn't knock up *any* women, the problem was obviously below his belt, not theirs.

Mom wouldn't have left me with him all alone on purpose, would she? Or would I rather that she had than think that Dad had *forced* her to leave in some permanent way? How well had I really known her anyway? Sarah probably hadn't believed her mom would ever run off on her.

A thump at the fence brought my attention jerking to the far end of the yard. At the sight of the massive form crouched on top of the white pickets, my stomach flipped over.

It was Xavier, poised like a tiger about to spring, with a menacing grin stretched across his face.

I dropped the bracelet, my dominant hand leaping to the gun wedged in the back of my jeans. Before I'd managed to raise it, Xavier pointed his own pistol right at my face.

"Hello, Mercy," he said like he had yesterday night, balancing on the narrow top of the fence without the slightest waver. I hadn't even heard him coming. For all his bulk, he was obviously agile and stealthy as well as strong.

Of course he was. How else could he have snuck onto the Noble property to leave me all his horrible "gifts" like the creepy drawing and the severed cat tail—not to mention the rest of the cat's corpse and the rotted body parts he'd dug up?

I could never forget that I was dealing with a total psychopath in him, someone who didn't operate according to typical human standards.

I kept my fingers curled around my gun, afraid to raise it in case Xavier shot me before I could shoot him, afraid to turn my back on him to run toward the house. I took one step backward, and he clicked off the safety.

"You're staying right there," he announced, so coolly and confidently I had no doubt that he'd put a bullet in my brain the second I made another move. Then he started to whistle an eerie tune under his breath, as if he were taking a casual stroll down the street.

There were supposed to be a couple of guards keeping an eye on the back of the house, but he must have managed to keep out of their view. I held myself still and considered my options, fear tickling up my spine.

"Don't even think of raising the alarm either," Xavier warned. "Or it's going to be a bloody massacre for not just you but all your pathetic followers. But I think you know a thing or two about that. Do you have any idea how many men you blew to bits tonight? Most of those idiots weren't even headed for Paradise Bend. But what do you care about the havoc you wreak?"

"The only person wreaking havoc around here is you," I said, pitching my voice just a little higher than usual so it wouldn't be obvious I was trying to catch the guards' attention, but loud enough that I could hope that they would hear me anyway. "And we're going to keep destroying the Storm's resources until he realizes it costs too much to stay in the Bend."

"Why do you feel the need to explain that to me?" Xavier asked in a taunting voice. "Oh, that's right." He waved the gun toward me. "Under all the pretense of a badass leader, you're a just a little girl with a gun. You're a weakling with no spine, and you have no idea what you're up against. So far, you've gotten real lucky, but that's only because I was toying with you. Now it's time to put you down for all the misery you've caused me."

"The misery *I've* caused you?" I retorted in a disbelieving tone, letting my voice get just a little louder. "I'd never have had anything to do with you or the Storm if you hadn't barged into my home. Maybe you're the weakling, scared of this little girl." If I got him angry, affected his focus, I might have the chance to take a shot after all.

But Xavier just snorted in response. "Scared of you? Oh, no. I loathe you. I loathe your very existence. You took away the only thing I've ever cared about."

Genuine anguish reverberated through his fierce voice. I frowned, racking my brain to figure out what he might mean. Had one of the Storm men we'd taken down been important to him? It'd never seemed like he cared about their lives.

"What the hell are you talking about?" I demanded.

Fury clouded Xavier's face. Unfortunately, his gun hand didn't dip. "You took Josey from me," he snapped.

My heart stopped. The words tumbled from my mouth before I could think better of them. "Don't you dare try to use my mother's name to mess with me."

Xavier shifted his weight. His voice came out thick with rage. "Before she was your mother, she meant much more to me than she could ever have mattered to you. She was my entire world."

"Stop fucking with me," I said, but my voice faltered. I gathered myself and put more force into my next question. "What the fuck do you mean?"

Had any of the men nearby caught on that I was in trouble yet? They might be sneaking closer to make sure they were in a good position before they jumped right into the fray.

And maybe I didn't want them to jump in yet. I wanted to know what connection this sick bastard had to my mother.

Xavier's pupils were dilated and the veins on his forehead pulsed as he began to speak. "Your mother and I grew up together, and somewhere along the line, we fell in love. Or at least I thought she loved me back until she ran off someplace too far for me to find her until years later. She said I was hurting her. As if I'd ever do anything that wasn't for her own good." His tone had taken on an odd rambling quality.

He laughed suddenly, the sound echoing around the backyard. He wasn't even trying to hide himself now. He dropped down on the lawn in front of me, and I instinctively drew a step back. Anger emanated from his every pore. His eyes were bloodshot, his face tightened into a mask of pure fury—all directed at me.

"She looked just like you," he went on. "Innocent and pure, and you wouldn't even suspect that she schemed behind my back to leave me. Took off one night while I was on a job—I came back to the apartment and found her and her things gone."

My stomach twisted. Maybe I didn't really want to hear this story after all. But I needed to understand—and to give any help that was coming time to get into the right position to take this monster down.

"How's that my fault?" I asked. "I wasn't even born yet."

"No." He gave me a dark look. "I spent a long time looking for her, looking for my answers. But it was only after she was completely gone from this world that I discovered where she'd ended up. She came here and decided to play house with that prick Tyrell Katz, got herself pregnant by him... I treated her like a princess only for her to become another man's whore. And then when I finally had my chance to get her back, she was already out of reach. All that was left was him and you, the two people she left me for."

He wasn't making any real sense. How could Mom have left Xavier for me when I hadn't existed yet? But in Xavier's mind, it was obviously my fault somehow.

He hadn't loved her. He'd been obsessed with her. He'd thought he owned her, just like Dad had thought he owned me. Josey had escaped one monster only to get wrapped up in another one's life. Maybe my father hadn't been quite as awful as the man in front of me, but they were cut from the same cloth, weren't they?

How could I doubt that she'd ever been with Xavier when she'd given Dad at least seven years of her life? She'd had a type, one that really wasn't good for her.

"You're lying," I challenged him, even though I didn't really believe that.

Xavier stared at me as if he wasn't really seeing me. Maybe he was imagining my mother superimposed on my features. "She would have come back to me. She would've come back where she belonged if it wasn't for *you*. She stayed so she could pretend to have her happy little family, and by the time I found her, it was too late." His voice cracked. "My Josey was dead."

He sounded so sure. "No," I said, shaking my head. "Maybe she got away from you *and* my dad like she deserved."

Xavier focused in on me again. His expression hardened. "*You* never deserved her. And you'll pay for stealing her from me. You'll pay and pay and pay some more. The Storm would have never cared about a pathetic little place like this if I hadn't pointed it out to him. I convinced him that taking over Paradise Bend would be a good investment. I wanted to get to Tyrell, but he was already dead before I got here. Now I've got the next best thing. I've got you, Mercy, and it's time for you to die."

He leaned forward, his aim steadying. Just as my muscles tensed to throw me toward shelter, a shot rang out from a different direction.

A bullet clipped Xavier in the shoulder. He flinched and ducked, his aim faltering. In that split-second, I jerked my own pistol up. But even as I pulled the trigger, the enormous man was vaulting over the fence and thumping down on the other side.

A couple more *bangs* of gunfire split the night. I dashed to the fence, hoping I could get in another shot, but when I scrambled up to see over the pickets, I couldn't make out his hulking form at all. He'd raced off through the yards.

Had anyone hit him more than that wound on his shoulder? He obviously hadn't been hurt enough to really slow him down.

Damn it. My teeth set on edge, but at the same time, I suspected I was lucky to simply be alive.

Claws men spilled into the backyard around me—half a dozen of them, Kervos among them. "I'm sorry, Mercy," he said. "We'd have taken a shot sooner, but we were afraid he'd kill you if we missed."

"It's okay," I said, pulling my spine straight even though my gut felt like jelly. "You got here in time. That's what matters."

"If we could have taken him down..."

I let out a shaky breath. "There would still have been the Storm to deal with. He's the real problem. But we definitely need more guards—all around the property."

"Of course." He strode over to the other men and started giving hasty orders in a severe tone. A couple of the guys hung their heads as he must have chided them.

I peered at the ground, searching the grass until I caught the glint of silver I was looking for. Bending down, I picked up the bracelet I'd dropped. As I brushed bits of dirt off the chain, my insides tangled up all through my abdomen.

Xavier was insane. But his story explained a few things: why he'd targeted me at the start, why he'd wanted to torment me instead of just killing me. Why he was attacking my home so viciously in the first place. This was all some kind of psycho revenge for events I'd had no control over. I'd been *six* when Mom had vanished from my life, for fuck's sake.

Kervos rejoined me, studying my face. "Are you okay?"

"Yeah," I lied. I was pretty shaken up, but I didn't want to show him that. I needed to process everything Xavier had told me—decide how much was true and how much insane ramblings.

Did Xavier really know what had happened to Mom, that she was definitely dead, or was he simply guessing?

11

Kaige

I TOOK A LONG SWIG FROM MY ENERGY DRINK AND GRIMACED at the bright kitchen lights. It'd been another long night with barely any sleep. My typical insomnia was only harder to overcome with the adrenaline that kept buzzing through my veins.

We'd pulled off so much in the past couple of days… but it didn't feel like anywhere near enough. And I had no idea what more we could be doing.

The other guys were pulling together a hasty breakfast, the smell of butter and burnt crumbs filling the air. Gideon chugged his precious coffee with one hand while he tapped on his tablet with the other. Wylder smacked a plate of toast on the island.

"Five more days," he said. "And Xavier's going as far as coming right up to Mercy's home. We can't let him get away with a move that bold."

My hand tightened around the energy drink can to the point that the metal started to crackle. I wanted to plant my fist in that motherfucker's face, and that was all there was to it… if I hadn't known he'd put a bullet in my brain before I got close enough. Asshole.

Rowan put on a calm front, but I could tell he was shaken by the danger our woman had been in too. "Whatever our next move is, we need to do significant damage. Maybe we should focus directly on Xavier. From what Beckett said, the Storm has pretty much given him free reign here. He's making the decisions."

"The rest of the troops will have trouble staying focused if he's out of the picture," Gideon said with a nod.

"Right," Wylder said. "We've wanted to bury that prick from the moment we found out he existed. So far, we haven't had any opportunities that panned out. It didn't sound like the kid has any inside line to info on Xavier's psychotic plans, so he won't be much help there. If we could just—"

Before he could finish that thought, two Noble lackeys rushed into the kitchen. "Mr. Noble," one of them said in an urgent tone. "There's —there's a problem."

I could see Wylder suppress a groan. "This early in the morning? Fine, what the hell is it?"

The men exchanged a worried glance. "We're not totally sure what's going on—or why, anyway. But a bunch of people are going around on the streets along the border between the city and the Bend smashing up stores and other buildings."

I frowned, and Rowan drew himself up straighter. "Is it the Storm's men?"

The other lackey shook his head. "It doesn't look like it. They seem to just be regular people—not trained at all, no weapons. Our guy down there reported that a few of them have been muttering something about Glory, so maybe they're druggies on a bender?"

Every nerve in my body jangled onto the alert. I hurled the near-empty can into the sink with a clatter. "Is that fucking crap making even more of a mess?"

The lackey who'd spoken flinched. "I'm not sure what they're talking about. But they also cracked the windshield of the Noble guy who spotted them while he was driving by. We just thought you'd want to know."

Wylder nodded with a jerk of his head, pushing aside his plate. "And it's good that you did, because we need to deal with this—whatever it is

—fast." And we couldn't count on Ezra to handle it well, he didn't have to say.

I wondered if the lackeys had come to Wylder rather than his father on purpose. The lower Nobles had to be picking up on what an asshat Ezra was being these days, right?

But none of that mattered if Xavier and his toxic drug were destroying the county even more than they already had. I flexed the muscles in my shoulders. "We have to go." Find out how bad the damage was. Beat whoever was responsible into a pulp. The Storm's people couldn't keep using Glory to manipulate the regular people of Paradise Bend—we couldn't let them all turn into junkies like my parents.

Wylder motioned to the men. "Gather a couple of cars of back-up, and we'll head down there to deal with it. And be quick about it!"

The two guys scurried off. Wylder adjusted the gun tucked in the back of his jeans and motioned us to follow him. As he strode down the hall and into the foyer, he called out to a few of the men we passed, ordering them to join us out front. He was already enough of a leader to know who he wanted supporting us out there.

The landing overhead creaked, and I glanced up to see Anthea and Ezra standing by the top of the stairs. Anthea's eyebrows had drawn together. "What's going on, Wylder?"

"We're going out to check on a disturbance," Wylder said. "Seems like a bunch of people are riled up—probably the Storm's involved somehow."

Ezra remained silent. He was watching Wylder with his mouth pursed. A fresh flare of anger rose up inside me. For as long as I'd been here, I'd seen Ezra push Wylder harder and harder to become the leader he wanted. He'd never seemed satisfied. I'd used to think he always wanted more because he was trying to hone Wylder's capabilities as much as possible.

But now that Wylder had finally stepped up to his role as heir and the men were responding well, something had shifted in Ezra. He didn't seem so happy about the turn of events. What the hell did the guy want?

All I knew for sure was that I didn't trust that asshole much more than I trusted Xavier, which was not at all.

We marched out to the garage, and I made a beeline for my favorite of the trucks in common use. It'd go faster than Gideon's surveillance van. As I jumped into the driver's seat, the other guys got in around me. Doors slammed as the other Noble men Wylder had called on got ready to follow.

I tore out of the garage and onto the street with a roar of the engine. "Whoa, there," Rowan said as we raced down the hill so fast my stomach lurched. "We'll get there faster if we don't crash on the way."

"I know how to handle a car," I growled, gripping the steering wheel harder, but I did slow down just a little so it was less likely some idiot cop would chase after me.

We flew through the city streets, already getting busy as the morning rush got going. Gideon made a faint noise when I blew past a red light, but I didn't care what he thought. His job was letting me know if there was anyone nearby who'd care about the traffic laws I broke.

Wylder was checking texts and looking at a map on his phone. "Right around here..." he said.

At the same moment, the sound of shattering glass reached my ears. I turned a corner and spotted the vandals easily enough.

They were spread out across a few blocks up ahead, at least a couple dozen of them. Some carried hockey sticks or baseball bats, others random debris like a broken tree branch or a length of pipe that they must have scrounged up somewhere.

They didn't seem to be working together, just focused on whatever destruction they could carry out on their own. A guy over there was smashing at a restaurant awning with a dusty board. A woman across the street from him was heaving what looked like a bowling ball through a barber shop window.

They seemed intent in their destruction, but the lackey had been right—they didn't look like the Storm's people to me. A few were teenagers, and others older men and women with graying hair. It was like a bunch of random strangers had suddenly decided it was time to riot. What the hell?

I parked the truck by the curb, and the other Noble cars stopped behind us. None of the vandals appeared to have noticed us yet.

"Jesus Christ," Gideon muttered under his breath.

As we got out, a middle-aged guy down the street yanked down a big inflatable sign outside a gas station and tore it open. Closer by, a teenage girl was scrambling out of a store through a smashed window, carrying what looked like a broken piece of the checkout counter. It was total fucking chaos.

Watching them, an uneasy shiver crawled up my back. There was an air of desperation to them, and a lot of them hardly seemed to notice *anything* going on around them except what they were doing with their two hands. I spotted glazed eyes and sweaty faces.

When I inhaled, I no longer smelled the asphalt road or felt the heat on my skin. Memories of drugs and pain washed over me.

I shook myself out of the momentary daze and concentrated on the present. I couldn't let my past eclipse what I needed to do.

I turned to Wylder. "They're out of their minds. They all look like druggies to me."

"All of them?" Gideon asked.

I squinted at the ragtag bunch again and nodded. "I'd say so."

Rowan frowned. "Why would a bunch of junkies be smashing up buildings like this? That's not going to get them more drugs. They don't seem like they're hallucinating—and Glory hasn't made people aggressive in the past."

I shifted my weight, restless and on edge. All I wanted to do was to barge in and set every single one of them straight, no matter how far I had to go to do that. But I'd messed up big time the last time I'd rushed in without listening to Wylder, and I'd gotten Mercy into trouble.

I trusted Wylder. I knew he'd run things right. Letting him call the shots and telling me when it was time for me to crack some heads wasn't really giving up that much control but showing I could control myself enough to be part of this team.

Thinking of it that way helped keep me focused.

Wylder walked up to the closest vandal and yanked the bat he was holding out of his hands. He waved it at the guy. "There's nothing you want here. Go home."

The man wobbled on his feet. "Why you got to go and do that, man?" he mumbled. "I just want some peace."

"Is this your idea of peace?" Wylder asked, gesturing to the mayhem around us.

The man coughed. "I just want Glory. I don't want no trouble."

"Then get going and quit smashing up other people's property," Wylder ordered him.

The man cringed, but he wandered off. Wylder shook his head. He motioned for us to follow him.

Up ahead, a man and a woman were punching and kicking at each other as they fought over what looked like a chunk broken out of a store sign. The woman hit the man in the ribs, and his grip on the hunk of plastic loosened, but before she could drag it completely out of his grasp, he snatched it back and slammed his foot into her shin. She hissed through her teeth.

Wylder glanced at me and tipped his head toward them. That was all the signal I needed.

I marched over and caught the man around the waist in one swift motion. He was so skinny he felt almost weightless as I hauled him over my shoulder. Rowan snatched up the sign piece that clattered to the ground.

The woman swayed from side to side, looking like she was still considering making a grab for the piece of trash. I wrinkled my nose at the BO wafting off the guy I'd grabbed and chucked him onto the opposite sidewalk.

"She's taking it away," he protested. "Don't let her take it away!"

I furrowed my brow. What the hell was he talking about?

Wylder advanced on the woman, looming over her with a menacing glower. He pointed at the chunk of sign. "Why do you want this? What the heck do you think you're going to do with it?"

The woman just sputtered furiously at him and ran off in the opposite direction.

"I'm not sure intimidation is going to work all that well on people this strung out," Rowan put in. "Let me give it a shot?"

Wylder motioned to the vandals still merrily wreaking havoc farther down the street. "Have at it, smooth-talker."

Rowan walked over to a young woman who was yanking at a plaque fixed to the side of a bank. He held up the piece of sign, and her head whipped toward him, her eyes widening as if he was showing her a lump of pure gold.

"You want this, don't you?" he said, keeping his tone patient and gentle in a way I could never have managed. "What's so special about it?"

The guy I'd grabbed scrambled up, looking like he was going to charge at Rowan, but I stepped between them with a glower. He backed down fast enough then and staggered off across the street.

The woman Rowan was talking to extended her hand toward the chunk of plastic. Her fingers opened and closed as if she thought she could snatch it up without even being close enough to touch it. "I don't—I don't know if I'm supposed to talk about it," she said weakly.

Rowan's voice softened even more. "We're not here to hurt you. We're not the cops, so you don't have to hide anything from us. We just want to know what's going on around here. If you can explain, I'd be happy to give you this. You can do whatever you want with it."

Her face brightened so suddenly it was almost funny. I swallowed down a laugh. And then any humor in me died as she rasped out her answer.

"The people who sell the Glory… they told us anyone who brings back a piece we can show we grabbed off some store or whatever in Paradise City, they'll give us a whole pound of Glory for it."

Wylder frowned, stepping up beside Rowan. "They asked you to bring a piece of a sign?"

The woman shrugged. "Anything, really. As long as they can tell we pulled it off a building here in the city. They said… They said the city people are too uppity and they want to see us bring them down a peg."

She was from the Bend, obviously. Even as my hands clenched, I could see how easily the Storm's men could have persuaded a bunch of their customers to take them up on their offer. A lot of them resented everyone who got to live on cleaner streets. I should know—I'd been one of them once.

"And you went along with it," I couldn't help grumbling anyway. "Very smart."

She winced, and Wylder held up his hand to quiet me. I reined in my anger.

That fucking Xavier. Using the people's emotions and their weaknesses against them to tear apart our home even more. My gaze swung around wildly, and I had to tense all my muscles to stop myself from pummeling the nearest utility pole to let out my frustration on something.

Rowan's expression had turned thoughtful. The wheels must have been turning in his head, because he tipped his head toward the woman. "What if I told you that you get to have a pound of Glory for doing absolutely nothing."

My jaw dropped. What was *he* on? We weren't going to go around handing out drugs... were we?

"What do you mean?" the woman asked, her interest obviously piqued.

"I mean you get to walk away from this and in return we give you what you want," Rowan said. He turned to Wylder. "We still have that stolen truck that we got from Colt, right?"

"Yes," Wylder said slowly. "I think I see where you're going with this."

"I don't," I snapped. "Are you insane? It's bad enough Xavier giving them—"

"Kaige," Wylder said sharply, and I managed to shut my mouth, my face burning almost as hot as the rage inside me.

My weaknesses were getting the better of me now. I forced myself to breathe deeply, hating every second of it.

"It's just lying around anyway," Rowan said. "Better that they get it from us in return for *not* destroying the city or listening to the Storm's people rather than letting the Storm keep the upper hand."

Wylder nodded and turned to me. "It'll only be temporary. We've got less than a week before either none of this matters or we've run the Storm out of town anyway."

I growled under my breath, but I couldn't come up with a coherent argument. Every bone in my body resisted the idea.

The problem was, I didn't have any better ones.

Wylder raised his voice to carry down the street. "Attention, everyone! I've got news about how you can get your Glory."

Several heads turned our way. Most of the vandals stopped what they were doing at the name of their drug of choice.

Wylder clapped his hands to catch even more of them and pitched his voice even louder. "We'll give you a pound of Glory right now if you back off and leave the buildings around here alone. And we've got *another* pound for you if you lay low for a week and we don't catch you messing with any other property or going to your usual dealers. That's all it costs. Chilling out and minding your own business. Sound like a good deal?"

Junkies weren't exactly the ambitious type. An offer that involved less work was obviously going to sound better to them. All along the street, the vandals set down their makeshift weapons and drifted toward us.

Wylder motioned to one of the Noble lackeys. "Go to the truck and bring over enough Glory to 'pay' all these good people so we can get them home."

As I watched the guy dash off, my stomach sank. Wylder caught my eye. He gave me a tight smile, sympathetic but unyielding.

He was the boss. The plan even made sense. I could deal with it—but only because I knew Wylder would only have run with this plan if we hadn't been pretty fucking desperate right now ourselves.

How much farther would we have to stoop before this war was over?

12

Mercy

THERE WAS SOMETHING A LITTLE WEIRD ABOUT HAVING Gideon in my bedroom—and weird that it felt weird, considering how intimate we'd gotten on multiple occasions. But this was the room I'd slept in since I was a child until very recently, and I'd never had a guy over here. I'd never wanted to expose any of the men I got together with to my father's unpredictable temper and the operations of his business through the house.

But Dad was gone now, and I decided what the rules were. And frankly, I liked being able to perch on the edge of my queen-sized bed next to the tech genius who'd proven to be so passionate under his analytical demeanor. He'd come in with his tablet already out, ready to get to work, but he paused for a moment to take in the warm violet walls and the maple dresser and vanity that matched the bedframe.

"The room smells like you," he said.

"It *is* my bedroom," I pointed out. "I guess that's to be expected."

A corner of Gideon's mouth quirked upward. "Mercy Katz's natural habitat. I have to admit I expected something more fiery..."

I rolled my eyes. "Just because I don't put up with any crap doesn't mean I don't enjoy getting to relax when, y'know, I'm actually trying to *sleep*."

His gaze homed in on a photograph on the dresser of me when I was eight, standing on the lawn with my legs apart and my hands on my hips in clothes a little too big for my skinny body. His smile widened. "You were a badass even back then. I need to show this to the others." Before I could protest, he clicked a photo of it.

I scowled at him. "I thought you had something important to go over with me. The druggies who were bashing up the stores haven't started up again, have they?" Rowan had called me to fill me in on the latest development in our war against the Storm a couple of hours ago.

"No," Gideon said, his expression turning sober. "But I took a bunch of photos of them while we were handing out the drugs to bribe them into laying low. Most if not all of them seemed to have come from the Bend. I wanted to run their faces past you in case you recognize any of them and know they're more than just some random junkie."

That made sense. I leaned back on my hands, my fingers sinking into the worn but cozy duvet. "Sure, I'll take a look."

He handed the tablet to me, and I crossed my legs to prop it on my lap. He'd already opened the Photos app. The first picture showed a haggard-looking man in grungy cargo pants. I flicked him away to study the next figure and the next, my stomach twisting with each image I dismissed.

They all had an air of desperation around them that I knew Xavier had taken advantage of. A lot of them looked as if they hadn't had a square meal in a month or longer. The youngest ones, teenagers with scruffy hair or wild eyes, tangled me up the most. They'd barely gotten started in life, and they were already way too far down a bad path.

Maybe we could change that once the Storm was gone for good. We just had to get on with kicking him and his men out of here.

Without thinking about it, I pulled my childhood bracelet out of my pocket and twisted it between my fingers. The memory of Xavier looming over me on the backyard fence flickered through my mind, along with an echo of the momentary helplessness I'd felt. It was hard to fully concentrate on anything with his words running through my mind. Especially the way he'd talked about Mom and her supposed death.

I shook away those thoughts and focused on the rest of the photos as well as I could. When I'd reached the last one, I handed the tablet back to Gideon.

"A few of them look vaguely familiar, probably from seeing them around town. I've never had a bad run-in with any of them—nothing significant I can think of." I paused. "Is Kaige okay? With the whole drug bribery thing, I mean?" I knew how much he hated seeing Glory distributed on the streets. Watching his own people hand it out must have been even harder.

"He understood why we're doing it," Gideon said. "He definitely wasn't happy about it, but he managed to keep himself together. It's only until this war is over with." He sighed. "I wish we could have gotten more use out of the tracker I placed on Xavier. He must have realized we used it to trace him to the Storm's secret facility, considering we blew it up the night after he went out there. It's still active, but it hasn't moved since last night. I think he's just stuck it somewhere to throw us off his trail."

"Figures."

He glanced at me. "I particularly wish I'd been able to see that he was heading to your house so I could have warned you."

I reached over and squeezed his hand. Gideon sometimes got it into his head that he wasn't doing enough to protect me just because his ways were with data and devices rather than kicking ass, but that was ridiculous. "It's not your fault. Anyway, maybe it's a good thing that Xavier had a chance to vent at me so I could find out why he's so obsessed with me and taking over Paradise Bend."

"Yeah." Gideon exhaled in a huff. "Him and your mom, way back when. Who would have thought?"

"Maybe we *should* have thought there was some kind of connection like that considering the way he was going after me." My thumb slid over the engraved panel on my bracelet, and a sudden inspiration sparked in my head. "Gideon, how difficult is it to dig up information on people who have been missing for a while?"

Gideon raised an eyebrow. "Do you have somebody in mind?"

I hesitated. I'd never talked about my mom much with the guys, and it wasn't as if knowing the truth about what'd happened to her fifteen years ago was all that urgent. "I don't want to burden you if there's more work you need to do to get ready for our next assault on the Storm."

"It's no problem," Gideon said. "I've already scoured the files the Long Night sent over at least a dozen times. Right now, we're waiting on Beckett to get back to us with more information before we commit to our next moves."

I clasped my hands together on my lap. "I'm hoping you can find my mom."

Gideon blinked, and then understanding lit his eyes. "You want to find out if Xavier's right about her."

"Yeah. All *I* know is that she took off... or something... when I was six—fifteen years ago. She just vanished one day, and my dad claimed she'd skipped town. I've never been sure whether that was true, but with the things Xavier claimed—I need to know whether she's out there, or if she's actually dead. Just to get the questions out of my head."

"Of course. I'll see what I can find." Gideon tapped through to a different app so eagerly that a rush of affection filled my chest. If anyone could get me answers, it was him.

"What do you know about her?" he asked. "The more details you can give me, the easier it'll be for me to narrow down the search."

I worried at my lower lip with my teeth. "Not much, unfortunately. I'm sorry. Her first name was Josey, although for all I know she'd have switched to a different name if she was trying to hide from both my father and Xavier after she left here. I never knew her last name. If she was with Xavier for a while before she came to the Bend and met my father, I guess she was living here maybe seven or eight years. She'd have been in her early twenties when she had me—my dad only went for younger women—so she'd be in her early to mid forties now if she's still alive."

Gideon's fingers flew over the touchscreen. "Anything else? Did she mention any places she liked? Did she have any favorite activities...?"

I thought back to those long-ago days as hard as I could. "She loved the outdoors. She always wanted to get out of the county to the state park nearby or places like that, but Dad didn't like her taking me too far away from him. He was probably worried she'd take off on him and he'd lose both of us. She had a thing for Indian food—that was how I first got to try it. I don't know how helpful that is. I was so little that I didn't really pay much attention."

"That's understandable," Gideon said, more gently than I was used to from him. "I'll see what I can dig up. It might take some time, but there aren't many people who can escape me if I put my mind to it." He shot me a grin.

The thought of just sitting next to him while he worked made me restless. I squirmed on the bed for a moment and then got up to see if anyone else needed anything in the rest of the house. "I'll be out there if you need me," I said.

When I pulled open the door, I found Jenner on the other side, a plate with a sandwich in his hand. When I startled, he smiled sheepishly. "I didn't mean to surprise you. I thought you could use some lunch. I haven't seen you in the kitchen since this morning."

"Thanks," I said, unexpectedly touched. There'd been a time when Jenner had been willing to kill me for the new allegiances he'd made. We'd come a long way since then.

I took the plate from him and headed to the stairs so I could eat in the dining room. Jenner followed. He stopped me at the bottom of the staircase.

"Look," he said, "I didn't mean to eavesdrop, but I heard a little of what you were saying to your friend there... You're having him search for your mom—for Josey?"

Any appetite I'd had abruptly fled. "Yeah. Did you know her?" I wasn't sure exactly how long he'd been working for my dad.

Jenner nodded, his mouth slanting at a pained angle that put my nerves even more on edge. "Why are you wondering about her now? It's been so long..."

I shrugged with forced nonchalance. "Xavier said some things about her—and, I mean, I've never really known what happened to her. Dad wasn't exactly super open with me."

Jenner glanced at the floor and then back at me. It was obvious he didn't want to say whatever was on his mind. He dragged in a rough breath. "I'm so sorry, Mercy. I thought you knew. You're not going to find her. She's gone."

All the air squeezed out of my lungs. "You mean dead."

He inclined his head, and even though I'd been prepared for that fact, it hit me so hard the plate slipped from my hands. It smashed on the floor, the halves of the sandwich falling apart. I ducked down, my legs a little wobbly, and grabbed at the pieces to clean up the mess.

"How do you know?" I asked, keeping my head low in case my eyes decided to spill over. I still needed to keep a strong front around the men working for me.

"One of the Claws men I was working with at the time helped Tyrell dispose of the body," Jenner said. "He mentioned it to me—and maybe a few other people, one of whom told Tyrell he was talking, because then we never saw that guy again either. You know how your father was when people went against him."

I inhaled shakily. "Is that why he had my mom killed? She 'went against' him somehow?"

"I don't know the details. I'd heard him complaining about her, that she was paranoid and thought someone might be after her, that she hadn't managed to get pregnant again, that she fussed over you too much." Jenner paused. "I didn't agree with any of that. She was a good mom to you, from what I saw. But Tyrell… Tyrell didn't really have that paternal instinct, did he?"

A choked laugh sputtered out of me. "No, he sure as hell did not." I straightened up with the pieces of plate and sandwich clutched in my hands and carried them over to the kitchen garbage can. All these years, somewhere in the back of my mind I'd held on to a little hope, but it'd all been for nothing. She'd been out of reach the whole time.

Jenner came with me. "I'm so sorry, Mercy. I wish there was an easier way to tell you. I assumed you'd already found out one way or another."

"Don't apologize," I told him, forcing myself to meet his eyes and willing back the tears that were burning in the back of mine. "I'm glad you told me. I needed to know. Thank you for being honest with me."

Of course Dad had killed her. Of course he'd never owned up about it to me. It'd been the most obvious answer the whole time, but suddenly I was more furious with him than I'd ever been before. I'd have given anything to bring him back to life just so I could kill him all over again.

She'd loved me, tried to look out for me, and he'd taken her from me like he'd taken so much else over the years.

I couldn't imagine eating anything right now. Shock was still surging through me, numbing the turmoil of my emotions. I headed back upstairs. There was no point in wasting Gideon's time with a search that would lead nowhere.

Gideon raised his head as I came into the room. At the sight of my face, his smile vanished. "What's wrong?"

"You can stop looking," I said, my voice coming out rough. "I got my answer. She isn't out there to be found. She's in an unmarked grave somewhere—wherever my dad had her dumped."

His eyes widened. He set his tablet aside and motioned me over. I sank down on the bed next to him, and he slid his arm around me.

"I'm sorry," he said. "That's awful. I—is there anything I can do? What do you need?" He peered into my eyes, so awkward but earnest in his desire to comfort me that it brought an ache into my chest.

Dealing with people's emotions wasn't something Gideon had much experience with. Usually he avoided them completely. But for me, he was trying his best. That meant more than any suave condolences would have.

I leaned into his embrace. "I'm just glad you're here. Having you with me makes it easier to deal with the news."

His expression turned doubtful, as if he couldn't compute how that could be the case. "Are you sure? If you want me to bring you back to the mansion so you can be with all of us..."

I reached up and touched his cheek. The jagged tufts of his blue hair caught the sunlight, turning it as vivid as the summer sky. He really didn't understand how much he meant to me. Maybe I hadn't even known how much he did until right now, in this moment, when all I wanted to do was fall into him away from the awfulness of my past.

He wouldn't pry for answers or demand I act in any specific way, just take me as I was. And if he could do anything to make it better, I knew he'd leap at the chance in an instant.

The feeling that had been building inside me since the first moment we'd kissed, only getting stronger when he'd opened up about his own past scars and shown me how far he'd go for me, filled my throat. I let it spill across my tongue. "You're enough. You've always been enough. I love you."

Something lifted in my chest when I said those words out loud. Gideon stared at me, emotion flashing through his normally cool gray eyes. His throat worked, and he brought his hand up to run his fingers into my hair. "I love you too. I didn't know I could feel this much about anyone, but I—I don't know what else to call it."

Joy bloomed inside me. I smiled at him. "I think those words work just fine." Then I leaned in for a kiss.

Gideon tugged me closer, his mouth capturing mine with all the intensity I'd come to expect from him and more. His tongue slipped between my lips, teasing over my own, and his free hand trailed down my side. Heat flared low in my belly. All at once, I wanted everything he could give.

I nipped his lip ring and tugged at the buttons on his collared shirt. A sly, knowing grin stretched across his ethereal face. As he started undoing the buttons, he leaned me back on the bed with him over me. With every caress he offered, more pleasure and longing washed away the grief that had filled me minutes ago.

When Gideon's chest was bared, I swept my hands over his smooth skin and the darkly divine figure inked on it. "My dark god," I murmured, and more lust flared in the tech genius's gaze.

He kissed me harder, splaying my legs around his hips so he could rock against my core at the same time. The press of his growing erection against my pussy had me desperate for more in an instant. He pulled back just long enough to yank off my shirt, and I pawed at his slacks, determined to have those off too.

Gideon proved just how many ways he could use those nimble fingers by stripping my jeans off me even as he sucked the tip of my breast into his mouth. Without raising his head, he flung the jeans aside, swiveled his tongue around my nipple forcefully enough to make me gasp, and kicked off his own pants. Then, moving his mouth to my other breast, he delved his hand under my panties.

The first stroke of his fingers had me gushing against them, pleasure surging from my cunt. I growled and yanked his mouth back to mine.

"I want all of you inside me now," I muttered against his lips, our hot breaths mingling together.

Mischief sparked in Gideon's eyes. "The queen of the Claws should get whatever she requires," he said, tugging my panties down. He spread my legs wide again and lined himself up. As the head of his cock rubbed over my clit and down to my opening, I noticed the faint raggedness creeping into his breath.

"We can flip over," I said, desire flooding my body as I remembered the time I'd ridden him. I didn't want him to strain his injured lungs.

But Gideon shook his head with a look of determination I'd become familiar with, though it was normally aimed at his computer screens. "You're mine," he said intently, "and I'm going to take you every way I want to."

I practically came just at those words and the intensity of his tone. He slammed his mouth into mine at the same time as he plunged into me all the way to the hilt, and my moan was muffled by that blissfully violent kiss. If this was what he wanted, I sure as hell wasn't going to argue with him.

Gideon snatched one of the pillows and shoved it under my hips to raise me to an angle that let him drive even deeper into me. With each thrust, a hint of a rasp sharpened in his breaths, but he showed no other sign of needing to slow down. He devoured my mouth and nibbled his way down the side of my neck, all the while pounding into me with enough force to send me soaring in a matter of minutes.

"Fuck," I gasped out, and then I was clenching around him, a shudder running through my body. Gideon groaned, thrusting even harder, with a stutter in his chest as he followed me.

He stayed braced over me as we came down from the high of our orgasms, kissing me more sweetly now. I wrapped my arms around his shoulders and pulled him down next to me so I could tuck myself against his slim but solid frame.

Right here, in the present, I was loved so thoroughly I didn't know how it was even possible. No matter what Dad had done, no matter what I'd lost, I knew I'd come out of this lucky in the end.

13

Mercy

I PLANTED A BOWL OF NACHOS IN THE MIDDLE OF THE COFFEE table in my dad's old office, and Kaige immediately dove in. From the way he gulped down the chips, he'd recovered from any lingering trauma of dealing with Glory earlier today.

I tsked at him. "Save some for everyone else."

"Want one?" Kaige mumbled around his mouthful, nudging the bowl toward Rowan, who laughed and shook his head. Wylder snatched up a handful and leaned back on the narrow sofa. Gideon finished arranging his tablet at the other side of the table to his satisfaction and straightened up to take a chair. When his eyes met mine, the gleam in them made me think of the words we'd exchanged earlier—and how thoroughly we'd proven them to each other after. I smiled back at him.

"When exactly are we expecting Beckett to call?" I asked.

"He left a message indicating that he'd try tonight," Gideon said. "Obviously he has to work around everything else going on in his life. We don't want him to get caught any more than he does. But it sounds like he was able to find some information on one of the Storm's business associates from the list of names we passed on that we got from the Long Night: Anderson."

"Anderson Cooper!" Kaige said with a triumphant air.

Wylder rolled his eyes. "It was Evan Anderson, you dork. He's a real estate guru, not a TV personality."

"The way the Storm's been tearing down the Bend, it's funny to think he's had that much interest in real estate *development*," I muttered.

"Hey," Rowan said lightly, "even Ezra's dipped his toes into that area. It's an easy way to pursue legitimate business activities once you've got some money to throw around. I'd guess a guy like the Storm, who's keeping his less legit activities super-secret, needs a legal front—or several—even more than any regular criminal organization."

"True." I waved a chip at Gideon. "You haven't found any evidence that this Anderson guy is involved in the underground stuff too, have you?"

Gideon shook his head. "He seems totally on the up and up. Lots of deals with prominent businessmen and public figures. I think there's a good chance he doesn't know anything about the Storm's other types of business."

Wylder smirked. "Which could be good for us. Exposing the Storm would be an easy way to attack him from a totally different angle. He needs to know that we're not letting up on him and that he can't predict how we'll strike next."

"But without the kid's guidance, we're going in mostly blind," Gideon reminded us. "We didn't get much more than the name and a few properties Anderson has managed for the Storm from the Long Night. No more than that for any of the other business associates he mentioned either. That's not really enough to make a solid plan."

"Beckett will come through," Rowan said confidently. "He wants this war over nearly as much as we do."

I nodded. "His information before was good. Let's just wait instead of getting all impatient." A shiver ran down my spine at the thought of what the kid might face if his dad caught on to how his own son was double-crossing him. Somehow I didn't think the Storm would see it as a loving gesture meant to protect his dad from getting into bigger trouble later, the way Beckett clearly intended it.

Wylder checked the time on his phone and sighed before grabbing more nachos. Kaige was still munching happily away. I sat down behind my dad's old desk and picked up the crystal paperweight so I could turn it over in my hands.

It felt strange sitting there. The leather of the chair bit into my ass, but Dad had always preferred not to get too comfortable. According to him, staying a bit on edge helped ensure you didn't miss anything when it came to important decisions.

Below the window, one of the Claws men moved through the darkened yard on his patrol. We had enough guards staked out around the house to be confident Xavier couldn't set one foot on this property again, at least not without taking several bullets in the process. Still, the evening shadows outside brought an uneasy sense of gloom over me.

A ringing sound pierced the air. Gideon jerked forward and tapped the screen of his tablet, which he'd connected to a burner phone to take the call.

"Hey, Beckett," Wylder said in his typical cocky voice. "I hope you've got something good for us."

Beckett's voice filled the room, slightly scratchy as if it wasn't the best connection. "I'm here."

Wylder frowned. "Perfect. Gideon said you indicated you've got something to share about this Evan Anderson guy."

Instead of answering right away, Beckett paused. After a moment of silence, Rowan cleared his throat. "Beckett, are you still there?"

"Yeah." The kid's voice had dropped to a whisper. "Yeah, sorry, I just—my dad has a lot of people in the house, and he's been restless, so I've got to be careful. Today was—today was bad."

Concern jolted through my nerves. "Why? What happened?"

Beckett let out a ragged breath. "Xavier came to the house where we're living right now. He was pissed off and going on about how my dad isn't supporting him enough. Ranting about how many people they've lost, insisting that he needs even more to work with if he's going to crush everyone in Paradise Bend. He sounded totally unhinged—I have no idea what he's going to do next. Or who he's going to do it to."

My stomach knotted. I wanted to be glad about how much our assault on the secret facility had thrown Xavier for a loop, but we had other things to consider too. Xavier definitely wouldn't go easy on Beckett if *he* found out that the kid had been in contact with us.

Which Beckett had obviously already realized, because the next thing he said was, "I kept freaking out that he'd realized what I'd done—how I helped you make that strike on the storage and training facility. He sounded ready to tear someone in half, anyone he was angry with. And I..." His voice got even quieter. "I don't know if my dad would be able to stop him. I don't know if he'd *want* to if he knew."

"You haven't seen any sign that he or your dad suspects you've reached out to us, have you?" Rowan asked.

"N-no. I think I've been careful." Beckett swallowed audibly. He sounded so raw and frightened it brought a lump to my own throat. "But who knows how it'll go in the future. I'm walking a perilous line here. I know it. I thought it'd be okay, that it'd all work out for the best..."

"That's what's important," I said, unable to stop myself from jumping in. Maybe we were asking too much from him. He was only sixteen. And I knew all too well what it was like to be afraid of your own parent, to not be able to trust that they'd have your best interests at heart.

We did have to end this war—for Beckett's sake too.

"You don't have to tell us anything else if you think your safety is at risk," I went on, ignoring the sharp look Wylder shot me. "You've already done a lot for us to help us shift the tide in our favor. Any time it's getting to be too much, you can back off. I promise your secrets will always be safe with us, and we're obviously very thankful that you offered your help at all."

Gideon's forehead had furrowed. "But, Mercy, he's the one who—" he started to protest.

I held up my hand and shook my head. The information Beckett could offer could make a huge difference to us, but it wasn't worth getting it at the expense of a teenager's life. I *wasn't* as brutal as my father, and I intended to keep what conscience I still had intact. There were lines I wasn't going to cross.

We could hear Beckett breathe. When he spoke again, he sounded annoyed with himself. "I'm being stupid. Freaking out like a kid."

I didn't think he'd appreciate me pointing out that he *was* technically a kid. "It's understandable that you're shaken up," I said. "Xavier's fucking terrifying, excuse my French. Being cautious around him is *smart*, not stupid."

"But nothing gets done if people are too scared to do it," Beckett said, sounding as if he was talking to himself more than me. He inhaled again with a rush of air. His tone got gruffer. "Sorry for melting down a bit. I want to do this. I *have* to do it, for me and Dad, for a better future. I'm not going to chicken out."

I wished I could reassure him more that none of us saw him as a coward, but I couldn't think of words he'd believe. I settled on, "I think you're going to make a great leader someday, Beckett."

The guys around me stayed silent, waiting as our conversation played out. I shot Wylder a grateful smile for his patience.

Beckett didn't respond to my compliment. There was a rustle as if he'd straightened his posture. More of the confidence we'd seen in him when he'd first come to speak to us came back into his tone. "Okay, I managed to overhear a conversation that Dad was having with one of the guys he does business with. Someone on your list—at least, his last name was Anderson, like I already told you."

Wylder leaned forward. "What were they talking about?"

"I was wary of getting too close in case he noticed me eavesdropping, but from what I could tell, Dad was pretty irritated. He was talking fast and telling Anderson how he wasn't happy about where he was taking the deal. It sounded like the guy wanted a better arrangement than he's been getting from Dad, and Dad was insisting he wasn't going to get better elsewhere and didn't like that Anderson was trying to squeeze him for more money—a higher percentage or something."

Kaige's eyebrows rose. He might not have been much of a strategist, but even he would be able to figure out that friction between the Storm and his associates could work in our favor.

Rowan spoke up. "And as far as you know, the kind of business they were talking about was all above board, nothing illegal, right?"

"Yeah," Beckett said firmly. "The only things my dad is directly involved in are totally legitimate. He's very careful about that, believe me. You're not going to be able to pin anything on him that way."

"That isn't quite what I had in mind," Rowan said.

"Okay. I didn't mean— I guess I'm still kind of keyed up."

"That's understandable," I said. "Is there anything else you found out that might help us?"

"I don't think so. I'm going to keep listening in as much as I can. I'll contact you again if there's anything. I should probably go now, though. I don't know how close an eye he's keeping on me."

"Thanks," Rowan got in before the line went dead.

"So," Wylder said, looking around at the rest of us, "the Storm is having trouble keeping his associates under his thumb. They're starting to want more than he's offering."

I wet my lips, an idea hitting me so abruptly that I felt almost giddy. "Your dad *was* getting into some real estate deals. Is there any reason we couldn't too? Maybe we could steal the Storm's business with this guy right out from under him."

Kaige frowned. "Are we really in the big leagues enough to approach some international real estate whatever-exactly-he-is?"

A smile was creeping across Rowan's face. "He doesn't have to know our background. We can control how we present ourselves and put forward a compelling offer. Then we just need to reel him in. Money talks more than anything else. We do have plenty of that to work with." He glanced at Wylder. "If you don't mind dipping into the Noble accounts."

Wylder waved a hand. "Absolutely, if you can pull this off. Let's steal everything that used to belong to the Storm that we can get our hands on. And this Anderson guy could be a great asset to have on our side in the future too."

Gideon cocked his head in thought. "Rowan negotiated the waterfront deal for Ezra. Ezra was very happy with how that went down—and he's hardly ever actually happy. Obviously we should have Rowan do the talking for us."

A hint of a flush colored Rowan's cheeks. He'd always been a little too modest to know how to take a compliment without getting embarrassed. "Of course, whatever you need me to do," he said to Wylder. "I do have the lingo down at this point."

"You shouldn't have to go alone," I said. "You can do most of the talking and fill me in on what I'll need to know, but this'll be a joint venture, Nobles and Claws. That way we can put more clout behind it. My dad left behind some capital I can access."

Kaige thumped his hands on the table. "In that case, why don't we all go? I'm in!"

Wylder raised his head, but I spoke up before he could encourage the idea. "I don't think we want to intimidate this guy. All of us together could be kind of... overwhelming. He's a regular businessman, not a gang lord we need to make a huge show of power with. I think this probably needs a little more delicacy."

"I can be delicate," Kaige said, but then he cracked a smile, because he couldn't even say it with a straight face. Gideon snorted.

"I think just Mercy and I would be perfect," Rowan said. "It's better this way and less messy. But all of that aside, I'm guessing it won't be easy getting to Anderson. Someone that well-connected and in-demand probably has meetings and events scheduled out months in advance."

Gideon had started furiously tapping away at his tablet. After a minute, he raised his head and grinned. "Well, we're just in luck. There's a charity fundraising auction happening tomorrow afternoon, and Anderson is one of the sponsors. You can meet him there."

"What if the Storm's there too?" Kaige asked.

"I don't get the impression he's paying enough attention to Paradise Bend to have bothered to find out what we even look like," I said. "He's letting Xavier handle everything while he pretends he's a regular business mogul."

Rowan nodded. "But events like a charity gala tend to sell out their tickets well in advance."

"Which is why it's always good to be friends with an expert hacker." Gideon jabbed at his screen some more and then rubbed his hands together triumphantly. "Your names are now on the guest list."

Kaige guffawed. "You're fucking magic, man."

"You are," I agreed. "Now we just need to figure out what these deals are that the Storm is getting pissy about so we can steal them out from under him."

"That's right." Wylder leaned back in his seat, crossing his arms over his chest. "We're going to show the Storm what it means to mess with us. He needs to know that if he keeps on attacking us, we're more than capable of taking away not just his men and his supplies, but his livelihood as well."

14

Mercy

"DON'T YOU LIKE IT?" ANTHEA SAID.

I realized I'd been frowning as I stared at myself in the mirror, examining the flowing turquoise dress she'd lent me. It clung to my curves, but not so tightly or exposing so much skin that it'd look out of place at an elegant gala, and it complemented my dark hair just like Anthea had said it would.

But I hadn't gotten dressed up like this since the guys had fully accepted me—since I'd come into my own as queen of the Claws—and I'd forgotten one thing I now took for granted.

"It's gorgeous," I said. "I just feel kind of naked without a gun. And there's nowhere to tuck one away wearing something like this, is there?" I motioned to my back where I'd normally have shoved my pistol into the waist of my jeans or sweats.

Anthea snapped her fingers. "I have just the solution for that." She went to the closet and popped open one of the built-in drawers. When she turned back to me, she was holding a gun no longer than her palm, bubblegum pink in color. She raised her eyebrows. "This is what 'proper' ladies carry in their purses."

I took it from her and turned it over in my hands, unable to hold back a snort. It was a third of the size of my usual pistol. "It's very cute."

"I know it doesn't look like much, but it'll get the job done," Anthea said. "A bullet between the eyes will still do the trick just fine, no matter how big a gun was shooting it. Hopefully you won't run into that kind of trouble at this fancy fundraiser, though."

I swallowed thickly. "Yeah."

Just the thought of being around all those posh businesspeople made my chest clench up. It wasn't likely they'd start firing shots, but they had their own ways of going on the attack that I had no experience with at all. It was so far from my scene, I might as well be traveling to Fiji.

I tucked the gun into the purse Anthea had also lent me and stepped into the stilettos that completed the look. Anthea stepped back to take in the full picture and nodded with satisfaction. "You look beautiful. You'll fit right in. Now go get those rich bastards."

I had to laugh, her enthusiasm loosening a little of the tension inside me. "Thank you. I'll do that."

Rowan was waiting outside by the car we were taking. He'd exchanged his usual silver Toyota for a sleek black convertible, and he'd upgraded his own look too. He always dressed pretty snappy these days, but this was a completely new level. His dark tailored suit and crisp white shirt fit him perfectly, and he'd slicked back the spikes of his blond hair with gel. I stopped in my tracks, drinking the image in.

I liked his usual boy-next-door vibe, but there was no denying that he looked particularly delicious right now. And definitely not as a boy but a man.

"Wow," he said, giving me a similar onceover and then a soft smile. "You look fantastic. I'll be beating guys off with a stick."

Another laugh spilled out of me. "Then you'll have to lend me the stick after so I can beat off the women who'll be drooling over you. Come on, let's get going." It was early in the morning still, but we had a long drive ahead of us. The gala was happening two states away.

Rowan took my hand as if I really were some kind of lady and led me around to the front passenger seat. As my fingers twined with his, I couldn't help admiring his profile too. He'd grown up so much, and for the better, I thought, even if he wasn't always so sure of that. He'd become even more confident and passionate, ready to fight for the people he cared about.

A swell of affection filled my chest. I had the urge to kiss him hard—I would have if it wouldn't have ruined the lipstick Anthea had painstakingly applied.

Had I ever really stopped loving Rowan? I wasn't sure. Underneath the anger and the sense of betrayal, I'd still held a candle for the first guy who'd ever won my heart. Now, the rush of feelings swept all the words out of me.

I'd told Wylder and Gideon I loved them. I should say it to Rowan too. But this didn't feel like the time, not when we were practically playing dress-up. I didn't want him to think I was only caught up in the moment or that I preferred him this way.

I'd tell him later, when we were back to our regular selves, because it'd be just as true then.

Rowan waited until he was sure I'd gotten my skirt out of the way before shutting the door for me, all gentleman-like. He got in on the driver's side but didn't start the engine right away.

"I wanted to show you something," he said. "I figured why not now, since we'll have a lot of time to kill."

My curiosity was instantly piqued. "What?"

He reached to the back seat and handed me a sketchbook. "I've been getting back into old habits over the past week or so. I thought you might like seeing the results."

He'd been drawing again? "Yes, of course," I said, my heart lifting. As far as I knew, Rowan hadn't done much drawing at all since he'd gotten involved with the Nobles. He'd told me that he didn't feel he deserved to have art in his life. I hadn't agreed with him then, and I was relieved to hear he'd changed his mind too.

As he drove down the driveway and onto the street, I flipped open the sketchbook. I lingered on each page, taking in every detail of the lines of pencil before turning to the next.

He'd started with random objects around the house, it looked like. There was a fruit bowl from the kitchen, a sitting room with armchairs and side tables drawn with every carved flourish in the wood, even a sketch of Wylder's Mustang in the garage. They all looked so real I could almost believe they'd spring right off the page. I ran my fingers over them, careful not to smudge the pencil lines. "Wow. You're really getting back into it, huh?"

Rowan looked abashed. "Just a little. It's felt good, exercising those old muscles again. And there's been lots of inspiration for me to use."

"Well, I'm glad you're getting your groove back so quickly," I said with a smile.

A few pages farther in, the pictures began to change, getting more ambitious. They were full scenes that filled the paper all the way to the edges, some of them with figures. I found Wylder and Gideon poised around the chess table, and Kaige lounging in his hammock. Rowan had captured their personalities perfectly with a few strokes of his pencil.

But most of those more expansive drawings featured me.

The first one showed a familiar building—an abandoned auto shop—and a woman who was suspended mid-leap. Then I was facing a few men, jabbing my finger at them, my hair pulled back in a ponytail and my face fierce with determination. Another showed a forest draped in dark shadows, with the flashlight in my hand bringing only the shapes within its glow into sharper focus. Toward the end, I found one that was just my face, a wide smile curving my lips as I gazed into the distance.

A lump rose in my throat. There was no mistaking the fondness in every line Rowan had drawn to depict me. He'd made me beautiful in a way not even Anthea could have managed—he'd made me *art*. And not just when I was wearing a pretty dress but when I was out there getting things done the way I needed to.

For a few minutes, I couldn't speak. Finally, I found my words. "Rowan, these are incredible. Really."

His gaze darted to me as if checking to make sure my reaction was genuine. His expression relaxed with a grin. "Thanks. I'm glad you like them."

I beamed back at him. "It's great to see you reconnecting with this side of yourself again. The gang doesn't have to be your entire life, you know?"

"I didn't really know that until you came back, Mercy," he said, his gaze fixed on the road again. "It's like you're my muse. There's nothing I enjoy drawing more than you. I hope you don't mind."

"Are you kidding me?" I said. "This is the most flattering thing anybody has done for me."

"Even more flattering than taking a three-hour train and getting you snow cones and cheesecake from Beach View?" he said, a teasing hint in his voice.

I punched him playfully on his arm. "Half of it had already melted by the time you came back."

"Sure, but that was also the moment when I realized how special you were to me," Rowan said, his face turning serious. I felt that familiar squeeze in my heart again and the words that I hadn't said to him in years, ready to burst out of me.

Wasn't it amazing that we'd been able to go back to our former selves, able to enjoy each other's company without the shadows of our troubled past hanging over us? I'd missed this vibe so much. I'd missed *him*.

I cleared my throat, pulling my mind back to the business at hand. "Should we go over our strategy? I want to make sure I'm totally clear on everything, since this isn't really my wheelhouse."

"Sure," Rowan said. "But I know you'll do fine. And I'll be taking the lead."

As we left Paradise Bend far behind, we went back and forth on our story, making sure we were in sync and polishing up our proposal. We weren't going to lay out all our cards upfront, but we needed to show enough for it to sound like a lucrative and appealing offer.

By the time we reached the city where the gala was being held, I was still anxious, but my nerves were under control after all that prep. I gazed up at the skyscrapers catching the mid-afternoon sunlight, twice the height of any building around the Bend. This was where the big players did their work, people like the Devil's Dozen and their associates.

In my earlier research to prepare for this event, guided by Gideon, I'd discovered that the building where the gala was being held was a hotel built in the late sixties that Evan Anderson had helped broker a deal around last year. The subsequent renovations had left it newly cleaned up and extravagant. The marble panels on the exterior were so polished they practically glowed.

Rowan gave the car to a valet, and we joined the current of attendees streaming into the building. Anthea had chosen well—we fit right in with our fancy clothes. I definitely wasn't overdressed. I saw a woman wearing a feather boa and another with a hat with so many whorls of fabric protruding from it I had no idea how she kept it balanced on her head. All the men sported fancy suits or even tuxedos. The place was all glitz and glamor.

Uncertainty clenched my stomach as we approached the door, but the security didn't give us a second glance as they checked us off the guest list and motioned us into the premises. The vast foyer inside was pristine white with gilded walls and marble floors.

We climbed a winding staircase to the ballroom already buzzing with the people inside. The air held a decadent mix of expensive alcohol and cloying perfume. Smooth jazz trickled from hidden speakers. The lights from the fancy chandeliers hanging throughout the massive room dazzled me.

"Quite the place," Rowan said, letting out a quiet whistle as he glanced around.

My heart thumped as I scanned the room for Anderson. It took a minute before I spotted him deeper inside the room, surrounded by a crowd who appeared to be hanging off his every word.

He wasn't afraid to make a style statement, that was for sure. The pattern on his suit resembled zebra stripes, but somehow it worked on him perfectly rather than looking out of place. His silver hair fell in sculpted waves to the tops of his ears, and a diamond stud glinted in one of his earlobes. He had to have tons of money, but he wasn't flaunting that part of his persona as much as a lot of the other patrons.

We needed to get him alone, and when he was in a mood to be open to offers. I studied him surreptitiously from across the room. "Maybe we should wait until after a few of the auctions have happened? If they go well, he'll be in good spirits."

"That sounds like a plan," Rowan said. "The program said the auctions would be scattered throughout the afternoon—in between refreshments and time to socialize, I guess." He nodded to a painting mounted on the stage set up along the far wall. "I believe that one's up first."

As if on cue, Anderson walked to the center of the ballroom, clapping his hands to catch everybody's attention. As soon as he had it, somebody handed a mic to him.

"Attention, everybody! We shall now begin the auction of our first item." He walked to the painting and flourished his hands at it. "First up is a 2012 masterpiece by one of the most celebrated artists of the United States, Augustine Cavallaro."

We wove through the crowd to get closer to him, and my thoughts whirled in my head. We weren't here to buy any paintings, but Anderson would also be more open to talking to us if we showed a willingness to open our wallets right away, wouldn't he?

"The bidding starts as ten thousand dollars," he said. "Do I have ten thousand?"

"Ten," I said, raising my hand. Anderson's eyes sought me in the crowd. He tipped his head at me in approval.

Somebody else called out, "Twelve thousand."

"Fifteen," I said.

"What the hell are you doing?" Rowan whispered next to me, his smile twitching with a mix of amusement and confusion.

"Just showing we can play with the top dogs," I said.

I tossed in another couple bids as the number quickly soared, but stepped back when there were still a few other bidders in the mix so there was no chance of the painting going to me. It was won by a short, balding man who looked very happy with the now one hundred thousand dollar purchase.

"A great showing for our first auction," Anderson said. "Remember that all our proceeds from today's event will go to charitable foundations that work with displaced children and veterans."

We circulated through the crowd, keeping an eye on Anderson and waiting out the next two auctions. I didn't bid again, but Rowan did in the third, picking up my strategy. After that was over, I noticed Anderson going over to the corner to consult with another man, maybe a colleague. The other guy hustled off, and for that moment, our target was alone.

"Come on," I said, tugging on Rowan's suit jacket.

We hurried over as quickly as we could while still pretending to be as posh and poised as everyone around us. Rowan grabbed a glass of champagne from a passing waiter and held it up in a cheers gesture to Anderson as we reached him. "The event seems to be going well."

The real estate guru looked us over. "It has," he said. "I'm sorry neither of you has scored anything you were interested in yet, but I appreciate you throwing your hats into the ring all the same."

Rowan flashed his smile, the one that always seemed to put people at ease. I simply stood there and looked pretty, which was my main job while he did the talking. I was totally okay with that for the time being.

"That's all right," Rowan said. "Obviously there are people here more fanatical for art than we are. But we had our sights on a bigger score."

Anderson raised his eyebrows, clearly intrigued. "What would that be? What line of work are you in, by the way? I don't think our paths have crossed before."

"Not surprising," Rowan said breezily. "We're venture capitalists, and we've spent the last two years hustling to expand our business to the point where we can compete on a national scale. We already have holdings in a few different states."

"Anything I'd have heard of?"

"For now, we mostly operate in smaller cities. Our most prominent business is based out of Paradise Bend."

Anderson showed no sign that he'd ever heard of the county, which wasn't surprising, considering that it sounded like the Storm kept his illicit activities very separate from his legitimate business ventures.

"But I take it you're looking to expand," he said.

"Yes." Rowan let his smile turn a bit sly. "We've cultivated a lot of... connections to keep us abreast of any interesting developments where we might have an opportunity. I understand one of your regular financiers is balking at agreeing to fairer terms—which seem truly deserved considering how much you've done for his company."

Anderson's gaze flickered, but otherwise he kept his expression impassive. "Who would have suggested a thing like that?"

Rowan shrugged. "I don't want to get anyone in trouble. I just wanted to let you know that if you're looking for someone who'll meet your conditions and give you the percentage you're worth, possibly even offer a little extra bonus as a show of trust in a new partnership, we'd love to talk further."

Anderson glanced at me, and I figured it was time I showed that I had a brain as well as a body. "We think it could benefit both us and you," I said. "We're impressed by what you arranged for this hotel, and we've seen several of your other projects. You clearly have a good eye."

"I'm not sure," Anderson said. "I don't like to make any kind of deal on the fly like this." But he was clearly intrigued.

"We're expecting a boom in the real estate business in our county and the surrounding area very soon," Rowan said. "With the right partnership, we could have a gold mine on our hands. We definitely don't expect you to commit to anything upfront, but I'd love to submit some documents to your office for you to look over. We'd just need to hear within a couple of days. We're looking to set up multiple investments, but we can't wait too long to get started."

An eager gleam had come into the businessman's eyes. He rubbed his hands together. "Yes," he said, pulling a business card out of his pocket. "This is the card I only give people I *actually* want to hear from. Send your proposal to this address, and I'll take a look right away."

As Rowan slipped the card into his suit, a couple of women dragged Anderson away, but not before he gave us another encouraging nod.

As soon as he was out of view, I turned toward Rowan. "We did it! I think he'll bite. You already have all the paperwork done up, don't you?"

"Yeah." Rowan chuckled, looking a bit dazed. "I spent all yesterday getting it perfect. We can contact Gideon as soon as we've left and he can send it before we're even back at the mansion. If Anderson bites—it'll be amazing for the Nobles and the Claws even without the fact that it's undermining the Storm's business at the same time."

"Then let's celebrate with a little partying, since we are here at this fancy party, after all." I grinned at him.

We drank a little more champagne and gulped down dainty hors d'oeuvres until we figured we could make our exit without looking out of place. We still had a long drive back to Paradise Bend.

Rowan put the top down on the convertible now that I didn't have to worry about messing up my hair, and the breeze washed over us as he set off. I texted Wylder letting him know everything had gone well, sent Anderson's contact info to Gideon, and kicked off my shoes to rub my aching feet. "Stupid heels."

"No more of them for a good long time," Rowan said with a laugh.

"I sure hope not." I glanced over at him. "You were really great tonight, you know. It's no wonder you managed to hook him."

"*We* managed to hook him," Rowan corrected me. "You were amazing too. Getting his attention with the bids was a great warm-up."

I elbowed him lightly. "Obviously we still make a great team."

I turned on the radio and leaned back in the seat, and the hours passed with occasional chatter and a few spurts of singing along when a song we particularly liked came on. The late afternoon darkened into evening and then night. By the time we reached the edge of Paradise Bend, it was totally dark, everything silhouetted by the harsh glow of the streetlamps.

Maybe now was a good time to speak up, while we were high on the victory, our hair wind-blown and our fancy clothes loosened. I looked over at Rowan. The headlights of an oncoming car deepened the brown of his eyes.

"There's something I've been wanting to tell you."

He glanced at me. "Yeah?"

"Yeah. I—"

I didn't get a chance to finish my sentence. The car that'd been coming toward us abruptly veered in front of us, just as two more roared up from behind. There was nowhere for Rowan to turn to avoid them. He hit the brakes, and the car behind us crashed into the back of the convertible.

We jerked to a halt with a screech and the distinct sound of safeties clicking off all around us.

15

Mercy

My head banged against the car window. I slapped my hand to my temple at the sudden ache, but there was no chance to do more than that. Doors were flying open on the three cars that'd surrounded us, armed men spilling out.

They had to be the Storm's people. It was only a matter of seconds before they started shooting. There was no way for us to drive away from them when they'd boxed us in like this.

My gaze darted to Rowan, confirming he was okay other than the fear paling his face, and then to the buildings beyond the sidewalk. A scruffy brick structure stood on the other side of a paved parking area patchy with weeds. It was our closest option for shelter.

The second I spotted it, I shoved the car door open. Rowan unsnapped his seatbelt and clambered after me. We bolted for the building without a word, both understanding the situation, keeping our heads low.

Someone yelled, and footsteps stomped behind us. We veered left and right as bullets whizzed through the air around us. Bits of gravel dug into my bare feet, and I almost missed the heels I'd kicked off. But all that mattered was reaching the shelter of the building in time.

As Rowan kicked the rickety door open, another bang pierced the night, and he flinched. The bullet had sliced across his upper arm, carving a channel in the fabric of his suit and the skin beneath. Gritting his teeth, he pushed me onward into the dark, dusty space.

It was one of the Bend's many abandoned warehouses, mostly one huge room smelling of old plywood and grease. The hulking outlines of various pieces of mechanical equipment showed in the faint streams of city light that drifted in through the high, grimy windows amid scattered wooden shipping crates, some stacked on top of each other, most of them yawning open. Whatever they'd delivered was long gone.

Rowan heaved the nearest crate in front of the door, ducking to avoid another barrage of bullets. The door's wood was already splintering—blocking it wasn't going to keep our attackers out for long. I groped around for anything to defend myself with and realized I'd left my purse with my shoes on the floor of the car. The pretty little gun Anthea had given me was way too far out of reach.

Rowan wasn't armed either, but he was creative. He snatched up a metal rod that was lying on the ground and wielded it like a sword, testing its weight. His expression had gone taut with tension. Blood was soaking down the sleeve of his suit from where the bullet had grazed his arm.

I grabbed his hand, ignoring the stinging in the soles of my feet. "Come on. Maybe there's a back door." The windows were too high to easily reach, and who knew what the drop on the other side would be like. My parkour skills might be up to it, but Rowan didn't have the same training.

As we darted farther into the building, the door exploded with a hail of bullets, bits of wood flying everywhere. We dove behind a couple of the crates. I spun around and noticed a vicious-looking steel hook dangling from a chain overhead.

If I could get that swinging, I could smash a whole bunch of skulls. I just needed to get to it.

Rowan was tapping out a message on his phone. He shoved it back into his pocket, his grip tight on the metal bar. Our enemies were fanning out through the building, shouting to each other as they searched for us.

"We're too far from the mansion," Rowan said under his breath. "I don't think anyone will be able to get to us in time."

"Then we'll just have to deal with these assholes ourselves," I said, my heart thumping. I could do this. The machine looming next to the crate should mostly block me from view—and bullets.

I dashed over to the machine and scrambled onto a crate partly wedged behind it. The hook was just within reach of my grasping fingers. I spotted a lever I could use to adjust its height on the wall just a few feet away.

But I also spotted a few of the men coming up on Rowan's hiding spot. If only I'd had my fucking gun. Grimacing at myself, I leapt up to grab the hook, meaning to whip myself right into them and kick them all square in the face.

At the same moment, Rowan charged out from behind the crate. He must have seen the guys coming and figured he'd do better with the element of surprise.

And maybe he was right. He caught one guy in the side of the head with a smack of the bar that must have shattered the man's skull from the crunching sound that followed. Rowan whirled and clocked another guy in the gut. I launched myself at them, bracing myself for a flying kick—

And several more men hurtled toward us, bullets exploding from their guns.

Rowan tried to jerk himself out of range, but he didn't have enough time. His body spasmed as if he'd been hit. His legs buckled. He fell to the floor, blood blooming around a wound on his upper chest.

No! The silent protest echoed up my throat. I flung myself onto the edge of the crate just above him, meaning to jump down and grab a gun from one of the fallen men, to try to stop the bleeding while I shot at the pricks who'd ambushed us. But the Storm's force was too overwhelming. I was only just starting my spring when a bullet tore into my flesh this time, ripping through the muscle of my thigh.

My leg shuddered, and the impact threw me backward. I tumbled onto my back in the bottom of the crate with a thud that sent pain spiking up my spine. Pain streaked through my body from the bullet wound like a bolt of lightning.

As I flailed to try to right myself, packing straw rustling around me, someone slammed the lid of the crate down, shutting out the thin light overhead.

I was alone. I was alone in the dark with the walls pressing in around me and blood smearing the floor beneath me.

A cry caught in my throat. My pulse rattled past my ears, and my lungs seized, my breath coming in ragged spurts. Panic rolled over me and sucked me under.

Not this. Not this again. I tried to focus on the reality around me, but too much of my brain was trapped in the pit in the Katz basement again, listening to my father walk away while I sobbed and scratched in vain.

Some distant part of my brain was aware of voices outside—a brief, hollered discussion about what to do with us, someone making a comment about "won't even be bodies to find." I had no idea what they were talking about. I groped in the darkness, my fingers scraping over the splintery boards so frantically the skin split. My breaths were becoming more choked by the second. My head spun with the lack of oxygen.

Then, with one gasp, a new smell prickled into my lungs. I whimpered and gagged, and recognition clicked.

Gasoline. It smelled like gasoline. Why—

Liquid splashed against the side of my crate, and the smell got thicker. There was a click and a hiss, and then a warbling sound that made my blood run even colder. I banged my fists against the boards wildly. "No, no, let me out. Let me *out*!"

The men just snickered as their footsteps thumped off. A hint of smoke tickled into my nose, and the rising crackle filled my ears. My pulse lurched twice as hard as before.

They'd set the building on fire. They were burning it down around us—leaving *us* to burn in it.

I knew that. I knew I had to get out; I had to get to Rowan; we had to run for it. If we stayed here, we'd die for sure.

But even with the smoke curling through the tiny crevices between the plywood slats and fiery heat starting to waft in with it, I couldn't shake myself free of the panic's hold. The old fear had dug its claws deep into my brain. I kept gasping and sputtering, my heart pounding so fast it dizzied me.

Come on, Mercy, I thought. *Come on, come on.* And in the back of my mind the concrete lid slammed shut over the pit again, just after I'd gotten one last glimpse of Dad's sadistic grin.

Something thumped against the outer wall of the crate. There was a ragged breath and a groan. "Mercy?" Rowan's voice said, weak and wavering.

Tears flooded my eyes. It took me a second before I could work any words out of my constricted throat. "Rowan. Are you—I can't—I don't know—" I couldn't even pull more than three words together into any kind of coherence.

Even as rough as he sounded, he managed to speak with the same warm assurance he'd always had. "Don't worry about me. You need to get out of there." He paused with a muffled grunt. "You—you can do this. Just focus on me. Focus on my voice. I'm right here with you, and I'm not going anywhere. I'll always be here."

His words sank in through the haze of panic just like they had all those years ago when he'd found me trapped in the cabinet in the museum, the day we'd really become friends. I gulped the smoky air and clung on to the sense of calm he was projecting as hard as I could.

"I'm trying," I said, noticing the pain in my thigh again, my body shuddering with it in the growing heat. "I'm trying."

"You're doing great. You'll get there. Just keep—just keep going, one step at a time, one thought at a time. You're in control. You can handle this."

My heartbeat started to even out, my chest loosening. I squeezed my eyes shut, seeing him slumped against the other side of the crate, giving everything he had to talk me through this moment. Resolve cracked through the rest of the turmoil that'd gripped me.

I *could* handle this, and I wasn't going to die here. I wasn't going to let *him* die. Those bastards weren't going to win.

I heaved myself upright, slamming my shoulder into the lid of the crate. The Storm's men had weighed it down with something, but it creaked at the impact. Ignoring the pain searing through my injured leg, I braced both hands against the scratchy plywood and heaved as hard as I could, up and away from where Rowan was sprawled.

The lid slid to the side with a scraping sound. I shoved again, and it toppled right off. Swallowing a whimper at the agony lancing through my thigh, I hauled myself up over the top and dropped to the floor next to Rowan.

He was lying right where I'd imagined him, his eyes closed other than brief twitches of his eyelids, his face sallow. His breath rattled in his throat. He'd passed out while I was freeing myself from the crate. Blood smeared the floor all around him.

The smoke was congealing thicker around us, my skin prickling with the heat. The flames had engulfed most of the crates around us. The inferno roared so loud my eardrums ached.

I coughed and smacked Rowan's cheeks. "Wake up. Please, Rowan, wake up!"

He didn't stir. Fresh tears stung my eyes.

I couldn't leave him here. No fucking way.

I hobbled around him, hissing every time I put any weight on my bad leg, and curled my arms under his until my elbows locked into his armpits. Clenching my jaw, I heaved us both backward. Again. And again. Dragging him toward the doorway slowly but surely.

More blood oozed out of his wounds. The sight of it and the limpness of his body made me want to lie down and give up. Pain screamed through my body, but the scream of refusal rang out inside me even louder.

I wasn't losing him again. I simply *wasn't.*

That defiance and the adrenaline coursing through my veins propelled me onward. The flames licked closer, scorching Anthea's lovely dress and singing my hair. I winced at the sting but kept pulling, Rowan's body jerking along in my grasp a couple of feet at a time.

The Storm's men had smashed the crate Rowan had wedged by the door as they'd come in. I was grateful for their destructive inclinations now. I smacked aside the scattered boards, some of them already sizzling, and hauled Rowan out into the cooler night air.

I couldn't stop there on the doorstep. The flames lashed after us, roaring up to the doorway. And Rowan needed help. I heaved him and heaved again, over to where the convertible was parked with its crumpled back end. The Storm people had driven off in their cars. The road was clear again.

"Hang in there," I pleaded. Rowan made no indication he heard me. "Please, stay with me."

A thin moan escaped his mouth as I hauled him into the back seat. I cringed, guilt stabbing through my gut at the thought that I might have hurt him more. "We're going to get you help," I swore, tucking him against the smooth leather as carefully as I could. "You're going to be okay." Oh, please, please, please, let him be okay.

I straightened up and nearly blacked out with the pain that blared through my mind. Somehow, I managed to hold on. With lurching steps, I stumbled around the car and fell into the driver's seat.

The key was still in the ignition. I murmured a ragged prayer under my breath while I turned it.

I'd never heard a more glorious sound than the engine growling to life. I swiped at the blood and tears coating my face, angled myself so I could set my foot from my uninjured side against the gas pedal, and took us into drive.

The car leapt forward. I gripped the steering wheel so tightly my knuckles were pure white, and trained all my attention on the image of the Bend's hospital in my head. I just had to get there. I just had to get there and let them take care of Rowan, because this was one injury Frank didn't have a hope in hell of fixing.

16

Mercy

The doctor flashed a beam of light over my eyes. "Look to one side and then the other," he said.

Irritation rippled through me. "For the umpteenth time, I don't have a concussion. The only place I'm really hurt is my *leg*, not my head."

The doctor looked at me disapprovingly, but to my relief, he finally stepped back. The room, like the rest of the hospital, smelled like disinfectant and bleach. But the stench of smoke that still lingered in my nose overpowered everything else unless I took a particularly deep breath.

"You and your friend came in here pretty battered up," the doctor said warily. "What happened exactly?"

I straightened my spine. They had been trying to crack me and get me to admit to some kind of criminal activity since I'd driven up to the emergency room doors, yelling for help. While they'd rolled Rowan toward surgery, I'd been detained so they could stitch up my leg, check my lungs, and up my fluid intake. Apparently the bullet had slashed across my leg but not sunk right in, but they could still tell it was a bullet wound—and Rowan's had obviously come from gunfire too. Those kind of injuries led to a lot of questions, which was exactly why the Nobles turned to Frank for this kind of treatment when they could.

"I'm sorry, but like I said before, it was official business, and I can't disclose anything," I said, trying to keep my voice neutral. Maybe he'd buy that I might be involved in some kind of work on the right side of the law.

From his expression, that was a no. "Right," he said, eyeing me skeptically. He looked like he was getting ready to pick up the phone and call the cops.

There was a knock at the door. Both of us looked up at the same time to see Wylder there.

Relief rushed through me. If he'd made it this far, that meant that he'd dealt with all the hospital formalities. Before now, all he'd managed to do was pass on a T-shirt and sweatpants for me to change into since Anthea's dress was no longer wearable.

Wylder's mouth pressed into a hard line. "Can I take her?"

The doctor frowned. "She should avoid straining her leg during the initial healing period, and she may have taken some damage to her lungs from smoke inhalation. I personally think she should stay at the hospital for tonight while we run more tests."

"I'm fine," I said. To make a point, I slid off the bed and stood up. Immediately, a shock of pain jolted from the wound on my thigh up through my chest and down to my foot. I grimaced but quickly covered it with a forced smile.

The doctor wasn't convinced by that performance either. "See, miss—"

"She's fine," Wylder said. It was a statement. Period. "We'll make sure she's well taken care of."

The doctor swallowed hard. When Wylder loomed on him, he took a step back. Either he knew the Noble heir by reputation, or he could tell he was dealing with someone he shouldn't mess with. "Yes, in that case, take her home."

"Thank you, doctor," I said.

Wylder gave me his hand, and I limped out of the room next to him.

As soon as we'd left the doctor behind, he turned to me, peering into my eyes with a storm raging in his. "You sure you're okay, right? Those bastards..."

I squeezed his hand. "I'm fine. Sore, but nothing that won't heal. I want to see Rowan if we can. Do you have any idea how *he's* doing?" He'd been alive when we'd made it to the hospital, but I didn't know by how thin a thread. What if he didn't make it? A lump rose in my throat.

"They're not letting us see him yet," Wylder said with a hard edge to his voice. "We'll wait them out until we can convince them otherwise."

He led me on down the hall toward the seating area where I could see Gideon and Kaige poised opposite each other on the rows of metal chairs, which were bolted to the ground as if the hospital was afraid someone might try to steal them otherwise.

"Did the doctors even say anything?" I asked Wylder. "How did the surgery go?"

Gideon looked up at the sound of my voice. His face was so serious that my heart sank. He got up and gave me a quick, tight hug that was so unlike his typical undemonstrative self that I got even more worried. "It doesn't sound great," he admitted in a low voice.

Kaige had stood up and hastily helped me into a chair with Wylder at my other side. He kept his arm around my shoulders. "They don't want to tell us much of anything," he grumbled. "We had enough trouble even getting them to admit that *you* hadn't taken any life-threatening wounds. I was starting to think I'd have to knock some skulls together."

I gave him a baleful look. "I appreciate your dedication, but let's not take that approach here. We need them putting their heads toward fixing Rowan."

"Fine," he growled. "Then I'll just settle for pummeling every single one of the assholes who did this to the two of you. There's going to be nothing left but a bloody pulp."

Wylder didn't say a word, but I'd never seen him so deathly quiet, not even when he'd found his brother's corpse. Cold fury seemed to engulf him as he stared down stubbornly at the floor.

Before I could say anything to him, a doctor approached us. "You're here for Rowan Finlay?" he said to the guys.

Wylder leapt up. "Yes. Is he all right? Can we see him?"

The doctor looked so solemn I wanted to punch him. As I hefted myself back onto my feet, he motioned to us. "You can, but only briefly. And I'll warn you, his current appearance may upset you. One of the bullets ruptured a major organ—we have him in a medically induced coma while we encourage his body to recover from the trauma. He's going to need at least one more surgery you'll have to sign off on."

My throat closed up. "Do you even know if he's going to make it?" I asked in a thin voice.

The doctor's expression told me he didn't. "We can't make predictions of prognosis in situations like this. We'll do our best for him."

Shit. My hands clenched tight as I walked with the guys down the hall after the doctor. He showed us into a small private room where a limp figure lay on a gurney in a hospital gown. Even though I should have known what to expect, it took me a second to process that the figure was Rowan.

His blond hair was stained with soot and blood. His face was so pale it looked like wax. He had tubes going into his arms and another into his mouth, and bandages protruding here and there all over his limbs and torso. I pressed my hand to my mouth to muffle a gasp. The pain in my leg suddenly seemed miles distant.

"Give us a moment alone with him?" Wylder said. "Then I'll sign your damned forms."

The doctor dipped his head and hustled out as if he couldn't leave fast enough. Wylder stood right by Rowan's head, gazing down at him. His stance had gone even more rigid. When he finally looked up, pure rage blazed in his bright green eyes.

"I'll tear Xavier limb from limb. He'll pay for every single drop of Rowan's blood that his men spilled. I swear it on my fucking soul."

Kaige smacked his hands together, intense in his agreement. "Oh yes, he will."

"And I'll be right there with you," Gideon said in a flat voice edged with his own anger. "I'll rip the Storm and his people apart every way I possibly can."

Their collective anger couldn't fill the hollow of grief and guilt in my heart. I wanted to see Xavier gutted, sure. But what would the price be?

Rowan had already paid for the war I'd dragged the Nobles into—he might pay with his life. Was this war worth it if it took away one of the people I cared about most? How much else would I lose before it was over?

I glanced between Kaige and Wylder. They looked ready to go after Xavier right this instant, guns blazing. Even Gideon's face was a mask of worry and frustration. How many more people would have to be sacrificed in my crusade to protect my home—a crusade that was seeming more hopeless by the day?

I'd never even gotten to tell Rowan I loved him. What if I'd lost that chance forever?

What was the point in all this fighting if everyone ended up dead anyway?

I closed my eyes against those awful questions and the horrible specter of Rowan's injured body. There was a rustling as the doctor came back in.

"I'm sorry to disturb you, but the operating room is open. The sooner we can get started, the better off he'll be."

"Of course," Wylder said gruffly. A pen scratched across a paper form.

I forced myself to open my eyes. I stared down at Rowan as the attendants wheeled his gurney out of the room. *I love you*, I thought at him, as if that would make a difference now. *I love you. Please come back to me.*

Wylder turned to the rest of us. "It sounds like there won't be any news for a while. We should let them work and get ourselves sorted out. It won't do Rowan any good if he survives only for the Long Night to cut him down in a few days' time."

I wanted to protest, but deep down I knew he was right. For a second, my pain seemed to cut right through the center of my being. Hanging around here was only making it worse. I needed to get away, to think, to figure out where I stood now that my world had been upended in a way I hadn't really been prepared for.

"Can I get a lift?" I asked. "I want to go home."

"You shouldn't even have to ask that," Wylder said.

He and Kaige supported me on either side as I limped out to Wylder's Mustang. Kaige stayed with me in the back seat. The sun had risen for the morning, blazing over the streets with a brightness that made me feel like I was hallucinating. How could it be *daylight* when Rowan was locked in darkness?

Wylder drove straight to the Katz house. He parked out front, nodding to the Claws men stationed on the lawn, who studied me with obvious concern. I was going to have to put on a brave face for them.

"We can come in with you," Wylder said. "Keep you company."

As much as I appreciated his offer, I shook my head. "I think I need to be alone for a little while to collect myself."

Kaige grunted. "Are you sure that's a good idea? Feelings can be quite a bitch."

My lips twitched with a hint of a smile at his blunt statement. "Yes, they can. But I think I'm having a few that I'll work through easier on my own." I touched his cheek. "Thank you. I'll call in an hour or two. Let me know if anything comes up."

I got out, careful of my injured leg, and walked up to the house as steadily as I could. Quinn and a couple of the other guys were hanging out in the living room.

"Hey," Quinn called out. "We hit the jackpot last night. Picked up some cars and cash we can put to good use."

"That's great," I said, my voice coming out stiff. I couldn't summon any enthusiasm.

Put them to use attacking the Storm people some more? Maybe I should tell all the Claws men who'd joined my cause that they should cut their losses and just get out of here before the Long Night rolled in to lay down his brand of the law. How many of them would die in the next few days if I didn't?

I limped on down the hall to the kitchen, not feeling up to handling the stairs. Part of me wanted to go out in the backyard and sit under the big oak tree, as if it would give me answers, but Xavier had ruined my favorite part of my childhood home the other night along with so much else. My teeth set on edge.

I paused at the sound of a high-pitched giggle up ahead and then pushed myself forward. Through the kitchen window, I could see Sarah dashing around in the backyard, letting the wind whip through a pinwheel covered in tassels. She had no sense of that space as dangerous—not yet, anyway. I was relieved to note the guards standing by the fence, keeping watch.

Jenner was leaning against the kitchen counter, gazing through the window too. A soft smile curved his lips. It amazed me that a man ruthless enough to be my dad's former lieutenant could be so loving with his daughter.

Without thinking, I stepped closer to the glass. Sarah stopped playing long enough to wave at me.

"She seems... happy," I ventured. It felt like a foreign concept.

Jenner nodded. "She's pretty good at finding joy in little things. Never made much trouble for me or her mom. It's one of the things I really admire about her." He glanced at me, taking in my off-balance pose and the lump of the bandage on my leg. "How are you?"

I didn't really want to answer that question. And somehow at the same time I had the sense that my answer lay just beyond the window. "I'm fine," I said, concentrating on Sarah.

She deserved all the joys she could find. She deserved to keep her home. What would happen to her if we all had to make a run for it? What would happen to Beckett—would the Long Night kill him too?

I'd wanted to make a better future for all the kids in the Bend, hadn't I? I didn't see how that was going to happen if I let the Long Night take over. I'd seen the cold ruthlessness behind his polite exterior.

Rowan wouldn't have wanted me to give up on my dreams, no matter what happened to him.

The mounting pressure on my shoulders eased. I was doing this for Sarah, and Beckett, and all the other kids. And for little Mercy who'd lost her childhood, and now wanted to make sure that others didn't have to suffer the same fate. Things *would* be better in the future than they were today. They were counting on me to make that happen.

Jenner let me hold my silence for a long stretch. Then he ventured, in a gentle tone, "We're not done yet, are we? What's up next, boss?"

The way he said "boss" set off a weird glow in my chest that burned away a little more of the anguish twisted around my heart.

"We're close," I said. The Storm people had to be scared, or they wouldn't have gone out of their way to track down Rowan and me like that. They'd tried to steal my best friend and my first love from me, but I wouldn't let them back me into a corner.

My resolve bled into my words, turning them firm. "We're close, and we're going to make the Storm pay."

My phone buzzed in the little purse of Anthea's I'd brought in with me. I pulled it out, seeing Gideon's name on the call display.

"Hey," he said when I answered. "Something's just come up with the Storm. I know you just got home. We can handle it if you need to rest—"

"No," I said before he could go on, my chin lifting. "Swing by and get me. I'm still in this fight."

17

Gideon

"What's going on?" Mercy asked, leaning forward from the backseat. "Why are we headed for the shopping strip?" Kaige was sitting next to her, his face caught in silent fury.

"The Storm's men have launched attacks on several Noble properties throughout the city and the Bend," Wylder said, his gaze intent on the road as he wove in and out of traffic. His irritation was only evident from the tightness of his grip on the wheel.

"Several—all at once?"

I nodded, tracking incoming text reports from Noble men scattered across the county. "It seems to be some sort of divide and conquer strategy. Thankfully with Ezra's permission for us to call on all the Noble forces, I don't think they're going to manage the conquering part."

"At most places," Wylder put in. "Xavier himself and the largest bunch of men have turned up at the old furniture store where we stashed the rest of the Glory and all the extra weapons we stole from them. He must have figured out it was important after we started giving out Glory to screw over his previous plan. He's trying to turn the tables on us—but no way in hell are we going to let him."

"There were guards already there, weren't there?" Mercy said, her dark eyes flashing with anger.

"There were five on the premises when the attack started," I said, confirming the data on the screen in front of me. "Unfortunately, a couple of them were shot in the initial skirmish—at least one fatally. The other men inside have managed to keep the building secure, but Xavier and his people have surrounded the place. The Nobles may not be able to hold them off much longer."

"We've called in reinforcements, and they'll follow us as soon as they can," Wylder said. "Unfortunately, a lot of them have gotten tied up in the other attacks. But I want to take this prick down myself. We'll give them something to worry about other than their little siege. How many Claws were you able to round up?"

Mercy glanced through the back window at the car following us. "We only had four who could come right away, but I told Jenner to put out a wider call. I'm not sure how far off the others are. How many people does Xavier have with him?"

I grimaced. "I don't have a clear report. The men at the factory haven't had a whole lot of time to chat. It sounds like quite a few."

And there were only eight of us to go up against them so far. Well, seven, really, when you considered that I wasn't going to contribute much other than sorting through the incoming data and filling Wylder in. I didn't even have the benefit of the full computer array in my van, since we hadn't made it back to the Noble mansion before we'd gotten the call about the attacks.

My stomach twisted. Ever since I'd told Wylder I'd be staying with him when he set off to deal with Xavier, there'd been a pang in the back of my head, like the start of a throbbing headache. Images of my last encounter with the psychopath flashed through my mind.

The last time I'd been close to Xavier, he'd nearly killed me. He *could* have killed me—I was just lucky he'd decided to wait and use me as bait. Who knew if I'd survive this time?

But I couldn't let my nerves get the better of me. We were down one man with Rowan in the hospital. Everyone had to pull their weight. I couldn't hide away in my office while my brothers-in-arms and my woman did all the fighting for me. Maybe I'd get the chance to take a shot or two that could help turn the tide.

We turned the corner, and Wylder eased to a stop. My heart sank.

It was a hell of a lot more than twenty men. Cars were parked all over the street from halfway down the block to the next corner, surrounding the old store and cutting off the flow of traffic. The Storm's men were hustling between the vehicles or staked out behind them, some taking shots at the second-floor windows that our men were using as a vantage point. At least one of our people was around at the back too, shooting anyone who tried to get to the back door.

Thankfully, the store's windows had already been boarded up. But the front and back doors wouldn't withstand a steady barrage if Xavier sent enough people in that the guards couldn't pick them all off.

The menace himself was standing on the roof of one of the cars near the back of the horde, apparently unconcerned about the possibility that anyone might shoot *him*. "Just you wait," he was hollering at the Noble men inside. "As soon as we get in there, we're going to chop you up like chicken liver. Why don't you make a run for it now?"

A bunch of men were hauling something out of one of the other vehicles, a large SUV. I squinted at it, and my pulse hiccupped.

"They've got explosives," I said, pointing. "They're going to blast the doors in—maybe bring the whole building down." I wouldn't put it past Xavier to care more about making sure *we* didn't have the drugs and weapons than getting them back for himself.

"Shit." Wylder pushed open his door. "We'd better deal with this fast, then. We can at least cover the front of the building so they can't bring the bombs close enough." He glanced at me. "You stay in the car, but keep the window down in case you pick up on anything you need to give us a shout about."

I tipped my head in acknowledgment, my gut full of a queasy mix of relief... and shame at the fact that I was relieved. But the relief part flooded me even more sharply when Xavier's head swung toward us.

A savage grin stretched across his face. Wylder's hand whipped up with his pistol, but the shot that would have hit Xavier smack in the face missed as the giant leapt down from the car at the same moment. He sauntered closer to us, moving between the cars so he could keep us in view with his body almost entirely shielded.

My heart thumped faster at the sight of him looming closer, some part of me clenching up with the urge to flee, to put as much distance between him and me as I could. I clamped down on that impulse, forcing myself to breathe slowly and evenly like I did when my lungs acted up.

This must be similar to how Mercy felt when she was trapped in a tight space—this irrational panic. Except it wasn't totally irrational, was it? We were both reacting to a reminder of a situation that'd been quite literally life-threatening.

Mercy, Kaige, and the four Claws men who'd joined us had gotten out too. They stuck close to our cars and a couple other vehicles belonging to regular citizens that were parked along this stretch of sidewalk. There was an empty space of maybe thirty feet between the horde of Storm vehicles and ours. I didn't think Xavier would risk trying to cross it, opening himself up to our fire. But we couldn't dash across it to get to the building without getting picked off by his men either.

As I'd expected, Xavier stopped before he passed the last of his vehicles. He leaned his massive arms on the top of the car, still grinning but tensed to duck if anyone aimed their gun at him. Wylder glanced past him and motioned to the Claws men. They opened fire on a few men who'd made a dash for the entrance with the explosives, and the bunch fell back.

"Look who's shown up," Xavier said in a drawl. "Why am I not surprised? The scared little kitten, the second-rate heir, and even the mouse who hides behind his computer screens most of the time." His gaze narrowed in on me, and my heart outright lurched. "I missed getting to snap your neck last time. Wouldn't want to lose the opportunity again."

He was just bullshitting, spewing out crap. He was nowhere near me. I knew that, but adrenaline kept racing through my veins all the same. My hands balled on my lap.

"Fuck you!" I yelled out the window, which actually made me feel a little better, even though Xavier just chuckled. Kaige aimed an approving grin at me.

Then Xavier turned away from us to call out to his men. "Bring one of the trucks right up onto the sidewalk to give us a clear path. These dipshits aren't going to stop us from getting what we want for long."

Damn it. Wylder and the others started firing again, forcing Xavier to jerk out of range, but the truck the Storm's men hurried to was sheltered by other vehicles around it. None of our force managed to pick any of them off. And as soon as they got it in place on the sidewalk, they'd be able to run the explosives right to the front door while it shielded them, nothing we could do about it short of charging at them straight to our deaths.

"In just a few minutes, we'll all be smelling baked Nobles," Xavier announced in a weird singsong voice. The man was totally deranged.

Even as my nerves jittered with that thought, something clicked in my head. Xavier made a terrifying figure, sure, but he shouldn't have been that much of a challenge. He was reckless and savage. All we needed to do was outthink his animalistic brain. How hard could that be?

What did I have around me that I could use?

I scanned the entire street, my physical symptoms of panic fading into the background as I focused on my new goal. My gaze snagged on a building at the far corner, beyond the Storm siege.

A huge poster of a man's slickly smiling face was posted in the window, the sign overhead announcing it was the office for one of the new mayoral candidates. I'd barely even noticed the election campaigning getting started a few months ago, it mattered so little to us. The Nobles lived above the law.

I doubted that dork had been doing much campaigning since war had broken out on the streets of the Bend anyway. But he had a loudspeaker system set up in the building, with speakers mounted all along the front of the structure. They should have some kind of control center that ran them from inside. If I could just get access to that...

"Wylder," I hissed, keeping my voice low enough that Xavier shouldn't be able to hear. "Hold them off as long as you can. I need a few minutes, and then I think we can send them running."

Wylder raised an eyebrow at me, but my best friend trusted me without needing to hear more than that. At his gesture, our men all started shooting again, one of them managing to shatter the back window on the truck. The warmth of his faith in me sped my fingers across the tablet's screen.

Xavier thought he could lord his strength over me, taunt me like I was pathetic. He had no idea what *real* strength looked like—or just how many forms it could come in.

The local network was still running inside the campaign office. I clicked on a device I'd stashed in the glove compartment that boosted my own range and disabled the security protocols in a matter of seconds, peeling them away like tissue paper from a present. A different sort of adrenaline coursed through me now, thrumming with confidence rather than quivering with fear.

I might not get far with a physical confrontation, but this was what I was made for. Xavier couldn't beat me at my kind of game.

He'd noticed I was up to something, though. He leaned against the car he was poised behind and cocked his head. "Look at the poor little geek, scrambling frantically to save his skin."

I let out a laugh, not even needing to fake it. A couple more taps—and there, I was in. I barely needed to look at the screen as I set up the final pieces of my gambit.

"You're the one who's going to be running scared in a moment," I shouted out the window. "You'll get going right now if you know what's good for you."

Xavier snorted. "Big words from a puny little man. Am I supposed to be afraid of this tiny band of resistance."

"Nope," I retorted. "But I don't know how much you'll enjoy dealing with our friends in blue."

I concealed the click of a button on my lap out of his view, and the wail of police sirens sounded as if in the distance. The truth was, it was a recorded sound I was playing through the loudspeakers, keeping the volume low to give the Storm's men the impression that the cars had only just gotten close enough to be heard.

Xavier's head jerked around toward the sound. Then he turned back to me with a sneer. "The cops wouldn't want anything to do with the likes of you."

I shrugged. "We've paid them off to look the other way plenty of times, and now we're paying them to crack down on the mess you're making on our streets. Every cop in a twenty-mile radius is headed this way right now, fully armed and ready to rumble."

A flicker of uncertainty crossed the big man's scarred face. I nudged the volume a little louder as if the sirens were getting closer.

"How would your boss feel about you getting into a massive shoot-out with the local law enforcement?" I asked. "Is that really what he sent you here to do? I'd have thought *he'd* want to get them in his pocket, not have you turn them into enemies. You know how the police feel about cop-killers."

I could tell I'd struck the right chord. Xavier's jaw twitched. A man like the Storm, someone who kept his own hands as clean as possible, didn't care how many fellow criminals Xavier took down, but he wouldn't want to set himself completely at odds with the police before he'd even claimed this territory.

Most of the Storm's men were listening now. Several had lowered their weapons. They looked at Xavier and each other nervously.

I increased the volume even more. It sounded perfect, like a whole swarm of cops about to descend on this street.

Wylder didn't know exactly what I'd done, but he was smart enough to play along. He set his hands on his hips and smirked at Xavier. "I look forward to watching the boys in blue mow you down."

Xavier cursed, but I could tell he was finally convinced. He pulled back, shouting at his men. I pushed the volume higher, as if the sirens were just a few blocks away now. It was almost hilarious watching the Storm men scramble into their vehicles and peel out like they had a pack of demons on their tails.

"Run, baby, run," Kaige hollered after them. Xavier gave us one last ominous look before he leapt into his car. The vehicles scattered into the side-streets, a few of them almost colliding with each other in their haste to get away.

As soon as they'd roared off, Wylder and Mercy waved to our people, and they rushed to the store. "Bring the injured down so we can get them out of here right away," Wylder called to the guards who'd been holding their ground inside. He shot a glance back at me. "That was fucking brilliant, Gideon."

Kaige glanced around. "There aren't any actual cops coming, are there? Because I don't think they see us as friends."

I chuckled. "It's just a sound effect I found online. Go get our guys out of there."

We'd beat Xavier even hugely outnumbered and out-armed. We would beat him again and again. For the first time, I could really believe that we'd take him and the rest of the Storm's forces down for good before our time ran out.

And I'd be right here fighting alongside the rest of the Nobles in my own way.

18

Mercy

I DIRECTED SAM AND HIS FRIEND TOWARD THE RIGHT corner of the room. They were carrying a wooden crate between them. "Put it there with the rest of the boxes."

They did as I asked and heaved the crate to the top of the last of the neatly stacked rows.

Gideon came in after them, carrying his tablet. He ticked something off on the screen. "That's the last one."

Beyond the garage-style door, Kaige waved off the truck we'd used to carry the stash from the old furniture store to a different Noble property where hopefully Xavier wouldn't discover it again. The factory had reinforced windows and doors in case it did face an attack. Wylder had gone to fill his father in and get approval to have a new contingent of guards posted here.

Kaige watched the truck leave and then came inside, dusting his hands as he walked. "So, that's all wrapped up."

I turned to Sam. "You guys must be tired. Thanks for your help."

He gave me a teasing salute. "Anything for the Queen of the Claws."

I laughed. "I think we're good now. Why don't you go back to the house and relax for however long we get before we have to be on the move again?"

He and his friend nodded, and they headed out.

"Probably won't be very long," Kaige muttered. "After the stunt we pulled off this morning, I'd bet Xavier is pissed. We humiliated him in front of his own men." He glanced at Gideon. "Which was a total genius move. I'm just saying… he won't be happy."

Gideon shrugged with a newfound assurance that I had to admire. "Whatever he throws at us, we'll be ready."

Kaige's gaze roved over the stacked crates—the wooden ones along two of the walls that held the weapons… and the few large plastic ones against another wall that held the remaining Glory. "At least the prick didn't get his hands on all this."

As if drawn by a magnetic pull, he walked up to one of the plastic containers, his expression hardening. Setting his hands on the edges of the crate, he glared at it as if he could incinerate it with the force of his eyes alone.

"Kaige," I said softly, "you can go now too. Gideon and I can finish going through the inventory."

He shook his head and straightened up again with a grimace. "I'm fine. I just hate that we have to be a part of this twisted system that's hurting so many people. Now *we're* the ones handing out Glory, getting the junkies even more hooked."

"It was the best option we had in the moment," I pointed out.

"Maybe. I wish we could have found some other way, any way except for this." The tendons on his neck flexed as he began to pace the room, his fists clenched at his sides. "You didn't see them that day, Mercy. Willing to break their own city just to get a hit. Those people… they're sick. And instead of helping them, we're only making the situation worse."

I dragged in a breath, my chest tightening. "I don't like it either. And I get why you're upset. Just remember that it's only for a few more days until we've gotten rid of the Storm, and then we can destroy any Glory that's left in the county. We'll support the people already hooked on it any way we can."

"Wylder and Rowan have already been working on that," Gideon piped up. "They were encouraging people to take lower doses than the Storm's men suggested so they'll start to wean off. I mean, we didn't say that's why, but it'll work the same way, and the people just think they're getting to stretch their supply longer. They didn't seem to notice any difference in the effect, so they were happy to go along with it."

"Well, that's something," Kaige grumbled, but he didn't stop pacing. "We should have figured out how to crush Xavier and all the rest of those Storm assholes by now. We only have a few days left. I just want to march right out of here and smash them all to pieces." He took a swing at the empty air.

"You'll get your chance to smash them," I promised, walking over to him. He came to a halt and let me wrap my arms around him, hugging him. As I bobbed up on my toes to embrace him more tightly, the wound on my thigh protested, but the pain was dulled by the medications Frank had sent over.

Their numbing effect didn't do anything to mute the thump of my pulse as Kaige stroked his broad hand down my back. He sighed and leaned into my arms, and an ache filled my chest.

Under his tough shell, Kaige had such a soft heart. He cared about the people not just in the Nobles but all of Paradise City and the Bend, and he wanted to do right by them. Maybe he didn't always show it in the most graceful of ways, but that was just who he was. I wouldn't have asked him to be any different.

I pulled back to look up into his warm brown eyes. His musky scent with its gingery bite engulfed my senses, and I closed my eyes to inhale it deeply.

I'd waited too long to confess my feelings to Rowan, and maybe I'd never get to now. I didn't want to lose my chance with Kaige too.

"What?" he asked in his sexy baritone voice, as if he sensed I was working up to something. His hands slid down to the small of my back, his palms rubbing soft circles there.

There was no backing down now, not from our war and not from the feelings I'd never expected to grip me so powerfully.

"I love you, Kaige," I said.

Kaige's eyes widened, shock rippling through him. I winced inwardly with a pinch of regret. I'd said it totally out of the blue, and it probably wasn't at all what he wanted to be thinking about right now. More words tumbled out of me as his grip on me loosened. "You don't have to say anything right away. I don't expect you to—"

"I love you too," he said.

I stopped talking, not sure I'd heard him correctly. "You what?"

He grinned. "I love you, Mercy. Would have said it a lot sooner if I hadn't been worried you'd sock me in the face."

A giddy feeling rose in my stomach, and I couldn't hold back a giggle. "Really?"

"You mean it hasn't been obvious?"

I swatted him. "As far as I can tell, you go around charming the pants off all the ladies you meet. How was I supposed to know I'm so special?"

He pointed at himself. "What can I say? This thing, it's a total machine. You can never turn it off." Then he sobered a little. "It's always been different with you. Felt like more with you from the very beginning. I'm all yours now, Mercy. Anyone else who wanted a piece of me is shit out of luck."

I beamed back at him. "Mittens might have a few things to say about that."

"Any other woman," he amended with a wink. "Cats are another story."

Kaige was back to his former flirty self. I was glad that I'd at least momentarily managed to distract him from his darker thoughts.

His hands circled my waist, and I looped my arms around his shoulders. As soon as I did, he jerked me to him so that the length of our bodies fused together. I could feel him harden almost instantaneously against my belly. "Now that we've gotten that all straightened out, maybe we should celebrate. We're finally alone."

He swiveled his hips, and I swallowed a gasp at the press of his cock. My eyes flicked to Gideon, who was standing near the door, tablet clutched in his hands, looking uncertain but not uncomfortable.

"We're not *completely* alone," I pointed out.

Kaige followed my gaze. He paused for a second as if debating with himself and then shot a grin at his friend. "Is that a problem? It wasn't before." Heat flared in his eyes, and I knew he was thinking back to when all five of us had collided in spectacular fashion in the back of Gideon's van. "Besides I think it's a lot more fun for you with extra company, isn't it, Mercy? The more the merrier?"

I couldn't deny that. I wet my lips automatically as I nodded. "You won't find me complaining."

Kaige leaned over and caught my bottom lip with his mouth. He sucked on it for a second before pulling me into an open-mouthed kiss. It was messy and hot and made my panties dampen in an instant. His insistent cock resting against my hip only urged on the desire surging through me.

Kaige eased back an inch and raised his eyebrows at Gideon. "Care to join us?"

Gideon shifted on his feet, and then a sly smile crossed his lips. The same kind of spark came into his cool eyes as when he'd been hit by one of his brilliant inspirations. Without a word, he yanked the garage door closed, set his tablet down on the nearest crate and walked over to us. He slid his fingers along my jaw and tugged my face around so he could claim a kiss.

Kaige swore under his breath, sounding so turned on it only made me wetter. I kissed Gideon hard, drawing his tongue into my mouth, swaying as Kaige's hands traveled over my body. Gideon caressed me too, cupping one hand over my breast and squeezing with just the right force to bring a moan to my lips.

Maybe we'd all needed this—a moment to let go, to get caught up in emotions we hadn't been able to spare much time for in the past few days. To celebrate the joys we had.

When Gideon released my mouth, Kaige dove in again. His tongue tangled with mine. He grasped my hips and hefted me into the air, and all of a sudden I was flying—until he set me on top of one of the crates.

I hooked my knees around his thighs instinctively, grateful to have my weight off my wounded leg. He leaned even closer, capturing my lips again. As he fucked my mouth with his tongue, Gideon clambered onto the crate and sank down behind me. He teased his hands around my chest to play with both of my breasts, pinching and tugging the hardening nubs until I whimpered with need. The heat from both men's bodies engulfed me with a heady sensation.

I trailed one hand down Gideon's arm encouragingly while I tilted my head into Kaige's kiss. Gideon nudged the hair away from my shoulder and pressed small kisses to my neck along the line of my shirt collar. His lip ring brushed my skin. I broke from Kaige's mouth to tip my head against the man behind me, sinking into his skillful touch.

Kaige took the opportunity to unzip my jeans and yank them off my legs, careful around the bandage. I groped for his shirt and tugged it up, and he tossed it aside without a second's hesitation. His eyes devoured me and Gideon's hands on me. "So fucking sexy."

Gideon took that remark as his cue to peel my shirt off me. Kaige moved in to make short work of my bra. He ducked his head and lapped my nipple into his scorching mouth, and I growled in encouragement as I arched to meet him.

We continued to make out like that, me pressed between their taut bodies, their hands and mouths roaming over every inch of my uncovered skin. Finally, Kaige's fingers slipped between my thighs. He rubbed up and down my sopping wet slit before flicking his finger against the overly sensitive nub above it.

At my back, Gideon continued to explore my body, laying kisses where he knew I liked it the most. He sucked on the curve of my neck and squeezed my breasts before gliding his fingers down to spread my thighs to accommodate Kaige. His own rigid cock bumped against my back.

Kaige watched us while stroking his cock, which seemed to grow impossibly harder. While Gideon slipped his finger inside my pussy, Kaige tore open a foil packet and rolled the condom over him.

Gideon didn't move away. Instead, he opened my pussy lips wide for Kaige who in turn started to rub his cock up and down the length of my slit. I moaned at the feel of him.

"Take my cock, Mercy," he groaned, and buried himself inside me in one quick jerk. My eyes widened, and I had to grip his shoulder tight so I didn't slip off the crate. My body felt like putty.

Kaige adjusted my legs around him before he slipped out, and then thrust right back in, his strokes shallow and fast at first. I cried out at the overwhelming surge of pleasure and sagged heavily against Gideon, who was panting at my ear. He and Kaige worked together with their fingers and cock respectively, stroking every ounce of pleasure my body was capable of out of me. I closed my eyes as the wave of bliss rose.

It wasn't quite enough. I groped behind me and curled my hand around Gideon's cock through his slacks. It twitched at the contact. He fumbled open his fly, and I delved inside his boxers to grip him skin to skin. As I ran my fingers along his stiff length, he groaned.

Kaige let out an animalistic grunt, his thrusts becoming erratic. I bit my lip as he hit a spot so good that my eyes almost rolled inside my head.

I stroked Gideon faster, determined to bring him with us, rubbing the sensitive tip of his cock before sliding all the way to the base and squeezing his balls. My breasts bounced in front of me as Kaige fucked me harder. Gideon reached around and kneaded them roughly, his breath ragged against my neck.

I crested the peak in one swift surge and moaned as my pussy walls began to convulse around Kaige's cock. A cry broke from my mouth, and at the same time Gideon's cum shot across my arm. Kaige came with a shout.

Kaige wrapped his arms around me while I settled into Gideon's lap. I trailed my fingers down his face and over Gideon's arm, spent and sated. We shared a private smile between the three of us.

I wanted to believe that no matter how many enemies we faced, no one could take this amazing connection away from us. But even with the afterglow rippling through me, my mind tripped back to the vision of Rowan in the hospital bed. The thought of losing Kaige, Gideon, or Wylder as well sent a dagger into my chest.

And we were running out of time before all our lives were forfeit.

19

Mercy

"AND THAT'S HOW I TRIPPED DOWN THE ROOF AND survived the fall," Kaige said. The dining room burst into laughter. I stood leaning against the door frame as I watched the Noble and Claws men bond and talk. The guys had swung by the Katz house this morning to discuss strategy, and somehow it'd turned into storytelling time while Jenner had whipped up a big breakfast for everybody.

"Yo, that's sick, man," Sam said with a shake of his head. "Was that part of your initiation?"

"Yep," Kaige said. "We all had to go through the trials. They don't make any exceptions, not even for Rowan. He saved Wylder's life when we were in school—took a knife to his chest and everything."

My smile faded. We still hadn't gotten any news from the hospital other than they were continuing to monitor Rowan's situation. He hadn't woken up yet. The waiting was killing me.

"He was always loyal," Gideon said quietly, catching my eye.

"And he always will be," I said. "Until the end, which hasn't happened yet."

Wylder's phone pinged with an alert. He checked his phone and tensed up, springing to his feet. "We've got to go."

I stood up too. "What's wrong?"

"Beckett just reached out. He says he found out his father's men are going after the waterfront property—they're planning on ruining the construction that's happened so far. They're already on their way."

"Shit." Even I knew how much that waterfront development mattered to Ezra. If the Storm's people succeeded in tearing down all the progress he'd made there...

I motioned to the Claws men around me as Kaige and Gideon leapt up. "We're going to need everyone who isn't on guard duty or injured with us to take them down. Are you with me?"

Jenner nodded without hesitation. "We've got your back. Come on, men."

"Grab all the weapons you can get your hands on," I ordered. "We won't have much time to strategize once we get there, but our primary objective will be to hold them off the property."

I didn't wait for them, hurrying ahead to catch up with Wylder, who'd already gotten Ezra on the line.

"Dad," he said as he yanked the front door open, putting the phone on speaker so he had more use of his hands. "We need our men in the Bend."

"What's going on?" Ezra said almost testily on the other side.

"Xavier and his men are gunning for the waterfront property. They want to blow it all up."

Ezra swore under his breath. His previous apathy disappeared, replaced by urgency. "I'm sending all the men not already needed in the city over. You'll have the full Noble force at your disposal."

Wylder smiled tightly. "I appreciate that."

"I want the property secured," Ezra said. "Nothing less."

"Of course, Dad," Wylder said in a taut voice. "You don't have to worry about it."

"And I intend to monitor everything that is happening there. Give the phone to Gideon."

Wylder seemed to debate on his decision before he turned off the speaker and handed his phone to Gideon, who looked surprised.

"Yes, Ezra?" Gideon said as we hustled toward the car that was parked outside the house. While Wylder took the driver seat, I slid in next to him, with Gideon and Kaige jumping into the back. Behind us, the rest of the Claws were already making their way out of the house, hollering and shouting, pumping themselves up for the big fight.

Wylder pulled away from the curb and tore off toward the river. My stomach tied itself into a knot. We'd been planning on getting in another hit against the Storm this morning as soon as we'd finished breakfast, hitting them while they were down. Our men had been out tackling any smaller groups they came across all night. Xavier must have rallied even faster than we'd counted on. Did he have any idea about the timeline we were up against?

Gideon made agreeable noises a couple of times while Ezra must have spoken. By the time the call ended, he was frowning.

"What did he want?" Wylder said, checking from the rearview mirror.

"He asked me to see if I can remotely fix the CCTV connection on the property. It went down when the cops marched in there the other day, and with everything else going on, no one got around to fixing it."

"Can you?" Kaige asked.

Gideon shrugged. "I mean, I can try, and maybe it'd be a good thing. Ezra needs to see first-hand how bad things are out here."

Wylder snorted loudly. "He doesn't care about that—or us, for that matter. He'll lose a ton of money if the existing construction is demolished, and it'll look bad to the investors. The only things Ezra Noble protects are his wealth and his reputation. He probably just wants to ensure that his development doesn't come to any harm."

"Yeah, no wonder he's sending in the entire Noble troop," I said, making a face. "He seemed awfully obliging all of a sudden."

"Exactly." Wylder's grip on the steering wheel tightened. "Because God forbid anything happens to his *property*."

I stayed silent. Wylder was right. Ezra cared more about the condos he was building than his own son's well-being.

"We need to turn this around," Wylder added. "Maybe with a whole army of Nobles and the Claws, we can come down on the Storm so hard he'll roll over. I want to see that Xavier psycho dead, whatever we do."

I nodded, my body buzzing with anticipation. We had to strike some kind of fatal blow, and soon. We had less than two days left.

I spotted the looming tower of the half-constructed project and the metal bars of the crane poised next to it. The rising sun blazed through the steel girders. The waterfront project was easily the tallest building in all of the Bend, surrounded by tall construction walls that the Nobles had reinforced after the Storm's people had broken in before to frame them for dealing Glory.

We weren't alone. Up ahead, engines roared closer as the Noble forces Ezra had called on converged with us. The Claws men behind us honked their horns.

But as we came around the last corner, a swarm of other cars racing our way came into view down the road. "Fuck," Wylder said, stomping on the gas. "They're practically here already."

He ripped across the asphalt and screeched to a halt outside the gates to the construction site. The other vehicles with us, Nobles and Claws alike, parked haphazardly around us. But our men had only just started pouring out of the vehicles, more still arriving, when the Storm force sped to meet us from the other direction.

A swarm of Storm men streamed out, already taking shots at us. We ducked behind the cars. I pulled my pistol from the back of my jeans and curled my fingers around the grip and the trigger.

Bullets were flying freely on both sides, making the air thunder and my eardrums ring. I eased up in time to fire at a few Storm men who'd made a run for the gate. They probably figured that once they'd gotten inside, they could pick us off from over the fence.

One of my shots caught a guy in the shoulder. Wylder took another down with a bullet in the side of his head. There was no time to think, only to react.

More men on the Storm side fell, but I saw a few of the Nobles and Claws men stagger and slump too. Anguish squeezed around my heart. We were fighting and some of us dying to protect the only home we'd ever had. What fucking right did the Storm have to come in and try to wrench it away from us? Wasn't his empire big enough already?

"Head around the back," Wylder shouted to a new contingent of

Noble men who couldn't reach us through the fray. "Make sure they don't sneak around that way!"

A few cars tore off around the side of the development. Others parked with the men leaping out, guns already in their hands. They blasted away at the Storm forces.

The front line of the Storm's men pulled back to a farther row of cars. We were starting to drive them off. Triumph surged up inside me.

They'd underestimated us yet again. We were so much stronger than that rich bastard in his mansion had ever imagined.

But the Storm's people had other tricks up their sleeve. I spotted Xavier poised in the back of a pick-up truck, wavering and hollering at the men around him. I couldn't make out what he was saying amid the rattle of gunfire, but his intention became clear soon enough.

"They've got fucking TNT," Kaige bellowed, his lips pulling back in a snarl. "They're going to try to blast right through the wall—or us—like they were going to at the store yesterday."

"Don't let them get close to the wall!" I cried out, hoping that enough of our people would hear me. I shot at the men carrying the explosives, catching one in the chest. He collapsed. Another dashed in to pick up his cargo, but a renewed hail of bullets from our side caught him too.

"That's right!" Wylder shouted. "Push them back! Push them right out of our county."

Just as hope started to unfurl in my chest, at least a dozen more cars roared into view to join the Storm's forces. I swore under my breath and reloaded my gun. "We've got even more to deal with."

Wylder's face hardened, but he kept his jaw firm. "We've still got enough manpower to hold them off. We're taking down more of them than they are of us."

That wasn't necessarily going to be true for long. With the new men joining the Storm's crowd, a different sort of gunfire reverberated in the street. A few of them held machine guns. They pelted our front lines, and several more figures on our side crumpled with blood spurting from their wounds.

"Take cover but keep shooting as much as you can," Wylder ordered, pitching his voice to carry through the chaos. "Keep protecting the wall!"

The air had gotten thick with the stink of hot metal and spilled blood. My gut churned. My ears must have been numbing with the constant barrage of noise, because it didn't sound so loud anymore. I shifted my weight to get a better angle to aim from and hissed as pain lanced through my wounded thigh.

These fuckers were responsible for that too. We'd come here to win, and that was what we'd do.

I managed to drop another man hauling explosives before he got close to the fence. Kaige was yelling something I couldn't even make out and shooting wildly. The Storm's people weren't pulling back any farther, but they hadn't made any progress pushing *us* back either. We were holding them off, by however small a margin.

All of a sudden, a strange movement caught my attention from the corner of my eye. My head jerked around in time to see a bunch of the Noble men who'd been fighting with us hurrying to the cars farthest from the fight.

"Where the fuck are you going?" Wylder yelled after them, his eyes furious. "You're needed here!"

Gideon jabbed at his tablet where he'd crouched next to the car, his gun beside him. "I can't see anything that could explain it."

The men didn't answer Wylder, didn't even look back. They dove into the cars, and five vehicles peeled away from the fray, leaving us that much more outnumbered. A chill washed through me. What the hell was going on? Why would they just *leave*?

I didn't have time to wonder for very long. Xavier let out a triumphant roar, and the Storm's men pressed in on us. I glanced at Wylder and saw the same flash of panic in his eyes that I was feeling.

We were absolutely fucked.

20

Mercy

Xavier watched the retreating cars and threw back his head with a raucous laugh that echoed through the streets. "Sniveling cowards," he roared, and swept his arm to urge his men onward in the battle. "Kill them all except the girl. She's mine."

"Not if I have anything to say about that," Kervos announced from behind the car next to ours. He raised his gun just as another wave of gunfire swept over us—and a bullet caught him between the eyes. He collapsed on the ground with a red blotch expanding over his forehead.

My mind froze, my thoughts seeming to stutter. Kervos's eyes stared at the sky, his body totally limp. Just like that, he was gone.

The first man who'd really supported my bid to lead the Claws was dead.

And not just him. Even as we fired back as well as we could, Nobles and Claws were dropping all through the maze of cars. I saw Sam's friend who'd helped us move yesterday's cargo fall, and then one of the men who'd been laughing at Kaige's story in the dining room just an hour ago. My vision swam, my body wobbling with a momentary dizziness.

Wylder yanked me down below the level of the car just as a bullet whizzed by where the top of my head had been. "What the hell are you doing?" he said, but he sounded more panicked than angry. "You're going to get killed."

Like everyone else was. I shook myself, willing my mind to focus. Forcing my gaze away from Kervos's lifeless body.

Too many men were dead—good men. And I didn't even have time to mourn them.

I had to make sure the ones still living stayed that way. That was my job as their queen. I hadn't come here to embark on a suicide mission.

The words stuck in my throat before I could propel them out. This wasn't how I'd wanted the battle to end. "We'll be slaughtered if we keep fighting," I said. "We have to get out of here, regroup, or the war ends here. With the Storm winning."

Wylder's jaw tightened, but after a moment, he nodded. "Damn it," he spat out, and then waved to the nearest men. "Pass on the word. We're cutting our losses and moving out. Get to whatever cars aren't boxed in and head back to the mansion—or Claws to their own headquarters. Keep firing at the Storm's forces to cover each other, but getting out of here alive is all that matters now."

"Are you sure, Mercy?" Jenner called over from a few cars away, but I saw his gaze catch on Kervos's body. Horror flashed across his face.

"We have to live to fight again another day," I said.

We took off through the maze of cars, bobbing up just long enough to fire at the Storm's men as well as we could. They were pushing toward the wall now. I didn't realize they'd already gotten some of their explosives there until the first *boom* echoed through the air.

The impact of the explosion shook the ground beneath our feet and threw me forward. I tried to twist myself into a flip to land more steadily, but my wounded thigh gave out. Instead I crashed to the ground, scraping my chin on the rough concrete.

Kaige grabbed my shoulder, hefting me up. "I'm fine, I'm fine," I insisted, but he stayed right beside me as we took off running again, Wylder close at my other side, Gideon right behind us.

I didn't even bother trying to shoot anymore. All that mattered was getting to the cars at the edge of the mess. My legs pumped under me, my teeth gritting at the pain searing from my wound. That doctor would have been *really* pissed if he'd known he was releasing me to get into this kind of trouble right after.

The Claws and Nobles who'd already been near the fringes made it to the outer cars first. A few tore off down the street in the vehicles they managed to grab. Others fell under the next barrage of bullets. We paused, panting, just a few car lengths from a Ford we could grab—as long as the driver had left the keys in it.

Just as we braced to make a final run for it, a furious bellow split through the air from behind us. The gunfire went momentarily quiet. I craned my neck around to see Xavier still poised on the pickup truck, his face now ruddy with rage as if *he* had any reason to be upset with how the tide had turned.

"You fucking cowards," he bellowed after us, spit flying from his mouth so wildly I could see it even at a distance. "Playing stupid fucking tricks. You'll find out what thieves get. I'm going to make you pay even more than I was already planning. No one will even be able to recognize you when we're through."

"What is he talking about?" I whispered to Wylder, who shook his head, looking totally bewildered.

We couldn't exactly ask the lunatic. At his urging, the Storm men charged straight at the rest of us, firing off whatever shots they could take as they closed in on our remaining forces. A couple of them leapt onto the hood of a car and mowed down three Nobles who'd just reached an accessible car.

Wylder grimaced and shot both of the assholes down with a few squeezes of his trigger. More cars were peeling away from the mass. We sprinted toward the Ford, my breath rasping in my throat. Gideon was starting to wheeze.

Just as we came up on the car, Jenner leaned over the back of the one next to it and spewed bullets from a rifle at the advancing Storm men. He bought us just enough time to dive into the vehicle, Kaige taking the wheel. He twisted the key that'd been left there, its original driver probably having fallen nearby assuming he'd be coming right back to it, and rammed his foot down on the gas.

I stayed crouched in the back seat next to Gideon as the car swung around and raced away from the waterfront property. I squeezed his arm in a soothing rhythm, and his breaths started to even out. He raised his head, meeting my eyes with a haunted look in his. "We lost too many men out there."

I choked up abruptly. "I know." I couldn't even say yet how many we'd lost, how many the Storm's people had killed that I hadn't even seen.

I sat up slowly, brushing shards of glass and bits of gravel from my clothes. My heart was still thundering, but we'd left the horrific scene behind. The street we were racing down now looked almost peaceful in the mid-morning light. I sputtered out something halfway between a laugh and a sob.

Gideon eased upright too, his gaze dropping to my leg. He sucked in a breath. "Mercy, you're bleeding."

I glanced down. Blood was seeping through my jeans from where I must have reopened the wound on my thigh. That was no surprise, considering the hell I'd just put it through.

"We need to rebandage Mercy's leg," Gideon insisted.

"Let's get the fuck away from those maniacs first," Kaige retorted. "Or we're going to need a lot more bandages."

I grimaced. "I'll be all right. I've already survived this wound once. I just—I need to put pressure on it."

I fumbled for something to use to staunch the bleeding, and Gideon whipped his shirt off as quickly as if he gave it up for use as a bandage every day. I offered him a grateful smile and balled it in my hand before pressing it hard against the wound.

"I don't suppose any of you have a clue what Xavier was ranting about?" Wylder said. "What trick did he think we played? How were we being thieves?"

I bit my lip. "I mean, obviously we've stolen Glory and weapons from the Storm in the past. But he seemed to get upset all of a sudden, not like he was still fuming about stuff that'd happened before."

"Maybe he was pissed off that we were... stealing his opportunity to take the waterfront property without a big mess?" Kaige said doubtfully.

Gideon shot the big guy a baleful look. "Somehow I don't think it's that. He sounded *very* upset. I saw one of his men talking on a phone and then passing a message on to him right before he started ranting."

He squirmed around, and I realized he'd managed to drag his tablet all the way to the car with him. It figured. "Let me see if I can find out anything," he muttered, waking up the screen with a tap.

An uncomfortable sensation coiled around my gut. "You don't think his outburst has anything to do with the Nobles who up and left out of the blue, do you? We don't know what was going on with them either."

Wylder frowned. "They're definitely going to be taken to task for fleeing their duty, you can count on that."

My voice hardened. "People *died* because of them." Images of the crumpled bodies rose up in my mind, Kervos at the forefront. I swallowed hard. I'd pulled him and the other Claws into this war, and I hadn't been able to get them through it. I hadn't even been able to salvage his body. Guilt snaked around my lungs, making it hard to breathe.

Wylder leaned past the passenger seat. "Mercy, you can't blame yourself. If anything, you should blame me. It was my men who screwed us over. And you've got to know that every man who was out there today was aware of the danger of the situation—of this whole life. They wouldn't have been in it if they hadn't come to terms with that."

"Still..."

Gideon cleared his throat, his hands tightening where he was gripping the tablet. He glanced at Wylder. "It isn't your fault either."

Wylder's eyebrows drew together. "What do you mean?"

"I think I know what happened. I'm seeing a new report from our typical communication channels that the Nobles captured a major storage facility in the Bend, one that belonged to the Storm—one of the places we were considering attacking earlier. It's where they've been keeping their supply of Glory once it's transported into the county."

Kaige's head jerked around, and he nearly drove us into a mailbox. "Say *what*?"

"I have to guess that's where the Nobles who took off on us went," Gideon said. "There wouldn't have been enough men available to take down the guards protecting it otherwise."

"Why would they up and do that of their own..." I trailed off before I finished the question, because I already knew the answer. The mission hadn't been of their own accord. My stomach twisted.

"My dad ordered them to," Wylder said before I had to, his gaze darkening even more than before. "That's got to be it. They wouldn't have listened to anyone but him after I'd already given *my* orders. *Fuck.*" He slammed his fist into the dashboard. "No wonder he sent all our troops to the Bend. He probably never intended to help us. He wanted us as bait against Xavier to distract him and most of the Storm's people while he took what he wanted."

"That's why he told me to make sure the cameras were set up. He wanted eyes on each one of us, Xavier included, so he knew just exactly when they would have to leave." Gideon worried at his lip ring. "Everything makes sense now."

"But why the hell would Ezra want to take the Glory?" Kaige demanded, his voice raw. "What the fuck was he thinking?"

"It could be just to stop the Storm from continuing to use it," I said tentatively.

Wylder met my gaze. "Do you really think he'd go to all that trouble and sacrifice the waterfront property if he didn't believe he was getting his hands on an even bigger prize? He's seen the power that drug has over people, how much they're willing to do for a hit of it."

A shiver ran through me. Yes, that did sound exactly like Ezra. For Wylder's sake, I had to say, "We won't know for sure until we talk to him."

Wylder sank back into his seat. His voice came out flat. "We do know one thing: He fucked us over by not informing us about his second, secret mission. He never intended to save the waterfront property. It—we—were only a decoy. He purposefully sabotaged us and left us for dead."

21

Wylder

I BURST THROUGH THE FRONT DOORS OF MY HOUSE. A couple of guards stared, uneasiness flickering across their faces, as I strode through the foyer with Mercy, Kaige, and Gideon at my heels.

I didn't say a word to the Noble underlings, just stalked up the stairs and onward into the hall that led to Dad's office. I hadn't paused for even a second since Kaige had parked outside the mansion. Fury burned in my chest and unfurled through my limbs, making my hands flex and clench with the urge to find something to punch.

The sight of the study door up ahead cooled my rage just a little. I had to get my temper under control to have this conversation, or Dad would just brush me off. I needed to be clear and incisive, not ranting and raving.

He wasn't getting away with his betrayal.

I stopped and dragged air into my lungs. Then I glanced back at my woman and my friends. "I think I'd better talk to my father alone."

Mercy frowned. "Are you sure that's a good idea? We know what he's capable of."

Kaige nodded, cracking his knuckles. "We'll back you up every step of the way."

I shook my head. "I'll get the most honest answers out of him if it's just family. I don't want him focused on anything but what I'm saying to him. You don't need to worry—I can handle it."

"We'll be right outside," Gideon said, quiet but unshakeable. He wasn't going to question my competence by outright saying it, but the implication was clear: if I *did* happen to need them, all I'd have to do was shout.

If this situation came to that... I didn't even want to think about it. I wished I didn't have to wrap my head around the things my father had already done in the past few hours.

Keeping an iron grip on my temper, I walked the rest of the way to the study and grasped the doorknob. I half-expected it to be locked, but it twisted easily in my hand. I marched in without preamble and kicked it shut behind me.

Dad was sitting behind his desk, his expression its typical impenetrable mask. "I expect a knock rather than you barging right in," he said, as if this was the time to be chiding me like a toddler.

I bit back half a dozen snarky retorts that leapt to my tongue and strode up to the opposite side of his desk. I braced my hands against the top, leaning slightly forward, and met Dad's eyes with a gaze I kept as firm and steady as my voice.

"You undermined our operation at the waterfront property. You ordered a bunch of the men who were supposed to be supporting us in defending it to leave—so they could steal the Storm's supply of Glory while his men were distracted."

Dad gazed back at me, looking so unruffled—almost bored—that it took all my self-control not to lunge right across the desk and sock him in the nose. "I'm glad that you were able to put the pieces together so quickly," he said. "Maybe that mind of yours hasn't gotten so soft after all. It was a perfect plan, as evidenced by the fact that it went off without a hitch."

A perfect plan? I couldn't stop a little venom from creeping into my tone. "Do you have any idea how many of our men *died* because of that plan? We were holding the Storm's forces off until we lost so much support. We could *all* have been slaughtered."

Had Dad hoped that even more of us would die? The thought struck me with a chill that cut through my anger. Maybe he'd wanted Xavier to mow me down like so many of the Noble and Claws men who'd fallen today. One disobedient heir off his plate.

Dad simply shrugged. "Our men know the risks of our line of work. Sacrifices must be made for the greater good."

Funny how those sacrifices had all been by the men he hadn't trusted enough to call on for his secret operation—the ones he must have known would be more inclined to stick with me. He'd played a move that would secure his goals and also eliminate underlings he thought could become a future problem without getting his own hands the slightest bit dirty.

But I still didn't understand what those goals were. I gritted my teeth. "The greater good? What about the waterfront property you've invested so much money and time in? We had to pull back—we were going to lose it anyway. Lord only knows what Xavier and the others have done to the site now."

Dad chuckled, a low humorous sound. "Well, I, for one, hope they took as much aggression as they pleased out on it. It'll be easier to claim insurance if I can easily prove that the damage was maliciously caused by an outside source."

I still couldn't wrap my head around what he was saying. "You had all these plans for it—you put so much effort into getting the contract—"

Dad waved aside my protest. "Plans change. We have to think on our feet and adapt to changing circumstances. Ever since the drug distribution incident, that property has become too much of a hassle to deal with. It's much more to our benefit to cut our losses and focus on a new business venture."

I stared at the face of the man I had once thought held absolute power in Paradise Bend. I knew that wasn't the truth anymore. He knew it too, and maybe that was why he was going off the rails like this.

"A new business venture," I repeated slowly. Something that to him was worth even more than the waterfront property. All the unpleasant suspicions that'd entered my head when Gideon had announced what he'd discovered came rushing back to the front of my mind. "Tell me you're not going to start selling Glory."

Dad gave me a thin smile. "Why shouldn't I? You've seen how avidly the people of the county are responding to it. We certainly couldn't leave it in the Storm's hands with the power it was giving his people."

"One warehouse full isn't going to last all that long."

"Which is why it's a good thing my men were also able to find information about the Storm's suppliers in that warehouse. We can set up our own distribution channels and take over the entire market. Even expand it farther abroad."

My mouth tasted as if it was full of ash. Images flashed through my mind of the desperate junkies smashing storefronts along the edge of the city, of the addicts wandering in a daze around the waterfront property when the Storm's men had been handing out samples there.

Dad wanted to keep those people in that fucked-up state? To make a whole county full of druggies who'd do anything for their next hit?

Come to think of it, that outcome might suit his power fantasies just fine. Junkies were easy to control, which was exactly why Xavier must have taken that route. But my father used to care about more than just holding all the cards. Staring at him with a pit opening in the bottom of my stomach, I thought I might have an inkling how Beckett felt about *his* dad.

The kid believed it might not be too late to get the Storm back on the right track. I wasn't so sure with Ezra Noble, considering how far gone he already appeared to be.

"This doesn't make any sense," I said. "Didn't you want to branch out into more legitimate business opportunities, not ones that are totally illegal? You've always said it's better not to get too involved in the drug trade specifically because of how messy it is. And yeah, I've seen the effect Glory has—it's fucking messy, all right."

An unsettling glint came into Dad's eyes. "I avoided this type of business because I hadn't found a drug that made it worthwhile. Amphetamines, meth, and the rest, they don't hold a candle to where Glory could take us."

He got up from behind his desk and walked over to the window, gazing out it over the lawn. "The world is a boundless well of possibilities, Wylder. I let my faith in that fact get shaken for a little while, but now I'm taking hold of the future of the Nobles with both hands. The Storm has barely gotten started with Glory, from what I understand. The distribution here was only a test run. I can take it to the heights it deserves and show *everyone* what the Nobles are capable of."

"This is crazy," I burst out, unable to hold in my frustration. "We've still got a war on our hands. We won't be around to sell even a gram of Glory to anyone if we don't focus on tackling the Storm. If you'd actually backed me up today, maybe we'd have turned the tables on them and ended this. Now we're down dozens of men and running out of time and options."

Dad swiveled on his heel, his tone going icy. "I think you're forgetting that I'm still in charge, *son*." He stressed the last word, but it sounded hollow to me. "You follow my orders, not the other way around. I'll handle my business as I see fit, and you can work on seeing through the agreement *you* made with this Long Night person. If you can't manage that—if you can't accept that I know what's best for our organization—then perhaps I'll have to do some clearing of the slate myself."

Those last words came out razor-sharp. The threat was so clear I had to restrain a wince.

This was what our simmering feud had come to. He was outright stating that he'd kill me if I kept disagreeing with him—definitely if I got in his way. While he got our men massacred and ignored the most pressing problem looming over us as if it'd go away if he pretended it out of existence hard enough with his dreams of future triumphs.

He was going to get all of us killed, even himself, and there was nothing I could say that would accomplish anything other than earning me a bullet in my heart. So I'd better get back to the real work rather than wasting my remaining hours here.

"Thank you for your time, Dad," I said. Without another word, I simply walked out of the office.

Mercy straightened up from where she'd been leaning against the wall. Gideon and Kaige raised their heads too, all waiting for me like they'd promised. Their gazes asked a question I didn't know how to answer.

If I was ever going to become the leader the Nobles needed, I was going to have to go through Dad. He couldn't have made it clearer that he was never going to step aside of his own accord.

I hadn't wanted to come to blows with him, but if that was the only way to set things right... I'd do what I had to do to maintain the Nobles' legacy and the security of Paradise Bend.

But for now, before I could even think about that problem any deeper, we had a deal to fulfill and a psychotic maniac to crush.

"Let's go to my office," I said. "We've got a war to win."

22

Mercy

When Wylder had finished filling us in on his conversation with his father, we all sat for a moment in shocked silence. Beyond the window, evening was rapidly falling, turning the sky an ominous shade of red.

Anthea, who'd joined us on our way over to Gideon's office, shook her head, her mouth twisting. "I'm sorry. I wish I could have helped, but I had no idea what my brother was planning."

"It's not your fault," I said. "Ezra was obviously keeping the whole thing as quiet as possible."

Wylder grimaced. "The fact is that Dad screwed us over, and he feels zero guilt about it. In fact, he's practically gloating about his new plans."

Kaige was scowling. "His new plans are shit. I thought the Nobles had a policy to keep a ten feet pole between us and drug dealing."

"We did," Wylder said. "And I'd have kept to that policy if it were up to me. But as long as he's still around, Dad's the one calling the shots."

"Fuck." Kaige slammed his fist into his other palm hard enough to leave a red mark on the skin. "This isn't what I signed up for. I don't want anything to do with spreading that crap around the city."

Wylder's voice turned deadly firm, his face hardening like I hadn't seen it since he first came out of his father's study. "You won't have to. I'm not going to let it come to that. But we've barely got a day left in our deal with the Long Night. We can't think about anything except tackling the Storm for the next twenty-four hours."

Anthea touched his shoulder lightly, regret still marked on her face. Her voice came out quiet but firm. "If I don't get another chance to say it before it matters—just know that I understand that you'll have to do whatever you have to do."

Wylder glanced at his aunt and nodded, a tiny bit of the tension seeping out of his stance. The coolness of her tone sent an uneasy quiver down the center of me. I didn't want to examine what she might mean too closely.

The Noble heir was right. We had to focus on the Storm for now.

"Could Ezra's takeover of the Glory distribution work in our favor there?" I asked. "That's how the Storm was funding a lot of his operations, wasn't it? Grabbing it out from under him has to be a major blow. Xavier was obviously furious about it." The thought of his raging face sent a shiver down my spine. I'd seen him purposefully menacing and hostile, but I wasn't sure I'd ever witnessed so much uncontrolled fury from the psycho.

"Not enough to get him to leave town," Anthea said. "We've been getting reports of the Storm's men still roaming all over. I'm not sure they're even finished demolishing the waterfront property yet." Her nose wrinkled as if she found all this overt aggression distasteful.

"We lost so many people out there," Kaige said. "He's got to know we're having problems too, right?"

Wylder sighed. "It doesn't really matter. Our time is up tomorrow night. We have to assume that the Long Night is prepared to rally his forces and set them on us as soon as the sun goes down. We need to move fast and figure out some final move that'll give us the best possible chance at driving the Storm's people out of Paradise Bend." He turned to Gideon. "I don't suppose there's anything in your surveillance of the city that's given you any brilliant brainstorms?"

Gideon rubbed his mouth, but his hand didn't hide his frown. "I think Xavier is the key. He's the Storm's figurehead here, and if we took him down, then the Storm would have to step up himself—which it sounds like he doesn't want to do—or admit defeat. The trouble is making that happen."

Kaige smacked his hands together. "Let me at him, and I'll take care of it."

Gideon shot his friend a bemused look. "It'd be hard to do that when we can't even be sure of where he is. He left the waterfront development not long after we did. The Storm's men who didn't stay there to work on demolishing it have scattered throughout the city and the Bend, and I'm seeing them constantly on the move. If we can't corner him anywhere, we wouldn't have a hope in hell."

I worried at my lower lip. "He *was* really pissed off about losing the drug stash, so maybe we could use that as bait somehow? Lure him over there thinking he'll have a chance to take it back?"

Wylder shook his head. "I wouldn't be surprised if Dad's given the men he's stationed out there orders to shoot anyone who tries to interfere, even if it's me. He thinks the Glory is his key to taking back the power he thought he already had in the world."

Gideon leaned back in his chair, his forehead furrowing. "It'd be a long-shot, but it's possible we could—"

A knock on the door interrupted him. Wylder sprang up as if he expected it to be his dad, arriving to announce more horrible plans, but he opened it to find one of the Noble underlings who'd stuck with us in the fray earlier today standing outside.

"Mr. Noble," he said with a dip of his head. "That kid who came around the other day is here again—he says he needs to talk to you right away..."

I leapt to my feet too. "Beckett? Of course."

I paused, because technically I wasn't in any position to give orders here in the Noble mansion, but Wylder glanced at me with a small smile and nodded to the guy. "Bring him up. And... don't let word get to my dad about this, if that's possible."

A shadow crossed the guy's expression, and I wondered if he was thinking of how we'd been betrayed by the Nobles loyal to Ezra just hours ago. He inclined his head and hurried off.

Less than a minute later, he returned, ushering Beckett to the doorway. At the sight of the teenager, my heart lurched.

"Are you okay?" I asked automatically.

Beckett stepped into the room with his shoulders slightly slouched. His face had turned paler since we'd last seen him, other than the dark circles under his eyes that suggested he hadn't slept well in days. He was wearing posh clothes like last time, but he hadn't seemed to notice that the collar of his shirt had gone askew. His gaze darted around the room as if he thought we might lunge at him rather than welcome him.

"I—not exactly," he said in a raw voice.

Gideon looked him over and reached for one of his spare mugs. "Coffee?"

The kid couldn't have known how rare it was for the tech genius to offer up his precious brew, but he managed a hesitant smile. "Yeah, that might be good."

Wylder motioned him to the chair the Noble heir had gotten out of and stood over him while Gideon poured the coffee. Kaige studied the Storm's son too. "You look terrible."

"Kaige," I chided.

"It's okay," Beckett muttered, a little of his usual spirit coming back. "Tell it like it is." He accepted the mug from Gideon and chugged about half the liquid in one go, not even wincing at the bitter flavor I could smell from a few feet away.

"Has something else happened at home?" I asked carefully. "It was a big risk coming all the way out here to see us in person, wasn't it?"

"I didn't know—it's hard to tell what's a risk and what's not even in the house these days." He took another gulp and stared morosely into the mug. "Things have gotten worse in all kinds of ways. Dad's on edge—he's freaking out over the trouble he's facing here and looking for people to blame. I don't really feel safe there anymore."

My heart squeezed. He *was* still a kid, really. It wasn't fair that he'd had to grow up so quickly.

Then Beckett raised his head, and I saw the man being forged beneath all the fear and uncertainty he was facing. He wasn't beaten yet.

"I think I know how you can force him to back down. For good. That's why I came here. I want this to finally be over."

Wylder perked up. "You have a plan?"

Beckett nodded, but I could see the hesitation on his face. "You have to really trust me on this one."

Gideon gave him a penetrating look. "More than we did before? What's so special about this time?"

The kid dragged in a breath. "You'd have to confront my dad face to face."

Wylder laughed for a second before it became clear to all of us that Beckett was serious. Wylder's eyes narrowed. "How do you expect that to work? We know how powerful your dad is. We've been having a hard enough time dealing with his underlings here on our home turf. It's not as if he's going to sit down for a negotiation with us."

The corner of Beckett's mouth twitched with a hint of a wry smile. "That isn't exactly how I'm picturing it. I can make it work—I'm your inside edge. I can get you to him in a way that'll put you at an advantage. You just have to promise you won't kill *him*. If you do things my way, he'll listen. It'll work; I'm sure of it."

Hope rang through his voice, but my stomach had clenched. The same resistance showed on the expressions all around me. We'd already come face to face with one member of the Devil's Dozen, and it hadn't been a reassuring encounter. If we followed Beckett's advice, we'd be putting our lives very literally in his hands.

"We need to talk about it," Wylder said. "Just us. This is too big for us to jump right in without a full discussion."

"I understand," Beckett said. "You don't trust me."

"It isn't just about trust. We're the only line between our men and their total destruction. We have to think this through." Wylder turned to his aunt. "Anthea, will you escort him outside? There were leftovers from dinner—Beckett looks like he might be hungry."

Beckett's mouth opened but closed again without a sound. His head drooping, he followed Anthea out into the hall.

As soon as the door shut behind them, Kaige whirled on us. "What the hell is he on? Going right up against the Storm head to head?"

"I don't think he's lying about believing this is our best chance at ending the conflict quickly," Gideon said. "I *hope* he isn't lying, because we need that."

Wylder nodded. "His heart seems to be in the right place, but I don't know how well he's thought through the possible fallout. And what if he's misjudged the situation? If we go into this confrontation, there might be no way to pull out before it's way too late to save ourselves."

"And we're going to be relying on his inside intel to guide us." Gideon made a face at his computer array. "I won't be able to confirm everything he says to be sure the details add up."

"We should at least hear the whole plan, shouldn't we?" I put in. "We can't make any definite decisions until we know exactly what he has in mind. We do need to do *something*, and fast."

Kaige let out a huff. "But what if he's setting us up to get assassinated? That'd be a quick way to end the fighting too."

Wylder raised an eyebrow at him. "Not really, considering it'd only take out us and not my dad, who's proven he's got a stake in this war now too. All the information Beckett has given us so far seems to have been legit. I can't imagine he'd have let us blow up his dad's secret base and undermine his real estate business just to set us up for this. The only person who's actually screwed us so far is Ezra Noble." A hint of bitterness crept into his tone.

"That just proves my point," Kaige said. "You can't trust anybody. How do we know the kid didn't set up the attack on Rowan and Mercy?"

Every part of me balked at that suggestion. I didn't know if Beckett's plan was solid, but I couldn't believe he was trying to get us killed.

"That doesn't make any sense," I said. "We weren't attacked until we got back to the Bend—which is where Xavier's been watching for us and attacking us all along, since before Beckett was ever in the picture. If going to that gala was a setup, then Beckett would have arranged for the ambush to happen before we got a chance to talk to Anderson and mess up the Storm's business arrangements."

Gideon gestured to me. "I agree with Mercy on that point. And from what I've seen in the street cam footage, the ambush appears to have been a spur-of-the-moment attack that was launched because several Storm men happened to be nearby when you were coming into the city. My best guess is that a sentry spotted your car and called them in just a few minutes ahead of time. That doesn't fit with a larger conspiracy."

"Fine," Kaige grumbled. "That still doesn't mean we should go along with some kid's plan."

"Do you have a better one?" Wylder asked dryly. When Kaige just glowered at him, the Noble heir exhaled roughly and looked at me. "I think that unless we hear something in his plan that sounds off, we should give it a shot. It's better for us to go down fighting until the end than to wait around to get slaughtered by the Long Night's people. The question is, are you and the Claws going to join us?"

I hesitated. Was I going to stake both my life and those of my men on this kid? Maybe I was being swayed by my instinctive sympathy because of his age, and he really did have malicious intentions.

I closed my eyes, and the flames in the old warehouse flickered up in my mind. I could still feel how helpless Rowan's body had felt in my arms as I'd dragged him to safety. See how broken he'd looked lying on that hospital bed. He hadn't come out of his coma yet. We didn't know if he ever would.

But he'd trusted Beckett. He'd been the first of us to speak up for the kid, recognizing something in him that he related to himself.

And I wanted to trust the kid too. I could see some of *myself* in Beckett: the rebellious teenager who'd spied on the Claws' moves and stored up my resentment of my father's treatment while wishing I could have earned his respect. Back then, before Dad and Colt had totally beaten any idealistic sense of hope out of me, I'd been able to imagine a future where conflicts could be solved by making deals and negotiating rather than through bloodshed.

What if I hadn't been wrong? What if we could make that teenage idealism real after all? Wasn't it worth trying?

"I'm in," I said. "I meant to set a different course for the Claws than the men who came before me did, and I'm going to start on that right now. I'm choosing trust over paranoia. The kid's been here for us the whole time, he's risked his life more than once to help us, and now we're going to be there for him."

Wylder smiled, and even Kaige's stern expression relaxed a little. Gideon stood up, brandishing his tablet. "Let's go hear this plan, then."

We found Beckett in the kitchen, scarfing down teriyaki chicken from the plate in front of him while he chatted with Anthea. She caught my eye with a sly glint in hers as we came in, and I had no doubt that she'd managed to find out a few more things about him without Beckett even realizing. Nothing that bothered her, though, because she simply tipped her head in acknowledgement.

"All right, Beckett," I said, tugging back a stool to sit next to him. "Tell us about your plan."

Beckett's face brightened. He set down his fork and looked around the island at all of us. "I know you're putting a lot of faith in me, and I'm not going to let you down. We're going to set up a meeting early tomorrow morning."

"First things first," Wylder cut in. "Everything else apart, what guarantee do we have that the Storm will leave Paradise Bend alone after this, even if the meeting goes in our favor? What's to stop him from changing his mind after a few days of peace and attacking us again once our guard is down?"

Beckett gave him a pained smile. "You don't have to worry. I know exactly how to take care of that."

23

Mercy

Walking into the lion's den felt exactly as it should. My heart thundered in my ears, and my mouth had turned to sandpaper. We'd driven two hours to reach a city I'd never visited before, and I felt totally out of my element.

As soon as we stepped into the small boutique mall, the air conditioning hit me at full force. The space was dark and empty, only our wavering reflections showing on the polished marble tiles. The mall didn't normally open for another hour anyway, but we'd ensured we'd have it to ourselves. Beckett had managed to send around a strategic message to all the businesses inside using his father's contact info, telling them that emergency work was being done today.

In a way, it was even true.

Our footsteps clacked against the floor as we walked down the cavernous main hall past the shuttered storefronts. At the far end, the ceiling lifted even higher into a huge dome with a honeycomb of skylights that loomed over the upscale food court. Gleaming tables with attached seating stood at wide intervals in the glow of the early morning sunlight. A broad terrace with more shops ran around the second floor overhead, their shuttered entrances visible through the gaps in the railing.

Kaige looked around and shuddered like he'd seen a ghost. "Seems like a weird place to have a business meeting."

"My dad and Anderson worked on this place together," Beckett said. "From what I've been able to gather, they often met in the buildings they invested in, so he won't think it's too strange." He motioned to a set of stairs that led to the second-floor terrace. "You'll want to have your men waiting up there. I picked this spot specifically so you'll have as much high ground as possible."

"We appreciate that," Wylder said in a dry tone, and motioned to the Noble men he'd trusted enough to bring along. I nodded to Jenner, Sam, and the handful of Claws who were with us too. Altogether, a dozen men tramped up the stairs to position themselves just out of sight around the terrace, their guns at the ready.

"What about us?" Gideon asked. "You suggested it was best for us to face him on equal ground."

Beckett pointed to a couple of thick, regal columns that stood at the far end of the food court. "We can wait behind those until your men have... subdued any opposition." He paused and looked at me and then Wylder sharply. "You did make it clear that they're not to hurt my dad?"

In that moment, hearing the fierceness of the question and knowing that he'd set this whole operation up to ultimately protect his father and their empire, I wouldn't have gone up against Beckett for any money in the world. If we made an enemy out of him, we might be screwed in the long run regardless. He obviously wasn't the type to forgive and forget.

"They have their orders," I said.

Wylder nodded. "The only way anyone's shooting at him is if he makes a move to shoot us. I assume you'll accept that as a reasonable exception?"

Beckett grimaced, but he tipped his head. "I don't think it'll come to that. He isn't stupid—and he'll want to get out of here alive if he can. But I won't blame you if you need to defend yourselves."

The five of us gathered behind the columns, Beckett with me and Wylder, Kaige and Gideon behind the other. Gideon was monitoring street cams on his tablet. "He's on his way. I'd estimate his time of arrival to be five minutes from now."

"Very punctual," Wylder muttered.

That was the whole reason we'd used a supposed meeting with Evan Anderson as bait. We were counting on the Storm being particularly eager to re-establish ties with his real estate associate after their recent dispute. Little did he know that Anderson had just reached out to us last night wanting to talk more about the proposal we'd sent.

It'd been hard to get excited about his interest when the man most instrumental in earning it was still unconscious in a hospital room. At least we had some hope of letting Rowan wake up to a world where death wasn't lurking right at our doorstep.

Wylder adjusted his earpiece. We'd agreed that he'd give the signal to all of the men above, both Nobles and Claws, to ensure they were fully coordinated. "Just a few more minutes," he said into the mic. "Stay alert."

I couldn't make out any of the figures through the railing. They were keeping well out of view like we'd discussed. My heart thumped even harder as the seconds slipped past us.

There was a distant squeak of hinges and then a soft rasp of several sets of footsteps heading our way. My back stiffened. I held myself rigidly still as the Storm and his usual contingent of bodyguards marched toward the food court. I had no idea what the man who'd rained so much terror down on the Bend even looked like, and in my mind's eye, I saw a shadowy figure like the dark god tattooed on Gideon's chest slinking through the grand hall.

"Planning on being fashionably late as usual, I suppose," a low, gravelly voice said at the far end of the atrium. I dared to peek from our shadowed position beneath the terrace.

The man who was just walking into the food court was nowhere near as intimidating as the supernatural figure I'd imagined, but the solid frame encased in his expensive gray suit had an imposing air all the same. He looked to be in his late forties, with thinning hair that was flecked with gray. I could have mistaken him for a regular, if powerful, businessman if I hadn't known better.

That was how the Devil's Dozen blended into society, I guessed.

He was flanked by eight bodyguards in darker suits. As they strode deeper into the food court, they fanned out a little amid the tables. Wylder was watching their progress now too. As the last of them came into the open area beneath the skylights, my fingers curled into my palms.

"Now!" Wylder whispered into his mic.

On cue, the men on the terrace leapt forward and opened fire. They took down most of the bodyguards in the space of a second, the men crumpling to the floor before they even had a chance to reach for their guns. The sound of the shots blared through the atrium and rang in my ears.

When the Storm and his two remaining protectors moved to make a run for the hall they'd come out of, our men fired several warning shots into the floor around them, as they'd been instructed.

"We don't want to hurt the rest of you," Wylder said, stepping out into view. "Stay where you are, and we can talk like civilized people." I followed him at a slower pace so that the limp from my leg injury wouldn't show. Gideon and Kaige joined us, leaving Beckett still hidden behind the column.

The Storm stared at us and then at the corpses around him, his face taut with horror. One of the remaining bodyguards made a grab for his weapon, and Wylder raised his own pistol to shoot him in the shoulder. "Next time it'll be your head," he warned.

In that moment, standing in front of the man who'd caused so much pain and bloodshed in my home, I wanted to put a bullet of my own between his eyes. My hand itched to leap to the gun tucked into the waist of my jeans. The only thing that held me back was the thought of Beckett and his pleas that we let his father leave here alive.

We'd trusted Beckett, and he'd delivered on his promise. Now we had to show we'd been worthy of *his* trust. We'd never have gotten this opportunity without his help.

"W-what is this?" the Storm demanded, his voice getting firmer with each syllable. He drew his substantial frame taller. "Who the hell are you, and what do you think you're doing here?"

I exchanged a glance with Wylder. The man didn't recognize us at all. He knew so little about the county he'd invested so much in taking over that he wasn't familiar with his main opponents. Somehow that both pissed me off and took the wind out of the sails of my earlier desire for revenge.

We were just pieces on a gameboard to the Storm, not actual people he'd been fighting like we were to Xavier. That must make it awfully easy not to think about the blood being shed—until it was trickling across the pretty marble floor all around him.

"We're the people whose territory you're trying to steal," I said, coming to a stop right beside Wylder. "Mercy Katz, leader of the Claws of Paradise Bend."

"Wylder Noble, heir to the Nobles of Paradise Bend," Wylder said, with a motion to his friends. "And my close associates. We're here to see if we can't come to some arrangement that involves *you* getting your men the hell out of our home."

A starker fear flickered in the man's eyes. He knew what was at stake for us now—and he'd already seen how far we'd gone to secure what was ours. "You won't get away with this," he snarled, but his bravado was obviously only for show.

"We already have," I said. "We got you here, didn't we? Ironically enough, you're now at our mercy."

Kaige snickered at my remark.

Wylder stepped a little closer to the Storm, leaving plenty of room in case one of our men overhead needed to take a shot. "Exactly. We've just proven that we have the means to overpower you. You could make a run for it and let the rest of your guards take the bullets, and *maybe* you'd make it out alive—though I doubt it—but then you'll be on your own again. And we're only getting stronger."

"We've damaged your operations in multiple ways," I said, picking up the thread, and folded my arms over my chest. "Ways you never expected we'd be able to, I'll bet. You thought your men could roll into Paradise Bend and crush us with a snap of their fingers, but it hasn't been anywhere near that easy, has it?"

The Storm's lips pulled back from his teeth. "Perhaps you've given me a little more trouble than I counted on, but you have no idea what you're up against, how much force I can bring down on you if I choose to."

"But should you choose to?" Wylder said with a quizzical air. "Do you even really want to? Is that tiny place that you'd never even heard of until, what, a few months ago worth so much to you that you'd refuse to cut your losses and move on?"

"Just how much do you want to lose while you keep fighting us?" I added.

"I couldn't possibly lose as much as you will," he snapped.

"We'll see about that." I motioned to the fallen bodyguards. "Looks like today the sacrifice was all on your side. *You* have no idea what else we might be capable of." Never mind that if we didn't succeed today, both sides would be wiped out. I wasn't going to tip him off to the Long Night's involvement. If he knew how closely his competitor was watching his movements here, his ego might balk even more at giving up.

Wylder shrugged. "Maybe it's not even your decision anymore, and you just don't want to admit it."

The Storm's eyes narrowed. "What are you talking about?"

"Xavier," Wylder said. "It seems to me that he's the one who's been in charge for a while now. He pushed for you to move on Paradise Bend in the first place, didn't he? And he's been badgering you into letting him take more and more control over operations there. I'd say at this point he's gone right off the leash."

"Bullshit. Xavier acts on my behalf—what he captures will be mine."

"Really? Or is that just what you want to believe?" I said. "Maybe your pride won't let you face the truth that you're no longer in charge. He's made himself the boss, and you know it, but you're too *scared* to stand up to him, no matter how much this war of his is costing you."

My taunt made the Storm bristle, but I caught a hint of doubt in his expression. His anger was starting to fade. At the end of the day, maybe he was simply a businessman at heart—finally realizing just how much of a liability one of his supposed assets had become.

"Nonsense," he said. "I can call him off anytime I want. I simply don't want to."

Wylder hummed. "It's hard to believe that when we've all seen him out there carrying out his own personal vendettas. What's in it for you anymore? I'm sure you've already made a fortune selling Glory. If you don't get out now, the losses are going to keep piling up. I can't see a man as smart as you risking so much unless he was frightened of the consequences of taking charge."

The Storm sneered at him, but he'd deflated a little more. "Of course I'm in charge. Maybe your little territory simply wasn't at the top of my list of concerns."

"Well, it should be right at the top now," I said brightly.

His gaze snapped to me. "You people have festered like an infected wound, refusing to leave."

"The feeling's mutual," Wylder said. He spun his pistol in his hand. "And we can finish this here, but only if you have the guts to do it."

The Storm stayed silent for a long moment. "And I'm supposed to believe that if we put an end to this war now, you'll let me leave here alive?"

I motioned toward the entrance to the food court. "Make the call to bring your men out of Paradise Bend, and you can waltz right out of here. We just want our home back. We can live and let live as long as you're doing the same."

The wheels appeared to be turning behind the Storm's dark eyes. I couldn't tell how much he was coming to terms with the situation and how much coming up with some new scheme. Whatever the case was, he raised his chin as if he still held the authority here.

"Now that I've given the matter more thought, I believe your pathetic county is far more trouble than it's worth. I have bigger prizes to pursue anyway."

He pulled his phone out of his pocket and dialed a number. As he held the phone to his ear, his stance tensed.

I didn't think our jabs about his fear of Xavier had been so far off the mark.

My breath caught in my throat as he started to speak. "Xavier. Yes. No, I don't want to hear about that. You listen to me." He swiveled, turning his back to us. "I want the entire operation in Paradise Bend scrapped. We're done there. Pull all the men out, and we'll discuss the next job I'll have for you tomorrow."

Whatever Xavier said in response, the Storm didn't quite contain a flinch. "I don't want any argument about it," he retorted. "Get your asses out of there *now* or I'll be having them served to me on a platter. Do you understand?"

His tone was cold enough to chill me to the bone. Just like that, I could imagine him sitting at the same table as the Long Night and their other menacing colleagues in the Devil's Dozen.

The two men talked back and forth a little longer, and then the Storm asked to speak to a couple more of his people who must have been high up in the operation. Finally, he hung up and turned to face us again.

"It's done," he said. "They're already packing up. Are we finished here?"

I might have trusted Beckett, but I sure as hell didn't trust this prick to keep his word. "And they won't be back? We expect to be left alone from here forward."

"Of course," the Storm said, way too easily.

Wylder cleared his throat. "Naturally, to ensure your cooperation, we're going to be holding onto a little something as collateral." He motioned toward the back of the room.

As Beckett stepped out from behind the column and walked over to join us, the Storm's expression shifted from haughty confusion to tight bewilderment. It took him a moment to speak. "Beckett?" His gaze shot to me and then Wylder. "What the fuck is my son doing here? Why did you drag him into this?"

"They didn't drag me into it, Dad," Beckett said with impressive calm. "You did."

The Storm sputtered. "What?"

"Beckett will be our collateral," I said, setting my hand briefly on the kid's shoulder. "As long as your son and only heir stays with us, that should be enough incentive for you to stay away."

"Fuck you," the Storm said.

"You have no choice," Wylder said. "Beckett walks out with us."

"Beckett," the Storm said, directly addressing his son. "I'll get you out of this. I'll—"

"I'm sorry, Dad." Despite his best efforts, Beckett's voice cracked. "But this is the only way. I *want* to go with them so I know you'll keep the peace and get back to focusing on what's really important. Just think of it as me doing my bit for the business."

Right then, I saw the father behind the hardened criminal—a look of the kind of anguish my father had never felt over my fate. "Please," the Storm said.

"If you want us to trust you to keep your word, then you should trust us to take good care of your son," Wylder said. "It's his decision anyway."

"Goodbye, Dad," Beckett said. "I'll still call. And maybe when things are back on track, I'll be ready to come home."

The Storm shifted on his feet. Wylder waved him off. "You wanted to leave here safely. Now go, before we change our mind about that part."

The Storm gave his son one last wretched look. Then he dragged himself away, trudging with his two bodyguards toward the hall. We waited until we'd heard the far doors bang shut behind them before we called our men down and headed out the back entrance.

Beside me, Beckett's posture was totally rigid. "Are you okay?" I asked him.

He nodded. "I didn't think it'd be easy, but... I didn't think it'd be quite that hard, either."

"He loves you," I said quietly. "I could see it. He'll keep the peace for you."

The kid gave me a tight but genuine smile. "I hope you're right."

So did I. I should have felt triumphant as we made our way out onto the sun-lit street, but tension stayed coiled tight inside me.

Gideon was checking his tablet. As we reached the cars and got in, he smiled. "I'm already seeing the Storm men driving off. They're not wasting any time now that the big boss has laid down the law."

Somehow that didn't relieve me as much as I would have expected it to either. "All of them?" I asked.

"I mean, some of them must have things to sort out first, but it's a good sign that any of them are already getting out of town."

Beckett stared out the window. After several minutes of silence, he let out a rough chuckle. "I'm starving."

Wylder laughed and relaxed into the driver's seat. "Let's put a little distance between us and your dad and then see if we can't—"

Gideon's curse cut him off. Wylder's head jerked around, and my pulse lurched. "What?" I asked.

Gideon looked up at us, his mouth tightening. "The Storm's men are continuing to head out of the county... but not Xavier. I've just caught him on a street cam. He's going totally crazy—rampaging through Paradise City, taking shots all along Main Street. The rest of the Storm's people might be willing to listen to orders, but it looks like he's a different story."

My heart sank. The war wasn't over yet.

24

Mercy

GIDEON TURNED HIS TABLET TOWARD ME WITH SOME OF THE footage playing. It was even worse than I'd expected after what he'd said. Xavier was walking down the normally busy city street with a large semi-automatic rifle in his hands. Most of the pedestrians must have already scattered, but he took random shots at people who were still dashing for shelter, at the windows of the stores on either side of the road, and at the cars parked along the street.

My stomach churned. I found myself grateful that the street cam feed didn't come with sound so I didn't need to hear the booming of the gun and the panicked shrieks that must have been splitting the air. Hearing them in my imagination was bad enough.

Sitting between me and Kaige in the back, Beckett sucked a breath through his teeth. I felt a quiver go through his body where his arm brushed mine. "Fuck. I knew he was a loose cannon but—*fuck.*"

"The Storm screwed us over," Kaige said, his voice harsh with anger. "He pretended he'd gone along with our deal—"

Gideon was already shaking his head. "I don't think the Storm ordered this. Most of his men are on their way out of the city as he promised. The kid told us that Xavier's been chafing against his leash. Seems like he's snapped it and gone totally rogue."

And yet the psychopath was walking almost casually down the street, as if he had all the time in the world to wait for what he really wanted. A chill ran over my skin. I knew exactly what that was—or rather, *who*.

"How is this going to affect our—" I cut myself off before I mentioned the deal with the Long Night, remembering that we hadn't told Beckett about that part. Maybe we should fill him in now that he'd proven his commitment to us, but I wasn't going to make that decision on my own. "We needed the war to be over," I said instead. "Everyone out."

"I don't know how this will factor in," Wylder said darkly, hitting the gas hard as the highway came into sight up ahead. "One thing is for sure—we've got to get back to the county quickly. It's time to put this rabid dog down."

He must have broken a dozen traffic laws zooming along the highway toward Paradise Bend, but thankfully there weren't many other cars taking this route at this time of day to get in our way. Gideon monitored the situation via the street cams the whole time, his frown pulling deeper and deeper.

"Almost all of the Storm men and vehicles I was aware of have left the county," he reported as Paradise City's skyscrapers came into view. "A few stragglers seem to have joined up with Xavier for whatever insane reason. Maybe just enjoying the rush of power. They've cleared the street completely, everyone keeping out of their way. They even took down a couple of cops who tried to intervene. It looks like the police are hanging back while they try to figure out a workable strategy... or maybe just hoping they can wait until he tires out."

"Useless as usual," I muttered. "That means it's up to us."

Wylder drummed his hands on the steering wheel and veered to pass another, slower car. "We'll head straight there and take the lay of the land. There's got to be something we can do. We haven't got any legal restrictions holding us back from taking him down, whatever it takes."

I glanced at Beckett, who'd shrunk in on himself with each glimpse of the street cam footage. "We shouldn't let him see you with us. He's already pissed off enough—I don't want to put you in danger like that. I'll get one of my men to take you back to..." I paused, not sure where the safest place was. But as long as Xavier was rampaging through Paradise City and I was there trying to deal with him, I didn't think he'd suddenly head to my house. "You can stay in the Claws headquarters in the Bend until we sort things out."

Beckett nodded with obvious relief. "Thanks. I—I wish I had some idea how you could stop him, but even my dad didn't seem to know how to keep him in line."

"Obviously," Kaige muttered, and let out a growl of frustration. "We can't let him ruin everything."

"We won't," Wylder said firmly. "This is our city, and we're taking it back whether he fucking likes it or not."

I texted the Claws who'd come with us for the ambush to confirm that they were sticking close by and then called some of the men at the house for additional backup and someone to pick up Beckett. Gideon had been coordinating with our Noble allies too. By the time we parked a few blocks from where Xavier was currently wreaking havoc, an occasional gunshot reaching our ears, we had five other cars joining us.

One of the Claws guys motioned Beckett over to him. I gave the kid a wave before they drove off. Then Wylder and I looked around at the assembled men.

"We need to try to kill Xavier before he can do any more damage," I said. "If you get a shot, take it. Same with any of the other Storm people still attacking the city. They've made their choice, and now we have to show them the consequences before they tear our home completely apart."

Wylder's mouth curved into a crooked grin. "You heard her, boys. Let's go prove to them what the true rulers of Paradise Bend are made of."

We hustled through the streets until Xavier's voice reached my ears. He was alternately mumbling and yelling. I could only make out the yelling parts, which were things like, "You're all going to pay!" and "Fucking coward!" I wondered if even he knew who he was talking to.

We got into position along some parked cars that could act as shields. A couple of the vehicles had already had their windows shattered by bullets.

Xavier was strolling down the middle of the road, almost carelessly. The other Storm men were sticking closer to the storefronts, smashing windows and shooting out door handles. As I watched, they burst into one building and ended up on the second floor, where they tossed furniture out onto the street just because they could.

My blood ran cold. What if they broke into a place that still had people inside? I hoped anyone who was still in the stores or apartments overhead had a back door they could escape through.

Xavier was too far off and weaving back and forth too randomly for anyone to get a good shot. A few of the guys darted closer along the line of cars, but even with his back turned, the monstrous man heard them. He spun around and shot at them before they could even start firing. As they ducked low, he sprang behind a van with the swiftness that'd startled me before.

Our men took a few shots at the Storm guys emerging from the building they'd broken into and had better luck there. One crumpled, clutching his wounded knee, and the next bullet caught him in the skull. His companion dashed farther down the street, aiming a couple of shots over his shoulder at us.

I pulled out my gun and flicked off the safety. My gaze traveled from the van where Xavier had disappeared to the other figures roaming the street. It caught on the sprawled bodies of pedestrians who hadn't gotten out of the way in time. Blood stained the asphalt beneath them.

A weight sank into my stomach. I was responsible for this carnage; I was the reason the city bled now. Xavier was never going to stop until he had me. He was always going to be one step ahead of us, destroying and killing everything and everyone in his path.

My legs wobbled abruptly, and not because of the healing wound. I sank down behind the car, willing my breaths to even out.

Kaige dropped down next to me, his gaze concerned. He grasped my shoulder. "Are you okay?"

"He's here because of me," I said. Another wave of gunfire nearly drowned out my voice. I couldn't tell how much was ours and how much from the Storm's men.

Kaige's brow furrowed. "What are you talking about?"

"Xavier. He came here because he wanted revenge on me and my dad. He won't leave because he hasn't gotten it, and that's all he cares about. I'm responsible for this mess."

"That's not true."

"He loved my mother, and my dad killed her." I shook my head. "That was the beginning of the end, even if I had no idea at the time."

Kaige's grip on me tightened. "Do you see what Xavier's doing now? This isn't about you—it's about him being fucking insane. Besides, you're not responsible for what your father did. You can't blame yourself."

"Maybe I should have figured things out sooner. Maybe I could have made a difference then."

"You still can." He gave me a little shake. When I looked up at him, his brown eyes were unusually serious. "Your dad is the only one to blame for his own actions, and the same with Xavier. Any way they try to pin this shit on you is just them looking for an excuse for what they want to do anyway. If what Xavier is doing was about love, it wouldn't end with all this violence. I know *that* much about love. I would move worlds to be with you, but if you asked me, I would let you go."

Something about Kaige's words sank into the place where my chest had started to constrict. My lungs loosened, letting in more air again.

I wasn't trapped by Xavier or anyone else, not if I didn't let myself be. I could still stop this horror—without losing my life in the process.

"We always have your back. *Always*," Kaige added.

"I know," I murmured, squeezing his hand. Then I pushed myself up, filled with a renewed sense of determination. I wasn't the one to start the war, but I would end it.

Our men had been spreading out along the street, trying to get closer to Xavier while he continued to take shots at them. The other Storm men were still firing away too. I added my own bullets to the fray—and then I saw one of the Storm's men take off down the street with a bundle of what looked like dynamite in his arms.

Shit. Did they have more explosives? How much else would they destroy if they got their way?

I didn't think any more than that—my legs were already in motion. Ignoring the throbbing of my wound, I threw myself after the man.

I shot at him as well as I could, but it was even harder with both of us in motion. One bullet dinged off a lamppost, and another embedded itself in a wall.

The man scrambled down an alley on the other side of the street, and I ran after him, gritting my teeth. The pain in my leg was slowing me down. As I hustled after him, a limp came into my gait. But I had to get to him before he blew up somebody's house and livelihood—and maybe a whole lot of people too.

The alley connected to a lane that ran down the length of the block between the streets. I veered around the corner and spotted the Storm lackey several buildings ahead of me. I took another shot and raced after him as fast as I could push my legs to go.

I was just passing one of the side alleys when an immense figure charged out of it, straight at me.

I was flinging myself backward out of the way before I even registered Xavier's face. My body instinctively hurled me toward the nearest passage—but when I spun around to make a real dash for safety, my heart plummeted.

The alley I'd stumbled into was a dead end, boxed in by buildings on either side that met several feet beyond where I stood, leaving no gap between them. And Xavier's hulking form filled the only exit.

I raised my pistol and pulled the trigger, but all I got was a hollow clicking sound. I'd used up all my bullets. My mind leapt to the tiny gun Anthea had gifted me, but that was in the purse I'd yet again left in the car. That little handbag wasn't the kind of thing it was easy to carry with you on tense missions.

Xavier gave me a sharp-edged smile. "Here we are again, little kitty. I think you've finally used up the last of your nine lives." He took a menacing step toward me.

I tossed the useless pistol aside—Wylder could get me another when I needed it, and right now I wanted both my hands free. My gaze darted over the brick walls around me. "Killing these people isn't going to bring Josey back. They've got nothing to do with it, Xavier. *I've* got nothing to do with it. It's not like I asked to be born."

"Oh, but you were," Xavier said, his smirk stretching wider. "And now you'll die."

"You're sick," I spat, backing up a couple of steps. "You didn't need to involve all these people. You want to pick a fight with me, then fight with *me*."

"I intend to." He raised his gun. "I think I'll start by blasting away those tricksy feet of yours so you can't run off again, and then I'll take the rest of you apart with my bare hands."

I took another frantic glance around me and spotted an open window on the side of the building two floors up. But I had to buy enough time to get to it first. I groped at my pockets, as if I might have brought a knife and just forgotten about it—and my fingers brushed the slight protrusion of my childhood bracelet.

My pulse hiccupped. I reached into my pocket and yanked out the silver chain. When I held it up to the streaks of sunlight that penetrated the alley, Xavier paused, frowning.

Every nerve in my body screamed at me to squeeze the bracelet tight and tuck it away where he'd never find it. I'd clung to this last concrete memento of my mother for fifteen years. But I didn't need it to remember her. I understood the full sacrifice she'd made for me now. And I knew with absolute certainty that Mom would have cared less about me holding onto it than about protecting me any way she could like she hadn't managed to before.

I wasn't really an angel anyway, little or otherwise.

"This is the last piece of my mother I have left," I said, closing my fingers around it. "If you want her so badly, you'd better go get it."

Xavier's eyes fixed on my hand with a sudden flare of longing. The next second, I hurled the bracelet into the strewn debris along the edge of the alley.

Xavier dove after it, nearly dropping his gun in his haste. I sprang at the wall. Using the uneven texture of the bricks to brace my shoes, I spun and launched toward the wall kitty-corner, bouncing back and forth between the sides on a diagonal. Sweat beaded on my forehead at the pain in my thigh I was ignoring.

Xavier let out a cry of triumph—and I flung myself in one final leap to grab the sill of the open window.

A roar echoed up from behind me. I didn't look back, only hurled myself through the window. Gunfire sputtered in my wake, chipping the ledge. I sprawled on the floor in a vacant apartment and shoved myself to my feet.

"This isn't over!" Xavier bellowed after me. "You're going to realize eventually that it's going to come down to you or me."

I met up with the guys by the base of the hill that led to the Noble mansion, my feet and my thigh aching. I fought the urge to sink down on the sidewalk. The somber expression on all their faces only made my spirits sink more.

"You couldn't stop him," I said.

Wylder blew out a frustrated breath. "We couldn't get close enough. The cops came by again and totally failed too. He's too smart and too fast."

"And has too much ammunition," Kaige grumbled.

"We'll regroup," Gideon said. "It's barely noon. We've got the rest of the afternoon to come up with the right approach—and we don't even know that the Long Night won't consider the deal fulfilled already."

I was pretty sure he wouldn't, but I couldn't bring myself to say that. "All right," I said, and limped over to the car.

I'd only just made it to the doors when my phone buzzed. I didn't see how it could be good news, but I pulled it out anyway. I didn't recognize the number.

"Hello?" I said.

"Is this Mercy Katz?" said the voice at the other end.

I hesitated. "Yeah. What's this about?"

"I'm calling from the Paradise Bend County Hospital. We have some good news for you. You're the contact for Rowan Finlay? He's just woken up."

25

Rowan

My chest felt as if it were being stabbed by tiny pins and needles, and everything around me seemed hazy. Somebody hovered to my side. "Mercy?" I said softly.

"No, dear." My vision cleared a little, and the nurse's face came into view. She was in her late forties and definitely not the woman I was looking for.

"Over here," came a voice from near the curtain. I whipped my head around so fast that the dull pain at the back spread into a pounding headache.

I winced and fell back against the pillows. Bandages were wrapped around my arms and torso. An IV drip was pushed into a vein on my right wrist, and monitoring equipment next to me gave off a quiet but persistent beep.

"Easy, dear," the nurse cooed. "You don't want to strain yourself."

Mercy hurried into view, her eyes wide with worry and her forehead furrowed. "Rowan, are you okay?" There was a smudge of grit on her cheek, a healing scrape on her chin, and strands of hair had come loose from her ponytail. She looked as if she'd walked through hell to get here.

"I've felt better," I managed. My voice came out creaky.

"Be glad you're feeling anything at all," the nurse announced. "You've been off in your own little world for almost three days."

Three days? I stared at her as she stepped aside to detach my IV, but my attention was caught by Wylder, Gideon, and Kaige coming up beside Mercy to circle my bed. I didn't mind. They made for a welcome sight, one that sent a rush of relief through me.

"*You're* all still okay," I rasped, my voice getting a little stronger and my mind a little less dazed as I regained my focus. "How is— Is everything—?" I didn't know how to ask the questions I wanted to with the nurse here in the room.

Mercy squeezed my hand. "We're still working on it, but we're almost there. You don't need to worry about that right now." She blinked hard. "I'm just glad to hear your voice."

Seeing her fighting tears, I knew without her saying it that she'd been afraid I was going to die. I had a vague memory of thinking the same thing myself when I'd been slumped in the warehouse with flames rising around me and pain radiating from the places where the bullets had hit me.

But somehow I was still here. That was some kind of miracle, wasn't it?

"How *do* you feel?" Gideon asked.

"Like a truck ran over me," I said. "Or maybe two."

"Wow, Rowan is cracking jokes," Kaige teased. "I think you should check for a concussion, nurse."

The nurse frowned at him, but Kaige only chuckled.

"Don't mind him," Mercy said. "That's just how we are."

That was right. We were a team.

Which brought to mind another question. "How—how did we get out of the fire?"

Mercy smiled bright but tightly. "You talked me through my panic, and I dragged you out of the building."

"But you—you were shot too." I remembered that clearly: the jolt of panic that'd struck *me* when I'd watched her fall.

"One way or another, we were both getting out of there," Mercy said stubbornly, and I caught a glimpse of the girl I'd seen that night.

She was my fierce angel, my savior. "Besides you're the one who saved me first."

"You both got out, and that's all I could have asked for," Wylder said with typical assurance, but his gaze held mine for a few beats longer than usual. "I expect you to put as much effort into healing up as you give to all your other work."

My lips twitched with a smile. "Aye, aye, boss."

The nurse motioned to the bunch of them. "You've said your hellos. You can't all stay in here at once. The patient needs room to breathe."

"Right, right," Kaige said. He gently tapped his knuckles to my shoulder. "You're tougher than me now, Finlay. No more showing off, all right."

I snorted, and he grinned before following the nurse out of the room.

Gideon dipped his head to me. "We've ensured, thanks to the Nobles' accounts, that you have the best room available in the hospital."

"Thanks," I said. "I appreciate that."

"Come on," Wylder said to the other guy, cuffing him lightly. "I think we should give these two a little time to 'catch up'." He winked at Mercy. "I'll make sure no one interrupts you for a good long while."

Mercy rolled her eyes at him and waved him off. They headed out, the door closing with a click behind them. Then it was just her and me in the small but private white-walled room.

Despite Mercy's reaction to Wylder's innuendo, I still wanted her as close to me as I could have her. With a wince I suppressed, I scooted over on the bed to make room for her to climb up beside me.

Mercy took the unspoken invitation and nestled against me. I wrapped my arm around her and kissed her forehead. Tension I hadn't realized she was holding in loosened as her body relaxed against me.

"What did you mean, we're almost there?" I asked quietly. "Today's the last day, isn't it? What's going on?"

"I really don't want you thinking about that," Mercy said, tucking her head next to mine. "You need to focus on getting better."

"I'm going to have trouble doing that if I have no idea what you all are facing out there."

She sighed and hugged me tighter but still carefully. "The Storm pulled his men out. Most of them have left. So we won in that way. But Xavier is rampaging around Paradise City, and we haven't figured out how to stop him yet." She nuzzled my cheek. "But that's *really* not for you to worry about right now. We'll figure it out."

I could hear the anxiety in her voice, and I didn't want to add to it. "I know you will," I said. "You and the guys have gotten through an awful lot."

"And so have you." Her breath grazed the side of my face, warm and sweet. "I'm so glad you're back with us."

"Me too."

I turned my head and found her lips bare inches from mine. Nudging closer, I brushed my mouth to hers. She was too damn magnetic for me to resist, and I'd been without her touch for way too long.

Mercy kissed me slowly at first, almost leisurely. Her hand came up to caress my cheek. I teased my fingers into her hair as I kissed her back. It felt even better than the day when we'd finally come back to each other after so long apart and so much turmoil and misunderstanding. I knew exactly how much we meant to each other, how far I'd go for her and she for me.

For several minutes, we didn't do more than kiss, until the press of her warm body against mine became too irresistible. With my cock hardening behind the hospital-issue gown, I skimmed my fingers down the side of her body. When I reached Mercy's ass, I couldn't help tugging her closer and kneading those taut curves. A pleased murmur escaped her.

When I tried to sit up more to catch her mouth at a deeper angle, Mercy pushed me back down on the bed. "Relax. Let me take care of you."

I might have protested if her next move hadn't been to peel off her T-shirt and her bra. My gaze drank in the creamy mounds of her breasts with unrestrained eagerness. Any pain I'd still been feeling had faded away.

This was my girl. My *woman*. The queen of the Bend. And even if she was trying to make this easy for me, I intended to show her just how glad I was to be back with her in every way she'd let me.

She leaned over me, and I reached up to cup her breasts. Her nipples pebbled at the swipe of my thumbs. My mouth watered, and my cock turned even harder. I hoped Wylder had done a good job of barricading this room, because once we got going, I didn't know if I'd be able to stop, even if a doctor marched into the room. I needed her too damn much.

Mercy leaned even closer so one nipple hovered right over my mouth. I latched my mouth on it and sucked hard. A perfect little gasp escaped her lips. Her palm flattened against the wall for support as she kept most of the weight of her body off me, but she rocked with the movements of my tongue. The brush of her thigh against my hard cock brought me to even stiffer attention.

I meant to make good on my silent promise to give as much as I took, though. I sucked and pinched, alternating my attention between the two soft mounds. Above me, Mercy started to moan. With my free hand, I inched closer to her pussy and fumbled with the fly of her jeans. As soon as they were unzipped, I tucked my fingers right inside. I caressed her slit, moving my finger up and down the length of it before curling my forefinger against her clit.

She moaned again, louder this time. I spanked her ass. "Shh, be quiet. We don't want anybody to hear us."

She whimpered in answer. A wicked idea took over me. I moved the flat of my palm over the soft curve of her ass before slapping on it again. Mercy's body jerked with a gush of wetness from her pussy. I spanked her lightly, careful not to be loud enough for the sound to echo around us while I continued to work at her pussy.

"Please," she said as she sat back down, adjusting her legs on either side of my thighs. "I need you."

I nodded, my own breath ragged with desire. She eased up the hospital gown and slid off her panties before bracing herself right over my throbbing cock. I gripped her hips, pulling her down over me.

Her slickness closing around me was absolute heaven. As she took me fully inside her, both of us groaned together. Mercy raised herself, squeezing my balls slightly as she went, before her greedy cunt swallowed my cock again.

She clutched my shoulders in an almost vice-like grip as she continued to pump over me, rotating her hips around my hard dick. "Fuck," I whispered, and her eyes rolled up in her head in answer. Suddenly an impulse gripped me that had nothing to do with lust.

"Look at me," I said softly.

Mercy lowered her gaze, her eyes dark with so much longing I almost came just seeing it. My cock pulsed with need, but I reined that urge in for now. I brushed her hair back from her forehead so I could have a better look at her, and said the words I'd said so many times before, but not recently enough. "I love you, Mercy."

The way she beamed at me told me it'd been exactly the right time. She leaned in, kissing me hard, and then spoke with her cheek resting against mine. "I love you too, Rowan. I don't think I ever completely stopped. I'm sorry I didn't tell you sooner."

At the choked quality to her voice, I hugged her to me. "Don't be sorry. I'm lucky enough to be able to say it after I almost lost you."

"I'm lucky to have you too. I'm so glad we found our way back to each other."

We held each other for a little longer, and then Mercy began to move over me again, taking my dick deeper inside her. She felt so hot and wet and perfect. I tugged at her hips to encourage her to go faster, knowing I could take it. Knowing she'd like it best that way too. An ache had woken up in the wound in my side despite the painkillers, but it was worth it to have this moment of connection with her.

Mercy gasped, following my guidance. She rocked against me, lifting and slamming down so I pounded into her. It only took a few more times before her pussy clenched around me, setting off a sharper flare of pleasure all through my veins.

Before I came inside her, she slipped off and eased down the bed to wrap her lips around me. With a few passionate swipes of her tongue, she brought me right over the edge, spurting into her mouth.

Smiling slyly, Mercy snuggled next to me. We stayed there in each other's arms until our breaths evened out.

"I did love you back in high school, Mercy," I said, feeling the need to clarify. "But I love you just as much the way you are now too—fierce and unstoppable."

"I'm not unstoppable," she said, her face falling.

"Yes, you are. No one gets between you and what you want. Your dad treated you horribly, but you've come out of it stronger. I couldn't be prouder to stand by your side, and I'll keep telling you that until I know you're just as proud of who you've become."

Mercy swallowed audibly and pressed a tender kiss to my lips. "Thank you." After a few more minutes, she sighed. "I want to stay here with you for the rest of the day."

"But you need to go deal with Xavier. I understand." I grimaced. "I just wish I could come with you to help instead of being stuck in here."

She slowly pulled on her clothes. "I'm sure you'll hear all about it afterward. And I did bring some things to distract you."

My curiosity stirred. "What do you mean?"

She fished into the tote bag she'd carried in with her. "I figured you might get bored, so I brought you drawing supplies." She placed my pencil case and a sketchpad on the table beside me.

I glanced around the room and let my tone go wry. "So much inspiration to draw on in here."

Mercy swatted me. "I guess you'll just have to use your imagination then, huh." She paused, and something about her expression made my heart skip a beat. She looked at me cautiously. "And your mom called."

My pulse outright lurched. "What?"

"I answered the call but then I didn't know what to tell her." She bit her lip. "She wanted you to call her back when you could. I brought her number in case you didn't have it programmed in, and here's your phone, even though I don't think you're supposed to have it in the hospital room." She slipped the phone under the sketch pad. "It's totally up to you, but if you ask me, you really should give her a call. She's never going to stop being your mom."

Mercy gave me one more lingering kiss before she left. I settled into the pillows, grappling with my emotions. The aches of my body were asserting themselves again, and part of me wanted nothing more than to close my eyes and let exhaustion drag me into sleep.

My hand went to the phone instead. I weighed it in my fingers for several minutes. Then I dialed Mom's number, my mouth going dry.

Mom picked up on the third ring. "Hello?" she said. When I didn't answer, she said, "Rowan, is that you?"

"Hey, Mom," I said slowly. "How are you?"

"I'm good. Just glad to hear from you after all this time. I know that's a mom thing to say, but... well, it's true."

Carina's voice carried from farther away. "Is that Rowan? He finally called?"

My lips twitched with amusement at her impertinent voice. "Sounds like someone else has been waiting to hear from me too. You can put Carina on—we'll talk more after she has a chance."

"All right," Mom said, sounding bemused, and handed the phone over.

"I missed you at my birthday," Carina announced first thing. "The present was nice, but I really wanted to see *you*."

Homesickness for the family I'd once had squeezed around my heart. "I want to see you too, kiddo," I said, using the old nickname that I knew made her grimace now. "I just..."

What excuse did I have, really? Life had dealt a hard blow to me, and the blows had kept coming. But after each one of them, I had come out stronger, just like Mercy had.

An unexpected sense of hope unfurled in my chest. I'd convinced myself that the life I was living made me toxic to the family I had left. But talking to Mom and Carina now without resisting their concern, I didn't feel like poison to them.

Maybe I could be both Rowan Finlay, one of the Noble elite, and I could be a good son and a brother at the same time. If they ever needed it, I could even protect them better from my position of power.

"You know what?" I said. "Never mind excuses. How about I catch a flight over there in a couple of weeks, and I'll make it up to you then."

26

Mercy

WHEN I REJOINED THE GUYS IN THE HOSPITAL WAITING room, their grim expressions swept away any lingering peace from my interlude with Rowan. "What?" I said, hurrying the rest of the way to them.

They were already getting up from their chairs. "We've received another report from the men who've been tracking Xavier's movements," Gideon said, keeping his voice low so the people around us wouldn't overhear. "He and the Storm's lackeys who've stuck with him have set up explosives around a building where there are a couple of families and some other civilians hiding out in the upstairs apartments. He's threatening to blow them all up if anyone comes close to him."

My pulse stuttered. Somehow I didn't think Xavier would hold back on the blowing up part no matter what anyone else did, if he got testy enough. He'd probably wanted this news to get to me so I'd feel even more horrible about running away.

But could I really believe that he'd stop his rampage even if I gave myself up? No, not for a second. He was reveling in the destruction, using his anger as an excuse, just like Kaige had said. Once he'd killed me, he'd start blaming all of Paradise Bend for stealing Josey too, and the Bend would be without a queen to defend it.

Wylder looked as if he'd gone through the same thought process. "You can't give in, no matter what he demands. We'll find a way to take him out that doesn't end with him getting his hands on you."

I inhaled deeply. "I'm all for that. But we're going to need help. Should we call together all our men—the ones we can count on, anyway—and see what we're working with?"

Wylder nodded. He turned to Gideon. "Contact all the Noble underlings who stuck with us at the waterfront property and survived. I don't trust anyone who's in tight with my dad to have our backs. Tell them to gather on the front lawn at the mansion—we need room for a larger group—and we'll be there in half an hour." He glanced at me. "If you're okay with bringing the Claws to my house, that is. I think it's best if we talk to them all at once."

"Agreed." I took out my phone. "I'll have Jenner assemble everyone."

"Tell him to bring the kid too. I'm not sending Beckett in to fight, but he's been instrumental in bringing down the Storm. He might know something about Xavier that'll help."

I added that note to my text message and sent it off as we hustled out of the hospital to the car.

We reached the Noble mansion just ahead of the Claws forces. A couple dozen men were already milling around on the lawn, Anthea in their midst looking like she'd had a hand in corralling them, but the atmosphere was tense. She caught my eye as we passed with a tight smile that was closer to a grimace.

As we wove through them to the front steps, Wylder catching people's eyes and nodding here and there, I picked up a few snippets of hushed conversation, things like: "bomb" and "psycho." It seemed that word about Xavier's current gambit had spread widely already.

Several of the men didn't quite meet Wylder's gaze. Apprehension prickled down my spine. When we reached the steps, we stopped at the base and looked over the crowd, including the few cars of Claws men that were just arriving to join the bunch. The men stirred restlessly on their feet, looking like they wanted to be someplace else.

"What the hell's wrong with them?" Kaige muttered.

"They're probably nervous," Wylder said. "Xavier's acting like a maniac, and they've got my dad breathing down their necks in a not-much-better state too." His jaw clenched. "But Nobles don't back down, not when our city is on the line. We'll get them sorted out."

I grasped his hand, tugging him a little apart from the others for a second, closer to the house. "You know you're twice the leader your dad is, right?" I said quietly, searching his eyes. "Ten times, even."

The slightest hint of a smile curled the corner of Wylder's mouth, even though his eyes stayed dark. "If you say so, then it must be true. Now we've just got to get them to believe it."

I glanced at the unsettled men who'd nonetheless turned up to hear what the Noble heir had to say. "I think they already do. You just need to remind them of why."

Wylder didn't say anything for a moment. His fingers tightened around mine. Abruptly, he leaned in to kiss me. I swayed into his touch, his intoxicating musk washing over me. Then he pulled back to meet my eyes again. "How do you do it?"

I raised my eyebrows. "Do what?"

"Always make sure I see reason while keeping me on my toes."

I tapped his chest teasingly. "I'm your queen, remember."

"You're my equal in every possible way. Maybe my better in a few, but we won't talk about that in front of company." He managed a small grin, looking a little more relaxed than before, and tugged my arm. "Are you ready?"

"As I'll ever be."

He dropped my hand as we climbed onto the front steps together, but we stood shoulder to shoulder—equals, like he'd said. Wylder clapped his hands, and the uneasy murmurs died down. Everyone turned to face us.

"I think you know why you're here," Wylder said, slipping effortlessly into his role as leader. His commanding presence had been impossible to ignore even when I'd first staggered into the Noble mansion months ago, and now he wore it with total assurance. Watching him stoked the flames of my love for him. "The menace that calls himself Xavier is tearing up our city's streets and threatening our people, and it's time we dealt with him once and for all."

"How the hell are we going to do that without *us* getting blown up?" someone asked from the crowd.

"That's what we're here to figure out," I said. "He's lost most of his allies. With all of us working together, we should be able to end his reign of terror."

"He's out of control," another guy said from the edges of the group. "There's no way to predict what he'll do next. We already lost a ton of people at the waterfront property, and now he's even crazier than before."

"Yeah," a third man piped up. "Let the cops deal with him for once. They can take the hits this time."

I didn't like the approving hum that spread through the gathering. Wylder scowled at them all. "Really? That's your answer—wait for the police to finally step up? Chances are that dozens more people will be dead before that happens, and if we don't act now, their blood will be on our hands. The last time Xavier got the better of us, it was because we were abandoned by those who should have been fighting with us. But we have the strength in numbers this time."

"He can't hold us all off at once," I added. "Once we're coordinated, we can find an opportunity to pick him off, and this war will all be over just like that."

The expressions in the crowd still looked doubtful. I spotted Jenner, Sam, Quinn, and several other Claws hanging back by the edges with Beckett standing among them. An impulse gripped me. I caught Beckett's eye and motioned for him to come join us.

The kid skirted the crowd and walked over to the steps a little hesitantly, but his shoulders pulled back and his chin rose as he came to stand next to me. He peered out over the gathered men as if daring them to challenge his right to be there. "What do you need?" he asked me under his breath.

"Just for you to be yourself." I smiled and set my hand on his back, pitching my voice to carry farther. "This is Beckett. Take a good look at him. How old are you, Beckett?"

"Sixteen," Beckett said, his shoulders stiffening even more.

Someone in the crowd snickered, and Kaige took a step toward the guy with an intimidating pose. After all his skepticism about Beckett, he'd obviously come around.

"This sixteen-year-old," I said, "is the reason we were able to take down the man behind Xavier and most of his forces. You've noticed that most of the men who worked with Xavier have already left town? It's thanks to Beckett that we were able to force the Storm to back down."

Wylder folded his arms over his chest, picking up my thread. "If one sixteen-year-old kid can make all the difference in tackling a huge crime lord, then the bunch of you should be able to manage one psychopath, don't you think? Beckett wasn't afraid to take action when he needed to, and we can't let ourselves cower either. We're Nobles, and Nobles fight for what's theirs."

Anthea nodded approvingly. The gathered men stared at Beckett. I saw flickers of shame and then resolve cross their faces. They stirred again, but this time the energy was more aggressive than uneasy.

"Right!" Jenner shouted. "The Claws are going to fight. We're going to put this asshole down like the mad dog he is."

"I'm going to be there going at him," Kaige said, flexing his arms.

Gideon gave a tight smile. "And me."

"Who else?" Wylder called out. "I only want people who are ready to go all in, who'll stick with us and not turn their backs when the going gets tough. I *thought* that was what you were all made of. If that's what you want the Nobles to be, then stand with us now."

The murmurs that rose up now thrummed with eager determination. "Hell yeah!"

"I'm in."

"Let's take that bastard down and show him who the real boss is around here."

"Wylder'll make him pay!"

I glanced at the Noble heir, knowing what an important moment this was for him. The Nobles were throwing their lot in with him, with no guidance from his father and even against what they might have suspected Ezra would prefer. Wylder had just proven that he was stronger than his father, with solid principles and a desire to protect everyone within this city, not just those who kissed his feet.

It might not be just Xavier we conquered today.

But we did still have to conquer the psycho. We waved everyone closer.

"We head out now," Wylder said. "We have the numbers to surround Xavier and his lackeys on all sides. Stay where you have some cover but get as close as you can without provoking him into setting off his explosives. When we have every possible angle, one of us will get an opening soon enough. Be ready to take it if it's you. I don't care how you do it—if you can kill him, make it happen."

The men let out a whoop and started streaming toward the cars. I didn't know if that plan would be enough to get us all the way there, but it was a solid start. We couldn't be sure exactly what we'd need to do until we faced Xavier on the turf he'd tried to claim as his own.

"Thanks," I said to Beckett, and sent him off to the Claws so Jenner could arrange transport back to the house for him while the rest of us headed downtown.

Anthea had ambled over. "I'll see about getting more weapons and ammo sent over there so you can handle a long stand-off."

"Perfect," Wylder said with a tip of his head.

"We'll have to set a specific boundary," Gideon started saying as we walked away from the house, but my attention was drawn away from the conversation by a movement at one of the front windows.

Ezra was standing in the living room, half hidden by one of the curtains, watching us. His lips were pursed and his eyes narrowed. When he realized I'd noticed him, he stepped back, fading into the shadows.

A chill pooled in my gut. Xavier definitely wasn't our only enemy.

But he was the one we had to tackle first. I yanked my gaze away and hurried over to join my men.

27

Kaige

THE STREET WAS SO EMPTY IT WAS EERIE. USUALLY AT THIS time on a late summer afternoon, music would have been spilling from restaurant doorways and masses of shoppers would have been ambling past the storefronts. Now it was all still and silent, as if frozen in time.

A pretty awful time. Several of the windows had been shot out, shards of glass glinting in the fading sunlight. A dead body sprawled across the sidewalk nearby, and I spotted another near a car down the street. Xavier had continued to leave a path of carnage in his wake.

But there were some signs of living humanity left. A few faces peered out of the windows on higher floors, pale with fear.

"He's been shooting anyone desperate enough to try to make a run for it," Gideon reported. "Hard to say whether they're safer taking that chance or staying put."

Mercy peered down the street. We could see Xavier and the two Storm men still with him a few blocks away, pacing by a small delivery truck they'd stalled in the middle of the road. As I watched, Xavier took another shot, shattering a second-floor window. Someone yelped, whether in pain or just fear I couldn't tell.

"Where's the building he's set up the explosives around?" Mercy asked.

Gideon gestured toward the distant figures. "It's that coffee shop on the corner. The upper floors are divided into three apartments, and several of the shop's customers ended up fleeing upstairs when the shooting started. Xavier's set up the explosives all along the front of the building with a trigger switch he hasn't moved more than ten feet from since he placed it. The Storm's men barricaded the back door so no one can escape that way."

"Who's going to try me now?" Xavier hollered, still pacing like a caged lion. He slammed his fist right into a store window, making it burst apart. "You want a piece of me? I'll tear *you* to pieces."

The guy was fucking insane. Not that I'd had much doubt about that fact before, but he'd somehow pushed the title of maniac to a completely new level.

A familiar burn of rage spread from my gut up through my chest. My teeth set on edge. This asshole had destroyed enough already. He'd tormented the woman I loved, smashed up the city I called home, and tried to kill the guys I considered family too many times to count. It'd gone on for too long. I was going to end the motherfucker and protect what was mine before he could do any more damage.

"Let's go," Wylder called to our troops. "Remember, keep low and don't make yourselves an easy target. Surround him as close as you can safely get and pick off him and his men as soon as you have an opening."

A few of the Claws men pumped their hands in the air. "For the Claws!"

"For the Claws!" Mercy echoed. "And the Nobles, and freeing Paradise Bend together!"

With a rush of energy, the men dispersed, some hustling along the sidewalks where the parked cars offered some shelter, some jumping back in their own cars to drive around and come up on Xavier from the other side.

The four of us stuck close together, moving down the street with our eyes fixed on Xavier and our guns ready. My free hand balled into a fist. I wanted so badly to charge right up to him and pummel his face into a pulp, but I wasn't reckless enough to give in to that urge, which would probably end with me dead before I got within half a block of him.

It was a good thing I didn't go dashing off into the open, because we'd only closed the distance by one block when bullets sprayed down at us from above. We leapt back against the nearest buildings, but one of the Noble men hadn't been fast enough. He slumped with the back of his head blown out.

"There's someone on the roof," I yelled out.

Wylder motioned everyone in view as close to the buildings as we could get, where the shooter wouldn't be able to take proper aim. The anger inside me churned even more furiously. Our job had just gotten twice as hard.

Xavier had taken notice of the activity at our end of the street. He let out a roar that sounded as enraged as it did triumphant and smashed another window with his fist. Blood was trickling over his knuckles, but I saw no sign in his wild expression that he cared. Then he let loose his own hail of bullets from his rifle, forcing us to drop low to the ground. Gunfire battered the sides of the cars and set off a couple of alarms.

But a few of our men had made it farther down the street to come at Xavier and his accomplices from the other side. With a *bang*, one of the Storm men next to Xavier crumpled. Xavier growled and jerked back closer to the safety of the truck, shooting indiscriminately all around him. We couldn't move any closer, not without walking into the path of a bullet from one direction or another.

"If we could just kill *him*, the other men would take off," Wylder muttered. "They've only stuck around because they've got him on their side."

"But how do we get close enough?" I asked. "Do you think the other Nobles—"

Before I could even finish the question, more of our men opened fire farther down. The other Storm lackey went down with a splat of torn guts, but Xavier had stayed out of range. Then he grabbed something he'd stashed under the truck and hurled it toward the combined Noble and Claws forces.

"Watch out!" Mercy cried.

I couldn't tell how many of the men managed to dash far enough for safety before the device Xavier had thrown exploded with an earth-shattering force. Two cars flipped right onto their sides with the impact. When the dust cleared, I thought I spotted a few limbs lying on the street with no body attached to them.

My stomach clenched with nausea, and my rage burned hotter. We couldn't let Xavier keep at this.

I aimed my gun around the side of the nearest car and shot at his head as well as I could, but it was too far. The bullet just dinged the truck's side mirror five feet to Xavier's left.

I glared at the buildings around Xavier as if it was their fault for not simply jumping off their foundations and burying him in rubble, and my gaze caught on the electrical wires running from post to post along the street. I grimaced. "Too bad we can't just shoot one of the wires and electrocute the fucker."

To my surprise, Gideon perked up. "I don't think it'd work that way, but the basic idea might have something to it."

I let out a startled chuckle. "I guess I can be smart every now and then, huh? Who'd have thought?"

Gideon studied the buildings, his face hardening with intense thought. I swore you could see the gears turning in his head when he got like this. "He hasn't smashed up that shoe store over there yet. I might be able to use it. But we'd need to get him to come over and make contact with some part of the building when I'm ready. I don't know if we can be sure—"

Mercy straightened up. "I'll do it."

My spirits plummeted. "No. You're not getting anywhere near that bastard." Gideon looked equally unnerved.

Mercy shook her head. "Xavier's here because he wants revenge. He wants it most of all from me. You're not going to get any better bait than that. I'm fast, even with my leg hurt. I won't get too close to him. But I can get him over to the store. You just have to make sure you don't electrocute me too."

"Here." Wylder handed her his headset and nodded to Gideon. "Stay in contact with each other, follow each other's cues. I know you've got this… but be careful."

"There's got to be another way," I said desperately, but even as I spoke, I knew Mercy had a point.

She motioned in Xavier's direction just as he sent another volley of bullets over the street. "Look at him. He doesn't care if he walks out of here alive so long as he takes everybody out with him. He hates me more than anything else, and that makes me his greatest weakness."

She was right. There was no other way. But it didn't mean I had to be happy about it. I pulled her in for a hug while I laid a kiss on top of her head. "Good luck."

She nodded and stepped away.

"I'll need someone to get me to the back of the building," Gideon said.

"I'll do that," I volunteered. "It was my idea—I should go with you."

Mercy set off down the sidewalk, walking slowly but steadily toward Xavier, braced to duck if she needed to. I stared after her until Gideon tugged on my arm. "Come on. I know you're worried about her—I am too—but Mercy can handle herself. We have to do our part."

"Right." I forced myself to follow him down a narrow lane between two of the stores and into the back alley that ran the length of several blocks. We had to reach the shoe store and get everything set up in time.

As soon as we were in the alley, we set off at a jog. Gideon's breath started to rasp within seconds, but he didn't let up his pace.

Just as we came up on the street between us and the next section of alley, a Storm man we hadn't spotted earlier stepped out to confront us, his gun pointed right at me.

I didn't think, just sprang at him, bringing my full weight to bear. The gun went off, the bullet ricocheting off the pavement. I slammed my elbow into his forearm, hearing the bone crack, and heaved him down onto the ground. With a swift punch, I crushed his windpipe. He sputtered and sagged, the life going out of him.

"And that's why I'm glad I brought back-up," Gideon remarked, sounding just a little shaken. "Let's go before Xavier catches on to what we're doing."

We rushed the last short distance to the back of the shoe store. Gideon had me bash the lock on the back door and then, once we were inside, punch holes in the walls here and there so he could get at the wiring. When he was satisfied, I left him fiddling with the wires and mumbling to himself as he worked out how to adjust the connections and lay his trap.

I peered out through the big display window at the front of the store. The awning outside shaded it, and with the interior lights off, you would've needed to come right up to the glass to make us out inside. For now, I kept well back just in case, but Xavier didn't appear to have noticed us. I could see him ranting and waving his gun around just a little farther down the street.

Then Mercy came into view. She'd crouched down as she got closer, staying hidden behind the cars. She had her gun in her hand, but I knew as well as she did that Xavier was moving around too fast and erratically for her to get a good shot in. Still...

"Tell Mercy to try to shoot him first," I said to Gideon. "Even if she misses, it'll be a good way to get his attention and get him pissed off. And maybe she won't miss."

"I'm trying to concentrate here," Gideon muttered, but he passed on my suggestion into his mic, following it with, "But keep laying low for another minute or two. I've almost got it..."

Xavier strode a little to the left and then a little to the right, taking more shots at the Nobles who were holding their ground farther away after the earlier blast. Then he went around the truck to where he was keeping the explosives. The hairs on the back of my neck stood on end.

"Hurry!" I snapped.

"I'm doing my best," Gideon hissed back. "If you don't want to end up electrocuted too, chill out for five seconds."

I might have been annoyed, except it seemed like it really was only five seconds later when Gideon moved to the hole I'd made closest to the window and snipped a wire there. Holding it by the insulated covering, he pressed the frayed end to the metal window frame. It stayed in place when he moved back.

"Okay," he said to Mercy. "All he needs to do is touch the window frame, and he'll get a good shock. The glass and the sidewalk should be safe. Just avoid anything metal."

Mercy murmured something and nodded in return. She cocked her gun, bobbed up, and fired off a shot.

As I'd expected, Xavier wove to the side just as she pulled the trigger. At the sound of the gun firing, he lurched even farther out of the way and spun around.

Her body rigid, Mercy stood up to show herself. Her voice carried through the glass. "Hey asshole. I'm the one you want, aren't I? So why don't you come and get me?"

In answer, Xavier snarled and spewed bullets at her from his rifle. Mercy leapt down with her well-honed reflexes, rolling to the far side of the store. Xavier marched forward, his expression getting fiercer as he came.

Our plan was working, but I hated it now. He was getting way too close to her. My muscles strained all through my arms. I could dash out there and punch the lights out of him...

Except I wouldn't get very far while he was still armed and totally aware.

"Missed me," Mercy taunted. "What's taking you so long?"

Xavier let out a wordless bellow and rushed at the car. Instead of hurtling around it, he leapt right onto the hood. Mercy dove underneath it, out of the range of his next spray of bullets. I winced at the thought of her limbs getting scraped on the asphalt.

"You're stuck now, pathetic little kitty," Xavier snapped, and jumped onto the sidewalk right outside the store.

The second his feet hit the ground, Mercy struck. She was fucking amazing, and in that moment, I couldn't believe I was lucky enough to call this woman my own. She whipped her legs out from under the car and slammed both of her heels into Xavier's calves with all the strength she had in her.

Xavier stumbled and teetered to the side. His heavy form crashed into the window. The glass shattered around him. As he twisted to the side to avoid the jagged shards, his shoulder smacked into the edge of the frame.

It wouldn't have mattered if we hadn't set everything up. He'd probably have bounced right back around, barely bruised. But Gideon had been fucking amazing too.

The second Xavier's shoulder hit the frame, a crackling sound hummed through the air. Xavier's entire body jerked and spasmed, his muscles jiggling like Jell-O.

He managed to break away from the frame, but he was reeling so badly he nearly tripped over his own feet. And that was my cue to jump in.

I fired off all the shots left in my gun as I ran at him through the broken window. At least two caught him in the chest. He swiveled around, staggering, and I sprang over the window frame so my own body didn't catch so much as a spark of the live electricity. Then I was on him.

I rammed into Xavier, shoving him to the ground. My fists connected with his jaw, then his nose, drawing a spurt of blood that added color to his scarred face. He twitched underneath me, and I pummeled him even harder, smacking his head back against the sidewalk, my vision hazing red.

This was for all the horrible "gifts" he'd left that'd freaked out Mercy. *This* was for every injury he'd ever given her. *This* was for killing our men, kidnapping Gideon, and siccing his lackeys on Rowan. *This* was for passing out Glory like candy and getting all those people hooked. *This* was for encouraging the Storm to set his sights on our home in the first place.

"Kaige. Kaige!" Mercy's voice reached me through my furor.

My mind started to clear. My hands slowed and then fell to my sides. I stared down at the ruin of Xavier's face, his features battered beyond recognition other than a few shreds of the scars clinging to what was left of his cheeks. His skull had broken open like a cracked egg leaking brains and blood onto the concrete. His body lay totally limp beneath me.

Mercy's arms wrapped around my shoulders. "He's dead. Xavier's dead. You did it."

I had. I blinked a few times, and something released inside me. Pushing myself off of the mutilated body, I turned and grabbed Mercy in the tightest hug I had in me.

She squeezed me back just as hard, a bit of a sob coming into her next breath. The other Nobles and Claws gathered around us, Wylder and Gideon pushing through the crowd to reach us. Someone let out a low whistle.

I forced myself to look at Xavier again and then down at my raw, bloodied knuckles.

I'd done that. I'd beaten the man into a pulp. It'd been brutal and horrific, but also so fucking necessary. He'd already hurt so many people. I'd just spared who knew how many more the same pain.

"The guy on the roof made a run for it when he saw you take Xavier down," Wylder said, clapping me on the back. "We managed to take him out before he got very far. They're all gone."

"It's over," Mercy said with an air of wonder.

A smile stretched across my face. Hell, yeah, it was. And I'd seen it through to the end, with my best friends and my woman with me every step of the way.

28

Mercy

My heart was still pounding double-time. Xavier was dead. My worst enemy was *dead*. I felt laughter bubble in my chest, but no sound came out of my throat.

"You're bleeding," Wylder said, pushing closer, and it was only then that I registered the stinging on my arm. I'd scraped the skin raw on my elbow when I'd hurled myself under the car to escape Xavier.

"I'll be okay," I said, taking one deep breath and then another. A smile started to curve my lips. "I'll be just fine." And it felt like I was stating a fact this time, not just a hope that the words would be true.

Gideon finished fiddling with the wires to cut off the electrical current in the store and hurried over. He brushed the loose strands of hair back from my cheek and looked me over. "I knew you could handle him, but I was pretty worried for a few minutes there."

The laugh finally tumbled out. "So was I," I admitted.

I glanced down at the broken body lying near my feet. Kaige had battered Xavier's head so badly that his skull had literally split open. The gore made my stomach churn, but a sense of victory gripped me at the same time.

This was the only fate that monster had deserved after the way he'd terrorized our city.

Wylder slipped his arm around me. "Come on. Let's get you home. Or to my home first. You played a huge role in taking down Xavier—you should be with us when we tell my dad the good news."

I nodded, exhaustion trickling through me. I'd been so keyed up for the entire week, and now it was over. The sun was only just sinking below the level of the buildings, streaks of pink and purple touching the sky.

We'd met the deadline. The Storm's presence in Paradise Bend was at an end. The whole future stretched out ahead of us, and it had to be better than what we'd just gone through.

I walked a little slowly, the wound on my thigh still closed but aching from the strain I'd put on my body. As we headed back to the car, I noticed a few people who were peeking out of the buildings giving us curious looks. None of them would know exactly what had happened on the streets today or who had saved them, and maybe that was for the best.

After I congratulated the Claws and thanked them for their help, I returned to find Wylder talking to Gideon. I didn't catch what he'd said, but Gideon tapped away at his phone texting while Wylder drove. I picked up the little purse that Anthea had lent me off the floor by my feet where it'd spent so much time in the past few days and tucked it onto my lap instead. The gun in the back of my jeans felt uncomfortably heavy, but I didn't want to set that aside until we were safe within four walls again.

Kaige noticed the purse and grinned. "Are you going to get all ladylike on us now?"

I snorted. "Not likely. It's Anthea's. I should probably give it back to her at some point."

"Can you even fit anything in there?"

I thought of the tiny gun tucked inside next to the lipstick tube and packet of tissues. "You bet."

I understood what Wylder had instructed Gideon to do when we walked into the Noble mansion and found Frank waiting for us in the foyer. "I'm fine," I protested again as he dabbed an antiseptic wipe against the scrape on my elbow and taped a bandage there. Then he gave Kaige's blood-splattered shirt a nervous look.

Kaige's grin widened. "Don't worry, this isn't *my* blood."

"Is my dad around?" Wylder asked Frank.

The older man shrugged. "I haven't spoken with him lately, but I didn't see him leave either."

There was no sign of Anthea either. I shot her a quick text, and she replied that she was tying up some loose ends as far as cleaning up the various bodies we'd left behind, but she'd be back at the mansion within the hour. She finished the message with a *Congrats!* surrounded by celebratory emojis that had me smothering an unexpected giggle.

Wylder motioned to us, and the four of us climbed the stairs and strode down the hall to Ezra's study. But the doorknob jarred when he tried to turn it, and no one answered his knock. Frowning, he led us to a few other spots he seemed to think his father might have been hanging out—one of the sitting rooms, the dining room, the living room—but we didn't find him anywhere.

"I guess he'll turn up eventually," Wylder said when we came to a stop near the bottom of the staircase, but his brow stayed knit.

Kaige stretched his arms over his head. "Oh well, I need a shower anyway. This dude really stinks."

"I should check up on a few things in my office," Gideon said. He already had his tablet out and was scrolling through some document on it.

I glanced toward the lounge room that held the big mahogany bar. "Why don't I mix up one of my custom drinks for us all to celebrate? I think I've got plenty of inspiration. You guys can meet us there when you're done."

Kaige's eyes brightened. "Yeah, we should totally celebrate! We deserve it after everything." His expression sobered momentarily, and I suspected he was rewinding the brutal events of today. I couldn't believe that in less than twenty-four hours we'd managed to both convince the Storm to back off and take down Xavier.

I was ready to nap for a thousand years.

"Are you sure you're up for it?" Gideon asked, his eyes scanning me.

"I'm okay, really. Besides, Frank didn't look concerned." It was barely evening, and I was still too wound up to think I'd actually be able to sleep. A euphoric sense of freedom was rising through me with the knowledge of Xavier's death. I had a few good hours before exhaustion eventually got the better of me. "Better sneak a little celebration in while we can."

Gideon and Kaige headed upstairs, and Wylder came with me into the lounge room. The gun at my back, the new pistol he'd given me after I'd had to throw away my other one earlier today, chafed at my skin. I set it on one of the stools, put Anthea's purse down on the counter, and went around behind the counter to eye the bottles lined up there.

"Any preferences?" I asked.

"Hmm?" Wylder said distractedly, dropping into the next stool over.

I leaned across the bar to poke his arm. "The booze? Remember?"

"Something that makes me buzzed," he said, finally snapping out of whatever thoughts he had been caught up in. "That'll do."

"Vodka then," I said. "With a little rum to even it out, and a few splashes of this and that." I started setting glasses out on the counter.

Wylder smirked. "It would be better if I got to taste it off of you."

I rolled my eyes. "Since when do you speak Kaige?"

Wylder just kept smiling. "You've changed me in more ways than you think." He paused, his gaze traveling over the glasses. I'd put out five. "Are we expecting Anthea?"

I paused before looking up at him. "I guess we could be. She said she'd be back soon. But I was thinking of Rowan, actually."

I started to put the fifth glass away, but Wylder stopped me. "No, pour one for him too. I know he's not here to celebrate, but he was equally responsible for our win—and for saving you."

"He has made a habit of rescuing people." I picked out the best brand of vodka on offer and poured a dollop into each glass, including the last one. "For Rowan."

Before I could move on to the other ingredients, Ezra sauntered in through the doorway. I stiffened at the sight of him. He was dangling a bottle of whiskey from his hand. When his gaze caught on us, he stopped in his tracks. The frown on his face deepened. "What are you doing in here?"

Wylder turned to face his father. "Celebrating. Want to join us?"

Ezra didn't look like he was in a festive mood. His eyes were clear enough, but his face was flushed and his mouth set at a sour angle. I suspected he was at least a little drunk. He took a couple of steps toward us, his gaze sliding between me and his son. "What the hell should we be celebrating for?"

"We took out Xavier for good and ran the Storm out of town," Wylder said. "Paradise Bend is ours again with no challengers."

Ezra took a long swig of the amber liquid. "Mine. Paradise Bend belongs to *me*. I'm still in charge."

"Yes, of course," Wylder said.

"Don't you dare use that tone with me," Ezra said. In a split second, he'd reached to his concealed holster and brought out a gun. He kept it pointed at the floor, but my nerves set immediately on edge. "I see what you're trying to do."

"Dad, put that away," Wylder said, calmly but firmly.

"You think I'm so gullible that I don't see what you're trying to pull?" Ezra hissed. I saw him note my gun where I'd left it on the stool on the other side of the counter, too far away for me to reach. My fingers itched for it. He shot me a cold smile and then focused on Wylder again. "You figure you can steal my empire from under my nose while I sit back and do nothing? Well, you can forget about that, son."

My heart lurched in my chest. I had the feeling that it'd only take one wrong move, and he wouldn't hesitate to shoot us.

"Dad," Wylder said, getting up carefully from his seat. "You've got it all wrong. I wasn't doing it for me. It was for all of us—for the Nobles. I was doing my duty as your son and heir, protecting our empire."

"My son is dead," Ezra said. Wylder flinched at his words. "You've undermined me at every turn. Even today, you gathered my men and tried to antagonize them against me."

I would have guffawed at the absurdity of that accusation if Ezra hadn't been in such an unstable mood. *He* was the one who'd constantly undermined Wylder and worked his underlings against us. Wylder hadn't said a word about his father when he'd rallied the Nobles to fight Xavier.

I eased closer to the counter and set my hand on its polished surface next to Anthea's purse. There was no way Ezra would suspect I had a gun in there, it was so small. I tucked my fingers through the opening, brushing the pistol's surface and sliding it into my grasp. Just in case.

"I was doing what needed to be done," Wylder said, an edge creeping into his voice as he no doubt had some of the same thoughts I'd had. "Someone needed to go up against Xavier—someone had to get everyone organized to defend the city. It isn't my fault that you decided that was all my job and washed your hands of it."

"It was all your fault to begin with," Ezra snarled. "Getting in with this slut and then allying with the Claws as if they could hold a candle to our power. But that was all part of your plan, wasn't it? Leverage as many men as you could against me and then with me out of the way, and you thought you would have the throne. Well, who's holding the gun now? Do you think if I was weak I could do this?" He brandished the pistol at us.

Wylder didn't reach for his own gun. His jaw clenched as he stared at his Dad, his hands raised in a placating gesture. If he pulled a gun on his father, it would come down to two choices—kill him or be killed instead.

I couldn't blame him if he was having trouble crossing the point of no return. My heart ached for him. Why had it needed to come to this? I knew what it meant to have your father as your worst enemy, and I wouldn't have wished it on anyone.

"Dad." Wylder took a step toward Ezra. He was still trying to deescalate the situation.

"Don't," Ezra warned, clicking the safety off. My fingers curled around the trigger of my tiny pistol as I glanced between the two men. Was there any way all three of us could walk out of this confrontation alive? The wildness in Ezra's face and voice reminded me of Xavier in the middle of his rampage.

"We can talk about it, Dad. Keep the bottle and put the gun away."

"Don't tell me what to do." Ezra's eyes hardened as if he had come to a decision. "*I* know what to do. It's time to start over, to build my empire from the ground up again. But first I need to get rid of the snake in our midst."

"You already have what you wanted," Wylder said. "Open your eyes, Dad. I'm the person you raised me to be."

"You're a fucking traitor," Ezra snarled. Then his gaze snapped to me. "But you're the real problem. You're the reason I lost my son. You spun your web around him, seduced him, warped his mind, and took him away from me. So you die first."

My pulse thundered in my ears. Ezra jerked his gun hand toward me, his grip tensing around it, and there was nothing else I could do. I yanked my hand out of the purse and pulled the trigger on the tiny pistol.

Wylder's hand shot up at the same instant, having snatched his own gun. Two bangs split the air simultaneously. I flinched, half-expecting to feel an impact as a bullet tore through my flesh. But no pain came.

Ezra fell, his grasp going limp and his gun tumbling to the floor next to him, unfired.

With my heart in my throat, I stepped around the counter. Wylder came up beside me. We stared down at his father. Ezra sprawled on his back, his eyes gazing at the ceiling unblinking. Blood streamed from two bullet holes side by side in his forehead. We'd shot him together.

We'd killed him together.

The knowledge took its time sinking in. I kept bracing for Ezra to blink, to sit up and start ranting at us again. But his body didn't so much as twitch.

He was really gone. No more snarky remarks about me and the Claws. No more belittling Wylder's contributions. No more insane power grabs that undermined his own people.

In a way, this was the moment we were finally free.

Wylder dropped his gaze, his mouth tightening. I gripped his shoulder. "I'm sorry. I know you didn't want it to end like this."

He sighed and leaned into my touch just a little. "I didn't, but I knew it was coming. It needed to happen. He was always going to force my hand, from the moment I started questioning his judgment. I just —" He shook his head, cutting himself off. "Maybe it shouldn't have been hard after everything he's done, but it still was."

"I think that just makes you human," I said softly. "But you're going to be okay. You've got Kaige, and Gideon, and Rowan—and me. I'll be right here with you as we rule Paradise Bend together. We'll tell a different story this time. We'll fix our fathers' mistakes, as many of them as we can. I give you my word."

Wylder tugged me to him and bowed his head, his forehead brushing mine. "And I give you mine," he said, and kissed me like he never meant to stop.

29

Two months later

Mercy

"We caught some guys poking around the former Glory supply house," Sam reported, standing on the other side of what was now my desk in my father's old study. "They said some shit about how they were going to pick up the trade if we and the Nobles didn't want it."

I leaned back in the leather chair and rolled my eyes. "There's nothing in there to trade." After Ezra's death—which as far as anyone outside his inner circle knew had been an accident, no matter how they might speculate with the body going unseen—one of Wylder's first decisions had been to dispose of every bit of Glory in the Nobles' possession. Kaige had gleefully joined in the destruction. "I hope you told them Glory is off-limits in the county and that we're going to crack down on anyone who tries to bring it in."

Sam nodded with a sly grin. "I put it to them very clearly." He waggled his fingers toward his gun. "They were hardly more than kids. I think they were bluffing anyway."

"Like so many others," I said with a bemused grimace. Since the Storm had pulled out of the county and the Nobles and Claws re-established ourselves as rulers of Paradise Bend, random small-time crooks kept coming out of the woodwork, trying to figure out if there were any scraps they could snatch for their own. I didn't mind them picking up a little business here and there where we'd left gaps, but Glory was a total no-go.

Quinn had just come in, waiting by the door for his chance to speak. Now he piped up. "There are rumors going around to the Steel Knights revival now. A few guys were spotted at the skateboard park wearing their old bandanas." He snorted.

I waved off that news. "Let them be. They weren't villains—they just ended up under the control of one. If anyone gets it into his head to come at us, we'll crush them then."

I wasn't concerned about this new development. I didn't need to be. The smaller street gangs were already lining up to swear fealty to me, and the Claws were getting new recruits every day. In just the past month, we'd doubled in size.

And most of them specifically wanted to work for *me.* People knew who the new Queen of the Bend was. They knew who had killed Colt and taken out Xavier. They were afraid, and they believed that I could show them how to conquer the things they feared.

For the first time in my life, I could be the woman my whole life had been preparing me for, whether Dad had wanted to accept the role I could play or not.

"Anything else?" I asked.

As the two men shook their heads, Beckett peeked into the room. "Just finished up my patrol."

I smiled at him, getting to my feet. The kid had been settling in here pretty well, although Anthea kept talking about how maybe she should bring him out to New York City and put him to work there. We hadn't quite figured out what the best position for him would be, and so far I'd just had him running what amounted to errands.

He hadn't shown any sign of minding, though. I got the impression he kind of liked getting to be a regular gang member out on the street, kicking butt and taking names, after all his years keeping up appearances by his father's side.

"All's well?" I asked.

Beckett shrugged, a glint of amusement dancing in his eyes. "I ran into some punk who was claiming that Wylder Noble is the only real power in the Bend and you just follow his orders. So I kicked his ass and informed him that those were my orders from you."

The other two guys cracked up, Sam clapping Beckett on the shoulder. "Good work, kid."

I tipped my head. "If anyone does more than just shoot their mouth off, let me know and maybe I'll make a personal visit to set a few things straight."

Beckett laughed. "I don't think it'll come to that."

The guys headed out. I checked the time and followed them. It was getting late, but I had one more thing to take care of before I turned to my other business of the night. I had a task ahead of me that'd been a long time coming.

Stopping in my bedroom, I picked up one of the urns I'd finally been able to collect from the coroner's office. I'd already scattered the other ashes in my relatives' favorite spots, saying a private good-bye. This final one, I carried downstairs.

Jenner met me in the hall. "Everything's ready."

"Good." As we tramped down to the basement, I glanced over at him. "How's Sarah doing?" After the chaos had died down, he'd brought her with him to his old house, since her mom had never turned back up. I wasn't sure he'd have handed Sarah over to her mother anyway after the way the woman had abandoned her.

"Oh, she's great," he said with a chuckle. "Loving this year's teacher. I swear she's excited to go to school—definitely doesn't get that from me."

As we came into the basement, his expression turned more serious. A couple of other Claws men were already there next to a huge tub of mixed cement. Jenner walked over and gave it a careful stir.

"Are you sure about this?" he asked me. "You're tying him to this house forever."

"That's fine," I said, shifting the urn in my arms. "The house is at least as much his as it is mine. But this is definitely the most fitting part of it to bury him in."

At my gesture, the other men heaved open the concrete slab that covered the pit where I'd spent so many tormented hours. I didn't shy away from the sight of the stains of blood and other bodily fluids that marked its base. A flicker of the old panic rose up in my chest, but I breathed through it.

Dad was gone. He would never shut me away in there again, and neither would anyone else. No one in the Claws would use that kind of torture under my rule—or ever again, if I had my way.

I opened the urn's lid and shook the gray dust of my father's ashes into the base of the pit. Then I helped Jenner heave the tub closer. Together, we poured the cement into the hollow. The gray sludge swallowed up my father's last remains and crept up the sides of the pit.

We had a little more than enough to fill it to the lip where the slab would sit. The other men shoved the slab back into place where it would bind with the new cement. Then Jenner sealed the edges with the last few dribbles from the tub. He smoothed the stuff out with a scraper, and just like that, the floor looked seamless, as if there'd never been anything cut out of it.

In the back of my mind, the distant echoes of a child screaming for help faded away. Both my father and the horrors of the past were truly buried.

"Thank you," I said to Jenner and the other men, and turned my back on my worst memories.

As I drove into Paradise City, my eyes caught on the distant spire of the waterfront development. Construction had started up again a few weeks ago, and they'd been making quick progress with the new plans, approved of and invested in by Evan Anderson. From the moment he'd left the hospital, Rowan had gotten to work coordinating with the real estate guru, and more modern office complexes and condo buildings were in the works on Noble-owned property throughout Paradise Bend and where Ezra had started to expand throughout the state.

If the Storm was pissed off that we'd nabbed one of his business associates as well as his son, he hadn't dared to complain.

Anderson wasn't the only new alliance we'd formed. We'd heard from the Long Night a couple of times since the Storm's departure, once to congratulate us and assure us of his continued support of our leadership, and once to connect us with a construction company looking for new contracts that he'd thought might be a good fit. I still wasn't sure exactly how he took his cut of the profits we brought in, but I was resigned to not knowing.

As long as he didn't mess with Paradise Bend, I could live and let live.

When I reached the Noble mansion, instead of pulling into the front drive, I parked the car a little way down the street and scaled the side wall. No one would have stopped me from walking in the front door, but arriving this way was more fun.

I sneaked between the trees to avoid detection, clambered up to the lowest level of the fire escape using a window ledge and a decorative ridge for help, and climbed the rest of the way up the metal structure to the room that was now my honorary guest bedroom in the house.

I slipped through the window to find I wasn't alone.

"You're late," Kaige declared, getting up from where he'd been lounging on the massive bed.

I rolled my eyes. "I wasn't supposed to be here in the first place."

Kaige smiled impishly. "But I was hoping you'd show up tonight." He hooked a finger around the loop of my jeans and pulled me closer. I put my arms around him and grinned.

The door opened, and Gideon came in, just putting his phone in his pocket. He tsked his tongue at me. "No matter how stealthy you get, that alarm is still going to go off."

"Who says I want to avoid it?" I said, leaning over to invite a kiss from him. "It told you I was here, and that's exactly what I wanted."

Gideon caught my mouth with his in answer. The flick of his tongue and the cool pressure of his lip ring combined with Kaige's solid arms around me had me wet in an instant.

"You've been busy," Gideon said when he stepped back. "Still keeping everyone in line down in the Bend?"

"There's always something going on, but I find ways of dealing with whatever comes up. And I can always squeeze in some time to drop in on my favorite boys."

As if summoned by those words, Wylder and Rowan stepped into the room, Wylder locking the door behind them. My heart still fluttered seeing Rowan walking so steadily, the crutch he'd needed for a few weeks after his hospital stay long gone.

"Glad you stopped by," Wylder said with a smirk. "I had to get in touch anyway. Rowan and I are just working out the details of a deal with Anderson. We're having dinner with him tomorrow, and he wants you to be there too."

I flopped down on the silky comforter draped across the bed. "I think I can fit that into my schedule. What are we building this time?"

"Some kind of entertainment center," Rowan said. "Movies, games, the whole shebang. I think it'll be really good for the county."

I laughed. "The more we can keep people entertained with things that don't involve guns or drugs, the better."

"I absolutely agree," Kaige put in.

Wylder came over, and the brawny guy let his boss tug me out of his embrace. Wylder brought one hand to my cheek and the other to my waist, dipping his head to capture my mouth.

He kissed me only at the edge of my lips, teasing me. Impatiently, I turned to face him fully and deepened the kiss. His tongue caressed my lips before coaxing its way inside.

I murmured encouragingly and slid my hands up his chest to loop them around his shoulders. Wylder pulled me over closer so our bodies were flush against each other. I could feel the others' eyes on us as their boss devoured my mouth, but there was no jealousy in any of those gazes, only a growing heat.

Wylder ground his hips into me insistently, his rapidly hardening cock pressing against my core. A groan escaped me at the promise of pleasure in that motion. Our kiss turned open-mouthed, our tongues tangling together, sloppy and glorious.

The others didn't stand back for long. Rowan's hands skimmed my back and kneaded my ass. He stepped in so I was sandwiched between the two of them. When he teased his fingers along my jaw, I broke my kiss with Wylder to turn toward him.

Lust hazed his dark blue eyes. He closed them before leaning in to steal a kiss of his own.

As our mouths crashed together, Wylder didn't let go of me. His fingers pinched my nipples through my shirt, making me gasp against Rowan's lips. If my panties hadn't been soaked before, they definitely were now.

As I kissed Rowan harder, Wylder continued to work over my breasts until my nipples were hard nubs, sparking with every touch. Then he bent down to suck them through the thin cotton of my shirt.

Gideon and Kaige came up on either side of me. Gideon slipped his hand between me and Wylder to undo the fly of my jeans. Kaige took it upon himself to tug up my shirt. The other guys eased back for just long enough for him to pull the tee right off me.

Gideon eased down my jeans, and Rowan took the opportunity to unclasp my bra. I let that drop to the floor too, standing before my men in nothing but my panties. Their eager gazes roamed over my naked skin, trailing heat in their wake without even touching me.

"You're a goddess, Mercy," Kaige murmured. The men surrounded me, and I relaxed into their combined embrace. They could do whatever they wanted to, and I'd enjoy being along for the ride.

I slipped my hands into Kaige's thick hair and kissed him, my naked breasts grazing his chest. Kaige put his arms around me and pulled me tight against him. My hands slipped down his muscular frame until I could squeeze his cock through his jeans. He groaned, his hands stroking over me even more urgently. His fingers slipped into my panties, and he curled a finger along the length of my slit.

I closed my eyes, resting my head on his shoulder as his finger continued to fuck me. The other three watched us in rapt attention. Wylder was stroking his cock through his jeans as he took in the sight.

Gideon and Rowan unzipped their slacks in unison, wicked smiles curling their lips. The idea couldn't be clearer. I eased back, letting Kaige step out of the confines of his pants. The rest did too, the sound of heavy breathing and zippers coming undone raising the tingle of anticipation in the air.

I knelt on the ground while the boys circled me, slowly peeling their underwear off until four beautiful and hard cocks sprang out of their respective confines. My mouth watered at the sight.

I reached for Gideon's first, wrapping my tongue around the base and tasting his precum before sliding up. I kept my eyes on him while my mouth greedily engulfed his cock. His hands rested on my shoulders, but he didn't move, letting me work on his shaft. I bobbed my head as I swallowed his length whole before letting it slip out of my mouth. The others pressed close with eager impatience.

Kaige wasn't as sweet as Gideon. As soon as I wrapped my tongue around his cock, he put his hands at the back of my head and rolled his hips so that my mouth was stuffed with his cock. I moaned in the back of my throat as I swallowed him down, squeezing his balls at the same time.

When Kaige's grip on me loosened, I moved to Wylder next. I teased him a little, flicking my tongue around the piercing at the head of his cock before sucking it into my mouth. Not to leave Rowan out of the fun, I grabbed for him too, alternating between sucking their cocks.

Drool trickled down my chin, but I didn't care, licking their shafts and swirling my tongue around them. All of them were panting now, the smell of arousal heavy in the air. My pussy was outright gushing.

I pulled back and gave them all a satisfied smirk. Kaige growled, and before I knew what was happening, he swung me up over his shoulder and carried me to the bed.

I landed with a thump on it. I pushed myself toward the headboard as I watched the boys divest themselves of their shirts. Their glorious tattoos came into view on their chests and arms. I had the urge to lick every single stroke of art.

Kaige crawled toward me and spread my legs wide. Before I could react, he dove into my sopping wet cunt. His tongue licked up and down the length of my slit before flicking around my clit. My back almost arched off the bed at the waves of bliss rushing through me.

The others climbed onto the bed with us. Wylder leaned in and brought his mouth to my breast, suckling it hard while Rowan took the other. Their teeth grazed the sensitive skin of my nipples.

Gideon climbed up near my mouth and kissed me. The sensation of being pleasured at all the sensitive areas of my body overwhelmed me. My eyes rolled back, my hips swaying to meet Kaige's skillful tongue.

The heat of their bodies consumed me like a furnace. I whimpered and keened, letting these wicked men ravage me.

Kaige continued to lick and suckle my clit. The force of an orgasm blazed through me faster than lightning. I screamed as my body bowed upward. My pussy continued throbbing as Kaige pulled away, and the unmistaken sound of foil being ripped open reached my ears.

Before I could recover from my orgasm, Rowan flipped me on my stomach and dragged me toward him. Sometimes he was still the gentle boy-next-door with me, but he knew I liked him fierce just as much. Pulling me up on my knees, he knelt behind me and thrust into me from behind.

I gasped at the feel of his hard cock stretching my walls. The remains of my earlier orgasm made my pussy even more sensitive, pleasure shooting through me as Rowan continued to stroke in and out of me. He rocked his hips into me before pulling out and slamming home.

Rowan groaned, and I moaned right alongside him. My pussy clenched around his cock almost viciously and before long, I felt him jerk inside me. My body shook as my second orgasm of the night tore through me.

Wylder replaced Rowan in seconds. He turned me onto my back again. I watched him, my eyes at half-mast as he nudged my thighs apart and rubbed the head of his cock over my entrance. The slide of his piercing against my clit made my hips twitch and propelled another moan from my throat.

My legs lifted, embracing his hips to bring him closer. He braced himself over me, his hands bracketing my face as he stroked his way inside. Our bodies jerked together as he stroked in and out of me. Wylder's eyes closed as he continued to fuck me, hard and fast before switching to shallow but slower strokes.

Kaige watched us, lust scorching in his eyes as he stroked his cock. "Let me have my fun now."

Wylder didn't move right away but gave enough space for Kaige to come up beside me. Kaige's fingers skimmed over my heaving tits and swirled down to my stomach before he pressed his palm against my sensitive clit.

Wylder pulled back to give Kaige a turn. The bigger man settled between my thighs and drove his thick cock into me. My wet pussy welcomed his girth with barely any resistance.

Kaige knew just how to pound me to my next peak, gripping my hips and finding just the right angle. He was already almost there too. The second I squeezed around him with another earth-shattering orgasm, he followed me over the edge with a little shout.

Wylder pulled me back to him, rolling over so I was straddling him. As I happily sank down over his cock, his gaze slid past me to Gideon. "Aren't you going to get in here? Haven't you been doing all that 'research' on ideal positions for sharing?"

A hint of a blush colored the tech genius's cheeks. He was always the most adorable when he got awkward. "I *have* found some interesting options. And I made sure to be prepared." He opened the drawer on the bedside table and drew out a small tube. "This lubricant has a warming effect."

I grinned at him. "I think I'm pretty warmed up already."

"Not everywhere." With Wylder's cock still buried inside me, Gideon teased his fingers down my spine to my ass, letting them graze my other opening. "I'd like to take you from behind this time. Both of us, together."

A giddy giggle tumbled out of me. "What are you waiting for, then?"

Gideon's gaze heated. He squeezed some of the lube onto his fingers and massaged it over the pucker of my asshole, his finger occasionally slipping right inside. True to his promise, a pleasantly hot sensation spread over my skin, relaxing my muscles faster than ever before.

I rocked over Wylder, taking him deeper inside my cunt and swaying into Gideon's touch. Gideon knelt behind me and rubbed his cock over my ass. When I shook my butt side to side, he slapped me. "Steady," he warned.

Somehow, the bossy tone of his voice turned me on even more. I waited with bated breath as he slid inside of me, slowly at first before pulling out. The feeling of being doubly filled was as intoxicating as ever. Gideon pushed into me again, going halfway. On the next try, he was almost completely in.

I held in a breath as I felt his length invade me alongside Wylder's. Rowan bent his head to lap the tip of my breast into his mouth, and Kaige stole a kiss, and just like that, I was completely surrounded in the headiest of pleasures.

"What do you want Mercy?" Wylder murmured in the most seductive tone I'd ever heard.

"I want you both to fuck me," I managed to get out.

Both men obliged by bucking into me. They gradually picked up their pace as they matched each other's rhythm. I whimpered as the pleasure unfurled through me, wrapping all the way around my bones.

Gideon's breath came in short rasps behind me, his sweat-slick chest smacking against my back. Wylder rocked up to meet me, his gaze holding mine with nothing but desire and love in it.

"Our woman," he said in a raw voice. "So fucking amazing."

"Damn right, she is," Kaige said, watching us with avid eyes.

Gideon came first, arching over me with a sputtered groan. With the last slowing pumps of his cock inside me, Wylder thrust into me even harder, and I shattered all over again. My body sagged over him, and he spent himself inside me with a hitch of his chest.

I settled onto the bedspread on my back, and my men tucked themselves around me, all of us perfectly sated. Our sweaty limbs tangled with each other until I was completely cocooned between them. The smell of sex still hung thickly in the air.

I let out a yawn, cuddling closer to them as sleep crept up over me. Being queen was pretty fucking sweet, if I did say so myself. My father might even have been proud of me if he'd gotten to see how well I'd taken charge of the Claws and the powerful alliance I'd made with the Nobles, both in bed and out.

Well, no, he probably wouldn't have been proud, because I still wouldn't have been what he'd wanted—but he *should* have been proud. It didn't matter to me anyway. *I* was proud of both myself and my men, and that was all I needed.

We'd fought for the lives we wanted and won, and no ghosts of the past could steal away the brilliant future we were making for ourselves.

OUR KIND OF PARADISE

A Crooked Paradise bonus epilogue

Mercy

"Are you sure this is the best way to make your grand return?" Kaige asked, frowning. "It seems awfully... legit."

Only Kaige could say that word like it was a bad thing—and sound totally earnest at the same time. I swatted his brawny arm where he was sitting next to me on the sofa in my living room, but Beckett's calmly determined expression didn't waver.

"It's the kind of move my dad will respect and appreciate the most," our hostage-slash-apprentice said, and shifted forward in the armchair he'd taken across from the sofa. "Maintaining a solid front of legitimacy over the less savory parts of the family business is hugely important to him. The property is a prime piece of real estate, and I've already seen at least one smaller syndicate sniffing around."

Beckett had been talking about scooping up a plot of land with a derelict strip mall a few counties over from Paradise Bend and developing it into an entertainment complex. With the way this part of the state had been flourishing in the past few years since Wylder Noble and I had taken over as head of our respective gangs—and run off the more destructive criminal organizations—it sounded like a good plan to me, but real estate wasn't my usual domain.

One of my other men had plenty of experience there. Rowan nodded where he was standing next to the couch, his hand resting on my shoulder. "Property negotiations are no walk in the park. If you can beat out the crooks and the above-board buyers, who can be real sharks too, you'll be making a strong statement."

Perched on one of the other armchairs, Gideon looked up from his tablet and gave Beckett an analytical glance. "Are you sure you have the resources to back up the kind of bid that'll be necessary?"

"That's not a problem," Beckett said. "I have plenty of funds saved up from the work I've handled for the Nobles and the Claws. I've already arranged meetings with a couple of investors who could fill in the gaps and often go in on these sorts of deals."

He spoke with the same air of confidence he'd held even as a sixteen-year-old scrambling to save his family's legacy. The aura of authority he could give off was still impressive three years later. It wasn't hard to imagine him taking over one of the thirteen most powerful criminal organizations in the entire world when his father, the Storm, was willing to hand over the reins.

Wylder leaned his hands against the chair he'd been standing behind with a glint of amusement in his bright green eyes. "Sounds like you've got it all figured out." He glanced over at his aunt, who'd propped herself against the doorway to the dining room. "You figure he's ready to leave the nest?"

Anthea smiled in her measured way. "I know men twice his age who aren't as cool under pressure. He picked up the ropes around New York just as well as he did when he was running around down here. I think anyone who decides to compete with the Storm once Beckett's back home is going to regret it."

"Go for it, then," I said to Beckett with a tip of my head. I didn't hold the ultimate authority in the room—if anything, Wylder, Anthea, and I shared it—but I knew he'd been waiting on my approval. It'd been me Beckett had answered to when we'd first taken him under our wing. He'd come to me before anyone else to ask about taking steps toward returning home.

After the disastrous end to his last campaign and the three years of peace since, I didn't think the Storm was likely to launch another attack on Paradise Bend even once he had his son back in the fold. Maybe especially once his son was there, pulling a fair number of strings himself.

Beckett beamed at me, and while it was a little hard not to think of him as being a kid still, I couldn't help reflecting that he'd probably be breaking a whole lot of hearts as well as skulls back home.

"Great," he said, his assurance turning a little awkward just for a second. "I wanted to run it by you, after everything we've gone through... I'll go start getting the details in order right away."

As he hurried out, Kaige chuckled and slid his arm around my shoulders, tugging me closer to his massive frame. "It's a good thing he's so damn respectful, or I'd be worried about him moving in on our woman."

I rolled my eyes at him and patted my bulging belly, which made me feel almost as massive if in a totally different way from his brawn. The baby, eight and a half months along, gave me a sharp kick that both reassured me that she was as energetic as usual and felt as if she'd put a dent in my liver. "I think it's *very* clear at this point that I'm already attached. And I sure as hell don't need any more trouble than the four of you already give me."

If anything, I felt almost maternal toward Beckett after the way we'd all guided him through his late teens in the dangerous waters we'd found ourselves in. Maybe mentoring him had been good preparation for motherhood.

Anthea smirked. "I'm looking forward to seeing these four trouble-makers getting wrapped up in Daddy mode. Did you need me for anything else? I was going to head back to Manhattan."

"Go get back to your life," I said, with a knowing smile in return. Anthea had confided in me a couple of years ago that she had three men of her own keeping her on her toes in the best possible ways back in New York City.

As she headed out too, my second-in-command, Jenner, peered into the room from the hall. The Claws men regularly came and went from the Katz home.

"Have you got a second, boss?" he asked.

I motioned him in without worrying about the company. The leader of the Nobles and his inner circle knew all the goings-on within the Claws ranks, just as they filled me in on everything happening with their own gang. "What's up?"

Jenner stepped into the room with a respectful bob of his head. "Just confirming that we took care of the squabble with the idiots downtown and everyone seems to have gotten in line. No major problems on the horizon. You should be able to take at least a little time off without having to worry that we're drowning without you." He gave me a crooked grin with those last few words to show he wasn't criticizing my concerns about stepping back from the helm.

"I'm not going anywhere," I reminded him. "I still want to know everything that comes up, even if I'm nursing an infant while you're giving your report."

He let out a light laugh. "You should take some time for yourself, Mercy. Lord knows you've earned it."

I guessed he had some idea what he was talking about, since he was a father himself. But I knew it was going to be a delicate balance maintaining my position as queen of the Claws while also adapting to motherhood. A few of the men serving under me were still a little uneasy about the whole female boss thing, and plenty of outsiders had seen my lack of literal balls as an excuse to challenge my metaphorical ones.

"I'll do what I can," I said, and Jenner ducked out, sensing he was dismissed.

Kaige rested his hand on my belly and grinned when the baby inside landed another kick. "She's going to be a fighter like her mom."

"No doubt," Rowan said, giving my shoulder an affectionate squeeze, but I thought I heard an odd note in his voice.

Before I could wonder too much about that, Wylder pushed to his feet, raking his hand through his auburn hair. "Well, come on, all of you. Stop hassling the mother-to-be, and let's get on with our own business."

He said it in his usual cocky way, but there was an abruptness to his movements and a tightness to the smile he shot at his friends that sent apprehension prickling through me. I'd gotten to know the leader of the Nobles pretty well over the years, and I could tell when something was bothering him.

"Has some new problem come up over in the city?" I asked, heaving myself to my feet. The temporary new shape of my body put me more off-balance than I was used to, but I was determined to get back to my parkour practice within months after the birth. My daughter was going to see that you could be a woman and a mother and still hold your own alongside any man in our kind of world.

Wylder brushed past Gideon to give me a quick but demanding kiss. "Everything's fine," he told me, holding my gaze with his hand cupping my jaw. "You worry enough about your business without taking on ours too anyway."

I hmphed at him, but he just cracked a more relaxed smile at me and motioned the other guys out of the room. I watched him go, my concerns slightly eased but the question still tugging at me.

Was he really okay, or was he trying to protect me from something?

It wasn't as if my men usually neglected me, but one of the upsides of pregnancy was definitely seeing my toughened gangsters become totally doting fathers-to-be. I still wasn't totally used to the pampering. Like having Kaige turn up at noon with a takeout bag from my favorite Indian restaurant. The moment I'd finished discussing new plans with a few of the Claws underlings, he dragged me upstairs for a private lunch.

"Gotta keep you *and* the baby well fed," Kaige told me with a wink, laying out the food on the table in what had been the master bedroom when my dad still ruled the Claws but was now a meeting room. I'd kept my childhood bedroom even though it was a little smaller, mainly because I liked the ability to make a quick exit through the window via the backyard tree—not that I'd been doing a whole lot of tree-climbing in my current state.

I raised my eyebrows at the sight of the spread he'd brought. "Me, the baby, you, and an army from the looks of this."

"Hey, I can put away enough to cover a whole army on my own," Kaige said with a laugh.

But as I picked up one of the pakoras, my phone rang. I checked the number and hit the answer button.

"It's Beckett," I murmured to Kaige, putting it on speaker phone. I hadn't heard from our protégé since he'd announced his plans for the entertainment complex three days ago. "Hey, Beckett, how are things going?"

"Hey, Mercy," Beckett said in a strained tone that immediately put me on the alert. "I've actually run into a little trouble… I was hoping to get your advice."

My heart sank. I suspected it was a lot more than a "little" trouble if he'd risked his dignity by coming to me for help during what was supposed to be his bid for independence. "Of course," I said.

Kaige set his elbows on the table and leaned forward. "I can contribute my grand wisdom too," he announced with a grin.

I kicked him teasingly under the table and cocked my head to listen.

Beckett sighed. "It's just that another party, I think associated with a bigger gang than the one I was already aware of, is pushing in on the deal. They're pulling out all the stops to win over the investor I was making progress with, which is fair, but they've also been intimidating the seller. Lots of posturing and unspoken threats, a little property damage… But nothing directly against *me*. And if I want to push back, I don't have the Storm's people at my disposal yet."

Well, that one piece I could help with. "If you need Claws troops to command, I can send people over to help. I'm sure Wylder would say the same about the Nobles."

To my relief, that was enough to make Beckett's voice lighten. "Okay. Good. Thank you. That would give me enough to work with. I should figure out the exact tactics on my own if this is really going to be my win, so I won't ask you for specific strategy advice, but—you *would* push back, wouldn't you? It doesn't feel right to just back off, but maybe that would be the smarter decision and I just want this too much."

"I could tell how excited you were about the idea," I told him, with a pang through my heart. "It means a lot to you to get this project off the ground, and it seems like the location and the setup already there are perfect for it. Sometimes to get to where you need to be, you've got to get your hands dirty." We all knew something about that.

"Yeah." Kaige thumped his fist on the tabletop. "Don't let those pricks jerk you around. You were there first. Blast 'em all away and see how they like that."

Beckett let out a soft chuckle. "I might go for a more subtle approach than that, but I have no intention of giving up while I have the chance. Thank you. It was good just to get confirmation—and your support."

"We're in this with you," I said, and hung up feeling satisfied—until I saw the way Kaige's face had fallen.

I knit my brow. "Hey, what's wrong?"

He rubbed his hand over the sheen of dark hair on his scalp. "Maybe I shouldn't have said that. I went right to murdering them. What kind of crappy advice is that? Obviously Beckett's not going to get very far if he just kills every person he's got any problem with right off the bat."

One corner of my mouth quirked upward. "Or he will, but with a trail of dead bodies in his wake."

Kaige made a face at me. "You know what I mean. If someone threatens me—or you or Wylder—I take them down. That's what I know how to do. But I realize it's not always the best way."

I got up and motioned for him to push his chair back so I could sit on his lap. Even with my protruding belly, his brawny frame could completely engulf me. I looked up at him, stroking his neck. "Why are you worrying about that now? I know who you are, and it's never bothered me before. Beckett took your suggestion with a grain of salt. It isn't a problem."

Kaige hung his head. "But what if it will be?" He rested his hand on my belly. "I'm going to need to be a role model for her. That's what a good dad should be, right? That's how my dad was when I was really little, before he turned shitty." He raised his other arm and rubbed the dog tags he always wore between his fingers. "I don't want to be like him. I want to be there for her every way she'll need me to be. But maybe I'll just screw her up."

My heart wrenched, and I pulled him into a full embrace. "You don't need to worry about that," I insisted, hugging him tightly. "The fact that you're worrying about it means you'll make sure you don't go too far in the wrong direction. And you've got three other dads who'll be contributing who can keep you in line too, not that I usually have any problem doing that myself."

"You're sure?" he mumbled into my hair.

"Completely sure, or we wouldn't be doing this," I said with total confidence. "We've got each other's backs, like we always have."

A rumble reverberated from deep in Kaige's chest, and then he was kissing me hard, his arm looping right around my extended waist. I opened my mouth to him, welcoming his passion. When his tongue swept past my lips, I made an encouraging sound.

We hadn't gotten busy all that often since we'd more generally gotten busy preparing for the baby's imminent arrival, but heat unfurled between my legs. I wasn't totally against a little action.

Kaige angled his head to deepen the kiss, stroking his hand up and down my side. He was just cupping my breast with a growl when he hesitated at a particularly emphatic jab from my belly. Snorting, he slid his fingers down to that much larger slope instead. "Someone objects to how much attention Mommy's getting."

As if in answer, the baby kicked again, right where his hand was. Or maybe that was an elbow or a head-butt—I couldn't generally tell. She seemed to take great delight in working all of her limbs to maximum effect, like she figured my uterus was her own private gymnasium.

I guessed I could expect her to pick up the parkour good and fast, then.

I set my hand over Kaige's and nuzzled his neck. "It does kind of kill the mood, doesn't it? But she can't tell what we're up to, I'm sure."

He chuckled. "Still. I feel like I'd be scarring her innocent little mind." He pressed another peck to my temple and let his voice drop low with promise. "We'll wait until she's gone back to sleep, and then I'll show you all the good time you could possibly want, Kitten."

I nudged him. "I expect you to keep that promise."

To tell the truth, I kind of liked being pregnant, as much as it slowed me down physically. There was something pretty special about the sense that I'd grown a whole new life inside me, one I knew would be cherished from the start by *all* her parents in ways I'd never been. But far too many of the lowlifes I needed to keep in line saw my current state as an excuse to be even more asshole-ish than they'd been simply because I had a pussy instead of a dick.

I got back to the house after a walk that was more of a waddle—my attempt at keeping myself in as good shape as possible even in what would hopefully be the last week of my pregnancy—and found a small cluster of guys barely out of their teens hanging around near the front lawn. One of my Claws men was glowering at them from the porch, but they mustn't have done anything obnoxious enough for him to feel the need to run them right off yet.

"There she is!" one of the strangers crowed when he saw me, swiping his hand over his acne-scarred face. "This is the girl who figures she calls the shots in the Bend? You should be in a kitchen making us sandwiches."

He and his three friends cracked up as if that were a super original joke. I came to a stop a few feet away from them and set my hands on my hips. The stretchy waistbands of maternity pants came with a few advantages, one of which was that it was particularly easy to keep a pistol tucked out of view beneath the hem of my shirt. I also had a knife in my pocket. But I suspected I could take these jerks on barehanded.

"Maybe I'll carve the bunch of you up and feed you to the Claws for dinner," I said with a scoffing sound. "What do you want, or are you just looking to get your asses beaten?"

One of the other guys snorted. The one who'd spoken before looked at me with narrowed eyes. "Like you're going to do anything while you can barely walk without falling over."

I smiled at him thinly. "Try me. Lots of other men have, and none of them were laughing about it afterward—if they were even alive to make any sound at all."

The guys' amusement seemed to simmer down a bit. I didn't go around shouting to the world about how I'd killed my ex-fiancé and taken down various other pricks who'd tried to screw me over, but word got around. It was unlikely anyone operating on the criminal side in the Bend existed here very long without hearing at least one story.

"These Claws guys have been hassling us over nothing," the apparent leader said, switching from patronizing to indignant. "We don't owe you anything. You don't own the county. If we want to sell some shit, that's our business."

Okay, now we were getting down to the real problem. "What kind of shit exactly are you trying to sell, and where?"

"It shouldn't fucking matter!" one of the other guys bellowed, flinging his hand at me, and I noticed a bruise mottling his cheek. From a recent tussle with my men? "We've got a right to make a living how we want."

I opened my mouth to lay down the Katz version of the law, but before I could say anything, a familiar silver Toyota skidded to a stop next to the curb with a screech of the tires. Rowan leapt out, the wind rippling through his spiky blond hair and his dark blue eyes flashing. His gun was already in his hand, close by his side.

"What the fuck do you think you're doing?" he demanded as he stormed toward the guys. "Get the hell out of here and be glad she hasn't already kicked all your asses the way I'm about to."

Panic flashed across the guys' faces. They clearly hadn't been prepared for their confrontation to take a turn like this—and honestly, neither had I. Rowan was usually the peacemaker among my men, the one who looked for ways to negotiate rather than attack. I'd rarely seen him this aggressive.

As he came to a stop on the sidewalk next to me, the amateur gangsters took off down the street. Rowan shook his head, his stance still tense.

I elbowed him. "I was handling it just fine. They weren't that dangerous. Did you get yourself possessed by Kaige or something?"

Rowan's gaze slid to me, and his mouth twisted. "I—sorry. I noticed them hassling you, and I just saw red."

"Hey," I said, grabbing his hand to give it a quick squeeze. "I'm not saying it's a problem. We look out for each other. But they were practically kids. I hadn't even figured out what their beef really was yet." I raised my eyebrows at the guys' retreating backs. "I guess they'll come around later—or else they'll fall in line because they'll have realized they really were being asshats."

"I don't know if we should count on the latter," Rowan said, but he looked chagrinned. "If you think I undermined you—"

"Seriously, it's okay. I might have already come on just as strong as you did if I wasn't hefting this around." I patted my belly. "Why did you come over?"

He ducked his head. "Well, I was actually just driving by on my way back to the mansion. I like to take the route that goes past your house just to check up on things."

Amusement and affection wound together in my chest. "And lucky you, you showed up just in time to be my knight in shining armor." But the whole interaction left me feeling there was something else going on. I patted his arm. "You know, I was going to swing by the mansion to pick up a couple of things Anthea said I could grab from her room. Why don't you give me a drive?"

"Sure, of course." Rowan pressed a kiss to my forehead and opened the passenger door for me, but his body hadn't relaxed yet. I could see the apprehension coiled through his muscles.

I gave the Claws guy on the porch a little wave and hopped in. After Rowan had driven a few blocks, I decided it was time to pry.

"So, what was that really about? You've seemed a little more on edge than usual in the past week."

Rowan was silent for a long moment. I knew he wouldn't lie to me —he was just sorting out his thoughts.

He shifted his grip on the steering wheel and glanced over at me when he stopped at a red light. "I guess it's just—you're almost due, and seeing Beckett heading off to do his own thing—I keep thinking about how we're going to raise our kids. The kind of world we're raising them in. I'm not sure this is what I'd have wanted for them. How are we going to keep them safe? Even *not* being brought up in a gang isn't a guarantee..."

He had to be thinking about his little sister—the sister my dad had threatened and then nearly killed, taking another child's life by accident in her place. I swallowed thickly, my chest constricting.

"That's the thing, isn't it?" I said. "There aren't any guarantees.

And maybe our life is more dangerous than most, but we're used to it. We know how to operate within those rules. We've got two armies of gang soldiers who'll do whatever it takes to protect what belongs to us... And unlike my dad and Wylder's, we're going to let our kids choose their own way. We can make sure they have whatever opportunities they need. Isn't that why you joined up with Wylder in the first place—so you knew you could protect your family when you needed to?"

The slant of Rowan's mouth turned wry. "That's true. I guess we just have to take it one day at a time."

"That's how I'm looking at it." I raised my eyebrows at him. "And what's with making it 'kids,' anyway? I haven't even popped this one out yet and you're already planning on more?"

A laugh burst out of Rowan, breaking the last of the tension hanging over the conversation. "Hey, I just assumed," he said slyly. "I mean, they'll have four dads to pick up the slack."

"Yeah, yeah. Let's see how the first one goes." But the truth was, the thought of a larger family, of at least two kids playing together in the yard behind the Katz house or the Noble mansion, brought a warm glow into my heart.

When we got out at the Noble mansion, Rowan reached to hold my hand again. "Are you sure you won't consider moving in here for at least the first couple of weeks after she arrives?"

I made a face at him. "I'm not abandoning my home turf just because I have a baby to look after. I'm sure between the four of you, one can manage to be around lending a hand at any given time."

"Obviously," Rowan said, interlacing his fingers with mine. "I was just thinking you could be a lot more pampered with all of us around."

"Right, because I'm *so* the pampered princess type."

He leaned close to murmur in my ear. "I'm sure we could make sure it was very enjoyable for you in whatever ways you'd like."

I bumped up against him. "Hmm, tell me more."

But as we stepped into the foyer with its grand wooden staircase, Gideon appeared on the second-floor landing. "Excellent timing," he said, sounding a little harried. "I need to run some things by you."

"Me?" I asked.

He nodded with a swish of the hair he'd recently dyed more of a dark turquoise than pure blue. "It won't take too long... I hope."

I gave Rowan a questioning look, and the other guy shrugged. Gideon was already striding back toward his office with his typical brisk strides.

We hustled up the staircase as quickly as I could manage and met him inside the dimly lit room. His aquarium was burbling away, and he had a fresh batch of coffee brewing, sending a rich bitter scent through the air.

Gideon had sat down in front of his array of monitors. He tapped impatiently at his keyboard and then spun to face me with an intense expression.

"I've been reading through all the newborn resources I can dig up," he said. "Some of the basics are obvious, but there's an incredible amount of conflicting information. I can't tell what the best method for encouraging proper sleeping habits is—or how long it's definitely ideal to breastfeed for—if you definitely *want* to keep nursing, I mean —and—"

I had to restrain a giggle at his nearly frantic tone. It seemed like all of my men were getting caught up in their own separate insecurities about the impending new arrival in our lives. Naturally Gideon's would involve how much data he could or couldn't obtain.

I walked over and rested my hands on the hacker's shoulders. "I think there probably isn't one perfect method, because there isn't just one type of baby, right? Just like we can't know in advance exactly how to deal with an underling getting insubordinate or a new gang making trouble. It depends on the people involved."

Gideon let out a disgruntled sound. "It's a *baby*. It's not that complicated. There should be concrete facts."

"I think the fact that there isn't shows that it is that complicated," I said teasingly. "But if you've absorbed all the possibilities, then you'll be ready to immediately suggest every possible strategy if we run into trouble."

His gaze slid back toward the computer. "There are a few options I think we can discount right out the door."

I grinned at him. "Then it's good that you've eliminated those along the way. Somehow I suspect you're going to be better informed than the vast majority of new dads, including the three who're going to be sharing the duty with you."

Rowan's chuckle showed he agreed with no offense taken. Gideon sighed and then knit his brow as he studied me. "How long have you been on your feet? You should give your joints a break."

"I'm *fine*," I said with a laugh, but the next thing I knew Rowan had come up behind me and slipped his arms around me across the swell of my belly.

"You know," he said to Gideon over my shoulder, "I think we've all been running Mercy ragged, getting her to take care of our troubles in the past few days. What do you say we give our woman a demonstration of how well we can still take care of *her*?" He dipped his head to gently nip the side of my neck. "If you could get into the mood...?"

A twinge of longing shot through my core. I reached back to run my fingers through his silky hair, my voice dropping lower with desire. "Already there. I won't be doing any acrobatics, but..."

"You don't need to do anything at all except let us take charge for once," Rowan murmured.

I couldn't bring myself to protest that suggestion. Rowan eased me into the other office chair and massaged my shoulders as he stood behind me. Gideon got up, an eager gleam lighting in his pensive gray eyes.

"I have read enough to know that intimate stimulation shouldn't have any negative effects on the pregnancy," he said, his matter-of-fact voice taking on enough heat to make the statement sound weirdly sexy.

I waggled my eyebrows at him, even though I was already twice as turned on as before. "Is that what you're going to do? Intimately stimulate me?"

His smile turned wicked. "I'll do a whole lot more than that."

He leaned over my chair the way I had with his a minute ago, except he bowed low enough to claim my lips. As we kissed, Rowan eased his hands lower too, stroking them over my impossibly full breasts. My nipples pebbled instantly at the contact, even more sensitive than usual.

From recent explorations, he knew not to up the pressure too much or the friction would go from delicious to painful. He rolled his thumbs over the peaks until giddy quivers radiated through my chest. I wrapped my arm around Gideon's neck to pull him into a deeper kiss.

The hacker wasn't content to focus on just my mouth, though. As he delved his tongue between my lips, he reached for the hem of my shirt and tugged it high enough to expose my bra. Rowan hummed approvingly and took the opportunity to slip his hands right under the cups.

I shivered with pleasure at the feel of his caresses skin to skin. There was nothing quite like being adored by more than one of my men at the same time. I'd done my own reading, and I knew that I wasn't likely to be "in the mood" or physically ready to enjoy this kind of interlude for at least a little while after birth, but I had no intention of losing out on this part of my life for too long.

Gideon released my mouth to nibble his way along my jaw. Then he sank to his knees, nudging my legs apart so he could get better access to the rest of me. "Let me at one of those," he demanded.

Rowan let out a low chuckle and dipped his hand around one breast to offer it up. As Gideon closed his lips around my nipple, Rowan continued working over the other with his skillful fingers.

I tipped my head back against the top of the chair, sliding lower as I melted with their attentions. My pussy was aching for relief now. I grabbed Rowan's sleeve to yank him around the side of the chair so I could enjoy his mouth too.

As we kissed, Gideon dropped even lower. He hooked his slim fingers around the waist of my pants and tugged them and my panties down together. I pushed my hips farther forward at the same time, welcoming his apparent intentions.

He hovered his face over my sex for a moment, just letting his warm breath wash over the folds that were throbbing for his touch. Then he pressed his mouth right against my cunt.

I moaned and arched to meet him as well as I could. He swirled his tongue over my clit the way he'd learned to so well and then lapped it between my folds. Every sweep of it sent fresh waves of bliss rushing through me.

I forgot the heaviness of my body and the uncomfortable aches that'd been creeping through it as I got bigger—everything except the heady sensations Gideon was conjuring in my body. And not just him. Rowan was fondling both of my breasts again, bending in to test one and then the other nipple with his teeth, teasing the tips of those teeth along my neck, urging another whimper out of me with a nibble of my earlobe.

I squirmed between them, rocking with the intensifying rhythm of Gideon's tongue and the fingers he thrust into me after it, clutching at Rowan as he spread the pleasure through the rest of me, gasping and growling for relief.

They didn't leave me hanging. Gideon sucked hard on my clit as he pushed a third finger inside me, curling them to hit the neediest spot in my pussy, and I exploded. I bit back a cry that would have rung through the whole mansion as my body shuddered with the glorious release.

Gideon kept stroking me with his fingers and his tongue until my tremors of ecstasy had subsided. Then he smirked up at me. "*That* is one area where I know exactly the right approach."

I laughed breathlessly. "If you get even half as good as fatherhood, I don't think you have any reason to worry."

Rowan nuzzled my cheek with a laugh of his own, and for that moment, all our worries seemed far behind us. Then the door swung open without a knock.

"Hey!" Gideon said sharply, and made an apologetic face at the sight of the intruder. "Sorry. I didn't know it was you."

I glanced over my shoulder to see Wylder standing in the doorway, taking us in. In that first instant, his expression looked oddly stormy. Then he shook his head as if clearing it and managed a smile that only looked a little tight around the edges. "Anyone else who barges in on you, especially when you're so well-occupied, feel free to blast them to Kingdom Come."

I was about to invite the leader of the Nobles to join in the fun, but without another word, he spun on his heel and left again, jerking the door shut behind him. But why had he come to Gideon's office at all if he hadn't wanted something from his friend?

My interlude with Rowan and Gideon and then the odd encounter with Wylder left me feeling unsteady in a different way from usual. I found myself tramping through the mansion to Anthea's bedroom and stretching out on one of the lounge chairs on her back deck rather than grabbing what I needed and immediately heading out.

As the late spring sun washed over me, I settled into the chair's padding, but I couldn't quite relax. The physical release had sated certain urges, but my emotions seemed to have tangled in my chest. I'd been trying to chill out for about ten minutes when my phone rang.

It was Beckett. I quickly lifted the phone to my ear. "Hey, how's it going?"

"Hey Mercy." To my relief, he sounded less anxious than he had during our last conversation. "I think it's actually coming together pretty well. The guys you and Wylder sent have been taking care of everything I needed them to… I've got one more trick up my sleeve that I think is going to make my main competitor back off."

"Sounds like you've got everything under control then," I said. "That's great!" So why did the knowledge send a pang that felt almost like loss through me?

"Yeah." Beckett paused. "I just had the urge to talk to you before I set this in motion. Maybe it's silly. I know I'm ready to step up and stand beside my dad as at least close to his equal. I'm *going* to be the Storm one day. But there's a part of me that can't help worrying that maybe I'm not actually ready, that I'm pushing for too much too soon and I'll fall on my face. I don't know whether the fact that I'm worrying about it is something I should ignore or some kind of warning sign."

I had a strange urge of my own, one that put the earlier pang in perspective. Part of *me* wanted to tell him not to rush in, that if he was uncertain he could stick around with us for another year and get even more confident in his footing.

Not only for his sake. So that I could be sure I hadn't failed him in some way too. But after the conversations I'd recently had with my men, I suspected the impulse didn't really have all that much to do with Beckett's competence. I *knew* he had it in him to take on everything this world might throw at him. He'd practically been ready when he'd first come to us.

I rested my free hand on my belly, smiling softly when the baby stirred within me. "You know, I think that's probably normal. You're trying to accomplish something that matters a lot to you, so of course you're going to have worries about pulling it off. Do you think *I* feel totally ready to suddenly become a mom on top of everything else?"

"You don't?" Beckett said. "You've seemed totally on top of everything from the beginning."

"Well, you should know that part of our line of work is putting on a tough front. Maybe even with ourselves." My smile turned crooked. "She isn't here yet. I haven't needed to put myself to the test. And you haven't either, not all the way."

There was so much I didn't know about the future. So many challenges I couldn't wrap my head around yet. Not just while our daughter was a baby, but as she grew up and had her own dreams too. Had I known how to guide another person even well enough to send Beckett off on the right foot?

But no one really knew what they were doing, did they? Like Rowan had said, we'd see how it went and do the best we could. I wanted to see our daughter grow and flourish, and I wanted to see Beckett come into his own too, whatever hand I'd had in raising him.

"I've seen you in action," I went on. "I think you've got everything it takes to step into that role. It won't be the end of the world if you make a few mistakes along the way, right? Just try not to make any really big ones."

Beckett laughed. "Fair enough. Same goes for you, huh?"

I stroked my thumb over my belly. "Same goes for me."

After I'd put away the phone, I couldn't help reflecting that there was one of my men I hadn't had a chance to hash things out with yet, and maybe that was why I couldn't feel totally at ease. I pushed to my feet and went off to find the Noble king.

It wasn't too hard. Wylder was predictable in his habits even if he wasn't in his temper. I spotted him in his favorite lounge room, sprawled in one of the leather chairs with his long legs stretched out, sipping his expensive brandy and glowering at the wall.

I walked over and plunked myself down on his lap without bothering to ask permission, and to give him credit, he showed no sign at all of noticing that I weighed a good thirty pounds more than I had until very recently. He slipped one arm around me and raised his eyebrows, turning the glass in his hand before setting it down on a side table. "You look like a woman with a mission."

"And you look like a mission I need to take up," I informed him, and prodded his chest. His warmth and the masculine smell of him was as intoxicating as ever, even less than an hour after two of my other men had gotten me off. "What's up with you? You've been in a mood ever since Beckett went off—don't even try to deny it."

He raised his free hand in surrender. "I know better than to argue with you, Queen Katz."

"So what's the matter, then?" I asked when he stopped there. "Are you nervous about becoming a dad? Because that's definitely going around."

His arm around me tightened, and the rough note that crept into his voice told me he meant his next words. "There's nothing I'm looking forward to more than being a dad—a way better one than I had. Especially with you."

I tipped my head against his shoulder. "Then what's the problem?"

His mouth tightened the way it always did when he didn't want to tell me something. I swung my legs in a gentle gesture of impatience and fixed him with a pointed stare. Finally, he sighed and lowered his head to press his lips to my hair.

"I want to be a dad to our kid in every meaning of that word," he muttered. "I want her to be *mine*. I know she'll be all of ours anyway, but if she comes out with Rowan's blond hair or Kaige's brown eyes, I'll know it wasn't me who did the deed, and I don't know how I'm going to feel about that."

Somehow I hadn't expected that admission at all and yet hearing it didn't surprise me. I trailed my fingers along Wylder's jaw. "You're worried you'll be jealous. Do you think it'd make it harder for you to stay committed to the family?"

I tried not to tense waiting for his answer, but it didn't take long anyway.

"I'm totally committed to you," he said without hesitation. "And the other guys—they're basically brothers to me. I wouldn't lash out at them. But I don't want to have any kind of venom in me, and I have no idea how it'll actually be—how I'll handle it… I don't want anything to sour what we have. Because what we've got is pretty fucking special any way you slice it, Kitty Cat."

My lips curved with a smile I didn't have to force. "Yeah, it is. And that's how I know it's going to be okay. We've been through a hell of a lot of shit worse than a little jealousy."

Wylder let out a strained guffaw. "No kidding. Whatever happens, happens. I *will* deal with it, and I'll do my best not to take it out on the other guys. Now…" He lifted me as he stood up. "You're coming with me."

There was something incredibly sexy about being carried like I was made of feathers, especially in my current state. I nudged Wylder's shoulder as he stepped out into the hall. "And where are you taking me, Mr. Noble?"

He simply let out a huff in answer, but his route made it pretty obvious. He pushed open the door to his bedroom and laid me down on the bed, turning me toward him as he stretched out next to me.

When he kissed me, his mouth didn't convey the fierce dominance he often claimed me with. It was a long, lingering kiss full of a sweeter sort of passion. Then he tucked one arm under my head to cradle it and traced the fingers of his other hand over my curve of my belly, gazing into my eyes the whole time.

"I love you," he said. "And I already love her. That's got to be enough, right?"

"It's more than enough," I said, choking up a little. "I love you too."

I tugged him into another kiss, perfectly happy to keep doing nothing but kissing as long as it brought all that determined affection washing over me.

I was starting to get a little concerned that I hadn't heard from Beckett in the two days since his last call. Then I walked into my office in the Katz house and found an unexpected but not unwelcome visitor waiting for me.

Beckett straightened up from where he'd been leaning against the desk that'd used to be my dad's. His smile immediately reassured me that this wasn't an emergency call.

"Hey," he said. "The guys let me come up. I guess they figured they didn't have to worry about me making any trouble."

I laughed. "Not for us, anyway. How's it going? Did you get that last problem sorted out?"

Beckett flexed his hands in front of him with a crack of his knuckles. "It took some doing, but when we were finished with them, the pricks who tried to bully me out of the way ended up on their asses. The deal's finalized—I just signed the paperwork this morning. I've already got a construction company lined up to start the renovations."

His face practically glowed with enthusiasm. It set off a rush of pride in me, even though I wasn't sure how much I'd actually had to do with his success in this particular situation. Then I noticed the scabbed-over scrape mostly hidden by the sleeve of his dress shirt. Whatever he'd had to do, he hadn't come out totally unscathed.

"Do you feel okay about how it all went down?" I asked, remembering our earlier conversation.

Beckett rubbed his forearm as if he'd realized what had prompted my question. "Yeah," he said, getting a bit more serious. "We had to come down on them pretty harshly, but I'm happy with the balance I struck. I want to be tough enough to get things done and not let anyone walk over me, but fair enough that the people who work under *me* know they can count on me to lead them well. Like the way you are with your men." His smile came back.

Maybe I'd guided him in more ways than I knew. "I try," I said, and clapped my hands together. "I think this calls for a celebration. I might not be able to drink it, but I've got some good wine around here somewhere for everybody else. I'll call in Wylder and the guys. And you should tell the men you took on for the job that they should come by and join in the victory party too."

"I'll do that," Beckett said. He hesitated and then stepped forward to grab me in a quick hug that I hadn't expected. "Thank you," he added as he stepped back. "I had no idea what I was really getting into when I came out here to Paradise Bend that first time, but I've never regretted the choice. I don't think anyone could have prepared me better for what's up next."

"We did what we could," I said, feeling awkward at the compliment, but as he hustled out, already raising his phone to his ear, a softer smile stretched my mouth. For the first time, I didn't have any doubts at all that I could handle this whole parental thing.

It didn't take long before the Katz house was vibrating with upbeat music and laughter from basement to rooftop. The men toasted to Beckett's success and shared stories about the most dickish opponents they'd ever had to take down. Cans and bottles clinked. Rowan had brought along some of my favorite soda so that I wasn't left out of the drinking altogether, and he and my other three lovers stuck close by as I circulated through the rooms, swaying a little with the beat of the music thumping from the speakers.

I paused now and then as a clenching sensation ran through my pelvis. I'd started having the pains while I'd been helping set out the food and drinks, but they weren't so intense that I couldn't easily breathe through them, and they were coming pretty far apart. They could be just what my doctor had called "practice contractions." He'd advised me not to bother coming to the hospital until I started feeling something I couldn't ignore. It was still a few days before my due date anyway.

In the middle of the living room, Kaige caught my hand and spun me slowly with the music before catching me by the waist and claiming a kiss. Gideon snapped a photo of us with his phone and then huffed when I insisted that he take a picture of all five of us as well as Beckett squeezed together, as if taking selfies injured his dignity.

Wylder was just passing me a plate of mozzarella sticks, like he thought there was some danger of me starving if I wasn't eating something every hour, when a contraction hit me hard enough that my fingers twitched and the plate slipped from my grasp.

I clutched the edge of the table and gritted my teeth, and all four of my men were at my side in an instant.

"Are you okay?" Kaige demanded, looking like he was ready to throw down, as if he could have menaced my body into taking it easier on me.

Wylder peered into my eyes, his expression steadier but no less intense. "Should we get you to the car? I'm parked right out front."

"Or we could call an ambulance," Gideon put in, his eyes unusually wide. "If it's urgent."

"Doctors said... first babies don't come that fast," I said, with a ragged breath as the pressure released. "I might be fine for a little longer. Let's just wait and—"

The next contraction squeezed my abdomen right on the heels of the first. I bowed my head again with a hiss through my teeth, and Rowan took my arm. "We're going," he said, calmly but firmly.

Wylder made some motion to Jenner, who redirected the attention that'd already shifted toward us with a rousing challenge to beer pong. Beckett caught my eye, and I managed to nod to him. He aimed a hopeful smile at me and mouthed, "Good luck. You've got this."

My men ushered me out of the house with a couple more pauses for me to wince at the tensing sensation inside me. Kaige practically dragged me into the back seat of Wylder's Mustang, Rowan squeezing in after us. Wylder was already in the driver's seat, gunning the engine. Gideon had whipped out his tablet and was checking the traffic cams.

"The clearest route is along Howland Street," he reported as Wylder tore away from the curb.

I was still with it enough to crack a joke. "Maybe we should have taken an ambulance. You're not going to be very happy if my water breaks all over your fancy leather."

"I don't give a shit about the leather," Wylder retorted. "Stop talking and do those visualization exercises or whatever so it doesn't hurt you as much."

I started to roll my eyes at him and had to stop with another wave of pressure. Shit. I'd been shot and stabbed before, but neither of those injuries had prepared me for a sensation this all-encompassing.

Wylder's back seat was spared. We screeched into the hospital parking lot, and I was just waddling up to the admission doors with my men flanking me when a gush of liquid flowed down my jeans. It spurred the guys on with even more urgency, hurrying me into the building with shouts ringing off the walls.

The rest of the labor was a blur. Waves of pain and sips of cold water, nurses taking my blood pressure and checking the situation down below, and the whole while my four men clustered around the bed, squeezing my shoulders and hands, offering encouraging words.

When one of the nurses tried to insist that only two family members could be in the room at a time, I gave a roar that sounded mostly incoherent to my ears. I must have gotten the point across anyway, because Wylder jabbed his thumb toward me, his usual cocky grin tight. "What she said."

It went on and on, Kaige stroking my hair, Rowan snatching Gideon's tablet before he could try to advise the doctor for the gazillionth time on some procedure he'd looked up, Wylder standing over me like a bodyguard. And then the pushing. Way too much pushing.

But when it was over, even though I was wrung out and sweaty and aching, nothing but joy filled my chest when the nurse lay my daughter against my breasts.

One of the nurses was filling out the birth certificate. I decided I'd let the guys hash out who'd end up in the Father slot. But when she asked, "What are you naming her?" all four of them looked toward me.

"Josey," I said, firmly and clearly. "Her name's Josey."

For the mother who hadn't gotten to be there for me anywhere near as much as she'd wanted to. For the mother whose love had stopped me from ever believing I was as worthless as my father had wanted me to think.

"Here," the nurse said in a subdued voice. "She'll need another feeding now."

I accepted my daughter into my arms, still working out the best position for her to latch on. The room's lights were dim for the night, and I'd managed to get a little sleep before Josey had woken up hungry.

As she started to suckle, my men stirred from where they'd finally crashed in the chairs around the room—and in Kaige's case, on the floor next to the hospital bed. They gathered on either side of the bed, gazing down at us.

My baby felt so delicate in my arms—fragile and precious but also shockingly full of life. A little murmuring sound carried from her throat, and I smiled, as exhausted as I still was.

No wonder people called birth a miracle. It really did feel like one.

When she'd had her fill, I just held her for a little while, taking *my* fill of looking at her. As I stroked my thumb over the fine dusting of hair that covered her little head, Wylder shook his head with a click of his tongue.

"Look at her," he said in a lightly teasing tone. "That dark brown hair. The light blue eyes. She took everything from you. That's hardly fair—now we're never going to know which of us did the deed."

Rowan elbowed him playfully, and I let out a laugh, cuddling Josey close.

"Infant eyes are almost always blue," Gideon informed us. "Then they can change color later on in the first year." He paused. "Not that it matters."

"It doesn't matter at all," Kaige declared. "She's all of ours."

Wylder smiled down at me and Josey, and I could tell none of the fears that had dogged him before were bothering him now. "Yeah, she is."

I sighed happily in the circle of their protective warmth. So many people had tried to tear us apart, but we'd always come back stronger. Now we were united as parents too, and none of my own worries seemed all that important.

We were going to be the best damn parents Paradise Bend had ever seen, or my name wasn't Mercy Katz.

ABOUT THE AUTHORS

Eva Chance is a pen name for contemporary romance written by Amazon top 100 bestselling author Eva Chase. If you love gritty romance, dominant men, and fierce women who never have to choose, look no further.

Eva lives in Canada with her family. She loves stories both swoony and supernatural, and strong women and the men who appreciate them.

Connect with Eva online:
www.evachase.com
eva@evachase.com

Harlow King is a long-time fan of all things dark, edgy, and steamy. She can't wait to share her contemporary reverse harem stories.

www.ingramcontent.com/pod-product-compliance
Lightning Source LLC
Chambersburg PA
CBHW020324030826
48979CB00022B/1005

9781990338663